ALSO BY NATE CLEVELAND

Bare Hands, Numb Skulls

NIGHT'S BELL BOOKS Ω

ISBN 979-8-9902631-9-2 (pbk)
ISBN 979-8-9902631-8-5 (ebook)

H E M I N G W A Y

A Novel

By Nate Cleveland

For my father.

CANTO I

"Come my friends, tis not too late to seek a newer world."

Tennyson

1

The first day of school that fall started like any other, I guess. Kids walking around in new clothes with fresh pens and notebooks going to classes where teachers stood waiting with seating charts and icebreaker activities and syllabi. The freshmen all had that deer in the headlights thing going on, while the sophomores were just relieved that they weren't freshmen anymore, and the juniors all looked pretty depressed because they were still looking down the barrel of a full two more years of this shit—all while the seniors could smell freedom wafting in on the other end of the school calendar, and walked around like they were kings and queens of the freaking kingdom. Yeah, everything was pretty much going on as it always had, like the first day of school was going all across the rest of Michigan, like all across the country. That is until during third period before lunch, when Rosalind Howard—a senior—cut class, walked out to the football field and blew her brains out on the fifty-yard line.

Rosalind, or Rozzy as she was known to the rest of us, was a relatively quiet girl with raven-esque skin, already properly inked with tatts and riddled with piercings, and hung out with a lot of hard-core druggies. Looking back on it, most of us recall her looking kind of sad and strung out a lot, but I think it's safe to say that we didn't really see her little field trip out to the football field coming. Apparently, the 38-caliber revolver she used was a gun that her mom's boyfriend kept in case of intruders or something. They believe she had the gun with her the whole morning in a small purse. Rozzy was last seen alive by one of the gym teachers that saw her walking out to the field from a distance. He said later he thought she was just sneaking out there to have a vape under the bleachers or something and before he could make it out there to bust her, she had already pulled the trigger.

As you can imagine, everything went ballistic after that (*sorry—sick pun*). Principal Carter came over the speakers and made a brief and somber announcement and then dismissed all of Hemingway's 1,956 students for the rest of the day. An army of counselors seemed to be all over the halls after school was cancelled, a trauma team was called in, parents started showing up roaming everywhere babbling about rumors that someone had brought a gun to school and had shot students. Cops and ambulances closed off all access near and around the football field, and somehow a Channel 8 News van was already in the parking lot getting footage of the chaos.

It's weird, but looking back on it, not many of us remember seeing anyone crying or overly upset. Don't get me wrong, we were all pretty concerned and kind of shaken up—and we totally felt bad for Rozzy's family, whoever they were—but most of us couldn't remember many scenes of huddled groups of students sobbing or seeing any kids off by themselves in corners sporting messed up thousand-yard stares.

Most students were back in class the next day. And you can bet there was a lot of chatter about Rozzy, why she did it, and what was going on with her. It was weird, but it was like the social stock totally went up of those who had had classes with her or knew her better than most. Finding those who were true friends of hers however, proved difficult. Like I said, for the last couple of years she had been hanging around kids that were frankly kind of scary looking to most of us, and they weren't really big on habitual daily attendance or talking to other students that they considered preps or jocks, which most of us were in their eyes, to varying degrees. So by and large, Rozzy's suicide was a mystery to most of us, and we were prepared to buzz about it maybe a couple more weeks and then be happy to let it slide to the back of our consciousness and get on with the rest of our school year.

After all, we weren't the one's dead.

Only later, much later in the school year would some of us recall that even though he had probably never talked to her in his life, that he probably didn't even know Rosalind Howard by name before her suicide, Luke Forrester did not return to school for nearly a week after that tragically surreal first day.

2

If you were to ask me to tell you what I knew about Luke Forrester before senior year, I wouldn't have had a lot to say. I mean, there would've been like an awkward silence and then I probably would've stuttered out an 'uh…' and then I would have told you that Luke Forrester is the big deaf kid that's really good at soccer and that would have been about it.

If you would've asked me if he was cool, I would've been like *nah, not really,* but it's not like he was a dork either. Because to be a dork you got to be made fun of somehow or in some way—and people really didn't make fun of Luke at all. Don't get me wrong though, Hemingway High has plenty of A-holes that are capable and willing to make fun of deaf kids or retarded kids for that matter, just for the sake of being mean. But no one made fun of Luke though. The A-holes were scared off because Luke was big and strong and could probably kick the crap out of anyone at school.

OK, sorry—saying Luke is big and strong is pretty general, so let me rephrase. Luke was built like a chiseled marble image of Achilles or some other golden god I forgot the name of from mythology. Seriously, he was athletic perfection. He had these totally powerful pecks that seemed to be molded out of iron and cased inside flesh and skin. He stretched out his T-shirts and his quadriceps were so pumped they seriously challenged the denim of his jeans. No lie, Luke Forrester was backed and stacked. I'm sure every coach wanted him for their sport—especially the basketball coach who couldn't understand a seven-foot kid that didn't play hoops—but he seemed content—I mean, absorbed/obsessed with soccer. Plus, he was hot too, and that also kept the A-holes from making fun of him. I'm telling you, he totally could've been a major player with the ladies. I mean he had everything a teenage guy could want in the looks department. A superhero jawline, perfect complexion, and eyes as bright as million candle flashlights. Seriously, most of the Hemingway girls were in creamville whenever they took the time to check Luke out walking down the hallways.

But here's the thing—Luke never went on dates. Hell, Luke never even talked to girls, he was just *man*candy to them. In fact, Luke never talked to anyone. I mean, he must have communicated with his soccer pals somehow and his coach and dad—but more on that later. The point is, if Luke had been normal—meaning if he hadn't been hearing impaired—he could've been cool, popular, and looked at as a *guy-who-has-it-all* type of guy. But because of his deafness, all his physical gifts and charms seemed to be canceled out and as a result we didn't talk to him, and he didn't communicate with us.

Plus, there was his tragedy too. See, when Luke was eleven, his mother and his eight-year-old sister were killed in a plane crash coming back from Atlanta where Luke's grandparents lived. Once everyone found out about the crash, that sealed the deal—he was totally unapproachable. Because there's just something about people who have suffered. Like there's this glow of untalked about sorrow that hovers around them like an invisible storm cloud. You know the glow I mean? Unless you're real close to the person with that kind of grief, the weight of all that makes every attempt at conversation awkward, everything's a struggle, and we of the HHS student body certainly didn't have the social know-how to break that barrier.

So, team up that kind of tragedy and deafness with someone like Luke, who seemed to be aloof and distant anyway, and *Bang!* There you go. You've got yourself a willing teenage social exile. He was a big, athletic, good-looking, deaf, tragic, neutral anomaly. It was like Luke was totally window dressing to the rest of us at Hemingway High School. We saw him in class and in the hallways, driving around with his dad around town sometimes, and even saw his picture in the paper occasionally after he scored a goal. Other than those kinds of sightings, Luke Forrester's existence had zero bearing on our lives. But like I said, all of this would change, *everything* would change, come senior year.

3

Jason

Fuck'em.
Fuck them, man.

This place is crawling with assholes from top to bottom, man. They don't care. They don't care about shit. They didn't know Rozzy. They didn't give a fuck about her when she was alive, so why are they so overfuckingwhelmed with concern now that she's dead? Bastards and bitches—they're all bastards and bitches. Rozzy got it half right—she just pointed the gun in the wrong direction. It's the rest of these fuckers at school that deserve to die. It's all these preppy ass-puppets whose parents get them everything they want so they get so spoiled they think they can treat people like shit and it's no big deal. Well, put a fucking bullet in their kneecap while they're gossiping about who's fucking banging who or what "cool" party all the "cool" people are going to and that will get their attention. If some asshole gets shot in the face right when he's bullying a kid—*that* will make them all sure as shit perk up. And I know who I'd start with too. That Dylan Sorensen fucker. I swear, if that jockstrap piece of shit, or any of his dick-patrol friends call me '*faggot*' or '*cocksmoker*' one more time I will fucking kill them. *Fuck!* I hate those assholes! I swear one more time, man. If he wants to call me queer, *fine*—I'll show him queer. I'll put a round in his chest, poke out his eye with a pencil and skull-fuck the shit out of that bitch. I hate those guys. I fucking hate them. I don't know if I could quite land an AR-15 or something even close to that heavy but fuck, I could certainly land me a piece in *the D* to get the job done. Or hell, my old man's chrome .45 would do just fine too. I know the combo to his safe where he keeps it. Piece of cake, man. But who am I kidding? I could just as easily walk right up to Dylan and slash his throat wide open with my serrated knife I got for my birthday two years ago. Damn, I hate Dylan. It'd be so easy to just walk up and baseball bat that bitch.

Fuck, Rozz. Why did you have to do that today? Damn it. Damn, Rozzy. I'll be getting fucked up in your honor tonight. My pops just picked up his delivery from Dre who just got it in fresh from his lab in Detroit, and I still have half a bottle of Jim Beam stashed in my closet under my dirty clothes. I'm going to get so wasted I can't see. Maybe you're the smart one, Rozzy. Maybe I'm the idiot for hanging around here. I mean, *fuck* man, really? What am I doing here?

Damn it, Rozzy.

4

When Luke Forrester finally returned to Hemingway, he had something new with him as he walked into Mr. Becket's Western Civ class. With a small green notepad flipped open to the first blank page, Luke scrabbled down a message and approached Mr. Becket at the podium. Becket glanced at the note and said something like, "Oh yeah… I guess you've been absent for a spell, haven't you…" and proceeded to give Luke a bunch of materials that he had missed since the first day. Luke jotted something else down. Mr. Becket squinted at it through his reading glasses and mumbled, "Uh, you're welcome."

And though this small mundane exchange really didn't grab anyone's attention there in class, a first step had just been taken, the first small tremor signaling the coming of a much larger quake, or like the first drop of water before the torrent that will break the rock, or like the… ah, forget it—anyway, the point was that Luke Forrester had just initiated contact with a teacher, other than his soccer coach, for the first time since he was thirteen. I mean, never mind who it was, it was amazing that Luke Forrester had just initiated contact with another human being at Hemingway High School—and none of us noticed a thing. But we would.

So, Becket broke his class into groups to work on timelines chronicling the highlights and lowlights of Mesopotamian culture. It was widely known that small group work wasn't exactly Luke's cup of Mountain Dew. He was usually unresponsive, did his own thing, and made most of us feel really awkward because we really didn't know how to communicate with him, and he really didn't help us either. I mean, Luke sometimes gave us these looks, stares really, that seemed to say, *Don't even think of trying to talk to me*. And I mean, it wasn't even like all that of a malicious look either—it was more like just this indifferent glare. So as a result, we took the hint—*OK, that Forrester kid's a rock. Fine*. We didn't even try. But today in Becket's class was going to be like the birth of a whole new nation, and Becket couldn't have made a better crack team for Luke and his new notepad to join. And so, this is how it came to pass that Luke Forrester joined Greg Forsythe and Jason Turner (yeah, that's right, Jason freaking Turner) as group number three in the back corner of the classroom.

Wow, you know looking back on it now, up until senior year, Jason Turner taught us the meaning of the vocab word *infamy*. I mean, we knew what popularity was of course—like whenever you said so-and-so is popular, it was usually considered a good thing. Popular meant people all knew who you were because you were hot, or a great athlete, or had a cool car, or were rich, or threw cool parties, or got away with something cool, or you had a number of these in any number of infinite variations and ratios. But as our high school years droned on, we realized that everybody knew who Jason Turner was, but like no one was envious of his popularity. I mean don't get me wrong—drinking, partying, and vaping a little of the wacky tobacky was definitely a checkmark in most people's cool book. But with Turner… I mean *wow*, man.

For us Jason Turner put the stone in stoner—the drug in druggie. And since each high school in this country probably has its subtle little discrepancies and stuff in how it defines the major stereotypes we all find so much comfort in, Hemingway's perspective on what a stoner or a druggie is, is one I should explain. At Hemingway the term druggie didn't mean that you had taken drugs every so often in your life—it meant that drugs *were* your life. Remember, drug and alcohol use were rampant at our high school, but Turner went well beyond use. Um, OK. If you'll stay with me, I'll try to use an analogy here. So here goes:

> If recreational drug and alcohol use at Hemingway
> was like the equivalent decibel level of a ditzy freshman girl
> humming the pop tart chart topper of the week between chews of
> bubble gum while she fixes her hair in the bathroom

then…

> Jason Turner's decibel drug use was a full-out thrash
> metal assault concert, complete with a mosh-pit of kids
> screaming, armed with swords and cannons going off on stage.
> We're talking unfreakingbelievable.

I mean we're talking common knowledge that Turner was into daily binges of hard liquor, pills of any/every kind, weed, meth, and rumors of crack. Seriously, Turner had blown through the proverbial gateway drugs with a bong-loaded bazooka and was now sacking all the castles made of cocaine. In the words of our grandfathers, you could say that Jason Turner was *heavy*, man.

And Turner also became well known at Hemingway, when he wasn't so drugged-up he drooled, for being at war with Dylan Sorensen and his ultra-prep/jock faction. Everything about their confrontations made most of the rest of us beyond nervous. So by and large, we tried to steer clear of their heated harassment sessions—but it was easy to see why there was tension between these two opposites. Where Dylan and his gang were groomed and hooked up with the freshest and latest fashionable clothes and colognes, Turner's wardrobe was all tattered and worn, as seldom washed as his body. Where Dylan's hair was styled with a variety of products, Jason's was longer and unkempt—free to do what it pleased. There were plenty of times when it looked as if Turner was on a particularly deep bender, where he had whiffable aura of vomit and b.o. about him. Just seeing Jason in this condition sent most of us running in the other direction or holding our breath in order not to breathe him in as if he was the source of an air-borne pathogen that could somehow creep into us and make us just as filthy from within.

And really, in all truthfulness, Dylan and his buddies on the opposite end of the social spectrum were just as intimidating as Jason was for most of us "normal" kids. But still, I mean except for the upper ranks of the most popular students and maybe teachers, coaches, and administrators—nobody really said *hi* to these guys for fear that they'd freeze you into an ice block with their coolness if you did. I mean, if you were a pretty girl, you might be fine—Dylan and his guys would flirt with you whether they knew you or not. But for the most part these guys were pretty hostile and self-absorbed, so if you got in their way, or made a social false move in front of them, they would be all over you. Death by sarcasm. It was like total Darwin: *the strong eat the weak so the strong get stronger*. But here's the thing, their aggression wasn't as out in the open as Turner's was.

They were underground. I mean, if Turner got pissed, he'd just haul off and deck someone, or yell with neck veins bulging for certain students, teachers, and sometimes administrators to go—uh ... go do something very private to themselves. Seriously, Turner was constantly riding the revolving door between the offices of the assistant principals, the police liaison officer to Hemingway, and even the big guy Principal Carter himself.

In contrast, the aggression that Dylan Sorensen and company unleashed was every bit as volatile as Turner's, and yet it was as invisible to teachers and administrators as it was present to all the rest of us, as oxygen. These guys sabotaged with rumor and mini scandal. They maimed with their scalpel-like, almost innate, understanding of how coolness worked in a high school setting and their awareness of their own place and potential in that system. I tell you—they smelled inferiority like a great white smells a bleeding dolphin. They were geniuses when it came to using the phrase, *I heard*. For instance, one of them might say to the person they were out to take down— "Hey, I heard you fill in the blank with the most violating, personal, exposing, and mostly untrue thing you can think of. The 'blank' was usually sexual, sometimes illegal, sometimes a healthy mixture of both. But always personal. Always damaging. If you pressed Dylan, or any of them on who said so, they would respond with, "Uh... I don't know, everybody. Everybody's talking about it..." Then it would hit the socials and you were toast. It was a perfect weapon really. No one to peg as the source and yet there was still this rumor, as unkillable as the air, like COVID or some other major plague I've already forgotten about.

It was early during junior year that Dylan heard a rumor about Turner, or maybe he made up, or embellished it—or whatever. But the point is that this rumor was their number one weapon against Turner. The story goes that Turner and his friend, and frequent partner in crime, Toe-Faux (the kid's real name is Toben, but he sported this faux-hawk haircut that he sometimes dyed green and so you know, a nickname was unavoidable) had brought acid to school and they were looking to get ripped right before 5th period. Apparently, they were wanting to get a little tripped out for their English class because they were watching a film version of *Macbeth* from like the 70's or something and there was supposed to be some freaked up scenes in there with psychedelic witchcraft and daggers flying around. Word was that the 70's director's wife had been totally slashed to pieces by Charles Manson and he was getting all his frustrations out through this bloody Shakespeare. So—it goes that they cut their 4th hour classes and met each other in the porta-john behind the school next to the Ag shed. Once they were both cramped in the porta-john, the rumor was that they took a couple of tampons, laced them up with acid, and then shoved them up each other's ass. I know—totally gross, but most of us believed it. I mean, we believed that Jason Turner was capable of any and all things criminal and Toe-Faux was just as freaky with his hair, nose stud piercing, and more eye-liner than most cheerleaders. And while most of us buzzed and whispered the rumor in Turner and Toe-Faux's wake—Dylan and his band threw it in their face. Seriously, from then on it was non-stop. Anytime Dylan and his friends saw Turner, they grilled him about if he was gay or just bi or thinking of going trans. They called him and Toben all sorts of names and things. They even shoved Jason around one afternoon after school in the parking lot. Toe-Faux had "Ass Bleeding Queer" printed on his locker with black ink. One of the janitors had it cleaned off by lunch—but a week later the same label was scratched on by a key or a knife or something.

It was also widely known that towards the end of that year, in the large study hall held in the lecture hall, that while Mr. Gibbons hunkered over correcting one of his geometry exams—Dylan and Kirk Wellington wrote out on a piece of loose-leaf paper a message and held it up for Turner to read. The message read:

TURNER
YOU CUM BELCHING FAGGOT

Well, Turner totally got pissed and blew up and chucked his pen at them and then threw another kid's laptop at them too as he was charging towards them. It was about then that Mr. Gibbons snapped to life and moved to stop what looked like was going to be a brawl of like 9/11 proportions.

"Come on! Let's go fuckers!" most kids remember Turner shouting.

"What the hell is your problem?" Dylan asked as he and Kirk stood up straight, waiting to see what Turner was going to bring.

"Jason! Stop! Stop now!" Mr. Gibbons yelled, practically sprinting up to Dylan and Kirk.

"Hey, I didn't start this shit, man. Ask them why they got to be flashing signs calling me gay. These guys are the problem. Ask them," Turner said to Gibbons.

Gibbons turned to Dylan and Kirk. "Let me see the note."

Kirk shrugged like he was clueless, and Dylan was like, "I don't know what he's talking about. We looked over at him and he's flipping us off, so we just did it back and he just went psycho."

"That's bullshit and you know it! Look, man, look through their stuff or have Officer Truman frisk them or something. But they're lying about that note! They got it, man," Turner pleaded to Gibbons.

Gibbons looked at Dylan and Kirk. "Is there a note?"

"No, he's lying—he's just trying to get us in trouble," Kirk said.

"That's it." Gibbons was sick of it. "Down to the office. All three of you. Go see Mr. Henderson or Principal Carter. *Now*."

Word was that Assistant Principal Henderson spent most of that meeting trying to get Jason Turner to speak calmly and appropriately about what happened. Turner never quite settled, and Henderson had to suspend him for profanity and threatening statements he made to Dylan and Kirk. After Turner was escorted off the premises by Officer Truman, Henderson gave Dylan and Kirk a warning about the consequences of harassment and then sent the two back to study hall. The note was never found, although there were about twenty or so of us that were in that study hall that day and did see the note. Not one of us was ever questioned about it by Gibbons or Henderson—however, I'm sure none of us would have said a thing about it if we were.

Well—yeah, sorry about the tangent there—I know, I sometimes hate it too when they give you too much of that kind of background stuff in books, but whatever. So anyway, back to Becket's class and small group number three in the back corner where Jason Turner is totally strung out and hung-over, reeking not-so-faintly of liquor, which apparently all of us students notice and most of our teachers don't, or don't want to notice enough. The elegant/deaf hunk that is Luke Forrester sits back in his desk allowing his long legs to sprawl all the way across the floor where he crosses his feet while he focuses his attention once again to his little note pad. And Greg Forsythe—poor Greg Forsythe. Greg was interested in getting good grades—you know, like visions of scholarships danced in his head. Somewhere inside that skinny body of his, covered by a sweatshirt over-a-collared-shirt, lived the orange dream of going to Syracuse University far away from Michigan suburbia. So, the sight of who he'd been teamed up with I'm sure filled Greg with concern while he's trying to read the Mesopotamian Timeline direction sheet Becket gave him.

Luke scribbles something and places his pad on Turner's desk and nudges it a little forward. He taps the slumbering Turner hard enough on the shoulder that Turner finally lifts his groggy head out from his arms. "What?" he goes, looking at Luke.

Luke nods towards his pad.

Turner glances down and tries to focus his bloodshot eyes on Luke's note that reads, *Are you OK?* After a confused couple of seconds Turner mumbles out something close to, *Yeah, I'm fucking awesome, man—jeeze, what the fuck*... and plops his head right back down in his folded arms.

This little exchange between his group partners starts to make Gregory a little anxious. "Uh... guys, I don't..." is all Greg gets out. The rest of us could totally understand Greg's plight. I mean, what do you say to the school's biggest druggie-psycho that's showing signs of getting pissed at the total brick-house anti-social deaf kid? I mean seriously, which one do you try to reason to? And keep in mind; at this point none of us truly understood that Luke could read lips perfectly (I'm not kidding either, he understood us whenever we spoke in his presence—whether we were talking to him or not.) So anyway, Greg does what probably any of us would've done—he marches right up to Mr. Becket and says that the three of them all decided they were going to work separately. Reportedly, Becket glances to the back of the room and sees Turner slumbering away and Forrester right across from him writing another note and then tells Greg, "Fine. But I still expect the same quality of work as if all three of you were still working together."

As Greg picks up his stuff and moves to another desk away from his estranged group mates, Luke makes another stab at giving Turner a note.

"What the hell, man? What's with this need for constant fucking updates about how I am?" Turner goes. Now it wasn't just Gregory—now the whole class was nervous with anxiety. Turner shoots Luke a look like a cornered cobra right out of the damn Discovery Channel. Luke just underlines his latest note *Are you sure you're OK?*

"I don't know what your deal is today, man, but I'm definitely not in the mood for it," Turner goes and walks up to Becket saying he has to see the nurse.

"The nurse? What for?"

"I'm sick."

"How sick?"

"Diarrhea. I got serious diarrhea. I think I'm about to get diarrhea all over the place—the walls, the desks, your shirt, everywhere, man. Can I go?"

"Get out of here, Turner," Becket goes. "But I'll be checking with the school nurse, and you better be excused on today's attendance."

And that's how the very first conversation between Luke and Jason ended.

We had no idea what we were in for.

5

Abby

I guess I wouldn't call it shock. I guess it was more like surprise than anything else. I didn't know even how to react at first. There were so many other things on my mind—you know? I seemed lost in a million worries before he came up to me out of nowhere in the commons area waiting for Peter to pick me up. I probably had that all-blanked out face people get when they're just sitting there zoning—you know, and their mind is totally somewhere else. In my defense I had good reasons to be a total zombie that afternoon—I mean I had just found out the day before that I was pregnant with Peter Calloway's baby for crying out loud, and I was thinking about telling him on the way home.

We had been dating for the last two years. I mean two years! God, it's just so weird it had been that long. I thought he was cute all of freshmen year. He had these super dreamy eyes and this caring kind of wide-awake expression that I found extremely hot. One of his friends heard from my friend, Amanda, that I liked him, but it took him all the way until the middle of sophomore year to ask me out. He was so nervous about it too—his face was all flushed and his voice was kind of crackly. He asked me in between the second and third periods of one of the hockey games. It was all loud around us and we were heading back through the crowd from the concession stand to our separate groups of friends on the bleachers. I remember it all in a kind of slow motion—you know, like how they do in the movies or in videos when something real emotional is happening. And that kook, Dickey Schwartz, was zipping around on the ice on the Zamboni with his screwball sombrero waving to the crowd to the tunes that the band teacher was pounding out of the pipe organ. And in all that crazy flurry and noise, when everything seemed to be dancing, Peter asked me out. I don't think I had ever been happier. I was smiling so hard my cheeks hurt. You ever smile like that? Anyway, it was beautiful.

Well, we didn't have sex until our junior year. It was both of our first times. We had talked about it for months. Talked, talked, talked. Our reasons, our concerns, our beliefs—everything came out leading to that mid-Saturday morning when I went over to Peter's house. His parents were going to be gone until late. His brother was already gone away to college for a full semester, and we would be alone. He said he bought the condoms at the BP station near his house. I wore the brand-new black bra and panties I got a couple of weeks before at a mall outside Detroit. Ugh—I can't believe I'm telling you all this. So, there we were as bashful as couple of unicorn ponies, all undressed and walking towards each other. He wrapped me up in his arms. It's weird I know, but I can still remember small drops of his armpit sweat smearing on my bare shoulder as we hugged. Both of us were so nervous, trembling. Kissing. Then flopping onto his bed. There was this gentle little tornado in my head making the room spin. I was suddenly warm everywhere and looking up into his eyes. I raised my hands and held the smooth and reddening cheeks of his baby face. *This is going to happen! This is going to happen! God! What am I doing?* was all playing on over and over in my head. What was Peter thinking? There was such a weird look on his face—like a little boy's face when he's discovered something really cool that he knows he's not supposed to touch. And then it happened. He was there. He was everywhere. Suddenly I felt like I had been shot down there or something—I felt warm and broken—regretful and relieved—full, yet somehow suddenly empty. It was so strange, so different than what I was expecting, I guess. I let Peter finish and then I quickly retreated to his bathroom. It was so weird being in their bathroom in the state I was in—seriously, there I was completely naked. And it was the nicest bathroom I'd ever been in—the décor immaculate and every fixture in it, from the sink to the toilet, I could tell was super-expensive. Seriously, the place glowed. I remember this oil painting they had above their toilet in a golden frame that showed a bright beach during a real peaceful looking morning tide. I remember thinking, as I stood there like ridiculously naked that I really liked that painting—I remember even thinking *I wish I were in that painting*. My mind was in a weird place, I guess. I felt both like an idiot for what had just happened, and yet I felt also wise somehow. Like, if I really were in that painting, I could see myself as an older woman, you know, like late-thirties or something, and I'd be looking out over that sea and thinking about all the hard truths of reality, you know, whatever they were...

So there, between thick red wipes of toilet paper and dabs from a wet washcloth, I took care of what was left of my virginity—my mind too much in freak-out mode to think coherently on anything more than just getting *clean*.

It took a few weeks, but I was ready to do it again, much to Peter's delight. And from then on it was easy. We got into a habit. Sex became our routine, like taking a cookie out of the cookie jar as soon as you get home from school for an afternoon snack. His car became our five-seat hotel room. We got so good at sneaking around I'm sure Peter and I could've made it into the CIA. Straight up sex, bj's, hand jobs, and all that stuff had all stopped being the mysterious forbidden fruit and turned into our daily bread, if you know what I mean. Sometimes I really liked it, and sometimes I just simply did it and tried not to think too hard why, and always, without fail, Peter was ready for it.

So yeah—by sometime in late August before senior year, we must have either went too many times in the same condom, or one broke and we weren't aware of it or made a big deal of it, but in any case, at some point Peter's XY hooked up with my XX and then...I mean in all seriousness, who gets pregnant in high school? Sure, all the trailer park girls, or the girls sleeping with all the gangstawannabes and maybe your occasional drunk hick chicks that don't know any better. But who else? Not girls like me. Not girls with good families. I was thinking that my mom would kill me when she found out and my dad would burn me to ashes after mom's done killing me. I thought, should I tell Peter in the car or wait till Friday when we have more time to talk? What should I tell mom? When should I tell mom? There's no way to hide this forever...or is there? Should I tell mom and dad together? When do I tell my little sister, Kate? Is there a way I don't ever have to tell Kate? Should I just do what that Rozz girl did and just shoot my head off? What about abortion? Seriously—what about an abortion? Can a girl just run in quick to a clinic and get one, no questions asked? Can I even still get one in Michigan? What am I doing?

And there you have it, one scared seventeen-year-old girl standing in the commons area at Hemingway High, zoning out—gazing out the window, thinking of a billion things at once, trying to figure out the most important and intense stuff of her life, when out of nowhere, Luke Forrester comes up to me and hands me a note.

"Whoa..." I think I said. But there Luke was all urgent looking, obviously trying to get me to take his note. So, I grab it, more out of reflex and confusion than anything else; and I feel everything getting weird—I remember looking around instinctively as if the whole thing could be a mean joke and some assholes are video-ing me with this clueless look on my face.

I finally looked at the note, but it took a couple of seconds before it clicked what I was actually reading:

I know this is crazy, Abby.
But remember way back that day when you
asked me if you had done something wrong?
I'm sorry I never answered you. But for what
it's worth, you didn't. It was all me and what
I was going through.

"Luke..." I looked up at him. I'm sure he saw utter cluelessness in my eyes. He looked back at me too for a second and then scribbled something else.

It was all me.
I just wanted you to know that.

By now I was tearing up and I didn't know if that had to do with Luke's notes and presence that I barely understood, or if it was about Peter and my whole deal, or my parents, of just everything all together—I even had a glimpse of that Rozzy girl all lying dead in the grass in my mind, and for the first time I truly thought about how sad it all was about her.

I guess I was like that for a while because I didn't notice right away that Luke was touching my arm gently and nodding at me again, you know—the kind of nod that adults sometimes do to like confirm you understand them. I just stood there with what must've looked like a dumb look on my face and then he just turned and walked away. A blaring car horn like suddenly snapped me back to reality though, and I looked out and saw Peter in his car waving me to hurry up. As I walked out to Peter with the fog of everything in and around my head, the sun clashed off his car's fresh wax finish and I could barely see where I was going because of the light totally searing my eyes.

6

It's pretty obvious to everybody now that at some point during his first couple of days back in school, Luke Forrester went down to the Tech Ed. wing, notebook in hand, to go talk to Mr. Darringer.

Darringer was the welding teacher and, depending on whom you talked to, he probably ranked as one of the coolest teachers in school. He was certainly one of the most interesting to us, if not outright the most mysterious. First off, he was so hot he got more girls to actually sign up for welding than otherwise would. With his long dark hair and baby blues and trim and fit figure sitting at thirty-something—Darringer was definitely not your average male teacher at Hemingway. When Darringer started teaching, the guidance counselors at first were totally perplexed by all these mallrat princesses electing to take Tech Ed. credit. But after seeing Darringer all decked out in his tight Carhart dungarees and worn blue denim shirts, it didn't take long for our counseling staff to figure out the freaking sea change.

And you know, Darringer just didn't act like other teachers either. He had a quiet, yet confident, way about him. No one ever heard him yell, and he rarely even joked. When he spoke, he spoke so calmly that his students would all shut up to hear him. Any of the kids that had him would all say he was super-alert, helpful, patient, and never seemed rattled by anything. He was famous for calling over students that were total screw-offs or kids that were serious injury risks and saying to them in a soothing voice, 'Fill in the blank, I just don't think this is the class for you,' and then he'd gently send them down to the guidance office to change their schedules. Plus, he had this sweet beat-up Jeep with honking tires that he drove to school always cranking old stuff like James Taylor, the Eagles, and some singer named Steve Earl.

It was also pretty obvious that he really knew his stuff when it came to welding too because in the summers, he would contract his services to shipyards and head out to sea to do underwater welding. According to the other Tech Ed. Teachers, Darringer could totally be making loads more money as a full-year contract welder—which all his students thought was cool and respected him for giving that up to teach them.

I guess Darringer might've been a little surprised to see Luke stride into the welding shop—I mean since Luke had already taken all the welding classes offered and couldn't really remember any real teacher/student bond that had formed between himself and Forrester.

"Well..." Darringer said and wiped his hands with an old work rag. "Good afternoon, Luke."

Luke scribbled:

Would you mind if I came in from time to time to weld?

"You mean after school?"

Luke nodded.

"I guess," Darringer said and shrugged. "As long as I'm here in the shop."

Luke jotted:

Good news. Because I'd like you to help me with something.
Darringer remembers being mildly amused. "Oh yeah? With what?"
Luke smiled.

My life's great work.

7

Isaiah

I can see him out my bedroom window. In the mornings he comes to play with his soccer ball. He can do all kinds of tricks and stuff with the ball. He comes in the morning just after Mom gets me up for school. He's out there almost every morning, except in the winter. My house is across the street from the big soccer field. It has lights and the high school plays their games there. That's probably why he comes to practice there in the mornings because it's the field he plays games on. Mom told me that she heard he's deaf and can't hear like we can. He looks really strong though.

He's been out there in the mornings since I was eleven. I'm thirteen now. Sometimes Mom gets me a bowl of cereal and I go out to the living room where Dad's bed is now, and I watch him out the front window juggling the ball with his feet.

This morning was cool because when I was watching him Dad told me to go out and check for the paper. I went out and he saw me from across the street. He stopped with his soccer ball and moved his hand telling me to come here. I was kind of scared at first. He didn't look mean, but when he practiced he always looked mad—like he was fighting; not playing soccer. But I didn't think he was going to hurt me or anything, so I went across the street to the field where he was. When I got up to him, he started writing something down on his little note pad he had. Then he showed it to me. *My name's Luke. What's yours?* I told him my name was Isaiah. Then he wrote down that he was deaf but could understand what I was saying by watching my lips. He said he likes to talk with his note pad, and I told him I thought that was cool. Then he wrote down that he had seen me watching him practice for a while. He said that was OK. Then he asked me if I played soccer. I told him I was on an U14 team this last summer. He asked me if I had ever come over to any of the high school games at night and I told him that my mom lets me sometimes and that I had seen him score goals before. He thought that was cool. He said his last season starts in a few days and said it'd be cool if I could come and watch him. I said I'd ask my mom. Then I remembered that my dad was waiting for the paper, and I told Luke that I had to go, and he said that he would be back again early tomorrow morning and that it was OK with him if I wanted to come out and practice with him. I went back in and told my mom and Dad about Luke and she smiled and even Dad did a little too. And Mom said I could go out there and practice some with Luke tomorrow if I got up and got ready for school quick enough!

8

The second week of school rolled by putting more and more distance from Rozzy's suicide and us. I guess it's kind of like the way stuff moves in space if it's not in orbit—it just goes, no stopping, no backtracking, like a rogue satellite that's jumped the rails or like that Voyager thing we shot out across the universe to look for aliens and other intelligences and stuff like that. That's how we were, moving away from Rosalind Howard—no stopping, no looking back, no orbit.

The hyper-ness of the new school year and the added adrenaline of a suicide on campus was wearing off, and we could all—students, teachers, administrators, office ladies, custodial staff, freaking lunch ladies—I mean everybody could feel that everything was about to finally settle down into the familiar school year routine. Classes were back on track and the homework was flying. Clubs and student council were starting to meet, and kids were already buzzing about Homecoming. Sports teams were starting their seasons and even the football teams were allowed to practice and play again on their field. Sure, it was kind of weird to watch the first home football game. I mean, everybody was making comments, teenagers and adults alike, about how sad and strange it was that just a couple weeks ago a girl did such a horrible thing to herself right there, yeah—right there, on the fifty-yard line.

"Such a shame," the adults said.

"That's so messed up," we said.

In school you could even hear some of the football players joke about it. Craig Matthews, a wide receiver, said something like "That psycho-girl's ghost has been helping us out there. I caught two passes last game that there was no way I should've caught." Tight End, Nelson Tremblehall, was even heard saying "Dude, I was totally picking pieces of brain out of my cleats the CSI guys must've missed."

Now maybe all of us didn't make jokes like that, but most of us that didn't still laughed. It seemed we were entering that last stage of it—you know, Rozzy's deal. Done with the shock, done with the wondering, the gossiping, we were ready to make light of it and let it go like a helium balloon given to the sky. Like I said, we were done with her. It was time to let Rozzy slip into outer space, to have her finally move out beyond our reach, to leave our galaxy and to find a new home in like the black holes beyond.

And then something started to tug on our attention. It took a while, maybe like three to four weeks into the new school year, but the student body at large started to notice through announcements and finally word of mouth that our soccer team was undefeated. Like we started to realize that our soccer team was actually good. And it just wasn't that they were winning—they were beating other teams that were really good. I mean, football rules—no doubt. But we'll cheer on a winner from home no matter who it is. And to be honest, our football team that year was going to be OK, but we all knew they weren't going anywhere. We were going to be fifty-fifty at best. It was crazy. Like freaking nature in reverse—soccer suddenly became bigger than football. We all kind of started showing up at the games. We all learned the players' names. I mean, jeeze, they even beat Rochester Hills who is state ranked and usually kicks our ass every year. Local press seemed to be covering soccer all over the place too and the attention the team was getting on the school's daily announcements was way more than usual.

A few of us seemed to be figuring it out though. To some of us it seemed that the administration, and even the town to an extent, seemed to be supporting the soccer team's success more than usual solely *because* it was in the aftermath of Rozzy's suicide. It's like the adults were all going, "Yeah! Finally, here's something positive for the grieving student body to band around. Yay, soccer!" Can't really blame them though—it was a good strategy. But you see, the main thing I think most of the adults didn't realize was that by and large we didn't really ever care about Rosalind Howard. We certainly didn't care about her, or know her, before she died. We were shocked but still didn't care too much when she died, and now we were even losing interest that she had died right here at school. But that didn't stop us from not starting to care about the soccer games though. I mean you gotta love a winner, right?

9

Coach Striden

The greatest compliment of my life came from my soccer coach and mentor at the University of Nebraska after I scored the game-winner in a 3-2 thriller against top-ranked Notre Dame. He said, "You're a comet, Elizabeth. Damn it all to a fine hell if you're not. Pure light on grass." I'm sure in that moment even I couldn't hide from him my widest of smiles.

And so, years later, beyond all doubt, Luke Forrester was my comet—pure light on grass through and through. I'd never seen a more committed, conditioned, technically sound, obsessed athlete—and I've been around some pretty great athletes in my time. He was a coach's dream in so many respects. He woke up before sunrise each morning to work his foot skills with the ball at our fields. Even in the winter he kept it going, doing his touches at six a.m. in the gym. In the off-season, Luke was religious about weight workouts and did daily sprints like a fiend working his lungs into generators that never seemed to shut down. He studied the game constantly and understood the idiosyncratic differences between the Barcelona style of play versus the Manchester United style. Of course, it helped my cause that Luke was silently obedient to all my instruction and desire for my team to push themselves to their limits. It also served my needs that Luke had zero social life to distract him from *my* mission. He was the complete soccer machine really and devoured everything about the sport. And when he played the game? Luke's eyes burned with the gleam of a zealot.

Now, I can't altogether plead ignorant to what Luke's home life was like in those days with his dad. I was also keenly aware of the toll Luke's hearing impairment had on his social development with his peers. And actually, I was pleased about it because it all added up to him focusing on his soccer development even more. The dude had no distractions. So—now that there's been some space and time to reflect, I do keep going back and forth on a couple of questions. For instance, should I feel any guilt in having fostered such obsessive devotion in Luke? Would he have been this disciplined without my encouragement? Or was Luke simply a mirror image of my own obsessive tendencies? I guess some honesty is in order here. You see, I've been driven to excel at the sport of soccer ever since I can remember. I am a daughter of Title Nine. Surrogate daughter of Julie Foudy and Mia Hamm. I grew up believing an athlete's destiny was mine. I'm telling you as a teenager my soul was ignited when I watched Carli Lloyd light up Japan in the World Cup final.

I was my daddy's pride and joy, and he fostered my athletic ambition all the way. High-end training camps, taking me to summer tournaments—sometimes states away, the latest in gear and shoes—you name it, my father did it for me. Soccer became our lifestyle. So, when I finished my senior season in high school, the natural next step was going on to play soccer in college at an NCAA Division One program. So that's what I did. Full ride to the University of Nebraska, Lincoln (*Go Big Red*!). After four more years of the best years of my life playing at a high level, I was at a crossroads. Either I could go for it and play for the U.S. Women's World Cup team—or start coaching. And after a near-miss try out with the U.S. National team in Colorado, I found myself coaching and jumping in without hesitation with both boots pointing forward.

So, when I got the job teaching Physical Education and coaching Boys Soccer at Hemingway, I thought nothing of it. I was ready to go—this all seemed the natural progression to me. But apparently it was a big deal to the coaching community here and the public in general. I guess I didn't really realize what a novelty I was—a twenty-seven- year-old woman coaching teenage boys.

In all honesty, I was expecting the boys on the team to push me a bit to see if I was for real or whatever, or if I was going to be a pushover and let them get away with whatever they wanted just because I was a woman. Well, I put all wonderings to rest when a cocky senior jokingly asked if I would go with him to Homecoming and said, "and by the way… I'm all about protection." So, without batting one of my pretty little eyelashes, I called for them all to line up for full-field sprint staggers. No lie, I ran those boys for near a half-hour non-stop at top speed. They were puking, two quit the team before we were done—and just about all of them threatened to quit, and after I stopped running them, I told the kid that made the remark to turn in his equipment and go tell his parents he was kicked off the team for sexually harassing his coach.

I haven't had a problem from the lads since.

But the thing is, I fully expected something like that to happen, and so, consequently, I had a plan. What I wasn't expecting, or prepared for, was all the attention from the local press, you know—the whispering behind my back from all the male coaches of the holy balls trinity (Football, Basketball, and Baseball) and the overall mystique that I was getting from just merely coaching high school boys.

I'll spare you the total bs I was put through at the beginning. After two threats to push sexual harassment on most of the football staff and staring down anyone that thought I couldn't handle a boys' varsity caliber program, I finally won some sort of legitimacy for my tenure here.

So eventually I came to peace with the fact that I'm a novelty. Fine. So be it, I say. As long as my team plays to win and plays my way. As long as they fight and bleed for me, I'm happy.

And so, by Luke's senior year, I was *very* happy. We were a team on the rise. We were primed. We were set and loaded to do what no other Hemingway soccer team had ever done. Make it to State. In addition to the monolith that was Luke Forrester we had a complete constellation of other stars surrounding the comet. I mean we had studs up top, studs in the middle, and studs on the back line. Not to mention big Patrick Durning in the goal. The kid had bones of oak and seemed to always be in beast mode during the match. Seriously, put Patrick and Luke in a pub brawl in South Hampton on game day and these two would come out whistling.

But anyway. I guess I tell you all this so that you will have some idea about what our team was like, so you can have a clearer idea about what happened to our team and why.

10

It seemed that Fall that when Luke wasn't playing soccer he was more or less stalking Jason Turner in the hallways. I mean, Turner would just be walking out of the caf after lunch and Luke would glide right up to him and flash him some sort of note and Turner would be heard saying stuff like, "Not fucking now, dude," or, "Hey! How do you say back the fuck up in sign language? Shit Almighty, man—get the hint." After which Luke would just walk away with a whatever look on his face.

For those of us that noticed these creepy little encounters it was pretty weird. In fact we were starting to realize that a lot about Luke's behavior lately was getting a little odd. You know there was stuff like him suddenly scribbling out these notes, talking (*in his way*) to people. Remember, we were used to Total Anti-Social Luke. Not the Luke Forrester writing the four closest kids sitting in his radius a *What's up* note at the start of each class.

Add this to the growing knowledge that Luke could read our lips way better than we could've imagined. Before I think most of us thought Luke could maybe just get the main idea of what someone was saying to him if they said it directly in his face and slowed down their speech. But now—as he would ask us in class questions about a math assignment, or he'd jot down a random question about how someone's day was going—we started to realize that he was catching every freaking word we were saying. He began startling us by holding whole conversations with us on his little pad. I mean it was getting surreal.

Then some of us began to wonder—how much had he heard us say in his presence? OK, not *heard*, but you get what I mean. How many private things could he have picked up on even across a crowded room or in the common areas around school? I mean, sheesh. Some of the sharper of us started to think, 'how much dirt does he actually know?' It floored some of us that the school's most visible deaf kid could tell what someone was whispering about someone else at a volume that nobody else could possibly hear. I mean *Dang Smokey*! It was almost too much.

There was a noticeable change going on within Luke—and we didn't like it. We were leery about any of our number who suddenly tried to change the stereotype, the image, or the function that we had gotten used to seeing them in. We didn't approve of social makeovers much. I mean, everybody let the trans kids do their thing without much public comment. It was our parents that freaked about that. But as far as our *stereotypes,* there was no changing lanes, much less direction, on the Hemingway Highway as far as we were concerned. I mean, if you were a hick, you didn't suddenly go all emo on us—that just wasn't done. So, to suddenly see Luke Forrester thawing out a bit and engaging us in weird and random conversations it was safe to say it creeped us out.

And nobody was more creeped out than Jason Turner.

Then one afternoon, Turner blew up, I mean just totally came unglued at Luke right between 4th and 5th period at the foot of the east staircase. Those that saw it got all jazzed up because they thought it could turn out to be the fight of the century—and yet everybody hung a little bit farther back than they would have for any other fight. I mean seriously, we didn't know what kind of havoc these two were capable of. Apparently, Luke was trying to give Turner another note asking how he was doing when Turner just snapped, threw his books down, shoved Luke double-handed in the chest, and shouted, "For fuck's sake! This bullshit stops right now! I don't care if you're a deaf retard or not! I don't even care if you think you're the toughest motherfucker up in here! But you will stop pissing me off with these weird-ass notes!"

The look on Luke's face was totally unreadable.

For like the first time like ever, we kind of saw where Turner was coming from for once. I mean there weren't any of us at that time that would've enjoyed the kind of messed up attention that Luke was giving him.

Turner jabbed his finger at Luke and kept ranting, "You better keep yourself and your malfunctioning deaf ears away from me from here on—got that!" He started moving his fingers in some sort of mock sign language while making what could only be described as like mongoloid-type moaning sounds. "I mean it. Come near me again with that note pad and you're fucking dead. I don't care if you can bench 260—you're still dead. There's more than one way to tear somebody a new asshole."

While Turner was going off, Luke was scribbling on his pad.

Sounds good. See you tomorrow.

Then Luke just turned and walked away like the whole thing was no big deal.

"Sounds good…? What the hell?" a bewildered Jason Turner said to himself and anyone else who was still milling around. "Fucking lunatic…" He said and turned to go up the stairs.

"I should baseball bat that bitch…" someone remembers Turner mumbling.

The standoff wasn't the hottest piece of gossip ever or anything, but Forrester and Turner did raise a few proverbial eyebrows that day. News of the confrontation got passed around. And by the next morning when Dylan Sorensen was told of it, at the corner table in the caf where he held court and downed multiple cartons of chocolate milk before school, he was heard passing this judgment: "Damn. I thought the big deaf fucker was just a soccer savior. I bet you Forrester was just looking for a queer piece of ass from Turner. I mean *wow*, huh? Who would've thought that underneath all those quiet good looks, Forrester's just a total psycho-fag?" And of course, without fail, all of Dylan's friends blasted laughter over that.

11

Abby

He seemed so confused the moment after I told him. Like what he was hearing from me, weren't words at all—more like annoying gasping sounds that held absolutely no meaning whatsoever. When Peter finally got what I was telling him, he was quiet for a long time.

We were in his car, parked in front of the park just a couple of blocks from my house. It's not a big park at all, just a row of five swings, two teeter-totters with rusty handlebars, a sandbox, a slide that got so hot in the summer sun it could give you third degree burns, a small merry-go-round. Pretty standard. But it was our neighborhood park and I loved it as a little kid.

So eventually Peter spoke up. He hissed the word *fuck*. I just looked at him for a sec and he gripped down hard on the steering wheel of the motionless car. I turned my blurring eyes to the merry-go-round.

Peter let loose then. Asking questions like how long had I known? And am I sure? Which time was it? Do you think it was that time in my hot tub when my parents were gone? He raved. He bawled about how this was going to screw up both our lives. He hinted that I should've been more careful—it was *my* body after all. He said *shit,* and *fuck*, and *goddamnit* a lot. Somewhere in all that, I completely lost where I was. I was no longer sitting in Peter Calloway's passenger seat, tears streaming, dripping from the cliff of my nose and merging with my snot that always comes sliding down all gross to my mouth when I cry. No, I was back on the merry-go-round with my best friend Beth Tillery, back when she had pigtails and still talked to me, and with little Angela Forrester with her pink Hello Kitty corduroy overalls on. Better times I was seeing. Times with my friends at the park.

But Peter's voice yanked me back to the car. Abby! Pull yourself together, he was saying. It's going to be all right. I couldn't look Peter in the face—there was something in his eyes, the shape of his mouth that made me queezy. Then he said the word *clinic* and how we could go there, and they could do things, and no one would have to know—not our parents, not people at school—and we could make it right. We could make it go away. Money wasn't a problem; he would pay if he had to.

We could get our lives back.

I think I was barely breathing at that point. I just kept nodding. I think I said OK. He tried to hold me. Gave me a weak kiss on the driest part of my cheek he could find. He started the car and slowly drove me home. I have no real memory of him saying goodbye and driving away, or of me walking, zombie-like, into the house and going straight upstairs to my room. I don't think either of my parents, or my sister, were paying enough attention to notice me, or the state I was in.

And like suddenly I'm like sitting at my dresser in front of my mirror. Out my window I can see the sun was setting and hear shouts of neighborhood kids playing on their bikes and big wheels or whatever. I can smell dampness and leaves.

I look at the car wreck that is my face. I do nothing to wash my tears or smudged mascara. I just keep staring at myself with zoned-out loathing. I think of nothing. I am nothing.

I know this is crazy, but I had this spark of a thought. I made a silent vow to God. I promised God that if I opened my dresser drawer and saw Rozzy's gun there, I would blow my head apart.

Then I check. Nothing.

I close the drawer again and pray. I tell God I'm serious, I'll do it. I tell him I believe. I tell him I'll take the gun into my mouth and bite down hard on its barrel for my sins and pull the trigger. I pray please, God—please let Rozzy's gun be there.

And then my younger sister, Kate, is suddenly knocking on the door saying something about dinner.

I pull open the drawer. Nothing again.

"Damn it," I go.

After a half-hearted try at cleaning up my face, I sit down with my family for dinner. It's stir-fry broccoli with grilled chicken and asparagus. As the fam digs in—forks flying, gulping iced tea, dishing out spoonfuls of rice—they start talking of things and their day, and as Kate drones on about something with her science class, the putrid smell of asparagus finds me and turns my stomach in knots. And suddenly it's all on me again—visions of me and Peter making out and climbing up on my family's dining room table. And while he strips me down all my family comes in to sit down—Mom, Dad, Kate, even my grandparents sit there, quiet and watching as my naked thighs are opened and I let Peter do it to me on the table.

Crazy, right?

I dry heave. My mother says something to me, but I can't hear it. I retch again, but nothing comes out because there's nothing in my stomach but the accidental little life coiling inside me. It feels like I'm screaming, but I can't hear it because the world is ending... Shut it all off, pull all plugs, because it's all ending, and I don't want to see what comes next.

12

You know, it's kind of crazy, Homecoming—you know, when you really think about it. Activities all week, pep assemblies, a girl's powder-puff football game, raffles, the Varsity football game, and then it all caps off with the Homecoming Court and dance on Saturday night. I mean, it's kind of nuts that high schools all over the freaking country pretty much all have some sort of Homecoming deal. I'm sure they all have their own little specific differences—but in the end, doesn't it end up with some hot boy and some hot girl being named as royalty and then everybody runs off into the night to drink and play hide and seek with the local P.D. till dawn? I mean it's crazy. Just imagine all those kings and queens of September all over the country from the hickvilles, to suburbs, to the inner cities—all of them ruling over their separate little kingdoms. All title, no power—all show, no go, for one night only. And just like at Hemingway, I'm sure every other school has their yearbook geeks working overtime trying to catch every smile, touchdown, dance move, and every burst and cackle of annual school spirit.

But what would turn out to be ultimately the most important and shattering moment for Hemingway High from that week wouldn't be photographed or documented, in fact, none of us would find out about it until months later.

It started with Jason Turner knowing something. What Turner knew was that his study hall teacher, Mrs. Branson, was no longer taking attendance. Mrs. Branson's study hall was in room 115, which held enough seating for sixty students. Well, after the few first weeks of *setting the tone* for the study hall expectations and attendance, Mrs. Branson simply went through the charade of looking over the epic seating chart and logging any students absent. Besides, I'm sure she was thinking she had better things to do with her time there. So, after testing the waters a bit and skipping a few times with no consequences, Jason Turner just stopping coming to his third period study hall altogether.

So, when third period came around the Monday morning of Homecoming Week, Jason slipped outside to go hide in the trees behind the Ag shed and smoke a blunt or pop a pill as custom.

What Jason did not know was that Luke Forrester had probably been watching him do this for days now without Jason knowing. So, you can imagine Turner's total bewilderment when he turned the corner behind the Ag shed to find Luke waiting for him with a note.

"Sonofabitch! Fuck this!" Turner goes and turns back towards school.

Luke grabs him by his long sleeve T-shirt's collar and yanks Turner back. "All right! Damn it. Fine. I'll read your fucking note—but get your paws off me!"

You seem to be someone capable of killing.
I bet there are some people at school here that you wouldn't mind killing.
Am I right?

Turner looks up from the note. "Yeah. So? What the fuck of it, asshole?"

I can help. You interested?

Turner shakes his head. He gets this sudden flash of himself and this big dumb mute striding the Hemingway halls blowing away jocks and hicks and thug-lifer-wannabes with AR's at will, blood splattering on lockers, the screaming of all the bastards and bitches. He sees Dylan Sorensen's brain matter erupting with shards of skull up to the ceiling tiles.

"How the hell you going to help me?" Turner goes.

Holding his pad firmly in the palm of his hand, Luke's pencil dances across the small page.

I'll let you kill me. And I'll help you get away with it.

"What? You bleeding insane? Why the fuck would I want to kill *you*?" Turner goes.

Because killing me will be practice. Killing someone's a big deal. Not everybody can do it. People freeze up or freak out at the last second. If you ever do plan to kill someone else don't you want to be sure you got the nerve to go through with it? Not everybody's a real badass. By killing me you would know if you have what it takes. I'll plan to make sure there's no way you could get caught. I don't mind dying. It's my time maybe. I'm cool with all this.

Turner's blown away. He starts pacing. "Hey, so you can like fucking understand everything I'm saying to you, huh?"

Luke scribbles back, *Yeah. As long as I can see your lips move.*

"This is fucked up. Totally fucked. Why would you just offer yourself to be snuffed? You suicidal or something?"

Got reasons. Leave it at that. I'll come up with the plan and how to dispose of my body. It'll all be clean and untraceable. You'll drive and not ask questions about reasons. That's the deal.

You badass or not?

Turner reads the note and tears it into tiny pieces. "You fucking serious?"

Luke nods.

"Let me think it over, nut-job. Crazy shit like this usually isn't my thing. But like you say, how will I know I've got the right stuff?"

Luke just stands there.

"When would you want to do this sinister shit, if it was really going to go down?"

Luke holds up the pad.

Saturday night.

If you're gonna kill me, kill me Saturday night.

Jason takes out his lighter and a blunt. "I'll let you know tomorrow, man. I guess you know where to find me, huh? Now if you don't mind, I'd like to take a little time here to *Enter the Dragon*, so I'd appreciate it if you'd get your crazy-assed self the prairie-fuck out of here."

Luke just nods and leaves Turner to get high behind the Ag shed.

13

Jason

I don't know, Rozz... I just don't fucking know. I don't know what to think of this guy. I mean, part of me feels sort of sad for him—you know, being a big deaf tard that wants to die and all. It's just so sad and sick. And yet most of the time I think the kid's a total fuckstick and if this is what he wants and I could actually do this and come out shit-stain free, then so fucking be it, he's gonna find out I'm down.

I kind of wish you would've asked me to kill you rather than you sneaking around and going through with it like you did all by yourself. Because if you would've asked me, I could've talked you out of it and then we could've killed the people that were messing you up. And I would've done that for you, Rozz if you would've asked me—I would've ended them. Each one. And still might, girl. I'm so damn sorry, Rozz. The world's fucking shit. I mean it's not just the third world wastelands where you see people dying and killing every night on the fucking news, but the shit's everywhere. It's sure as hell here, I mean, I swear, I fucking swear on any holy textbook they put in front of me that Hemingway's the corn-hole of the world, man—it's just that everybody's so good at covering it up with total smoke and mirrors bullshit like test scores, and sports, and all sorts of ball-washing achievement. This place is a burning hell, man. And it feels like there's nothing that can be done about it and nobody really cares.

And it's getting to where I don't care either, Rozz. It's just so damn hard without you here. It's just too hard. I don't want to do anything anymore except get wasted. Get fucking trashed and think about you.

Rozzy, girl, I'm so fucking sorry. So sorry I can't stand it.

I'm thinking I'm going to do it. I'm gonna help that deaf kid die. I'm gonna snuff him out. Kill him fierce and get away clean and see if I can't feel some kind of real rush again, see if I can't get some of this FUCK-ALL rage out. Maybe this is exactly what I need to pull it back together—or maybe it will finally push me over the edge. Either way, it's got to change. I need a change, Rozzy. Just hang on, girl. I might be joining you sooner than you think. Wouldn't that be something?

Anyway, I'll let you know how it goes. And who knows? If this goes good and it turns out I'm good at cold-blooded shit, maybe I'll take out Dylan Sorensen before I'm all done. Now that thought's making me fucking smile. Yeah, Dylan deader than shit by my own hands—yeah, that shit's coming in like sunshine right about now. I'll let you know, Rozz. Stay tuned.

14

Tuesday that week was the pep assembly. We all filed into the gym and stood up in the bleachers while the cheerleaders bounced and flaunted and yelled out cheers at us. The band boomed out the usual loud pep tunes. The student council announced and introduced the Homecoming Queen nominees and they all walked out to the center of the basketball court each cradling a red rose. Finally, a group of senior boys came out and did the annual male pom-pom routine. This was always a highlight, or lowlight, depending on who you were. We all went nuts in the stands. The guys came out with their pom-poms with pink T-shirts with the word TACO printed in blue across their chests. Dylan Sorensen and Kirk Wellington lead them all out. Word was it was all their idea. A few teachers winced and all of us seniors went proverbially ape-nuts while the hip-hop beats blared from the gym's big speakers and our senior guys moved and gyrated, screaming in unison, "Eat Pink Tacos!" at the end of their routine. It was priceless. Droves of ninth graders whispered that they didn't' get it and I don't get it and what's going on? Principal Carter looked just as clueless, while teachers like Mr. Darringer just shook their heads.

But unfreakingbeknownst to us getting away with being totally inappropriate in the gym, something was going on outside behind the Ag shed that would've chilled all of our blood had we heard it.

Away from the gym and adult supervision, Luke Forrester took Jason Turner through his pain-staking plan. Luke had thought of it all. Jason listened—or read, actually—better than he had in years in any of his classes. Luke had written it all out in morbid detail. And even Turner could see that if they did it according to plan, it was flawless. Turner realized that Luke had thought of everything. There was maybe a two percent chance that Luke's body would ever, *ever*, be found and zero percent chance that Turner could be charged with the murder. It was perfect. There was only one thing that was confusing to Turner though.

"Why not use a gun, though? I mean I can get one if I try. Easy, man. My pop's got a shitload of them."

Guns can be traced. This is better. Trust me. Don't want them dredging a lake and finding a gun. Too many risks. Besides, if you can do it this way, there's no way you can't do it by simply pulling a trigger. This is how I want you to kill me.

"Well, fuck it, man, whatever you want then. It's not like I was bringing this up cause I was too pussy to snuff you out, it was a common courtesy as far as pain was concerned, but whatever."

Just be there with your car at the right time.

"Okay, man," Turner goes. "You can fucking bet on me. So, go have your last hurrahs and shit or whatever. I'll be there."

Back in the gym we were whooping and yelling. Yeah, man! Go, Pink Tacos! We were idiots. We were assholes. How could we know what we were in for?

15

Isaiah

Tonight, Mom took me to Luke's soccer game across the street. There were so many people there tonight! Some had on green and black paint on their faces that matched our team's uniforms and some of them went running around the stadium bleachers trying to get everyone to cheer loud. Mom said it was their Homecoming Week and all the high school kids were excited.

The game was pretty good. Hemingway won 3-1. But Luke didn't score. I didn't want to tell Mom, but it looked like to me that Luke just wasn't playing good. It had been almost a week since he last came to the fields in the morning. He didn't run as hard as I knew he could run. He didn't do all the moves I knew he could do. He took one shot from way too far out and the ball went way high over the goal onto the other fields in the dark. I kind of felt sad for him. He kind of looked like he knew he wasn't playing the way he should. But everyone else was loud and excited and one of Hemingway's strikers got all three goals, which really got the crowd going crazy.

When we got home, Dad was still awake in the living room. "So how did it go?" Dad said, "I heard a lot of cheering out there."

We won three to one, I tell him. Mom said the kids were crazy because of Homecoming.

"How did Luke do?" Dad asked.

"OK," I said. "He didn't score though."

The TV was on, but the sound was so low I don't think Dad's really been watching it. He reached for a bottle of pills from the little table that has all his pills. "Hey, Izzy, can you go get me a fresh glass of water?"

I went into the kitchen to the sink. Mom was wiping up the table a bit. 'After you say good night to Dad go get ready for bed, OK sweetie? School night,' she says.

I took Dad the water and he swallowed down two pills. It looked like it kind of hurt to swallow them.

"Come here, Izzy."

I moved closer to the bed. Dad hugged me to him and kissed my head. "I love you, boy. Night."

"Night," I said.

Up in bed I can kind of look out to the soccer fields. I love to do this on nights after games because sometimes the stadium lights are still on as the teams and fans leave. But sometimes, like tonight, the lights are already off—but it's still cool because the big light bulbs still glow a bit after they're turned off. I like that glow. And I sometimes lay on my pillow sideways looking at the orange glow of the stadium lights and it makes me think of the nine planets, like Jupiter and Neptune, and deep space and other galaxies with way far away suns. It sometimes makes me wonder about how nice it would be to be able to sleep in space far back enough to see the just turned off glow of the sun.

16

If Hemingway's seven-game win streak wasn't signal enough for the rest of the conference, and the state, to take notice—the boys soccer team's 3-1 win over Afton Falls on Thursday night would finally sound the alarm. We packed the stands and went rabid when Trevor Morehouse tallied in a hat trick. He and Erik Volgstaad were everywhere, crossing into space and running onto through-balls like fighter jets. And Morehouse's shots on goal were like live artillery. I mean we're talking full on thunderous.

So, when it came to Friday night of Homecoming, there seemed to be a million parties going on everywhere which left many of us creeping from party to party trying to find where the coolest spot was at. It was then that word was spreading pretty quick that a wild one was cooking at the soccer team's *Meet the Players Party* out at Volgstaad's family cottage in the woods about thirty-five miles out of town.

Erik and the team held the party every year about mid-season, but it was usually a pretty secret and low-key affair involving the team (except for Luke), a couple of player's girlfriends maybe, and a few twelve-packs and that was about it. But this year was like a whole new animal with cars and kids everywhere in and around Volgstaad's cottage. It was getting a little later and the remoteness of the *Players* party meant that there would be a less likely chance of getting caught, so partiers were droving in like moths to a freaking flame. As people kept pulling in bringing more beer, liquor, and girls, most of the soccer team couldn't believe their luck. Their recent success and newfound popularity had suddenly turned Volgstaad's cottage into a Homecoming Hot Spot.

"Dickie! Dude, I'm gonna need you in a minute on the drums!" Erik was yelling to Dickie Schwartz while strolling around the living room of his family's cottage like a freaking king. Volgstaad was already four beers and three celebratory whiskey shots into the night as he tried to rustle up all the soccer players for the annual *Meet the Players* Promenade.

"Ryan! Ryan! We got everyone?" Erik yells to Ryan Leone across the crowded and bustling living room that Erik's parents would have seriously freaked over if they had seen it right then.

"Naw, man. We're missing Linus and T.J. for sure, and I thought Morehouse was in here, but I don't see him now," Ryan goes.

Erik shakes his head all dramatic. "Dude, go outside and find 'em. We gotta get this *Meet the Players* thing done before people start leaving or passing out. It's getting crazy around here."

"Yeah, yeah..." Ryan goes, way under impressed and headed out the screen door.

Erik takes a sec to look around the room. He sees kids from school here he barely knows but knows they're cool. He sees a couple of underclassman girls he's never even talked to before totally checking him out and whispering in the corner of the room. He sees six or seven unopened cases of beer stacked in the cottage's kitchenette sink and on the floor. There's five full gallon bottles of different whiskeys and two more unopened bottles of Everclear on his kitchen counter. Kids are talking all around him, some dancing to his music, some huddled on couches near the TV. His parents are staying overnight in Detroit and have no idea that he had his own key to the cottage and therefore will have no knowledge of this night. *Ever*.

And Erik is smiling. Big time.

"Holy shit, Dude, is this awesome or what?" Trevor Morehouse screams in Erik's fricking ear.

"Where you been?" Erik goes.

"Fuck, bro, all over. Do you realize how much snatch is here?"

"Yeah, so much it's off-the-hook ridick, dude."

"I know." Trevor laughs. "Stay sharp, man. Cause if we play it right, we're all getting laid tonight. A lot of these kids are not pacing themselves at all. Like *at all*. It's like they're not saving anything for Homecoming tomorrow and blowing their whole wad tonight, bro."

Erik scans around. "Did you see Maddie O'Leary and her gang show up?"

Trevor nods and takes a sip of beer. "Yeah. They're outside. And without the Dylan Sorensen crew."

"So—they finally done now, or what?" Erik goes.

"Fuck if it matters, dude. You know she's damaged goods now. Oh yeah by the way, Linus is a little indisposed, cause Janice is giving him a blowjob right now in his dad's Lexy."

"Get the fuck out... Hell, is anyone video-ing it?"

Trevor laughs. "Hells yeah! Teege has been taking video from the backseat *AND* with Janice's total fucking consent, dude! Linus is all posing like a pimp, winking and shit while Janice goes to town on his little lolli-pop dick. Ridiculous, man."

"Well, where's Teege then? Teege! C'mon, boy, where you at?" Erik yells across the room.

Teege walks in as if on cue. "Forget Linus for a while boys. Check this out, dude," T.J. goes and holds up his device. "He's getting his balls blown and there ain't no way he's coming in right now for a team photo-op."

"What do I care about fucking Linus?" Erik goes. "Bench warming little turd don't deserve the power of a good shit! Let's go then!

"OK, then, good people. Fuck!" People almost shut up. "It's totally all good, then." Erik looks out and sees more at the *Meet the Players Party* than all the three years combined.

Dickie Schwartz takes his place at the full drum kit set up in the corner of the room and tips his head to Erik signaling he's good to go.

"What the fuck, *Mutha-Fucka's*! Sit the fuck down and listen to the straight up shit!" Erik yells at the top of his *F-ing* lungs into a mic hooked up to a karaoke speaker. "Cut the tunes a minute here. Cut the TV too, ya'll!"

A kid sitting with the gang huddled on the couch in front of the TV starts slurring, "But dude, it's Sports Center. They're showing the Lions' last—"

"Screw the Lions!" Erik goes. "What's the Lions' record right now? Like one and go-fuck-yourselves last time I checked. Naw, turn that shit off and let's talk about a team that's about the business of winning! Can I get the men of the Hemingway High Soccer Association to please rise! Yeah! Stand the fuck up ye fine gents, yeah!"

Those of the team present stand—although Ryan Leone and Troy Jensen look slightly pissed back at Erik.

"All right then," Erik goes. "And now if you would rightly get it the fuck on, Mr. Richard a.k.a. Dickie with the drum roll *puh-leeze!*

With the cue, Dickie shines his trademark gap-toothed goof-ball grin and kicks up the rolling thunder on the snare all while Volgstaad riffs out the *Twentieth Century Fox* Anthem on the kazoo tied to a string around his neck into the mic.

The crowd cheers and wheezes.

"And right about now, ladies and gentlemen," Erik goes and staggers a little, "Your Hemingway Men's Soccer team! First up, at left midfield, number eight—that's right, lock up your sisters and your sheep cause here's Ryan Leone!"

Ryan barely raises his hand and heads out of the cottage.

Erik takes a sec to register his friend and teammate leave the room. "I don't know what to say folks—it looks like the cat's got Ryan's crotch tonight, but we'll look for him to be back in fighting form next week against conference rival Ann Arbor next Tuesday. And next up, at right defense..."

It takes about another seven minutes or so for Erik to go down the team roster, and then everyone goes back to partying pretty hard. Then it starts to get even more nuts. Volgstaad's got T.J. running around trying to get everyone to shoot all the rest of the hard liquor. That's when football stud, Nelson Tremblehall, and goalkeeper, Patrick Durning, start to get into it about who can outshoot who when it comes to whiskey.

"Hey, man—I gotta take it easy. I've got the Homecoming game tomorrow!" Nelson goes.

"So what are you saying?" Durning goes back. "Come on—you brought all this up. Put your money where your mouth is. You can't puss out now. My bet is you can't drink half the crap you talk."

Well now the whole crowd that hasn't left yet in the living room is getting mildly into it and starting to agg Nelson on. And before you know it, they're both sitting down to the table.

"Teege!" Erik yells. "Get over here with the whiskey! We got ourselves a rightly match of drinking manhood over here."

Both Nelson Tremblehall and Patrick Durning are huge guys, and the remaining kids start making bets all around.

One shot down. Everybody claps.

Two shots down. Somebody unmutes Sports Center.

Three shots. Fellow football Stud tells Nelson to slow down and think of the game. Nelson shoves his teammate. "Not till I put this lawn-fairy down."

Trevor Moorehouse is seen slinking out of the cottage with a couple of sophomore girls with reputations for being uh... physically *recreational*.

Shots, four, five, six. It appears we were making no headway here.

It's about now in the party where all the rest of people begin to leave by the carload or settle in for the night—but most are leaving, or trying to.

Shot seven. Eight.

The music's off and there's no one outside the cottage anymore except for cars peeling out of the driveway.

Shot nine. Ten. Eleven.

"Teege! Open a fresh bottle, dude!" Erik orders.

Shot twelve. Nelson's got two of his teammates begging him in the name of god and football to stop and let them take him home.

Shot thirteen.

I remember bringing my own car.

I remember really thinking at this point that *I* should be heading home—but *I* had five bucks on Patrick drinking the football guy under the table—so *I* just keep hanging around the table with Erik Volgstaad standing next to me with '*Teege*' on the other side playing barkeep to our two whiskey heroes.

I take this time to lean over to Erik and go to him, "Hey—it make you nervous about the clean-up for a gala like this? I mean, aren't you a little nervous about missing something and getting caught?"

Erik just takes another sip of whatever's in his cup and fidgets with his kazoo in his other hand. "That's my master stroke, bro. I hired a professional maid service for tomorrow."

"Clever…" I go.

"Oh yeah," Erik goes. "They deep clean everything up—no questions asked. My parents'll never know, or ever need to know about these shenanigans."

Shots fourteen and fifteen. Nelson Tremblehall starts turning a shit-shade of green.

"Who's the lawn-fairy now," Patrick slurs.

And it's just about now when Nelson totally barfs prompting Erik to tell his Football buddies to make sure he gets home safe, and Patrick announces with flammable eighty-proof breath that he calls the sofa to crash on, and I collect my five bucks from one of the football studs, that something happens. Something strange and kind of incredible, and pretty disturbing in a way—and I'm so *glad, glad, glad*, I was there to see it.

Because it's then that Luke Forrester strides in looking as cold and as pissed off as I've ever seen him. And right away all the soccer guys kind of perk up a bit calling Luke's name in amazement and start making gestures welcoming him in.

Luke heads right for the table where Erik's sitting.

"As I piss and breathe, Luke Forrester! How the hell are ya, buddy? Come to join the festivities? Want a beer?"

Luke stops in front of him and scribbles out a note.

What the hell are you doing?

Erik takes the note, scans it, looks up. "What, man? What's it look like we're doing? It's *Meet the Players*, bro."

This isn't the way it's supposed to be. We signed a code.
We gave our word we wouldn't do this.

"The hell you talking about?" Erik goes. "Signed a code? You talking about the Hemingway's Sports Code? Nobody follows that—it's a joke! We've been doing this for years and you never cared before, so what the hell's the crisis now? Come on, man.

This is our senior season. It's time to fucking reap the fruits of our labor, bro. So relax. Have a shot. Go outside to the fire pit and vape up with the stoners back there or whatever. Get laid. It's the springtime of our glory, man. This is what it's all about!"

Luke writes on the pad again and then leans on the table, sliding his next note just under Erik's nose:

> *Our glory? You kidding? If this is what it's all about, then our whole season, our whole identity is built on shit. Wake up.*
>
> *This was our last chance to do it right.*

Erik shakes his head. "You going nuts or something? Our season is going awesome! We're fricking dominating! This is our chance to make it to State! We *are* doing it right! What the hell, man?"

Luke straightens up. The football guys are next to him—but Luke looks bigger, leaner, and more dangerous than all of them put together. He motions to T.J. to hand him a half-full bottle of whiskey. It takes Teege a sec to figure out what Luke's actually asking for and then he hands Luke the whiskey. Luke takes the bottle in his big, knuckled fist and raises it up to his mouth and guzzles a few powerful swallows of straight Kentucky whiskey—and then without warning, whips the bottle full throttle against the wall behind Erik, shattering the glass and denting the drywall in a thudded blast.

Me, Volgstaad, Teege, the football guys, everybody in the vicinity all duck from freaking shards while Luke turns and scrabbles a final note before flipping it behind him like it's a piece of trash and then kicks the cottage screen door open to march out into the night.

"The fuck, Luke? You just blasted my parents' wall!" Erik goes.

"Holy crap," goes one of the football guys, "What's that dude's problem?"

I bend down and pick up Luke's note off the totally glass-strewn floor.

"What's it say?" Teege goes.

I look at it while everybody looks to me and listens as I read Luke's words:

> *Fine. To hell with all of this then.*

17

We just didn't know what it meant; you know? Not me, not the soccer team, certainly not the student body at large—none of us at that point could've known what Luke had already set in motion.

We crammed the stadium that Saturday to hopelessly cheer on our football team as we got annihilated 41-10 (with absolutely no help whatsoever from a sick and wobbly Nelson Tremblehall) while totally unfreakingbeknownst to us bad things were afoot in the shadier corners of our student body. We didn't know what a dark night it would be as we dressed up for the Homecoming Dance—all the guys in black liquorish tuxedos and the girls all in gowns the colors of exotic frostings and sherbet ice creams. We were in blissful ignorance, absorbed in our teen spirit, all headed for the big dance to watch and whisper about each other in our gymnasium turned to a dreamscape of streamers and mood lighting. Phones flashing, awkwardly dancing to the music blasting from monolithic speakers, laughing yearbook-ready laughs, taking sips of liquor in the restroom stalls, priming ourselves for the real parties to come—asking our dearest friends if they could spare an extra condom package, and finally crowning our royalty. Dylan Sorensen never looked sharper—his queen Maddie O'Leary smiling bright as usual even through the public awkwardness of the moment (being as she and Dylan broke up a week ago.) Yes, here in the gymnasium, Homecoming had made things appear again as they should. Order seemed to be restored. It wasn't a perfect peace—but one we'd gotten used to. But that night, other things were going on that would eventually impact us all in varying degrees.

Jason Turner's Saturday started at the crack of 11:30 in the morning. He'd been up half the night binging in his room, listening to tunes, toking between drinks, thinking mostly of Rozzy and what it was gonna be like killing Luke and shit like that, while his dad was in the next room with Alexandre and his thug-lifers delivering the next shipment and going over the week's traffic on their laptops.

Well, Turner got up and grabbed some cold pizza out of the fridge and downed a big *Lord of the Rings* collector's glass from Burger King full of apple juice. His dad was still passed out on his EZ chair in the living room with the TV going on full-tilt volume about some kick ass bass fishing tactics. After breakfast, Turner hooked out the day's jeans, slipped on a T-shirt, zipped on his hoodie, and left a note on his dad's gut saying that he would be sleeping over at Toe-Faux's and would be back Sunday sometime.

By dusk Turner was half-drunk/half-high and waiting at the far end of the Walmart parking lot at the arranged time when Luke came pulling in. Turner just kept sitting in the driver's seat smoking a cigarette with the window down looking all badass when Luke got out of his car and motioned for Turner to open up his trunk. Turner popped the trunk and Luke tossed in a hatchet, four rough looking cinder blocks, two lengths of chain, a big green tarp, and two master locks.

"Holy fuck in hell... You're not joking, kid..." Turner goes.

Luke slams the trunk home and tears off a note.

I drive there. Pay attention so you know how to get back.

Turner exhales smoke. "Whatever, Mr. Fucking Chauffeur. But make sure you take it easy on the clutch, yeah?"

The doors slam and Luke tears Turner's Honda *Civic* out of the massive parking lot and accelerates into the falling night.

Luke holds his pad against the middle of the steering wheel and scribbles a note while driving.

Your boy solid?

Turner reads it. "Solid as a shit brick, man. Toe don't know the full scheme just like we planned, but he understands that's part of the deal."

Luke swerves the car a little as he jots another note.

He better. He's the weakest link. If he caves and spills—he's the only angle where suspicion will head your way.

"Look," Turner goes back, "he's well aware of the gravity here without being fucking privy of the skinny, you know? I mean the last thing I asked him before I left to meet you was, 'All right, Toe, underfuckingoath in a cocksucking court of law, where was I tonight?' And he raised his left hand and shit and says, 'I swear your fucking Honor, Mr. Turner was kicking it at my house getting lifted and watching fucking *Talladega Nights* for like the millionth time, man.' So don't fucking worry, Deafy. I got my shit covered."

They keep driving, winding and what not, chasing the headlight's beams. Turner snuffs out the butt of his cigarette in the car's already overflowing ashtray and lights another. He sees a couple cold dead French fries on the floorboard and grinds them under his shoe like they were loathsome ants on a sidewalk.

Luke rounds a corner and the headlights hit a huge possum chilling in the middle of the road. Without warning Luke pumps the break and swerves around the animal.

"Shit! What the fuck, man?" Turner goes. "What's with the cardiac arrest? If it were me, man, I'd run the beady-eyed shit out of 'em! Ugly Fangoria-looking motherfuckers! It looks like a piece of old white shit with hair."

Luke just shrugs and drives on while Turner takes out a plastic flask and gulps down some *whateverclear*.

But Luke takes one hand from the wheel and grabs Turner's wrist.

"What? Come on, man. I'm trying to regulate myself here. Unless you want me to have a terrible case of the shakes when this deal goes down, I gotta have at least two more hits from the flask, man. Get it?"

Luke just keeps driving, his face unmoving.

Turner lifts the flask to take another swig, but Luke rips the flask away and then tosses it out the driver's side window.

"Fuck all!" Turner goes, staring daggers.

They keep driving.

They emerge on to Highway 25 heading north up the coast of the seemingly black waving water of Lake Huron. The two are like silent as they cruise up the lakeside, a distant lighthouse the only sign of life other than Turner's headlights. Some clouds shift and crawl away from the moon like some massive and airy dying animal glowing all eerie above the lake and everything—the water, the moon, the lighthouse—suddenly looks like a *Magic of Michigan* postcard.

Turner lights up yet another cigarette. He stares out the window. "Kinda looks cool..."

Luke says nothing, writes nothing.

Eventually, Luke turns off High 25 and hauls down a dark wooded road for what seems to Turner at least another half hour. The trees get thicker. Turner knows they're getting closer, nearly there. His palms start to sweat, his fingers twitch. He looks over at Luke again and sees that the big guy doesn't even seem nervous at all. Just serious.

They take a left down another deserted road and Turner started to imagine how it will be. He tries to get his nerve up. Imagines Luke's skull caving in. He plays the deathblow in his head over and over again, sees it in different camera angles, plays it back in slow-mo. He wonders what kind of stuff will come out. I mean, blood of course—but what else? Chunks of brain? Turner imagines that there might be some milk-filmy stuff that could ooze out, but he's not sure—he's never seen this kind of stuff for real of course. Turner suddenly shudders and fills the car with a fume of alcohol. He puts his ear buds in, scrolls his playlist and pushes ***PLAY***. The music comes blasting in like holocaustic gunfire juicing Turner up, feeding the hate. Closing his eyes, he tries to concentrate on Dylan. *This is all just practice for fucking Dylan, man.* He cranks the volume up, invoking his nastier demons. He conjures all the vicarious violence he's ever seen with the speed of a racing digital stream letting the waves crash into him—he joins its flow, drowning willingly in the carnal images—and then unbelievably, discovering he's got gills and cannot drown. Eighteen years of images sear through his brain from all the movies and vids he's ever gorged gore on. Until tonight there's always there's been screens separating him from the blood spatter—until tonight he's always been trapped outside the terror—but no more, *not tonight, motherfuckers!* I'm gonna split that screen to oblivion with a nuke-powered hatchet stroke, he thinks. *Dylan and his ass-puppets...* Turner grins with rancid breath, creating his greatest hits list—*Kirk Wellington, Nelson Tremblehall, that Brian Wilhelm fucker, Peter Calloway, Cunter* (if he could ever find the bastard), *maybe even fucking Officer Truman or Dre while I'm fucking at it...* on and on it goes, he sees the prep/jock faces of the damned, the asswipe druggies and dealers from his dad's biz, all names destined for body-bags and coroner-tied toe tags.

The car stops. Turner opens his eyes and presses ***PAUSE***.

They're here. The spot.

"This is a pretty creepy looking place, man," Turner goes and looks out over Harper Lake. I guess mostly fishermen and canoe-ers used the lake, off deep into the Harper Woods, way back in the day. But apparently over the years though the place hadn't been too well kept. Turner remembers trash scattered the shoreline and people had dumped big stuff like ratty carpets and old refrigerators in the woods close to the water. Somebody even abandoned a crap pickup out there that was now rusting in the weeds.

Luke and Turner start hauling out their gear—and Turner spies the old rowboat Luke promised would be out there sitting right where the shore meets the water. It hits him then—this is for *real*.

"Hey—yo," Turner calls out. "You sure you still want to do this, man?"

But Luke just keeps setting up, nearly done, probably didn't even know Turner was speaking to him.

"Fuck..." Turner goes. "This is all just so fucking diseased, fucking asshole doesn't even care." Turner looks up but there's no moon to be seen anymore—the tree cover's too high and thick and there's no sound but the weak waves that barely splash on the shore as the smell of a bloated fish wafts in from the small lake.

No one to see, no one to know, Turner thinks.

Finally, everything seen to, Luke turns and hands Turner the hatchet and note wrapped around the handle. Turner takes the hatchet and clicks his flashlight on so he can see Luke's final words.

Jason,

I give you the power of this moment. My life is yours to take should you want to take it. I have no regrets. No bad feelings. Dig deep now. One way or the other it's my hope that tonight will give you a glimpse of what you are truly capable of.

P.S. Remember to burn this note with your clothes.

Turner looks up from the note and Luke nods to him, as if to endorse what he's written or something. Then, Luke turns away from Turner and the car's headlights, faces the dark lake, falls to his knees on the tarp and closes his eyes, ready for his deathblow.

Turner grips the hatchet. He looks over and sees the chains, the cinderblocks, the rowboat. He breathes deep—the power of death in his hand. *This is it. The point of no fucking return, man. All right man, fucking do it. I mean, there he is just waiting for it,* he tells himself. Turner stares wide-eyed at his willing victim kneeling before the dead pool, its filthy water spawning stink. *Come on. Focus. Split this fucker open now. It's his choice, man! The kid wants to die. This is like doing him a fucking favor. Imagine it's Dylan's head, man. No hesitation, no mercy for that fucker! Come on, man! You can't fucking hesitate like a pussy if it's Dylan, man! So do it now! Remember this kid wants to die—it's like suicide, he'd probably do it himself at home if you didn't do it for him now. The deaf kid's crazy and wants to commit suicide—he's just using you as the weapon, man. So do him now, man. Remember it's suicide, man, just like Rozz. Just like Rozz.*

Gripping the hatchet all white-knuckled behind Luke's head, Turner shouts out in a cloud of cold breath.

"Fuck! Fuck it to hell! See Dylan, man!"

Luke remains kneeling, head bowed as if in some long prayer.

"See Dylan, damn it!" Turner's screaming now, ranting at the back of Luke's head. "This is fucking your fault, man! You lied, you deaf shit! 'This is all about Dylan' you scribbled in your little shit-ass pad. Fucking liar! There aint no Dylan now. Not when it really counts!" Turner looks up to the black sky. "See Dylan, damn you."

But there, in his mind's eye, there is no Dylan. Instead, against his will, totally uninvited at this moment, is Rozzy. Just Rozzy. Rosalind Howard. All in slow-mo, looking at him with that look of hers—that look he knows was just for him—and the weight of that look along with the reality that she's gone, long gone—and not the broken skull of one crazy deaf kid or the broken skulls of a million Dylan Sorensen's would ever bring her back—instantly brings Turner to his knees.

Dazed and crazy-eyed, he's dumb silent for a moment. And then the tears begin to come. Big tears like drops from a fireman's hose. The tears turn into uncontrollable sobs, total gushing really, as Turner's heart seems to break apart and everything that was in there just starts to run out of him and thicken in the mud beneath his knees. He finally drops the hatchet altogether and falls further down, both hands over his face wallowing into the shore. Pile driving his screams into the mud, he writhes around like an outcast worm that can't seem to push a hole into the earth. Dirt and mud begin to cake and cover his hands, wedge between his fingernails, smear his face and hair.

The total groveling is only interrupted when Turner occasionally rises to his knees for another chorus of open yelling to the sky, the universe, to the black beyond, or God maybe, or whatever. He collapses again and lets the doom of it in—large drunken sobs and convulsions, his face still in hands he grinds into the dirt.

Finally, Turner passes out right there on the shore. Eventually Luke wakes him with a tug on the shoulder. All groggy and hazy, Turner looks around and realizes that the engine's running and Luke's put everything away and is shining a flashlight on a note right in front of his face.

Come on, man. I'll drive you home.

Turner squints at the note for a bit and bobs his head, *OK*. Luke pulls him up and they tear out away from Harper Lake towards home.

Turner rests his head on the passenger window and sleeps the whole way back.

Once they're pulling into Turner's driveway, Luke wakes him. They get out of the car and Luke throws Jason the keys.

Turner blinks, all puzzled. "You know where I live?"

Luke nods.

Turner starts walking to his house but turns. "Hey wait, man, how you gonna get home?"

Luke takes two fingers and walks them on his other palm.

"Aint that a long way back to your neighborhood? Aw hell, wait—your car's all the fuck back at Walmart. I mean, you aint gonna walk all the way back there are you?"

Luke raises his eyebrows and kind of shrugs.

"You know," Turner goes and hacks out a cough, "You're one crazy, deaf sonofabitch."

Luke smiles and scribbles a note.

See you Monday, man.

Turner just bursts a half-assed snicker as Luke walks down the street. He holds the note up above his head like it's a white flag or something and goes, "Yeah, Monday, man. *Whatever*... fuck." Then he staggers into his lightless house and collapses on his bed as used up and dead as a frozen lab room cadaver.

18

Coach Striden

So. It's Monday morning after homecoming and Luke Forrester comes down to see me in the gym before school. I look up from collecting the flag football gear for the day and go, 'Good morning Luke,' and he writes back, *Good morning, Coach. Need to talk to you about something*. And of course, I go, 'Well, what's going on? What is it?' And that's when he springs it on me. He writes that he made this bad decision on Friday night. Says he broke the athletic code.

So, there I am reading and re-reading it—completely baffled. I shake my head, totally stupefied, for what probably seemed like minutes before finally saying, 'What?'

Luke shrugs and gives me this kind of shit-eating grin and looks down at his note as if to say, *Hey, it's all there...*

"Luke, I don't understand. Were you busted for underage by the cops this weekend and you're just telling me now before I find out from them or the administration?"

But he just shakes his head and writes that he was wrong and wanted to take ownership of it. He says he was aware he was going to be suspended for some important games and that he was sorry about that.

I couldn't have been more blindsided than if Luke had pelted me in the head with a whiffle ball bat. I mean it made no sense to me at all. It wasn't just the inconceivable fact that a teenager was willingly turning himself in purely on principle, but that it was Luke—Luke-Completely-Focused-On-Soccer—Forrester here that had gone and jeopardized his senior season and possibly landing a Division One scholarship by drinking. We were in crazy territory here.

"All right, all right, all right," I say. "Let's go. We need to go talk with Mr. Steinholtz for a minute and get this processed."

Jerry Steinholtz is our school's athletic director, and we leave the gym and cross the hall over to his office. Luke and I both sit down at his desk, and I show Jerry Luke's note and watch the stupefied look that I had been sporting five minutes ago fall on him.

After staring at the note for a while, Jerry finally looks up to us and says, "Is this a joke or something?"

Luke and I shake our heads.

"Luke, son, did you get busted by the cops or something?" Jerry asks.

Luke shakes his head again.

Jerry shifts in his chair. "Uh, is your dad putting you up to this? Did he catch you in his liquor cabinet or something and now he's the one making you come forward? Is that it?"

Another headshake.

"So—you're just turning yourself in because you feel bad about breaking the code?"

Luke shrugs, then nods.

Jerry's silent. I sit there motionless. And then I start thinking, well, there goes the season… or at least the conference championship. Maybe even our shot at State. And the prospect of pulling off an undefeated season? Gone. Totally and completely. All because of what? This kid and his weird sense of conscience that's seemed to have kicked in out of nowhere? Is he doing this just to piss me off? Did I do something to make him mad? Is he doing this to get back at someone on the team? Really, what's been the deal with Luke lately anyway? I thought back to all his erratic behavior during the season. For instance, like him finally reaching out to his teammates and writing all those notes, even smiling and joking around for the first time in his high school career. And then I thought of our last game—and how he played the worst game I'd ever seen him play. Not only that, it seemed he was back to his old pissed off looking and withdrawn self. And now *this*. Suspended for drinking before the Ann Arbor game, our bitter conference rival. No way, I thought. There's just no way we can beat Ann Arbor without Luke Forrester. I just couldn't see it—and there I was, sitting there in Steinholtz's office getting pissed and at the same time feeling ashamed of myself for being so pissed, so selfish, so blatantly concerned with winning.

I couldn't help myself.

I couldn't stand myself.

Not my best moment to say the least.

"Well, OK," Jerry goes. "You'll be suspended from all competitions for the next two weeks. So, that's how many games?"

"Two," I answer. "He'll miss Ann Arbor Huron and Harper Hills."

"All right then, two games. After that you'll be eligible to play. Now, I've got to write up all the paperwork, let administration know—of course I'll have to call your dad—and then this will all be a done deal," Jerry goes, sitting back in his chair and Luke and I get up from our seats.

Jerry says to Luke, "Thanks for your honesty, son. A conscience like that is a rare gift. You keep close to it. Liz, can I have a quick word?"

"Sure," I say and turn to Luke. "We'll talk more about this after practice tonight, OK?"

Luke looks at me—a look that I'd like to think meant *I'm sorry* and goes out of the room.

Jerry sighs and holds up his hands. "All right now. So, what the hell was that all about?"

"No idea," I go. "The kid's always been a bit of a mystery—even to me. But it's a hell of a time for him to find a conscience. Frankly, I don't think we have a chance against Ann Arbor this week without him."

19

Before the first week after Homecoming senior year, Luke Forrester usually ate his lunch outside near the loading docks behind the school if the weather was nice. Sometimes, he'd drive off campus and pick something up at a fast-food place or eat in his car while he drove around for thirty minutes. But that Monday after Homecoming here's Luke, brown bagging it and walking through the crowded cafeteria and taking a place at a lonely table where Jason Turner and Toe-Faux sit looking all contemptuous and pissed at everybody.

"Whoa, back it the fuck up a sec—what's all this?" Turner goes. "What? Are we fucking friends now?"

Luke scribbles, *Yeah, pretty much.*

Turner laughs. "Unbelievable."

Toe-Faux gathers his stuff. "Hey bruh, I gotta jet to gym class. But I'll catch you later, man."

"Yeah. Later Toe," Turner goes, but keeps staring at Luke.

With a mouthful of turkey sandwich, Luke waves a grand *adios* to Toe. Toe grins and goes, "Yeah. Uh, later *Luke*."

"So friends, huh?" Turner goes. "Just like that? Saturday night's all done and why the hell not be buddies now?"

Luke keeps chewing. Nods back to Turner.

"No way, man. Not a fucking chance," Turner goes. "That's just not happening."

Luke just laughs, puts down his sandwich and writes,

Hey—you might as well just get used to it. I'm not going away now. Like it or not we're gonna start hanging out.

"Oh yeah?" Turner goes. "Well, let me tell you, dude. You got a fucked-up way of making friends, man."

Luke shrugs.

"You are something else, man. Balls beyond belief if you ask me. Look though, man. No matter what you got planned, or you think is going to come of you and me hanging out—I gotta tell you, I'm not talking about Saturday night. OK? I don't want to talk about it—I don't even want to fucking think about it right now, OK? Not a word about it—got it?"

Luke writes,

That's fine with me, Jason. We can talk about it whenever you want—or never—it's up to you.

Turner sits back. Luke finishes his sandwich, swigs some water, opens a bag of pretzels and nods for Turner to take some. For a second or two Turner just sits there considering the bag… then dips in and grabs a few.

"Thanks, man." Turner goes and they both start munching away.

They stay quiet like that for a while, eating pretzels and finishing their lunch like this kind of thing happens every day while a few of us at nearby tables notice this odd pairing that we don't quite know what to do with. I mean, weren't these two like openly fighting in the hallways a couple weeks ago? But none of us are too outspoken when it comes to awkward things like this—so we don't say anything to them at all—and we try not to stare too much.

Luke finishes his lunch, gathers his trash and stands up ready to go, but jots Jason a note before he leaves.

See you around.

Turner looks up. "Do I got a choice?"

Luke just smiles and walks off. But before Luke can leave the cafeteria area, he's totally accosted by an obviously pissed-off Erik Volgstaad who drags Luke by the T-shirt into the commons.

"What the hell, Forrester?" Volgstaad goes. "What's this crap I'm hearing that you turned yourself in for partying this weekend for chrissakes? You trying to sabotage the team or what? You tell them it was my party? I mean, what's the deal? You ticked at me for some reason? This got something to do with why you put a freaking crater in my parent's wall?"

Luke writes,

I'm just trying to do this the right way.

"What's that supposed to mean?" Erik goes. "What do you mean, *the right way*?

Do you know what 'honor' is?

"What? Like a dictionary definition?" Erik goes. "Yeah. Honor is...you know, like honor. Like 'I'm a man of honor.' Or the when they say the fricking Marines have honor. Like to be good or whatever. Who cares?"

Luke flips to another page and jots.

I know. That's it. Nobody cares. Hell, I didn't even care really until a few weeks ago. But I woke up. I totally woke up, Erik. And so should you. The whole team should.

"What? Why?" Erik goes. "Wake up and get some honor? I'm not getting this, bro. Why the hell do we need some freaking honor?"

Luke grins, writes,

It'll make us a better team.

"Yeah. OK. That's great, Luke," Erik goes and pulls Luke by the shirt out the front doors into the school's front courtyard. "How's that going help us win more soccer games, huh?"

With honor our victories will mean more. If we lose, we'll be able to come back from them quicker, fiercer. We'll unite better as a team. We'll just flat out play harder for each other. Make us fearless and more fearsome. It'll make us stronger, Erik, in every possible way.

"OK. Fine. Let's pretend for a sec that I don't think what you're saying is total bullshit. And let's say we all start playing with honor and we get so much honor we got honor coming out our asses. What does this got to do with you turning yourself in for drinking? How is it honorable if what you're doing totally hurts the team? I mean christ, Luke—we got Ann Arbor this week!"

Turning myself in is just a start. A start at getting it all back. See, we all lost something somewhere over the years by partying and tons of other stuff that was against the spirit of the team or the athletic code we signed and gave our word to uphold.

"Dude, you sound like a freaking teacher or a brown-nosing honors student. So, what are you saying? That you're turning yourself in to get our *honor* back? Is that it?"

No. I turned myself in to get <u>my</u> honor back. The only way the team can get its honor back is if the <u>team</u> turns itself in.

Erik takes a step back as if Luke's just burped up a soggy gym sock. "The hell you talking about? You want *us* all to turn ourselves in? Are you freaking out of your mind? No way! Not a chance in hell, Forrester. Yeah, sure—over the years I'm sure just about all of us have probably broke code. Some of us more than others. But hell if we're just going to turn ourselves in. I mean that's what you want right? For all of us to just walk right in to Principal Carter's office and just turn ourselves in all so we can get our *honor* back?"

Yeah. Pretty much.

Erik shakes his head. "You need to have your head examined because this is nuts. I mean, come on. Nobody takes this code crap seriously. Just because you sign it doesn't mean anything. Seriously, kids sign it because they want to play a sport or whatever and that's it."

No, Erik. What you're saying is that <u>your</u> <u>word</u> doesn't mean anything. Come on yourself, 'bruh.' When we all sign a pledge knowing full well we have no intention of following it, it's not the oath that's meaningless—it's our word that's meaningless.

"Fuck you, Luke. This is the real world. And what you're asking is bullshit. You need to get your head out of your ass before you do anymore damage to our senior season. We're so close—damn it. So close," Erik goes and then storms back through Hemingway's front doors.

20

The thing about drama is it gets into the air. You can smell it way before a word of it is spoken, you know? I know there's a lot of people out there that just assume getting all dramacidal is a girl thing. And no doubt a gaggle of teenage girls do drama as good as anybody. But that doesn't mean a gang of guys can't do drama. Oh, believe me they can, y'all. They just do it different than girls—but make no mistake, they do it.

So that afternoon Coach Striden could smell it on her team as they came filing in for soccer practice. She was pretty sure some of them were aware of Luke's true confession earlier that morning—but she could tell just by looking at them not all of them did. Which all meant this whole situation with Luke's suspension was about to powder-keg and she was mentally preparing to defuse the nuke as best she could.

Luke was one of the last to arrive. And right away Ryan Leone and Erik Volgstaad lunge up from the patch of grass where the rest of the guys were busy putting on their socks and shin guards to rush Luke at the gate.

"Luke," Ryan says, "Volgs told me why you turned yourself in and what you want us all to do. And I'm on your side. I think we should do it."

Luke flips open the evergreen pad.

Great. We're going to need a team meeting. Just the players. OK?

"All right, I'll go tell Coach and get it all set up. Hang tight," Ryan goes and runs off in the direction of Coach Striden.

Erik and Luke look at each other.

"Look, I still think this is nuts. But Leone went ape shit for your idea when I told him. Apparently, you're not the only one who thinks we lost ourselves somewhere along the way."

Luke writes,

So, does this mean you're in?

"Oh, hell no," Erik says. "Not by a long shot. But I'll wait and see what the rest of the team thinks."

After they are all dressed out, Coach Striden dismisses the JV to their field, while she calls the Varsity squad to gather up. "OK, guys. Listen up. We've had some drama today. And believe me, playing on girls' teams all of my life, I know that if handled the wrong way, drama can kill a team like cancer. I've seen drama between players totally derail an entire season. It doesn't matter how much talent we have. You guys are the most talented crew I've ever coached. But if we don't put the drama beast down and realize that we need to play for *each other*—more than victory, more than personal glory, more than anything else—if we don't realize this, we could go right down in flames.

"So, I'm going to step back and let you iron out whatever it is you need to iron out. Your captains will lead you to the team room to talk. And when you're done in there let me know what's going on so we can get practicing. We got Ann Arbor this week boys and you know what that means."

Ryan and Erik lead everybody into the team room at the end of the soccer stadium and close the door.

"You want me to explain, or do you?" Ryan asks Erik once everybody's all seated on the team room benches.

"No, you go ahead. It's all you," Erik goes.

"OK. Here's the deal," Ryan stands up straighter, raises his voice just a little bit. "We all pretty much broke code by holding the *Meet the Players* party last Friday even though none of us got busted. Well, this morning Luke turned himself in for drinking at the party."

Immediately the place erupts in an uproar of *'What?' 'Why?' 'Narc-ed?'*

"Whoa. Wait, guys." Erik raises his hand. "Listen to the rest of it. Wait till you hear what else he and Luke have to say. You think you're shitting a brick now—"

Ryan glares at Erik a sec, and then continues. "Look, Luke did this because he thinks we've lost ourselves a little bit as a team. That we've lost our *honor*. So... what Luke thinks we should—I mean—Luke thinks we will actually become stronger as a team if we turn ourselves in too."

Again, a total chorus of *'No way!' 'Is he nuts?'* and *'Screw that'* from the rest of the team until finally Patrick Durning booms, "What? All of us?"

Everybody shuts up a sec and looks to Ryan and Luke sitting next to him. Luke kind of grins and then nods to Patrick. And then Ryan goes, "Yeah. All of us."

Trevor Moorehouse stands up and stares down at Luke. "Not a fucking chance, Forrester. No way."

Pauly Thompson chimes in, "Yeah, hey, come on. I haven't even had a drop of alcohol like ever."

"Yeah, but you were still *at* the party. That's against code too," Ryan goes.

"Who the hell cares if I was there?" Pauly goes back. "Point is I don't drink."

Troy Jensen taps Pauly on the shoulder. "So, what if you don't drink, you've still broken code before. Remember a couple weeks ago we were in Walmart, and you lifted that pack of batteries?"

Pauly scoffs. "*What?* Are you serious? Come on, everybody knows it's not stealing if you steal from Walmart. Besides, it was just freaking batteries, man."

"Pauly, that kind of attitude is like exactly what we're talking about here," Ryan says.

"Whoa—just back up a sec here," Linus goes and stands up next to Moorehouse.

Teege stands up all fired up too. "Can somebody just explain again to me why we would ever want to turn ourselves in and how that would make us a better team? Because the way I see it, we'd only be getting in a lot of trouble, losing two big soccer games, and be the biggest joke in school."

Ryan's about to respond when Erik reaches over and taps his arm. "No, hang on Ry, I got this one. Look it's real simple, Teege. See, Luke and Ryan here have really thought this out here. See, what we do is turn ourselves in *and then* we lose two games *and then* after that we get like a total *Summer's Eve* fresh start."

"The hell's a *Summer's Eve* fresh start?" Patrick goes.

"*Summer's Eve*. It's a douche. Anyway, we—"

"What's a douche?" Pauly goes.

"You kidding me?" Erik goes. "You're a freaking douche. Look, these two want us to always tell the truth, not play selfish, and start going to church on Sunday. I mean, doesn't that pretty much sum it up guys?"

"Quit being such an ass," Ryan goes.

Luke keeps grinning like Erik's explanation was good enough more or less.

"Oh, I'm an ass, huh?" Erik fires back.

"Hey, you've been acting like one for a while now. Seriously, I've never seen you act more like a drunken ass than at the party last Friday," Ryan goes and steps closer to Erik.

"Oh really? And since when did you get all high and mighty, Ry? It's not like you haven't been drunk before. You always were—"

"I know I have. That's part of the reason I'm up for turning myself in. I want to make it right. I'm with Luke. We've lost something."

"Look, guys," Trevor pipes in again. "Nothing we do now is going to change anything you did in the past. That's stupid. Ryan—uh, Luke—if you guys feel bad about drinking and breaking code, then don't break it again. But not all of us feel bad about it. So let those of us who want to party or whatever just do what we do—and we won't tempt you guys to break code or talk bad about you behind your back. Does that sound OK?"

T.J. and Linus quickly second Moorehouse. Linus adds, "Yeah. I mean as long as we don't get caught, why would anyone else even care? Seriously, my parents know I party. They even brag all the time about how they did when they were our age. Really—this shit's no big deal, guys."

"This isn't really about what's right and wrong about drinking. It's about our promise to follow the rules while we're on this team," Ryan goes.

"They're not *my* rules. They're school rules and school rules are bullshit," Moorehouse goes back.

"No kidding," Teege says getting Moorehouse's back. "Look this is totally gay that we're debating this at all."

"Don't say gay," Erik goes.

"What?" Teege goes back.

"Say this is bullshit, or horseshit, or any animal shit you want, but don't say—"

"Whatever," Teege goes.

The team center blows up again in hailstorm of raised voices and pointing fingers. While some bicker, some sit in nervous anticipation, wondering where this is going, all while Luke fishes out his pen and pad. He writes something and gives it to Ryan.

Read this to Trevor:
How important is giving your word to you?

Ryan reads it to Trevor, and everybody quiets down a bit.

"I don't know…" Trevor looks back and forth from Ryan to Luke, not really sure which one to address. "None of this keeping-your-word-shit counts right now anyway. We're still teenagers for chrissakes."

Luke tears off another note for Ryan to read to Trevor.

What about in a couple of years?

Trevor starts laughing. "What? Man, in a couple of years my drunk ass will be living it up in college and splitting as much wet snatch as possible."

Ryan reads more of Luke's words.

That's sounds great, Trevor. But what about after that?

"What do you mean?" Trevor asks. "I'll go on with my life. I'll do whatever I want. Look, this is so stupid we're even talking about this. Come on, let's go tell coach we're ready for practice."

Ryan immediately objects and suddenly the yelling starts again while Luke writes on his pad again. He finishes a couple of small pages and bangs his soccer cleat against the bench. Hard. Everybody shuts up. Luke motions for freaking everyone to sit down with his eyes and they all do except Trevor and Ryan. He hands the written pages to Ryan to read and begins writing more. Ryan clears his throat and then begins to read.

What then?

Do you all just expect to wake up one fine morning and suddenly be the man you've always thought you would be? Seriously. Imagine for a second. Imagine waking up one morning and suddenly you're thirty-five. You're at the peak of your power. You're a total man. Reliant on no one. Whoever you were becoming until now—you're it. When you get there, to that point—who do you imagine you'll be?

Think back to when you were a kid and played make-believe. Who did you pretend to be? What superhero did you love? What did you want to be like when you were finally BIG? Did you ever want to be the Good Guy? I know I did. I still do—I had just forgotten.

Ryan looks up from Luke's notes a moment. The whole team stares back at him. Luke writes feverishly at his side. Ryan continues.

So how do we get it back? Freaking magic? I mean are we gonna just wake up some morning after spending our lives doing whatever the hell we want and getting away with whatever the hell we can and then suddenly turn into the men we'd always hoped we'd be? Is it that easy? Can you go from a selfish bastard prick to your best self as fast as a flick of a flashlight?

<u>We can't continue to think that way</u>. Because if we keep thinking that, we're gonna wake up all right. We're gonna wake up and be the thirty-five-year-old version of the clueless assholes we were in high school—or worse—we'll realize we're total selfish pricks pretending to be what we once hoped we'd become. And you know what then? We'll be OK with that—because we'll have accepted being ghosts of our former potential.

I'll be real honest. Until this fall, I didn't care about any of you. I haven't for years. I cared about myself and winning. I cared about landing my D1 scholarship. I cared about putting ink on the stat page and making the All-State team. I really wanted to obliterate the school's scoring record—and if that meant not passing the ball off to you, Volgs, or you, Trevor, then I was fine with that. All you guys were means to an end for me. I saw you all as my supporting cast. That's all.

Ryan finishes reading the page and Luke almost instantaneously rips another off his pad and hands it to Ryan. As Ryan lifts the next page to continue reading, the room of guys is totally silent except for Luke's violent scribbling.

So Yeah... Maybe I didn't technically break code ever until Friday night. But I've been breaking a more sacred code in my heart against all you guys for the last three years—maybe even longer.

I am so sorry.

I've been so selfish. I've been closed off to all of you when I should've been open. I haven't been a teammate. I've been a traitor.

But I don't want to be like that anymore. I can't be like that anymore. So, I've been trying to change. Maybe some of you have noticed.

Half the team lets out a snicker over that. "Yeah, Luke. We kinda picked up on some changes," Troy Jensen goes.

A lot of guys laugh more and nod heads in agreement. Patrick Durning goes, "Dude, you've been acting like you've been totally off your meds. I mean, for years you never tried to communicate with us at all—and this year you're freaking writing us *knock, knock* jokes on that pad of yours."

Luke smiles. Then shrugs. He sets back to writing. Ryan continues reading:

Well, I'll tell you all— the more I try to change—the better I feel. Lately when I play with you guys, you know what I feel like? I feel like I did when most of us were all twelve years old playing club soccer together. Remember that summer we won that shootout at that tournament in Blaine, Minnesota? We played that team from Dallas and they were freaking good. Should've beat the crap out of us. They had that forward that's up on the U 18 U.S. team now. Remember? But we played like little lions. They scored first—but we didn't give up. With two minutes left Erik got that goal and they couldn't believe it. And in the penalty kicks Patrick made those two unbelievable saves. I'm getting goose bumps just writing this. And then we all dog piled Troy when he nailed the winning penalty kick. Remember?

All the senior guys that were on that club team all burst into reminiscence.

"Yeah, that ruled," Matt Glendening goes.

"That shot was so lucky, Jensen," Patrick goes.

"Up yours," Troy goes back to Patrick, "That was the shot of my life, man."

"I remember hearing about that game," Teege chimes in.

"It was classic, bruh," Trevor says.

Ryan tries to regain order. "Guys—shut up. Come on, Luke's not done. I got like another two pages yet."

"OK, then everybody shut it—" Erik goes. "Let Ryan finish. Or Luke, or whatever..."

Remember that? I felt like we were gods back then. Like anything was possible. Like everything was so pure. It was the time of my life, right when I needed it most after my mom and sister died. And I suspect it was the time of some of your lives too.

But somehow, somewhere over the years, we've lost something. I hope you all can sense that too. We lived and died for each other back then. I felt like you were my true brothers. And now... now that we're all big stuff in high school, I think we've lost some of that. But here's the thing:

We can get it back.

I want to be gods again with you.

I want to ROAR again with you like when we were twelve. For you younger guys, I want to roar with you for the first time now. Because that's the right way. This is what I'm talking about when I talk about honor. And we can get it back, boys. Get it back right. Back before the beers. Before the bullshit. Before we became cool-crazed, selfish jackasses.

By turning ourselves in as a team, we make a stand as a team. We get a clean slate as a team. A fresh start where anything is possible.

So what do you think?

Are you with me?

Ryan finishes and looks up the team. For a second there's no response from any of them, although clearly by the looks of their faces, some of them have been stirred.

"No one's ever done anything like this before," Ryan goes. "And I for one, think we should do it. We should turn ourselves in and start new again."

"*Geesh*— Troy Jensen goes. "It's a bold move to be sure, fellas. It's gonna take a set of balls on our part."

"Jupiter-sized," Patrick goes.

"I still say no way," Trevor goes. "I mean I can't believe I'm hearing this. It's like fucking suicide. I'm not admitting to anything. Come on Linus, Teege—for chissakes, Erik—where's my back-up here?"

"This is bullshit. I'm with you, Trev. I'll never turn myself in," Linus goes.

Teege pipes up too. "No kidding. Come on guys, this is *baked*. Let's quit wasting time listening to this crap and practice."

But Erik is still silent. Hesitating. Everybody's looking to him; finally, he asks, "Will we really be gods again?"

Luke writes a quick answer. Ryan reads,

Yes.

But before you can be a god,
you gotta die to yourself.

"Sounds painful," Glendening goes.

Anything really worth having always is...

"Then I'm in," Patrick Durning goes with his voice all booming and deep.

"*What*?" Trevor Moorehouse can't believe it.

Patrick stands up and goes, "You guys all know I don't mind having an excuse to drink. Hell, I've been partying hard since the eighth grade. Most of you guys have probably seen me with my buds *Jose*, *Jacky D*, and *the Captain*. And really, I don't still see much wrong with drinking in and of itself. But still, I think what Luke and Ryan are getting at is bigger than drinking. I never thought of this honor stuff much until now—but I have to say what Forrester said about how we were and how we are is starting to sink deep with me, lads. I'd like to be the kind of guy that doesn't bullshit anybody—but I can't be that, I guess, if I'm two-faced about the code just so I can get shit-faced and sneak away and play soccer too. I got to stop bullshitting myself first. I suppose in the back of my mind, I kind of knew it was pussy trying to get away with it—so it makes a lot of sense when it's kind of said out loud—or read out loud, or whatever. Anyway, if it comes to a choice of playing soccer or drinking while I'm in high school—I choose soccer. And turning ourselves in is the balls-*iest* thing I ever heard of."

Now you could see guys really nodding in agreement. The whole vibe in the room suddenly glowed different.

"Should we put it to a vote?" Ryan goes.

"Don't you guys understand? We'll forfeit the games with Ann Arbor and Afton Hills if you guys turn yourselves in!" Moorehouse goes.

"Yeah—that'll suck losing those games, but we got some season left to make up for it," Ryan goes.

"I'm not turning myself in no matter how your bullshit vote turns out,"

Moorehouse says and takes a ballot.

"Yeah. Me neither," Teege says too.

Ryan ignores them and announces, "just write down a *yes* for turning ourselves in or a *no* for not. Then fold them and pass them back up."

The team votes. They turn in their folded pages in. Luke counts them and marks down the tally and hands it to Erik to read. Erik looks back to Luke like *why me?* and then looks up to the team and clears his voice all awkward.

"The final vote is turn ourselves in: *fifteen*. Not turn ourselves in: *three*. I guess we all got a set of Jupiter-sized balls."

Trevor stands up again. "Screw this! I am not turning myself in. You dickheads do whatever you want."

"Fine, Trev. *We'll* turn you in," Patrick says.

Trevor looks at Patrick like he can't believe what he just said. With like total bewilderment, Teege rises again beside Trevor and goes, "What? You're gonna narc us out then?"

"If that's what it takes, Teege," Erik cuts in.

Trevor turns all struck and pissed at Erik, "What the hell, Volgs? You stabbing me in the back for this bullshit?"

Everybody tenses up a bit more. They almost can't believe it—that their two star forwards are actually going head-to-head against each other.

Erik stares right back at Trevor. "You need to re-define your definition of backstabbing, Trev-O. This is what the *team* is for. I am part of the *team*. So, I go as the *team* goes. So, if you want to remain part of this *team*, you can either turn yourself in with us—or we'll turn you in ourselves. But like it or not, the *team* is going down together."

Trevor looks around the room at his teammates—trying to get a feel if this is really happening or not. He finally looks back down to Luke still sitting on the bench.

Luke gives him a huge grin and shrugs.

"Or we can say 'fuck it.' And ditch your crazy narcs," Trevor goes.

"Yeah," Erik goes. "Or I guess you can play it that way too."

Trevor slowly starts nodding. He realizes it's done. Sees that somehow, some way, that big deaf kid has brainwashed them all in a matter of minutes to do the unthinkable. "Fine, but I'm not hanging around for this."

"Yeah—me neither." Teege gets up. Linus follows him.

"I hope you guys get your asses royally kicked—you bunch of fucking narcs," Trevor goes as he, Teege, and Linus push past Ryan and Erik, out of the team room and head for the parking lot.

Outside by the training field sideline, Coach Striden absent-mindedly kicks at a bag of soccer balls, waiting. She looks up and sees Trevor Moorehouse, T.J. Brandt, and Matt Linus walking toward their cars and the rest of the team jogging double-time up to her with Luke, Ryan, and Erik in the lead.

"So's she gonna a kill us or what?" Erik mumbles as they jog.

"Probably. But hey look, Erik," goes Ryan, "thanks for staying with us. I know you and Trevor were—"

"Just shut it, dude. I'm a soccer player. I love playing this game more than anything. Besides, just because Moorehouse and I *had* been hanging out lately doesn't mean... I mean come on, Ryan. Wake up, numb nuts—*you're* still my best friend."

"*So, lads...*" Striden goes all suspicious as the team comes to a halt. She looks way over to the guys in the parking lot and then back to the team. "What's the story?"

The team kind of looks at each other and then they all look to Ryan and Erik. Ryan and Erik then look to Luke. Erik says to him, "Hey, this is your team now, man. *You* tell her."

Luke looks at Erik and Ryan and then to Coach and clicks his pen and starts to write down what indeed is *the story*.

21

I guess it's pretty safe to say that Coach Striden didn't quite realize ahead of time what kind of implications the team meeting would end up having. If she thought she was shocked earlier that morning by Luke turning himself in, then she was outright electrocuted when the rest of the team informed her they would be doing the same this afternoon.

So, the next morning Luke and the remaining fifteen Hemingway Varsity soccer players found themselves in Athletic Director Steinholz's office, who immediately marched them all, Head Coach Elizabeth Striden included, into Principal Carter's office where they all crammed in around his desk explaining that they wanted to all be put on athletic suspension for drinking.

I guess 'totally flabbergasted' doesn't really do justice in describing how Principal Carter reacted to the whole deal. I mean you really had to feel for him here. Talk about uncharted waters. Here he was looking at retirement in two years and had spent a better part of twenty years as a school administrator punishing kids for drinking, dealing with enabling parents quick to call their lawyers, interrogating guilty students to ferret out names of other guilty parties. *And Now…?* How could he not feel this was a put-on, a jibe at his expense? Who could blame him for looking around for hidden cameras to catch his punch-line reaction? The fact that he made Erik and Ryan go through the story twice, word-for-freaking-word, before he would make a comment on it really let you know just how alien he thought this all really was. And as Carter finally hears the last of it, (again,) holding one of the ends of his glasses in between his lips all like he's orally fixated, doing his best Sigmund Freud, he swivels his chair to look at Coach Striden and Jerry Stienholz who both shrug and hold out their hands like they want to wash'em in Pilate's sink.

So, Carter turns back to the fifteen of Hemmingway's finest and asks, "So is there anything else?" And that's when the team makes it very clear that they have no intention of giving the names of any other Hemingway students, were indeed sorry for breaking the code of conduct, they all accept the consequences of due process, and that they vow never to break the code ever again during their time at Hemmingway High.

"OK then…" Carter says after a moment. He instructs Athletic Director Steinholz to prepare the paperwork to suspend the remaining fourteen student athletes for the next two conference matches just like Luke.

Everybody's quiet again, and Erik, who apparently has had all the awkward silence he can take, stands up to leave.

"Sit down," Principal Carter goes. Erik sits back down.

"Boys…" Carter goes, "To be honest, I don't know yet how to take all this. You've given us all a lot of food for thought here. I can tell you on the one hand, it is incredibly disappointing to know that you all willfully broke our school district's activities code—and further, I'm sure you have knowledge of others who chose to break it as well and you refuse to bring their names into the light.

"However, that being said—I am not so out of touch, or ignorant, to realize that our code is probably broken every weekend—if not every day, by someone at this school. Therefore, the act of you all coming forward like this, in what seems in all sincerity, is an expression of accountability that is sadly rare indeed."

"Thanks, sir. We won't fail again," Ryan says.

"You're welcome," Carter goes. "But can I ask one more thing?"

"Sure—shoot," Erik says.

"Good, because forgive me, it still feels like I'm missing something here. Can I ask *why*, exactly?"

All the guys just start looking around at each other to see who's gonna be the one to answer. Eventually all eyes fall on Luke Forrester. Luke, looking as proud and satisfied as I guess a first-time father would, nods to Erik.

Erik clears his throat and goes, "Well, uh… I guess… honor, sir."

Principal Carter eyes boggle. "*Honor*?"

The team starts nodding, grinning at each other. They can't help it. They pass on gazes like torches. Erik answers, "Uh yeah. I guess, you know…we kinda want it back."

Well, it didn't take more than thirty minutes after the soccer team's "closed" meeting with Principal Carter before the chatter-fire had spread through the whole school. Through word of mouth, flurried texts, and everybody's socials—the soccer team was making serious buzz again, although this time not for being undefeated, or not for holding the sickest party of the Homecoming season, but for actually *turning* themselves in for having it. Later that night socials came alive with tons of rumors, theories, and specs about the team's motivations.

Comments and questions shot out across the student body like:

WTF???? what kind of retards host a huge kick-ass party and then totally go and turn themselves in for it?

NK!! they must still be drunk. HA!

or still cheeched out!

did they narc anybody else?

no—but I heard they made trevor morehouse, matt linus, and t.j. quit the team cause they wouldn't go along with this shit…

I heard morehouse is pissed and is looking to get some payback.

I heard they give each other blowjobs in the showers.

I heard they made a suicide pact to kill themselves at the end of the season.

no way!!

that's the word.

GTFO—that's total BS...

And so on, and so on, and so on. It was totally ridiculous. And it wasn't just the students that went crazy over the subject. Parents freaked. Groundings abounded for the boys of the Hemingway High soccer team. Patrick's dad was completely thrown and grounded Patrick not because he drank, but because he did something so stupid as to turn himself in. Patrick's dad then called the school to see if he could appeal the violation by saying his son didn't know what he was talking about and that Patrick lied about drinking just to get back at him for other family stuff. It was crazy. Of course, there was no appeal, and Patrick more or less told his dad to shove it where the sun don't shine.

One other cool thing that happened the day the team turned themselves in went down in the halls during the bustle right after school. Kids are usually slamming lockers, scrolling phones, and scrambling to get to their ride home—and it was right about then Luke, with a total Devil-may-care look all over his face, quite literally bumped into Abby Browne. They both stopped dead in a sea of swirling student traffic. They just stood there, sharing a pregnant pause. (Sorry about the pun—but it was irresistible.)

"So, I guess you and the team are having quite the day..." Abby says.

Luke flips out his pad. *Ah... Not such a big deal. You look nice.*

Truth is though, Abby looks nervous, near panicked. She looks Luke right in the eye and just blurts, "I'm pregnant."

He writes, *Whoa.*

"I'm sorry," Abby goes. "I'm so sorry, I don't know what I, why I..."

No, it's fine. Really. Relax, don't worry—it's not like I'm gonna start running around and yelling it out or anything. You and Peter then?

Abby sighs. "Uh yeah. Me and Peter, teaming up..."

Gonna be a lucky kid, Luke writes.

Abby just looks at him. Luke says nothing but smiles.

"Luke, I..."

Abby, I'm here.

Anytime you want to talk. Anything. I'll drop everything in a second if you need me.

She reads it. She nods. "Thanks," she says all awkward, yet somehow relieved. "I gotta go, but… I'll talk to you soon?"

Luke smiles, nods to her, his eyes beaming.

Abby remembers wanting to hug him in that moment—but she doesn't—she just walks away feeling warm.

22
Isaiah

It was so cool today. After school I got home and showed Dad the good grade I got on my Math homework when all of a sudden the doorbell rings. And it was Luke and two other guys with him. It was Erik and Ryan. I didn't recognize them at first because they weren't wearing their numbers. But it was them! They were dressed for practice though and Dad said they could come in. Well, Luke and Ryan and Erik said their names, and they shook hands with Dad being so sick and in a bed right there in the living room, which made me feel good.

Luke started writing on his pad and gave to my dad a note that said they wanted to come in and talk to us and apologize. Dad was kind of confused and said, "Apologize for what?" And that's when Ryan said, "We know Isaiah is a big fan of ours and comes to all the home games. Luke's told us too about how Isaiah even comes out some mornings to train with him. Well, recently most of us on the team broke our school's athletic code by hosting a party with alcohol. It was a poor choice on our parts. We weren't thinking about the consequences, or all the people we were letting down, like your son, for instance. So we'd like to say we're sorry—and we promise to be better role models for your son, Isaiah, from here on out."

Luke wrote another note saying that he hoped that my parents would still let me come to the games and workout with him in the mornings if I still wanted. At this point my mom came in too, and Dad seemed like he didn't know what to say at first—but then said that it was OK. Dad said, "Thank you, boys. And thanks for being so considerate of my son who looks up to you. I remember this kind of stuff when I was…" then he kind of trailed off but came back and said, "Thank you."

But the best part was out on the front porch before they went to practice. Luke handed me a note. Ryan said, "I'm sorry. We'll make it up to you Isaiah."

Erik just held out his fist and said, "Pound it, little man." I pounded it. And then he said, "I'm sorry. Don't do as we did."

And then they left. But I rushed up to my room, closed the door, and then flipped open Luke's note to me. He wrote all neat and clear:

We won't fail you again, Isaiah.
I promise.
You keep me on the truer path.
--Luke

ERIF AND THE AURA-MAKER

A Story by Luke Forrester

Come with me. Through and back and beyond. To a place where there was once a large mountain. And within this mountain there were many caves, but the biggest cave was at the very top of the mountain. This particular cave's entrance was so big it could be seen from below like a dark yawning mouth at the peak of the mountain's head. All that lived in the Great Mountain's valley, from every wood and mortar shed to wood-planked manor, knew this cave as the Crack.

Since long before anyone could remember a dragon named Erif lived in the airy darkness of the Crack. I don't think I'm giving anything away by telling you Erif was an evil dragon, destructive and cunning–given to flying throughout the country sides and kingdoms, laying waste to whatever was his whim. Nor do I believe I am spoiling it if I told you that long did Erif hold all the lands in terror.

Nowhere else was the terror of Erif so alive than in the village of Thorn which sat almost baby-like in its defenselessness in the valley of the Great Mountain. Thorn was a simple village of farmers and craftsmen who lived in fingers-crossed homes of clay, straw, and wood.

So now you may ask–*Why did the people of Thorn remain at the base of Erif's mountain?*

Well, because it was their home.

Point of fact, the people on the outlaying kingdoms were more at risk to receive Erif's random wrath than Thorn.

But again, you may be tempted to ask–*But why would Erif not swoop down from his mountain on high and once and for all destroy a village that presented such easy pickings?*

Good question, but tricky to answer. You see, the first thing you need to remember is that this dragon was an *evil* dragon. He was not some terrifying animal just interested only in finding food like the grizzlies that roam in the dark recesses of the woods or a shark that hunts the ocean deeps. No. This dragon could talk, reason, scheme–and therefore knew full well what was right from what was wrong. And this dragon chose to do wrong, chose to do evil—-and not only that, but also doing that evil with saliva dripping from his immense jaws.

The second thing you need to know is that long, long, ago the dragon made a deal with the village Elders of Thorn. As they cowered in the village's square outside the Great Hall one winter's night, Erif told them that he would not destroy the village but let them live in peace as long as they sent a child every year up to the Crack to be devoured as a willing sacrifice. Legend says that the Elders all shuddered at the prospect, and as they talked it over amongst themselves with their chilled words steaming above them, Erif waited in the shadows and snow at the far end of the square, blue heat huffing out of his great nostrils with each breath. Finally, the Elders came back with their terrifying answer: *yes.*

And so, that's how it came to pass that Erif let the village of Thorn go untouched year after year. But year after year, some family lost one of their young sons or daughters as a sacrifice, and each year the wails of family after family went up to the sky so that Thorn was allowed to endure.

Now, I get it— I get that it might be hard to understand why the Elders and the people of Thorn would go along and live with such conditions. But remember that Thorn was their home. For generations and generations, Thorn had been peopled by the same families—-and to just suddenly up and leave and try to re-create a new village elsewhere would take a lot of time, a lot of sweat, and lots and lots of blood. Better to find safety in a system. True, not a perfect system. But are we all not creatures of routine? Don't we all function best under a schedule? So, try not to be so hard on Thorn accepting Erif's grim offer. They were just humans acting like humans usually do. And in this regard, if I may be so bold, perhaps the people of Thorn were no different maybe than *you* or *me.*

23
Jason

Rozzy you need to help me. I can't fucking see straight. I'm fucking equalizing on Jack and coke and can barely keep it together enough to write this. I mean, I'm really, really losing it here. Fuck that, I mean I've already lost it, man. I'm the most helpless piece of shit floating around in the whole goddamn bowl.

I couldn't kill the deaf fucker. I don't really want to go into why. Just, it's that it was just so messed up, Rozz. The whole fucking scene, man. All of it was so clusterfucked. But here's the nuts of it though—just because I can't kill some deaf nut-job in fucking cold Capote don't mean I can't kill his Majesty, King Cock-Jock Dylan Sorensen, man. But that's part of it too though. What if I did kill him? I mean, where's that fucking get me? Screwed. Either I get caught by the law or blow my fucking brains out right after I kill him. Or, what if I fucking do Sorensen, get away with it, and keep living this shit-ass life like it never happened? Then how's killing some eighteen-year-old kid asshole gonna sit with me when I'm fucking fifty? Odds fucking are when I get to be some old adult-diaper-shitting fucker I'll probably have a shit-load of regret issues anyway, knowing me. So, I'm screwed big time. That's what I fucking get for my troubles. I don't know.

And to fucking make it worse, Dre pulls me aside all secret as he's leaving tonight and is all like, 'Yeah, Lil Pops, I know y'all's been crystal so far but what would you say if I could use you as a cabbie sometime?' I mean, fuck! Are you kidding? I mean, Rozz, you know the one fucking point me and the old man agree on is for me to stay fucking crystal. And I don't know why the fuck Dre's gotta all of sudden be asking me to cab for him, my big guess would be maybe Kid T's been either slipping or skimming a little, but who the fuck knows?

Point is, I wouldn't even be tempted by this shit if you were here, or if I thought I was really going to go down in a blaze of glory and fucking cap Dylan to fucking death. But shit Rozz, you're not here. And you know my ass is as broke as a joke. I know my Dad would shit a cat if I started dealing behind his back, but fuck-all I could sure use that money to split this shit-ass scene before it kills me.

I don't know. I don't really fucking know one goddamn thing about anything. And that frustrates the complete and total hell out of me! You know, Rozz! You know me! You know I don't want to be like this! You saw me, girl. You saw the real me. I just want to make you somehow proud one day about something, anything, I fucking do. It's just I feel *sooooo* shitty about what happened to you, and my part in it. You know I feel it's all my fault. I mean when you boil it down, when it's all said and done, it's all on me—because I'm the one who could've fucking stopped it. Stopped all of it. Shit! There are times when I feel I'm the biggest pussy on the planet. Rozz, I hate myself so bad sometimes. I really do feel like I should die too.

But I'm still here. I mean this is what I'm talking about, girl. What the fuck should I do? Fucking kill people in a total rage? Deal drugs to make some green and

GTFO? Or what? Kill myself? I wish you were here, Rozz. Or I could at least talk to you from across all darkness to wherever you're at. I miss you. I miss you. I miss you.

24

I have no freaking idea why I signed up Mr. Malory's *"Great Works"* Honors English class. I guess I must've thought it would look good to colleges on my transcripts. In my total naiveté, I was even kind of excited to read some of these *"Great Works,"* some of which I had heard titles of countless times brought up by smart characters in movies and TV shows I'd seen but, as for myself, had no idea what they were about. But by October, I was pretty much ready to shoot myself. I was pulling a D and it was only then that I remembered I had *never* liked reading. Seriously, I don't even think I made it through *Where the Red Fern Grows* back in seventh grade because I found coon hunting so damn boring. I found all reading in general boring. In fact, I remember thinking that's what Malory's class should really be called, *Professor Malory's voyage into the "Great Bores" of Literature*.

Not only was it the reading that was killing me though. No, at least the reading could've been ignored, not read, and then you could've avoided any lasting scars. It was Mr. Malory himself. I mean, I had heard from some of the seniors in the class ahead of me that he was a little odd, kind of a goofball, that he'd say weird-ass things in class, and was a pretty stiff grader when it came to papers—but geesh!

I mean for starters Mr. Malory was tall and lanky. Straight gray hair, with a length just flirting with being unruly, but bald on top. He wore like basically the same outfit every day, but he varied the colors and patterns a bit. Chino slacks, button up shirt with a lame-ass cardigan vest over it, reading glasses were like perpetually slinging around his neck, and for footwear...*New Balance* running shoes (I mean, WTF, right?). As far as his age, he looked like he was fit for being late forties (?) but who really knows. And I don't know for sure, and I couldn't really say why, but it looked to me that Mr. Malory ate a lot of fiber cereal and gourmet soup, and I'm pretty sure he casually smoked pot—or at least did a lot back in the day.

And it was Malory's fifth period class, the day after the soccer team turned themselves in, that a very interesting discussion took place. *I* know this because *I* was there, sitting in the fourth seat of the third row, two seats away from Erik Volgstaad.

We were still droning on through *Dracula*, which had started out pretty cool, but got real lame and boring in the middle of it, which I kinda Swiss cheese skimmed and skipped through and then was real surprised the next day when Malory would talk about all this hidden erotic sex stuff that was in the book.

Well anyway, at the start of class we were all buzzing about the soccer team and everyone in class was like totally pumping Volgstaad for details about why they would do something so stupid.

"Dude, are you guys like out to prove something, or what?" Peter Calloway goes to Erik from the back row.

"I don't know, maybe," Erik goes.

"I mean, from what I'm hearing, people be saying you guys all think you're all that and better than everybody else, or something," Dallas Douglass goes.

Erik kind of smirks at that. "Well, that's all BS—and maybe you should stop listening to what 'people' are saying, because they don't know crap."

Dallas sits back in her seat.

"Well, whatever, dude," Calloway goes, "whatever you guys are doing it for, it's totally post."

"Now, I hear *all that*," Basketball stud, Philip Lukas goes and slouches just a little farther into his seat.

Maddie O'Leary, sitting at the desk to the right of Erik, leans in and goes all quiet, "Well for what it's worth, I had a good time at your party..."

"You did?"

"Yeah, for the whole ten minutes I was there. Why didn't you come talk to me?"

"Uh, I... I was busy with the whole *Meet the Players* intro thing, you know."

"You looked like you were drunk off your ass," Maddie goes.

Erik winces. "Well, I was. And if it makes you feel any better, I'm making sure I'm getting in trouble for it."

And then—*bam!* Mr. Malory descends into the classroom like a highly caffeinated angel of death. "Hallo everybody! Are we all ready to talk about the gurgling death of Renfield and willing rape of Wilhelmina Harker? Ha *ah*!"

"Aw naw, we ready to keep talking about Erik and his crazy teammates turning theyselves in for partying last Friday night," Philip Lukas goes.

The whole class pipes down a bit to see if Malory will take the bait to engage on an off-the-topic-of *Dracula* discussion. Which was always a safe bet. Malory was almost legendary about his off-topic tangents and rants on a wide variety of subjects.

"Ah yes, yes! I heard of your little act of atonement. Well done, my boy, well done." Malory extends his hand to Erik. "So—what will Coach Striden do with Ann Arbor tonight? Is it just a straight forfeit?"

"No. The entire JV squad's been called up to play in our place. We'll all be in the stands watching them tonight for a change," Erik goes.

"Wow, they're gonna freaking get killed," Peter Calloway goes.

"No kidding," Dallas goes too, "My little brother's best friend is on the JV team and they all freaking out about it. You know, like they scared they gonna get beat 10-0, or worse."

"Well, that might happen—Ann Arbor's pretty much the schniz," Erik goes.

"Seems to be the price of honor, then, eh?" Malory says, twiddling with his reading glasses. "It's a tried and true motif that honor seldom comes without an act of sacrifice."

Peter scoffs. "Yeah, well it sounds like you're just setting up those little ninth and tenth graders to get their butts kicked to me. I mean, if you really feel you have to turn yourselves in, why not wait till after you play the biggest game of the season? I mean, *duh?* Right?"

Erik turns around and faces Peter in the back row. "Man, it turns out it just don't work that way. I wish it did—but it don't."

"*Wow*, Erik," goes Gray Cahill, valedictorian wanna-be and all-around brown-nosing know-it-all. "Grammar aside, that was the most interesting comment you've made in here all year."

"Ah, Mr. Cahill—are you being serious, or addressing yet another of your fellow students with your patented brand of sarcasm?" Malory goes.

"No, sarcasm this time," Gray goes, trying to hold his pen in the most thought-provoking posture possible. "I'm just sincerely intrigued at this whole situation. I mean, at a school where the code is blatantly ignored by just about everybody that signed the thing. And for the code to suddenly be held in such high regard from someone like Volgstaad here, well, it's kinda refreshing..."

"And kind of suspicious," Maddie goes.

Philip Lukas raises his hand. "Whoa, whoa. Yo, I just wanna say if it was ballers in this whole here situation—well, uh—a true baller wouldn't say nothing about whatever a fellow baller does in his down time. I mean, because there's like a deeper code, *see?* Like the code to respect your fellow teammates and what they want to do off the court, especially if it don't concern you, see? And pressuring guys to turn theyselves in for something they don't feel bad about ain't right, y'all. No way."

"I hear that," Peter pipes up and so do a couple other guys—even Dallas was nodding her head a little. But there's this whole bunch of us in class that don't want to seem like we have an opinion either way—like me, Greg Forsythe, and Darian Thomas. I mean, for Greg and Darian, all they wanted to do was keep their heads down, do their homework, get to college, and forget high school altogether. As for me, I just didn't know yet where I stood with this whole deal. I knew, like everybody else, that being cool meant getting away with stuff and never really breaking the teenager/adult code of silence about certain issues. But here's the soccer team, all of a sudden, throwing everything out the window. And the thing was, there was nothing special about these guys really. (Well, other than Luke—that none of us understood anyway.) In fact, some of them were bigger partiers, and in some ways, cooler than most kids at Hemingway. I mean in all seriousness, I was at the *Meet the Players* party—I saw Erik totally drunk, bragging about how his maid-service was going to make sure that his parents never found out about the whole soiree. So, to see them doing this now, gave all of us in the middle between cool and uncool, *pause*.

"Yeah, yeah, yeah," Erik goes to Peter and Philip. "I get what you're saying. In fact, I felt the exact same way four days ago. Like *exactly* the same. But something happened, you know?"

"And what was that, exactly?" Gray goes.

Erik sighs and looks to Mr. Malory. Malory just holds out his hands to Erik and goes, "The floor is yours, my boy."

Erik looks to Maddie O'Leary sitting next to him.

"What are you looking at me for?" she goes.

"OK. You know, *whatever*. Look, I know this is going to make me look as un-winner as possible, but I'm going to actually try to say something real here. You see, it's Luke. And contrary to the freaking rumors going around, he's not our cult leader. And *no*, we're not gonna all drink a bunch of cyanide Kool-Aid after graduation. But in his own messed up way, Luke's made me realize that we're not, you know... grown-ups yet. You know, that there's still stuff we got to do—that *I* gotta do, to get there. I mean look, I don't always want to be as self-conscious as I am right now. I don't want to be as shallow as I am right now. Or as distracted. Or as lazy—I mean seriously, Mr. Malory, you know I've only been reading bits and pieces of *Dracula*. It's all over my crappy quiz grades. It's not like a secret that I'm barely applying myself. And the thing is that my BS amount of effort isn't just here in class—it's like in every part of my life. And Forrester's making me realize, making the whole team realize, it just doesn't have to be that way, I guess. I want to be able to do stuff, like good stuff, you know? I want to know things, be curious about things. Be able to say stuff, like when it really matters. And the whole point of turning ourselves in—is how are we going do all that until we practice it?

"And, I guess that's pretty much it. We're just trying to do things the right way. And if that means we get ripped on the rest of the year, or called narcs, or gay—then so be it—*whatever*. But for now, just understand I'm new at all this, so—you know, lay off."

The classroom goes dead quiet.

Finally, Mr. Malory raises his eyebrows. "Well, I believe that was well said for now, Mr. Volgstaad. It appears you have silenced the throng for the moment."

Everyone starts shifting in their desks, when finally, Mr. Malory mercifully directs us to get out our copies of *Dracula* and turn to page whatever.

In all the shuffle of kids flipping pages and getting out notebooks, Maddie leans over to Erik and whispers, "Well, I'm gonna have to take back some of the things I thought about you."

"Like what?"

She grins. "Wouldn't you like to know."

Meanwhile, I'm like jotting down like a fiend on my notebook as Mr. Malory approaches my desk.

"Ah—Mr. Caxton, whatever are you writing down with such fervor? I haven't started lecturing on the day's notes yet."

"Uh—just writing down some ideas," I say all distracted. I remember wanting to get down everything Erik had said. At the time, I couldn't have told you why it was so important for me to write down all of it, or what specifically I was feeling at that moment until Mr. Malory goes, "Feeling inspired, are we?"

I finally look up at him. "Maybe..."

"Well then, good luck with that, Will," Mr. Malory goes and starts to blather on about vampires and sex.

25

Last year's Michigan State Champion, Ann Arbor Huron, currently ranked number two in the state, came strolling into Hemingway's soccer stadium with the same kind of freaking swagger I'm sure the ancient Romans were capable of when they invaded like Gaul or any other of those helpless no-name loservilles they conquered. I'm telling you—beyond cocky. I'm sure they already knew about the suspensions and that they'd be playing essentially Hemingway's JV team. Not that they needed that knowledge to be cocky. You see, we were in their regional—so in order to win conference, or go to State, you have to take out Ann Arbor first. And doing that was rare. Ann Arbor Huron was our regional's representative to the Michigan State Soccer Tournament the last seven seasons out of eight. I mean you could see it all over their faces—they were used to winning and winning big time.

The HHS student body were moths drawn to like any other flame other than the soccer match. And who could blame them? All the Varsity All-Stars were suspended. Morehouse, Linus, and T.J. had all quit. The undefeated season was over as far as everybody was concerned—and plenty thought it would be social suicide to show up to such a spectacle now. And speaking of suicide—that's totally what most of the *former* JV squad thought they were committing as they stepped onto the same field with Michigan's defending State Champion.

The opening whistle blew, the Ann Arbor offense was let loose, and it was 1-0 within two minutes. If Coach Striden was rattled, or embarrassed, it didn't show. She still marched the sideline, arms crossed sporting her usual scowl. She yelled out names and intense commands like she always did—but I'm sure she must have been sick to her stomach to see her chance to grab a Conference Championship hopelessly slip away under the futile play of her JV squad against such a powerhouse.

By the sixth minute mark, Ann Arbor's All-State striker, Alan Shuremaker, had made it 2-0 with a dipping cannonball inside the near-post goal. Immediately, Coach Striden started chewing out the defense about tightening up and not giving Shuremaker any more looks at the goal. As the Ann Arbor team sauntered back to the center circle, more than a few Hemingway JV-er's heard Shuremaker say to his teammates, "Yeah, how's that taste, bitch," as he looked over at Coach Striden.

Of course, his mates all laughed which prompted Ann Arbor mid-fielder, Connor Livingston to say, "Now she's got *kind* lips. You know, the *kind* that would feel good wrapped around my dick."

"Keep it in your jock, boys. Keep it in your jock. We got more ass-kicking to do before this half is over," Shuremaker was heard to say.

"I would've had that," goes Patrick Durning in the stands.

"Aw hell, Pat—he would've never got the shot off if I was back in sweep doing my job," Troy Jensen goes.

The entire suspended Varsity team sits together with little Isaiah Walker in the stands. Besides the Ann Arbor fans and the scattered Hemingway JV parents—there's no one else here. Compared to every other home game this season, the place is a graveyard.

As the onslaught continues on the field, Luke sees something that pleasantly surprises him. Like out of nowhere, Turner and Toe-Faux creep out from the darkness at the north end of the bleachers looking all badass in their hoodies and start to come up to where Luke and the team are sitting.

Ann Arbor gets another goal, and their team just turns back to the center without any signs of celebrating. The goal gets barely any response from the bleachers either.

"Wow, it's like fucking *Dawn of the Dead* up here," Turner goes.

"No kidding, this place looks as exciting as a morgue," Toe-Faux chimes in.

"Come back next week, man. You'll see an amazing turn around," Erik goes.

You can tell the team has no clue what to make of Jason Turner's presence. They seem to slide, all subtle, inch by inch away from Turner and the mascara wearing Toe-Faux. Ryan is not the only one that notices that Turner and Toe-Faux smell of an unholy mixture of body spray and alcohol, but he's the only one that looks Toe-Faux in the eye.

Turner uncaps a plastic water bottle and takes a huge chug. "*Waha!* That's refreshing," he goes.

"So, what's in the bottle?" Erik goes.

Turner and Toe-Faux laugh. "Want some?"

"No—I better not," Erik goes.

Turner laughs again, "Yeah, I guess you better not. I'd hate for you guys to have to narc yourselves out again."

Patrick clears his throat. "That's pretty funny, dude. So what are you guys doing here?"

Turner returns Patrick's stare, uncaps his bottle and takes another swig. (Now any sensible guy would see that Patrick Durning is nobody to mess with physically. Besides Luke, there's nobody else in school that actually looks like they were *born to kill*. But does this stop our intoxicated hero from pressing his luck? *No*.) Turner wipes his mouth with his sleeve and caps the bottle all while staring back at Patrick, his eyes full of popped blood vessels. "Just catching some soccer, man. Heard you guys were the shit lately. But from the looks of that scoreboard over there—*well...*"

Patrick's jaw sets rigid, and he starts to rise when Turner suddenly relaxes back and starts playing it off like, "Whoa, whoa, man. I'm kidding. Seriously. Shit, man. Just playing, that's all. Can you believe these guys, Faux?"

Toe-Faux kind of laughs, but you can tell this whole scene is making him feel way out of his comfort zone too.

"Look, honestly, I got to tell you guys, I admire what you're doing, seriously," Turner goes. "I mean, I thought my reputation was shitty, but you guys done replaced my ass on the bunghole rung of the HHS totem pole—I mean, I'm here to tell ya'll. Nobody hates nobody as much as a narc, man."

Patrick clenches his fist, about ready to do some violent business if you know what I mean, when Ryan grabs his wrist and whispers, "Patrick, don't. He's drunk, he doesn't know what he's saying."

Luke rips off a note, stands and hands it to Turner.

Great to see you guys here.
Hoping you'd show up here sometime.

Turner scoffs. "He's glad we're here, man," he goes to Toe-Faux. "Hey, man—don't like get too over-fucking-joyed. We're on our way to Toe's and tearing through the soccer fields is like a total short cut. We just thought we'd come up and see what's what while we were passing through."

Turner keeps talking while the three of them descend the bleachers. Luke hands Turner another note and Turner gets a little more serious suddenly and says something to Luke that nobody else can hear up in the bleachers. Then, quick as that Turner and Toe-Faux start heading back on their way.

"What an F-ing drugged up couple of boozehounds," Erik goes. "Oops, sorry Isaiah—I should have said *earmuffs* or something."

"What?" Isaiah goes.

"Forget about it, bad joke. I'm trying to watch my language better when I'm around you. My bad."

"What was with all that?" Troy Jensen says as Luke comes back up the bleachers.

Luke kind of absently shrugs and scribbles out and shows everybody,

He's a work in progress.
No need to get all pissed at him.

"Who was that? He looks kind of weird," Isaiah says as Luke sits down next to him and writes.

That's just a buddy of mine. His name's Jason.

"*He's* your friend?" Isaiah goes.

Luke chuckles.

Yeah, he's my friend.
He just doesn't know it yet.

By half time it's 6-0 in favor of Ann Arbor Huron. Ann Arbor's coach is at least subbing his superstars liberally—but still, his talent is deep; it's part of the reason that they are defending State Champions.

In the second half, the lights come on and the moon comes out. The ball seems to glide across the wet grass. Ann Arbor continues to pass unobstructed for whole minutes at a time around the Hemingway JV's. Even from the bleachers you can see Striden's jaw clinch tighter.

You can also tell the Ann Arbor players are treating the whole match as an extended joke. They keep sneering and smack talking the Hemingway players after each pass, each time they burn by a Hemingway player on the dribble. And the sexual ripping on Coach Striden is never-ending. Nobody but the players out on the field can hear it, but the young Hemingway JV's felt there was nothing they could do to stop it. You could see the helplessness all over the faces of the Hemingway players—*except one*.

The freshman had had enough. As the Ann Arbor defensive line passes the ball nonchalantly, yet accurately in the backfield—Tristan Marigan *chases*. It's futile, of course—and yet he chases them. As the Ann Arbor back four played keep-away from him, Tristan still chases the ball as if his life is forfeit and all that matters is that he dies heart bursting, chasing down that ball.

But finally, Hemingway's other forward and outside mid-fielder both decide to leave their marks and crash forward to pressure the ball and help the dying Tristan.

Suddenly, if only briefly, there's finally pressure on Ann Arbor's back line defenders. You can see all four of them recoil in shock. Like *What's this?* totally goes across their faces. Under the out-of-nowhere feverish pressure of Tristan, the center back plays a sloppy-weak ball to his right defender. Tristan goes into *shark mode* and yells "*Double!*" to his teammate on the flank.

The Hemingway mid-fielder follows the order and he and Tristan rush the ball as if they are frothing with rabies. Both of them blast into the Ann Arbor defender at the same time as the ball. Everything collides at once—ball, shins, sweat, forces of will.

The ball's suddenly loose three feet in front of Tristan rolling towards the goal. The Ann Arbor goalkeeper steps off his line for a 1v1, and that's when seventy-seven minutes of straight getting-your-assed-kicked frustration wells up in Tristan's soul as he lunges at the moment to finally strike back.

The Varsity squad all bolts up from the bleachers.

"I don't believe…" Erik mumbles.

Tristan blasts the hell out of the ball sending it into the goal's net just as the goalkeeper smashes the hell out of Tristan when they collide.

The Varsity guys howl in defiance—the first time all night that life seems to be in the sparse bleachers.

Tristan's slow to get up. His knee and shin are bruising fast—but he's all smiles as he stands.

"Who is *that* kid?" Troy goes, as all the Varsity guys are still cheering.

"Tristan something," Patrick goes.

Luke passes Erik a note,

You thinking what I'm thinking?

"Hell, yes," Erik goes.

The final score is 9-1. Mathematically speaking, it's the worst defeat in Coach Striden's career. Ann Arbor celebrates like nuts because it clinches a conference championship for them. They parade around the field with their shirts off, take photos with all of them holding up their #1 middle fingers, and chant:

WE ARE WHO?
HU-RON!

over and over again while they jump around in a banshee circle.

Coach Striden goes through the ranks of her JV team and compliments them on their grit and honor during the match. The Varsity guys too, descend down to support the JV guys who played in their stead. Tristan especially gets congratulated for his effort and goal. Erik and Luke walk up to Coach Striden and Erik says, "Coach, Luke and I have been talking and we think we've found Trevor's replacement to play forward with me."

"You have, huh?" Striden goes. And all three of them turn their gazes to the freshmen, Tristan Marigan, who's over by the bench stuffing his sweaty socks and shin guards into his bag totally unaware at that moment he's just made the permanent Varsity starting line-up.

26

Abby

It really came down to two certainties at that point:

A) I knew I did not want to have a baby in high school.

And

B) There was no way I could abort it.

Which pretty much left putting the baby up for adoption. Understand, my decision was not really based on like strong religious grounds (my family used to be Lutheran, I guess—and I believe *every* woman should call the shots when it comes to her body's health) but dealing more with the fact that I just couldn't stand an unborn fetus taking the hit for my mistake.

My mom and I visited a couple of adoption agencies just outside Detroit. They were real excited to see us and said that they would have absolutely no trouble finding a good home for my baby.

I mean, once the decision was made to have it, suddenly everything became a frantic schedule of appointments. I went to the hospital and started my checkup program and everything. It was super-scary and intense the first time I heard the baby's heartbeat *wah-wah-ing* through the sonar and really pounded home that this was *really happening*.

The toughest part about it by far though, was that if I was going to put the baby up for adoption, then that meant everyone, and I mean *everyone* in my universe would know that I had gotten pregnant. This is what Peter was dreading too and was the big reason he had been laying low in the couple weeks after I had told him that day in his car.

So, the day after I had my first sonogram, I broke the news to my friends at school with them all huddled around me near my locker.

"Shut up, are you serious?" Gabriel Altman grabbed me by the wrist. You could tell they were beyond shocked. My other two friends Jena Meyer and Amanda Segal stood there with their omigod faces.

"You're kidding, right? I mean this is like a joke, right?" Gabby still couldn't believe it. "Uh—God! You're not, Oh my god!"

Jenna said something like she had noticed I was gaining weight, but she just thought it was stress about Peter and I having problems and I was just eating my way through it or whatever.

Anyway, by telling them, I knew I wasn't *just* telling them. I was announcing it to the whole school. I knew that once Gabby knew something like this, it wouldn't be long before all of Hemingway would know. And understand, it's not that I thought at the time, that Gabby was a backstabbing bitch and would tell people about Peter and me to be mean—but she would tell others just because she couldn't help it. Gabby couldn't keep a secret to save her life. Well, and now that I think about it, neither could Jenna and Amanda either.

And just like I thought, once it was out, it didn't take long at all before everyone knew. Even though not many people talked directly to me about it, you could tell they knew. I could see it in the way they looked at me, the way a classroom, or an entire hallway would go all hushed when I entered it.

The worst part wasn't just that people knew I was pregnant with Peter Calloway's baby—but the fact that they knew for sure that I had had sex. And I don't know if it was just me being paranoid, or weird, or if there really was something to it—but I felt like people, especially boys, whenever they saw me in class, or in the halls were like imagining me naked and having sex. Like they were seeing a private porno in their head of Peter and I—or maybe just me, and it freaked me out. What made it worse is that I didn't just think this about most of the boys at school, but also some of the male teachers. I mean, my Physics teacher, Mr. Rutz, already gave me the creeps anyway—but now, it seemed ten times worse! I realized it might be unfair too, and that maybe none of these guys were even close to thinking this stuff, but the point is, I *felt* like that was what was going on, even if it wasn't rational. I felt exposed in so many ways that it was hard to even try and express it.

And it wasn't much better when I tried to imagine what the other girls were thinking of me. I mean I was driving myself crazy those first few days after I knew the secret was out. Every girl I made eye contact with, I couldn't help thinking, *Does she think I'm a slut? Is she judging me? What about her? Oh my god! And her? Do they think I'm a whore?* I was near insane.

Even when someone would say something nice, or encouraging to me, I couldn't help trying to see through it. You know, like maybe there was something artificial or negative waiting just beneath the surface. Like when Mrs. Brandt pulled me aside in AP Calc and said, "Abby, I know this has got to be a trying time for you. I want you to know that if you need anything, or want to talk, I'm always here. And by the way, I was so proud of you when I heard you're planning on giving the child up for adoption. Such a brave and noble choice, dear…"

I mean, what do you say to *that*? I guess she was sincere, but my mind-set at the time was to question everything, and like I said, I felt absolutely paranoid about everyone judging me.

Even at home I felt everything was getting all surreal. I had conversations everyday now that felt out of place, you know? Like they were conversations from out of the future from when I was married and was ready to start having babies and a family and a house with a two-car garage of my own, but I was forced to have these conversations *now,* during my senior year of high school. For instance, talking to my thirteen-year-old sister, Kate, about what it's like to have a fetus alive and growing in your uterus.

"So, what's it feel like? You know, like really?" she asks one night when we were hanging out in my room.

"Uh… you know, weird," I say to her. "The biggest thing so far is I'm like tired, hungry, and nauseous like all the time, and all three like all at the same time."

"Weird," Kate goes back.

"Yeah, like just yesterday, I was in the study lab and Mrs. Watts, the lab lady, comes around and like offers me some hand sanitizer, and as soon as she squirts it on my hand, I get a big whiff of it and *immediately* my stomach does a flip and I have to just get up right then, without explaining anything to her, and jet to the bathroom before I like puke all over my laptop. It's crazy, Kate," I tell her.

Like that's the kind of conversation, like me describing about being nauseous because I'm pregnant, that I should have with Kate like ten years down the road, not like *now*, you know?

I mean, I had gotten to a point where I was no longer going so nuts that I fantasized about killing myself, like I did the day I told Peter and he freaked. I was so past that stage at least. But I was still miles away from being mentally calm about the whole thing, or being at peace with my whole situation, you could say. I was totally self-conscious and paranoid about what everyone was thinking, and about how crazy my body was getting, and worried about how crazy and bloated my body was going to get! Seriously, in those early days of October, I had nightmares where I was walking halls wearing huge spandex pantaloons and weighing over three-hundred pounds! I woke up screaming sometimes; it was awful. What made it worse too was at that point I was convinced that Peter was going to dump me. The fact that he hadn't called or come over since he found out seemed a pretty obvious hint to me that we were done. The one time I tried to talk to him in the halls at school, he just said that he needed time. And when I had made the choice to have the baby and put it up for adoption, I thought for sure he'd call me that night and freak out on me because all the kids and teachers at school would know he was the one who got me pregnant and all. But he didn't call. Which I just took as *well, he doesn't even care—it's over.*

The fact is, during those chaotic, paranoid, surrealistic weeks, the only time I had felt any real sense of relief was the moment I blurted out to Luke Forrester that I was pregnant, and he had said, or uh, written, *Abby, I'm here…* I couldn't explain why, but as strange as it was that Luke was talking to me again, him going out of his way to talk to me again, was extremely comforting to me. Luke was comforting like my grandmother's old orange and green afghan that I used to love and wrap around myself when we visited my grandparent's house, and the family would all gather in their living room with the lights off and watch Holiday specials during Christmas break. Like I said, I couldn't explain it, but Luke was comforting like that. And to tell you the truth, at that point, I really didn't want to think too much why I found so much relief in Luke. I didn't want to deal with what I might find out there if I thought about it too much.

So, for the time being, I was just trying not to think too much about Luke Forrester and his sudden comfort and concern. Which was hard to do if you want to know the truth. But trying to do my AP Calculus homework helped—cause I'm here to tell ya, if you're concentrating on Calculus, you can't really think about anything else.

In fact, it was when I was up in my room slaving away on Calc that my phone rattled on my desk next to my notebook. It's a text from Peter:

look out your window

My stomach flutters and it's got nothing to with hand sanitizer this time. I get up and go over to window and look down to the street. Peter's there, standing in the sidewalk with his phone in one hand and he waves to me with the other.

I texted a

?

I see his phone glow and then I see his fingers splay all over his screen like spider legs.

My phone rattles.

come down. talk

I send him an OK, and scurry downstairs and slip through the kitchen to the back door, the whole time thinking, *is he going to break up with me now?*

By the time I make it out to the sidewalk, Peter's phone's out of sight and he's leaning on his car. He looks all calm, which could be a good thing or a bad thing. I get up to him and we just look at each other for a minute. *Let him be the first*, I think.

"Hey."

"Hey." I go back like an idiot.

"Abby... I—I'm sorry for being so, you know, upset and all, the last couple of weeks. Stupid of me. I guess I was just kind of in shock with it all too, I guess."

"Yeah."

"Yeah, took me awhile to figure out how to tell my parents. Ever since I did, my mom's been really worried about how to talk to your parents. She wonders if your parents are mad or upset with her or my dad, you know—for whatever."

"Yeah—I mean *no*," I go. "My parents aren't upset with your parents. In fact, my parents aren't really, I guess, *upset* with you either. They're disappointed with both of us a little, I guess. But they're not freaking out really. They're ready to deal, move forward. They've actually been really great. It helps I think that it's going to be adopted and not with us permanently, maybe."

"Yeah, I guess that might help," he goes.

It suddenly gets all quiet again between us which freaks me out—but then he saves us.

"It's been quite the last few days at school, huh?"

"Yeah. It's been a beast, not gonna lie. We've been quite the talk of the town, I think."

"Yeah, for reals," Peter goes. "Some of the guys have been calling me 'big daddy Calloway' and stuff like that. A lot of *stud horse* comments. It's been pretty relentless."

He goes on talking and kind of smiles as he does which I all take as a good sign. I get more and more confident that Peter isn't going to dump me.

"So, do you think we had as much gossip as the soccer team got for narc-ing themselves out, or the Rosalind Howard deal from the beginning of school?" I go.

"Yeah, maybe," Peter goes, moving in and wraps me up in his arms. In auto-mode now, I raise my lips to his.

Peter comes up for air. "So do you forgive me?"

"Yes," I coo.

He grins now all in slo-mo. "Good. So... how about going for a little drive with me? I know there's a little friend of mine that hasn't *felt* your mouth in a long time."

This catches me off guard.

Peter sees my confusion. "Abby?"

Say something. Duh... Earth to Abby! Come on! I go to myself. Then. Something. Clicked. Something in me realizes. Real small at first—like when you turn on something big and electrical that needs time to boot, like a computer or a massive cooling system, you know—there's that low hum before it gets going, that *HMMMM* noise before it really like kicks into gear. Yeah, at that moment with Peter, that's exactly where I was at, at that moment out there on the street in front of my house.

"Wait. Hold on," I go. "Peter, did you just like suggest for me to give you a blowjob right now?"

It's Peter's turn to freeze. Then he stammers out the most evasive "*What?*" in history.

"*What?* Are you kidding? Like seriously?" I go.

"Huh? Yeah, I'm kidding, I mean, I'm not kidding about going for a drive, you know talk some more. Yeah, but that *little friend* thing was just a joke, you know? There'll be plenty of time for that kind of stuff later, you know... I mean, *jesus christ*."

There's this weird moment of silence then and I finally kind of just cough and laugh at the same time and shake my head. "Well, I'm glad you came over and we talked like this. Really glad, actually. I mean I was really kind of worried what was going on, and this has been good."

"Yeah, I'm glad too," he goes.

"Good, yeah," I say. "But I think I'm gonna go back upstairs and finish my Calc. But maybe we can go out sometime soon? Like *real* soon, you know?"

"Yeah." He takes a step back towards his car. "Yeah, you know... I'll see you in school, then?"

"Yeah, I'd like that."

"All right. Well, we'll see you tomorrow." He opens the door.

"OK. Good night, Peter," I go and cross my arms, shivering.

He's already getting into the car, but he suddenly pops his head back up. "Hey—you know you're still the sexiest girl in the world to me *OK?*"

"OK," I go back. "But we'll see if you still think that in six months!"

"Ha! I guess we'll see!" Peter goes and then pulls away from the curb and I watch his sports car taillights zoom down my street.

I walk back to the house my head swimming with *yes* and *no—no* and *yes*. *Dark clouds nestle lightning, black is all colors at once and white is no color at all.* I mean *yes*, Peter still seemed to be interested in me. And *no,* it did not escape me that he did not kiss me goodnight.

ERIF

II

It's amazing what people can learn to live with. They can scrape and struggle to find the 'normal' in almost any horrible situation. And so it was with the people of Thorn.

After the annual traditional week of mourning following the Lottery and the giving unto Erif the child sacrifice, the village tried hard to return to normal living. They did this by plunging themselves into their work and daily chores. But this was not enough—they also needed their distractions, something to divert and to make them forget, if only briefly, about the vile dragon and the children they sent up to him in the Crack.

One way they did this was to hold festivals. *Lots* of festivals. They held a fall festival, during which the village square would be packed with harvest fare: rough-grain breads, bloated ripe pumpkins, and robusty spiced ale. The autumn fest always wrapped up with a prestigious competition between the realm's greatest weavers to see who could make the best life-sized wicker animals.

And for the winter's festival, the town's menfolk would construct a large ice hall out of snow packed into bricks. Inside that frosty hall, many fires would be lit in holes dug out of the floor and more ales (of course) would be served—except unlike the fall ales, the yule ales always had heavy helpings of peppermint mixed in. Once all sheltered and warm, the people of Thorn would give hand-made gifts to each other, and gobble down mincemeat pies by the handful. Then at the end of the evening, the whole community would sing in unison *The Old Song* that had been sung by the people of Thorn since before time out of mind—and certainly before the coming of Erif the *Wing-Swift*. It was a bright song, full of hope, whose melody was so graceful no one could finish it without their face flooding with tears with the beauty of it.

Then came the spring. The thaw. And this was the season of the biggest festival of all: *Mayodon*. This grandest of festivals came with the bloom and the blaze of the wildflowers, with the filling of the rivers by early rains and mountain snowmelt. It took weeks for the townsfolk to decorate Thorn with banners and flowers. They erected tents and constructed stages and sent exotic orange and purple streamers and flowers up the Spring Poles to dance in the wind.

For the seven days and nights of Mayodon, the village square came alive, highlighted by big steaming mutton dinners and minstrels constantly playing flutes, fiddles, harps, and drums. The very air smelled of fresh mud and life emerging. Every man, woman, and child of Thorn turned up for the nightly dances and cheered on as they watched the various tournaments of archery or wooden-sword sparring. It was during the massive spring festival that Thorn was invaded by acting troupes, puppeteers, and other performers of the stage. In the days of Mayodon, Thorn's daily droog turned to *Carnevale Deluxe*.

It was during one particular Mayodon, that two sisters walked among the thronging hordes of festival goers on a bright and blue-skyed day. Both were bright of eye with full hair flowing. The eldest, Annabella, being sixteen, was starting to show all the grace of full womanhood and she looked at everything with a skeptic slyness. She turned the heads of all the boys in Thorn with her lithe beauty and firefly wit.

But even with the conventional beauty of Annabella, it was the younger, Angel, who struck all who looked upon her into a stillness. To look on the lightly freckled face of Angel, to sink into the calm ocean of her eyes, was to see a girl that glowed with an understanding that went well beyond her mere eleven years.

But anyway, like all in Thorn, the sisters loved the festivals. These festivals, Mayodon especially, gave them a break from the harsher realities of their lives. Even though, as of yet anyway, the casualties of Erif had not directly touched their family, they had lost their mother to the fever four winters prior. Since then, the responsibilities of the home fell hard on the sisters. Their father, Vidgis, though he worked hard in his field, began to pull further and further away from his daughters, and deeper and deeper into the ale, since his wife's death. He had been rendered motionless by a grief too long into healing. It fell to Annabella to look after Angel—and in time, it also fell to Angel to be a source of support and love to her older sister.

So sorry for my bramble... but let us look again to the sisters walking through the Mayodon. As they walked through the crowds, they were drawn to the sounds of amused laughter and applause from a rabble surrounding a particular stage, showcasing a peculiarly handsome young man of eighteen winters. The boy was dressed in a rough tunic of the deepest purple and had apparently just finished a trick of magic.

"And for my next amazing feat, I shall juggle for you fine, fine folks," said the youth.

But groans erupted from the crowd and a man's voice called, "Aw come off it now, we seen plenty o' juggling before! Boo with ya!"

The youth held up his hands. "Good people! Good people now! Now, that's all right and good that you've seen some mad juggling before—but folks! You haven't seen someone juggle as I can juggle."

"Well, what are you saying then?" called another disgruntled man. "That you can juggle blindfolded or something? Cause we seen that a' plenty too!"

*Boo! Murmur...*went the rabble. *Boo! Murmur...*

"No, no, not blindfolded—that's a peck tricky to be sure, but no," said the youth. "I was thinking more of—"

"*Boo!*"went the crowd again. "*He can't even juggle blindfolded!*" voices called out.

Angel started giggling. "He's funny, Anna."

"Only because he's being the biggest of dorks," Annabella said.

"Fine folks! Good, fine, venerable folks!" The youth picked up a beaten leather satchel from the stage and motioned for quiet again. "Now, good and epically fine people of Thorn, what I am prepared to juggle for you today is none other than these three ale mugs!" he said and pulled three mugs form the satchel; all three seemingly filled to the brim. "See," he appealed to the crowd. "They still have their foamy tops and everything!"

"Fake!" screamed a man from the crowd again. "Them ale mugs is fake!"

*"Boo!"*the crowd erupted again. *"Cabbage him!" "He's shite!"*

"See, Angel, he's a dork. Those ale mugs, the froth on them, are obviously made out of something solid to look like real foam. His act is as a lame horse," Annabella said.

"Yes, sister, but I do believe he's dorking on purpose. He's making fun."

Indeed, the youth seemed to barely be taking himself, or the situation, seriously. However, he continued to try and silence his audience. "Good people, I say! Oh, I do beseech ye all now! Fine folks, what if—I say, what if I juggle something else? Something of your good choosing?"

A man with a nose like a rotted mushroom yelled above the rest, *"BAA!* Yer shite, boy! Stale shite right out o'a sick mule's arse! Off the stage with ye!"

"Whoa, *whoa*—good people now—I can't believe there's nothing here you'd like to see me juggle?"

Annabella raised her hand and yelled out, "Very well! Make him juggle sheep shards!"

The boy turned and locked eyes with Annabella.

Annabella just tilted her head, narrowed her eyes, and looked right back.

'*Yeah! Sheep shards!*" yelled the crowd, *"Juggle sheep shards, boy!"*

"Get him a shovel o'shards!" yelled the man with the mushroom nose.

"*Get three shovels!*"cawed out another.

*"Yeah!"*boomed the crowd. "*Three shovels of shards!*"

The rabble went nuts as the youth tried in vain to control their outbursts. Presently, a sheepherder and two of his young boys came up to the stage; each with a shovel piled high with sheep poop.

"Ere we go!" said the shepard. "Fresh from me flock this a'morning!"

His oldest boy snickered as he raised his shovelful for the youth's inspection, "And this a'pile's still steaming!"

They dumped the moist feces into three separate mounds on the stage and retreated back into the crowd. The youth stared at the poop and then looked back out to the crowd. The crowd burst back with jeers and laughter.

"All right," the youth said. "All right now. You want to see me juggle a little sheep shards then?"

"YEAH!" the good people of Thorn yelled back.

The youth then looked to the blonde-haired sisters and grinned. "Very well... How can I deny such a request from such an adorning–and shall I say, *adorable* crowd?"

Annabella recoiled from that and sent the youth a slap to the face with her eyes.

"I like him," Angel said. "Let's introduce ourselves after the show, sister."

"We'll see if you still want to meet him after he gets those shards all over himself," Annabella replied.

The youth stood straight and closed his eyes. He held arms straight out from his sides as far as they would go and turned up his palms. The crowd quieted a little then. They all went even quieter when everyone realized that the boy was humming at a lowly pitch.

"Ughmph! He's puttin' it off," yelled the man with the mushroom nose. "He's stalling cause he don't want to put the shards in his hand!"

"Quiet!" The youth startled the crowd with a yell that sounded more like the growl of a bear than a teenage boy.

The youth resumed his low humming.

Then suddenly, though slightly, something began emerging out of the palms of the youth's hands. The crowd let out a series of quiet gasps.

Annabella squinted her eyes and leaned forward from where she stood.

"It's light," whispered Angel.

The bluish-purple light coming out of the youth's palms began to arc and expand until it looked like he was holding two bluish crystal balls in his hands the size of cantaloupes. The youth opened his eyes and the crowd gasped. He looked to the crystal in his left hand, and it rolled off his palm and floated in the air!

"*No way...*" the man with the mushroom nose mumbled.

The floating crystal hovered downward, like a bath bubble, while another arc of light began to emerge from the youth's left palm. Then the crystal ball in his right hand dropped and floated too. By the time a third crystal dropped from the youth's palm, the other two crystals had expanded and enveloped around the two outside mounds of sheep shards. The third crystal made its way to the mound in the center.

The youth then brought his hands together, as if he were about to lead his spectators in prayer, when he raised his hands again, palms up in front of him. *He was bidding his crystals to rise,* it dawned on the crowd. And rise they did; but to everyone's amazement, the piles of sheep turds rose too within the crystals.

Without actually touching the crystals, the youth went through the pantomime of juggling while crystals went around and around above his head. The poop piles fell apart as he juggled them faster and faster, but the shards never left the crystal they were in.

The crowd then began to *Oooo* and *Ahhh*. He increased speed until the crystals were blurring flashes of light twirling above him like a tornado of rabid lightning bugs. Roars of applause rose up as the crowd lost itself in the spectacle.

The crystals stopped just above the youth's head and hovered; he bowed graciously to their applause. As the ovation continued, one of the crystals broke away from its station and zoomed out into the crowd. The flying crystal found the man with the mushroomed nose and hovered above him a second. Bewildered, the man looked up at it. Then it suddenly popped into oblivion, spilling the ample mound of sheep shards onto the man's face and in his mouth.

The good people of Thorn erupted into an even higher fevered state of rapture.

After a grand bow upon the stage, the youth ambled off to receive his wage from the Master of Ceremonies, as the crowd broke up, all in a general good cheer after such a dramatic and unexpected display of showmanship.

Angel saw the youth stash a coined purse into his satchel and scan the crowd. "Look, sister!" she said. "He's coming right for us!"

"Oh my—remain calm, Angel—no matter what nonsense he conjures."

The youth walked with a certain kind of goofy swagger as he approached. "Ah—good and fine ladies—"

"Ah yes, are we to hear more endless *goods* and *fines* from you throughout eternity, then?" Annabella said.

The youth winced a little. "Perhaps so—but know, gentle ladies, that I actually *mean* them when I address such beauties as yourselves."

Annabella rolled her eyes yet again, while Angel giggled and asked, "Good sir, where did you learn to make those, um..."

"Auras, you mean? They're called Auras. I can conjure them at will, I'm afraid."

"So, you mean they're *real*?" Angel squealed. "Not a trick or anything?"

"No, my dear, they're quite real," the youth said. "Just ask my new friend over there." The youth nodded to the man with the mushroom nose splashing his beshitted face with water from a rain barrel.

"So–you're a Yonderling, then?" Angel said. You see, Yonderlings were a small number of people that carried within them the bloodline of an old and distant race of wizards. They inherited at birth from their mystical ancestors all manner of magical abilities such as necromancy, shape shifting, mind reading, and corporal transporting, just to name a few–and of course, and in the case of the youth, Aura-making.

"Why yes, I am–and I am quite at your good service, I might add," the youth said and bowed.

"Oh, that was grandly said," Annabella said. "Hmm. So you can levitate sheep shards and juggle your balls–*uh sorry*, I mean your *crystal* balls. Not the most amazing Yonderling gift I've ever heard tell of."

"Sister be nice." Angel frowned. "He's the first Yonderling we've ever met."

"My fair maiden, I am sorry if my *balls* offend. They were the only gifts I was given I'm afraid."

Annabella arched her brow.

"And now, good ladies, I believe tis high time I heard your names."

The two girls introduced themselves–Angel with enthusiasm and courtesy, Annabella reservedly.

"And pray, what might your name be then?" Annabella asked.

"Ah, now we come to it. You may call me Prince."

"Scoundrel Prince, more like," Annabella said.

"Very well then, the Scoundrel Prince if you like," said Prince. Both he and Angel giggled at his retort. "Would you permit me to escort you fine ladies through the fair?"

After a half-serious objection from Annabella, the three of them began to amble through the Mayodon. They laughed and joked while they walked past flame blowers and two ale-soaked farm hands doing a spirited dagger dance. Angel beamed with questions for Prince about his life of travel, while Prince and Annabella seemed to take turns stealing glances at each other. Prince took out some coins and bought them all roasted squirrels on a stick. Angel squealed at the deliciousness of hers–she had always been fond of the one's seasoned with paprika and cinnamon.

While they walked through the crowd, Annabella continued to playfully make fun of Prince's hair, shoes, rough old tunic, ears, even his gift of making the magical Auras–"making your little bubbles," she said.

But there arose a disruption. A man came running by them, pushing his way through the crowd, followed hotly by a group of men in metal helmets wearing black capes and armed with daggers and crossbows.

"Clear the path!" one of the armed men ordered.

Everyone scurried back from the running man. One of the caped men shot a bolt into the running man's thigh. The man fell to the ground with a howl and clutched at the arrow in his leg. Seven caped men encircled the fallen man when another man emerged from the crowd. This man was tall, thin, looked to be just beyond his fortieth winter, and was bald—no hair on his head whatsoever, not even eyebrows. He wore a long black robe, making him look like some kind of whacked-out monk. This man stood, statuesque, over the man writhing in the dirt.

"Thievery is punishable by death here in Thorn, man," the bald man said.

"I—I have done nothing!" the wounded man cried.

The bald man looked to one of the armed men in capes. "Check the inside of this man's vest."

The soldier knelt, threw his hands into the wounded man's vest roughly and then produced a golden ring.

"Yours?" the bald man asked.

"Uh—yes! Of course, my lord. I can prove! The ring is an heirloom of my very family. It was my yester-uncle's, Feogarrd's!"

The bald man continued to stare at the wounded man. The bald man did not blink—just glared down with eyes of a shark. "Pray," the bald man called to the kneeling solider, "reach into this man's pants, near his wretched crotch, and pull out what you find."

The order drew shrieks from some of the women looking on in the crowd. However, the soldier obeyed and yanked out something red in his fist and handed it to the bald man.

"I am a dead man," the wounded man hissed.

The bald man's eyes gleamed at the object and then held it up for all to see. "It's the Eye of Erif! You have all witnessed that this man here has been caught stealing this sacred ruby from Thorn's Great Hall!"

"What's that?" Prince asked the girls.

"The Eye of Erif is a ruby that the dragon gave the village elders the day they agreed to the Lottery. It's a kind of symbol of the bargain. They keep it in the Great Hall where the Lottery is held each year," Angel said.

"Take this man away," said the bald man; and the caped soldiers picked the wounded man up to carry him off.

"No—wait. It's not possible! How did you know I hid the jewel there! No one could've seen me! No one could have witnessed!" the condemned man began to wail as he was being taken away.

The crowd then began to go back about its merrymaking business, when the bald man approached Annabella, Angel, and Prince. "Greetings, Annabella, and young Angel. I hope our little display of justice has not upset you. I do hate making arrests in such a public place—but it was quite unavoidable in this case."

"Elder Cyvilard, on the contrary," Annabella said. "I believe it is most agreeable, and refreshing, to see the hand of justice administered so in the light of day,"

"Well said," Cyvilard said and nodded towards Prince "And who have we here?"

"Ah, very well, yes. I am a roving squire and showman. Prince is the name." Prince gave a respectful nod.

"A showman, eh?" Cyvilard raised an eyebrow.

"And a Yonderling! Prince can make the most wonderfulest Auras with his hands!" Angel cried.

"Is that so?" Cyvilard's face instantly turned even more serious. "Mind yourself then, Yonderling. We take to no tomfoolery here with magical trifles. Are you here long in Thorn?"

"Ah no. I leave with the Mayodon, sir."

"Ba!" Cyvilard broke into a laugh. "They always do—don't they? Any visitor of Thorn is sure to tuck-tail and run after the closing of the Mayodon. May I guess that you have no stomach for our Lottery, then boy?"

Prince stared back at Cyvilard. "I do not, sir."

"*Good,*" Cyvilard barked. "It's our lot, you know, our curse. We prefer to bear it all unobserved anyway. Much easier for everyone involved." Cyvilard looked again to the two sisters. "Uh, and how then is your father these days?"

"The same, my lord," Annabella said.

"Well then, tell him, as always, I send my regard. It's a pity that having the loveliest daughters in the Thorn cannot pull good Vidgis from his grief. Good day."

"Good day, my lord," Annabella said.

And with that, Cyvilard turned and followed his men back to his headquarters to deal with the thief.

"What was that all about?" Prince asked.

"That was Cyvilard and his Tarrenbacks," Angel said. "He's a village Elder and the Tarrenbacks are the village guard."

"It's the job of Cyvilard and the Tarrenbacks to conduct and oversee the Lottery," Annabella added.

"Hmm. Well, they seem, um, rather *intense*," Prince said.

"As for me, anytime I meet Cyvilard's stare, I feel my blood chill," Annabella confessed, and then the trio continued their way through the fair.

27

Jason

Holy fuck in heaven and Jesus and all his sweet-winged angels if this wasn't the bitch-all of all decisions, man. I almost got wasted tonight, Rozz. And not *STONED* either, man. Like fucking killed. My hand's still shaking like I'm locking down in one of your total grand mals, Rozz. Gotta regulate. And what did Dre say? *You gotta think.* Anyway, I just downed about half a bottle of Jim Beam from my closet just so I can fucking steady my hand, man. And I've got just my little lamp on here while I'm sitting against the wall with my pillow behind my back, sitting on some of my ratty clothes, with my notebook and pen, man. Gonna try and get this all accurate and shit, Rozz, so I don't forget what a bad idea this was, man. See if I can't figure out what the hell happened. Or like what fucking *is* happening, man.

See, I had just dropped off Toe at his house after school. We couldn't hang today like we usually do because he had to go with his dad to help his uncle move this furniture to some guy's house or some shit. Anyway, I haul ass home because I don't got nothing better to do. Basically was looking to get lifted or trashed and watch some TV or dick around on online. So I park in our driveway when like from fucking nowhere a car screeches to a tire-burning stop behind me.

You remember Kid T, right? That fucking dropout glass & coke cabbie that pushes it for my pops? Well, like fucking *duh* on me, man. Of course, you know him, Rozz—because he's the bitch that got you all hooked up with Dre and his crew. But anyway. So that fuckhead pulls up in his piece of shit Mitsu and lets down his window saying, "Hey, yo—Lil Pops, Dre wants me to see if you down. Do one little camelback? What do you say, yo?"

I'm just standing there in the driveway, Rozz. Just standing there knowing full fucking well I should just flip the white trash g-bang'n-wanna-be fucker off and get my sorry ass into the house. But I don't.

"Is Dre here? Is he in town?" I ask instead.

"Yeah, bitch. I supposed to take you to him first."

Get in the fucking house, man, part of me says to myself. "Let me go inside and check on something first."

"Yo, Pops don't need to know, *ya* know?" Kid T goes. "Dre says Pops don't need to know."

"Hey, fuck my dad—dickhead. He aint even home right now anyway."

Kid T gets all *whoa—back the fuck up* and says *fine*—but tells me if I don't get in the car like *right now*, I can forget the serious cash I could make like in an hour's time.

"Really?" I go. "An hour?"

"More or less, dog," Kid T goes. "Then you can get back here and get high and jack off and shit or whatever you were gonna do in there before I pulled in."

Before I fucking know it, man—I'm fucking getting into that scrawny white-skinned, baggy-clothes-wearin, trying-to-grow-a moustache-but failing, lame-ass hat-to-the-side glass cabbie's car.

And the whole time we're driving I know the only reason I'm going on this is for the cash. Yeah, I just sat there in Kid T's car *cash dreaming*, man. I was thinking that if I did enough of these camelbacks in a few months I'd have enough of my own green to get gas. Gas to get my ass out of this shit-ass town. Maybe even this shit-ass state. Get the fuck out of Michigan before the winter really hits its motherfucking prime, man. Leave this corn-hole and go someplace where there aint no fucking Kid T's, or Dre's, fucking white trash drug dealing dads like my pops, or even big weird deaf fuckers doing things that don't make any goddamn sense.

I got in, Rozz. Even though I hate all those dealing motherfuckers for how they treated you—I got in. I got in to try and fucking *get out.*

So Kid T drives us out to fucking AL SKID'S Bowling Alley for godsakes. You know that dive out off the access highway past the ghetto Burger King? I mean I've seen the outside of that dump a million times, but this is the first time I'm actually going in.

"Seriously?" I go.

Kid T shuts off the car and just starts laughing. "Yeah, dog. Dre's got like a permanent table in the pizza joint in the back."

Fucking cheese and rice, Rozz, you should've seen the inside of this place. But then again maybe you *have* seen the inside of this place—like before we started to hang out. But anyway, the place reeked like they hadn't opened a window or turned on a fan in like twenty years. Seriously, everything smelled like socks and puke. The guy behind the bar/shoe rental counter had these honking gray muttonchops looking like some elderly *Wolverine* motherfucker. So he looks up from whatever bullshit he's doing and gives Kid T and me a look like *fucking kids these days* while we stroll by.

Anyway, there's a trio of burnouts playing cutthroat at one of the pool tables and a few morons are bowling on a couple of lanes. A couple of them look familiar—like I've seen them in the halls at Hemingway but I'm blanking on their names. Kid just keeps walking, and we go through these double doors at the end of the alley into Pazzaro's Pizza Parlor. The parlor aint much cleaner than the alley either, man. Like the first thing we pass is the men's bathroom and the door's all open and there's this guy with like a baker's apron on with a mop leaning against the sink and he's dumping a bucket of ice into the urinal. You know—so they don't have to clean it as often, I guess.

Fucking sick.

We get into the main part of the joint and the only people there are Dre and his crew sitting in a booth. I mean you can hear people working back in the kitchen and there's the asshole in the bathroom—but other than that, the place is fucking *Deadsville.*

Tagger and Sin-Dawg suddenly stand up looking all badass at us and then sit back down at the small table across from the booth. Dre nods for me to sit down.

And suddenly like right then I'm filled with fucking rage, Rozz. I mean at that moment I'm like totally regretting I don't have one of my dad's pieces. Because if I did, I'd like to think I would've pulled it out right then and there all super-fast and put a round right in Dre's throat. And then before they could draw their nines, I'd blast Tag and Sin too, man. Then with their fucking brains oozing out all over the pizza parlor's floor I'd take a few seconds just to stand over Dre as he's choking on his own blood, fucking gurgling and shit. And say something like, 'this is for Rozzy—bitch,' and put the final blast through his skull.

Seriously at that moment, man—that's all I wanted, Rozz. Even though that supreme asshole, Cunter, wasn't there which would've made my split-second fantasy of wasting these fuckers complete.

"Yo, you holding a piece, Lil Pops?" Dre goes like he can fucking read my mind.

I just shake my head like he's a total dickhead for even asking.

"Come on, Lil Pop's—I gotta ask. I mean, fuck, dawg—you should see your eyes sometimes. You always looking like some psycho muthafucka these days," he goes and starts laughing.

Sin reaches in from behind me and frisks me just to make sure. I sit down in the booth across from Dre who's just got a huge-ass glass of iced tea in front of him. I notice that Kid T moves over and tries to sit at the table with Tag and Sin. Tagger like fucking immediately tells Kid T to stand his cracker ass back up and wait for further fucking instruction.

"So now Lil Pops," Dre goes. "You finally ready to pop your cherry, dawg? You ready to break that crystal bubble you got round yourself? Or should I say that your Pop's is got around you?"

"Yeah, fucking whatever, man. How much for the camelback?" I go.

All three of the crew start laughing—even Kid T joins in. "Alright now! Lil Pop's aint wasting no time!" Dre goes.

"How much?" I go again.

"Three hundred bucks, Lil Pops."

"Bullshit. For one camelback?"

"No bullshit. But hold up, yo. Let me explain this shit so you can get the lay," Dre says and takes an overdramatic sip of fucking tea. He sits back in the booth all slow and sinister like he's the Darth Vader of drug dealers.

"Now looky here, normally I wouldn't tell no cabbie shit except where a camel got to go to drop his hump. But since you Pop's boy and since you got to have at least some muthafucking understanding of how your old man's business works, I'm gonna tell you some shit that will make this whole camelback go quick and easy like Sunday fucking morning—if you can feel me, dawg. So *can* you feel me?"

I swear I really didn't know what the fuck was going on. I mean the way Dre was launching in to all this shit, it seemed like he was trying to prime me for the fucking deal of the century. Again, Rozz, part of me was like telling the other part of me to just say *Later* to this shit and just get up and bolt out of Pazzaro's fucking Pizza and run home—Kid T's ride be damned. But again it all came down to *THREE HUNDRED BUCKS.*

"Yeah, I fucking feel you," I go. "So get on with it."

"OK. So here it is, Lil Pops. I know you know we work out of *The D.* I also know that you know we come out here to supply your Pops with the fucking holy trinity: glass, cocaine, and party psychos. Now I'm muthafucking sure your Pops is also dealing some weak-ass grass too—but that shit's not from us so I don't give a fuck. Now you know we don't have to be here *bizzin* with your Pop's, right?"

"Yeah. Right. I realize you would be just fine sticking to your crack ho's or whatever in Detroit. I'm pretty fucking sure my dad realizes that shit too" I go.

Dre nods and then takes another sip. "So now, Lil Pops, why do we take the time to be here *bizzin* with your Pops?"

I shrug. "Make more money?"

"Now come on, Lil Pops, wake up now. There's more money to be made in *The D* than in the subs, recession or not. A fucking crack ho's always got to eat and so does her junked-out pimp. Ha!"

This gets a laugh riot from Sin and Tagger. Kid T only braves a couple giggles.

"No Lil Pops, it aint the money, dawg. So what is it then? Why do me and my crew spend any muthafucking time and resources operating out of this here cum-stained Pazzaro's Pizza connected to Al Skid's muthafucking Bowling Alley?"

"Don't have a clue , Dre. You're the fucking drug dealer—you tell me."

Again, I get laughs from the whole crew.

"*Diversitize*," Dre goes. "We diversitize, Lil Pops. Like they do on muthafucking Wall Street, yo? Create market diversity, is what I'm saying, dawg. Instead of relying on one really big-ass market, stretch out and get a couple of different markets in different environments with like totally different fucking forces at play see, Lil Pops?"

"Uh, yeah—sort of."

"Yeah—so like when one market has like a fucking unknown variable suddenly fuck-up our ebb and flow, we can chill on that market and concentrate on another for awhile. You still feeling me, Lil Pops?"

"Yeah—I think I'm still feeling you. But this is starting to sound a lot like school, man."

And again, they go a'fucking howling. Sin Dawg even pats my back like we're old buds or some shit.

"Well—that's good, Lil Pops. That's good. Now listen up, cause class is still in session now, son. Now take Detroit. The biz is good right now even with things being the way they is. I mean, looky here—half of fucking Detroit is out of work, which means that other half that's got stuff better look out, yo. All things go in cycles, Lil Pops. And once you see the cycles you can ride them. Like waves, dawg. And that's the way it is right now. Times like these, crews like us thrive. We surf the wave, yo. Niggaz get paid. Peeps can't find work, get they welfare check. Fucking folks gotta chill. Niggaz get paid. Folks can't make rent no more, can't get food money no more, they knock off a liquor store. Dawg, we the first place them thugs go. Niggaz get paid.

"But that's the muthafucking thing, Lil Pops. I know how this cycle ends, dawg. It ends with a muthafucking crackdown. Always does. The Law-Dawg's gonna fall and fall heavy on *The D* after it's gotten bad enough. Some pre-Trump-Giuliani-type *clean house muthafucka* gets elected mayor, more cops in the streets and the risks go up. That's the cycle. And it's coming sooner than later, yo. So we diversify. So when the law hits, we out making bank somewhere else till the fucking chill. That's why we *bizzin* with Sunrise—to stay ahead of all these amateur fuck-ups that think you can make it on fucking cocaine and guns alone. You gotta think! *Think*, Lil Pops, and that's why we enlisted whitebread's like your Pops. To sell to the trailers and the junkies, and party kids in the subs. And that's why I want you going with Kid T on this camelback."

"That's all great, but can you tell me the *why* part again? Because I think I missed it," I go.

Dre looks all confused. "Which *why* part?"

"Jesus Christ, Dre… Fucking why you want *me* along?"

"Oh right, right. I got four very specific reasons why I want you on this camelback, dawg. You ready for them, yo?"

"Yeah, man. Fucking lay it on me, *dog*."

"All right, looky here. One. You use all this shit we push, and you still got more brain cells than most of the mutha's in this biz."

Tagger smirks at that. "Yo, Dre that was more like *two* reasons at once, dawg."

"Bitch—I aint got time for you to come bargin in tryin to correct me and shit while I'm about the biz, yo? You just concentrate on your job, pullin triggers and dumping bodies," Dre goes all playing around and shit.

"Yeah, but hear me out, you said he uses the junk *AND* he's also kind of smart. That's two reasons, yo," Tagger keeps it up.

Sin and Kid T start laughing. Honestly, I couldn't for my fucking life see how this shit was funny. Maybe it was an inside joke for drug dealers or something.

"I mean, yo—you know. If you want to project a mastermind persona, dawg—you gotta get this simple math shit down, yo?" Tag goes.

"Alright—it's a fucking two-*fer*. Now can I continue you overpaid hyena muthafuckas?" Dre goes and looks back at me. "Now as I was on the path to saying, Lil Pops. Two. You're one psycho looking muthafucka whitebread. Young as shit, but psycho. And since the camelback is with some sorry-ass whitebread trailers, your psycho's gonna help keep them muthafuckas in check, yo?

"Three. You Pop's boy and because of that you're the only other whitebread I trust. Other than Kid T here, I don't trust any of these cabbies Kid's got pimping at the Hem-way or anywhere else in the subs. Anyone of these muthafuckas we got camelbacking would fucking rat out the Kid, your Pops, and whatever else they think they know in two pumps of a pimp's dick if they ever got pinched by the five-O, yo? But you, Lil Pops, I trust. Because you got blood that's *all in*. Which means you *all in*, feel me?"

He was talking about dad of course. And since I would never rat out my own dad, Dre was banking I'd never rat out him or his crew neither.

"Yeah, I feel you," I go. "What's the fourth reason?"

Dre sits back again. Fucking sucks some more tea. Tagger moves his toothpick from one side of his mouth to the other. Sin Dawg fidgets with his gold watch. I steal a glance at Kid T. And you know, even though he's like fucking twenty years old or so, at that moment he looks like he's ten standing there. Maybe it's because he's so close to Sin and Tag and those guys are like huge or maybe it's because Kid wears clothes that are *waaay* too baggy when he's already a bare-assed skeleton to begin with.

"All right, the fourth and major reason to have your ass out with Kid T on the fucking mutha of all fucking camelbacks is because these trailers ordered a hundred and five grams. Which basically be thirty 8-balls."

My jaw hits the ground and comes back up to my mouth slapping my bewildered dick on the way, Rozz—I fucking swear.

"The shit you say?" I go.

"That's right, Lil Pops. Thirty 8-balls in the bag."

"That aint no camelback, it's fucking *Miami Vice*, man," I go.

"So these trailers," Dre goes, "they bought from Kid T plenty of times. All glass. But till now they just buying a party at a time, dawg. I mean they junkies, but they just been buying in three-day to week quantities. But now *this*. So here's the deal, trailers that are pipers, they creatures of habit. I mean *HA-BIT*. They don't order up this way. They got fixed income, fucking welfare, so they can't afford a big deal like this. So for them to order this big—well it's got my red lights flashing, Lil Pops. Chances are they just fell into some extra green somehow. Either by legal means—or stealing some shit somewhere. Point is, yo. Even though they loyal customers, we need a little extra manpower to make the drop. They know Kid T is your Pops's cabbie but they don't know we *bizzin* with your Pops and that we got Kid on payroll too. Hell, they don't even know we exist—and it gonna stay that way. They just know that your Pops feeds them the best glass in town. They don't know it's because he getting it from our fucking labs in *The D* and not some fucking local Sudafed-and-dogshit factory around here. So looky here, I don't give a fuck if they robbed a candy shop or a fucking hair salon. I just want one extra cabbie that I can trust to deliver the product, yo? You feel me? And that's why it's $300 for the drop. So you get it now? You ready to break that crystal, dawg?"

"Yeah, I'm ready, man," I go. "Just one fucking thing—I know why I don't want my dad to know—but why don't *you* want my dad to know?"

"Oh he gonna know—sooner or later," Dre goes. "But here's the thing, he fought a long time to keep you crystal. Even tried to keep you off all this shit you know—when you was younger. But even now that you on all our shit, Pops always wanted you clean from the fucking deal, from the biz. But you're right. He gonna know about this—and you best get ready for that conversation. But mean time—like tonight and for the next couple days or so—it probably best for all of us he don't know yet. That makes sense, don't it?"

Yeah. That fucking made sense. My dad might be a lot of bad things, man. But at least he always fought like a crack-crazed gorilla to keep me from selling drugs, man. I mean he'd let me do them, fucking let me do whatever, (except drink—which never made any goddamn sense) but never let me know the biz, man. Always tried to keep me away from the biz. Now here I was, man. Leaving the bowling alley with Kid T with a backpack of thirty 8-balls worth of glass in our possession heading out to some pipe smoker's address on the East side.

28

Isaiah

Please, dear God, please help my dad right now. Please God, be with him. Be with those doctors downstairs to know what's going on and to fix it. Fix him, dear God.

Everything was going fine. Dad even seemed like in a good mood and stuff. We were in the living room—all of us, me, Mom, and Dad. We were watching the Chargers and the Raiders on Monday Night Football, and my mom had just made us all popcorn and hot chocolate and it was just another half-hour till my bedtime when all of sudden Dad just started coughing. Except it was bigger than coughing. More than coughing. Suddenly really white stuff came out of his mouth—stuff that was too thick to be spit but too white to be throw-up. And then blood. But this blood was like purple, almost black. I got real scared and Dad couldn't talk and Mom got on the phone quick and called thc hospital or someone.

Before I knew it there was sirens outside our house and lights flashing into the windows and I could hear Mr. Reese, our next-door neighbor outside asking questions in a voice like he was scared too, and then these hospital guys were in our living room and moving all fast and loud. They started doing stuff to Dad and then I got really scared because his eyes were starting to look real bad like he was leaving inside or something and I started crying real, real hard. Mom looked almost as white in the face as Dad did and even though she wasn't crying I knew she was close. I've seen her cry a lot before.

She told me to go up to my room for now and that she would be up when she knew what was happening to Dad. I think I cried even harder then, but I started to go upstairs. Right before I made it all the way up the stairs Mom popped up at the bottom of the stairs and said, "And pray, Isaiah. Pray for Dad up there. I'll be up there soon, sweetie. Try not to worry."

But I am worrying, dear God. I'm worried about him. I know he doesn't have long. He had a long talk to me about that a while ago. But please, God! Please just give me a little more time! He's the best Dad in the world! I love him SO, SO, SO much!

So I pray, dear God. I pray and I write, and I try not to hear all the scary sounds coming from downstairs and I just pray, dear God. Oh, dear God, please don't let this be the night that my dad dies.

ERIF

III

As the sun began its slide below the Great Mountain, the Mayodon was lit with torches and the nightly dance kicked up in the village square. Prince and the sisters strolled towards the sounds of music and the shuffling people of Thorn dancing away and kicking up thin clouds of dust. Ale was passed freely, and the men *whooped* and *hollered* as they twirled their sweethearts while the band played spritely airs. It didn't take long for Prince to start taking turns dancing with each of the sisters—Angel diving in whole-heartedly, and Annabella more reserved at first, but obviously still enjoying the opportunity to cut loose all the same.

With Angel, Prince spun her around and around in the most ridiculous circles to her shrieks of delight. To Angel's eyes the torches swirled into vibrant circles of light making her feel the exhilaration of a speeding planet orbiting a warm sun, the other dancers sparkling around her like stars.

But with Annabella, Prince danced as if part scarecrow with legs all hay and no bones. The pair of them drew bewildered stares from the other dancing folks and spectators alike. All flopping and dorky, dancing with Prince like that, Annabella couldn't help herself from laughing—laughing from deep within her gut. By the end of the song, poor Annabella was crying with laughter, doubled up—barely able to stand, fully aware that she was embarrassing herself in front of the others who saw her. Merrymaking and letting loose was surely expected at the Mayodon dances—*but this?* She could almost hear the next morning's gossip *'Did you see Annabella dancing with that Yonderling boy—how queer they were.'* Staggering with raucous joy with this strange boy she had only just met, red-faced with tears, about one more giggle away from pissing her dress, with clear snot running down her nose—Annabella realized somewhere in the back of her mind that she had never had such a good laugh since her mother's death.

And *WOW* did it feel good.

After a few more dances, Annabella realized that it was probably time for her and Angel to head home for the night. Prince, of course, offered to walk them as far as he could and then bid them good evening. They walked through the dirt streets until coming to the crossroads where Russler's Alley lay at one side. This was the area designed for all those visiting Thorn for the Mayodon to set up their tents and keep their carts.

"I regret we must now part company for now, my goodly tent calls me to slumber," Prince said. "But it is my hope that I will see you ladies at the fair again tomorrow?"

"Well, we will of course be there, it's the last day of the festival," Annabella began. "But as for seeing you, good sir, *well...*"

"Of course, we would be delighted for the pleasure and look forward to seeing you!" Angel cut in.

"Ah, splendid. Till tomorrow then, ladies," Prince said. "And good evening then to you both. Angel it's been a pleasure to meet you. You've the beauty of a beaver and the charm of a horse apple."

Angel snickered and replied, "Thank you, good sir, and may I say that you have the wit of a donkey's tush and the charm of a shovel!"

Prince laughed at once. "Ah, well said, and if you permit me, a little kiss on account!" and Prince bent down to kiss young Angel's hand while ripping a perky fart at the precise moment his lips met her knuckles.

Angel erupted into the most powerful stream of giggles that her eleven-year-old frame was capable of.

"Uncouth! Uncouth to the core!" Annabella railed above the squeals of her sister. "Come, sister. We must now part company with this mystical barbarian-boy and go home to our beds to dream of purer companions!"

"But wait!" Prince pleaded. "Before you ladies retire, Annabella, surely you will gossip with your troops of friends tomorrow of your time with me tonight, no doubt?"

"Perhaps," Annabella said.

"Ah, I thought so. And come—-I bet I know exactly what you will say: *So, I went to the Mayodon with my sister yesterday, just to see the sights of the season when suddenly I was set upon by this most unmannered boy who hung about me like some loathsome disease. His breath smelled of the toilet hole and his face was alike to a moldy cabbage. And to hear him laugh and talk so endlessly one might think he had been kicked in the head by oxen at an early age. Oh, his attentions were dreadful. Dreadful!"*

"Perhaps that is what I will tell them," Annabella said. "Yea, that about tells it, sir."

"Ah yes, I'm sure, my Annabella. But do you know what I should like you to say?"

"What?" Angel answered for her sister.

Prince arched a brow. "I should like you to say: *Well, I was suddenly approached by the most dashing and sophisticated of young men. I felt on the brink of complete swoon every time he looked my way or opened his mouth to make brilliant commentary on the evening. Oh, I dare not know what I will do if I should see him again. Surely, it was all I could do not to grab him by the tunic and acquaint my inexperienced and trembling lips to his firm and bold ones. Oh! Oh my!"*

"That's beyond outrageous," Annabella said.

"So is true love. Or so I've been told," said Prince.

"I'd have to have been devouring dozens of the forbidden mushrooms to say something like that," Annabella continued.

"Huh? What are the *forbidden mushrooms*?" Angel asked.

"Never mind," Annabella said. To Prince she said, "You're a dork. In all the world, how can you be so... so, *weird?"*

Prince whipped out his best roguish grin, made even more ridiculous by the way the street-torch's shadows flickered across his face. "I must say, I find your insults as comforting as any compliment I've ever received from any other girl."

"And have there been many other girls?" Annabella asked.

"Quite a many actually," Prince said. "Some with your eyes, Annabella—but none of your tongue. And none of your good stomach, dear Angel!"

And before either of them could respond, Prince turned and began scampering off toward the camp of Russler's Alley, calling out *Goodnights!* and *See You Tomorrows!* until he was out of the sisters' sight.

Once back to their modest two-room dirt-floored home that lay on the outskirts of Thorn, Annabella and Angel immediately fell into their well-rehearsed routine of lifting their passed-out father from his wooden chair before the fireplace, replacing his ale mug to the mantle, removing his boots, and laying him down on his cot by the door. The sisters did this wordlessly, and then retired to the small back room where they slept.

Once in their own space, with some candles lit, they began to speak again, going on and on about the Mayodon and Prince, and the thief, and dancing, and everything, simply everything about the evening.

"So sister," Angel finally was ready to ask. "Do you like him? You know *that way?"*

"Angel—that's so absurd. *He's* so absurd."

"That's not an answer, sister."

Annabella took a moment before flinging herself to join Angel on her bed. "He's not like any boy around here, is he?"

Angel giggled. "No, surely he's not like any other boy anywhere."

It was Annabella's turn to giggle. "Perhaps not, perhaps not... But anyway, sister, it's time for bed and we'll see our young Prince tomorrow then! But to sleep with you," she said and hopped off the bed.

"You're not coming to bed yet?" Angel asked.

"I'm going to have a bath first. The dancing has surely dusted up my hair. But I'll not keep you from your dreams," Annabella said, and blew out her sister's candle, pulled the curtain divider between their beds and went to the next room to fetch the big basin and hot water.

Outside Annabella's small window, was an old poplar tree not ten steps from the house. And on that tree was a particular branch that was dead even in height to Annabella's window. Furthermore, on that branch sat an old raven, black as the night that surrounded it, riding the night breezes, while it looked in through the window.

Inside, Annabella had filled the basin with the hot water that always hung above the fireplace. She placed her one candle on the rickety old night table that lay beside her bed, grabbed the tattered washrag, and took off her dress.

The raven watched. Now, the thing about this raven was that had it had complete control over its raven-brain, it probably wouldn't have stayed on that branch so long, watching Annabella begin to gently bathe herself. In fact, if this raven had complete control of itself, it would've never landed on that particular branch, on that particular poplar, in front of that particular window. But you see, this raven was controlled by a certain Yonderling. A Yonderling that possessed the ability to *splice* into the minds of certain birds, and to see what they saw from afar, and to make these birds do his bidding. And this particular Yonderling had kept his abilities to use birds thusly a secret. He knew it would be in his best interest as a village Elder and the head of the Tarrenbacks to keep his full powers hidden. And so even though he was physically back in his quarters in Thorn's Great Hall, Cyvilard was able to see Annabella through the eyes of his surrogate raven.

He gazed long and hard at the whites and pinks of her flesh. Watched as she stood in the basin she had bobbed for apples in when she was Angel's age. Watched as she dipped her mother's old washrag into the water and lifted it, dripping, and slowly pressed it to the skin of her left arm, scrubbing over her belly and navel, the warm water running through her fingers and hair.

And while the raven's eyes were open, Cyvilard watched far away in his room with his eyes shut, standing with hands clasped as if in prayer. And as he took in these stolen glances of Annabella's full beauty, he vowed with his black heart to do all within his power to possess her.

As for Annabella, despite the steaming, near scalding, quality of the water—she, inexplicably, still could not rub out the chill she felt in her blood.

29

Jason

"Yo, like check it," Kid T goes and pulls onto the access highway. "Dre's *bizzing* deep with some big-time heavies, dog."

"Like other biggies out of Detroit?" I go.

"Naw, man—bigger than that, dog. He's buying his party psychos and coke like *factory direct*, man. We're talking about international fuckers, man."

"Shut the shit up, man," I tell him. "The fuck you saying? Like Dre's hooking up with cartels or some shit?"

"Man, either that, or motherfuckers that are close to the cartels. He's meeting with mugs in suits and shit. Speaking in weird accents, dog."

I start shaking my head. "Fuck that, man. And Dre just opens up and tells lowly cabbies like *you* this shit?"

Kid T like cocks his head back a little. "Well, yo. Like not directly to me, but I hear it by the fucking way, dog. So be fucking rest assured. You stick with Dre a while, you gonna get paid some serious green, man. Because he's as smart as he says he is and he got connections from the top of the food chain to the fucking trailer bottom, man. And that's exactly where we're fucking going right now, yo."

"Whatever, man. So where'd you get your intel on these 'international connections,' man?"

"Uh—you know, dog. Tagger told me."

"Bullshit. Tagger's way too smart and invested to talk to a motherfucking lackey like you. So who's spilling to you, man? Like for real?"

Kid squirms around in his seat like he knows he's just been called. "Man, Cunny told me, dog. Last week we was in *The D*, when we was on the set of one of his movies, yo."

Fucking Cunter. Rozz, just hearing that snake's name always flashes me red like I'm a motherfucking bull ready to charge. Matador's sword be damned, man. One of his fucking *MOO-VEES*. That's the way those bitches always say it too when they talk about his vids, man. His fucking *MOO-VEES*.

Damn it, Rozz. I'm so fucking sorry. I'm blinding myself here with tears. I keep trying to write it. I keep trying to put it in words what I feel here without you and how sorry I am. Just trying to make some sense. And here I am—getting into Kid T's car, fucking camelbacking for Dre having to hear that that fuck, Cunter, is still out there doing that fucking sick-ass video shit. I'm sorry, Rozz. I'm sorry for getting in his car today. Should've known the day'd turn to shit the second I left my driveway. Anyway, I gotta finish this, Rozz. Let me write this down while it's fresh. So I can make sense of it when I get fucking in a right mind to think about such shit. Let me finish then I'll pass out and you can come to me again. You can come haunt me again in my fucked-up stupor like you've been doing. Just let me finish.

So yeah, we're in Kid T's car and he tells me Cunter's been spilling to him about Dre's connections and shit and that's what Dre was referring to back there when said some shit about *Sunrise* or whatever the fuck. But I must've got all quiet and pissed looking after he told me because I don't remember us talking for a while and then he like finally goes, "Yeah hey man, I heard about Rozzy, man. Sorry, dog. I know you two were tight. That shit aint right, man. Aint right at all."

At that point I'm just trying to be calm, you know? I took out my flask and just took a gulp and go, "Yeah, man—whatever. It sucks but it's OK. Now who we going to see here?"

So Kid T tells me about this heavy tweeker, Lester. And how Lester's this goony fucking white-trash type that buys glass from him on a weekly basis and shit. Says he always seemed pretty harmless—but you could tell he was getting deeper and deeper into the glass which means you get more and more paranoid and unpredictable. Kid goes on about how he and Lester usually met in the movie theater parking lot for their camelbacks but that he'd made a house call for Lester once, and now that's where this deal was going to go down.

I ask Kid T how this is supposed to play out. He goes on about how it should be real easy and quick. He said that *I* would do the dealing, while *he* stood behind me as back up. I told him that's fucking post since he's like the experienced mother fucking drug dealer and I'm supposed to be only an experienced druggie. But he goes, "Hey, there's nothing to it, dog. You just stare them down. Calmly ask where the money is. Fucking look at it for a sec to make sure that it's really cash, and we leave. There shouldn't be any real discussion about it, yo. Besides, this is what Dre wants you to do. See, they know me, but they shouldn't know your ass. They see you there for the big deal, they might think you're my boss. It'll throw them. Hopefully enough to keep them all in check until we leave with the green, dog."

"But don't they know my Pops is running the high-end glass in town?"

"Yeah, dog. They know *of* your Pops, but they don't *know* your Pops, see? They've never seen him. They only contact's been through me. That's the way it works, man. So by that fucking rationale they should have no way in shit of knowing who the fuck you are, dog. You feel me?"

"I fucking swear, Kid, I already answered that *do you feel me* shit too many times today. So don't put nothing that way the rest of the night, man. Besides, when you picked me up after school this afternoon didn't you say this shit'd only take an hour? Look how dark it is asshole. You can kiss all that *this will only take an hour* shit goodbye."

"Yeah well…" Kid goes and starts laughing. "I had to get you in the car somehow, dog."

I don't know why but I start laughing a little too, Rozz. I think it was my first laugh of the day too—maybe in the last few days. Anyway, no matter what the circumstances, it felt good to laugh even if it wasn't gonna last.

I start to notice that we're on the Eastside. The houses are just as run down here as they are on our streets—except worse. And another thing—there are more houses that are *empty*. Whether it's the recession or because this is the fucking armpit of the town, I don't know. But the fact is this place was fucking *eerie*.

Kid T pulls over to the curb next to a shit-ass house that's got all these Halloween decorations on the run-down porch. Skull posters on the windows and cheap-ass orange and black streamers on the porch rails. Even has a lame R.I.P. plastic gravestone stabbed down in the front lawn.

"OK. We're just a block away," Kid goes. "Lester already knows the price is three and a half-grand. Dre said it would be OK if he tries to jew you down to three-grand. But that's the hard-assed line. If for some reason he decides not to pay three—we walk. No discussion. We just fucking walk."

"Wait, man," I go. "If we walk will I get my three-hundred bucks?"

"Yeah, dog. Dre wouldn't do you like that. He'll pay, and so will fucking Lester, eventually, dog. But it'll just take more time. But don't worry Dre's good about this shit. You'll have cash tonight."

"OK, man," I go. But I'm still getting pretty nervous.

Kid seems to like sense my jitters, man. "Dude—you ready for this? You ready to break that crystal? Because now it's for real."

"Yeah, I'm ready. Just need a hit to stay sharp, man." I pull out my small Tupperware of coke. I dash a small mound on my finger. Kid T totally asks if he could have a hit too and I'm like *sure*. I dab a fucking little on his finger and he snorts it and pulls a piece out of his jacket. It's a fucking SIG. Like its right out of one of my dad's gun mags he's got stacked right by our first-floor shitter. Kid pulls out the clip, checks the mag and clicks the clip back into place and cocks it like he's fucking John Wick or some shit.

"Just in case, dog. Now grab the shit and let's fucking do this," Kid goes, and we pull out and turn the corner.

I reach back into the back seat and grab the backpack of glass. All fucking one hundred and five grams worth. "Cheese and rice, man. We get caught—we are well beyond fucking possession."

"That's right, Lil Pops. We deep into an *eleven-three-eight-seven* we get caught with this shit," Kid T goes and fucking winks.

We screech to a stop in front of some shitty house. We hop out of the car. Man, the first thing I notice is the other houses on the street. I mean, the one we pull up to is lit up like it's Christmas. It isn't a trailer home. It's like a real house even though it's like surrounded by trailers. But what gets me wasn't that some are trailers, man. It's that none of the houses on Lester's half of the block are lit at all. There's like no lights on in any of them. Not inside, not outside, nothing. Now that could've been because they're deserted—which is fine, I guess. But what if they're not? Also, there's this random patch of woods at the end of the street like the whole goddamn neighborhood just stops and gives way to fucking forest, man. Like we had just entered the neighborhood at the end of the world if like the world was, you know, flat or whatever.

But there's like no more time to think about that shit because here I am, following Kid T across the lawn then up the front porch stairs and knocking on the front door.

A couple seconds later a door opens and this guy with rotting teeth is standing in front of us.

"Hey!" the guy goes, blowing rancid breath through his browning rotten chompers. "My fucking main man, Kid T! Come ye the fuck in, fine gents."

"Hardy, fucking har, har, dog," goes Kid. "What up, Lester?"

We step in his living room I guess and Lester's all smiles for Kid T, but he gives me a fucking less-than-thrilled look. "Who's this, man?"

"This is A-Sac, dog. He's here to seal our deal, man."

I shoot a glance at Kid T. *A-Sac? You fucking serious?*

Kid just gives me this shit-eating shrug.

"The fuck you say?" Lester goes. "*A-Sac*, huh?"

I swallow my jitters and put on my best psycho-glare.

Lester's a couple inches taller than both Kid T and I. He's about forty years old or so, thin hair up top, a little longer in back, not quite a fucking mullet but getting there. He's wearing this beyond ratty T-shirt that's got ROCHESTER COLLEGE printed across the front. The guy's a sure hard-core tweeker, looking all skeletal in his sagging jeans that look fucking like they've been pissed in and dried and not washed.

"Yeah. You can fucking call me, A-Sac, *Lester*," I go, getting into character.

Lester wipes his amused-ass smirk off his face and just keeps staring at me for a spell. In the meantime, Kid T backs up and stands behind me, facing Lester over my shoulder and with his own back to the front door.

"So—like, A-Sac. Is it safe to say then that, uh, Kid T's your *bitch?"* Lester goes.

I look back to Kid T and grin, fucking enjoying this part for the moment. "Yeah. It's safe to say the Kid's my bitch. Now are we dealing or what?"

You could see something on Lester's face change. Like he was ready to take me seriously from then on.

"*OK* kids. Righty *ho-ho-ho*!" he goes and looks at my pack. "Is that the shit then?"

"Yep," I go and unsling the back and put it on the stained and shredded carpet.

"May I?" Lester goes.

"Sure," I go, and look back to Kid. Kid just nods like *yeah, man—this is how it's done.*

Lester drops to the floor with the bag and unzips it making sure the glass is all there. Meanwhile I take in the rest of the room. On my right's a sofa with a girl sitting on the far end. She looks about fourteen or so. She's trashy, thin as a cracker, greasy blonde hair that don't look too frequently washed, man. She's got grimy short shorts and a shirt on that looks like she got it at Salvation Army. She must be cold in that get up because it's fall now. Anyway, she's texting on her phone. She looks up once and we like lock eyes, but her stare is vacant. I can't tell if she's stoned, zoned, or just a fucking ditz.

She goes back to texting like a fiend, all thumbs, man—and I look across from her and there's a TV tuned to some glitzy poker game. Then it like registers with me—the TV's like a fucking huge brand-new HD plasma screen, man. I mean, the rest of the house looks like shit, but they got a brand fucking spanking new plasma? I mean, the thing was nicer than our TV and my dad's the biggest fucking drug dealer in town, man.

I see they got plastic all stapled over the windows. Like every window I can see. Which isn't too uncommon for Michigan—but in October? Maybe it was early for it—maybe it wasn't. I didn't know, I never put that plastic shit up and neither did my pops.

"Righty ho-ho-ho," Lester goes and stands back up after checking our goods. "Well, man—I mean, sorry—*A-Sac,* if you please, what do I owe ya?"

"Three and half grand," I go. *What the fuck's with that smell*? I say to myself. I mean, I'd realized it smelled like a pipesmoker's pad in here upon entry, but the longer we stood there… I mean, *fuck* –the meth smell was getting stronger it seemed.

"Scotty! Yo! Scotty, man!" Lester yells over his shoulder into what looks like a filthy kitchen.

Footsteps come pounding down some stairs somewhere and someone steps into the kitchen. Then like out of nowhere this guy shows up behind Lester and goes, "*Yeah*?"

And *this* guy… Fucking cheese and rice, Rozz. This guy looks like a fucking beat-to-shit zombie, I mean living dead beyond dead, man. Sunken eyes and browner teeth than what Lester was sporting, man. Seriously. Each of his teeth look like tiny turds stuck in his slimy gums, man. And this guy's peering into the living room from the kitchen waiting to see what Lester wants, his eye twitching multiple times likes he's fucking seizure-*ing*. And skinny as Lester is, this Scotty guy is skinnier. Thin as an anorexic credit card if that's possible. He's got his push-button flannel shirt tucked in just above his huge-ass belt buckle—as if to make the fashion statement, *yeah big buckle means a big dick beneath, ladies*. Which is shit, because everybody knows a lifetime pipe smoker couldn't get a solid boner to save their life.

"Scotty—go get these boys their money," Lester goes. "I think the case is upstairs."

"Yeah, fucking-*A*. I know right where it is. Be right back, dudes," Scotty goes but stays an extra second to lean in and shoot a look to the girl over on the couch. She looks back at him and then he darts back through the kitchen goes back upstairs.

The girl just fucking goes back to texting.

So now we're just standing there. Lester with his back to the kitchen. Me facing him with Kid standing right behind me.

Something bumps the floor beneath us like there's someone screwing around in the basement.

We all heard it, but Lester doesn't say jack shit.

"Yo, what's going on down there? Sounds fucking lively," Kid T goes.

"Just my kids. Probably wrestling around and shit. Rowdy little fuckers," Lester goes. "Say, now that I really look at you, *A-Sac,* you look like you're just a kid too. I mean don't fucking get me wrong Kid T's always looked like a primary school motherfucker too. But you look like a fucking babyface next to him. Huh—*A-Sac?* You a baby*?"*

I start to fucking freeze up, Rozz. I didn't understand the fucking change in tone of the whole scene, man. And it wasn't just Lester's tone changing. It was fucking Kid T's too. Because suddenly he goes, "Oh yeah, Lester—you genius—*whose* baby does he look like, huh?"

"*What?*" Lester goes.

"You know who this is?" Kid T keeps pressing. I feel him get closer like right behind me, his voice in my fucking ear.

"What the fuck you on about? Do I fucking know *A-Sac* or whoever the fuck this is? How in the holy shit should I know who this is—you fucking brought him!" Lester goes.

And suddenly it just all hits me, Rozz. All the shit that didn't make sense and felt all wrong about this whole deal just comes stacking up in my mind super-freaking fast like my mind was like trying to send my body one last warning to get the fuck out of there ASAP, man. The dark neighborhood, the beyond amped up smell of glass (that I had finally figured out that was coming not only from the kitchen, but more likely the basement), the plasma screen, and the fucking fourteen-year-old chick texting *someone*.

And now here comes Scotty bounding down the stairs presumably with our cash but before Scotty can make it to the kitchen door Lester suddenly smiles all weird and twisted, flashing those shit-stained teeth, grinning like he's the motherfucking methed-up rabbit that just out foxed the drug-dealing gangsta-wannabe fox.

And that's exactly when I see Kid T's arm come out and extend past my shoulder and point his loaded SIG out at Lester. Lester's got just enough time to drop his goof-ass smile before Kid T pulls the trigger and sends an ear-blasting round right through Lester's ROCHESTER COLLEGE T-shirt and into his chest.

Blackish blood starts pumping out of this small hole and soaks down Lester's shirt as he falls dead as shit back into the kitchen and I barely have time to scream *what the fuck* to Kid T before the world suddenly blows up behind us.

I mean, we're talking *BOOM!*

Shards of glass, bits of wood and metal from the front door just rocket into the house. A shitload of hell plows into Kid T's back. His jacket just rips and disintegrates along with most of his T-shirt. You can tell a bunch of it rips right into his skin too because of the way he screams.

Kid crashes hard into me and we both fall to the floor just in time to see Scotty run into the kitchen—only that bastard's not carrying a case of our money—he's got a motherfucking shotgun. Then behind us like on the front porch somewhere we hear the unfuckingmistakable sound of another shotgun *CHH-CHH* another round into the barrel ready to fire.

Kid T raises up off me and starts firing rounds at Scotty in the kitchen before he can fire at us.

I fucking pissed my pants, Rozz. I fucking did. Right then, man.

And then I get hit in the head with a cereal bowl.

It breaks right on the top of my head. Milk and fucking Cheerios everywhere, man. I whirl around and see that fourteen-year-old chick chucking dirty dishes from the windowsill at us yelling blue murder the whole time.

Kid T twists and shoots out of what used to be the front door to keep that other unseen motherfucker at bay.

But that's when that hidden fucker blows the big living room window apart with another shotgun blast.

Pulverized glass rains in everywhere, you can taste it in the air. No kidding Rozz, you could taste glass in the air.

The screaming chick's blown back to the sofa showered with glass. I don't think she got too chewed up by the buckshot, but I couldn't be too sure. Anyway, she looks alive, scared shit-stone still and streaking blood from like everywhere. Her legs, arms, face. Man, you name it, Rozz. She looks like fucking *Carrie* on prom night, man.

Scotty fires a Hail Mary from the kitchen basically demolishing the kitchen doorframe sending wood frags out to the living room. Smoke's everywhere. You can taste it.

Finally my body starts hearing what my mind is screaming for it to do—which is *GET THE HELL OUT!*

I stand up and pull Kid T up with me. He's still screaming. Blood's streaming all over his back and that's when I realize how bad a shape the poor fucker's in.

I take the SIG from him and drape his arm over mine like in those fucking buddy-buddy war movies and start moving us toward the huge opening that had fucking lately been the door to this shithouse turned warzone.

But before we cross step outside I send a bullet out into the dark hoping to send the mystery gunman running for cover.

Then, convinced that we're gonna get blasted in half by shotgun blast at any second, either from the front or from behind, I charge us out into the night and practically fling us down the porch stairs into the front yard.

Sure enough before we can get up and head to Kid T's Mitsu—a blast comes from a crouching figure at the corner of the house. Lucky for us the fucker aims too low and the buckshot mostly tears into the front lawn. Grass and fucking soil and some small rocks fucking did a mini-mushroom cloud in front of us and then showers down on us. Unlucky for us we still got bit by some shit from the shell. Some shot tore into my left leg and I roar in pain and get a seriously potent shot of adrenaline. Kid T however is even more unlucky, taking some shot into his upper thigh area now ripping his jeans and into his flesh.

While I'm still roaring, I fire the SIG multiple times at where the crouching figure was. I really didn't see the target because of all the dark and the haze of the blast, but who gives a fuck at this point?

I stop firing and manage to drag us the rest of the way to the Mitsu.

I fling the passenger's side door open and dump Kid T in—even though he's screaming in pain at how rough I'm being.

I run around to the driver's side. Scotty emerges from the doorway with his shotgun across both hands. I fire the rest of the SIG's clip at him and he dives back into the house.

I see him point the shotgun barrel out of the door and fire a blast into the night. Fucking harmless though. The buckshot doesn't come near us.

Before I can slide into the driver's seat, I think I hear some belabored moans coming from the darkness near where I thought the mystery shotgun man would be. *Good. I hope you fucking die, shitbag.* I remember thinking. But then again maybe I didn't hear any moans at all. Maybe it was just the ringing in my ears from all this fucking gunfire.

"Where are the fucking keys?" I scream to Kid.

"Right here, right here, man! Let's fucking go!" Kid screams back.

I crank the ignition, hit the gas, and we screech out of there blaring past all the pitch-black houses and back into the streets of light and life, man. I slow the car down after we get a few blocks away—but my heart and balls were pumping a mile a minute, man.

30

Coach Striden

Well, after our drubbing (oh let's just face it—it was an all-out ass kicking by Ann Arbor Huron) we piled up in the team bus and marched into Harper Hills for a Saturday conference match. My promoted JV squad lost again 3-0—but I didn't even care. Each one of those kids fought as valiantly as their skills would allow. Again, Tristan Marigan continued to impress, and it was clear that we were going to need him to play on the full Varsity squad—maybe even as starting striker in Trevor's old spot.

I didn't allow any of the suspended Varsity guys to travel on the bus with us to Harper Hills—although they were there to see the JV boys off, wishing them luck, telling them no matter what the score, to *give'em hell.* You could tell the younger guys really appreciated it too. Like even though the JV kids knew they were in all probability about to get slaughtered—they had the support and the respect from the older kids, and you could tell that meant something to them.

I didn't tell the suspended guys to do it either—they just did.

What I really wasn't expecting, and what was probably, up to that point, one of the most memorable things I've ever seen as a coach, was to see the same older players: Luke, Erik, Ryan, Patrick, Troy—all of them, still there four hours later in the parking lot waiting for their stand-in teammates to return.

The older boys cheered as we pulled up even though they already knew we lost (some of the JVer's texted them the score after the game). They formed a line as the younger boys got off the bus, shook the JV guys hands, patted their backs, and said *thank yous* to them.

I even heard Patrick Durning say to Tim Felton (Patrick's backup JV Goalkeeper) "Thanks for cleaning up my mess, Tim. And hanging in there. I know keeping against those teams wasn't easy, man. But don't worry about it—you'll get'em back next year when you're full Varsity."

Tim nodded his head and smiled at Patrick's encouragement.

They then ushered the JV guys over to the tailgate of Troy Jensen's pick-up truck where they had a couple of towers of hot pizzas and a cooler full of Gatorade and soda. The parking lot suddenly turned into our own private Mardi Gras. Erik even started up his kazoo riffing "You Really Got Me" by *The Kinks* which the whole team eventually started to howl together.

I was beyond stunned, to say the least.

Usually in high school sports programs you have two distinct teams: your Varsity All-Stars and your JV Misfits. They usually practice separate, bond separately—and in some cases the kids on these teams sometimes never even know the names of those on the other roster.

But what was going on in that parking lot—what had been going on all that week at games and in practice—was anything but divisive. It was the pinnacle of unity. It was

all so incredible; so unexpected. And if I'm being honest here, I'd have to admit I really had
nothing to do with it. This was all *them.*

The party in the parking lot signaled the end of the suspension for the Varsity players. We had only one conference game remaining—which was essentially meaningless now. Losing two straight games kept us out of contention of winning the Conference Championship. So we would have another week of practice before the playoffs would start.

As we practiced in the coming days for our last conference game there was a noticeable change in the tone of our practices. It was a coach's total dream come true. First off, I was always last to arrive to practice because of my teaching duties—and before the suspensions, there were always guys milling around, half-dressed, some lingering around behind the Team Center taking a piss. But after the suspensions, I'd pull in and all the lads were dressed, jogged, and stretched. I mean, talk about *wow.* My assistant, Dan Vogel, goes to me as I walked up on one of those afternoons, "Get ready, Libby—the boys' are amped up again today…"

We nailed through drills with the utmost intensity. Their focus was singular; unshakeable. They were silent when we gave them instructions. You could see on their faces, their minds grinding at the concept we were drilling. It was just a ridiculous 180 degrees from where we had been in our practice effort.

They bled sweat like their pores were water-wounds, their effort sprayed and shredded the turf with their intensity. And yet, even with all this newfound ferocity, there was also such a *playfulness* about them. You know what I mean? Smiles abounded even when they were hunched over in exhaustion after I had just killed them sprinting 120's. They ribbed each other between drills still—but the usual amount of grab-assing was gone. There was no horseplay, no bitching, no nonsense—and yet—the gleam in their eyes, the passion with which they did the most commonplace skill drill—you could see it all over the practice field. You could practically breathe it all around you, it swirled around them, around Coach Vogel and even me, like some unseen warrior spirit sent to lift up those who were soon to go into battle.

And then it hit me as I watched Patrick with his big old keeper's glove tousle Tristan's hair as he rifled in a goal during shot drills, or after Troy picked up Pauly off the turf after a bone-crunching tackle and Pauly just tapped Troy's shoulder, wincing—but still like sincerely smiling and saying "*Nice* hit, dude. You keep hitting people like that in the games and guys are gonna be running scared from us. Seriously." And as I saw Luke grinning at it all, grinning at his teammates in a way I had never quite seen before from him, or anyone, in a practice, a look more like true brotherly love than anything I had ever seen on a soccer field. That's when I knew what I was seeing.

Joy.

Pure joy.

No other words for it.

Joy unbounded. The joy of struggle—pure and true, you know? The joy of a deep and righteous fury.

WARRIOR'S JOY.

Beethoven's 9th couldn't even touch what I was seeing out there.

Unbelievable. I mean, unbelievable. I could barely even conceive it. OK. So, first Luke turns himself in for drinking. Moorehouse, T.J., and Linus quit. The team turns themselves in for drinking, for godsakes. Then non-stop school gossip. Students, teachers, yadda, yadda—we get socially crucified. Negative press fallout—*I* nearly get crucified. Followed by a catastrophic drop in fan attendance at games. And then getting our butts kicked in two straight.

And all *that* turns into *this?*

Seriously? I get unbridled joy out of them? *You gotta be kidding me…* I'm telling you, it was at that moment that I became ridiculously aware of how much I didn't know jack about how to coach team chemistry.

Our final regular season match came. Watching us you would've thought we were playing a World Cup Final. Our opponent, East Kentwood was a solid mid-tier team—but they must have been completely taken aback at our aggressive play right from the opening whistle. Especially throughout what, by all accounts, should've been a meaningless throw-away game.

For whole segments of the match, we dribbled and passed around the Kentwood players as if they were vapors, rather than real athletes of flesh and bone. We won by virtue of four beautiful goals—the crowning jewel being an explosive header by Tristan, our new freshman phenom. And the celebration after was, well, immaculate. They swarmed the freshman, with Luke lifting Tristan up above the mass of teammates as if he were weightless.

Our modest crowd went crazy with applause. We were down to mostly just parents for fans at that point. But who cared? Their faces beaming, some moms nearly weeping at the joy of seeing their sons not only thrive on the pitch—but also emerge as human beings. The parents had noticed the same growth at home that I had seen on the field in practice. These boys were noticeably *changing.* Over beers later that night in my backyard around the fire circle, Coach Vogel, just shook his head sitting back in his lawn chair and put the change into words perfectly in his slightly Scottish accent, "Libby, they're not just boys anymore—they're becoming men. Ah, Libby—it's a sight to see."

When the Kentwood game was finished, I went and shook hands with the opposing coaches and then turned back to look at the bleachers where my team was meeting with their parents, and that's when I saw the sign. I hadn't noticed it during the match—but I saw it now. You see, I grew up about as tomboy as they come, and I'm usually not prone to quick emotional responses—a couple of past boyfriends had even used the phrase "emotionally frigid," but maybe it was because of the moment, or my hormones on the day, or whatever, but when I saw the sign Ryan Leone's dad was holding, I have to admit I felt a slight lump in my throat. I realized that we were, all of us, truly experiencing something special here.

The sign read:

Forget Dream Teams.
We Got The Redeemed Team!

31

Jason

There's curious fuckers all peeping out windows and a couple of brave-assed souls out on their front lawns wondering what the commotion was as we rocket past in Kid T's car. I covered my face as best I could and didn't worry about them seeing Kid T—he had already leaned his seat back as far as it could go and was writhing on his side in like supreme pain, man. And blood was flowing out of him, like everywhere. We were gonna like have to burn his car, or fucking dump it in a lake, or something.

Aint gonna be long before the cops get wind of this shitstorm, I remember thinking. I was also betting some of these fuckers were getting a good goggle at this car and its motherfucking plates, man.

"Think!" I actually say out loud and pound the steering wheel.

Kid T has like no response because of the pain he's in. I just keep driving like a madman and think how he's screwed. How I might be screwed too.

"What the fuck, man! What the fuck! What the hell with fucking blowing Lester away, man?" I go.

Kid just moans while I keep driving, hauling ass.

"Answer me motherfucker! What the fuck about snuffing out Lester, man? What kind of deal was this *really* supposed to be? Why'd it suddenly turn to shit? And if Lester's place wasn't a fucking renta-lab I'm a tina's asshole, man!"

I mean, I was going ape shit, Rozz. No wait, ape shit doesn't even cut it, man—let me re-phrase—I was full-blown going *King Kong* shit trying to get Kid T to fucking enlighten me ASAP on what the hell just happened.

"Get my phone, man. Fucking get Dre, man," Kid goes.

"What? Naw, man—screw Dre. We need to get your ass to a hospital. You're way too fucked—"

"No hospital!" Kid T goes. "No fucking hospital! You fucking hear me? Dre! Get Dre on the phone. *Now,* goddamit—" Kid digs his phone out of his pocket and flings it at me. His blood's smeared all over it like melted chocolate, man. "Press **Dad** on my contacts," he goes, and keeps writhing.

At this point I'm freaked for him (I mean, Rozz, I'd never seen someone shot for real, much less seeing gushing blood, ripped up skin all pink and pulpy and shit—not to mention seeing little glimpses of bone that was all coming out of his legs) and at the same time, I was also fucking fuming like a roided Incredible Hulk at him for not telling me what the fuck was going on with the deal and why I almost died and while we're at it, why he wasted Lester in cold fucking blood back there.

The whole thing was beyond fucked but I start getting a grip. I start thinking again.

I squeal down another dark street and steer straight for a park I know and park along the curb. I can hear sirens pretty far off in the distance. Heading towards Hotel Lester, no doubt.

"What the hell? Call Dre." Kid T goes, his voice getting weaker.

I take out my flask and chug a gulp. Leaning over I lift the flask up to Kid's mouth so he can down the rest of it.

"Kid," I go. "Here's the deal, I'm sorry as hell you're shot up and chewed to christ right now. And I really hope you don't die. But before I call Dre or do any damn thing on your behalf, you're gonna answer a few of my questions. OK?"

"Whatever, dude—just get Dre like fucking pronto, man."

"You gotta another clip to the SIG?" I go.

"Yeah. But what's that got—"

"Give it to me."

"Dude—stop playing around and call Dre. OK? He'll know what to do. He'll make sure I get patched up—"

"OK, OK, I'll call him for fuck's sakes. First give me your extra SIG clip."

Kid T looks at me as clear-eyed as he can. "Why do you want the clip, man?"

"Fucking *Duh*, man. Did you get shot in the fucking head? The cops are probably storming Lester's crib as we speak. You thinking they're just waiting around there to go on record of what went down there, man? Seriously? With a body on the carpet? Doors and windows blown to shit, eighty grams worth of glass in some backpack, not to mention a probable Walmart-lab they got all rigged up with fucking duct tape and Junior High School Science beakers down in that basement of theirs? I mean, talk about a bunch of JV B-team drug dealing motherfuckers. Come on, T! Use what fucking brain capacity you got left and fucking think, dude. It doesn't take an Einstein motherfucker to suppose that what's left of the Shotgun Brothers are cruising around these neighborhoods looking for your goddamn Mitsubishi Eclipse, avoiding cops the best they can and looking for some motherfucking payback. Does it? So fucking give me the SIG clip so I can reload our ass and then I'll call Dre or Pazzaro's motherfucking Pizza for delivery or whatever the fuck you want."

"OK, OK. Fucking christ. Here, dude," Kid goes and hands me this sharp rectangular clip from his coat pocket. "But call Dre like right the fuck now, man. He'll know what to do with my sorry ass without messing with the fucking ER."

I hold up the SIG, eject the empty clip like it was nothing, and clip the new mag in where it clicks and I get this rush all of a sudden. A fucking surge, man—like my pussy dick goes suddenly *Die Hard*, man.

"All right now, Turner," Kid T goes. "Fucking hold up your end, dude and call Dre like fucking ASAP, dog."

"Not just yet, Kid," I go. "First, you're gonna tell me all of it, man. From the fucking the lips to the motherfucking ass what the hell happened tonight."

But Kid can't take anymore I guess and just goes ballistic on me. Yelling and screaming that he's dying and shit, that if I don't call Dre, I'm gonna be a dead man myself no matter who my dad is. He screams out a ton of shit.

But Rozz, that's when I let the little roided Incredible Hulk lurking inside of me really go. I knew right then that Kid T wasn't gonna say shit till he knew he had to truly deal with me before Dre would be able to help him. I knew he needed to know that if he didn't tell me all the shit I wanted he wasn't ever gonna make it to Dre because his ass was going to be dead.

So that's when I just freaked on him.

Without fucking warning, man—I just start slapping him totally open handed in the face. Like *hard*, man. It totally takes Kid off guard too because he was still like trying to scream orders at me when I start wailing on him. Then I clench my fingers that griped the SIG and fucking clock him. Not *too* hard but hard enough to get his full fucking attention.

I open the driver's side and storm over and open his door and drag him out all rough and one-handed, so his body landed on the grass near the curb of the park. There were no close houses near us, except the park—so we were basically alone with only the playground equipment you could see all deserted in the distance.

Looking back on it now, I kind of hate I did it, you know with Kid T already fucking howling with pain from the shotguns—but I just started kicking the bastard then on the grass. Kicked his stomach, fucking legs, I think even once on the back of the head—I'm not totally sure, you know? I was really getting into it. He made some sick and hollow sounds and spat up some sick looking blood as I grabbed him back up by what was left of his torn-to-shit jacket and slammed him up against his Mitsu and then put the fucking muzzle of his own SIG up to his temple and looked like the fucking Devil's Bastard right into his eyes—And in that moment, Rozz—I thought, *Fucking Hell Yeah!* Maybe I can do this! Maybe I can trigger the fucking life out of someone. Maybe that Forrester kid was all full of shit with his psycho mind-fuck games like that night out at Harper Lake.

Maybe I am the psycho-killer Dre thinks I can be. Because I was rushing, Rozzy—and with that muzzle right up to Kid T's head felt way different than holding the fucking power of life and death like I had with Forrester out at the lake. With him it ended up feeling impossible with that hatchet. But it wasn't the same tonight with the trigger and Kid T and fucking all that pent-up adrenaline from almost getting blasted from fucking time at space at Lester's.

Fuck, Rozz—maybe rushing on adrenaline, Everclear, and coke with a trigger at your finger is a pretty fucked up math equation, man. No wonder the life expectancy of heavy camelbackers sucks to shit—especially here near *The D*.

But I didn't shoot him, Rozz. I scared the shit out of him that's for sure. Even scared myself a little. So yeah, I didn't shoot him. But I sure as shit continued my line of questioning.

"Fucking Kid! You need to listen to me now. I don't want to but I'm ready to whip you to death right here with the butt of your own fucking gun and leave your sorry ass here in the grass for the pigs or the dogs to piss on if you don't tell me what the fuck all of this is about."

You can finally see it in Kid's eyes. He realizes, Rozz. He realizes he's good as dead if he doesn't talk.

"It was Dre, man. Dre didn't trust Lester. He was pretty sure Lester was gonna start selling glass on his own. You smelled it in there—yeah? If that wasn't a fucking factory cooking down there in Lester's basement tonight then I don't know gold from shit, man."

"So if Lester and his shotgun crew were gonna start selling their own fucking meth, why order huge-ass from us?"

"Dude," Kid goes, "to fucking take us out, dog. Get rid of the competition, that's why, man."

I shake my head. "Don't those tweeked fuck-ups know—they take us out Dre'd come in from Detroit and—"

Kid T groans. "No, man. They don't know Dre exists, man. Those tinas think it's mostly just a bunch of kids cooking and running the local glass."

"Well, what about my Pops? They know he exists—or were they thinking of taking him out too?"

"Yeah, maybe... I don't know, man."

"OK, dickhead—then if you knew if might turn into a fucking bad night in Baghdad, why the fuck bring me in? Put me in front for chrissakes?"

"Come on man," Kid goes. "It was all Dre's idea, man. Ask him."

I raise the SIG again up to Kid's face. "Why did Dre want me fucking face to face with Lester at that deal, man?"

Kid winces hard core. I think he really believed I was gonna blow him away right then. "Dre wanted to see if Lester recognized you. If he did, then that would mean he'd probably been to your pop's place, it would mean for sure that your pops and Lester had like talked, yo. Dre's just trying to see if Pop's is trying to play two ways, man."

"The fuck you say?" I go. "That my dad's looking to push Dre's shit *AND* shit from Lester and the shotgun tweekers too?"

"That's what Dre was trying to find out, dog. He don't know though. And obviously, Lester didn't have a fucking clue who you were. So can we now—fucking please—call Dre?"

Well, Rozz—I swear I didn't know what to make of all this shit Kid was spouting but the way he was saying it made me believe Kid believed what he was saying. Whether it was true or not.

I ring Dre and tell him quick what happened and where we were. I was super-pissed and wanted to blow up on Dre on the phone for setting my ass up—but didn't. Dre tells us to lay low at the park and he and his crew would be there as quick as they could.

I hang up and tuck the SIG in the back of my jeans. Then I lean down and try to help Kid T up. I was all done going all psycho on him and he seemed to trust me again now that he'd told me the truth about the camelback.

I hear more sirens in the distance and know it would be damn risky just to leave Kid T still all bleeding and shit in the Mitsu, under a fucking streetlight no less, where a patrol car could just roll up to us and that would be that, man, *GAMEOVER*.

"Come on, Kid," I go. "We gotta get you hid till Dre gets here man."

So we move with Kid T groaning all the way. Takes a while but I drag him over to this deserted playground to hide. It was one of those playgrounds that's made to look like a castle. There's ladders you have to climb up to get into this like kid-fortress to get to all the slides and swings and monkey bars and shit.

The little castle is like a perfect hideout because it's dark as a motherfucker in there and I'd be able to see the street out from the thin window of the fortress.

So I lay Kid T down as soft as I can on the wood-chipped covered ground. We just wait like there for a while. I can hear Kid T coughing through his weak-ass breaths every once in a while, so I know he's still alive with me there in the dark.

From time to time I'd glow the castle up with Kid's phone just to check the time. And sure enough, one of the times I did, a fucking patrol car like totally rolls real slow down the street where the Mitsu's sitting. I shove the phone down my pants and shit like my third cat of the fucking evening, man.

Kid whispers, "is it Dre?"

"No—shut up, man. It's the cops. Just shut it and chill, man."

The cop car slows down and looks at the Mitsu and pulls back, parks by the curb behind it and just idles.

Shit, fuck, and Jesus, Rozz.

The cop just parks there forever. I mean *for fucking ever*. They must have been running Kid's plates for sure, man.

"Kid—" I whisper. "How's your driving record these days? Any unpaid tickets? Fucking DUI's?"

"No," he goes back. "I'm crystal traffic-wise, man."

Suddenly the patrol car's side-search light lamps up and the cop scans it over the dark playground. My god, Rozz. Here it comes—the pig motherfucker's gonna come over here with his light, see us move—or hell, smell Kid T's stinking rancid blood, call for back up—and *Bang*, Rozz—we're done. I'd probably get shot on accident trying to surrender when I held up the SIG because knowing my shit-ass luck the cops I'd get would be the twitchiest fuckers on the force.

But that doesn't happen. It's a miracle—or maybe you're an angel now looking over me or something like that because the cop just clicks the light off and drives the cruiser off.

Talk about breathing out one of the top-ranked sighs of relief of all time, man. Cheese and rice, Rozz. Fucking cheese and rice.

We wait again. And I think at one point Kid might've just fallen asleep. It's all quiet as fuck for a long time and I realize that I could probably just get up—like right then—and sneak home safe and sound. I could just ditch Kid T in the castle and walk home in the dark. I could be careful and watch for fucking cops and still be home in less than twenty minutes I figure. Maybe fifteen if I booked it.

But I don't go. Even though it was probably post to just hang there because surely the cops would come back to check on the Mitsu. And even though I didn't feel I owed it to Dre to explain anything since he'd pretty much like knowingly set me up in a situation where I could get shot. And fuck the three hundred bucks now—although, maybe that's part of the reason I stayed in the castle a little longer. Just so I could confront Dre about this bullshit and see how he took it if I fucking demanded my three-hundred bucks.

But mainly, Rozz, if you wanna know the truth, I think I stayed for Kid T. I think I knew like somewhere deep down it'd be wrong to just ditch him. Now, I know you know as goddamn well as anybody, I do wrong things all the time and I'm usually fucking fine with it. But I don't know. This just seemed different. Like it would be a mortal sin or some shit for me to ditch Kid in this state. You know, like it would be a huge act of dishonor on my part or something. I mean, it's really hard to put into words what I was thinking about it. I just got this bad sense in my head, like I heard this little voice say, *Hey, you do this, you ditch on Kid right now, and you cross over the line with them. Them. The fucking Dres, and Dylans, and fucking Cunters of this world. Even your Dad for chrissakes.* I mean, what the fuck, right?

So I get to thinking about other stuff, like even the playground castle we're chilling in and how little kids must think this fucking place is the balls—which gets me to thinking more about how boys probably play around on it pretending to be knights and warriors with sticks for swords and go around slaying imaginary dragons and saving fucking maidens from the tower by escaping down this huge spiraling slide which also gets me thinking, you know, about like real knights, ones that wore real armor and shit like way back in the fucking days of yore or whatever. Back when guys fought with some kind of code and had that chivalry shit oozing out of their armor like it was some kind of righteous diarrhea, about how all those stories with heroes and wizards wearing robes and carrying staffs the size of petrified elephant dicks, and how those stories are such bullshit fantasies. But that's probably why geeks flock to that shit—because it's so fucking ideal and unrealistic as hell.

Then I wonder if, like back in the dark ages, they had shit like meth and other traffic to fight over if knights would still fight with nobility, or if their fucking code of honor would all just crumble away and fall into the shitty moats surrounding all their limp-dick castles. And then I think that's why all castles these days have to be fake and tales about knights and dragons are all fantasy bullshit. Because there can't be knights and fucking honor in a place and time where there aint no good guys and there aint no bad guys. Seems to me there's only just guys and like the *really bad guys,* you know? Like evil fuckers like Cunter. Fucking psychos that enjoy cutting people into pieces for fucking fun and no other reason. And I thought about how there aint no Light and Dark these days—it's that everyone's more or less just fucking gray as goose shit when it comes down to it. Everybody's just looking out for themselves, just rotating each day between either being a clueless idiot or a fucking pain in someone else's already bleeding ass.

Honest to fucking god, Rozz, I thought all that stuff while I sat in the darkness of our play castle with Kid T's head practically in my godamn lap.

Well, finally his *Un*-Holiness, Dre shows up and I call out as he and Tagger and Sin-Dawg hop out of Dre's Rover.

I wake Kid up and help him stand but he was in some serious-ass pain if he even moved an inch.

So they run up to meet us and we're struggling out to them and Dre like orders Tagger and Sin to haul Kid T to the Rover, but Sin goes, "But the Kid's bleeding bad, Dre—"

Dre says it didn't matter because they had to haul before the fucking *Five-0* starts putting together the two and two, man. Once they get Kid in the Rover, Dre yells for Tagger to get the Mitsu and follow them.

Dre looks back at me standing in the wet grass like directly between the cars and the castle in the dark. "So you coming, Lil' Pops, or what?"

I swear, Rozz, I feel the SIG tingle between my belt and my back. "You fucking set me up."

"Well now, I see how it is now…" Dre goes.

I just stare back at him thinking about Kid's SIG tucked in at my back. "That really the way you want to play this, Dre?"

Dre looks like I amused him. "Looky here, Lil Pops—it aint personal, dawg. But I had to get the know on this Lester muthafucka and his band of tinas."

I don't say shit. Just look back at him.

"I had to know, dawg—whether they was just ordering and spending they life savings on the load of the tweeking century—or if they was looking to get into the biz. If it was the biz, I knew it might get fucking sporty, yo? But like I said, dawg—I had to know."

"I almost got fucking destroyed out there, man!" I go. "Kid's shredded to fucking hamburger. The fuck, man? If you knew it might get 'sporty' why not go blazing in there yourself? Between you, Tag, Sin, and your other boy, Cunter—you guys got enough muscle to take out Lester and his shotgun goons!"

"Lil' Pops, you aint seeing the big picture, dawg—the full canvas, yo. The only peeps that can know about us in this town is Kid, your Pops—my Pazzaro's boyz and you—and that it, yo?"

"And fucking Rozzy," I go. "She could know."

Dre all rolls his eyes and steps back like I just gassed out a silent killer of a fart.

"Oh now, looky here—there aint no reason to start going there, yo? Look, you need to stay focused on the present. You need to start thinking real hard about what comes next for you in this situation—because now we got some fucked up drama that gonna have to play itself out in these here subs."

My hands ball into fists. "And part of this drama is you think my dad is in with Lester?"

"Damn, dawg!" Dre goes. "How much shit you get out of Kid, yo? Serious? You like stick a lollie-pop of sodium pentothal up his ass while you two was hiding out in your little playhouse over there?"

"Well, Lester didn't recognize me, bitch. Kid T'll tell you the same, man."

"Yeah, dawg—I know," Dre go. "I know Kid'll tell me everything, yo."

"You know, whatever, man. The fact still is they don't know my dad, man," I go.

"You're right—maybe they don't, Lil Pops. Just because they didn't reckernize your pasty ass don't mean they's never bizzed with your pops."

"Yo, Dre—we got to split, dawg," Tagger yells from Kid's car.

"No shit—" Sin seconds out the Rover's window. "I be bugging here and Kid ain't good. He needs to go, dawg. Like right the fuck, Dre. Let's go, man."

"All right. Goddamn, y'all! I be right the fuck there. Chill," Dre goes and turns back to me. "I need to pow-wow with Pops—you tell him that. And remember you aint crystal no more neither, not in my book. Understand, Lil Pops? You like in live play now. So you need to think real hard about how you navigate from here, bitch."

"But why would my dad fucking biz with Lester when he's already got you?" I go, ignoring his bullshit.

"Looky, I aint got the time—so I'll just come out and make this real plain for your ass now. It's all about high-end/low-end, dawg. See our glass comes from like serious labs and chefs that know what the fuck, yo? So that means your Pops is selling quality product to good people for the most part in the subs. And that's been fine as wine for a long time, yo. But see, now time's getting harder—less cash, more junkies just want the jolt and don't give a shit about quality. So that's where these Lester fuckers see a niche in the market, yo? See? They looking to be Walmart while we be fucking Target, looky?

But if your Pops be bizzing with this Lester and his shotgun posse too, then he'd be getting slices from both ends—getting good glass from us and discount glass from those low-rent psycho-cookers. And the straight on this is we ain't too keen on competition in these subs—at least not on the scale this dead Lester fucker was hoping for."

More sirens are coming howling over the roofs of the nearby houses.

"Where's my three-hundred bucks," I go.

"Where's my camelback?"

"It's at fucking Lester's, man. The place turned to a war zone and I had to fight for our lives, man."

Dre keeps his eyes on me like he's got a built-in lie detector test tucked away in that paranoid brain of his, probably thinking I could be lying, but not sure.

"Dre! Let's go!" Tagger shouts.

Dre starts backing away towards the Mitsu and the Rover—but keeps looking right at me. "This ain't done, Lil Pops. We got us some fucked up drama here. That was a shitload of product you and Kid just lost—and *I will* get it back." He turns and runs to the Rover and they speed off.

I run back past the castle through the park and pull my hoodie up and run ninja-mode all the way home.

Dad wasn't around. Still isn't. Don't know where the fuck he is, Rozz. But I ain't looking forward to talking to him about any of this, you know? I don't know what to do now. I'm in fucking deep shit, I guess. I don't know. But I got a SIG Sauer now with a full clip. Don't know if that's a good thing or a bad. But anyway, I'm fucking spent. I'm drunk and I'm tired and my fucking hand is cramping like its fucking got PMS for fuck's sake.

Haunt me tonight, Rozzy girl.

Haunt me. Goodnight.

32

The closest Erik Volgstaad ever got to expressing his like totally true and amorous feelings for Maddie O'Leary was on Valentine's Day in Mrs. Kovoloski's Fifth Grade Class. It was afternoon, just after the Lunch recess and studies had been like suspended for the afternoon so that all Mrs. Kovoloski's little angels could haul out their hand-painted and magic markered shoe-box-Valentine-mailbox-for-a-day contraptions and place them on their desks so that everyone could get up with their stack of pink envelopes containing cheesy-assed, but sometimes heart-felt, cards with assorted Disney characters, race cars, and Spidermans and Barbies on them. Each card probably had that standard BE MY VALENTINE! with hearts and stuff, and if you were lucky, a Hershey Kiss might be attached to it with Scotch tape—or duct tape, maybe, if it was from a boy.

Anyway, you probably remember the total awkwardness/giddiness of this messed up ritual at your own elementary school with a kind of amused clarity. You probably remember how you wrote funny little inside jokes on your friend's cards and how you just pretty much signed your name on any kid's card you hated or just plain didn't know well. But then there was that *third* kind of card. You know, fellas—the card to *that girl* (or girls!) that you just happened to think was cute—or maybe you had even talked to a couple of times and didn't manage to sound like a total geek, and you might be thinking if you just wrote down exactly the right thing on that cheap card that that might just be enough for her to *like* you back or even make her want to be your girlfriend a couple of years later—you know, by the time you would actually have some sort of clue how to sound cool talking to a girl and might even have a couple of hairs starting to grow on your balls. The world was like totally full of romantic possibilities if—that is—you could nail down the right thing to scribble onto that special card with Mickey and Minnie Mouse on it.

Erik stayed up well past his nine o' clock bedtime going back and forth what to put on Maddie's card. He'd had a puppy-eyed jones for little O'Leary since Kindergarten and by the grace of the Primary School gods, he had the good fortune to be in each and every one of her classes at Grover Elementary, with the one exception of third grade, which had been a hell on earth for poor Erik and he habitually asked his teacher, Mrs. Anderson to go to the bathroom promptly at 10:25 so that he could catch one faraway glimpse of Maddie as her class, led by her teacher, Mrs. Birthington, went traipsing in single file to the gymnasium for their Phy Ed. period to play dodgeball or whatever. Erik would stand by the water fountain as Mrs. Birthington's class walked by and would sip water until Maddie passed by him, suspecting nothing, and then he would stare—blatantly, longingly at the back of Maddie's head. Taking in everything there was to take in about her auburn/blonde curls, her earrings dangling from her small tender lobes, if she was wearing them (he liked the green one's the best) and how soft she looked in her long-sleeve cotton shirts.

It's safe to say by the time he was in fifth-grade, Erik Volgstaad had it bad for little Maddie O'Leary.

So there he was up in his room, tapping his pencil on his small table where he usually did his homework—or pretended to, trying to figure out what little message to write on Maddie's Valentine card. He had like long since finished the rest of his class' cards and licked their nappy envelopes and stacked them all neatly together and even wrapped the pile in a thick rubber band. But what to write, what to write? Why couldn't he think of anything cool? Poor Erik wracked his eleven-year-old brain. Maybe he should just sign his name like he did with all the other girls in his class and just be on the lookout to talk to her later.

But then inspiration hit him. *Or sorta*, I guess. Anyway, Erik scrawled Maddie a special message and licked the envelope as gentle as if he were licking one of her earlobes and tucked it in with the others.

The next day at school when Mrs. Kovoloski announced everyone could get up from their desks and deliver their cards, Erik felt so nervous he was going pass out as he went from desk to desk, dropping the envelopes into each of his classmate's shoeboxes.

"What's wrong with you?" Ryan Leone asked him as he sees Erik walk past him as freaking pale as a glob of Elmer's glue.

"Ugh," is about all Erik could slobber out as he came up to Maddie O'Leary's box. He glanced behind his shoulder and saw that Maddie was safely across the room, dropping her last Valentine in John Priebe's box and then headed to the dessert table for some heart-shaped cookies and punch.

With a throat as dry as a crusty gym sock, Erik steeled his nerve and dropped his special card into Maddie's box.

The events that followed the next day were much hazier—and turned out to be more painful.

It started almost immediately while all the kids waited for the doors to open by the fifth grader's entrance.

"HA! Erik Volgstaad loves Maddie O'Leary!" It was Sabrina Dostel. "Maddie said she wrote him this huge creepy love letter!"

"Yeah!" Gabriella Altman said. "He wrote how he wants to kiss her, and kiss her, and kiss her! And lick her tonsils!"

"Yeah! Tonsil hockey!"

"He totally has the HOTS for her!" some other girl said.

Then some of the boys broke in: "What? Volgstaad wants to hump Maddie?"

"HA! Erik loves Maddie!"

"Erik's got the creepers for Maddie, *HA*!"

Erik totally protested in panic. He couldn't believe it. Maddie was nowhere to be seen yet. He continued to deny it.

He got pissed.

He told some of the kids to shut up.

Where were the teachers right now anyway? Isn't anybody gonna stop this?

Where was his best bud, Ryan Leone, to like totally come to his aide? Erik looked around all panicky and didn't see his best friend anywhere yet. (During grade school, Ryan was famous for showing up late—it was back when his parents were recently separated and there was always confusion about who would pick him up and drop him off.)

Kids were still laughing at him.

"Look! He's got a boner just hearing about it!" screamed some other random kid.

Erik involuntarily looked down towards the fly of his pants—he knew he didn't have a boner, but he couldn't help checking to make sure his pants weren't puffing out that way.

The fact that he looked down at his crotch made them howl even more.

Erik finally saw Maddie's mom dropping her off at the Grover Elementary turnaround. As soon as she jumped out of the mini-van, Erik sprinted around to the back of the school, tears streaking from his eyes.

What the hell happened? He asked himself. *How did it get this way? What did Maddie say to Sabrina to make her say all that?* Erik even wondered if Maddie had even let anyone else see his card at all.

Well, Erik kept a pretty low profile most of the day, not saying much to anyone in class and keeping his head down a lot.

Ryan crept up to him at milk time and asked, "What's the deal with you and Maddie? Kids are whispering all about it."

"Nothing. Forget about it," Erik said. "It's all a bunch of BS. It's just Sabrina Dostel being major a witch."

Ryan looked confused but didn't say anything for a while. Until, "So do you like Maddie, or not? It's OK if you do—she's cute and like really nice."

"No!" Erik hissed and then stormed back to his desk.

The rest of the morning he kept trying to glance at Maddie to see if she would look at him, or even like in his general direction. But she didn't. In fact, she looked pretty serious—kind of mad even.

At Lunch, Erik sulked over his sandwich and Fritos thinking about what a moron he had been for even writing anything on Maddie's Valentine card in the first place. I mean, what an idiot he was! What did he think was going to happen? Stupid. Just freaking stupid, he said to himself.

Ryan ate his apple and sucked on his juice box next to him all quiet—knowing better than to even try and talk to Erik when he was like this.

At recess, Josh Priebe threw a snowball at Archie Mcleisch. Archie threw one back and hit Carrie Young who was standing next to Gabriel Altman and they just happened to be standing by and flirting with David Plath, Jake Stafford, and Nelson Tremblehall. *Well*, the two girls screamed, and the three boys then started unloading on Archie. At that point, Josh Priebe continued chucking snow at everybody: Archie, Nelson, David, Carrie, and Jake. Seven kids at most just starting a little snowball skirmish in just one small corner of the schoolyard, right? *Right*—until eleven-year-old Dickie Swartz saw what was going on all the frick'n way across the playground and yells, *SNOWBALL FIGHT!* And like freaking immediately, the whole recess went bananas. Kids charged from all over, snowballs in hand, to where Josh Priebe was still pelting Carrie Young and the other boys were letting snow fly like grenades.

Soon there was thirty or forty screaming kids whaling snowballs around like its D-Day at the North Pole. Teachers were all over the place trying to calm the mob—but it was no use, at least not right away. We're talking SNOWBALL RIOT! Boys, girls, hell—even Mr. Doogie, the school's custodian took a break from his shoveling the walkways to lob a few into the fray, laughing away the whole time.

And Erik was right in the middle of it. Except Erik was freaking packing his snowball like it's a shotput. While all the other kids were the freaking epitome of indiscriminate frenzied throwing joy—Erik had a hit list. He wanted to hit that witch Sabrina Dostel in the face with his cannonball. He was looking for those dicks who were laughing at him in front of the doors this morning.

But the schoolyard was just too chaotic. Too much snow flying, too many bodies running, diving, somersaulting over snowbanks. But then he saw Maddie O'Leary. Maddie was just giggling away throwing fluffy snowballs at any of her random classmates that might happen to be in her range.

And suddenly the rage that Erik had been feeling all day falls on Maddie. Was all this humiliation her fault? Was she blabbing around to kids that he had a crush on her?

He kept adding snow to his already heavy snowball.

The teachers were finally starting to gain a foothold of control.

Erik looked around—no Sabrina in sight. Didn't have much time, he knew, and then the chaos would be over—besides, maybe all of this was Maddie's fault anyway.

Why did she have to tell everyone what he wrote on her card? And why did she make it sound like he wanted to kiss her?

Erik stepped up close behind her. His snowball now practically a freaking softball of ice.

Teeth clenched, he hauled off and slammed the ice ball right into the center of Maddie's back.

Her scream was heartbreaking.

Everyone stopped all at once and looked in Maddie's direction as she fell to her knees shrieking in pain with each breath. Teachers totally converged on her to help. Any kid still holding a snowball dropped it.

Those who weren't looking with a terrified sympathy to Maddie, were looking up to Erik with a whole lot of contempt.

Erik suddenly realized that what he had just done was wrong. *Uh—like way wrong*. Some of his classmates looked at him with something close to hatred. Erik looked around all stunned-like and caught Ryan's stare.

Ryan looked all wide-eyed back at him like, *dude that was so not cool. Not cool.*

Teachers raised Maddie to her feet, her face red and throbbing with tears. She never once looked Erik's way—just let herself be led away, whimpering as she went.

Erik didn't have time to watch long, because he was yanked hard by the arm by Mr. Doogie, who started dragging him with a brute-like strength straight to the principal's office.

"What the hell you thinking, kid? Nailing some sweet girl in the back like that. What's wrong with you?" Doogie said through his rigid jaw.

Eleven-year-old Erik had no answer to that, of course.

By High School, Erik had pretty much got over it. Got his first kiss out of the way at the end of Eighth Grade—a sloppy affair with Angie Flannigan that ended up tasting vaguely like peanut butter for some reason. After that, he sorta went steady with a couple of girls, if you could call it that—but those flings only lasted less than two months.

He'd been pretty much stag his whole junior year and now into his senior year and was pretty happy with that. Erik had his buds—his soccer pals and Dickey Schwartz to raise hell with. But even though he tried to hide it, any time he even caught a glimpse of Maddie O'Leary he felt a jolt as if his heart was all rigged up to a taser.

Another thing about it that made it so hopeless too was that by the time Maddie got to High School she was like immediately hit on by all the rock star senior guys and was pretty much catapulted into the total *member's only* ice box of cool at Hemingway. She had dates and made out with these older guys and hung out at parties with almost exclusively cool juniors and seniors. Erik watched all of this from a distance as he slowly had to build his coolness just like the rest of his mortal ninth grade classmates.

But it wasn't like Maddie was a bitch about it. Her magical rise to popularity didn't turn her into a stuck-up snob that never looked back on her classmates. Erik sometimes thought it would've been a lot easier maybe if she had. But no. Maddie still talked to everybody—even him, with the same nonchalant, un-sarcastic grace that she always had since she was a little kid. It was impossible to hate her.

> (That is if you actually knew her. Don't get me wrong though, plenty of other girls that didn't know her at Hemingway hated her on sight, just because of what she represented on the surface—you know, to them Maddie was the queen of all things *prep, cool, pretty, desirable*.)

The fact was that Maddie O'Leary was the perfect storm of looks, brains, clever sense of humor, and a freaking social ease that people the world over would kill to have.

And so, surely it wasn't just Erik's heart that plummeted deeper into the cellar of *Heartbreak Hotel* when, at the end of junior year, Maddie started going out with Dylan Sorrensen—the Uber-Stud. Dylan Sorrensen the Basketball star. Dylan, whose dad was a consultant for a major Detroit accounting firm and therefore made sure Dylan was adequately supplied with a sports car, designer clothes, colognes, and other accessories and expendable income that would be necessary to become the Dark Lord and Master of Everything Cool at Hemingway High.

And now he had Maddie O'Leary.

How the hell could she go out with a guy like that*?* Erik would think in his bed at night. Having tortured conversations with himself that he would never dare have with anyone else—not even Ryan Leone.

School hadn't even let out for summer before word was out that Dylan had banged her. By fall of senior year, Dylan was bragging about doing Maddie and giving like intimate details of it in the locker room after Gym class.

"I'm telling you, bruh. Her pussy is amazing. I mean *A-MAZING*! Serious. It's like riding a slick and tight waterslide, bros. Or sticking your dick in a warm banana peel like for days. It's just too bad she's not as tight as she was when we first started." Dylan said and chuckled. "I must be widening her out with my stud-horse dick!"

"*HAA*!" went all the jock-asses listening to him.

Anyway, Dylan and Maddie didn't last. Maybe she finally saw the light or heard some of the crap he was saying about her, Erik thought. But by Homecoming she had broken up with Dylan—or he broke up with her, depending on who you listened too.

According to the buzz that was coming from Dylan and his crew, he apparently dumped her after she finally let him uh…do her up the *caboose* and now he was tired of her and ready to move on totally single heading into college.

The buzz coming from Maddie though? Well, there wasn't much. Only she had broken up with him. That's it. No reasons coming from Maddie, or Maddie's friends. She never looked mad, scorned, or upset. In fact, once in Mr. Malory's English class Erik had overheard Dallas ask Maddie about it. And even though he didn't catch all of it, he thought he heard Maddie shrug it off saying, "yeah—It was just time, you know?"

That's when Erik got up enough courage to like tell her about his *Meet the Players Party* and said that she and her friends were like totally invited. He even scribbled out directions on how to get out to his parent's cottage.

In the days leading up to *Meet the Players*, Erik had all sorts of fantasies of Maddie showing up, and them talking casually, him being funny and clever and her being beyond beautiful and laughing. But that all backfired because half the freaking school showed up that night to party. Erik was the rock star of the moment for a change. That night *he* was getting looks from tons of girls. And he got drunk. He got ridiculous is what he did.

By the time Maddie and her friends showed up to the cottage, he was busy whipping the crowd up and introducing the soccer team in a drunken flourish. No wonder she didn't come up to him. No wonder she only stayed ten freaking minutes.

Ryan was right. Erik was a total jackass that night.

The night that Luke changed everything.

But now in the days since the team had turned themselves in, Erik had felt something *happen* inside him. He was still processing it and he really had never been good at putting such things into words—but *it* was happening. Since Luke's speech to the team and then the team bonding together in a way Erik never would've thought possible—other aspects of Erik's whole life seemed to re-emerge in new ways that he barely recognized. And he was thrilled. It was like Erik could suddenly see how much BS he was surrounded by and how much he was actually guilty of contributing.

What also amazed him was how quickly he felt things happening, *changing* in himself.

Erik looked for ways to try and express this new feeling welling in him. In his Eastern History class, they did a small unit where they took a look at Sun Tzu's *Art of War*. Up until a couple of weeks' prior, Erik couldn't have cared less about anything covered in any class. But now he was completely captivated by the title of one of Sun Tzu's chapters: *Attack by Fire*.

Hell, yeah… Erik thought. *Attack by Freaking Fire*. That's exactly what Erik was thinking—what was exactly going on in his heart. Even though it didn't make much logical, or grammatical, sense—Sun Tsu's words summed up Erik entirely.

He was so enthralled that he began replicating the Mandarin Chinese symbol for "Fire" on his middle knuckle with a black Sharpie. He kept it constantly fresh, always having his Sharpie on hand during the day.

Erik snickered a bit at his newfound habit. It was like some weird thing that Luke would do. Just a few weeks ago, Erik knew he'd probably laugh at some kid marking his knuckle the way he was doing now.

He began looking for other subtle ways to express his *awakening*.

Erik literally began to greet each day with a growl every morning the second he woke. *Attack by Freaking Fire, baby.*

So maybe it was because of this new burst of whatever pulsing in Erik that compelled him to stop Maddie O'Leary as he crossed her path in the hallway between fifth and sixth periods.

"Whoa—Maddie. Hey," he goes.

"Huh? What?"

"Uh, you know what?"

"What?" she goes back.

"Yeah. You know you should probably come to our playoff game Saturday."

"Hmm. Uh, OK. That was like out of nowhere," Maddie goes.

Erik shrugs. "Um, yeah. I guess I'm kinda an out of nowhere guy these days."

"I'll say. You *and* your soccer buds seem a bit out there lately. And what's with all the stuff you say now in Malory's class? You like actually reading the homework now?"

"Oh yeah. *Dracula*, dude. Righteous read, IMO. Really sinking my teeth into it, you know?"

"That was pretty lame."

"The pun?" Erik goes. "Yeah, I know—it really *sucked*."

Maddie shakes her head like she's trying to wake up from some weird dream. "OK, Random. Uh, I'm late. You know? So later, I guess?"

Erik yells down the hall after her. "OK, then! So great! We'll see you at our game this Saturday then?"

Maddie wheels around. "Are you for reals right now?"

"Yeah, you know, I guess I am. Like finally, you know?"

"Stop yelling in the hall," Mr. Becket barks at Erik from his classroom.

Maddie just does that thing again where she spazzes her head like she's trying to wake up and turns back and walks away for good.

Erik just stands there, watching the back of Maddie's head, thinking about what her hair might smell like up close and how soft her neck looks—and suddenly it's third grade all over again. Except that snowball's long gone, Erik knows. He grins. The bell rings. He's late. Erik could care less as he saunters down the hall.

Yeah, that snowball's melting into pure puddle now, man.

He kisses his middle knuckle.

Attack by Freaking Fire, baby.

33

You know I learned, or at least kind of remembered, in my microbiology class that the human mouth is like a freaking orgy of living bacteria and there are millions of microscopic centipede bugs crawling around your tongue and all sulking around your teeth and like totally chewing and boring into your gums at freaking will. Our Bio teacher, Mr. Stankowitz, even said the interior of the average anus was probably freer of unknown bacteria and micro-organisms than the human mouth.

It totally grossed me out when I saw some footage of them, and I still remember Beth Tillery sitting in the desk next to me dry heaving and convulsing like she had just been slapped with a rusty iron pipe hard in the gut.

The only reason I bring it up now is because Jason Turner's mouth must have been crawling with those bacterial micro-bug bastards the morning he woke up, mouth freaking opened, with those zombie-acrid filmy lips and baked dry whiskey-cracked throat the day after his and Kid T's run in with Lester and the Shotgun Brothers (as he was now calling them).

Jason staggered out of his room and realized his dad was like finally home but like in no freaking condition to talk yet on account of being totally passed out on the couch. There was his pipe and Zip Lock bag of glass on the coffee table and a mostly drunk 40 ounce can of Bud Light sitting next to it and Jason just put together the two and two on how his pop's put the finishing touches on his evening. So, Jason turned to the kitchen to start the day off right with a bowl of cereal.

Might as well, Jason thought—he'd need his nutrition for the father/son conversation to come.

Sometime before one in the afternoon, Turner's dad got up to take a dump or a piss, maybe both—who knows. By that time Jason was surfing around on the computer just looking around at random stuff, not really caring too much because he was way more nervous and concerned about the talk he was going to have with his dad about Dre, the camelback, Lester and shotguns—you know, everything, man—all of it.

Well, Turner's dad must've turned the whole bathroom trip into a shower too, which made Jason even twitchier having to wait longer. So when he heard the shower going full blast he jumped upstairs and took a quick swig of what little was left of his Jim Beam and then bolted it back downstairs to flip through some channels on the couch.

Finally, his dad emerged from the bathroom wearing a towel that probably hadn't been washed in a couple of months and made like he was headed for his room.

"Where were you?" Jason goes.

Like he's just remembered he's got a son that lives there in the house with him, Tuner's dad turns around towards the living room where the couch and TV are at.

"What time you'd get up?" Tuner's dad goes, leaning on the entryway to the room.

"The fuck you care?" goes Jason. "Earlier than you."

Turner's dad huffs a laugh. "Yeah, guess so..."

"Where were you?" Jason asks again.

"Out. Just out, man. Something wrong, or something?" Turner's dad goes.

Jason turns off the TV and chucks the remote to the EZ chair.

Turner's dad then rubs his temples, kind of groans a bit, and then comes walking all the way into the room. "What's the problem, Jace? What's eating at your nuts, boy?"

"You know a guy named Lester? Hangs around with a bunch of tweaked out skeletons. One of them named Scotty? They got a thing for shotguns. You know those guys?"

"Uh—yeah, I know those guys. But what the fuck do you know about them for? You hanging around them white fucking trash trailers? I told you—"

"Hey, man, fuck what you told me, man," Jason stands up. "How do *you* know these guys?"

Turner's dad's muscles tense and twitch like freaking live amp cords for a bit, making his old tats move around on his arms and chest like they were laying on the surface of some choppy water. "Look. I mean, look, Jace—if they tried to make you buy something—or did those no-bit tweakers try to hurt you in any way? Did they come at you and Toe?"

"No, man—Toe wasn't even there, man," Turner goes, still pacing. "Look, Dad—tell me how you know these guys."

"*Jason—*"

"No!" Jason screams. "Tell me how you know Lester first, then I'll tell you everything. I'll tell you every little fucking thing you want to know, you fucking *I need a God's-eye-view-of-everything* jackass."

Turner's dad steps back a little. "OK, Jesus. Let me see... Uh Lester's a guy I got Kid selling to pretty regularly every week or two weeks. It depends on the dude's flow, you know? Sometimes he's got the money to party, and sometimes he's just scraping."

"He ever *see* you? Or do you always just send Kid T on the camelback?"

Turner's dad shakes his head—nearly laughs. "What are you up to, you little shit? *No,* this Lester guy—he never sees me. I always send the Kid. That's the way you do business."

Jason says nothing.

"OK, Jace. What's this all about? Spill, little man."

"As far as you know Lester and his dudes just buy glass from Kid from time to time and that's it? You don't know if they biz stuff around or like pull off heists or shit?" Jason asked.

Turner's dad looks down and tightens up his towel around his waist and goes, "Yeah, man—that's pretty much it. Kid tells me this Lester and his buddies—Scotty and this dude called Maintenance Man—just order up glass about once a week and it's usually an in-and-out thing. You can follow it right as rain in the books—which I'm sure Dre does every week when we synch up our laptops on the weekly take, man."

"*Maintenance Man*?" Jason goes.

"Yeah. Kid T never knew the other guy's name, but he knew he worked maintenance somewhere because he was always wearing those coverall zip-up Dickies or whatever. As far as them knocking off joints, I don't know shit about that and don't really care just as long as they stay loyal customers."

Jason nods, says nothing.

"Fuck, Jace! Enough of the fucking suspense, man. What happened with you and these guys?"

Jason looks down at his sneakers. "Sorry, Dad. I should've never done it, but I did. I went with Kid T on a camelback to this Lester guy's house."

"Oh what the fuck, Jace—"

"I did it because we met with Dre and his crew beforehand at Pazzaro's. Dre like promised me three hundred just to be with Kid at the drop. Well, we get there..." and Jason suddenly turns ten years' old. He can't help it. I don't know, maybe every son has some built-in reflex when they're coming clean to their fathers. Even if their fathers are messed up criminals. Who knows? The point is that Jason starts tearing up while he continues, " and while we're there Kid T makes me do the talking, and at first I didn't understand why and Lester sent Scotty upstairs to get our money and suddenly he comes down with a shotgun out of nowhere, so Kid shoots Lester in the chest. Just wastes him. So, Scotty starts shooting and then suddenly somebody's blasting a shotgun into the house from outside—probably this fucking maintenance dude and Kid gets shot up pretty bad and it was just nuts in there and somehow I get Kid to his car and we go tearing out of there. But we left the camelback of glass at Lester's—"

"Whoa, whoa, whoa—Jason, slow down, son," Jason's dad goes. He grabs Jason by the shoulders. "Are you OK? Did you get hit anywhere? Are you hurt at all, man?"

"No, no—a few scratches on my legs, nothing, Dad. Anyway, let me finish, man—just fucking let me finish. So we meet Dre and they take Kid to go patch him up somewhere, but Dre is like super-pissed at me for not getting his huge-ass load of meth. And not only that, the whole thing was a set up. A fucking set up all the way. All Dre wanted to know was if you were *bizzing* with Lester and cutting Dre out of trailer profits from them pushing shitty junk."

"*What?*"

"I'm sorry, Dad—I should've stayed crystal. I should've just stayed crystal like you said."

"Whoa, whoa—let me get this straight. Dre thinks I'm *bizzing* with trailer meth behind his back and he fucking used *you* as bait with this Lester asshole?"

"Yeah—I'm sorry, I—" Jason doesn't get to finish his sentence though because his dad suddenly bitch-slaps him across the face.

Jason's dad turns from his son and totally roars. He kicks over the EZ chair. The towel loosens and falls from around his waist.

Jason's eyes are still wet—but he's no longer crying, just staring at his father panting naked across the living room.

"That was—*that* was for breaking your crystal, kid. That's all that was, OK? That was it."

Jason says nothing.

"All right," Turner's dad goes. "OK. The first thing we gotta do is pow-wow with Dre. Till I get this fucking stench out of the air, you gotta sit tight. You go to school. You come home. That's the fucking drill until further notice—got it?"

"But what about these shotgun guys? There's two of them still out there and they know what I look like." Jason goes.

"You let me worry about that. Dre and I will sort those fuckers out—no matter how this shakes it's in both our best interests for Scotty and his maintenance pal to get laid fucking low now."

Turner's dad bends down, picks up the towel and puts it back on.

"What about Dre holding me responsible for the lost camelback?" Jason goes.

"I'll take care of that when I talk to Dre. Regardless of what he says—you're going back to being crystal. I'll make damn sure of that."

Turner's dad makes for the stairs. He looks down to Jason who has still not moved since being slapped in the face. "Look, Jace—don't be scared, little man. I'm going to keep my blood safe, got it? I know it's been crazy around here lately with the heavy Dre traffic, and now all this Lester shit and I know you're still hurting like hell after losing Rozzy—I mean we all are—and I know it might be dancing around in your head about what it might be like over in Buffalo. But I *garunfuckingtee* you this. You're sure as hell much better off with me than with that alchy slut mother of yours scraping over in Buffalo. *OK*? I'm gonna keep my blood safe," he goes and lumbers up the stairs.

In the time it takes for Turner's dad to dress himself and load his chrome .45 revolver, Jason sits on the couch and turns on some random something on the TV. Maybe it was even some more poker action on ESPN2. He doesn't remember exactly.

Pops Turner comes downstairs wearing jeans and his badass leather jacket and some random black long sleeve T-shirt. Jason watches his dad but makes no move from his sitting position on the couch.

"Oh," Turner's dad goes right before walking out the door, "there's a little coke left in a Tupperware in the fridge behind the sandwich meat. And you can help yourself to a hit of glass on the table if you're in the mood. But if you do any of it, don't go anywhere. And it's OK if Toe comes over, but that's it. Got it?"

Jason says nothing—just watches his dad go out the door, slamming it shut behind him.

34
Isaiah

I think hospitals are sucky places to sleep and spend the night. There are too many lights everywhere for one thing. Another is all the noise and moving around and the weird smells everywhere. Every room smells like a brand-new plastic toy.

My dad didn't die last night. He was close my mom said the doctors said. Too much blood got into his stomach, and he was too weak to cough it all out on his own she said. I was so scared. All night, I was scared. Once Mom asked if I wanted to just go home and try to sleep in my own bed, but I said no. I mean, what would the point be? I would have still been scared and it would have taken longer for me to find out if Dad was going to be OK or not.

I know my dad is going to die. Everybody's been real clear about letting me know that it will happen soon, and it doesn't all have to be a bad thing, and we all die, and the main thing is that Dad doesn't hurt too much when it happens and he loves us and all of that. It's just I've had to know that so long now. It's been for too long now, I think. I don't want my dad to die, like ever. And it's not like I want him to die soon so all these serious talks with Mom and doctors and, whatever Mrs. Farris is, will all stop. But I hate this. I hate waiting for the worst thing of my life to happen.

The best part of everything right now is hanging out with Luke in the mornings, going to the practices with the team and helping Coach Striden and Vogel get stuff and shag balls. I love the way Erik screws around and jokes with me and lets me play his kazoo, even though it's kinda gross because his mouth is on it all the time and I think he spits *waaay* too much into it when he plays it. I also love the way Coach Vogel says to me in his funny Scottish voice, *ah my wee lil' lad.* And the way that all of them make me feel like I'm part of the team and laugh with me, and never, ever make me talk serious about my dad dying. They know he's sick. They all know he's going to die too. But they don't ever make me think serious about it. And I love them for that.

I've just been in to see my dad for the first time since the horrible coughing started last night. And now I'm back here in this way too bright waiting room, sitting down to write down what my dad just said to me. I need to write it now, so I don't forget a word, not one thing he said to me. God please don't ever let me forget my dad! Please don't let me ever forget what he sounds like! The way he hums to himself in the car! The way his arms feel when he hugs me. Please God. Always let me remember.

I went into his room holding Mom's hand. We all three talked for a while. The whole time Dad was still acting, like he always does, that none of this was a big deal. He tried smiling and even laughing at some of his own bad jokes. But I kept wishing he wouldn't joke though because I was scared of him coughing and the blood that comes up from too much coughing.

Well, after a little while, he nodded to Mom and Mom told me she was going to go take a walk in the halls and that she'd be back in a little bit. Then the only nurse who was in the room messed with some buttons or stuff on Dad's bed and took her clipboard and left.

So then it was just me and Dad.

"Hey Isaiah," my dad said, his voice all cracky and weak. "You remember me ever telling you about the big buck I shot when I was hunting with your uncle, Karl, back before you were born?"

"Yeah, sorta," I said. I kinda remember that he and Uncle Karl used to be big hunters and did a lot of hunting up north and I knew Dad had killed like a really big buck up there and it had made the papers and everything.

"Well today, I want to tell you that story," my dad said. "OK?"

"OK," I said. I don't know why, but for some reason right when he said it he kinda shifted in his bed and all of sudden it seemed real important. I mean, everything seemed real important. Like if I didn't pay attention, I was going to miss something, or I even got a quick super scary feeling like talking like this was my dad's way of saying he was about to die. Or worse that he sent Mom away just so he could die right now, and I could be with him. I felt a rush of energy in me, and my heart was pounding in a bad way like when we were driving on vacation late at night and I was asleep in the back of the car and Dad had to swerve out of the way of another car and I was shook awake and super scared and couldn't fall back asleep the rest of that night.

"So, your Uncle Karl has this cabin up in the U.P. past Munising way up there by Lake Superior. Where there's just woods and rivers and cliffs and waterfalls. The most beautiful stuff you ever saw. Can't believe I never took you up there. Always meant to, Izzy. Your Mom's been a couple times. I've always told Karl to never sell the cabin. But anyway, about ten years before you were born and your mom and I were just starting to date, Uncle Karl and I went up to his cabin to bow hunt. We loved to stalk. You know what that means?"

I shook my head.

"Means you move around, try and track the deer down. You don't just stay up in a tree stand or something and just wait for one to walk under you. Anyway, part of the fun for your uncle Karl and me was to just wander out into the woods near that huge Great Lake and stalk and camp and stuff. We wore backpacks that had all our gear, you know like our food, sleeping bags, canteens, matches—knives and hatchets, you know—bows and quivers—all that stuff."

I didn't know what "quivers" was, so I asked him, and he told me it was the thing they kept their arrows in. Dad kept talking about how he and Karl stayed out in the wild for like five days and hadn't seen one buck. But they didn't care cause they were having the time of their lives hanging out, camping, telling stories at night, smoking cigars. Real guy stuff, he said.

Dad looked up a lot as he told me this story. Looked up at the white ceiling tiles above his bed, but you could tell by looking at his eyes, he didn't see tiles. Even I could tell Dad was seeing the woods, the huge sunsets they saw slowly diving into the huge Great Lake. It even seemed to me he felt the sting of these black flies that they ran into when he told me about them.

He said to ask Mom to pull out some old pictures of he and Uncle Karl from that trip and he said I'd get a big kick at seeing them both with these huge bushy beards.

I started smiling just imagining my dad looking all scruffy and tough and even a little proud that he was like that once, even if it was so long ago.

"Anyway, on our sixth day out," Dad said, "I see Karl stop dead-still on the trail ahead of me. It was raining and I didn't even notice what had got his attention at first because I had my rain hood on. But then I saw it. Grazing, with its head down, not more that forty yards ahead of me in a small clearing of tall grass was this grizzly of a buck."

Dad's eyes lit up as he used his arms and hands to try and show me just how big this buck's head was even without the horns. He went on about the long and thick white, almost gray, fur that hung from this thing's huge, thick neck.

I got even more excited because I could tell my dad was getting really excited telling this part and I hadn't seen my dad like this, like, you know with this kind of energy, or glow for like days, or maybe even months.

"So, I slowly tried to un-sling my bow from my shoulder and get an arrow from my quiver. I looked over to Karl to see if he was doing the same, but he wasn't. He was too far ahead on the trail and knew I had the better shot. He just nodded at me. Well, I kneeled real slow and tried to sling off my backpack as quietly as I could. Then I flipped off my hood and let the rain just drizzle over my face. I notched the arrow on to my bowstring and took a breath. You see, Izzy, I couldn't shoot him from kneeling on the grass—that just would've been impossible. So, I knew the only way to get off the perfect shot was to stand, aim, and then fire and do it quick or the buck would take notice and be off in a flash."

Dad hunched down his head in his bed, pretending like he was back there in that wet grass. And I think his eyes were getting brighter and brighter as he told this part. I thanked God that I was wrong to think that Dad was calling me in to watch him die—cause it was real obvious nobody this happy and into a story just suddenly dies.

I can't describe it. I felt *so, so, so* happy for my dad as he told his story, especially this part.

"So I dared to take one last little peek over the grass to make sure he was still there, I took one more tiny breath to steady my nerves—and then as quick as it takes to tell, I stood, I aimed, and let loose. And WHAP!"

Dad stopped, moved his face down close to mine and smiled. A huge smile that stayed still so long on his face he could've been frozen or made of wax like those big life-size fakes of famous people they have where people go on cool vacations and stuff. "And the rest is history, son. I hit him straight in the neck. He dropped like he'd been struck by God's lightning."

"He didn't feel any pain?" I asked.

"Well, if he did it was real, real quick," Dad said. "I'd like to think he didn't feel a thing."

"Wow, cool," I said.

He sat back in his bed again. "Yeah, it was *cool*. Your uncle and I were local legends for a long time. The buck was a new Michigan Bow Hunting Record. Twenty-point rack, total score of 221 and 7/8 inches. We made papers all over the upper Mid-west. Even got a few photos of me and the buck in a couple of magazines and all over online."

"Was Uncle Karl ever jealous?" I asked.

"Sure, a little, I guess—but I've bought the beers every time we've ever gotten together since."

"That's cool," I said again because I didn't know what else to say. I was just so happy Dad was happy after such a terrible night and having to stay in a hospital bed.

My dad sighed and seemed to calm down a bit and then looked at me for a minute. "Hey…"

"Yeah?" I said.

"You want to hear something about that story that I never told anyone ever before in my life? Not to Karl. Not even to your mother?"

Of course I did! "Yeah…"

He motioned me closer again. "The moment I saw the arrow hit the buck…"

"Yeah?" I said.

"Well… *I pissed my pants*."

"What!" I couldn't believe it.

"Yeah—" Dad said. "I just totally peed my pants big time. And not just a little squirt of pee. No, no, no. We're talking my whole bladder went. Like a water balloon bursting! I peed myself like a little baby does his diaper, Izzy. Is that not crazy or what?"

I couldn't stop laughing and neither could he. I think I started crying I was laughing so hard. "But why, Dad?" I finally said when I could talk again.

Dad shrugged his shoulders. "I dunno. Nerves, I guess. I've never done anything like that since either."

"Well, how did Uncle Karl *not* notice?"

"Izzy, it had been drizzling all day. We were already drenched. And you can bet I made sure to 'trip' into a puddle before I got close to Karl again."

We laughed more. After some time, we both calmed down again,

"But Izzy…" he said and looked right into my eyes again. "Son, here's the thing. That story I told you is one of my greatest achievements and one of my most precious memories. But here's the deal, all of it, the record, the little bit of fame, the memory of it, you see it's all nothing compared to one single moment I've been blessed to have with you, boy. *You're* my treasure, Isaiah. The moment you were born—the second you opened your eyes, breathed in the first air of this world—is my greatest treasure. You are my most precious memory, my greatest achievement, every day with you, to see you grow, to see you become the boy you are, has been my life's joy. My joy. The twelve years I've had with you have been the best of my life, son. *Know that*, boy. There's no regrets when it comes to me and you. None. And even though our time together is going to come up short—just know the time we did have has been perfect. Perfect, Izzy. I love you so much, so much …oh my boy. My sweet, sweet son…"

I had to stop writing for a while. Mom took me home. The doctor's say Dad is doing well and if he stays that way he can come home tomorrow. When I was writing about Dad in the waiting room, I started crying pretty hard I guess trying to get it all down. Nurses came to make sure I was OK, and one of the dumb ones even wanted to send me to the Emergency Room. If I would've been able to keep writing I just would've wrote about how I told Dad I loved him too and would never forget him, never forget today, and that I would always love him. I would've wrote how hard we hugged and cried and how Mom came back and we just all hugged each other and cried and didn't need to say anything.

At first when Dad got really sick and all the doctors were sure that he was going to die they made me start seeing Mrs. Farris, which I guess is a doctor too, but her job is to just talk to me. It was her idea to have me write things down. You know, about what happens and how I feel and stuff. And at first, I thought she was so stupid and that doing all this writing was so stupid. But I don't think that now. I will never, never, never lose this journal. I still think Mrs. Farris is weird and smells like flowers and dish soap, but I will thank her the next time I have to meet with her. But for now, this is all I got to say.

So anyway, there's a big week coming up. I'm really, really tired and I need to get my rest. Dad's coming home tomorrow and then the team's got their last practice before playoffs. So, it's time to get ready to KICK SOME BUTT!

35

Jason

WHAT THE FUCK! I don't know what the fuck is stopping me from going up to Dylan fucking Sorensen and fucking blowing his weak-ass brains out all over the hallway floor. The little bitch. The little stretched-ass whore. All's I got to do is haul out that motherfucking SIG and pull on that tiny trigger and BLAMMO! His ass and brain are fucking history. Dylan. Dylan! That fucking asswipe today just about sent me homicidal. So I do all the coke that my dad left in the fridge. Then later I go to school like a good little boy. I fucking tuck the loaded SIG in the back waistband of my fucking jeans. And then that fucking ass with a glamour-boy face has the sac to throw a full can of Mountain Dew at my fucking head in the caf while I'm trying to catch some sleep at lunch? What the fuck, Rozz? First of all, it hurts so bad I need to cry—but I don't cause that's like fucking reputation suicide. But the whole cafeteria is either laughing or getting quiet like I'm gonna fucking blow and for a second, I thought I was, man.

Part of me just wanted to haul out Kid T's SIG and fucking put three rounds in Dylan's skull right then and there and watch as everybody scattered and ran like rats to the nearest hole for safety. Cheese and rice, what a bunch of bastards and bitches. I still dream sometimes of just going in with fucking fully automatics and rocket launchers and just blowing everything and everyone to shit and bloody shreds, man. Fucking blown apart flesh, man. AGHHHH! That's all I want them all reduced to. I don't know why anymore. Rozz, I fucking don't. I don't know why I don't just blaze Hemingway down or put a peace-ending round in my own brain like you did. There's so much shit. So much drama going on right now. I mean, holy shit on a fucking shit pile! My dad's gone to fuck know's where in Detroit, into the den of Dre and Hell and what the fuck-ever. I got fucking Kevin Wilhem today asking me where the hell Kid T is—and if not where the fuck my Dad is, cause supplies are drying up like the fucking desert suddenly and can I get something for them to tide this whole shit over! I mean what the fuck!? FUCK! FUCK! FUCK! I mean, what the fuck do these party kids think I am? Some sort of cure-all? A panacea fuck-house for all to get high on the shit of their choice? A fucking Meth-Gandalf? FUCK YOU, YOU FUCKING BUNCH OF FUCK-OFFS! And fuck my Dad while we're at it—that twat piece of shit old man. Fuck him—*protecting his own blood*. I should SIG his ass before I'm done too.

And to top it, that fucking deaf jack-off invited me to his lame-ass soccer team's pre-playoff party, which is sure as shit to be sober. They're watching some retarded war movie from the 80's or 90's to get'em all psyched for the fucking playoffs—but I feel so pissed right now, Rozz—maybe I should just take my SIG and just light them all up. Just blast big deaf Luke's brains out all over the fucking wall and then jack off right there on his fucked-up corpse while the rest of those chicken-shit teammates of his all go run off to safer places. BLOOD! FUCK! SKULLS! FUCKING SEVERED BODY PARTS! SHIT ON THEM! PISS! FUCK ALL HOLES, MAN! RAAAGHHH!!!!!! BRING ON THE END, MAN!

SHITFUCKDAMNITMOTHERFUCKERSACROSSAMERICA!

F U C K'N! DIE! DEATH! DEATH! PLEASE!

Please, dear Rozz, if you're up there, give me the grace, the fucking wisdom to blow my own brains out like you did before I seriously hurt someone. Got the SIG to my motherfucking head as I write here. Oh god! I'm so messed up right now, Rozz. *I CANNOT KEEP THIS UP!* Give me the strength to take my own life like you did. I got the SIG, I got the reasons, give me the fucking balls.

Please. You know I love you, Rozzy, girl. Let me go too. Let me do it. Before I go crazy. Before I kill lots and lots and lots of people. Fuck what happened or didn't happen with that deaf fuck at Harper Lake.

ERIF
IV

Dawn hit Russler's Alley in a swift rising of haze and swelter. The festival rovers awoke and prepared for the last day of the Mayodon. For many of them this would be their last day in Thorn until next year.

Prince, flung open the flaps of his tent, stretched out his back, groaned, spat, adjusted his testicles, and then looked to his breakfast fire with a grin.

After his meal and hot drink, the lad put on his day's tunic, secured his purse of coins to his belt, and walked up the main of Russler's Alley wondering where in Thorn he should best station himself to come across the most agreeable sisters he had spent most of last afternoon and evening with.

Prince did not have to wonder long. Annabella and Angel we're waiting for him in much the same place he last saw them, at the gate of the alley both looking as radiant and blonde as he had seen them in his dreams during the night—each sister in a modest, yet pretty dress of off-white.

As he approached, Prince began a foolish stagger, bumping into a merchant's breakfast cart, squinting through his eyes as if they'd just been scorched by the sun. "Oh, oh, I say! Mine eyes! Are my throbbing visionary orbs deceived? Or is it an Angel and her sister that hover in celestial radiance before me? Agh! Mine eyes!"

Prince spasmed and knocked a tomato and a hard-boiled egg off the merchant's cart.

"Oh come off, now!" the woman yelled. "Come boy! Ye knocked off a couple of me wares!"

"Baa! A million apologies, good sir! Here's for thy pains!" Prince chucked a couple coins at the old woman behind the cart and straightened his gait as he came up to the sisters.

"I see the night's repose has done nothing to remedy your manners," Annabella said.

"No, miss. I believe I am very much in a fevered state when I'm in your presence," Prince replied. "And good morning to you, sweet Angel."

"Good morning, to you too—our fine Prince." Angel bowed.

"And what do we have here, ladies?" Prince noticed the basket clinging to Angel's arm and another larger bag slung around Annabella's shoulder.

"Being that this is your last day in Thorn, we thought you might rather spend a day picnicking in the fields with us instead of bumbling through the Mayodon," Angel said.

"What say you, Prince? Did we guess right? Or would you rather be about the bustle of Thorn's people one more day rather than in our good company?" Annabella asked.

"No, no—ladies you have guessed my heart aright. I had very much rather picnic in the fields with you than any company in the world," Prince said.

"Hooray!" Angel cheered.

"Lead on then, good ladies," Prince said.

The trio let out beyond the gates of Thorn past the sisters' house and onto the path that led into the fields of tall grasses in the valley of the Great Mountain. There, among the yellows and purples of wildflowers and thistles they laid a blanket down to sit upon. The sky above ruled bluer, and the clouds whiter, than any painter could stroke with any brush. They merrily ate their victuals of fruits, bread, and dried meat—conversing and laughing all the while between mouthfuls.

After a while Angel began to collect flowers and chase clouds of butterflies along the clear, green shallow creek that ran over smooth pebbles that cut through the field flowing toward Thorn.

Prince and Annabella stayed put on the picnic blanket and lounged. The eldest sister reached for her long bag and pulled out a drawstring and bow. As she bent the bow and tied the string to it, Prince watched with an impressed arch of brow.

"It's my father's," Annabella answered his gaze. "Anytime Angel and I venture out here I take his bow and some arrows just in case we see any deer wandering into the fields in search for a drink."

"Has this habit been fruitful?"

Annabella smiled and took an arrow from her quiver. "More than a few times I've been able to put some meat on our table."

"Ah... So, you are a bit of a huntress?"

"Yes, I guess I am."

Prince snickered and looked up. Above he could see the mountains all around as well as the great dark opening of The Crack where the dragon lived. Looking back to the sky, he thought he spied an eagle hovering low, scanning for prey. He thought it was mildly odd how close this eagle seemed to swoop ever-nearer to them on the blanket. But then again, Prince had seen stranger things from his experience with beasts.

As the afternoon drifted on muffled noises from the Mayodon rose all soft and indistinct where Annabella and Prince sat on their blanket. Not that they paid the noises much notice. They continued their sparing and laughing with one another while Angel continued her romp collecting flowers and butterflies, only stopping to refresh herself with handfuls of water from the creek.

Prince conjured up a couple of Auras and set them up first twenty, then thirty, paces away. Annabella took aim and tried to burst them with her arrows. Anytime she hit an Aura directly, the arrow would ping off as if it had hit a plate of armor.

It did not take many lighted arrows for Prince to realize that Annabella was a crackshot within forty paces, so he moved his Aura ever-so-slightly on one instance, resulting in her arrow to go sailing far, far, away into the tall grasses.

"Hey! You cheat, Scoundrel Prince! It will take Angel and I a month to find that arrow."

"Hence the name 'Scoundrel.'"

"Well then, this game is over." Annabella gathered her long bag to put her father's bow away.

"Wait," Prince said. "Try just once more. I promise, no *scoundevilry* this time."

"All right—one more shot then."

Prince concentrated and produced an Aura from his palm and sent the bubble floating nearly a full fifty paces away.

Annabella notched her arrow to the bowstring; pulled back and raised in one motion. Closed one eye and aimed.

She loosed.

The arrow shot true, dead-on. Except this time the arrow did not ping off when it reached its target. Nor did it go sailing off because Prince did not move it. However, something was different.

This time as soon as the arrow reached its target the arrow stopped and hovered in mid-air.

"What happened? What did you do?"

Prince just laughed and curled his fingers into a come hither. As soon as the Aura came to them Annabella could see what Prince had done—though she scarcely could understand how.

There before them, in the center of the Aura, the arrow hovered, captured into the middle.

"How? The other times I hit them the arrow just ricocheted off as if it had hit a bear's skull."

"Well, you see dear Annabella, I can change the Aura's shell from that of stone to that of a soap bubble at the mere flick of my thought. See?"

And then the Aura *popped!* into nothing and Prince caught the arrow in his waiting palm.

Annabella giggled. "So then, you really do have complete mastery of your balls..."

"Yes, it appears I do. Just as it appears your endurance for that joke knows no limit."

The two laughed and then helped themselves by dipping their cups into the creek on their way back to the blanket. Between sips of the cool water Prince thanked Annabella for the last two days. He told her truly, without joke or guile, that the brief time he'd spent with the two sisters was some of the best-spent hours he could ever remember.

Annabella was a little surprised at Prince's sincerity and candor. She felt a sudden tug of sadness in her at the reality that Prince would have to leave Thorn tomorrow. Life was about to return to normal. A normal that harbored the reality of her father and the ale mug, the Lottery and its horrors, and the harsh fact that all of them in Thorn were ruled daily by fear and despair—ruled by the ever-present viciousness of Erif the Wingswift waiting in the Crack, waiting for his feast of innocence sacrificed.

She must have dwelled on these things a long time because when Prince put his hands on her shoulders, she felt like she had just been roused from a dream.

"Annabella... Anna, my sweet. I am drooling run-mad in *like with you*, is that not strange?"

Annabella was vexed. "In *Like?"* she said, tearing up. "You're in *like* with me?"

Prince looked down into Annabella's eyes. "What if I simply did not leave? Or better yet, what if you and Angel just up and came with me?"

Annabella shook her head. "It's madness you speak—"

"No. What if I took you away from this place? Took care of you. Took you and Angel away from that wretched Crack up there and the demon that lurks inside. Took you to a place where you could both be safe and live your lives."

"Impossible. *How*?"

"I could smith, set up a shop in the chain of villages near the coast. I could take you and Angel with me during festival season in the summers."

Annabella wiped her tears. "You could make enough?"

Prince nodded. "Aye. More than enough. I could take care of your father too. He wouldn't have to work. He could rest and get better. We could all make our living on the coast. Have grilled fish and scrambled eggs for breakfast on the beach every morning, Anna. Eat our fill—I *promise*."

She pondered this as she let Prince continue to rub her shoulders. Annabella couldn't believe this was all happening. Did she really feel the same for this boy she hardly knew? Was all this nonsense he was spouting possible? She didn't know. She just didn't know. Especially when she thought of her father. *Some wounds just don't heal* she heard her soul say.

She sighed. "*Dreams*, Prince. It's just—they're all dreams you weave here."

"Precisely. I mean really, Anna—aren't dreams what we—"

"I'm afraid."

Prince held her and she did not resist his holding.

Not long after that Angel returned to them and they packed up their things. By the time they made it back to Thorn it was getting to be late afternoon. Most of the side stages were winding down their final acts and people were thronging to the meal fires and ale huts. Prince bought them each a plate of mutton and a mug of spiced ale. Angel wolfed hers down with her usual relish while Annabella just picked at hers, distracted with her thoughts.

Just like the evening before, Thorn's streets came alive with torches and everyone gravitated towards the square to dance the last dance of the Mayodon.

But Prince and the sisters did not stay to dance. Instead, the girls escorted Prince once again to Russler's Alley and he once again began to bid them goodnight.

"Sister," Annabella said. "Could you please get a head start back home? I'll catch up with you in a bit. I have a few fast things to say to our dear Prince first."

"But sister, surely you can profess your love for him in front of me," Angel protested.

"Hmm... surely. But it is not of my love that I wish to speak to him about. Now off with you, then. And I'll catch up with you soon."

Angel kicked the dirt. "All right then, sister. But I will see you at least one more time tomorrow before you leave—right, dear Prince?"

"Of course, my Angel," said Prince, and then kissed Angel's hand. "I could never leave Thorn without a goodbye from its most beautiful citizen. Good night, sweet Angel."

He hugged her and when Angel finally let go of him, she began to wander towards home.

"Think on what I have said, Anna," Prince said.

"I fear it were impossible to dream of anything else tonight," Annabella said.

They stared at each other for many breaths.

"Sweet damnation, if you're not the prettiest damsel by torchlight," Prince said.

Annabella smiled; glowed. "Can you really make all your *what if's* come true?"

"I can die trying, my sweet."

"Then if that be true, good sir—you will have outdone all of your best Aura-making."

He approached her and kissed her forehead. "Good night. And I'll look for you on the morrow."

"And so you shall," Annabella said, and Prince turned and walked back down the alley towards his tent.

Annabella strolled through the torch-lit streets with music swirling in her head. She replayed in her mind the feeling of Prince's lips on her forehead, recalled his voice in perfect pitch *I am in drooling run-mad in like with you*, and conjured the image of his face—his eyes as he looked at her in that way of his.

She noticed nothing as she passed through the gates of Thorn and veered off on the path that would take her home. She was only a few paces from her house when she heard a rustle in the darkness a few arm-lengths at her side.

"Who's there?" She said, shocked out of her Prince-drunk thoughts.

"A friend—" came a deep and cracked voice. Cyvilard emerged before her like some kind of conjuring, his arms folded ahead of him in his robe.

"Elder—what brings you out near our house this late? No pressing town business, I hope?"

A sound came from Cyvilard that could only be described as a stifled laugh. "No, no, my dear, Annabella. I'm not about town business tonight. But make no mistake, I am here to talk business with you. Of that be sure."

Dread began swelling in Annabella's chest. "I must go, sir. My sister—"

"Your *sister*? Ah yes, you're quite right to worry about your sister now," Cyvilard said, stepping closer.

"What is your meaning?"

Cyvilard said nothing. Just stared at her with owl's eyes.

"So—you have strong feelings for this Yonderling boy, eh?" Cyvilard finally spoke again. "He makes your insides all a flutter?"

"I don't—I'm sure I don't know what you mean, Elder."

Quick as a striking snake Cyvilard spread his arms out from his robe and grasped his talon-nailed hands around both of Annabella's shoulders and started to undulate them under a sinister rub.

The breath left Annabella's lungs in a gasp; her whole body frozen solid in his grip.

"What is it, my Annabella? Isn't this how he hugged you? Oh wait, that's right. He did it from *behind*." In a swirl of a robe, Cyviard *whooshed* behind her, while keeping his hands' grip about her shoulders. "That's better, now—isn't it?"

Annabella was too petrified at the moment to speak, much less move.

"Now let me tell you how this will play," Cyvilard said, placing his chapped lips next to her ear. "At first light you will go to your Scoundrel Prince and you will tell him to leave Thorn immediately—and to leave forever. You will tell him you see through his lies. You'll banish him from your heart and your life. And you'll be convincing, my dear. Because if you're not and the boy stays even one hour after you see him, I'll have the Tarrenbacks arrest him for thievery and when I produce proof of it—be assured I will, my dear—he'll hang in the village square by sundown. Understand?"

Annabella nodded.

Cyvilard moved one of his hands from her shoulders and grasped his fingers around her throat. She could feel his sharp nails slicing into her skin.

"I'm not finished," he hissed. "After you send the boy away, you'll go back home do your chores and then bathe yourself. At nightfall, you'll sneak out under the cover of darkness. You'll sneak through Thorn to the back of the Great Hall where I will show you to my chambers. There, you'll let me set upon you in every passionate embrace I can devise."

He pulled her even closer.

"Ah yes, my sweet, sweet Annabella. You will let me ravage you to my liking tomorrow night. You know why you will allow this?"

Annabella shook her head through her tears.

"Because if you do not, I will fix the Lottery in such a way as to name your sister to be called to sacrifice. That's right, Annabella. Do not one thing I am asking you and Angel will be chosen for the Lottery and taken to the Crack. Believe me, girl! Send the boy away and come to my bed tomorrow night or Angel will be rent to pieces by Erif, set to flame and devoured. Do you understand?"

Annabella writhed to be free of the Elder's grip.

Cyvilard clenched his free hand into a fist and hit her in the kidneys.

Annabella's head whipped back in pain.

"I said, *do you understand*?" Cyvilard repeated.

Exhausted, Annabella finally nodded.

"Good! Tomorrow night, then. Do not fail me!" And just like a swift-moving tempest, Cyvilard and his clutching fingers were gone, leaving Annabella on her knees panting in the darkness on the dirt.

36

The night before their first playoff match, they all met at Ryan Leon's house. They all markered their knuckles with the Sun Tsu insignia that Erik had adopted. They howled and roared together. Got their blood up for bloody deeds. The next night the match wasn't even close. 4-0 victory versus poor Westingham. They got their first goal in the third minute. Erik pounding one in the back of the net off a pass from Tristan. Pure poetry. And it got more poetic from there. Coach Striden was smiles from ear to ear. We could even see that from the bleachers—well, those of us who showed. I counted about thirty-five people or so for Hemingway. Parents mostly, as usual, and some of the JV team of course.

Even with the win I'm sure Erik had to be a little disappointed scanning the bleachers afterward. Maddie didn't make it.

Two days later Hemingway hosted the second round against Walled Lake. The final tally was Hemingway 2, Walled Lake 0, but the game was not as close as the box score indicated. We scored both goals in the first half which allowed Striden to rest most of the starters. The main highlight was probably the impromptu somersault that Isaiah Walker did on the sidelines after the first goal. Our modest crowd went more ape-nuts for that display of joy than the goal itself. You could tell the kid was a little embarrassed by his antics—but he couldn't help it, you know? He was *that* excited for the boys.

The home crowd was still by no means big—but it had grown in numbers thanks to more Hemingway students making it out. And Maddie O'Leary was there this time. She and Thora Berkholder, Jessie Wyland, and even Dallas Douglass—who Maddie had just kind of started hanging out with. There were more of the JV guys there this time too—and they were louder.

Things got a little more tense the following Tuesday. It was the Sectional Semi-final Playoff against Rochester Adams. And Rock Adams was good.

Win or lose, this would be the last home game of the season. Their regular season record had been so good that it won them the first three rounds of the playoffs at home—and if they had beaten Ann Arbor Huron during the suspensions, they would've been awarded home field advantage throughout the playoffs leading to State.

The game started off fast and the pace just never let up the entire eighty minutes of play. Rock Adams had two skilled forwards that were always on the prowl for the counterattack. Couple them with two outside defenders and one midfielder that were definitely worth a damn, if not two damns, and it was a recipe for a tight affair.

Hemingway took the lead about midway in the first half off a corner kick header goal by Luke. It stayed 1-0 until halftime and then early in the second half we got a second goal, which should have been enough for all the Hemingway faithful to breathe easy.

But it wasn't.

Not more than a minute after our second goal, Rochester counterattacked, and they put an absolute firecracker past Patrick to make the game 2-1. The goal gave

Rochester a huge swing in momentum, and they gave our boys heck-fire for the rest of the game.

The match was finally put on ice though once Ryan sent Tristan on a run up the right flank and Tristan sent a one-touch cross up to the top of Rock Adam's goal box where Erik was waiting. Erik had time to give himself a set-up touch and then he blasted a right-footed shot low to the corner past Rochester's keeper at the near-post.

Relief was all over the Hemingway players, coaches and fans at that point. The match ended up 3-1. Those of us in the stands let out huge cheers when the ref blew out the whistle to signal the end of the game. Rock Adams players fell to the ground, or hung their heads—realizing despite their hard, spirited play, their season was over. The Hemingway guys were real good though about shaking their opponents' hands though and even helping a few of them up to their feet. It was cool; despite it being such an intense game both teams seemed pretty congratulatory after.

The crowd in the stands had again grown from the previous two games. Whether it was because it was starting to be at least a little more socially acceptable to cheer for these bunch of narcs, or more Hemingway kids were just morbidly curious about what was going on with soccer—who knows?

Erik would again be pleased since Maddie and her crew were again in attendance looking all glammed out. You can bet he made sure he went over there to say *'hey—thanks for coming'* and all that before they left the stadium.

There was another gaggle of girls too that showed up about the middle of the second half that caught my attention. Mother-in-waiting, Abby Browne showed up with Gabby Altman, Jenna Meyer, and Amanda Segal. I mean, granted—all four of them seemed to be on their phones most of the time either talking or texting, but they were there.

There were a couple of other attendance surprises too. Like first for instance, seeing Trevor Morehouse, T.J. and Linus slink to the top corner of the bleachers about ten minutes into the match. They didn't holler, or cheer. In fact, they mostly just chowed down on the McDonald's they brought.

I would just kind of glance up there from time to time and just saw them shaking their heads a lot and whisper what I imagined were a bunch of sarcastic and bitter put-downs about their former teammates and coaches—I don't know, I'm sure they all had to be full of sour grapes and vinegar piss to see the team doing so well after the suspensions. I bet they were there hoping to see a train wreck—but they just weren't getting it.

They left at half-time, leaving their trash just sitting up in the bleachers. Later, when the Booster Club parents cleaned up after the game one of the dads would also find a few empty beer cans up there along with the McDonald's bags and plastic *To-Go* cups.

And the second attendance surprise—and probably the most shocking—were the two kids standing by themselves just past the sound shed just underneath one of the massive light posts—both of them with hoods over their heads watching the soccer action. I nearly did a double take when I saw them. Jason Turner stood with Toe-Faux just watching the game. And when we got our third and decisive goal, I even saw Jason raise a fist in what can only be described as a cheer. I mean, what else could it have been? There wasn't a middle finger attached to it. He shouted no obscenities to accompany his fist. His whole body language seemed totally content and pleased. So, it had to be a cheer, right?

So anyway, they snuck away back into the darkness as the announcer counted down the last ten seconds.

After thanking their parents and fans for coming out, Striden called her team back to the field's center circle. They all huddled around her as she gave some spirited words causing them all to yell and cheer in affirmation. They chanted a "TEAM!" and then Striden and Coach Vogel withdrew, leaving the team together to chant and sing their theme song.

It all ended with a lot of howling and hand clapping, not to mention a lot of kazoo craziness compliments of Erik Volgstaad.

When they were heading back towards their bench to get their stuff, Coach Striden looked up from her phone. She had just gotten the result of the other game in their sectional. "Well—the table's set lads! Ann Arbor Huron just beat Afton Hills 3-0. We got our rematch!"

This news was met with even more yells and shrieks from the team. Patrick picked up Isaiah and hurled him in the air and caught him. High-fives abounded. The rematch was set. This coming Thursday, the day after Halloween, the recharged lads of Hemingway would get their shot at making State for the first time in school history and they'd have to take out the defending State Champs to do it.

37

Jason

Rozz, I woke up this morning with only one fucking intention today—and that was to blow my brains out. That was it. Like priority one, man. A one-item checklist: put bullet in head.

So that kid I almost killed, Luke, well, he basically kidnapped me and made me drive to this other kid's house where all the soccer guys were chilling watching movies and shit. Well, I stayed for about a half hour and kind of hinted to Luke that he might not see me again. Any fucking way I drove home pretty much like dead-set to either kill myself or Dylan the very next day. But the more I thought about it the more I knew, it wasn't gonna be Dylan, man. Rozz, I hate that fucker more than anything, but I was realizing that snuffing him really wasn't gonna do jack shit. And depending on my mood killing him might not even feel good. I mean, fuck! I'd have to be coked or tweaked out to do it proper and by the time I got home that night I was just too tired to think of it anymore.

Really the only thing that kept me from snuffing myself out with Kid's SIG that following morning was I was still curious about where my dad was and how he was dealing with Dre and those trailer assholes that tried to kill me. Well, that and also I told Luke I'd try to at least wait a couple of days before I decided what I was going to do. I realize Luke didn't know what the fuck I was talking about but for some reason (I can't really explain it, you know?) but I wanted to at least wait a couple of days just because he asked me to as a favor. I know—weird, right?

I don't know, Rozz. So, I get up, do a little coke, sip a little vodka in my OJ, snag a Pop Tart and fucking head off to school. I didn't know what else to do.

Well, I was fucking regretting showing up like the second I got there, man. I mean, I got a pass during first period to go to the shitter and like as hell would have it there's Kevin Wilhelm in there waiting for me. Kevin's still all busting my ass for a hook-up because Kid T still hasn't shown back up with treats for trade. And not only that—but now Kevin's figuring if Kid's on the low, or relocating, maybe he can be Kid's replacement.

"Just set something up where I can talk to your Pops, man," Kevin goes.

And I'm like, "Fuck that, man. I don't even know where my Pops is these days. Besides that, this aint my biz—so fuck off, dig?"

But that Kevin, man—he's a dense fucker and worse yet, he thinks he's ready for the biz and wants in big time. "Look, man—" he goes, "this can't keep going on this way. There's got to be a source available. There's just too much green for the taking for this tit to go dry, man. Your Pop's gotta know this. And all I'm saying is, is if Kid can't do what Kid's been doing anymore—I can do it. I know all the same people pretty much. I'm a quick learner and I can *sooo* be trusted."

"Look, man—save that fucking resumé shit for someone else," I go. "I already told you I don't know what the hell's going on with all that. My pop's fucking MIA. And he don't tell me shit anyway. So why don't you go pop some fucking pills, smoke a bowl, or fucking steal one of your dad's beers in the meantime to tide you over. Because I'm sure before too long this mother's gonna get all hardcore for you again and then you can go job-seeking to people that give a rat's cause they always need lackey's in the biz, man."

And I just left him and his weasel-nose and two snake-eyes there in the bathroom, Rozz. I mean, talk about a nightmare way to start your day.

Well, I made it through second hour, but after that I just fucking lost the will. So I cut out and went home and just got in bed, man. I just slept and slept.

I woke up and it was dark. I felt like death. I was sore from sleeping on my back so long and I just laid there in the dark for a while. It was the most alone feeling I think I ever felt just lying there. Like I was the only person left on the whole deserted planet.

I sat up and thought about putting in my earpods but the thought of all of my music depressed me. I like suddenly got sick just thinking about it. I mean, seriously who gets sick thinking about their favorite music?

I went downstairs. Fucking dark everywhere and even though I was feeling wicked depressed I still didn't turn any of the lights on. It was like I was getting off on my feeling low, you know Rozz? Like I was letting the sadness, the utter fucking hopelessness in. *Just take me*—I was saying to it.

The fridge and the microwave lights were the only lights that shined as I made a shit-ass melted cheese sandwich. We were just about out of food, but I didn't care. I ate the sandwich on the EZ chair in the living room. Left the TV off. Just sat there chewing in the dark as slow as a fucking cow, man.

When I was finished, I crawled back up to my room and gulped down what little was left of my whiskey and the last fifth of my vodka and laid back down in my bed and waited for it all to hit.

Rozz, as I laid there just fucking fading away, I think I started to cry. Not sob or anything— I think just hot tears just started flowing out of my eyes as my mind slowly hazed and unraveled.

I could taste the tears. Or at least I hoped it was my tears. Hot salt and wet. It was either my tears or some invisible asshole was hovering above me pissing lightly on my mouth.

The last thing I remember is just slurring out loud, "I die tomorrow. That's it. *Tha-Tha-Tha-That's all, folks*."

I was settled on it. I even told you in my mind, I was coming to see you. I was ready. I would wake up in the morning, get out the SIG and end it. Bang.

Woke up this morning and rose out of bed my bones creaking like they were made out of rotting tree limbs.

True to my word though I pulled out Kid T's SIG from between my mattresses and clicked the safety off and just stared at it in my hands. Man, this is it, I thought. And that's when I hear the front door swing open. My dad comes back right the fuck then. I can hear his heavy boot steps clogging all dramatic on the floor announcing his arrival, man.

You gotta be fucking kidding me, I say to myself. I like consider the SIG in my hands and I think for a second about just running down stairs real quick and plugging a couple of rounds in my dad's head and chest and then calling shit a day before my own grand finale.

But I hear him belt out, "Hey you little shit—I'm home! Where the fuck are you, boy?" and for some reason I think better of it and just shove the gun back between the mattresses and waltz downstairs to see what the deal is.

"Uh, there you are," he goes and takes off his jacket and chucks it on the sofa. He looks like shit just like I thought he would. Like he's running on no sleep for days and scraping by on meth and the Taco Bell dollar menu.

"So what happened?" I ask. But he just keeps stalking into the kitchen and basically makes me follow him in if I want to know the answer to my goddamn question.

He throws some junk mail on the table and then heads to the sink and slaps handfuls of cold water to his face and into his hair until he's like dripping all over the floor. He finally turns it off and wipes his face with the bottom of his T-shirt and leans back against the sink for like support. He just breathes like that for a while, zoning out, staring at the random envelopes and pizza delivery ads on the kitchen table. "Didn't you ever check the mail while I was gone?"

I ignored his question. "So what fucking happened talking to Dre, man? What's the deal?"

"The deal is—*little man*, that you're back to being crystal. You got that? And don't worry about the money from the camelback, OK? I took care of it and that's all you need to know, Jace."

"Well, what else?" I go.

"*What else?* There is nothing else—that's it, kid."

"No, I mean that can't be all of it. Like what happens now, Dad?"

He rubs his hand all over his dragging face. "What happens now is that I get some fucking rest. That's what happens now."

I was starting to get seriously pissed. "So that's it? You're not going tell me anything?"

"Look—I told you all you need to know. All right? You're fucking crystal again. No more fucking bizzing for you, *Lil Pops*—got it? You see Dre and his crew again you run the other way. Or better yet you call me and then run the other way. Got it?" he goes, getting pissed too and walks over and throws open the fridge door.

"So what about Scotty and that fucking maintenance dude, huh?"

"Dead on sight," he says over his shoulder. "That's the policy—both crews."

I shake my head. "You don't have a crew."

He looks back at me for a sec, "Not yet..." he goes and then like fucking chuckles.

"Fucking unbelievable—" I mumble to myself. "So those psychos are still out there cruising around looking for payback or whatever?"

"Don't worry. Keep your eyes peeled and you're pretty much safe. Those fuckers aint gonna last long. Any common sense those tinas had was smoked out them long ago, man. Besides they probably split town the night Lester bought it and aint never coming back. Probably off in the trailers of Detroit somewhere never to return, you know?"

"How's Kid T?" I go.

Dad pulls out what's left of a two-gallon of milk. "Who knows? Didn't see him."

"Did Dre say how he's doing? Say where he's holed up?"

He shakes his head. "Didn't say. Kid didn't come up—wasn't on the agenda. Besides what the fuck do you care? You two friends all of a sudden? Anyway, he's probably out of the scene too. But just to be safe—you see Kid T around you stay away from him too. Got it, Jace?"

I just stare at him. I'm sure this is the point of the conversation that fucking Kevin Wilhelm would have given me a blow job to mention his name to my dad as a possible stand-in for Kid but I sure as shit wasn't gonna say anything about it. Fuck him. Fuck all of them, man.

Dad flips off the cap of the two-gallon and takes a huge chug of milk. "*PLOOAHH*! Fuck!" he howls, spitting the milk into the sink. "The hell? Fucking curdled, man! Fuck, Jace? What's with keeping rotten milk in the fridge?"

"Hey fuck you too, man! Why don't you stay up to date with the groceries and maybe shit like that won't happen." I have to admit though, I thought it was pretty hilarious seeing him gag like that.

He gulps down water out of the sink and swishes it around getting all the rancid dairy out of his mouth. He wipes his mouth with his shirt again and heads toward the stairs. "I'm fucking getting some sleep. Don't disturb me for nothing. And hey—aren't you supposed to be at school right now?"

"Yeah, whatever," I go. "I took the day off cause I was worried about you."

He scowls a sec at that. "Yeah, well, OK—but just for today, all right? Now I'm not kidding—don't bother me while I'm sleeping," he goes and starts climbing the stairs to his room. "And hey—" he calls down one last time, "you got a letter down there."

I hear his bedroom door slam and I look on the kitchen table where he put the mail. I'm expecting the letter he's talking about is some bullshit from school, like a failure notice, or a fine slip or some shit like that but it's not of course.

Because Rozz, you know exactly what it is.

My blood freezes when I see it and pull it from the pile.

Your fucking handwriting on the envelope.

You wrote my name. My address. Yesterday's date stamped on the envelope.

My hand starts shaking, Rozz. Like the letter was electric, man. It's like I needed a drink to steady my shaking hand but remembered I was out of booze in the house.

I don't know how you did this.

How did you send this to me? I mean, there's no way you're alive, right? You've been dead for way over two months now. Or is somebody seriously fucking with me? But I swear to God this is *your* writing. I don't know. I'm scared as hell, Rozzy girl. I can't open it. Not yet anyway. I can't read it yet. I just can't. I'm just too damn scared.

I can't die either—at least not now. No, you're seeing to that. I don't know what to do, Rozz. I know you want me to read whatever's in there, but I'm just so scared of what I might find. So scared, Rozzy. Give me strength.

I'll open it soon, I promise. Just give me a little more time, girl.

38

Abby

It was around the time that the boys' soccer team was in the middle of playoffs that my mom and I started going down to the adoption agency to look at potential adoptive parent profiles for the child I was carrying. I remember going into the office-type cubical with my mom and Nancy, our adoption agent, where they had a few chairs, a computer, all these legal pads and pens all laid out on this rectangular desk. On the walls were all these cheesy kind of posters of sunsets and people holding up babies and that kind of thing.

Nancy showed us how to get started on the computer and how to go from profile to profile of all the couples of prospective parents they had in their database. Once she felt we knew what we were doing, I guess, Nancy left us to it.

Mom and I went in with kind of a mental checklist of the type of parents we were looking for: financially stable (of course), a married couple, people that were having trouble conceiving on their own—you know, things like that just to name a few. I was blown away about how many applicants there were. It was unbelievable about how many people want to have a child but for whatever reason just can't.

Even though I was barely even starting to show at the time, I couldn't help touching my belly from time to time as we surfed through the database. Thinking as we scrolled through photo after photo of couples, *so will this be your mother, little one? Will she? Could these be your fathers?* It was strange thinking back on it. My mom kept asking me as we kept going through, "Abby, you're still sure you're OK with this?"

"Yeah. I'm fine. This is good," I remember saying. I guess it was odd but as we were going through all the prospects, I didn't feel cold feet at all. It still felt like exactly the right call to give the baby up for adoption. If anything, I left the agency that day even more resolved that I was making the right choice. It was only at school, walking in the hallways, hearing little whispers in my wake that I ever felt like I might be an idiot for not just going and getting a quiet abortion in whichever state would have me.

I guess you could say that Peter and I were going strong again after that little awkward period where I didn't know what to do about being pregnant. Although it was a little different. I mean, we weren't doing much physically at first. Sure, some kissing and stuff but that was about it. Plus, Peter's weird kind of hint about maybe giving him a blow job and then him like totally backtracking and saying he was just kidding was still giving me some pause. Don't get me wrong—he seemed supportive and was constantly calling and checking up on me and real attentive and stuff—but it was still different on so many levels than what our relationship used to be before the pregnancy and everybody knowing. It was just really hard to get a handle on, you know?

Anyway, one night, Gabrielle was over and we were doing our toenails in my room. It was already past 9:00 and Gabby had the bright idea of seeing if she could just sleep over. I think fat chance since it's a school night and my rents were never big on sleepovers anyway, even on weekends.

So I say to her, "Hey, call your folks and if they say yes—I'll go ask mine. But I wouldn't like hold your breath, Gabby. It's like a school night, *duh*?"

Gabby hops off my bed and scrambles over and snatches her phone. Within minutes of saying please in her eight-year-old-*gimme-what-I-want-I'm-so-cute* voice, she hangs up saying it's A-OK with her parents if she stays.

"All right—hold on, I'll go check with my mom," I tell her but still had like serious doubts this would fly. But to my total shock, my mom says *sure.* I think mostly because she must have thought I needed some extra stress relief with everything that had been going on lately and just how exhausting it had been at the adoption agency pouring over people's profiles and weighing all of that and stuff.

So Gabby and I spend the next couple of hours in my room with the lights off and a movie on; but mostly we just talk and not watching as we lay on my bed with pillows under our chins.

"So like say after you give the baby to these like random people, you start to wonder what he/she looks like? Do you ever get to see your kid or what?" Gabby asks.

"Yeah, that's the kind of thing the adoptive parents and I and I guess our lawyers will like work out once we get to the next stage," I go. "But in all honesty, once I give the baby up, I don't know if I really want to see him/her again, you know? Not because I don't care, or anything, but more out of just respect for the situation and this idea that once the adoption happens it means that everybody's got to move on from there no matter what."

"Ugh—that's all so crazy, bruh," Gabby goes. "I mean, what if the kid like years down the road or something wants to know who his real mother was? What if he like comes stalking you later? How nuts would that be? I mean, you're walking out of the supermarket or whatever and as you're trying to load up your bags in your car you see this kid just eyeing you from across the parking lot. Seriously, aren't you always going to be thinking: *Is that him or her? Is that my baby?* Talk about freaked up, Abby! You ready for that?"

"I don't know… I'm trying not to think about that, you know? I mean, who knows how I'll feel years down the road? But I gotta believe, this baby's gonna be better off right now with a family that really wants him and can take care of him like right now, you know?" I go.

"You think he'll look more like you or Peter?" Gabby goes.

"I don't know—he'll probably look pretty much like both of us, I guess," I say.

Gabby lifts her head up real quick and groans. "Yeah—but what parts do you *think* will look most like Peter?"

I just start laughing. "I don't know? How would I know that? I guess, if it were a boy he'd be doing all right if he got his daddy's eyes."

"You're right—they are like dreamy stars," Gabby goes.

"Hey—watch it," I say, "that's my boyfriend you're talking about there."

"No—" Gabby goes, "that's your baby daddy I'm talking about there!"

That kind of nonsense girl-talk goes on for a while until whatever movie we're watching (honestly, I don't have a clue now what it was) was over and we finally settle down to go to sleep. But for whatever reason that night—I couldn't. Gabby sure didn't have a problem though. When I look at my phone and see it's almost one-thirty in the morning, Gabs is like snoring all soft like a little piglet or something.

But I'm totally restless.

So I get up and creep downstairs to the kitchen. I have a small glass of milk and chow down what was left of a bag of blue tortilla chips out of the pantry and munch between sips. I was just kind of zoning out, snacking thinking about how Gabby was really kind of an airhead even though she was kind of like one of my better friends at the time, and about how I guess I was kind of an airhead too—even though I didn't feel like an airhead, especially when it was just me thinking stuff to myself. Anyway, out the window I can see the bright full moon and I get the sudden urge to go outside and just look at it and maybe walk around.

I grab my dad's leather jacket that's all worn-out and soft and wrap it around my pajama top and feel around the bottom of the mudroom closet till I find my flip flops and sneak out the back door to the driveway. I remember it was crazy chilly out there. You can easily see your breath. No breeze, bright moon. The kind of night that your breath just rises like steam from a hot tub. The other houses down the street are all still and dark. The neighborhood dogs usually went bonkers if they saw anyone walking down the sidewalk, but they must have been all nestled up somewhere, because it's all graveyard quiet as I walk down the street.

It had been a long time since I had just taken a stroll down the sidewalk of my street. It seemed ever since getting my driver's license I barely walked anywhere anymore. But walking down that cracked sidewalk of my home street that night in my pj's and my dad's jacket—it was like walking back in time, you know?

Wasn't long before I made it all the way down to the Forrester's house. I look up to Luke's window. All dark. Was he in there sleeping? Probably. By the looks of things I am the only one on the entire block that's awake. But then I notice a small glow coming from the side of the Forrester house. I hate to say it, but I crouch low like a total creeper and sneak around the cedar tree in their front yard to the side of the house. I had been in their house plenty of times years ago, before the plane crash, and know the room that the light's coming from is the dining room. As I creep slowly, leading with one foot and then the other like a shaky trapeze artist inching her way across a suspended rope, I remember hoping that I was about to score a peek of Luke like sitting at his kitchen table eating a piece of leftover pie as a midnight snack or something.

But no.

Instead, I catch sight of Luke's dad sitting at the dining room table reading. Just reading. Sitting there with his reading glasses on, looking older than I ever remember seeing him. I can't tell what the book is—but not that I care. That's not to say I didn't care about Mr. Forrester at all—I certainly did, I mean how could you not feel for a man that loses his wife and eight-year-old daughter on the same day? Not only that—but then to have your remaining son go deaf like out of nowhere? I could only image, sitting outside in the dark watching him, what it must feel like to know that kind of loss. That kind of hardship. That kind of pain.

After a minute, or so, I sneak away and give the man back his privacy. But then I like see this dim light coming from a room at the back of the house. I creep close to the window and the room is just lit up by a lamp and the light of a computer's screen saver. And there's Luke writing. Not on the computer—but at the desk where the computer's glowing its screensaver light, writing on what looks to be sheets of like old fashioned paper. I watch him for a bit. My old friend Luke. Writing like he's in a trance or something. With that same intense look you see on his face when he's out on the soccer field. I think just ever-so-briefly about tapping on the window, somehow getting his attention—saying *hi*, whatever. But I don't. I just let him continue to work all obsessed looking. As I make my way back out to the sidewalk, I think a little more just about Luke and how weird it is that we are, you know, 'talking' again and just how cool it kind of is that even though he seems so different than how he's been for the last few years. In fact, if I really think about it, it seems that the way Luke and I were communicating now seemed more like how it was between us when we were eleven in a lot of ways—I mean, minus the crash and him going deaf, I guess.

Thoughts of Luke eventually turn to like memories of Angela. Little Angela Forrester. I loved Angela. I was three years older but that didn't stop me from hanging out and playing dolls with her, or hopscotch or drawing crazy animals with our sidewalk chalk. In fact, I was probably friends with Angela way before I was ever comfortable hanging out with Luke. I remember Angela and I cruising around the street—me on my scooter, her on her hot cycle when we were little. We hung out a lot even before Kate was old enough to even come out much. I could still see her so vividly in my memory. Little golden Angela. With those *Hello Kitty* overalls and a laugh like music. I'm not kidding. Seriously, her laugh was *that* pretty. It really did sound like music.

Suddenly I realize that I'm at the end of street, the corner of Birch and Cherry. There ahead of me is the closed down and boarded up donut shop. *Dream Cream Donuts*. The palace of my childhood. The palace of all our childhoods, really. I remember thinking: *How long had it been closed?* It seemed as if it closed the morning after the plane crash in my shattered memory, but it couldn't have been exactly like that, I realize. I must've zoned out staring at the place, because when a lone car passes me cruising down Cherry Avenue, I get all startled like I had just woke from like a dream or something.

Enough, I say to myself and turn to walk back the length of Birch Street all the way back home.

But the ghosts of childhood stay with me. I was back with Luke walking home from school when we were in third grade. I was back twirling with Angela in the park as we sang stupid pop songs from teenage pop princesses that were now well into their adulthoods and rehabs.

I twirl with my imaginary Angela below the full moon in my pajamas with my flip-flops and my dad's leather jacket flipping about me as I go. I skip. I hum. I frolic by myself as I head home. If anyone had seen me out there, they would've thought I was nuts or on crack. But I don't care. It felt good to be out there in the cold somewhere between night and dawn below a white moon. It felt so refreshing. Like I was taking a break. A break from all the stress, you know? All the crap at school. All the reality of being pregnant, of being with Peter—of trying to stay with Peter.

Oh, just to be back there, I think. Just to be so young. So clean. So free. I couldn't think of what else I was trying to say. I was losing the thought—losing the feeling. Truth was, I was starting to feel cold. Maybe I was starting to feel lame.

I took in one more big breath of cold air. I couldn't feel my toes—they were totally pins and needles at that point, I'm sure. And so, I go back in the house. Back up to my room and Gabby's snoring—only to wake up super-stressed in the morning and dragging ass all the way to school.

39

The bus rocks with song and claps.

"Oh my Lord, Lord, Lord, Lord! Mmm-hmm!"

The clapping forms a steady beat.

"*Mmm-hmm!"*

"Oh Lordy, we come to you this evening," Erik rises to the bus's center aisle. "We come before you on our way to the den of lions! Into the heart of Ann Arbor, dear lord! Into the great reeky bowels of our enemy!"

"Amen!" the chorus shouts.

"Mmm-hmm!"

The claps keep time.

"And Lordy, though the odds be great and though the price may be costly, give us the strength to fight! Fight, dear Lord! Fight to the last man if need be! Fight till there be nothing left but our blood! Our sweat! And our unbreakable love for our teammates! Our love for our coaches! And our love for our, *uh*—manager! Oh, dear Lordy!"

"*AMEN*!" goes the team.

Striden shakes her head up front.

Isaiah beams with pride.

"Give us the will!" Erik shouts. "Give us the focus to realize—*THIS IS IT!* Give us the lust for combat—*TO BE SO DEVILSH!* And no matter what—win, lose, or shoot-out, let us all look at one another and know—that *we*, brothers all, gave it all! To the last man! In victory! In death! WE ARE ONE! ONE TEAM!"

"YEAH!"

"ONE HEROIC HEART!"

"YEAH!"

"ONE FIRE!"

"*YEAH! OH MY LORD! LORD! LORD! LORD!*
OH MY LORD! LORD! LORD! LORD!"

The chant continues all the way into Ann Arbor. All the way through their opponent's parking lot. Out the bus, up the sidewalk, through the stadium gates, across the field to their visiting bench. The chant continues.

The stadium is still empty at the final glimmers of dusk. Still an hour and fifteen minutes till game time. Only the Ann Arbor Booster Parents are there to hear it, the chant, as they set up the concessions and the facility before the game. The Ann Arbor players and coaching staff aren't even at the field yet.

An hour and fourteen minutes later the stadium lights shine down through the November night on the two teams standing rigid at mid-field as two well-bundled girls from the Ann Arbor chorus sing the National Anthem. I can feel butterflies standing up in the stands. I can't imagine how Luke and the guys must feel. I look around and see that the bleachers are packed. There's all the parents, the whole JV team, a huge Ann Arbor crowd of course, but there's also Dickie Swartz in his honking sombrero with his crew without shirts and painted chests. I see Maddie and her friends here, but no Abby Browne tonight.

The referee blows the opening whistle and right away you can just tell. Within seconds of the game starting there's hard body-to-body contact. I mean *hard.* And it just keeps coming. Shin to shin. Shoulder to shoulder. Shoving. Pushing. Tackling. Some of it legal—most of it not. Like I said, right away you could just tell. These two teams *do—not—like* each other. Like big time.

The first twenty minutes are all rough and tight and tense with both teams pushing and playing tight defense. That is until Luke breaks free and pings a shot just over the Ann Arbor goal post.

The crowd *OOO's* and groans. Some stand. Cheering and yelling. One Ann Arbor fan yells, "You gotta pick up that guy! No daylight for him! C'mon now Huron!"

A few minutes later Ann Arbor's star, Alan Shuremaker, makes a run too—and fires a total heat-seeker towards the goal. But Patrick catches it off a sprawling sideways dive.

Not long after that Shuremaker's running alongside Troy. They're both shoulder to shoulder as their chasing down the ball. Shuremaker takes a dive. The Ann Arbor crowd goes nuts; they want a foul. Our crowd goes nuts because we want Shuremaker to get called for faking. The ref doesn't buy it for a second and yells for everyone to play on.

Troy looks down on Shuremaker and smiles. "Get up number ten. You ain't playing our JV's anymore."

Ryan wins the ball around midfield from a rare Ann Arbor bad pass. He takes two left-footed touches and sends a fifteen-yard pass to Luke across the carpet-like grass.

Forrester dribbles a yard—he cuts past one Ann Arbor defender with a razor of a step-over move and cut. Now he's got serious attention as two more defenders lunge toward him. That's what Luke's waiting for. As soon as the defenders commit to him, he sends the ball diagonally into space to the left corner.

Erik's there to run onto it. He jukes his defender at full speed and angles toward the Ann Arbor goal.

The rest of the Hemingway forwards and mids tear into the goalbox like it's a freaking jailbreak.

Erik launches a right-footed bender of a cross. High. Soaring above the Ann Arbor goalkeeper and defenders, above Luke and Knox Fullenberg crashing the six-yard box. But the ball, finally dipping, collides with the diving forehead of Tristan Marigan who nails it inside the far post into the back of the net.

We Hemingway faithful erupt.

Hemingway players on the field and on the sideline jump. Coach Striden pumps a freaking celebratory fist. Knox, Ryan, and Luke immediately converge on Tristan, hugging him and jostling him around.

"Hey—" goes one of the larger of the Ann Arbor defenders, "That's that little faggot from the JV team we crushed. That little bastard scored on us then too. Well, that shit's all done now."

"Yeah—your luck's all run out now, kid. Come back into our box, I'm gonna break your legs," goes another defender.

"Don't listen to these A-holes, man. Best revenge is to put another one down their throats ASAP," Erik goes and messes up Tristan's hair.

With the score 1-0, the game just intensifies. And even though Hemingway's got the lead, it's Ann Arbor that seems to pick up a physical edge. Every 50/50 ball's an all-out war. You can hear all of the colliding in the stands. The high school kids from both schools love the contact. They call out for blood.

Ann Arbor Huron starts to carry possession. Even rifle off a couple of dangerous shots. Patrick saves them, but he's got to extend to get to them. Tense stuff.

Shuremaker begins to show why he's so dangerous. He gets the ball on a run right up the gut and pulls a Messi-like spin on Knox Fullenberg which nearly splits Knox's shorts he's so turned around by it. Then with Fullenberg dusted, Shuremaker's clear to shoot and he sends a rifle past a diving Patrick that luckily goes careening off the right post and out of bounds. But *WOW* that shot had reverb—and all of us in the stands know we were lucky.

Patrick screams out at his team about all the open marks.

"Get organized now!" Coach Striden screams from the sideline.

Coach Vogel just watches, arms crossed, stone-faced while Isaiah chews on his knuckle looking like he's about to wet his pants.

The ball pops loose after a sloppy trap from an Ann Arbor mid-fielder.

Matt Glendening springs after it. Too bad for him two other Ann Arbor players are thinking the same thing and are going in *hard.*

Matt senses the space around the ball closing. He's almost there. He's not gonna be first, unless…. He stretches out his left leg as far as it will go. He swipes at the ball with the tip of the outside of his foot just as the two Ann Arbor players slam into, and on top of his extended leg.

A strong tree limb suddenly snaps in half—or what sounds like one anyway.

Matt Glendening screams. I mean freaking *SCREAMS.*

Play stops before the referee can actually blow the whistle.

"Oh my god. Matt!" Ryan yells.

The two Ann Arbor guys get up and step away while Glendening writhes in total agony. He holds up his leg, and the bottom half just flops over broken nearly in half.

The physical trainer and the Hemingway coaches sprint out on the field, out to where the referee stands above Glendening while he wails.

The timekeeper stops the game clock. The crowd hushes. The Ann Arbor players all huddle together on their end while the Hemingway boys kind of huddle together closer to Glendening.

It seems like years before the ambulance arrives. Severely broken leg. Nobody in the entire stadium has any problem diagnosing that. The paramedics drive that sucker right out onto the field. They work fast. Strap Glendening to the collapsible gurney, even haul out an oxygen mask for his face if he starts to hyperventilate.

As they start to get him ready to load, Striden says something to him and Glendening, done screaming now, says something back.

And suddenly this middle-aged lady comes out of the stands followed by a guy—Glendening's parents. Everybody claps as they hoist him up into the ambulance and Matt raises a feeble hand in response. Meanwhile his mom just gets into the back of the ambulance with him and the paramedic guys while his dad shuffles out of the stadium, presumably to follow them to the hospital in the family car.

Everybody watches the ambulance take off in a blur of red, blue, and yellow lights doing 360's on top. They hit the siren as soon as the tires touch pavement—and just like that, Glendening's gone.

Striden throws in sophomore, Dave Jerome, off the bench and the ref whistle's for a drop ball where play stopped.

Ann Arbor's vicious assault doesn't let up once play resumes—at all. The last seven minutes of the half are a barrage of Ann Arbor pressure. And finally, Alan Shuremaker brakes through into the box, burning past Troy Jensen, and hits a well-aimed low shot past a diving Patrick into the goal.

The Ann Arbor fans come unglued. The game announcer yells, "*GOAL!* Coming off the foot of number ten, Alan Shuremaker!"

The referee calls for half-time and each team hustles to their bench—Ann Arbor visibly looking more pumped and confident.

"Any word on Glendening?" Ryan goes to Coach Vogel the second he reaches the bench.

Vogel shakes his head. "I told his dad to call us when they know just how bad it is. It broke my heart to have to text him when they scored."

"Listen up lads," Striden goes as the team grabs water bottles and shuffles near her. Those that just came off the field huff and suck in air as sweaty steam lifts off their drenched jerseys and hair. "You had them early—but somehow, we've let them have us towards the end of the half. They've stolen this game from you. They have out-physical-ed you. Knocked you completely out of it mentally. I know, believe me, I know—seeing a teammate go down like we saw Matt go down is tough. It gets you out of your game because you're worried about him—and you want to see some payback. But you got to pick it up now, lads. They smell blood. They are not going to stop coming at you."

"So start marking tighter. Double Shuremaker when he's near the box like he was on that goal!" Patrick goes.

"Exactly," Striden continues. "But don't just go after Shuremaker that way. Go after *them all* that way. Like I said, they're not going to stop. So start going at them twice as hard. If one of their guys comes in hard, then two of us go in on him harder. Legal—*but hard.* Play it without fear, boys. I know if Glendening were here, he'd tell you to play hard no matter what the cost. What are you willing to risk tonight? How far are you willing to go for each other?"

Striden's lads start to look up from their zoned stares and look at her. Look at each other.

"This song you've started singing, these brave words you guys have started shouting to one another before games—are they just words? Something cute and cool to make you guys sound tough? Or do you *believe* them? Or can you even go further than belief and actually *live* them? Over the last two weeks you guys have shown me more heart and character than I thought you had in you. I completely underestimated you. I stand in awe of you now. You sure showed me. I thought I knew you before, but I was wrong. You guys are so much more than I thought you were. Now look at them—"

Striden points over to the opposing bench.

The team all looks over to where the Ann Arbor players sit half-listening to their coaches. Everything about their body posture screaming cockiness and entitlement.

"You get forty minutes to show them how much they underestimate you. To show them what's at the heart of what you're all about. Don't shy away from this opportunity! Don't shrink away from the physical and emotional cost of a chance like this! So get your gloves on, boys! Lace'em up tight! Cause it's time to battle, baby, and let them know with every hit off a 50/50 ball, every lung-bursting sprint to a through-ball, every chance for a slide tackle, that you'd rather die tonight on this chosen field than lose! Now get up and fight!"

The team roars to their feet.

"Come on, men!" Erik goes, circling them up.

"Everything now. Everything!" Patrick yells too as he puts his gloved hand in the middle of them.

They all put their hands in.

"For Matt," Ryan goes. They all lean in close.

"*For Matt*!" a bunch of them echo.

Luke says nothing, of course. Just looks around the circle at his teammates, beaming. When he locks eyes with Erik, he nods.

Erik nods back.

The siren goes off over the loudspeakers signaling the teams to take their places on the field.

The crowd comes back to life. All of us fans from both schools. On our feet and cheering.

"*Here we go*," Erik goes. "Everything you got. Save nothing, boys. Let's go—team on three. ONE, TWO, THREE!"

"TEAM!"

40

They take the field, and the second half comes alive with the ref's whistle. Just like the start of the match, the beginning of the second half's a collision-fest. Bodies flying everywhere. Fouls abound, but the referee still hesitates to card anyone. The fans come unhinged with each violent challenge that goes without a red card. The play with the ball is not as crisp as it was in the first half—the game decidedly fueled more by the enraged heart than tactics now.

"Pick him up! Shift! Damn it, Troy! *Shift!"* Patrick screams at the defense as an Ann Arbor forward moves towards the goal line with intensions to send in a deadly cross.

Troy gets there just in time to slide his leg in front of the ball on impact. The ball goes off him and out of bounds, setting up a Huron corner kick.

"C'mon! Cover! Cover! Knox! Watch number five, coming in back post!" Patrick directs.

The ball goes off a Hemingway defender. The Ann Arbor player steps over to take the corner kick. Man, it's a scorcher of a cross.

Every player in the box jockeys for position. Patrick's the first there but he can only punch it away with his fist. The ball bounces off the top of the head of an Ann Arbor player. Troy jumps up—tries to clear the ball out. Misses.

The ball falls to the ground. Everyone scrambles for it. The Hemingway guys are trying to clear it out—the Ann Arbor guys are just trying to drill it forward into the goal.

It's freaking bedlam. Like a rugby scrum—or mosh pit. Maybe a pig wallow.

Patrick dives hands-first into the middle of the mass. He sees a chance to grab the ball outright and disappears into a cloud of kicking bodies.

Most of us who were sitting in the bleachers stand up. It's too hard to tell what's going on in the free-for-all in the box.

The referee looks like he's about to intervene when suddenly a couple of guys go flying back out of the fray and the ball kind of ricochets off a few people and then off the left post and trickles past the goal line.

The assistant referee on the side-line signals an Ann Arbor goal.

Ann Arbor goes nuts. Their fans, their players.

The announcer goes crazy. He screams *goal* but hasn't a faint idea who got it.

As the Ann Arbor players run back to the center, Patrick finally rises out of where the dogpile was bleeding from the lip big time.

"Seriously!" he goes to the referees. "I just got jacked in the face and you guys are gonna count that as a goal?"

The ref just motions for the trainer and the Hemingway coaches to come out and attend Patrick.

"I got kicked twice in there!" Patrick keeps protesting while the trainer tries to put some gauze to his gory lip.

Some of the Ann Arbor fans turn to us and rifle off a bunch of taunting remarks.

"Hey—it ain't over yet, morons!" Dickie Schwartz yells back to them, shirtless and wearing green paint across his chest. His massive sombrero jiggling with each word.

"Ha!" goes one of the rowdy Ann Arbor students. "Check out the pasty Mexican boy with the green tits!"

Play resumes with Ann Arbor Huron up 2-1. And you can tell that Ann Arbor is now trying to preserve the win. They pull their mids further back into a more defensive posture. Their intention is clear. Get the ball out of their end at all costs—and take the counterattack when you can.

It makes for tough watching for us up in the bleachers. Ann Arbor knows how to keep a lead—that much is obvious even to those of us who don't watch that much soccer. And as much as our boys keep passing, keep pounding through, it always seems Ann Arbor has plenty of guys in place before we can get through into the attacking third of the field.

The Ann Arbor guys start doing little things to waste time. Milking the clock on every throw-in and goal kick. Long, drawn out unnecessary substitutions. Jacking the ball miles out of bounds. And dribbling the ball to the corners whenever possible to sap time and cause a throw-in. Not pretty soccer—but effective.

Hemingway boos in the stands.

The Ann Arbor Huron fans are emboldened by them. "There is the scoreboard!" one of them starts the cheer.

"THERE IS THE SCOREBOARD!" a bunch of them cheer back.

"There is the winning team!" he points to Ann Arbor Huron bench.

"THERE IS THE WINNING TEAM!" they point too.

"There is the losing team!" he points to the Hemingway bench.

"THERE IS THE LOSING TEAM!" the flock points too.

Patrick Durning looks over to the bleachers during this and then yells to Troy who just won the ball after a lame-duck Ann Arbor throw-in, "Troy! Ball!"

Troy looks a little startled, but quickly passes the ball back to his goalkeeper's feet.

"Up!" Patrick yells to his team and starts to dribble. "C'mon! Everybody up!"

Less than two minutes left in the game.

"Up!" Patrick yells again and quickens his strides on the dribble.

"Well, get him!" yells one of the Ann Arbor central-mids to his forwards.

As the Hemingway goalkeeper dribbles nearly to the center circle, the Ann Arbor forwards stand still—dazed, like they don't know what's going on.

"Shuremaker! What the hell?" goes the Ann Arbor mid again. "Get the keeper! Get the ball!"

Finally Shuremaker starts to come at Patrick, but he's too late. Before he can stop him, Patrick sends a beautiful chip to Luke just left of the center of the field, in Ann Arbor territory.

Luke thigh-traps it perfectly and turns and sends the ball forward to Tristan, who passes it lightning quick back to Luke who's moved diagonally into more forward space.

"Get him!" yells the Ann Arbor goalkeeper.

A defender charges Luke.

Luke fakes. The defender shifts. Gets stuck flatfooted. Luke cuts inside. Burns the defender. He sprints with quick touches on the ball into the Ann Arbor goalbox.

In the stands we hold our breath.

Luke poises to shoot. Fakes the shot and dishes the ball with the outside of his foot to the left.

And somehow Erik's there. He shoots a laser beam.

We all grab on to someone next to us—*hard.*

The ball bounces off the goalie's diving hands. He saves it.

We all have heart attacks.

But wait.

The ball bounces out to the six-yard line to the right of the goal. Right in front of Ryan Leone.

Ryan slams the ball into the net so hard it looks as if it might rip.

We scream our lungs nearly right out of our mouths. We're deafening. We're defiant. We're still alive!

Our boys slam into Ryan as he runs to the corner flag. He kisses the *Fire* symbol that Erik had them all marker on their knuckles and points to us in the stands. Erik jumps on his back. Luke somehow picks them both up off the ground.

41

With the game tied at 2-2, regulation ends with both teams heading back to their benches.

"OK, OK, lads," Striden goes, striding among her troops like an Amazonian warrior queen. "No let-downs. Stay tight defensively. Don't let that Shuremaker kid breathe. And most importantly somebody—*please*," she goes and tightens her hand into a boxer's fist, "deliver the sermon, baby. Deliver the freaking sermon!"

"AMEN!" the boys roar.

"Let's go! This is *ours*, boys!" Patrick yells as they take the field again.

The overtime starts, and here we go—right back at it.

The trash-talk on the bleachers tones way down—both sets of fans way too interested in the game now to be bothered by anything else.

Coach Striden was right to keep using boxing imagery to describe the match, because that's exactly what the game looked like now—two spent fighters circling each other, taking turns summoning up enough strength to mount an attack and then pulling back to regain defensive composure.

The first overtime comes to a close with few chances for both sides and both teams looking fatigued. They go to their benches for the last time for a two-minute water break and final feedback from their coaches.

Isaiah hears Coach Vogel's phone buzz. "It's Glendening. They're getting ready to set his leg. Wants to know the score."

"Tell him we're gonna win it for him," Erik goes, and a bunch of guys nod too.

Coach Vogel texts him back while Striden gives the team some final instructions. Vogel's phone buzzes again.

"What's it say?" Isaiah goes.

"It says, *Love you guys.*"

Luke then suddenly wraps his big arms around the guys closest to him. Everybody follows suit till everyone's got their arm around someone else in a tight circle. Luke looks around to them all. They all look back.

Luke reaches and pulls Isaiah into the center of the circle then takes Vogel's phone still glowing with Glendenning's text and gives it to Isaiah to hold. Everybody pulls in closer. No one speaks for a moment, just breathes. Luke makes an'*L*' sign with his hand and looks at them all with the utmost intensity. But nobody's getting it.

"*L-Loser*?" Erik goes.

Luke shakes his head and throttles his 'L' shaped hand in front of them again, then reaches down and kisses Isaiah on top of the head and points to the text. Isaiah looks confused, but excited.

Finally, it dawns on Ryan. "*Love.*"

Luke smiles and nods, pulls everyone even tighter.

Suddenly everybody gets it. Glows with it. Washes in it. Lets it in all around them.

"L-word on three, boys." Erik's face is calm. And without direction, without any further instruction about how to do it, on three the entire team quietly, but confidently, unashamedly goes in unison, "*Love.*"

They break their circle, and the starters take the field. Erik grabs Isaiah and kisses him on top of the head. So does Ryan. Troy also smacks him with one.

"Hey! What's with everybody kissing my head?"

"I think you just became a good luck ritual, lad!" Coach Vogel goes and then kisses the top of Isaiah's head too.

Then the rain starts coming down. Not a total downpour, but a steady misting.

We go nuts in the stands. The ref's about to whistle the second overtime to life and here we are stomping on the bleachers, the rain soaking us, the field, the players. We can feel it.

It starts and Luke Forrester will not be denied. He's everywhere—putting on pressure, winning balls, making perfect passes, even as the field is turning into mud soup. Ann Arbor Huron just cannot slow him down.

"C'mon! Keep it up! Keep pressing!" Patrick goes from the backfield.

Luke passes it back around the centerline to Knox. Knox traps it and takes a touch to his left, looking up field.

"Knoxy! Hit Volgs! Right flank!" Troy calls out from behind, seeing the play open up.

Knox doesn't hesitate, just passes, trusting Troy's vision.

Erik runs onto it in stride, looks up and sees Tristan making a run across the box.

"Yes! Hit Tristan!" Ryan Leone's dad cries out from the stands.

We all tense up. *Could this be it?*

Erik's about to send it, but an Ann Arbor defender jumps into Erik's intended passing lane. He pulls the ball back. Pulls off a behind-the-heel move and looks to dish the ball off somewhere else.

Another defender comes sliding in on the wet grass. The ball and Erik go flying.

No whistle. No call. It looks like another busted play.

Alan Shuremaker comes back and corrals the loose ball and turns to take it up the field. The Ann Arbor fans all cheer and a few of them yell for him to just dribble it all the way—as if he can just burn through all the Hemingway players.

But Luke flies in front of him from out of nowhere.

Shuremaker feints to his right and then pulls out a step-over and tries to cut back to his left. To his credit, it's a heckuva move and his speed and timing of it is totally *sharpish* by any soccer lover's standards.

But at the move's zenith, Luke jams his foot down on the ball, stuffing Shruemaker, sending the All-State striker flipping over to the ground.

Suddenly, it's Luke who's got the ball at his feet, less than twenty-five yards from the goal.

He looks up. Sees that the Ann Arbor keeper is a little too far off his line. Luke brings up his arms. His eyes focus on the ball, looking to hit it dead center.

The goalkeeper is only midway through shouting *NO SHOT!* just as Luke's foot blasts into the middle of the ball.

The sound of the strike is unmistakable. All laces, baby. That sucker rises swiftly to seven feet and stays there, zooming in a straight trajectory towards the upper right corner of the goal like a Stinger missile out of a launcher.

Luke smiles before he even looks up.

There are no doubts. *None.*

Alan Shuremaker knows too. He sees the ball rocket towards the goal from where he sits in the mud. He closes his eyes so he doesn't have to see it go in.

The keeper makes a go of it, but his dive looks in slow motion.

The ball blasts in and pushes the net out nearly three feet.

It's as if all of us breathe *in* for half a second. Silence. And when we breathe *out*—joy. The noise of victory triumphant. We become a nuclear detonation of cheering.

It's all so loud. So fast. Every green jersey on the field and from the team sideline jumps and runs at Luke, burying him in a dog-pile of pure thrill. Every white jersey-ed Ann Arbor Huron player hits the ground as if they'd been simultaneously hit by lightning.

And those of us in the stands? Well, we lose our minds. Suddenly all of us are running out on the field—despite the calls from the stadium announcer for us *NOT* to do so. And I mean all of us—JV's, students, parents—all of us are out there circling the team. Hugging them. High-five-ing them. Hugging each other. Seriously, I get kissed and hugged by at least three different random moms I don't know—and one dad. Dickie Schwartz picks me up and roars joy in my face and at that point I've never even hung out with that kid in my life yet. People are sliding in the mud like it's old freaking footage of Woodstock, or something.

I look off and see Luke and a bunch of the Hemingway players shaking hands with the Ann Arbor guys. I see Coach Striden looking as dignified as ever talking with the Ann Arbor coaches. I see class. I see Luke put his hand on Alan Shuremaker's shoulder and hand him a note. I see Patrick Durning give the opposing goal-keeper a hug of understanding that I suppose only goal keepers understand. I look at our boys and I see that newfound honor Erik was trying to talk about in Malory's English class.

And when the team returns to us—their muddied, joy-drunk, tear-soaked faithful few fans, we all make a ram-shackle circle together. Ryan and Erik both say a few words of thanks to all of us for coming out and supporting them. Then Coach Striden says a few words too.

And it was *then*, that I started to understand that what was going on here was more than enthusiasm after a playoff win. That maybe there was more at work here than just our soccer team's berth to the state tournament. That perhaps there was something about *how* these guys did this that had been the reason I had dragged myself out of my house to watch this—to join in *this*. That maybe all of us were celebrating something more—that we were becoming one with something rather than just merely watching our team win. I didn't know all of what all this was at that point—but I knew I wanted more of it. And I could tell, just by looking around at the faces of that muddy circle, whether I knew who they were or not, that they all wanted more too.

ERIF

V

"Get up! Rise, Prince of words! Get up, Prince of lies! Awake!" Annabella shook at Prince's blanket after storming into his tent.

Prince bolted upright, unsure of what was happening.

"You must leave! This very morning, Prince! This very instant! I can no longer abide in your being here!"

"*My—!* Annabella? Why are you here? And so early?" He looked up at her. He could see her earnestness lining her face as she crouched in his small tent. He spied a glimpse of morning haze outside the flap behind her.

"You must leave Thorn. Today, Prince. *Now*, as soon as you are able," she said.

"But why?"

Annabella rubbed her tired eyes before answering, "Because I realize now that besides your intensions and even my own feelings toward you—-what you proposed last night cannot be. It just cannot. Our place is here. Our father's place is here. He cannot leave—-not with all his infirmity—-with his *curse*."

"But Annabella, why can't you and your family not come with me? How is it so impossible?" Prince asked, staggering to his small stool.

"There are so many things that root me here that you cannot know. I shudder to tell you of them. Do not ask. If you truly *like* me as you said yesteryern, then leave by all graces. Leave Thorn and do not return. At least not until next summer and even then, under extreme caution as to disguise yourself."

Prince looked dumb. "What? Why? Tell me more. How could I ever leave you on such terms? Who's put you up to this?"

Annabella broke into sobs. "Do not seek further! Do not stay if you do love me! To stay a moment longer is to say you do not love me. That you do not care for our Angel. You must have faith in me that I know what must be—and that is for you to go my Prince. Please pack your moveables and leave the dust of Thorn to those of us doomed to live here."

"I will not leave you so wretched. Not for—-"

Annabella slapped Prince's mouth before he could finish his oath-making.

"Leave at once, foolish boy! I cannot love you, you *dolt*! Idiot child! Can you not conceive of the harsh ways of the world? Are you not aware of its spiked tread? This place is not for you. Weaver of dreams. Spinner of fantastical poisons. Conjurer of toy bubbles. *Go*—-and leave Thorn and its doomed souls at a distance to your back!"

Annabella kicked the tent's center pole over, bringing the whole kit down on Prince's bewildered head and fled back through Russler's Alley—-sprinting as fast as she could go in her summer's dress so that Prince could not see her streaming face and how it so betrayed her breaking heart.

Severely confused and hurt, Prince knew not what else to do other than to mindlessly pack his things. And as he did so, all of Russler's Alley was busy doing the same. The Mayodon was finished. The last dance had been danced. The last ale had been drunk. Nothing for the festival folk now but to pack up and leave until next spring. And so, Prince joined them in the festival-ending ritual. Not that it took him long. With his tent rolled and tied to his backpack, all Prince had to do was visit the well at the end of the Alley and fill his canteen. He waited his turn in line then hoisted up the dripping bucket and splashed some water on his face before filling up his canteen and then slinging its strap around his neck.

Merging into the pilgrim caravan Prince left the gates of Thorn and began the long road out of the valley of the Great Mountain—-the whole time Annabella's words of chastisement swirling in his brainwater like schools of barracuda unleashed.

Tearing hurt. Gnashing bewilderment. And finally, severing anger chewed through Prince's heart as he trudged along the road. He almost thought he could hear Annabella's voice echo off the huge mountains as loud as if Erif himself were leaning his scaly neck out of the Crack and bellowing them out—-"*Dolt!*" "*Idiot boy!*" "*Toy bubbles*!"

"Damn foolish!" he blurted aloud, kicking the dirt ahead of him on the road. "*Damn foolish*!"

42

We know at some point Luke Forrester opened his locker and a folded piece of paper fell out from between the locker's center vent inside the top. He probably looked at it on the floor all curious and whatever for a second and then snagged it up. It was from Abby. It said this more or less:

Congrats on making State!
I wish I could've been there to see it.
Sorry.
Peter and I will be there this Thursday though!
Talk to you soon, hopefully...

None of us know for sure, but there probably was really no way by looking at Luke's face right then to see if he was pleased about getting the note or not. You probably couldn't tell if he was glad she was planning on making the trek down to State to watch him—or if he was just barely feeling a jealous claw at his gut at reading Peter's name. You couldn't tell any of this because Luke was probably sporting the same easy-going, mildly amused face he'd had on most of the school year so far. He was probably looking pretty chipper, pretty amused.

In fact, it's safe to say all the active members of the Hemingway Boys Soccer team were looking particularly chipper this morning after their big win over Ann Arbor Huron. They all strutted around almost like they were floating and giving each other high-fives and tackling one another in the halls when they crossed paths.

Even the kids who could care less, or hated them, had all heard the news by then. It was like impossible to ignore. All over the paper, the local TV news, school announcements—it was getting press and buzz everywhere. And they were the only local fall sport still going in town. Football had been knocked off for weeks now and every other sport was finished too. Basketball, Hockey, and Wrestling had all just started their pre-season practices, I guess—but they wouldn't be in action for almost a month.

The buzz even made it into the *Great Works* Honors English class where most of us sat in our desks gabbing in the usual pre-class absence of our teacher, Mr. Malory.

"Aw, now—check him out now." Philip Lukas watches Erik come into the classroom and sit down. "One of the studs of the soccer world. Yo—ya'll goin to State now, huh, dawg?"

"Yeah. We're getting our shot. It's pretty cool," Erik goes back. "Maybe you *hoops* guys do well, you'll do the same and we'll come watch you in March, eh?"

Lukas just laughs. "Yeah. You got that right." He then tilts his head all laid-back-like towards Peter Calloway sitting in the back next to him.

"Hey—Volgs..." Peter calls up the aisle. "Hey, I hear you guys got some pretty cool cheers you do together. Like I heard you chant how much you like love each other and want blow each other after the game. Is that true?"

Erik just shrugs up in the front row and gives a *whatever* look. "Yeah, that's pretty much it. We all chant out how gay we are and then run out on the field with boners."

Philip and Peter laugh some more.

Maddie O'Leary turns around. "You know, Peter, you should really shut up if you don't know what you're talking about. It makes you sound pretty much like a lame-wad if you don't."

"Uh-oh, Petey—" Philip goes, "you a lame-wad, bruh—"

"Well, better a lame-wad than a gay-wad, I guess," Peter goes back.

"I don't know, *Petey*—how will you know for sure if you don't try?" Erik goes. "Say, the team and I are playing a few rounds *Soggy Biscuit* tonight and it'd be great if you and *little Philly* there joined us. I think you'd really fit in you know?"

Peter and Phil both stop laughing and just stare back at Erik and Maddie.

"What's *Soggy Biscuit*?" Dallas Douglass goes.

"You don't want to know," Gray Cahill mutters back.

"All righty, class!" Mr. Malory bursts in like some cracked-out game show host and starts making us take out our paperbacks and notebooks. Malory doesn't let up at all either—just keeps lecturing about Renaissance literature and freaking Chaucer like his teaching license depends on it. He even shoots down Gray Cahill's two attempts to get him to go on a meaningless tangent about the hardships of the current European economy and just keeps driving us like freaking cattle down the road of our own education.

But in the flurry of notes and scribblings about the *Canterbury Tales*, I do hear Erik lean over to Maddie and say, "Thanks—"

Maddie grins. Writes down more notes. "For what?"

"You know," Erik goes. "For having my back there."

"No problem. It's one of my pet peeves," she goes.

"What is?" he goes back.

"Seeing helpless soccer players being victimized."

Erik grunts out some involuntary noise that sounds somewhere between a wet cough and an obscenity.

"Why, Mr. Volgstaad—" Mr. Malory stops his fevered lecture. "I say, are you all right, dear boy?"

"Ugh—yes. Yes, sir. Uh, just a sudden… burst, sir."

"*Burst*?" Mr. Malory goes.

"Yes—of, from somewhere. I apolo—*sorry*." Erik goes.

Philip and Peter start snickering. They're not alone though. Maddie joins them as does the majority of the class.

"Do you require a sortie to the facilities, Mr. Volgstaad?"

"No—I believe I'm clean—I mean, I'm OK. I'm fine, sir."

"Good then," Malory goes. "Then let us continue. And by the way, everyone, if anyone does in fact need to use the restroom, please just ask. I would hate for any of you to have an accident, or a near accident, like Mr. Volgstaad here just experienced. Now let us turn our attention for a moment to Italy—and the lasting influence Francesco Petrarch would have upon the sonnet form…"

So, yeah—other than the soccer buzz, there wasn't much else happening. Kind of your typical early November day for most of us otherwise. You know, the sky was getting pretty much gray like all the time now; everyday it rained, or seemed it was about to. It was too far away to start looking forward to getting off for Christmas break, but Thanksgiving was starting to get on people's radar. It was one of those kind of in-between times in the school year and I'm sure some people had their own individual deals going on—but otherwise everything was just kind of *blah* around.

The only other thing that happened that day of note was when some of us noticed Jason Turner slither into the school through the doors at the far North end of the building. It was during the passing time right before 7th period, the last class of the day, and Turner was looking particularly loaded. To those few of us that saw him, he was disheveled as usual, but his face had a more wasted quality about him than usual. Word was too that he wasn't making too much school recently either—so the money was good that he was getting high, or drunk, or both pretty much 24/7 these days. His glazy eyes seemed to be scanning for someone in particular and their whacked-out sheen almost came close to some kind of clarity when he spied who he was looking for.

Luke Forrester.

Forrester was just walking seemingly without a care to his last class of the day until he felt a sharp ping in the back of his head. He stopped and turned around—not mad so much as suspicious probably, maybe as if he half-expected to see a hovering bee behind him that had just stung him or something.

Turner slung another penny between his fingers and hit Luke in the throat this time. It must have stung like a bastard, but no one remembers Luke wincing in pain or anything—but he sees Turner laughing at him and nearly falling over in a stupor over the whole deal.

"Hey, man—come on. Can you split this period? I gotta talk to you," Turner goes getting all serious now.

Luke stares at him and then just shrugs.

"Then come on," Turner goes. "I got my car parked right out here."

Luke stays put.

"Aw, come on, man. I promise we'll be done in time for you to go to practice with your team of lawn fairies, man. I promise. It's important, dude."

Finally Luke nods toward the door and they both head out the doors to Turner's Honda *Civic*. Turner suggests they go to the soccer fields since Luke's gotta go there for practice anyway. Luke just nods and away they go. Turner speeds the whole way and pulls into the complex's parking lot and squeals to a stop. Tuner turns off the ignition and pulls the key out. While Luke leans over and pulls his little notepad and pen from his back pocket.

After the other night at Volgstaad's thought I might not see you again.

Turner reads it. "Yeah, well—I took your advice and gave it a day…"

Glad you stuck around…

"I bet you are. Look, I was thinking we could hash some of this out on the phone or something but then I felt like a stupid asshole on account of, you know, you being fucking deaf and all and probably don't have a phone."

Right. Deaf fuckers like me don't have use for a phone. Besides not being able to hear we also can't, for some weird reason, read or send text, or watch video.

Turner crumples up the note and rifles it back at Luke. "Well, fucking *HA! HA!* on me then, you prick. Give me your fucking number, asswipe and I'll text you next time."

Luke writes his number down and tears it off for Turner. Turner takes it, but as he does his hand starts to shake. Luke just watches him, and Turner gets all conscious about it and slams his hands on the steering wheel all hyped up. Then he starts scratching the back of his head with both hands looking down and then snaps his fingers while looking back up to the soccer fields.

"OK. Let's stop beating off around the bush then and get to the fucking point. Look, here's the deal, man—I was gonna blow my brains out the other night. I was pretty fixed on it. That or waste Dylan Sorensen and then go blow my brains out. Either way, I'm done. I'm out. Get it?"

Luke stares at Jason. Jason's eyes are still red and rheumy or whatever but also, I like to imagine they're intense and like pleading. Pleading for Luke to make some sense. To shed some light about what was going on. So Luke looks down to his pad and starts writing.

I'm glad you didn't kill yourself, Jason.

Turner looks at him all suspicious. Snaps his fingers a little more then and rubs his left eyebrow. "Fuck it, man—I don't know. Still feels like you're holding out on me, bruh. You wanna know what stopped me?"

Luke nods.

"A letter."

From who?

"Why don't you take a guess, man?"

Luke scribbles a question mark.

"No, man—fucking guess."

IDK

Turner shakes his head, snaps more fingers. "No fucking dice, man. No—you gotta guess."

Luke just keeps looking all statuesque at Turner.

"I fucking knew it, man. I fucking knew it." He hits the steering wheel again. "You fucking with me? Why you fucking with me, huh?"

Luke doesn't move, doesn't freaking blink.

"You fucking *are* crazy. Crazier than shit. You think I'm playing games?" Turner hauls out the SIG from behind in his jeans. "What the bleeding hell, man? What is this to you? You just a bored deaf-psycho like everybody says playing your lawn fairy games and just looking for ways to fuck with people's minds? I mean, goddamn, kid! What the hell's your deal? You're stalking me for weeks and then all your bullshit about wanting to be killed then like wanting to hang out like it's all, you know, *whatever*! And now this shit? I mean, why would you ever want to fuck with someone like me? Huh? I mean, what's the rationale, dickhead? Seriously, it's not like you need to be a lab tech looking at the results of my urine test to know I'm one drugged-out and drunk motherfucker! It's not like you don't know I got some serious anger management issues or that if you keep antagonizing me, I will fucking flip and eventually kill your ass, Harper's Lake episode be damned! So what the fuck, kid? Get writing, man. Come on! You at least owe me some sort of answer."

What did the letter say?

"Oh, fucking— goddamn, asshole. How about you tell me what it said since you wrote it."

Jason, I don't have a clue what it said.
It's for you. And you only.

"She wrote it to *me*… How did *you* know her? How did you know Rosalind Howard?"

I didn't know her. I never talked to her in my life—ever.
But I know you did.

Turner puts his head in his hands like he's trying to fight off the mother of all freaking migraines. He sets the SIG up on the dash and puts his hands back over his open mouth while he just stares blankly back outward ahead of him. Luke sees Turner's red eyes begin to water up a little.

The both of them just sit like that awhile.

"Did you," Turner starts again, "write that letter pretending to be Rozzy?"

Luke shakes his head.

"But you knew I was going to get a letter from her soon after that night that you dragged me over to your soccer buddy's?"

Luke nods *yes*.

"How is that possible? How's any of this possible? Especially since you say you never knew her?"

Luke scratches his head as if he were thinking about how to get the wording of his next note just right.

I sent the letter to you. It was given to me sealed and addressed to you with instructions about when to mail it.

"The fuck you say…? Who gave it to you?"

Well, I guess you could say— in a way—Rosalind did.

Now it's Turner's turn to just stare like stone at Luke. After a moment he finally goes, "Come ye the fuck again? How'd she do that, man?"

ERIF

VI

Annabella took the time walking back to her house to regain herself as best she could. At the threshold of their rotting door, she took one more deep breath to cool her flushed face.

"Sister!" Angel said. "Where have you been to? Surely you did not go to see Prince without waking me?"

"Enough now, Angel. I'll tell you all later. For now, let us see to breakfast." Annabella made for the fireplace.

"All right—-but let us eat quick, sister. I do so want to spend as much time as we can with Prince before he must leave," Angel said.

Annabella stoked the embers at the hearth. "Angel—- I'm sorry, but he has already gone."

"What? How can that be? Did you go see him? But I cannot believe he's gone. Surely you trick, sister. And it is mean of you. Awfully mean. *Awfully.*"

"I'm so sorry, dearest. But it is no trick. I'm sorry, but he has left. But he did wish you well. He said he wished so much to see you one more time, but he could simply not tarry any longer in Thorn."

"Lie! This cannot be! Why would you say such?"

"It is no lie—-he had to leave. Angel, dear—-"

"No! If he is gone then it was you who sent him away! I know not why—-but I do know if he's gone it was your doing!" Angel screamed.

Annabella's face dropped. "Please, Angel—-understand—-there was nothing else I could do. For your good safety did I do it."

"My *safety*? Do you really take me for such an ignorant child? How could sending away the best person we've ever met somehow be for my good safety? Sister, tell me the truth. That, or let us hasten after him! He cannot have gotten too far from Thorn so quickly—-"

"No!" Annabella said. "It cannot be. I won't let it. You cannot understand yet, Angel, but in time you will. You'll see that life is not all festivals and Yonderlings making useless little Auras, glorious sunlight and endless fields of wildflowers. That every night is not just a heaven's show of angelic shooting stars sent by the gods for your wondered amusement. You'll see that with the daylight comes a hard day's toil and sometimes night begets true darkness, darkness that threatens to devour all that's good in the world or even a body's soul."

Angel merely stared a moment at Annabella. "Sister," her voice barely above a whisper, "do you not think that I don't know this already? How can you say that I am ignorant of the darkness when I have stood with my hand in yours through all that we have endured here together? Do you not think I *know,* truly, where our mother is? Do you honestly think I have no idea what lurks up there in the Crack? How can you discount me so?"

"Angel—-I—-"

But Angel swiped their father's large ale mug from the mantle and heaved it with all the strength her eleven-year-old body could bestow at the fireplace beside Annabella. "How can you?"

The crash was enough to finally raise their father from his cocooned slumber on his cot. "W-What the blazes?"

"Father—" Annabella said.

"Girls...what be ye up to—? Baah! Yer father's mug! A bust and cracked! Devil's piss upon me!" He rubbed his saggy face seeing the shards of his ale mug. "Baah and blast it!" He staggered up and kicked at the remnants.

"Daughter..." he slurred to Annabella. "Where's your father's purse now?"

For Annabella, now all was full despair. All was loathsome. "Here, father...*here*." And she handed him the purse.

Their father cradled the feeble purse as if his fingers themselves could divine the amount of the contents inside. The fingers must have been satisfied, because he said no more than this: "Keep away from mischief me lasses. Yer father's a goin' out to work today." And he closed the door behind him.

Their father's absence left his daughters in their separate silences.

Annabella, haunted by Prince's offer just the day before, suddenly burst into inconsolable tears.

Angel, for the first time in her life, torn about how to tend to her sister's grief, ran from the house. Ran to the solace of the fields and the calm of the twisting waters of the brook—-lost in her own throes of loss and longing.

By late afternoon, Annabella walked alone through the deserted plots of Russler's Alley. All of Thorn's festival visitors were now gone. None had ever stayed after the Mayodon to witness the loathsome Lottery. And why would they? They tucked tail and took flight before Thorn's great burden was levied upon it—-not wanting the village's curse to somehow rub off on them.

Annabella wandered the abandoned scene, kicking remaining scraps of trash and charred firewood as she went. She sat on a rotted log near one of the ashen fire pits and glazed in thought looking at the gray and black splatterpatch in the dirt, waiting for nightfall. Awaiting her horror. Her sacrifice at the hands of a corrupt villain to spare her sister from the jaws of the dragon.

Breaking out of her reverie, Annabella spied a bone-skinny cat rummaging through the Alley's scattered trash. In despair, she actually envied the cat's wretched existence. Better to be a lone animal sometimes concerned only with cornering the next meal than to know the full extent of the gut-wrenching anguish and complexity of human relationships, Annabella mused.

The nightstreetsmen began lighting Thorn's common torches, signaling that the time had come for Annabella to make her way to the back of the Great Hall and Cyvilard's chamber.

She rose and began to walk.

How could she have ever told Angel of this?

Slinking through the shadowed streets, Annabella wished she'd had a large mug of ale, or perhaps the lightest drop of *godsmercy* to dim her wits before sneaking to Cyvilard. She wanted no clear memory of what was about to happen to her and silently cursed herself for not making those preparations.

She approached Thorn's Great Hall. The large structure was the sturdiest building in the village, made of solid bricks, massive logs, and crude mortar. Two large pillars supported its front canopy and wide staircase. Annabella crept around the front, unseen by the Tarrenbacks standing guard at the base of the stairs—-and made her way to the darkness behind the Great Hall.

Once there, she saw no one. No lights. No entrance. She waited. She breathed. For a sterling moment, Annabella actually started to let herself believe that no one was coming—-that Cyvilard had changed his mind, or could not come—-or even better yet, *what if he had been somehow stricken, or killed during the day by a stroke of luck?*

But the sudden and unwelcome sound of a heavy metal latch un-clacking doused her hope. Before her, a door she had not perceived in the darkness opened from the wall ahead of her. Two Tarrenbacks with torches and crossbows stood in the entryway and ushered her within.

"This way—-" one of them said taking her by the arm, while the other one took the lead. The passage was narrow and crypt-like cobwebs and excessive dirt gave away its infrequent traffic. Eventually, the passage led to a small opening where the base of a slender spiral staircase began. They ascended in single file, with the one Tarrenback tightening his grip on Annabella's arm, lest she try and kick him down on the way up. As they began to trudge farther up, Annabella's spirits plummeted.

At the top of the staircase, they took her through an arched door into a dimly-lit chamber.

Cyvilard waited within.

"Leave us," he hissed to his Tarrenbacks.

They closed the door behind them leaving Annabella alone with the robed Elder. He stood on the opposite end of the circular room watching her with his bald head slightly bowed forward that out in the daylight would seem almost lowered in courtesy—-but here, alone with him, in this torch and lantern-lit chamber his gaze could only be likened to a predator in wait.

"So, my Annabella, you come to me."

"What is this place?"

"This is my aviary."

Annabella looked around the room. She knew already from the climb up the spiral staircase that they must be up in some sort of thin citadel atop the Great Hall. But now, the full details of the room were upon her. Lined up close to the wrapping wall were multiple perch-stands. Upon the perches were many birds, all still and silent, mostly ravens and owls—watching Annabella with wide indifference. On the floor was a ring of birdshite, crusted and caked around the room evenly, inches from the wall. Scattered among, and within, the feces, she could see little cracked skulls and remnants of rodent bones bleached white. She felt a sickening stab in her stomach and looked up to a small opening at the top of the room's arched ceiling—-the singular vent where the birds were able to enter and exit the room. A fragile waft of nighttime air descended to her—-the room's only comfort.

In the chamber's center was a circular table that a small company could dine upon, however, there were no chairs pulled up to it. Nailed to the tabletop were four leather straps at precise intervals. Not far from the ominous table was a crude piece of shelving that showcased various instruments and items that Annabella had never seen before. She could not, and would not, conceive of their intended usage—-not even the short knives lying there on top, knives with curious and menacingly curved blades.

Cyvilard took a step toward her, the table and the shelf still standing between them. "Are you ready to win your sister's freedom, my dear?"

Annabella's hands turned to fists. "Only if we do indeed have an accord freeing Angel from the Lottery."

Cyvilard took another step closer and smiled. "Surrender to all the pleasures and pains I can devise for you here in this room, and your sister will be the safest citizen in Thorn come tomorrow's Lottery, my child."

Annabella closed her eyes. She saw Angel running through the wildflowers. Annabella raised her eyelids and looked upon her ravisher. "Come then—-and do your will."

The Elder approached her producing his gnarled hands from his robes and motioned to the table. "Then please lie—-my sweet—-with thy back upon my table."

Annabella took Cyvilard's hand and allowed herself to be set down upon the rough table. The Elder took her right wrist and raised her arm above her head. She made no protest.

Cyvilard bound one of the leather straps around her wrist and secured it tight.

Let him, she thought through her repulsion.

With both of Annabella's arms fastened to the table above her, Cyvilard stood up to look down on her. He savored the sight of her surrender—-her hopelessness. So many nights he was reduced to just watching, to waiting, lurking in the shadows of his desire. And now here she was—-finally, strapped down in his aviary resolved not put up any impediments to his lusts. Here she was willing to suffer tortuous pains, wave after wave of his hideous pleasures.

Cyvilard licked his chapped lips. The only thing separating them now was the formality of strapping down her legs and the mere fabric of her dress.

He crouched down and began to kiss her.

She closed her eyes.

Let him.

His kiss turned to a grotesque licking. His tongue mapped her cheek, neck, her ears, her hair.

Let him.

He felt down the length of her body.

For Angel.

He began to raise the hem of her dress. Raised it to the curve of her thigh. His claws still roved but she didn't struggle. She let him as he started to make animal noises taking in large breaths and then heaving out drafts of putrid air.

Annabella fell back into her mind. She sees Prince and tries to stay with him, but she can't. She slips into darkness and sees her mother. Her mother when she was barely alive and near her fever's end. She sees the unstoppable sweat pooling out of her forehead, that basin that was constantly filled with her coughing blood. And then later, her mother's wrapped corpse... her father's tears at the gravesite... his endless rounds of ale for weeks and weeks after their mother's burial... Angel hugging her, consoling her, even though Annabella knew it should be the other way around. And finally, Annabella sees the twisted future before her. She sees her father's corpse now... his mouth opened in a horrid grimace, his teeth and gums all rotted from drink. She smells the rot of flesh and the soured ale all coming up from her father's decayed pores as she and Angel try to wash his body before burial. And finally, the worst of all, Annabella sees herself, walking up to the center of her mind's vision. She looks so sad—-defeated, near-dead herself—-but wait, there's something else... And then she sees. Annabella sees herself, her belly swollen and bloated with the weight of Cyvilard's child.

"*No—*" She shook back to reality. Annabella clamped her legs together, trapping Cyvilard's head between her thighs.

He raised his head as much as he could and tried to yell, but her knees crushed in on either side of his throat.

Keep pressing! Annabella told herself.

Cyvilard tried to pry her legs open with his hands. Spit burst from his swelling lips, veins pressing up all over his bald head.

Annabella held fast.

The Elder's face began to turn a pale purple while sweat streamed from Cyviard's head and flew into the air as they struggled.

She gasped and grunted, willing herself to keep the crushing pressure on his throat.

Cyvilard's eyes bulged like fish eggs about to hatch. His mouth contorted to a loathsome, breathless gasp. The Elder twisted and convulsed, sending the entire table crashing on its side.

Sprawling on the floor, Annabella still held Cyvilard fast between her knees.

He writhed. He spasmed.

Knives and tools were strewn everywhere on the aviary floor as his legs kicked.

Don't let go! Annabella told herself, even as she was starting to see black dots appear inside her own eyeballs too.

And with one last seizure-kick, Cyvilard went completely limp.

It took a couple moments for Annabella to realize her assailant was no longer moving. Once she did, she slowly released the tension in her knees.

She felt supreme cramping in every muscle in her legs and groin. Still, she was able to summon up another surge of strength and kicked Cyvilard in the face, hurling his motionless heap a little farther away from her.

She took in a well-earned breath but did not rest. She looked around. She knew she did not have long.

Lying part way strapped to the table and part on the floor, she spied one of the curved blades within touching distance to her right foot. Stretching out, she was able to snag the blade with her toe and drag it closer to her torso. By shifting her weight, Annabella realized she could turn the table, like a wheel. She did this and twisted her right bound hand close to the blade. With fingers splaying to their limit, she inched the hilt of the curved blade to her finger and finally into the palm of her hand. Biting her lower lip, Annabella raised the blade and was just able to tuck it under the leather strap binding her wrist. In a see-saw motion she moved the blade against the leather strap—-fraying it at first—-then, finally, cutting into it.

Saw-saw, went the blade.

Annabella huffed with effort.

Her eyes darted from Cyvilard's body to the aviary's door that she was convinced would open at any moment.

The blade was cutting through the leather but was also cutting painful grooves into her wrist.

Blood trickled over the leather strap, dripping into small splotches on the floor.

But she kept sawing.

Finally, the leather snapped in two. With the blade in her free hand, she made short work of the other strap. Annabella stood up. Breathing hard she noticed all the birds, still silent, watching her. She felt nothing but hatred for them all. She wished she had her bow and a full quiver with her so she could dispatch them all for pointing their cold gaze upon her.

She turned to the body of Cyvilard. His chest rose and fell weakly beneath his robe.

She crouched and put the blade just under his chin. She pressed it into the edge of his flesh. All she had to do now was swipe it across his throat.

Do it. He'll kill you and Angel if you don't.

Her hand trembled.

What are you waiting for? He deserves it!

But something else, deep within Annabella told her to pause—-to think.

"Not this way," was all she could mutter, and she ran out the door.

She quickly twisted her way down the staircase. No Tarrenbacks—-she was amazed.

She darted down the passage she had come. Un-latched the door. Fled out into the night and still no crossbow bolts rained down on her—-no Tarrenbacks carrying torches running after her as she crept in the shadows through the village.

Only when she was within paces of the village gates did she allow herself to think again.

What have I done?

As she sprinted toward her house, she knew there would hardly be time to explain. She would have to rouse Angel and her father, gather what they could and leave Thorn forever.

And where would they go?

Annabella had no idea.

43

Coach Striden

That year the Michigan State Soccer Tournament was held in Grand Ledge. And we had made it. The first time in Hemingway history. And then we lost, 2-1. To Caledonia. I'd love to say we were robbed or that we fell on a ton of bad luck sent down by the soccer gods and we were totally snakebit. But that just wouldn't be true. The fact is as good as we were, Caledonia was just better. But despite the loss I still couldn't have been more proud.

I mean right up until that final whistle our boys fought. And the way they fought—with true love in their hearts—I mean they were glowing with it out there. And on the sideline too. It was special. That's really all I can say about it. It was special.

At one point in the second half when the action was tense, I remember turning back to the bench and seeing Izzy. I remember thinking, wow. His dad's dying back home and he's here. With us. This means *that* much to him. How could we ever possibly be worthy of that kind of gift? I was blown away by it. I think that was the moment when I felt it. This—this *release.* It's hard to explain but I felt this calm, this new perspective just wash all over me.

The final whistle sounded just as Tristan tried to dribble past two Caledonia defenders much larger than him. The challenge left him sprawled out on the ground just as the referee finished signaling the end of the game and our season. Tristan just stayed there on the grass, looking all spent and lifeless.

Of course, the Caledonia players and fans celebrated wildly at the victory, which was completely their right to do. And our boys fell into a quiet exhaustion seeking each other out to console each other.

Coach Vogel and I went and shook hands with the Caledonia coaches and wished them luck on their next match. I looked back to the field and saw Patrick, Knox, Matt, and Troy packed in a group hug. Ryan was making the rounds, apparently hugging everybody. Erik was walking around to everyone too, petting heads and patting shoulders, with one arm around Isaiah.

Back on the field Luke went up to Tristan who was still lying in the grass. Luke picked Tristan up and hugged him. By the time they made it to the bench you could see that Tristan's eyes were beyond red and swollen from crying.

"I'm so sorry, so, so sorry. It's my fault there at the end, guys. I'm sorry I missed that shot—"

Luke pulled the freshman close again and just looked down on him and smiled.

"Trist, dude—don't worry about it." Ryan said what all of us were thinking. "You played your guts out. You were freaking awesome. No worries, man. And that goes for everybody. There's nothing we need to be sorry for. We fought to the last man tonight, boys. To the last man."

"Bring it in. Come on, tight," I tell them.

And everyone brings it into a tight circle.

"I am so damn proud of you guys," I tell them. "There's not a one of you that I am not proud of right now. From starters, to substitutes, injured reserves, to Izzy—you guys were all incredible tonight. Tonight, I saw a team in every conceivable meaning of the word. A team that bled for each other, a team that supported one another no matter the circumstance, or outcome. In all my years as a player or coach—"

And then I lost it.

Not once had I ever choked up in a soccer setting. Not once as a player, after a tough loss, or even the end of a season. Not once as a coach had I ever shown this kind of emotion. In fact, until then, I had gone out of my way *not* to show this kind emotion in front of my teams. I viewed it, as so many coaches do, as a sign of weakness or a crack in the rock of my leadership. But not that night.

I told them that I had never been prouder to be a part of a team. I told them you did it, lads. You did it.

Luckily, I could tell through my tears I was not the only one getting a little misty. Most of the faces looking back at me were wet in the eyes as well, especially Coach Vogel, thank God.

"If you haven't yet, hug a senior before you pack up your stuff and head over to see your fans and your parents. And remember, *We got class, so leave no trash, or I'll run your... how's that for poetry?"*

I started packing up my stuff to head to the bus when I looked up and saw all the seniors approaching me, Erik leading the way.

"Coach—we just want to say thank you. We know we made things rough there for a bit. But thanks for sticking with us."

I fought back choking up again. "No— *thank you*, lads." I grabbed Erik by both sides of his face, brought him down a little and kissed him on the forehead. One by one, each of them came up, most of them with tears in their eyes, and I did the same thing. Now, I'm sure some people would probably think that a gesture like that between a coach and her players could be seen as a little foolhardy or inappropriate—but with those boys, on that night—it seemed *exactly* like the thing to do.

Luke was the last to step up. I looked at this boy, turned man that had been the spark of our team's transformation. (Or was it an evolution? I'm still not quite sure. But his eyes at that moment spoke of a knowing that I have never seen in eyes so young. Certainly, I've never seen it in the mirror.)

"Thank you, Luke. Thank you for this," I said, letting it flow. "*For giving my heart back..."*

He bowed and I kissed his forehead. I have never seen such a face.

Riding the bus back home sitting in the darkened quiet on those uneven and squeaky vinyl seats that smelled heavy of ammonia and bleach—I thought of my old soccer coach at the University of Nebraska. I thought of his face. His close-cropped steel gray hair, the sincerity and fierceness of his blue eyes. "*You're a comet, Elizabeth... pure light on grass...*" And then I imagined my own face, years from now, well-worn to perfection from a lifetime of experience and the humility of what it means to coach, to mentor, and I thought to myself, *Yeah, I'll take more of this. I could make a life of this. Now I'm ready to make a life of this...*

44

When the team bus got back to the Hemingway Student Parking Lot late after the State game Luke was one of the last ones to finally get off and get all of his stuff over to his car. He had milled around giving all his exhausted teammates and coaches a last round of pats on the backs, personal notes, and bear-hugs, so by the time he made it to his car door, the lot was all but empty—even the bus had pulled away slowly with its amber fog-lights flashing.

Luke opened the driver's side door and tossed his bag into the passenger seat and the smell inside probably hit him immediately. It's funny to think the reek probably struck Luke as a mixture of all things putrid: as if someone had taken a week-long dead cat, doused it in cheap whiskey, lit it aflame until it was a charred mess and *then* chucked the whole pile into his backseat. Luke's eyes likely followed his nostrils to the backseat where a passed-out Jason Turner was lying sprawled out on his stomach, his mouth open and oozing out a foamy fluid flowing out to the edge of the seat and cascading into a yellow-greenish waterfall, dripping down to the floor mat.

I like to imagine that Luke saw this and simply stared at Jason for a moment

before rolling his eyes toward the stars in a partly grossed out, partly amused beseech.

CANTO II

"Come away, O human child
To the waters and the wild
with a faery, hand in hand,
For the world's more full of weeping
than you can understand."

Yates

1

When Turner awoke, the first thing he was aware of was the unfamiliar smell of clean sheets. The next thing was the sun's rays blazing in from the window. The smell of fresh bed sheets told him that he was not buried underneath the covers of his own bed, while the sunlight told him that he was late for school—if it was a school day that is. Turner sat up and looked around the neatly kept room he'd been dumped into and noticed the array of stuffed animals that lined one wall and seemed to be staring at him. From pink stuffed rabbits to an assortment of bears, to other soft creatures that were totally unfamiliar—they were all looking at him with the same un-blinking and glassy-black eyes. Next to a huge pink dresser, Turner noticed a tiny table and chairs with a miniature tea set, all of which were just the right size for some seriously small children or some pretty big dolls.

"*The fuck…?*" Sitting up, Turner realized he'd been sleeping inches away from another stuffed animal, this one a smiling blue monkey with Velcro patches on his feet and hands. He groaned another curse and swatted the little primate away with the back of his hand as if it had fleas or something.

Turner scooted out of bed and grabbed his shoes and hoodie that had been placed at the foot of the bed for him. He realized he was on the second floor of a house and found a bathroom soon after making it into the hallway. He took a long piss and while he did so, he was able to appreciate the overall cleanliness and un-clutter of the room. It looked nothing like the chamber of horrors he used back home that he and his dad both simply called *the shitter*. Seriously, in here it actually looked as if they scrubbed the bowl from time to time. They even had toilet paper hanging where it should—not random rolls tossed wherever, and there weren't piles of old newspapers and magazines laying around everywhere either.

When he was done, he headed downstairs where he heard the shuffle of feet and the smell of a cooked breakfast and strong coffee.

"Good morning, Jason." Some heavy-set middle-aged guy in a tie with glasses holds a cup of coffee. "Care for some breakfast? There's a plate of scrambled eggs and bacon over there. We got cereal too, if you want it—and Luke's got a pitcher of orange juice on the table if you want to grab yourself a glass over there."

"Uh…yeah. Thanks. I'll take some of that coffee though if that's OK. You know, only if you got any more that is—" Turner takes a plate from the kitchen and goes into the dining room to sit with Luke at the table.

Luke waves *good morning* to Turner with a friendly-looking raised eyebrow and takes a sip from a big-ass glass of orange juice.

"Yeah… fucking *what up*, man." He picks up his fork and looks at it a sec, as if in his hungover state he's forgotten what the hell it was for.

"Here you go, Jason." Mr. Forrester sets a full mug of coffee down in front of him. "Uh, Jason," Mr. Forrester goes and walks around to the middle of the table and leans down a little so he can look Turner in the eye. "Luke's told me a little about you and, I guess, some of what you're going through. Certainly, I don't, of course, know everything—and I—anyway, my point is, you're welcome here. Any time. Literally, day or night. You need a place to stay, or to get away, or if you ever need anything—or whatever."

Turner just stares at Luke's dad as the steam rises from the coffee cup in front of him.

"Well, I got to run to work. Somebody's gotta pay the bills around here, eh? But yeah, it was good to finally meet you," Mr. Forrester goes and walks over behind where Luke's sitting and kind of squeezes his shoulder and then says to him on his way past, "See you tonight."

Luke gives his dad a wave.

Turner hears Luke's dad pull out of the driveway and reaches for his mug. "So," he says and takes a quick sip. "What the hell was that all about? I mean, what'd you tell your old man, anyway?"

A huge folder stuffed full of paper sits on the table next to Luke's plate. He pulls out a sheet with handwriting on it and turns it over on the blank side to rifle out an answer.

The basics. You're having a rough time kicking some habits and that your dad isn't being supportive. You know, that kind of thing. And oh yeah, and that we're like friends now.

Turner nearly spits out his coffee reading that one. Takes him a sec to figure out which part to respond to first. "The fuck you say? Look, I don't know shit about any habits I'm looking to kick, and where did you hear that my dad and I aren't getting along? You hear that from Rozzy somehow, or something? This another one of your tricks where you say you're getting bullshit information from her about me? Huh? Where you getting this shit from?"

Educated guesses. How's about I ask you some questions? If you aren't looking to kick any habits or looking for any help with anything, then why are you breaking into my car in the middle of the night and passing out? Why are you here right now? Why do we keep talking?

"I keep talking to *you*? I fucking keep talking to you, huh? So, I'm the one bothering you now? That the fucking way you see it? Cheese and rice. I never asked for no help from no one, man. Fucking *help*, for chrissakes. What a joke. Aint nobody helped me with a damn thing since Rozz. Seriously, where do you get off asking me stuff like that, man?"

Why were you in my car last night?

"Fuck, man—" Turner goes and looks around as if he could find the answer in the corners of the Forrester's dining room.

Luke underlines the <u>Why</u>.

"Goddamn it! I don't know—" Turner rubs his temples a bit with one hand and cradles his mug with the other.

Luke watches him, says nothing.

"I'm tired, man. I'm just fucking done, you know? Exhausted as hell, man."

What do you want?

"I don't know." Turner takes another sip of java and looks toward one of the dining room windows looking like he's the oldest teenager in the world. "Maybe not to feel so fucking *spent*... you know? Not to feel like I ain't got the gas to go one more mile. But beyond that, man—I don't know."

Mind if I make a suggestion?

Turner reads it and gives a half-ass snicker. "You can do whatever the hell you want, man. It's your house, dude."

Luke gives a little shrug like *thank you* and then jots:

How about you get your wits back? Start there, you know?
Get clean, get your energy back, see what's what.
What do you think?

Turner reads Luke's note and tries to snicker again—but this time his eyes nearly break tears. His hand involuntarily starts quivering a little, so he snaps his fingers all rapid-like to hide his quakes. His eyes keep darting back and forth to the window and he takes another hit of coffee, more out of nerves than thirst. "Damn—your dad sure likes it strong. This is the best fucking cup of joe I've had in a while. I'll tell you that."

Luke just sort of smiles and keeps staring right at Turner.

A moment passes as the two guys just sit there and stare at each other from across the dining room table. These two guys. Luke and Jason. The soccer stud and the druggie. Luke, who never utters a word but could stop you dead with his silence and Jason, whose mouth could blaze with rage so blisteringly hot it could set off fire alarms. *These* two—who had never communicated until that day in Beckett's Western Civ. class, who had barely even been aware of each other's existence before September. One, who had known and loved Rosalind Howard in life, and the other, who never knew her name until the day she died. *These* two, who had that dark, dark night at Harper Lake between them and all that unsaid weight that went along with it. And here they were—skipping school, having breakfast together, and sharing a silence as if nothing else in the world were more important than finishing their conversation.

Finally, Turner takes in a big breath, lets it out. "Get clean, huh?"

Up to you...

"Yeah." Turner takes a gulp of coffee. "Hey, ain't you supposed to be at school right now?"

Nah. Taking the day off. I'm still all tore up about last night's game. Figure I'll just learn hooky from you.

"You know, I hear you get kicked off the honor roll for truancy."

Luke shrugs.

Turner just laughs and takes a bite of bacon. Luke starts laughing too then takes up his glass of orange juice and raises it like he's toasting Turner. Turner goes along with it and raises his coffee cup too and toasts Luke right back. "As I live and fuck," he goes.

They just simply called it the Blue Room. The Blue Room down in the basement. Not long after they moved into their house Mr. Forrester wanted a place where he could sing, play his guitar, and dabble around making recordings. He was really into old blues stuff and classic rock and the story went he had even been in a band when he started dating Luke's mom. The room was set apart from the rest of the basement by an old wooden door. The house was an old colonial and the Blue Room had probably been a root cellar or something a long time ago. The reason the room was blue was on account of the blue carpet Mr. Forrester put up, not only on the floors, but even on the walls to absorb the sound. Luke's dad didn't have Pro Tools or whatever, probably because this was like back in the day and when he had were old school track recording tapes and things like that.

Luke was pretty young when his dad set the room up with all his recording stuff along with a serious collection of microphones and amps and he had memories of hearing his dad wail away down there on his much freaking beloved Les Paul trying to play a solo by some guy named Johnny Lee Hooker. He remembered laughing with his little sister when their mom got all annoyed making dinner and yelled down there for him to wrap it up but after realizing he couldn't hear her, she stormed down there and had to slam on the door to get him to finally can it. Ah, good times, good times—back when the whole family was still alive and well in the Forrester household.

But the Blue Room had been out of use for years by the time Jason Turner made it down there. It seemed Mr. Forrester lost most of his interest in playing and making his homemade demos after his wife and his daughter died in the plane crash—and not too long after that is when Luke went deaf and that like totally seemed to seal the deal for him, I guess. I mean, *why play music now?* he must have thought. He still kept his Les Paul, but he sold his acoustic and most of his mics and recording equipment. Now, all that was down there were a few old mic stands, some beat-to-crap amps, a few harmonicas lying on the homemade shelving next to some of Mrs. Forrester's seriously ancient jars of canned vegetables along with some thick-as-yarn cobwebs collecting flies.

"If I'm gonna do this—we're doing it my way," Turner had said. It was his idea to go all out and get clean cold turkey. Even though Luke and Luke's dad both strongly suggested to Jason that there were easier and safer ways to break free from addiction like getting admitted to local rehab facilities and even multi-step programs, one-on-one counseling sessions—all these options the Forrester's showed Turner online—and mentioned if cost was a hang-up for him, they would more than willing to pay. But Turner was having none of it. As far as he knew he didn't have any particular leanings toward Catholic faith and practices; however, he seemed intent for his detox period to have a penance-like quality to it. He was pretty much adamant about quitting *all* of his drug and alcohol abuse freaking cold turkey and holing up down in the Forrester's Blue Room for the duration.

He told Luke and Mr. Forrester that staying at his own house while trying to dry-out and turn-off just wasn't an option. I mean, how could he possibly detox living in the same house as the biggest drug dealer in town? It just wasn't going to happen living with his pops he told them. So *OK*, the Forresters said. Luke's dad told Turner he was welcome to stay in their house as long as he needed or wanted to stay—especially while he kicked the habit or *habits*, actually, in Turner's case.

Turner had it all worked out in his mind how he was going to get it set up too. First, he went back to his house to grab some clothes and some of his stuff. He of course popped in during a time of day that he was pretty sure his dad would be out of the house. After stuffing his backpack with what he needed, Turner lifted Kid T's SIG from between his mattresses and then buried the gun near the bottom of his dirty clothes hamper where he used to stash his liquor. Turner even dropped a little trou and leaked some piss on one of his T-shirts at the top of the hamper just to ensure that his Pop's wouldn't snoop around and find the SIG. Turner's dad never did Turner's laundry anyway—and there was no way he was going to just up and start with a load that smelled like mellowed piss. No way. Not a chance, Turner thought.

They set him up with a cot down there. Duct taped a small camping pillow over the one window near the top of the basement wall and put a shade lamp near his bed so if he ever wanted light, the light would be *soft*. Next, they lined up a dozen lime-flavored Gatorade bottles and another dozen water bottles on a low shelf for when Turner got thirsty. He had two family-sized boxes of Saltine crackers if he ever needed an emergency snack and then two plastic salad bowls just in case he got sick during the night and needed to throw up.

The first night wasn't that bad. Turner watched the Lions game on Sunday Night Football with Luke and Mr. Forrester and then went down to the basement to his cot in the Blue Room but couldn't fall asleep. He was just too jittery—too wired. Too sober.

The next morning, Luke went to school and his dad went to work, while Turner stayed at the house and tried to just calm down enough to rest. But his hands and his legs were beyond restless with their spazzy twitches and shakes. By that evening his stomach started to ache and his mouth went dry. Turner lost his appetite and didn't join the Forresters for dinner up at the dining room table. He just lay on his cot and listened to his ear pods. Track after track trying to lose himself in the chords and the rhythms, the shouts and the screams.

Then things got weird. The sweating started. The diarrhea. And finally, the delirium. Jason embraced the darkness then, boy. Man, did he ever. Lost track of it all while his body cried out for him to regulate, *regulate, man! Gotta regulate!* Stomach feeling like it had a Phillips head screwdriver stuck in it up to the handle. The Blue Room. The Blue Room with its blue carpet spinning and spinning around. The world goes by in whispers and it whispers, *Jason, Jason wherefore art thou?* You can't tell where the floor begins or ends when the blue carpet's all around, and around, and around. Are you going up? Or going down? *Jason, Jason wherefore did you so? Wherefore do you so?*

Truth is for a couple of days there Jason Turner doesn't remember much. Fragments of stuff at best. He remembers the sensation of being lifted, turned over—of being scrubbed lightly with a damp cloth, of being tucked in. He remembers his own stink and streaking sweat, feeling paralyzed like he couldn't move or do anything as he drools and sees only with blurred snap-shot vision the dented aluminum duct work snaking along the ceiling of the room above him like some psychedelic mechanical octopus.

He knows he shit himself many times—just doesn't remember with like any certainty exactly when or how long he stayed soiled before either Luke or his dad, or both of them together, came down and cleaned him up.

Apparently, it's pretty common for people going through the first stages of acute substance withdraw to have some kick-ass hallucinations and stuff. But if Turner did, he really can't remember them. The only thing he sort of recalls that was close was a kind of dream where he's like in the grip of a serious thirst. Like a seriously deep thirst. Thirst like a freaking vampire would have who hasn't sucked a virgin blood-sac dry in too many moons. Anyway, he remembers feeling like the inside of his body was like super-dry like the exact opposite of what you feel like when you were a little kid and you dreamt you were so full of liquid that your bladder felt like it had Lake Ontario sloshing around in it you had to pee so bad. Turner remembers he was thirsty and he's working in some hot field like planting wheat in the dirt or some crap like that. He's got his shirt off, he's sweating rivers from his pores and stands up straight to take a break. Down at his feet he's got this two-gallon milk jug—but the cold and condensing liquid inside it isn't milk. He lifts the cool jug to his lips and starts to drink, not ice water but the sweetest chilled whiskey he's ever tasted—and he just tilts his head back and chugs and chugs, gulp after impossible gulp. But that's it. That's the only dream-like hallucination he remembers.

Nothing like the visions that would come to him later.

Mr. Forrester remembers most of the events of that week a little more clearly but not necessarily with a lot of fondness. He recalls he and Luke coming home from work and school and dutifully heading down to the Blue Room to change Turner's nasty sheets, underwear, and other clothes while Turner blathered on in an unconscious stupor. It got so bad at one point when Turner's fever climbed to a hundred and four degrees that Mr. Forrester was ready to haul Turner off to the hospital emergency room where he could enter the care of professionals—but Luke put the brakes on that, reminding his dad that they had promised they'd help Turner the way that he wanted and that they should give it one more night to see if his fever came down.

It was on the night of the fourth day that Turner's dad showed up like super-pissed wanting to see Turner. He screeched his truck to a halt and bolted out, storming up the Forrester's front lawn yelling. Well, it didn't take long for Luke and his dad to come out and open their front door—while every neighbor within earshot peeked out their front windows to see what was up.

Turner's dad just comes unglued with questions and curse words once he sees Mr. Forrester and Luke. Luke's dad holds up his hands and tries to calm the whole situation down, but Galen "Pops" Turner yells all above that and stops just short of climbing up to the Forrester's front stoop.

Luke says nothing while the two dads continue their mockery of communication.

The ruckus must be loud enough to reach the Blue Room and crack through Turner's near-coma because suddenly there's Turner himself, looking like he's just resurrected from the rank dirt-nap and brushing the two Forrester guys gently out of the way so he can see his father.

Galen finally shuts up at the sight of his son.

"Hey—go home, man. I'm all right here. I'll be home in few days. But go home. *OK*?"

"*What?* No. No—get your ass down here, Jace, cause we're going home now. You have any idea how much goddamn time I've wasted tonight looking for your sorry ass? What the fuck about leaving me that note that you'd be at Toe's all week and then I get over there and he and his old man say they don't know shit about it and ain't seen you all week? I had to learn from Toe that you might be here staying with your new *soccer buddy* or some shit. And I'll tell you, I had a hell of time finding this place. You know, they ain't the only Forrester's in town? Come on—we're going."

"*No*." Turner nearly collapses and grips Luke's arm for support. "I'm staying, Dad… I'm staying."

For like the first time since Jason showed up at the door, Turner's dad like really takes a look at his son. "What's wrong with you? You sick or something?"

Turner's eyes nearly roll to the back of his head, and he sways just a little bit before answering, "Go home, dad. I'll be home in a couple days. These guys are taking care of me right now. OK? I'm OK. Go home."

Turner's dad looks up to Luke and his dad. He looks kind of confused, trying to figure it out. "You know," he goes to Luke's dad, "I could call the cops. You got no right here, man."

Before Mr. Forrester can even respond, Turner forces himself to laugh hysterically triggering a nasty cough too. "You hear that? Hear that, folks?" Turner barks out to all the faces peering through their shades all along the street. "My dad—the biggest meth dealer in town, the fucking *Target* of the drug trade. My dad, ladies and gentlemen—who's looking to put together an armed hit crew and blast away his Walmart competition—he's gonna call the cops!"

"What the fuck, Jason. What the fuck," Galen goes and starts to back off.

Turner still tries to laugh as he staggers and coughs while Luke and Luke's father must steady him to lead him back inside the house.

"I'll give you a couple more days," Galen goes and walks backward towards his truck. "And then you're coming home."

The Forrester's are barely able to get Turner back down to his cot in the basement before he passes out again, mumbling words Mr. Forrester doesn't understand, and Luke can't hear.

Turner slumbers away, exhausted and spent by his duel with his father, and except for forcing himself to use the basement toilet in a small stall next to the washer and dryer, he won't leave the Blue Room for nearly two more days.

ERIF
VII

By the time Annabella made it home, her father had already passed out in his chair before the fireplace, the jug of ale he had bought at market lying on its side where he must have dropped it. She passed his snoring lump to see if Angel was in her bed in their small back room of the house.

Angel scurried off her bed at the sight of her sister and leapt into Annabella's arms. Annabella was overcome with so many spinning thoughts at once that she held her sister tight and kissed the top of her head. Each sister told the other she was sorry for their fight that morning and said how much they loved each other.

There was no time, Annabella knew; there simply was no time. She let it all go and told Angel everything. Told of Cyvilard cornering her the other night and his threats. His demands to send Prince away and to submit to his lust. How Angel would be named in the morning's Lottery if she didn't meet those demands. She told Angel how she hated yelling at Prince and scolding her afterward. She explained that it was the only way she knew she could protect them both from Cyvilard's treachery. As innocently as she could, Annabella explained being taken to the aviary atop the Great Hall's tower and her struggle there with Cyvilard and how she could not kill him before fleeing.

She entreated her sister that there was no time to waste; that they must gather up what they could, rouse their father and go—-*go now.* Flee Thorn and never return. That Cyvilard had surely regained himself by now and would be at their door any moment with a detachment of Tarrenbacks to make their arrest.

After hearing all, Angel did her best to calm her older sister. She put her hands upon Annabella's shoulders and lightly squeezed them—-just like she had done last summer when she had stumbled across a lost fawn in the grove on the far east edge of Thorn. She had picked the trembling baby deer up in her lap and held it just tight enough to let the little thing know, *you're all right—-I'm here for you as long as you need, sweet one—-you're not alone.* Angel held the fawn until it stopped trembling and let it go. Before vanishing behind a dense curtain of ferns, the deer turned and gave Angel a last, big-eyed look. When Annabella had finally ceased *her* trembling, Angel spoke. "Sister, dear sister, where are we to go at such short notice that Cyvilard and his Tarrenbacks will not easily catch up to us? Listen to me now, here is what you must do. Go and seek Elder Quindarius. Hear his good counsel on what to do next. Here with our father will I stay, and say I know not of you if Cyvilard comes. If anyone is able or knows how to deal with the evils of Cyvilard, noble Quindarius must. If you can, come to me in the morning and tell me his plan. Otherwise, if I hear not from you, I will wake Father and go to the Great Hall to witness the drawing of the Lottery like we are all to do. But keep yourself hidden till then, sister. Tis the only way to keep all of us safe until something can be done."

Annabella reluctantly agreed and ventured back out into the night to seek the house of Elder Quindarius. Creeping from long shadow to long shadow through the sleeping streets of Thorn, utter despair began to well in Annabella's heart. She realized that this plan of her sister's was really just a wild hope of saving any of them. Further, she couldn't help thinking that maybe they should've run away with Prince as he had offered. *But Cyvilard would've just followed you...* she told herself—-and now, much too late, she realized the full extent of what kind of malice Cyvilard was capable of. The most frightened, weakest part of herself shrieked inside her head, *Why, oh why, did you not just slit his throat when you had the chance?* She punched her thigh with the thought while she crept on, certain that the next turn of the corner would find her face to face with a troop of Tarrenbacks, or worse, Cyvilard himself.

But instead, she found herself arriving at Quindarius's door uncaptured, and presumably, unseen. Annabella knocked timidly at first, not really allowing her knuckles free force against the large oaken door. But after reminding herself of what an emergency, what a true and dangerous predicament, she and Angel were in, she allowed herself to knock with more gusto, till finally the door opened and a servant lady appeared with a roused, disheveled face and a taper in hand.

"Please! I must needs speak with the Elder! 'Tis a matter of gravest emergency. A matter of corruption and treachery here in Thorn!"

The lady stared at Annabella. At first it seemed that she would never respond to Annabella's request. It was during this awkward silent moment that Annabella had a flicker of thought about how odd it was to see such a mature woman answering the door at the house of the highest Elder in Thorn. All the nobility in Thorn had servants in their households of course, and even though Annabella certainly was not accustomed to calling on them as if they were her dearest friends and ale-mates, she knew enough to know that the office of doorman usually fell to, well, a *man.* And usually either a very young manservant, or a very old one—-but it was definitely a man's position. So, to see a woman, easily of forty winters there at the threshold a mere hour or so from dawn, gave Annabella pause, even if it was a pause of the briefest of moments.

But before the lady could utter a response, Quindarius himself opened wide the door in his nightdress holding not a taper but an ornate torch before him. "What is the meaning of this parlay? Do ye not know the hour? Come quick now, lass. Why upon my doorstep?"

Annabella swallowed and bowed her head. "My Elder Quindarius, I apologize for the intrusion. But I have intelligences that you must needs hear. My life and the life of my sister, Angel, depend on it."

Quindarius lifted his gray brows and investigated the dark ether past the girl at his door. He saw no movement, but the scowl upon his wrinkled face still bespoke his caution. He raked his free hand through his white beard. "What is this about, lass? And be quick with it."

"My lord—-this very evening I was detained and attacked by Elder Cyvilard in his aviary atop the Great Hall. I was lured there under the threat of him deliberately drawing my sister's name in tomorrow's Lottery."

Quindarius shot a frantic look into the darkness. He spied up to the rooftops and then to the branches of the cherry tree to the west of his house. Huffing a great breath into his chest, he answered, "Child! What is the meaning of this? Are you not aware of the punishments that may fall against the slander of an Elder of Thorn? What mean you? *Go*—-and speak no more of this to anyone, citizen or stranger alike. *Baa*! Begone! Before I give my words the teeth of my office. Cyvilard is not to be so mistreated. And at my doorstep nonetheless!" And with that, the elder slammed the door.

Wretched tears streamed from Annabella in messy sobs as she ran from the Elder's house, taking no heed in which direction she was going. She rounded a corner and collapsed to her knees and wept in the street. After a few pitiful moments, Annabella rose and began again towards her house, determined now to steal away with Angel in the few remaining hours they had left before the Lottery.

Before she could make it back across the village, in that final hour of darkness before the breaking of dawn, she heard a footfall behind her and whirled around to see a dark shape stride out from an alleyway.

That's it—-I'm done for, she thought.

"Daughter of Thorn..." the figure called out. "You must come with me. Quickly, if you wish to even have a prayer of saving your sister, you must come..."

"But who—? How?" Annabella then recognized him as Samuel, Quindarius's son of eighteen winters. And although she had never really spoken to him before, she had seen him many times through the years and had known he was the son of Thorn's most renowned Elder.

"All will be explained anon," Samuel grabbed her by the hand. "But now we must away!" he said and led her back towards the house of Quindarius.

When they arrived, they stole behind the great house and entered through the small window into the kitchen. Once inside, Samuel led her past the large brick ovens and baskets full of breads and stacked sacks of barley and wheat and flour. He lit a taper and guided her through the rest of the lower floor of the dark house to a small hatch in the floor that was hidden under a rug. Samuel flung the hatch open and held the taper so that it revealed a narrow ladder leading down into an underground chamber of some kind. They descended and walked through an ale and wine cellar with the dozen or so massive barrels of various ales and hanging wineskins. Eventually, Samuel led her to a well-lit room with earthen walls and a large rough-hewn desk surrounded by a few chairs. Quindarius himself sat in one of the chairs at the center of the desk.

"Well done, Samuel! You may leave us now, boy," the Elder said.

Annabella noticed there was nothing of his authoritative puffiness in his voice now as there had been when she had last seen him at the main doorway. She sat herself down in the chair across from him as Samuel left them, presumably back to the upper floors of the house.

"Forgive me," Quindarius began, "for my manners at the door before. I will explain all. But first, what is your name, lass?"

"Annabella."

"Ah—that's it. The daughter of Vidgis, is that right?"

Annabella nodded. "And of the late Pricilla."

"And of the late Pricilla, his wife. Of course. I remember her. She was a beautiful lady—-you've her look about you. And your sister's name is Angel, then—-is it?"

"Yes, my lord," Annabella bowed her head. "You have remembered us."

"It appears I have," the Elder managed an approving grin, shifting in his seat as if for the moment he was turning gears in his mind on how to best proceed.

During the silence, Annabella noticed the many parchments and globs of dried wax from years of melting tapers and dripping official seals pressed upon the desktop.

"I conduct my most important affairs down here," Quindarius seemed to guess her thoughts. "There is little to disturb me here as well as very little danger of being observed—-which I believe to be paramount when having a discussion very much like the one we are about to have, my dear."

Annabella's only response to that was a nod; she was now more than willing for Quindarius to steer the conversation to the matter she had brought to light earlier at the threshold of the Elder's door.

"I know," he paused and then started again, "I know so very well that for years now our Elder Cyvilard is most corrupt and possessed by the very blackest of hearts."

"Then if that be true, then how can he have gone unchecked for so long?" Annabella marveled, raising her voice. "How's it possible? You're the lead elder on the Village Council—-how could you have let Cyvilard go on so long as he has if you've known?"

Quindarius raised his hand. "Child, listen to me. I will tell you all, but you must be patient and hear me. Only by hearing all will you truly understand what is going on here in the shadows of Thorn."

For the moment, Annabella found her silence within her and waited for the Elder to continue.

2

And just like that, *boom*—Jason Turner is awake.

Like really awake. Like out of a coma awake, you know? Like for a few moments he doesn't even know where he is, or even like who he freaking is, you get what I'm saying? But after a few big breaths, he gets it. He remembers. He feels like he's just coming up from a dive beneath deep, deep waters.

The air purifier next to his cot's cranking away its steady hum as Turner sits up, his eyes focusing on the dark Blue Room. He sees the red digital numbers glowing from the clock they had set up for him.

6:10

Turner's mouth smacks as he opens it. It's so dry it feels like an old sock puppet had crawled on top of his tongue and died. He's got no clue whether it's six in the morning or night—but it doesn't matter, either way he knows it's time to get up.

He takes a long leak in the toilet next to the washer and dryer and heads up stairs.

Nobody else appears to be up. It has to be morning then, he guesses. He looks out the window. It's all misty and still—the pavement and grass are wet, but it still looks chilly out. Turner mills about the downstairs a little, not turning on any lights, just grooving on the stillness of things and then goes back into the kitchen to get a pot of coffee going.

He waits out the minutes to the first cup then wanders back out to sit at the table in the dining room. Within two soulful sips of coffee, Turner's whole body starts to tingle, the caffeine doing its job.

From his chair he's able to half-stand up and lean over to the wall and flick on the dining room chandelier. Sitting there, Turner sips his coffee and replays what he remembers of the hazy confrontation with his dad at the Forrester's front door. He can't quite remember everything, but he recalls the gist. He knows there might be some hell to pay when he gets back home—but whatever.

Turner drinks his cup down to the dregs.

He toys with getting up for a fresh cup when he sees Luke's manila folder full of papers lying on the table within arm's reach. It's the same folder that he remembers Luke scribbling stuff into the first morning he woke up in their house—and not only that, but Turner also recalls other instances since, seeing Luke walking around with this same lame-ass folder under his arm. He can't tell for sure, but it seems the folder's grown in considerable thickness in the time since he's last seen it, since before his long stint in the Blue Room.

Turner just zones out staring at the folder and then finally reaches over and drags the thing over. It's really not his intention to read the damn thing, he's just curious at what it could be is all, so he flips the folder open with his fingers. He picks at the hand-scrawled manuscript just like you'd pick at a scab that you initially had no intention of ripping off.

He reads a bit.

"Ugh—cheese and rice." He groans. "Don't tell me he's into this fantasy shit too." Turner sours as he skims over something about a dragon chowing on kids and burning shit and something else that seemed a lot like freaking magic or wizardry or some crap like that.

Turner hears someone galloping down the stairs.

Luke emerges all dressed and smiling. He gives Turner a big ol' *good morning* nod and sits down across the table.

"So what is *this*, man? You wrote this, right?" Turner goes. "This like your version of the fucking *Hobbit* or what?"

Luke grabs his pen off the table and rips a small piece from one of the sheets of paper in the folder.

Oh, just another project of mine.

"Another project? How many projects you got going?"

A few.
Speaking of which... you up for a field trip today?

"Sure. But don't you think I should probably show up to school again one of these days before I get blasted as truant?"

It's Saturday.

"Really?"

Luke smiles, nods.

"Well, I guess let's fucking roll then, man."

Once they get out to the garage, Turner notices Luke's dad's SUV is gone. Figures maybe he had to go to work on the weekend or something. But *wow* that would've been an early start time, Turner thinks. They hop into Luke's car that still ever so faintly smells of Turner's puke from over a week ago. Turner feels a little pang of embarrassment but doesn't say anything.

Luke rolls them out of the driveway and flicks the headlights on. The morning mist hasn't quite lifted but it's getting lighter out, everything turning light gray. Luke pulls into a gas station and points out the obvious to Turner by tapping the fuel gauge.

Turner nods. "Hey, I'm gonna go in and get something to eat. You want anything?"

Orange juice. Granola bar.

Turner rolls his eyes and nods.

Inside, everything's all bright lights above isles of shinny packaged snacks and standing coolers lined with armies of plastic bottled drinks. Turner grabs Luke's stuff and stops like freaking dead in his tracks when he comes across the packages of mini white powdered donuts.

"Hell *yes*." Turner grabs two packs.

Up at the counter he's shanked with the same ravenous stab of desire when he spies the huge library of cigarette packs and cartons back behind the cashier. Hits like freaking lightning. Turner's practically salivating like a hound for a cigarette suddenly. In fact, he can't recall ever wanting one so badly before in his entire life.

"You can have your fucking organic, save the planet shit. Fucking cigarettes and donuts, man," he goes to Luke getting back into the passenger's seat. "God never took a finer shit than this."

Luke starts the car and cruises back out onto the road. He looks at Turner with the powdered remains smeared all over both sides of his mouth, clearly in *Hostess* nirvana.

They chow down their breakfast and move past the scenery of their suburbia—past rows of homes and landscaped trees, all stripped of their leaves, past the sprawl, and merge onto the Interstate.

After devouring both packages of donuts, Turner fires up a cigarette and sucks down a deep drag. None of that new-fangled vape shit for him. He rolls down his window just enough to create a looping jet stream of cool air to lift the ghostly wisps of smoke out of the car. There aren't many other cars out. The sun is just now starting to appear out of the hazy clouds and mist. Turner stares out at the morning and nearly smokes half his cigarette before he remembers that he has no earthly idea where they're going. He finishes the cig and flicks the butt out the window.

"Where're we going?"

Luke just stares at him and turns back to the Interstate.

"OK. Whatever, man. You don't want to tell me yet, that's fine."

And it really was fine, Turner thinks. Truth be told he can't remember the last time he'd seen the sun actually come up, at least not from a moving car, all pretty like this. He lights another cigarette. *God,* these smokes are awesome all of a sudden. The *fucking cat's tits, man!* Turner thinks. He realizes he's just glad to be up—off his stanky cot, out of that freaking Blue Room—feeling better than he's felt since—since *whenever,* man. He suddenly wishes he hadn't forgotten his phone for tunes. As a consolation he moves to turn on the car's radio.

"You don't mind, do you?" Turner goes and starts flipping through stations.

Luke just turns and arches his eyebrow like, *are you serious? Do I mind?*

Turner gets the humor. They both start laughing.

"Yeah, I guess not then, huh?"

Luke shakes his head.

Turner finds a radio station playing mostly metal and hard rock out of Detroit.

They continue to cruise west.

"We going to Lansing or something?"

This time Luke goes for his pad while he rocks the cruise control, he holds the pad and his steering wheel and jots a note while keeping his eyes on the road.

Not quite. We're going to see a friend of Rozzy's.

ERIF
VIII

Quindarius began his tale. "What I am about to tell you only a handful of souls know. You are too young to have known my late wife, Gwyndeva. What are you? Sixteen winters?"

Annabella nodded.

"So—-my wife died nearly two years before you were born. But she was just about your age though when we married. She was so young, so full of...*everything*. Light. Passion. A playfulness. And I, I was not the old man you see before you now when I married her. I felt much younger too. Seems a thousand winters ago now. She was so beautiful."

Watching him speak, Annabella noticed the old man seemed to glaze over; his face looking as if he had just taken in the first bite of the sweetest chocolate truffle, a bite he meant to savor for as long as it would last.

"And even though it was a marriage of arrangement," he continued, "we were very much in love from the beginning. I tell ye, lass—-my Gwyn took my breath away with a mere glance. I had just been named an elder of the village and now I had the bride of my dreams. It seemed my life was becoming the richest of fantasies. Truly, I did believe myself to be the happiest of men in those blessed, blessed days.

"After working with the Council and attending to various affairs of the village during the day, Gwyndeva and I loved to spend the early evenings riding our horses along the various paths that cross the fields and groves of the valley. We had many a spot where we'd ride and spend out the sunset watching for the first lights of the stars in the purpling sky. Oh, it was soul music, those rides. Such music...

"But it was not to last," he said, sobering up. "It was early autumn when Gwyn took her fall. We were returning from the field of long grasses and wildflowers north of the village. We had tarried longer than usual, and the sky nearly held the full darkness of night about it as we rode. Gwyn was riding her mare ahead of me when something low, out of the grass, spooked her horse. To this day I still don't know what it was. A badger maybe? A frightened fox? I have no idea; but it's no matter now. Her mare reared and Gwyn was thrown off backwards, her precious head landing on a jagged bed of stones with such force—-"

Annabella thought she saw the first misting of tears in his eyes.

"She lay as if dead in all but breathing for many weeks and then into many months. At her bedside I stayed, day and night—-month after month, vigilant for the least bit of change in her station. We took no visitors. I hired more servants to care for her and brought in physicians from far off towns that knew of newer and stranger remedies than our modest doctors and apothecaries here in Thorn. I was desperate to try anything that would bring my bonny Gwyndeva back to me full-witted."

Annabella listened but could not help herself from becoming impatient with Quindarius. She felt in some way bad for feeling this way—-the old man was obviously reliving some pain as he told this tale of his long dead wife—-but she still could not see how all this had anything to do with the pressing danger of Cyvilard and what he undoubtedly was going to do once the Lottery was held at the Great Hall in only a couple more hours. Her left knee bobbed up and down under her dress as she endeavored to hear Quindarius out.

"But nothing worked. You must understand how loathsome I was at this time, lass. How vulnerable my wits and my heart. I was in such dire need of comfort, of reassurance of love. I could not sleep o' the nights. I could not stomach a proper appetite. It seemed I was withering away at the same rate as my poor un-waking wife. In resignation and despair, I sent away all doctors, I released all servants save two–Cornelius, who had served my father and tended our livery–and Leonella, who I had hired to be Gwyn's bed servant after her fall. As the wretched months dragged on, I began to rely more and more on Leonella's company–increasingly more for companionship in my woes than even to care for Gwyndeva herself.

"It is hard for me to tell you how tragedy can bind those souls who suffer it immensely. How people seek a communion that even overreaches our desire for adhering to laws—-or even vows. And so, it had become of Leonella and myself. It is hard now to tell you this. To utter the words aloud. And I shudder to guess what you must now think of me, but you must know all, lass. We fell in love of sorts. I–because of Leonella's understanding and listener's spirit, and she–because of my dark melancholy needing a breast for its weight to befall. I know such things must sound cursed to you, Annabella. But judge us not. We were plagued enough with our own consciences as it was, even as helpless as we were not to indulge our hearts into one another's arms."

Annabella knew not what to say. She still was very conscious of the precious moments that seemingly were being wasted by this narrative—-but utter shock with Quindarius's revelation for the moment rendered her completely speechless.

"To my shame, I took knowledge of Leonella many times. Once, even in the presence of my ever-sleeping wife. But you must understand those days had become such a whirling cyclone to me that my whole soul became engulfed in a dust storm of strange thoughts and deeds—-everything strewn, nothing fenced or restrained.

"Leonella became with child. We knew not how to take such tidings. Surely such scandal would mean the end of my Eldership. Leonella was convinced we would have to leave Thorn altogether, create new identities for ourselves. We would say she was my wife, of course, and tell everyone that Gwyndeva was my invalid sister." Quindarius's voice began to crack like the ice over a frozen lake bearing a weight it could not long support.

"But before this desperate plan could be put in place, Gwyndeva came back to herself. I went into her bedchamber one morning and collapsed to my knees, when upon entering I saw her eyes opened and did hear her in the feeblest of voices creak out my name! Leonella came running in and we all collapsed in prayer to the gods—-although I could see a hint of anguish twist, dagger-like, into Leonella's face.

"What were we to do? And the *child*... what were we to tell Gwyn of the child?"

Annabella stared back at Quindarius as if she'd been mortared to her chair.

"The next few months were of the bitterest torture to me. I lived a double life for a time. I was the attentive husband to my wife's recovering sick bed, all while scheming to protect my lover, the soon-to-be-mother of my child. Alas, I began to spread report all over Thorn of our good fortune that my wife was awake and recovering. Not only that, but she was indeed so healthy that she was also swollen with child to boot. I allowed none to my house, however; and Leonella and I took good measure to keep Gwyn innocent as to her bed servant's true condition.

"But this was still only mere goodly delay. Leonella and I both knew that it was impossible to keep this dread secret forever—-that eventually my wife would realize, or that in time the people of Thorn would begin to suspect scandal in my household the longer we kept them all from ever seeing Gwyndeva. That was unless—-unless something dreadful were to take place that would secure us all from public filth and scandal."

Quindarius rose from his chair—-his tale igniting him with a fit of jittery energy that belied his years. He paced before Annabella and seemed vexed about how to continue.

"But we were spared," he began on an awkward breath, "Leonella and I, from these baser thoughts taking a firmer root in our impaired imaginations. Because, you see, as quickly as Gwyndeva had awakened to us out of the void of her injuries—-she also just as suddenly *died*. Just like that. As if life itself was as fickle as a puddle of shallow water that can evaporate under the slightest change in the direction of a sunbeam." He stared at the flame of a taper for a long moment. "I found her one suppertime, lying in bed, motionless with a most frozen and terrible look on her face.

"I sat by her corpse all night numb in every sense about what to think and as to what to do now that so much had been lost—-and so much had been lifted. Round about dawn at the end of that horrible eve, I drew my dagger and contemplated thrusting the blade through my chin and up my throat. The only thing that kept me from doing so was the thought of my coming child hidden within the womb of Leonella.

A week later, Samuel was born. We subscribed to the whole village that Gwyndeva died in childbirth and made for a quick burial. And there it ended. All our shame, our secrets and self-inflicted wounds of the heart were laid to rest. Buried deep with the bones of my fallen wife.

"All of Thorn was so kind in their sympathies to my loss and bittersweetness of my joy in having Samuel. Leonella and I took comfort in the appearance that no one suspected anything was amiss—-and I began to sleep through the night for the first time in what seemed years.

"Leonella and I continued to live in this house alone—save Samuel and his newly hired wet-nurse, whom we of course did not really need, keeping the outward roles of Lord and servant, keeping separate quarters. We resolved that we should never tell poor Samuel the truth of his full parentage. A decision that has always fallen very hard on Leonella, I think."

"Then that woman that came to your door when I knocked?" Annabella said. "That was *she*?"

"Aye. That was my Leonella."

"And does Samuel still not know? After all these years?"

"No—-he does not. But let me finish, child. I can only imagine what you must think of me now—-but you must hear the end and then you will know all. Then you will know what it is you and your sister are up against."

Annabella calmed herself and waited for the Elder to conclude. But Quindarius was right—-there was no way to ever see him the same way. The venerable, noble, wise Quindarius she always assumed him to be was gone. In fact, as he kept weaving his tale, he seemed to have withered with age in front of her with the telling. She thought she could actually smell the disgrace and the fear wafting off him.

"Before Samuel was even three months old, I was returning from his nursery to retire in mine own bedchamber, when suddenly a cloaked figure stole out from behind one of the large tapestries. My heart knocked upon my ribs, and I leapt back drawing my dagger at the sight of the intruder.

"It was Cyvilard. Even then he was bald—-though he was just an upstart back then really. He hadn't been named an elder yet—-he was only a Tarrenback himself at the time. But there he was—-standing in my hallway, grinning at me like some hungry mongrel that's cornered a family of baby shrews.

"'What is this?' I was finally able to stammer.

"'The beginning of a very fruitful relationship—well, for me at least, my dear Quindarius,' the villain said.

"'Whatever are you on about? How did you get in here?' I was still in shock as to his presence. I could scarcely think straight.

"And then he said to me, 'Right. I'll be about it then. I know as certainty that Samuel is the child of your servant Leonella and yourself. And decidedly *not* of a union between you and your late wife.'

"I was stunned silent at his knowledge of this.

"'You know as well as I, Quindarius,' he went on, 'that I could ruin you with this intelligence. Now, I'll cut to what I want of you. I have many intrigues I'm looking to plant myself in here in Thorn. There are many purses here I'm looking to lighten and many beds I'm looking to warm—and I must lay many dark preparations so that none may stand in my way. So—-my sweet lecherous Quindarius—-I'll be asking favors of you anon.'

"'Favors?' asked I.

"'Yea, *favors*,' the viper repeated. 'Mostly to pluck out your conscience's eyes like you have so deftly done in trying to conceal your own affairs. I'll expect that same courtesy be turned to me when anyone questions my good name to your office. The first thing you will do is plead the cause among the other elders that I be named an elder.'

"'What?' I couldn't believe it.

"'That's right–I'm to be made an elder before the month's end. Not only that, but you will also petition for me to be given charge of a force of Tarrenbacks and for me to become the overseer of the Lottery. I will be more specific about what else I'll need of you when the situation demands it. You will comply with my every whim, sir. Or I will bury you with the truth of your scandalous treatment of your wife and the deceit you've swaddled your child with. And if that's not enough to win you to do my black graces—-then rest assured that when the time comes, I'll use the appointment of my office to make sure your Samuel is chosen in the Lottery the first year he's of age. Of that be certain. If you care not to save yourself from disgrace and embarrassment, think of your child given to the grinding maw of Erif and what a meal his young flesh would make.'

"And with that, he stole away, leaving me in horror in the corridor of mine own house."

"What? I don't—-I don't understand," Annabella said. "Are you saying that you knew—-that you have known for years about Cyvilard's villainy and have done nothing?"

"Listen to me, child," Quindarius said and moved toward her. "I have tortured over this for years, sick is my soul with it, but listen: Cyvilard cannot be stopped. The reason he was able to spy upon me so completely is because he is possessed of a Yonderling power. He can see through the eyes of the birds of the air—-that much I know. But here's what I can only mightily suspect. That besides seeing with the eyes of any bird he wishes, Cyvilard can also possibly shape-shift *into* a bird. I do not believe he does this often, but I have come to believe he is able to do it. I think that he was able to gain access to my house by turning into a bird and then shifting back to himself upon entering. It is my firm belief that he has used this strange power for years creating secret leverage on every elder in Thorn so that he can conduct his elaborate feats of devilry and satisfy the hideous demands of his lusts."

Annabella's eyes widened. "What then are we to do? How can you help me now to save my sister from unfairly being plucked for the Lottery?"

"That's just it, child—-*I don't know*. By now Cyvilard has a death-grip on every elder in Thorn—-not just me. *Run*. Save yourself. Take what you can and leave Thorn. But if Cyvilard is intent on choosing your sister this morning for the Lottery, there's nothing I can do to stop it—-even though I wish the world I could."

Annabella couldn't believe her ears. Was Quindarius really saying this? After his whole sordid story? After bringing her back from the alley was *this* all he had to offer? What Quindarius had told her was awful. *No*--it was more than that too. It was shattering. Her illusions of what their beloved elder was really like were gone. Not only that, but he had no answers either, no solution to her very pressing problems.

"What rot is this?" She stood up with clenched fists.

"My dear, I'm sorry," the old man looked up to her—-his bottom lip suddenly starting to quiver. "If Cyvilard fixes the scales to her doom—-then she must stay and bear the weight for us all. For all our sins. No matter if she's chosen by treachery or not—-Erif still requires innocent blood for our survival. I'm so sorry, my child. So sorry!" he began to weep.

Annabella was suddenly hit with visons of the night terrors that plagued her in the months right after her own mother's death. Nights when she would wake from horrific nightmares only to find herself on her cot with her nightdress soaked in urine—-in terror-piss. She would flounder in a haze, momentarily wading in her own stink, reacting too slowly about how to fix the situation and get clean.

That's the way she felt at this moment here in Quindarius's earthen office, underground with his vats of wine and candles, trying his best to escape the spying raven's eyes of Cyvilard she now understood. Again, she felt submerged in piss—-in mess—-mired in the slime and mud of scandal and helplessness. But a rage began to well up in her. What was Quindarius's point? What was it? Just to warn her further? Confirm her fears, *yep—you're right, Annabella-—Cyvilard is a demon incarnate?*

"Why tell me this and offer no help? What are we to do? What are we to do? Answer me!" She slapped his head.

Quindarius did his best to block her blows and rise. "Be still! Please, child!" He tried to restrain her, but Annabella lunged away and knocked a couple of tapers to the dirt floor.

"If you had no help to offer, if you had no scheme of escape from Cyvilard's vile clutches then why tell me all? Why give light to me, of all people, the darkness of your past sins? Why tell *me* above your own Samuel? Tell me, Quindarius—-what manner of man are you?"

"I know all too well what I am, lass! I am sick at heart of my wretched duplicity! I am flayed alive every day, I live with guilt of my filth and wretchedness!" Quindarius spat, bursting like a dam of rotten logs. "I cannot endure myself any longer. I am a flayed man! To the bone, I tell you. I cannot bear to look my Samuel in the eyes! I shrivel like a corpse when I am reminded of my treachery against my village, my wife, my son—-my very self! Even Leonella has lost her taste for my tears of self-loathed woe. There are days when I am so near ending my own life or exposing myself and going willingly to punishment—-but I know that that will do nothing now to rid Thorn of the canker of Cyvilard and his unshakeable grip on this village. I oft look to the skies and ask, 'is it not enough to have one devil who waits in the mountains for us to deliver our own children to him to devour that we must also harbor yet another among us, coiled and set to strike if we dare try to expel him?'"

"But why tell me? Especially now? And waste my precious hour that I could have used to at least *try* and fly my doomed sister from this diseased village!"

Quindarius stared at her for a moment, huffing for breath, oozing spittle from his mouth to his beard. "Because... because you showed up here. That was the only spur I needed. Now go and save yourself."

"You are a foolish, sad, and sick old man. What care I of myself? I'd burn this whole world to dust if I could just to save my sweet Angel from the horror of this place." She spat and turned back to the cellar.

Throughout the streets above, the bell of the Great Hall began its tolling, calling every man, woman, and child of Thorn to its steps to hear the reading of the year's Lottery.

Spring had come—-and the Mayodon with it—-and dried up the winter's snow and moisture, making Thorn as dry and brittle as a tinder. And now the world was on fire. And as far as Annabella was concerned, it was Quindarius that had ignited it. Not Cyvilard, not Prince, nor even Erif the Ever-Present waiting in the mountain above them like a fiery noose. It was Quindarius and his spineless complicity to the darkness of this world. *That* was the true and blackest of evils.

"Where is it you go?" a broken Quindarius called after her.

Annabella yelled her answer but didn't turn back to face the elder, "*To find Samuel*!"

3

If nothing else, Luke was teaching Turner patience. Turner didn't freak out hardly at all when he pressed Luke further about this supposed 'friend' of Rozzy they were going to see, and Luke's answer was just another blank stare and more silence.

Oh sure, Turner was still pissed at continually being kept in the dark and being strung along like a runny-nosed toddler on a wrist leash—but it was like a *whatever* pissed. Not a *I'm-gonna-baseball-bat-you-in-the-head-bitch-if-you-don't-tell-me-what's-going-on* pissed. So yeah—you know, progress. Patience. Personal growth for Jason Turner.

They continue driving east on I-69. The suburbs give way to fields. The morning's finally turning sunny—but cold with some serious November bite. And out in that farm country with nothing to obstruct it, the wind comes in gusts from the north and hits Turner's side of the car, like shoves from an invisible and incredibly pissed off monster.

Luke exits. Driving north now into what appears the main strip of a small town. Jason notices the sign as they pass it: NOW ENTERING THE TOWN OF BATH.

They blow by several fast-food chains and an oil change place. Turn at the Walmart and leave the commercial zone for a more rural looking area full of farms and fields. A few more miles down the road , Luke flicks the blinker and pulls into a gravel driveway to a lonesome property, heading up to a farmhouse with a Quonset hut and a couple of other buildings behind it. The mailbox sports the name BELMONT on it in white spray paint stencil. In the front yard two elm trees barren of their leaves stand watch, but other than that, the rest of the lot's all flat and sparse. An old, mostly brown, Ford pickup sits outside the house.

Luke eases the car up beside the truck and turns off the ignition.

"Are you fucking serious, man? I mean, you ever gonna tell me straight up what we're doing here?"

Luke just opens the door and gets out.

Turner follows him. But slams his door.

Luke leads them to the front of the house where they go up the stairs to a big porch with a porch swing facing the front of the property. Luke rings the doorbell.

After about a minute the door swings open. An old man, tall, heavy about the gut, wearing frayed and faded denim overalls stands before them. He just stares at them with these eyes behind glasses thick as storm windows. He kinda strokes his gray-whiskered chin like his mind is slow-cooking trying to figure out just what to say—or trying to figure out why they're on his porch.

Turner remembers thinking the old coot looked fricking senile and about ready to dump a shot put of shit in his geezer diaper.

"So now. Here we go, then. You gotta be Luke by the look of you—and that then would make you Jason." The old man steps back to give them room. "Well, let's not all stand here and freeze our balls off. Come on in, boys."

A couple of cats dart out from somewhere and rocket past Luke and Turner's legs and out the door.

The old guy leads them through the house and Turner notices the smell first. It's like classic nursing home reek. You know, that smell that some old people have. I mean some of them just can't help it, I guess. And that's what the Belmont house smells like. Old man breath and sanitizer and soup that's been left on the stove too long.

The house isn't messy—but everything's old. Like antique store old. It's orderly but musty. Like the couch for instance. The thing's a relic—I mean, Turner recalls thinking that he wouldn't go as far as to call it 'ratty'—he's seen and slept on worse. But the sofa's seen some years, no doubt about it. Also, the old guy's got like a flat screen and all but it's like sitting on top of this dinosaur looking TV that you can tell doesn't work anymore and probably pre-dated remote controls even because there's this circular dial on the front of it and it takes Turner a few to even realize what the crap it is because he'd never seen one before.

"Come on through here," the old guy goes. "Through the kitchen here. We'll talk in the sunroom."

They go through the kitchen where everything's tidy and in its place—but despite the neatness, the room's still thick with old looking stuff on the walls, the counters, and shelves.

The kitchen steps down into the sunroom that's of a completely different tone than the rest of the house. It must have been an add-on to the original farmhouse the way that it juts out. Also, the room is totally uncluttered and as clean as a chapel. Windows set on all three sides look out to a massive Quonset hut with old farm machinery lined up against it and a barren field beyond. Besides a small table and chairs the only other thing in the room is a stool tucked in one of the corners with a thick wide leather-bound book lying on top of it.

"I think I might have some cider squirreled away if you're thirsty. Could also boil up some hotdogs if you fellas are needing some lunch too."

Hot dogs and apple juice? What are we—in fucking third grade? Turner thinks but doesn't say. Instead, he just shakes his head *no* along with Luke.

"Suit yourselves." The old man sits down at the table with them.

So, the three of them just sit there awhile all quiet, which drives Turner completely bat-crap. He'd kept his cool about all this up to this point, like I said before, just rolling with it. Not getting too pissed when Luke was messing with him, not telling him anything. But now Turner's really starting to get to the end of his newfound patience. From a wall in the kitchen, a crazy antique looking clock that looked more like a freaking birdhouse than a timepiece ticks and clacks and ticks and clacks—*cheese and rice*— catching Turner's attention and further annoying the hell out of him.

"Ugh—fuck this. So am I supposed to just—"

"Hang on there, young fella," the old guy cuts in. "I want to show you boys something here you might be interested in." The old dude stands up and gets the big leather book off the stool in the corner and creaks the sucker open on the table.

He looks at Luke. "So, you can understand me, eh? What I'm saying? Reading my lips or whatnot?"

Luke nods to him.

"Hmm. I'll be damned," the old guy goes and turns through some of the album's pages making sticky sounding flips as he does it. "Here. Take a look at these," he says and slides the album across the table. Luke paws it around so he and Turner can get a good gander at them.

The photographs are all old and black and whites. Some of them have even turned all tan as if they'd been totally dipped in coffee at some point. All of them look to be like just family pics from *way* back in the day. A lot of them are of children wearing weird, almost pioneer-like looking clothes.

"This—I mean, these—are like all of your family?" Turner goes.

The old guy nods.

"All taken around here? On your farm?"

"That's right. Long ago…"

Yeah, like no duh, man… Turner thinks.

They look at a photograph of a middle-aged guy on a tractor. Another of two kids—a young boy and a younger girl sitting on a wood plank fence smiling. One of a mother in a long dress and a short haircut cradling a baby on the front porch swing. Another one of a large extended family sitting at a crowded table for a big feast—probably a Thanksgiving or Christmas dinner. There's a photo of a dog—a collie, sitting next to a boy standing in overalls and a tight wool baseball cap.

Turner still doesn't know what any of this has to do with anything whatsoever, but still can't help being captivated by some of the old pictures totally against his will. There's just something about them. Maybe it's that everyone seems so happy, or close, or that the photos are just so old it seems like he's looking at something that should be like in an exhibit at a museum or some crap so that he automatically feels like he *should* be compelled by them. But whatever the reason, he finds himself staring at them, totally enraptured or whatever, almost as open-mouthed as Luke is sitting next to him.

The two of them just stare and flip from ream to laminated ream.

The old guy clears his throat and reaches across the table just enough to flip the album to a certain page. "If I may," he croaks. He turns to a page showcasing a portrait of a man and a woman in front of their house. It kind of reminds Turner for a moment of that classic painting you see all the time with like the farmer holding a pitchfork standing next to his wife, both with like total dead-serious looks on their faces.

"These are my parents. David and Lucinda. Got married young. Before Dad went off to the war. Mom was barely sixteen. Dad wasn't much older. They bought this place after dad got back from the Front in France. Clem, my oldest brother, was just eight."

The old man turns to another page. "My name's Carver by the way, Jason. And these," he points to another photograph, "are my brothers and sisters."

There are four of them. All sitting on what looks like a wooden bench, or church pew—crammed in, shoulders touching—except for the baby that's in the arms of a young girl sitting between her two older brothers. The young girl's all smiling to beat the band, as old timers like Carver would say. She looks so proud to be the one holding the baby. The two brothers look pretty happy too. One, obviously the oldest, a teenager just starting to shed his boy body's awkwardness and take on the handsomeness of a young man. The other looking like your typical awkward fifth or sixth-grade boy probably all prickling with the first tingles of puberty. At the bottom of the photograph, underneath all the grain hand-scrawled in the white boarder: *August 1926.*

"Cheese and rice.... So, which one's you?" Turner goes.

Carver starts chuckling all full of coughy old man breath. "I hadn't been born yet, son. Wouldn't poke my head around for a few more years."

Turner finally does the math in his head and is blown away about how many years old this guy really is.

"Here... that's me," Carver goes after flipping to another photo. It shows him as a baby all swaddled up in white frilly blankets chilling in his mother's arms.

"Shit. You were a real cutie, man," Turner goes.

"He always this funny?" Carver goes to Luke.

Luke just makes a *meh*-face.

Carver flips it back to the kids on the bench. "I was the youngest. See? I was the baby. These are my older brothers and sisters. That's Clem—the oldest. This is Buddy. He's about twelve there. And Olivia. She's eight here. And the baby Oliva is holding is Sara. She's a little over a year old the time this was taken."

Olivia looks familiar to Turner. He can't place it at first. Something about her hair. Or maybe her freckles. Then it hits him. Olivia looks just like that girl from that *Kill a Mockingbird* movie he saw in class sophomore year. I mean she's the spitting image, Turner swears. Scout her name was. He never really read the book but he sure as shit remembers the movie though. All that *Boo Radley* shit. Maybe it was purely because they both had short jet-black hair or maybe because the movie was in black in white too. But *damn* if Olivia Belmont didn't look like Scout freaking Finch.

But Turner doesn't say anything about his little revelation though. Instead, he goes, "Look, fuck—I'm sorry, man. This is all kind of cool in its own way and all, but I don't have a clue what we're doing here. Luke, come on, man—this guy don't know Rozzy and you damn well know it. Why you gotta play it like this? No offense, old timer—"

"Carver."

"Yeah, OK—*Carver*. No offense and thanks for the history lesson and all, but I think my deaf friend here—"

"Rosalind—" Carver starts all deep and serious, stopping Turner in his verbal tracks, "Rosalind Howard. Yes, yes, yes." The old dude gets up and hobbles up out to the kitchen and out of sight for about a minute and comes back with something in his hand. Tosses it helicopter-blade style so it lands flat on the table in front of Turner and Luke. Rozzy's name and return address up in the left-hand corner in her unmistakable scrawl.

In the center of the envelope MR. CARVER BELMONT followed by the address and road to the sunroom where they are all sitting now.

BATH, MI.

Turner looks up to Carver, over to Luke. Luke looks back like *Hey, I told you—man.*

"I guess you could say me and your miss Howard were pen pals of sorts, old sport," Carver goes and sits back down.

Turner stares back down at Rozzy's handwriting. "I don't—"

"Know what's going on?" Carver goes. He looks over at Luke and the two of them share a little laugh. "Yeah, well hell." Carver eases back. "I barely do myself.

Barely at best, boys. Thing is though, Rozzy knew. Knew something anyway. She saw this. Or at least was hoping for this."

Turner breaks out of his trance on the envelope. "For what?"

"*This*. The three of us, sitting here like this. She wrote me months ago. Out of nowhere. Told me things there's no way she could know about me—about my family. So, I wrote her back. We wrote a few letters back and forth. On her last one to me she said a guy a like Luke would contact me. She said that he'd bring himself and *you*, Jason, here—to my farm. And now here you are."

"But—*why*?" Turner goes. "What for?"

"I think she wanted very much for me to tell you about my brothers and sisters, Jason. About my family. About my town. About Bath Consolidated School."

4

Carver Belmont flips to the back of the huge photo album and slides out a black manila-looking folder from the album's cover sleeve. There's a modestly thick stack of more photos in the folder. On top is this black and white photograph of a building.

"This here's the school. Bath Consolidated. Brand new when it opened in the fall of 1922. Two hundred and some odd students. First through twelfth grade. All one site for the whole region at the time," Carver goes.

The building was a long two story rectangular. All brick. On the front were two proud doors in the middle with forty classroom windows—twenty per floor. Brand new flagpole cemented into the courtyard. Newly laid brick path leading up to the doors. Groomed dirt for a lawn. The grass hadn't even been sown yet at the time the photo was taken.

"Yessir, the whole kit cost a pretty penny. All out of taxes. The county had to pass a referendum vote to get it. To hear my family tell of it, it passed pretty handily. Although there was a fair amount of concern too about how much it was gonna cost. I mean after all, there was the cost of the building, which was substantial as it always is, but also the cost of trucking them kids around. You know, carting kids to and from the schoolhouse—that was the hard sell. Need to understand boys—back in them days this kind of notion of school was all spanking new. They were all used to one-room schoolhouses. So, to suddenly have to shell out for buses too on top of a new building—well, I guess it made for some spirited open forum meetings in the Bath Town Hall. But like I said, after some debate ,it passed, and the school was built."

Turner sees Luke quickly glance down at the image of the schoolhouse and back up to Carver, so he didn't miss a word, presumably. Turner was still at like a complete loss about all this. He couldn't believe it—this old coot had a freaking letter from Rozzy for cheese and rice sakes. He was dying to know what she could possibly have written to him but was content for the time being to just sit back and let the geezer get his story on and then ask to see the letter later. And if the old guy wouldn't let him read it outright—then Turner wasn't above just fricking stealing it if he had too.

"The town bought six busses—one of them just a modified Model T pickup that they could take off the body in the summers and use for municipal maintenance work in town. They also set up this two-horse wagon with a canvas cover over the top of the trailer and potbellied stove to haul kids around in too. I remember they still had that deal my first year of school. Us kids loved it. Being drawn by horses to school. A nice warm fire going in the stove while you jostled along the way down some farm road or on one of the town's main streets. Pile of wood stacked up for the older kids to feed into the stove while some farmer drove the team." Carver glazes over a bit remembering that wagon.

"Anyhow—it was pretty big doings right after they opened up the school. My brothers and Olivia were so excited about going and learning and seeing so many kids their own age at school every day. They'd come home each afternoon brimming over according to Ma. Couldn't wait to tell her and Dad about their studies at suppertime. Especially Olivia. The girl was a firecracker. Practically hugged her schoolbooks and tablets. Most excitable eight-year-old-you ever saw to hear Ma tell it. *Little Miss Lightning if you please*, that Olivia.

"I know parents aren't supposed to have favorites amongst their own children—but Clem and Buddy both swore up and down that Dad loved Olivia the best. Oh, he tried to hide it, they said, but you could just see. And the boys didn't even get sore about it neither on account of how much they loved their sister too. See boys, she lit them all up."

Carver turns back to a picture of just Olivia, and Turner is hit with *Mockingbird* all over again. The old guy's right—Olivia's smile was total light incarnate shining right through the black and white film revealing the vibrancy of truth. *I mean, shit—how could you not love a face like that?* Turner remembers thinking.

"So, by the spring of 1927 Clem was seventeen and about to graduate. Buddy was in the seventh grade and Olivia was counting down the days of second grade so she could start bragging she was a third grader. It was May. A Wednesday. Only two days left before the end of the school year.

"When my family woke up that morning, a rainstorm was just finishing up. My dad and two brothers did their chores in the barn before dawn broke as usual, and you could still see flashes of lightning sparking in the dark, I was later told. Most of it was done by breakfast though.

"My dad had recently bought a 25 Tudor Ford Model T—so he had given over our old aught ten jalopy to Clem to drive himself, Buddy, and Olivia to school in. *Here*—I got a picture of them all in that broken-down monster somewhere." Carver scans through his album.

"Here. Here's Clem and the car at least…"

Luke and Turner look at a pic of Clem sitting in this ancient car looking like something out of an Al Capone movie or whatever—his hair all slicked back wearing a pair of weird driving goggles sitting next to some pretty brunette that sure wasn't his Ma.

"Who's that he's with?" Turner goes.

"Emma. Em Gershwin. Clem's girl back then. She was in the same grade. This was taken earlier that same May in fact. Good girl, I was told. Ma liked her. Wished Clem would've married her."

Carver sits back again. Clears his throat. "Anyhow, that's the old ten. Had to crank the thing something awful to get it to start. But Clem sure loved it. One of the only older kids that drove himself to school back then.

"So that Wednesday morning he and Buddy and Olivia piled in and drove up to the schoolhouse. It was the last day of exams. All grades. Except some of the twelfth graders were already done and didn't need to be in the building all day. Clem was among some of the lucky kids done with his exams. The morning had turned sunny by then and it was about as perfect a May morning as you could ask for. So, he was waiting with a few other boys in the front yard of the Methodist church across the street from the school. The church was going to be the site of the graduation ceremony the next day and the seniors were all expected to help with setting up the chairs and decorations. Clem and the boys had to wait though because Superintendent Emory Huyck and a couple other teachers were with the valedictorian and the salutatorian practicing their speeches at the church's podium to make sure they were up to snuff. So, somebody scared up a football from somewhere and Clem and the other boys started tossing the pigskin around, happy to pass the time.

"Clem's girl, Em and some of her friends didn't have exams either so they ditched the boys to go pick flowers in the graveyard just past the south end of the school grounds. As they picked dahlias and tulips, Em gossiped with Josephine Dahlman about some of the other boys and girls in their grade and who was getting fresh with who, I guess. You know how girls are."

Luke and Turner look at each other a sec and then back to Carver.

"But that still left all the other grades stuck inside that morning cranking away on their final tests. They were all anxious to get them done and just relax. Buddy told me it was tradition that after lunch on the last day, classes were to be suspended and the whole school was to be involved in the big students-versus-teachers softball game on the diamond in back of the school. Buddy was especially excited, not just for the game itself, or that that class was done for the day—but also the school cooks always whipped up more lemonade and cookies than anyone could possibly eat and drink. Buddy said you could always get so stuffed you couldn't walk afterward. He said the boys always had little contests to see who could eat the most cookies.

"So anyhow, Buddy was stuck in his classroom starting his final mathematics test at his desk, trying to concentrate on multiplication and long division and the like, instead of chocolate chips.

"I imagine Olivia was hard at work on her test too. I can see her going at her test like a little madwoman. Her tongue sticking out she's scribbling her answers so hard with her pencil. All her little second grade classmates probably doing the same.

"*Yessir*. Bath Consolidated School was humming like a hive that morning. Running about how the good taxpayers hoped that it would when they passed the referendum. *Yessir*, indeed. Our school was a model of the times. The future of education had come to Bath," Carver goes and then gives a weird laugh. "And so, it was then—at 8:43 AM it was determined—that down in the school building's basement, a timed detonator ignited the blasting caps rigged to a large cache of dynamite and pyrotol, causing a massive explosion."

5

"The boom was immaculate they said. Like the coming of an angry God, they said. The blast could be felt like an earthquake all through town as if the earth were opening up and was about to swallow the Town of Bath like an ordained holocaust right out of the Old Testament or something like that. *Joshua, Judges, Ruth*—boys. You follow me? *Boom.* In the houses in the surrounding neighborhood windows shattered. Clocks stopped. Felt and heard before it was seen for most people. The opposite of lightning and thunder."

Carver opens the black manila folder again. He fishes out another photo of the school taken obviously after the explosion.

"Mother of shit—" Turner hisses.

"Emma and Josephine saw it all from the graveyard. They said there was the boom along with the biggest blast of smoke and dust that come up from the school's basement you ever saw. Like a dust storm from hell had just been let loose under the building. Swirling up like a mad genie out of Ali Babba or something. Then the roof of the entire north side of the school rose above the dust like the building was alive and taking in a humongous breath and then suddenly fell. Collapsed with a wrath of blown brick, glass, and blasted wood all in a hell-rumble. Like the crumbling of the walls of Jericho. And suddenly Em and Josephine couldn't see anything. Just smoke and dust and ash. Couldn't even see each other. Dropped their flowers and bumped into each other in the haze. Hard apparently because Josephine would later realize she had chipped a tooth.

"Clem and his buddies didn't even get to see that. With the blast all the boys hit the ground like they had all been struck by lightning and fell instinctively into the fetal position to cover themselves best they could. By the time Clem remembers looking up, everything was in a cloud so thick you could taste it. Like fog in from the ether of an ocean or Lake Michigan.

"Superintendent Huyck came running out from the Methodist Church with some other horrified teachers trying to see through the haze to where the school was."

Turner looks back down to the photo of the wrecked school. The entire left side of the building collapsed to rubble. The right side looked fine. But if anyone had been in that left side—cheese and rice—Turner just didn't know, you know? I mean how anyone could survive *that?*

"And then, right after the blast, Clem said there was the longest moment of silence ever. No sound. No screams. Nothing. The dust started to lift. Not even a whisper. And then. Just like that—it was over. And the screams began. But muffled on account of being buried underneath all that debris and the smoke and the dust.

"Olivia's classroom was on the first floor on the south wing of the building. Her little desk was right next to one of the open front windows. That one right there.

"Well, no one needed to tell her what's what. She scattled up and jumped out that window before the dust settled apparently. First one out of the building. She yelled for her classmates to follow and some of them did. Her teacher they say was in shock and just stood there for a bit not moving or doing anything till some of her students started pulling on her hand to get her out of it.

"Buddy though and about sixty other kids in the north wing weren't so lucky. Buddy's classroom was up on the second floor on that side of the doomed building. His whole classroom literally fell through their floor and crashed on top of the first- grade class below them.

"They were all buried under rubble. Most of those on the first floor were crushed to death upon collapse."

"Jesus Christ—" Turner hisses. "How many, man?"

"Forty-three dead by the end of the day. Thirty-eight were children," Carver goes.

"Fuck-all, man. And you said this was all rigged? Like a bomb?"

"Not *like a bomb*, Jason. It *was* a bomb. Planted there in the basement."

"Well, what kind of a fucking sonofabitch'd do something like that, man?"

"Bastard's name was Kehoe. Andrew P. Kehoe. And he was Bath's School Board Treasurer."

6

The old tan once-white headline clipping reads:

HELL COMES TO BATH

MAD MAN BLOWS UP SCHOOL, KILLS 43

Carver's got over a dozen newspaper clippings in the black folder. One has a picture of the destroyed school in the background; in the fore are rows of small bodies lined up lying on some kind of tarp. Their torsos and stuff are partially covered by a sheet. Black-colored blood is batched on them everywhere. Below the sheet are the dead children's legs. Most of their feet are bare—Carver says that their shoes were blown off during the blast. Some their skin and flesh rubbed right off their bodies to the bone.

The pictures make Turner sick.

"*Madman. Maniac. Crazed Killer* the press called him," Carver goes. "They might have been partly right about the man. But not in the way that the goddamn press put it at the time."

Who was this guy? What was his deal? Luke writes.

"No matter who you talked to, or how much stuff you could read on the guy, Kehoe was a hard one to peg down. He moved to Bath with his wife Nellie to take over Nellie's family farm. Kehoe was supposed to be an electrician by trade but tried his hand here as a farmer once he got himself to Bath. Turned out he weren't no good at it. Folks said his planting fields were not well tended for. But turns out the bastard sure was good with machinery though. He made more cash fixing engines and rigging up electrical work for folks than anything that ever came off his farm at harvest. That much is well known for sure and certain. And he was a crackerjack with numbers too. That's what made him a shoo-in as school board treasurer when he ran."

"This him?" Turner goes, looking at one of the newspaper clippings. There was a print of an old photo of a mostly silver-haired gentleman dressed neatly with a sports jacket and tie holding a lit cigar in his hand like he was the real old school prince of style. He was sitting at a big wooden desk. The room looked like an old-time study or something. Neat bookshelf behind him like he was showing off his library or whatever. Sitting next him with super-upright posture was a thin, almost skeletal, woman. She had a sewing in her hands. She looked bored as hell too. Almost like she was forced to sit next to her pompous ass looking husband in what looked to be a folding chair while he sat all regal behind his fancy desk like he was trying to look real hard like some oil tycoon from the Roaring Twenties.

Carver was right. Kehoe sure didn't look like a farmer. And there was something about his face. Turner thinks there's something real familiar and all wrong about Kehoe's face. In the eyes maybe. Or his weird-ass forehead. *Fuck knows*...he thinks.

"His wife there—Nellie," Carver goes, "She was a sick woman. Kept having to go back and forth to stay stints at the hospital in Lansing. Most folks were never quite sure what it was she had. I think it must've been degenerative though whatever it was. I seen other pictures of her only a couple of years before this one here was taken, and the poor woman looked fifteen years younger. She's turning into a scarecrow here."

"So yeah—like Luke said," Turner goes, "what's this guy's deal? Why'd he blow up the school?"

"Well now, that's the big question. Isn't it? Anytime there's something so big, so awful, so damn evil folks can't wrap their minds around it themselves, they ask others and go, *why is that? Why'd this happen? Here? To us?*" Carver starts laughing again, but Turner's pretty sure it's the kind of laugh you hear people do when something is the freaking polar opposite of funny.

"The nice and tidy answer," Carver continues, "the answer the papers and history books would have you believe is that Kehoe was going broke. In fact, he was about to lose his farm on account of not keeping up with the payments. Plus, there were Nellie's medical bills from whatever she was suffering from. It didn't help matters that all about the same time there's this referendum needing passing for the new school that's gonna raise everybody's taxes. So, even though Kehoe was on the school board, he was also one of the loudest opponents for the referendum to pass at the open forum meetings. Apparently, he made some compelling arguments to vote '*No*' to consolidation and swayed a couple of other folks. But at the end of the day, he was still easily outnumbered. So, like I said, if you read up on this disaster at all, every story will tell you that Andrew Kehoe blew up Bath Consolidated School because he blamed it for pushing him over the top into financial ruin. He took his revenge on the innocent children and the schoolhouse itself. *Bam!* End of sad story."

"Well did the fucker go to the chair for what he did? Or did he try to make it to Canada?" Turner goes.

"Oh no. Not Kehoe. Men like this never run. It wasn't in him. Men like this chain themselves to the stake and take all comers frothing like mad dogs till the fat lady sings, boys. *No.* Here's what Kehoe does. It takes about eight months for this bastard to plan the bombing. Eight months to gather all the dynamite, blasting caps, fuses, wiring, and pyrotol to do the deed. There was no passion about this. This was done in blood as cold as Lake Superior in October, boys. And since he's on the school board and doubles up as the school's maintenance advisor, of course Kehoe's got keys to the building and plants his explosives two weeks before he planned on detonating them. The man had all the time in the world to rig the place up to blow.

"So, it finally gets to the night before the bombing. Tuesday, May seventeenth. He had just picked Nellie up the day before from a week's stay in the hospital in Lansing. So, it's just after nightfall in the Kehoe farmhouse and Nellie's probably just getting settled back in after being gone. I can imagine her husband going out of his way trying to make her comfortable. Makes sure she's sitting down in a chair. He gets her sewing out. Maybe gives her some mail to read or a newspaper she's missed since she's been away. Maybe he even makes her some tea. Who knows? But what is known is that at some point on that Tuesday night, Kehoe sneaks up behind his wife and bashes the back of her skull in with a hammer or a hatchet or something, killing her on the spot.

"Then he drags her body out into the dark. Out to the back of the house and ties her legs to the axle of a wooden cart used to haul hay. He douses his whole house with gasoline and diesel fuel. Ties his two horses fast in his stable. Stuffs his chicken coop so full of hay it nearly bursts. The next morning as he pulls out leaving his property for good and all, he's got the coop and house rigged up with enough dynamite to blow them to hell and back. Set on a timer to go off exactly when the bomb under Bath Consolidated is set to erupt.

"And so, it does. At the same moment innocent children and teachers are being blown up and crushed under mountains of unforgiving debris and God knows what—Kehoe's property blows sky high—house and all, while his wife's corpse cooks to black char strapped to that wagon and his horses ride the apocalypse trapped in his blazing barn, burning to death."

7

"So's this end with him going all suicide-by-cop or what, man?" Turner goes.

Luke holds Jason back in his seat.

"Hang on, kid," Carver goes. "I'm getting there. Well, right after the explosion at the school, Superintendent Huyck and Clem and every other able-bodied person ran to the half-demolished schoolhouse. By then kids was pouring out of the south wing, like Oliva and her class had done through the windows and such. Clem caught sight of Olivia and grasped onto her tight. Hugged her something fierce he said. But she wouldn't let him hug her long. Olivia started screaming that Buddy's still in there. Under all that broken up building. She screams to Clem to get him out. To find him. To save him.

"Well, it's chaos at that point. Children that were alive and OK, that had the good fortune to be in the part of the school that weren't blowed up, were crawling out of any window they could find. Those were the ones that were mostly unhurt anyway—and once they was out of danger they started crying and screaming for their parents.

"There just weren't enough adults there at first. Even most of the teachers weren't much use at first on account of them being all wounded and traumatized too. Mr. Piedmont, a guy who taught the older grades History—well, I guess he come out with glass sticking out gushing blood from his balding head yelling, *it's the fucking Keiser. That fucking Keiser!* like he was back in the trenches. There was no real order to assist the wounded and scared students. Superintendent Huyck tried to get things in order by telling all students who could walk and hear to gather across the road to the lawn of the Methodist church.

"So while's he was doing that, Clem and a few of the older boys started digging into the smoky rubble of the school, looking for survivors. They didn't have to look long though. The haze of the blast was clearing up around the destroyed north wing. Clem said there were kids laying all over the front lawn. Some were conscious and sitting up in shock, disoriented, while some were dead where they landed—and still others were just lying there unconscious, knocked out by the blast. All of them with various wounds and injuries. These kids were all literally *blown out* of the school when it exploded.

"Clem went around making sure none of the kids in the grass was Buddy before he and another big kid—Charlie Coniff, I think it was—tore in and started flinging debris up to get at the muffled screamers they heard beneath. It was hard, scalding, work though. Clem cut his hands to shreds after a couple minutes. Some gashes left scars for life there. Jagged bricks, glass. Blasted splintered wood. And those metal desks. *Those christforsaken things,* Clem would later say of them. Those desks were a pain in the ass clearing out. There were so many of them and the metal was white-hot from the blast or blown full of holes with jagged edges like serrated knives. The Coniff boy had to quit after a while because so much of his skin on his hands and arms got singed right off by the metal. Skin peeled right off his flesh like cellophane, so it goes.

"Clem pulled out a little first-grade girl that was alive and mumbling but had a deep gash on her head among other wounds. Well, he led her out of the pile aways and set her down in the grass. By this time Em and a bunch of older students were on the spot helping clear debris in the rescue effort, or helping the teachers gather up the wounded survivors.

"Nobody was touching the dead yet.

"Clem got back to it. He was getting frantic by now. Hoping like hell to find Buddy. And yet at the same time scared he would find our brother but find him all tore up and dead. He dug down to where it was just this pile of crumbling bricks. Every time he picked one up though, he noticed they all had blood and little shreds of flesh all gobbed on them. One after the other with unspeakable patches of gore plastered on them. Then finally he started to see that under the bricks was a body—more or less. He could see white skin and clothing. So he keeps taking away the bricks piece by piece. Revealing horror like some murderous jigsaw puzzle. Clem was trying to ready himself that this might be Buddy in pieces under there. But it wasn't. It was a boy though. A little younger than Buddy. It was one of the littles. One of the first graders. The poor boy'd had both his legs blowed off. What was left of him below his waist was hanging on him in shreds. Clem cleared the remaining debris off him and realized the child was still alive. He had this terrible but calm look in his huge eyes. Like a baby deer's eyes, Clem recalled. Like the kid was looking up past the haze and stink of the massacre, away from this ordeal he'll never live through, farther up, past the clouds somewhere's and seemed to be trying to will himself up there somehow. He never looked at Clem once. Clem doubted the kid ever really knew he was there. He opened his mouth a few times though. Trying hard to breathe, I guess. But Clem thought it was more than that. My brother said it reminded him of a dying fish. Like when their mouths open and close when they're gasping for water after you haul them out. Like they're saying *O, O, O* while they're suffocating to death. There was blood coming up all over the kid's mouth too. Welling out of it all winter-slow. Like a tree leaking sap, Clem said. My brother didn't know what to do with him. He didn't want to try and move him—thought that might make it worse—maybe even kill the poor boy. So Clem just moved a few paces away and started digging for Buddy all over again."

Turner and Luke can do nothing but watch and listen to Carver.

"Eventually, people from town start to show up. At first, it's just a dozen or so housewives from the near-by neighborhood. Then storeowners and businessmen from downtown arrive. Bath only had six policemen total on the force back then, but one of the two that were on-duty that day shows up sometime during the first fifteen minutes after the explosion.

"It's still pandemonium at that point though. Clem doesn't notice the other people at all. He just concentrates on finding his brother. And finally, underneath a barricade of desks, miraculously he comes across Buddy.

"Buddy's unconscious and has black residue all over his face and arms. Turns out most of his shirt was blown off him. But he's alive. Before Clem can lift him up to safety though, he notices Buddy's left arm is crushed. It's broken and nearly pulverized where the weight of a desk and a support beam crashed down upon it.

"Clem lift's Buddy up into his arms carries him toward a safe spot on the grass. As he does, Buddy's ruined arm dangles unnaturally like a hangman swaying on a gallows.

"Olivia sees them from a distance and comes running. When she gets to them Clem loses all strength and kneels with Buddy and Olivia kisses them each over and over as the Belmont children mass in a huddle of blood and tears.

"Well, it's Superintendent Huyck that breaks up my siblings. Although he mentions he's glad as hell they all made it through. But Huyck tells Clem they really need him to take Mr. Grogan from the Bath Goods and Emporium back to his shop to retrieve as many medical supplies and work gloves as they can. Huyck tells Clem he's ideal for the job on account of his car.

"Clem says *sure, of course*. It's the least he can do now that his brother and sister are accounted for. And besides, Clem thought, Buddy was going to need medical attention as soon as possible, and Grogan's store might have some things that could tide Buddy over till real doctors arrived from Lansing.

"Clem told Olivia to stay and watch over Buddy and of course she says she would.

"Old Grogan and Clem jumped in the aught ten and pull out heading to Grogan's store. Well, Clem cranked her more than he ought to and gave her a little more gas. Your adrenaline really flows when you're in the midst of life and death like that."

Turner nods at that and gets a quick flash of he and Kid T hauling ass away from Lester's house in the Mitsu.

"It was the worst of timing because about halfway there the engine blows. Clem couldn't believe it. The engine she just goes. Bang! There's smoke and oil stink coming up from the hood. Clem pulled over to the side of the street as far as he could and he and Mr. Grogan get out whiles this guy pulls up in his car and said something like, 'Hey! You boys know anything about the school being on fire?' 'Oh, aint no fire,' Grogan says. 'School's been blowed up!' Well, that shocks the guy's socks right off and Grogan tells him to give him a ride so's to get the supplies that Huyck wanted from the store. Grogan tells Clem he might as well run back to the school on account that they'll be able to fit more supplies in the car without him taking up space in it.

"So Grogan drives away with the man in the car and Clem starts heading back to school in a slow jog. And that's when this truck comes peeling around one of the street corners. Clem raises his hands in hopes of flagging the truck down for a ride back to the school on account of its heading that way. But the truck just keeps going right past him. Clem recognized the driver. It was Kehoe. And as he passed my brother on the street, Clem could tell even with the profile view of the man's face, that Kehoe was laughing. A big laugh. Not some chuckle or nothing. No. This was an open mouth *Ha Ha Ha* that makes your shoulders jump up and down so hard you nearly cry with joy at the power of it."

8

"By this point the disaster scene was swarming with Bath townsfolk. More and more people showed up by the minute. Most of them parents, mothers really, looking for their children. Combing the place in panic. The place became awash of mothers and screams eventually. More and more adult men showed up and immediately took over the task of rummaging through wreckage of the north wing looking for survivors. Most of the surviving and less-grievously injured students and staff were gathered just outside the Methodist Church. And Emory Huyck was doing his best to coordinate the whole effort. He was the school superintendent, and he was only twenty-eight at the time of the bombing. Quite a few had natural concerns at first that a man that young could handle such an administrative position. But Emory had a steady and intelligent way about him. And had more schooling and such in the education area than anyone else that applied for the job. And really everybody seemed to remember thinking two years into his tenure they had the right man for the job.

"Even on that most horrific of mornings, most people remember Huyck remaining composed and measured. In charge that's for sure. He was directing where everybody was to go but without yelling and carrying on so as to be swallowed by the enormity of the tragedy. Oh sure, some folks remember sweat rings forming under the superintendent's arms soaking through his oxford shirt and taking off those round wire-rim glasses of his to wipe the sweat of his brow off the lenses. But he kept his tie and suspenders on and still just carried on, exuding leadership during that first half-hour or so of that day's aftermath.

"People remember Huyck had just instructed a couple of older boys to go get a couple pails of fresh water from the church and scare up some cups for those working on digging for survivors when Andrew Kehoe pulled up on the school lawn right in front of him.

"Huyck saw Kehoe and his truck but didn't acknowledge Kehoe at first. And why would he? There was no reason yet to suspect the man of anything. Why wouldn't a school board member be concerned and pull up right in front of the school in the wake of such a catastrophe?

"But then Kehoe reached out the truck, waved his arm and honked the horn.

"Huyck looked at Kehoe still sitting at the wheel but then turned to finish saying something to someone else.

"Kehoe let go a second honk.

"That's when a few other folks started noticing Kehoe. Something just didn't look right about him sitting in that truck some would recall. He looked *off* they would say later. Almost feral. Wide-eyed, mouth opened, breathing in great huffs.

"Huyck looked back to Kehoe, clearly annoyed with the repeated honking. Kehoe beckoned the superintendent to approach the truck with his hand. So Huyck finally came over to see what the man wanted.

" 'We got our hands full here, Andrew. Sure could use your truck now that you're here,' someone remembers Emory saying as he got near Kehoe's vehicle.

"Well, the two men began a conversation presumably about the bombing. At first Huyck must've felt he and Kehoe were still on the same side on account of Emory putting his foot upon the truck's rail board as he commenced to keep talking to Kehoe through the driver's side window.

"Kehoe must've strung Emory along for a while playing innocent. Maybe acting shocked and horrified about the disaster. Maybe giving credence to a bogus theory that the boiler blew or that there must've been a gas leak that ignited or what not. That kind of talk went on till Kehoe decided he couldn't keep the sham up any longer and stopped abruptly and commenced to laughing.

"Folks heard the commotion in time to see Huyck look confused at Kehoe going all hysterical. Huyck was incredulous about what the man was on about. Anyways, all that must've set a light on in Huyck's head because the next thing he was heard to say was, 'Do you know something here? Do you? What do you know of this?'

"To which Kehoe said, 'It's a hell of a thing, isn't it? A hell of a thing…'

"Kehoe started wiping the hysteria from his eyes with his thick fingers of his left hand while his right started rummaging around in his suit coat.

" 'You should know when you're bested, Emory,' Kehoe says.

"'*What*?' Huyck says back.

" 'You should know when you're bested…' Kehoe says one last time.

"What happened next was real hard for everyone to remember with the exact sequence of events. It was like one second Huyck, Kehoe and the truck were there, the next second they weren't. *Whoosh!* Gone—" Carver snaps his fingers. "Just like that."

"What happened?" Turner asks.

"Kehoe must've pulled a revolver out of his suit coat. Turned to his back seat and fired his weapon. He had stacks of pyrotol back there. Dynamite. Over 200 pounds of scrap metal from his farm and coffee cans filled with rusty nails. The blast from the gun ignited the explosives. The truck exploded in a white flash followed by a storm-thrash of jagged metal spitting out in all directions like godforsaken dragon fire.

"Some witnesses recall the blast as if reality had dipped itself in a molasses of sorts, slowing time down to a lethargy. Some saw Emory's body rise then completely disintegrate first into a yellow, then pink haze of light. Most of Kehoe's left arm blew and ripped from his torso entire, landing in the street. After the initial flare from the blast, survivors would find other pieces of the two men commingling all over the place. Large dripping tangles of intestines twisted in the tree above the wrecked truck like streamers launched at New Year's Eve. They found what was left of the hollowed skull with most of Kehoe's face still intact blown clear into a ditch over fifty feet from where the truck exploded. The man that found it was about to crush what was left of Kehoe's teeth, eyes, and nose with the heel of his boot when a policeman stopped him and collected the remains as evidence.

"I don't know what Olivia was doing there. No one later was able to recall with absoluteness what she was doing that close to the truck. The best that was reckoned was that she'd been talking to Huyck about something. Probably concerning Buddy. Maybe to see about getting some help to move him over to the lawn of the Methodist church.

"See, when the truck blew, it sent two daggers of hell-sent shrapnel into Olivia's belly and chest with the urgency of lightning. She didn't die at the outset. Folks who were with her through her entirety say she didn't scream but choked and cried something awful. Her eyes rolled and her body shook with death spasms. Blood flowed from her mouth and the undersides of her eye sockets.

"She was dead moments before Clem showed up breathless from his run. Buddy wouldn't know she was gone till the next day when he was conscious and in right mind."

Turner and Luke say nothing. Just sit looking at Carver as he tells his tale.

Outside the farmhouse it starts dusting snow all blowing and aimless. Or at least that's how Turner remembers it.

9

"By the end of the day the population of Bath had tripled in size. By the next day at noon, it would be impossible to enter Bath by road or major thoroughfare due to the lockup of traffic. We were beset. First with police and medical personnel from Lansing and other towns. Next with journalists first from across Michigan then from the nation-wide. And finally, the vultures. Folks that just wanted to smell the tragedy up close, I suppose. The gawkers. The head shakers. The legions of ghouls wanting to see a body. See a dead kid. Steal a brick or two from the school, or rummage around and see what was left of Kehoe's farm. So many vultures descend at the whiff of something so horrible.

"By the third day after the bombing some of the funerals started. However, there wasn't but one funeral parlor in Bath, and not enough even in the surrounding areas to accommodate every family of a dead child. People started making do. Doubling or tripling up on one funeral time. Town folk just wandered from funeral to funeral. You'd go and preside over your own child's funeral, interment, and then sit witness to someone else's dead child right after.

"Ma wanted to wait on Olivia's till Buddy could come. He had to stay in the hospital in Lansing near a week before they'd let him come to Olivia's service. They had to sew up and clean up proper where'd he lost the arm.

"So, Oliva laid in wake at home. Lot of folks had to go back to that on account of there being no space anywhere else. She lay in our dining room—just right back there where you boys came in. Dad and Clem moved out the regular table so's they could haul in a table they made in the barn special to hold up Olivia. For three of those days and nights Olivia didn't have no casket. So, she set in state just right back there on the table wrapped in perfumed blankets. They held a visitation for her a day before her funeral and we had mourners over. Some vulture press got wind of it. The house was packed with folks giving condolences and whatnot and one of them got in with his big camera long enough to flash a photo. He got chased out of there something quick. But not before her photograph made some of the papers across the country."

Carver rifles through the black folder again. He takes out an old photo.

Luke and Turner lean in and look.

Through the veneer of aged film and paper you could see Olivia lying in peace on top of the table there in the Belmont dining room. Her pure ivory face peeked out of like shrouds of white wrapped real tight around her small body. Just a little of her jet-black bangs could be seen just above her eyebrows before the cloth hooded the rest of her head.

Turner thinks of *Snow White* sleeping the deep sleep of the drugged and betrayed.

"This was the photo that got picked up in newspapers everywhere a week after the bombing. Dad filed a lawsuit. Nobody did that back then. Never came to trial or nothing, I guess. But Dad said none of the papers ever ran it again. He also got an anonymous envelope a few days after his lawyer filed the suit with a typed apology and negatives of the print saying they was the originals and couldn't ever be duplicated if Dad didn't want. This copy we're looking at here is the only one left as far as I know.

"For near a week, every news organization in the country, and plenty abroad, had a feeding frenzy with the disaster and its depraved mastermind. They made a temporary airstrip out of Tobias Harmer's winter wheat field and paid him plenty for it just so reporters from *god knows where* corners of country could come in and get their story. And the public at large ate it up. Just like they eat anything up that's tragic and rancid and reeks of the underwing of the devil.

"And then, just as quickly as the news vultures and tourist-ghouls had come— they were just as quickly gone. Five days after the bombing, another Michigan Man usurped the throne of international attention away from Andrew P. Kehoe. Charles Lindbergh flew his *Spirit of St. Louis* across the Atlantic landing into Paris. And America's interest in a heap of dead school children done dwindled to a puff of smoke in the blow of a candle, boys. You never seen such a tuck tail and goodbye of press in your life my family told me later."

Turner's confused. "What? Why would the press take off because of some guy flying across the Atlantic?"

Carver just looks at Turner a sec. "Because Lindbergh was the first sonofabitch to do it. Don't they teach you that in school anymore?"

Turner looks at Luke. Luke looks back at him like, *seriously?*

"Well, maybe I heard something about some *Spirit*... plane, maybe. But fuck if I remember," Turner goes.

"Anyways, it was a big deal, Jason. Lindbergh came back to a hero's welcome in New York with the biggest parade this side of Thanksgiving. He was not just a national hero. But worldwide. He became a symbol. An icon of not only what America could achieve, but humankind.

"*What man can do.* Clem was always quoting what they all said in the papers and on the radio about what Lindbergh did. *What man can do.* The country, the world, celebrated another giant leap while back here in Michigan we still hadn't buried all our dead. We had no school. Bath was left in waste. The angel of death had come to our doors and taken more than just firstborns. Clem was always disgusted with the pictures and filmstrips of Lindbergh in Paris. The crowds. The fanfare. The tickertape. The unqualified heralding of the limitless potential of man and all his cleverness. He couldn't stomach it, I guess. The juxtaposition. How folks worldwide could so effortlessly ascend with Lindbergh to the celebrated clouded heights and so brainlessly make a man a god after just getting a glimpse of the oceanic darkness that lay beneath Bath and its child-slayer Kehoe. Clem once says to me, *What kind of shit are people made out of to change notions so fast?* I really didn't have an answer for him then.

"His feelings on this matter stayed with me through the years so's when the day came where Armstrong dropped his boot to the moon and the world heralded again the magic of such a moment, I couldn't help wondering who—*who* at this very moment was in the grip of a loss so heavy that they were weeping now while's the world cheered? Who in this wide world had died and who mourned for them so bitterly that it had all so sickened the well of the world's joy of landing on terrestrial orbs beyond our own planet? *What man can do....* Behold the depths and ascensions that man can surely attain. Alas. Huzzah.

"Well, history moved away from Bath leaving us to fend. Some folks moved. Most stayed. But a pall had fallen over the town. A restless silence. Families had a few more babies. I was born. But the town never got back to where it was. How could it? No matter how many babies it bore. The Volstead Act was still law. Then *The Depression* hit. I don't know how much we really noticed. As far as the drinking goes, it's pretty much known fact Prohibition wasn't enforced at all in this town. No police, no agency was gonna walk in here and tell these quiet grief-stricken farmers they couldn't drink themselves eye-shut so's they didn't have to lay all night wakeful thinking of their dead children. The Township of Bath ran rapids with Old Grand-Dad 'medicinal' whiskey and good goddamn to the Volstead.

"Here on the Belmont homestead, the damage of losing Olivia was total. Even with my arrival, the bright light of our family had been rent away as if with a knife. I was raised in the shadow of my sister's grave. I guess I didn't think anything of it at the time. I didn't know no better. But something happens to you when you grow up around pictures of the dead. When your mother and father and brothers slip into hallowed silences and observances you're just too young to understand. Home starts to turn into some serious and solemn cathedral. As I grew older, I spent most of my time outdoors. And alone at that. My sister, Sara, felt similar and grew up pretty solitary as well. I guess you could say we had each other, but then again, we didn't. I know that doesn't make much sense. But that's how we felt."

Carver grabs the photo album again and slides out another photograph. It showed an older Buddy, missing his arm wearing a denim-looking shirt all sewed up at his arm's nub. At his side was Sara looking to be eight or nine or so and little Carver in kiddie-overalls holding Sara's hand.

"I remember feeling the presence of Olivia in our house, around parts of the farm, in the barn or even out in the fields. Up in the branches of our trees. I remember feeling her presence well before I heard what a *ghost* was. Sara and I used to speak of it. We were too afraid to ask Ma or Daddy about it for a long time back then. Although Sara finally asked Ma while's we were at the table once if Olivia was a ghost and around with us here on the farm. But Ma just gave us a grown-up-like smile and told us to go back to eating our meatloaf and potatoes or whatnot. But we knew that meant *yes*—there were such thing as ghosts and hanging around in the twilight between this life and the next.

"Well, during my ninth summer, Dad had his heart attack walking to the house from the barn and Sara and I came running with Ma not far behind. He was grabbing at his chest while we hovered over him. Both Sara and me were scared and crying. I think he was trying to motion us two kids back but then gave up on it and just lay back staring up at the summer blue beyond. Ma kept calling his name, *David! David!* over and over like that. But he was falling into the next realm at that point. Then he mumbled out *Olivia. Oh, Olivia.* Later, Sara would maintain Dad saw Olivia at that final moment hovering like an angel or some such beckoning to him. But I never quite came around to that at first. At the time, I thought more like Dad knew he was at his last and just wanted to say his favorite child's name one last time. I thought his mind just naturally went to his most comforting thought when he knew he was about done. Her name was his last words.

"My brothers came back for the funeral. Clem had been working in Detroit but decided to stay on and work the farm as best he could and to help Ma out with Sara and me. He was a full-on drunk at that point though and getting worse. Buddy had just finished school in Ann Arbor. He stayed for Dad's funeral but then headed off to

Wisconsin with his fiancé to help run her father's tractor business. Except for his wedding and Ma's funeral much later, I would only see Buddy a handful of times ever again. He died about ten years back. I think he wanted very much to put Bath behind him and never look back. It's all right though. All these years I never held it against him.

"But everybody gets theirs. And that was ours."

Turner looked confused. "*Gets theirs* what?"

"Family tragedy," Carver goes. "Ain't no one exempted. Even old Lindbergh, that world-beating sonofabitch as Clem called him, finally got hit by life's grand shitstorm himself when someone kidnapped his little one-year-old boy. They were calling it the *Crime of the Century*. You should've seen it. The vultures were all over it. You couldn't watch a newsreel, turn on a radio, or flip a newspaper without hearing about the kidnapping. It was horrible. The kidnapper stole little Charles Jr. out of his crib and climbed down out of the second-floor nursery window of Lindberg's large estate in the woods of upper New Jersey. A ransom of fifty-grand was made. The press went madman over it. The Lindbergh's made public appeals to the kidnappers to give back little Charles. Cops, even J. Edgar Hoover and the FBI for chrissakes, went completely bloodhound trying to scare up leads and find the boy. It turned out though by the time they caught the guy who took him—some kraut hiding out in New York City—the boy's remains had been found. The bastard had stole away with Charles junior that first night and brained him with a hatchet not two miles from the Lindbergh's home in the Jersey woods and buried the poor child's corpse too shallow. The coyotes eventually got at him and unearthed him. The milkman found the boy one morning lying in a field.

"Clem took a sickly delight in the whole saga. He cut out every clipping he could find of the story and kept them tagged up on bunch of old corkboards in the tool room we had out in the barn. He'd sit nights drinking and looking at the clippings along with all the old news stories and photo prints he kept of the Consolidated School disaster. It was like on some twisted level Clem in his stupor shifted some of the rage he felt at the long-dead Kehoe over to Charles Lindbergh just because the guy had the gall to become a hero just days after we had lost our Olivia and Bath had lost its innocence, along with its soul in the bargain.

"Well, as Sara and I grew up, Ma became more and more distant. Like many her age in Bath who had had children in the bombing, she grew into an old and haunted woman. Clem was the same in some ways, but different in others. Where Ma continually wore her sadness like moth-ridden shawl she refused to take off, Clem was in a mystical state of rage over what had happened on May 18th, 1927.

"Ma would often spend some evenings on a rocker in the upstairs bedroom that used to be Olivia's. After Buddy and Clem moved out, the rocker was the only thing in the room. Other than clothes, and boxes of stuff in the closet, and framed pictures of mostly Olivia on the walls. It's the room just above the kitchen there, boys. In fact, I keep that rocker right where Ma left it. Looking out the tri-pane windows. Out to the fields. She'd just sit there and rock. Sometimes with a kerosene lamp at her feet. Sometimes just setting there in the dark.

"Clem had to get himself another job in town at a tire shop and we rented use of the fields to a corporate farming outfit stationed outside Lansing. But his drinking was getting worse. In fact, by the time Sara had graduated high school and moved out to Ann

Arbor, I was starting to find not only bottle after empty bottle of Old Grand-Dad everywhere, but also syringes Clem'd been using to get doped up something awful on. He was picking up junk from Lansing and sometimes driving or taking a bus out to Detroit for days on end before he'd show back up. So, eventually he lost his tire shop job too, and then I went to work with a construction crew to make ends meet for Clem, Ma, and me.

"One night I come in late after having some drinks with some old school pals of mine. It was the summer of 1949, and I hadn't seen one of my buddies, Scottie McFerren, since he had left for the service before the end of the war. Well, I stumbled out of my truck and tried to navigate the dark house so's to not rouse Ma or Clem. I got to my room and just plunkered down on my bed. I must've slept for a few hours passed out like that when I had a dream. The strangest thing I ever dreamed up to that point anyways. I was dreaming I was in this large basement. Didn't seem like it was a house. I was working on something. Standing on a small wooden stepladder working with something between the pipes up on the basement's ceiling. Then I realize I'm working with wires and the like. Putty. Then fuses. A contraption that I'd never seen before but somehow in my dream I know it's a timer. It was the damndest thing. All of it, boys—I tell you the truth. Then it all switches up and I'm driving this old truck down the streets of Bath. But it don't look like it did in 1949 though. And I slowly start to realize that my own hands upon the wheel don't look like my hands. And the tune I'm whistling ain't a tune I rightly know or ever heard ever in my life. It's a sunny morning. My window's down and the grass and road all smell of a freshly fallen round of rain. And then I hear a boom. A loud and deep concussion that hits me in my ribs and pulls at my balls if you know what I mean, boys. Up above the houses in the direction I'm driving, I start to see upward billows of smoke. And I just keep whistling this tune I aint never heard. I know in my dream that that's Bath Consolidated School I just heard blow. I know on some level deep in my head and heart that there's kids' dead and dying where that smoke is. I know my sister Olivia's there and my brothers' Clem and Buddy. And I ever so slowly realize that if I drive real fast. If I try real hard. Maybe, just maybe I can reach them and save them. But I can't. Cause there's a part of me that's happier than hell the school's blowed up. I realize that I'm practically pissing myself I'm so excited. The part that's in control. The part that's driving the car. The part that's so thrilled I can't stop smiling like a jackal coming across a plain full of leftover sun-fried carcasses. The part that can't stop whistling that song I ain't never heard before.

"And then *poof!* All up and sudden I'm awake. I'm me back in my bed on a hot August night in 1949. Lying in my bed drenched in sweat. But I can't move. Boys, I'm here to tell you—I felt stone-awake, but I could not lift my head or move my extremities to save my life. I tried to yell out to Ma or Clem, but my mouth wouldn't make no noise. Paralyzed in the dark. So's I started thinking I was having a stroke of some kind. But then I sense something, someone's standing just inside my doorway. I can't really see them because I can't move my head. But I feel them there. They take a few slow steps toward me in the dark. Now I know someone's in there with me. I just know it ain't Ma or Clem. I can see this dark shadow of a figure walking slowly up to my bed. I know that this close I should be able to tell who this is even in the dark—but I can't. The shadow seems to know I'm powerless to move. I try to scream out again, but my mouth only opens in a palsy contortion making no noise. The shadow stands just over my head.

It reaches out a hand. Covers my mouth. My eyes get to bulging. All sudden there's gobs of spit leaking out of my mouth. I can feel it oozing out against the pressing fingers of the dark stranger. The shadow starts to bend its head down. I brace myself for a vampire's kiss. A savage tear at my throat. Instead, I feel hot breath at my ear and a girl's voice whisper: *See…see beyond the veil into the mirror.*

"Then, like some sort of ignition, my brain fills with searing light, boys. Like my mind's been split like a log by the radiance of God. And I see the hammer of a revolver slam down and a flash of muzzle fire. Then, more light. Exploding stars of it reaching out like the epicenter of a great firework. Complete absence of dark, gray or fog. Stretching out, centersun-like. And then it climaxes—all this light. Then it recedes like an evening tide into the smell of smoke. Now flames. And finally, I see Clem lying on a floor, arm's crossed, coins atop his closed eyes, the whole of him on fire.

"The hand of the shadow lifts off my mouth. She stands straight and takes a step back into the darkness that swallows her up.

"And then I can move. I sit bolt straight up in my bed. I breathe in like a man that's been too long under the lake. I tear off my covers and turn on the lamp at my bedside. Nothing. I jump up and notice the flickers of light out of my window. There's smoke too. The barn's on fire. Damnation, I think. *The barn's on fire*. I jump down the stairs and out the house running towards the barn and kick open the door to the tool room. And there's Clem passed out on the dirt floor, whiskey bottle on its side near empty, belt around his arm, junk-shooter's on the table and flames from where his lantern's fallen and busted up and catching fire to the boarded walls of the room.

"The first thing I do is pull Clem outside by his legs and drag him out to the grass near the house. Next, I sprint like hell to the bucket near the well spout. I run back in and douse what I got but I can see right away it ain't no use. The flames have gone and multiplied at this point all over three out of the four walls and climbing into the hayloft. I knew once those flames touched one hair of that hayloft, the barn was done. And so it was. I turned to get out of there. But as I did, a swirl of papered ash flung up to my face and I clamped it down to myself as I made my final exit from the barn. Once I was out, I could see what I already knew. The whole of the barn's roof was on fire lighting the August night up in brilliance.

" '*Carver!*' called Ma from the front porch in her nightdress.

" 'I'm all right! Clem's all right. Ring up the volunteers.' I yell to her. She looked scared but nodded and went in to make the call. I moved my hand from my chest where I'd smothered the flaming debris that swirled out at me. The huge bonfire that was now our barn let me see the image in my hand perfectly.

"You know what I saw there, boys?"

Luke and Turner shake their heads, mesmerized by Carver's tale.

"There in my palm was what was left of two photos. A portrait of Olivia smiling, burnt in such a way that it did not destroy her image, but connected itself with another portrait of little one-year-old Charles Lindbergh junior. Clem had cut out the boy's picture from a glossy *Life* magazine. The edges of these two were burned to black wreck and char but their faces merged side by side, unmolested. These two children. Olivia at eight, the apple of my father's eye and baby Charles so chubby-cheeked and brand new looking—totally oblivious about how much pain and publicity his fate would engender. I let the image eat me up right then. I let both flood over me. I think I wept there, boys.

As I held them there like that in my palm, a hot gust came from the burning barn and blew Charles away out of my hand. I held Olivia fast for a moment longer though. But then I could hear Clem coming to behind me. I knew he'd need tending. So's I let Olivia's photo go too and went to go help my brother. The volunteer fire crew showed up not too long later and kept the blaze from spreading to the rest of the farm. The barn was a complete loss though. Couple of years later we were able to put up that Quonset there.

"Clem held on for another seven years. But by October '56 they found him dead in a motel room in Lansing. I identified the body. He'd had more junk in him than a poisoned rat. Truth is though, he was just another victim of the bombing of Consolidated School. He never recovered from that. Never recovered from not being able to bring Olivia home safe. *No*—Kehoe killed him too far as I'm concerned. Just took Clem longer to die from his wounds."

10

"So… there she is," Carver goes.

"What do you mean?" Turner goes.

"I mean, there's my story, kid. Believe it or not that's what you boys came for."

Turner growls a bit under his breath and sits back in his seat, exhaling all long and slow. "OK, OK… so what's the real reason somebody blows up forty-four kids?"

"Come again?" Carver goes.

"Kehoe," Turner goes. "You said before that the *nice and tidy* answer is he was super-pissed about paying taxes. But the way you said it made it seem like that wasn't the right answer. So what's the real answer, man?"

"Well, I sure don't think he was pissed about taxes or the fact that he was behind in his mortgage," Carver goes.

"Crazy then?" Turner goes.

"Let me ask you something, Jason." Carver leans over the table. "You crazy?"

Turner kind of grins. Looks over to Luke. Luke looks back at him and arches an eyebrow. "I ain't crazy. *I'm* fucked up. But that ain't crazy. There's a difference, man. My rather large deaf friend here on the other hand—now he's crazy. No offense—"

Luke just smiles like *none taken*.

Carver sits back again in his chair. "OK then. I don't think Kehoe was crazy either. I think he was probably how you say, 'fucked up,' in some ways. Maybe a lot of ways. But not the *madman* or *crazed killer* the press or history felt comfortable labeling him. In fact, right after the bombing there was so much horseshit flying around about what made Kehoe do it and what pushed him over the edge and whatnot, that it seemed the papers and folks just couldn't stop with the speculation. There was even this article—Clem kept it and I read it a few times—but this article was all about how these fancy professors over at the University in Ann Arbor were studying the remains of Kehoe's skull to see if he was some kind of throw-back to Cro-Magnon times. Like he was some atavistic caveman on account of the thick heavy brow the guy had. That it was all because Kehoe was really some left-over from a more primitive age of man that led him to eventually kill the weak around him and thin the herd of Bath as it were.

"*Horseshit*—Clem and I always thought."

"So, if all that wasn't it, then what was?" Turner goes.

"Well, I don't think there was any doubt that Kehoe had rage. Loaded brim full of it. No doubt about that. And I ain't saying that rage can't make a body crazy. But with Kehoe I don't think it was a hot rage. Meaning that when most of us get that mad, we burn like flame real quick and vibrant but then can just as quickly burn out. I don't think that was so with Kehoe. Now understand, I'm just going on growing up with the story, with hearing about this man all my life from my family and the people I grew up with every day here in this town. But that said, I still feel like I *know* this man. At least as well as anybody around here ever did or ever will.

"But my point is, kid, I don't think Kehoe's rage was hot. I think it was cold. Solid-like. Like an iceberg. And I believe an ice-rage harbored in a man like Kehoe is a dangerous mix. Because that man was cold at heart anyway. I don't think he ever cared for nobody the kind of way that makes a soul warm. I don't think some people can feel quite the way most people should, or as much, about other people. And when you add the lack of that warmth with a cold and indifferent rage, I think you get a man like Kehoe. And people best bewares that come near to him.

"I don't think he hated Emory Huyck all that much more than he hated anyone else. If he did—why didn't Kehoe just drive up to Huyck's house and shoot him dead? Or if he really wanted to blow him up, just blow him up alone? It would've been easy to do compared to planning and taking the pains to blow up a whole school.

"Clem and I used to talk it over endlessly. Talk over the bombing and Kehoe. Back when I was almost done with high school and even when I was working construction, he and I would stay up nights sometimes talking it all over sitting at the kitchen table with just a lantern for light, drinking Old-Grandad out of Ma's canning jars. On and on about this bastard that had killed our sister, maimed our brother and whose loathed spirit haunted every godforsaken nook and cranny of this town. And you know what we come up with, boys?"

Luke and Turner wait for his answer.

"Movie screens. All countrywide. Newsreels is what he wanted. Headlines of what he'd done. What he'd accomplished all alone while not one of the shallow fools in Bath ever even suspected him until it was too late. That the world would know the name Andrew P. Kehoe now and for ages after and the glorious wrath he had wrought. See boys, Huyck wasn't his enemy. Even Bath wasn't his enemy. The wide world was, and every godforsaken pissant in it that didn't see what kind of genius was alive in the mind of Andrew P. Kehoe. And when it's the world that's your enemy—well, then—there's weak spots galore to attack it at every turn."

Carver fishes out another clipping from the folder. "See this?"

Luke and Turner look down to an article with a photo sitting in the middle of it. The photo shows this placard all tied to a barbwire fence.

"This sign was strung up on Kehoe's fence at the front of his property. He knew people'd find it eventually after they went over the rubble of his burnt farm and found his what was left of his wife," Carver goes.

The small placard reads: **MONSTERS ARE MADE NOT BORN.**

"Can't say it's the most original thing I ever read, but that's all the world would get out of Kehoe as far as what he'd done. Him basically saying it was the world's fault he done it. The world's fault he turned into a monster. Like it wasn't his choice to turn monster in the first place. Anyways, I don't even think Kehoe would argue that expressing himself with words wasn't his strong suit. It was his actions he was relying on to do his talking."

"So you think he did all this just to get some attention?" Turner goes.

"Not attention, son. *Credit.* A little overdue goddamn recognition. Like this was forced attrition for the rebuke of his unrecognized genius. And now he's gotten his version of immortality, maybe."

"Cheese and rice," Turner goes. "What's with using all these big fucking words?"

Carver bursts into chuckles. "Sorry there, kid. I guess really when you boil it all down, what I'm saying is that it wasn't madness, or rage really as to why Kehoe did this as much as it was simply *evil*."

"Well duh, man. Like no shit Sherlock," Turner goes.

Luke fumbles for his pen and quickly writes,

Carver—

what do <u>*you*</u> *mean by 'evil?'*

"I mean, I think Kehoe had crossed over beyond just holding a grudge, beyond just being enraged. I think he crossed over into evil probably years before he ever came to Bath before he ever even married Nellie. I can't be sure. It's just me guessing but I think people can cross over into it—and that you have to willingly cross that fjord, boys. And further, that a body *knows* when they make it too. And I do believe that Andrew P. Kehoe was evil, and by the time he reached Bath, there was nothing anyone could've done about it.

"You boys ever hear that old expression? 'Evil is old of date and lurks in shadows long.' I suppose some would say it's the devil, but I come to believe evil's older than him too and that the devil's just one of the first to cross that fjord. Because it's evil that's cold. Not hot like madness, or love, or hate, or even joy or fear. It's evil that's cold and large as a stone-jagged mountain and lives well preserved in those who are best open to receive it."

Carver sits back again and his wooden chair creaks at the glued pegs that hold it together. He laces his fingers together over his gut and looks at the two boys.

Luke and Turner are quiet. Outside the snow continues to blow, blurring out of the gray sky somewhere all indistinguishable.

It's Turner that snaps out of the silence first. "So—that's it then?"

Carver nods slowly. "That's it. That's my story as far as what Rozzy wanted you to hear anyways."

Turner groans. "Ugh, yeah, OK. So now tell me why exactly she wanted us to hear that?"

"Why don't you tell me?" Carver goes.

"You serious? So now you're a smartass, old-timer? Let me read that letter," Turner goes.

Carver snatches the envelope up. "No."

"What? Why the fuck not?"

"You got some mouth on you, son," Carver chuckles.

"I aint your fucking son. Now why not?"

"It's not for you. I understand you have your own letter from her. What she wrote for me was for me. Just like what she wrote for Luke there was for him. And just like what she wrote for you was just for you. I'm sorry I can't give you more answers and that's mostly because I really don't have many, Jason. I don't know how Rosalind knew the things she did when it came to me and my family. And I don't know why she did what she did to herself. I'm sorry as hell about that by the way. I am. I'm sorry you lost your friend. I don't know how this all works. But I do know that somehow, sometimes, things *transcend*, boys. That sometimes the dead aren't completely dead. That sometimes those of us living are given eyes and ears to the workings beyond the periphery. Especially when we are in the grip of the tremors of things."

"*Agh*—I don't believe this shit. I can't understand what you're even fucking saying, man," Turner goes. "*Cheese*—" He stands up. He looks down at Luke. "You know why the fuck we're here? She write *you* why we got to see this guy and listen to all that?"

Luke writes nothing.

"*Agh*—fine. You know what? Fuck both you guys. I need a smoke," Turner goes and storms out the kitchen door out to into the dusty snow.

Carver and Luke watch Turner's back and shoulders hunch up all cold and tense while he smokes looking out in the direction of the Quonset and the fields.

"He's something else. Your friend there," Carver remembers saying after a while.

Luke smiles, nods.

"Did you know Rosalind well?"

Luke shakes his head.

"Funny, then."

Luke grabs his pad. Rips off a note.

What's that?

"Nothing," Carver starts. "Just how it all works. How things come together, I guess."

They sit watching Turner puff a little more.

"Say—" Carver goes again. "Were he and Rosalind… were they steady?"

Carver remembers Luke taking his time with the question. He remembers the big teenage boy just looking at him for a sec before jotting a reply.

I don't really know.

Luke and Carver see Turner walk out of their sight. A small alarm beeps back from somewhere in the kitchen and Carver gets up to fumble around in one of the cabinets over the sink. The old man shakes out a couple of finger-tip size tablets out of a flypaper-colored bottle and swallows them down with a guzzle of tap water.

Carver comes back to the table. "Another thing Rosalind and I share."

What's that?

"Our ailment. I don't know exactly what she was taking for it though. In your letter—she must have said enough too, eh?"

Luke just stares back at Carver.

Enough to what?

"Enough to believe," Carver goes.

Luke shakes his head. He writes.

She said enough for me to act.

Do you believe?

Carver chuckles again. "Oh yes. Count me in. I'm a *believer. Veils and mirrors*, she said to me. We're all veils and mirrors. Behind and underneath it all, we're all part of the same whole, kid. And rightly heard, all tales are one. Rosalind showed me so, and I believe."

11

Cars are starting to flip their headlights on zooming past them on the opposite side of the interstate. Luke turns his on too. The dashboard glows all blue making both of them look like they were glowing underwater or something. They've said nothing since leaving Carver Belmont's farm.

"Hey—" Turner goes.

Luke just keeps his eyes focused ahead of him.

"Hey," Turner goes again.

Luke turns to him.

"I ain't like that Kehoe guy, man," Turner says. "I ain't."

Luke nods back to him like, *I know…*

"I mean I'd never do something like that. You know?"

Luke nods again.

Turner looks to the road ahead of them. After a bit he taps Luke on the shoulder and goes, "Do you think that's why Rozzy wanted me to hear that old guy's story? You think she thought I was turning into that guy? That I was going to lose it so bad I'd do something like that?"

Luke looks like he considers it a sec then shrugs his shoulders.

"Hey, man—" Turner goes, getting all pissed now. "What do you think?"

Luke gets all intense-looking and merges off, pulling over into the first cracked up asphalt lot he comes to. Turner watches as Luke hauls out his notepad and fires off a note.

I don't know, Jason. No clue. The bigger question is what do you think? You're the one that's supposed to have the answer for that. I was just supposed to get you there—to Carver's house.

"Cheese and fuck, man. I don't know. That's why I'm asking you to help me figure it out. I mean you're the one that seems to have some weird-ass lifeline to Rozzy, man. You gotta know something that will help me get my head around this. So spill, dude."

Seriously—I don't have anything on this. I don't know why she wanted you to hear all the Bath bombing stuff. What's your letter say?

There's quiet between them with the roar and the hum of the overpass above.

"I wouldn't have fucking gone through with it, you know," Turner goes. "I wouldn't have done it, man. That night at Harper Lake. Course you probably already knew that going in, I guess. Killing Dylan too, man. I couldn't have done that either. Not when it comes down to it. I couldn't have. I wouldn't have."

Luke writes, rips, puts her in drive and gives Turner the note as he tears the car out of the lot.

Dude—it's time you read your letter from Rozzy.

12

Abby

You know like every teenage kid, and I don't care who you are, every kid has fights and different little frictions with their parents. Some definitely more than others but everybody's had to go a few rounds with their *rents*, right? Even the straightlaced angel types too. I mean, if anyone tells you they never had a tiff with their parents over something, they're lying to you. They gotta be, you know?

And I gotta say that up to this point, my parents had been doing pretty good with the whole pregnancy deal. Way better during those first few months than I thought they would.

I mean, my mom was always kind of good with dealing with the big stuff. Not always the case though with the smaller things. You know she would totally like freak out if somebody didn't do the dishes right or leave the stupid porch light on all night or something dumb like that. But usually if it was a real crisis—Mom was pretty clutch. Like when Kate fell off her bike and broke her arm and hit her head really bad in the driveway when she was like seven or eight. I was scared to death that Katie was really going to die when I saw her hit the pavement so hard. I was balling, screaming for Mom to come out. And when she did, she was so quick, so assertive to get Kate in the car and calling the emergency room. She made sure we were buckled. Little details like that in such a crazy situation. And I just remembered feeling Mom was in control. It made me feel better. Like taken care of, you know?

So, like I said, I wasn't too surprised that my Mom handled the news of me getting pregnant with Peter pretty well. The surprise was just how well Dad took it when it all you know, like came to light. Because usually it was my father that was the hothead. He's the one that was always quick to bring the smack down, if you know what I'm saying. Our dad, Kate and I always knew, was always super quick to defend us or punish us. But that night after dinner when I told them, there was no smokestack lighting from him at all. In finding out about his daughter's premature pregnancy, he seemed to adopt my mom's crisis-mode *we-support-our-daughter* demeanor. I mean he was obviously still like affected on a totally emotional level. Seriously, you could see heartbreak all over his face—but as bad as his heartbreak was over my mistake, you could tell he was feeling more love and for his daughter at the time. Like he knew it was more important than anything at that moment to show support for me. Most of what I remember from him at the end of the little convo where I told them everything after freaking out at the family dinner table was him hugging me and saying over and over, *We love you Abby, we love you… no matter what this is going to be OK.*

But in the months after them finding out, starting the whole adoption process, and seeing his daughter start to really show, it's like you could just see Dad starting to change his attitude about the whole thing. He started to get more and more short with me about like everything. And he kept referring to the whole thing as my *predicament*. Or *Abby's predicament.* Or if it wasn't for *your predicament* such and such would be different. It felt to me like out of nowhere Dad wasn't supportive anymore and just totally became edgier about the whole thing and more judgmental. It's like as soon as I was having to change my wardrobe and everybody from strangers to friends and relatives could tell on sight I was *knocked up*, that's when he started in with lectures about my poor choices and all these huge choices about how my life was now going to be forever different even with me giving the baby up for adoption. It just seemed endless from him all of a sudden.

And it was starting to tick me off.

And one night I got home from hanging out with Gabby and Jenna and Mandy getting smoothies or whatever, and Dad calls me into the living room for a family meeting. And he's got Mom and Kate on the sofa while he's all standing up directing things. And then he just starts launching in, "Look, Abby… now that there's been some time to really take in this new reality our family finds ourselves in, I think there's somethings we should discuss quite openly. Especially for Kate's benefit. You know, so she can avoid some of the pitfalls of your choices…"

What! Even now I can't believe some of the things he was saying. I mean, now that there's been some time between then and now—I guess I understand a little more where he was coming from at least. I mean, I understand. He *hated* the fact that his oldest daughter was sexually active in high school. That I hid that fact for so long about Peter and I's relationship before I got pregnant. That he *hated* that everyone knew his daughter had had sex and got pregnant and all that went along with that and that he wanted to make absolutely sure that his younger daughter didn't end up the same way. I get all that, I really do—but at the time I just felt I was being continually judged for the same decisions over and over like on a never-ending spin-cycle or something.

My thought was, 'hey—I already told you. You know I'm sorry. I'd totally do it differently if I could. So, what's with all the stewing and the anger and the freaking laying on the guilt trips *now?*'

Well anyway, I don't remember everything that was said—but I remember the meeting ending in Dad and I arguing and Mom trying to get us all to calm down while Kate probably just snuck off to her room.

When the worst was done, I told my parents I needed to cool down and asked Mom for keys to the car so I could drive to a park or something to think. Then instead, I drove to Peter's house.

His parents were out with some rich friends at some fancy place having dinner, so we went back to his bedroom.

Peter just let me vent and vent about my dad and how much it just kind of sucks being pregnant and how it seems everyone just judges you on sight for being a teenage girl and pregnant no matter where you are. Like you can almost hear their sneering little thought aimed at you like, *doesn't that girl know about freaking birth control? What a waste, what a shame. Serves her right.* All stuff like that. He just listened and nodded and agreed that it sucked and let me go off.

At one point I just asked him to hold me. He scooted closer to me on the bed and just put one arm around me. It felt good. I put my head on his chest. We just sat there like that for a while. And even though we were still technically together, we hadn't really done anything physically with one another since finding out about the baby. I mean, other than Peter's weird little request for a blowjob, there had been no hint or pressure from him at all. So, to have his arm around me, my head on his chest, his fingers starting to go gently through my hair—all of it felt so good. So reassuring. Especially after all my dad's guilt trips.

And then he starts to stroke my arm up and down. And then we seem to be falling down and lying on the bed facing each other. Part of me had thought that Peter might not want to do much with me after our awkward conversation in front of my house. I even thought he might start to get freaked out about my body once I started showing. Until that moment on his bed, I guess I wasn't even sure what to think about being physical with him again.

But then he was kissing me. Open mouth kisses. Lip-sucking kisses. And I started to melt. Then Peter's hands started their familiar roving. Caressing me up, down, everywhere. Everywhere *except* for my slowly growing belly.

Erif

IX

"Sister!" Angel squealed upon seeing Annabella run the path towards their simple house.

Annabella did not stop in her running until she collided with her younger sister, swept up in the tightest of embraces. After lifting her up off her toes, Annabella kissed her sister's cheek.

The bell beckoning for the Lottery kept up its tolling in the middle of the village. The tolls became angry with waiting.

"Angel," Annabella said. "We have no time. We must go to the Great Hall. But sweet sister, we *do* have a plan. Come, and do not fear. Where's father?"

"I'm here, lasses..." their father emerged from the doorway. Bloodshot, but as sober as he got in the mornings these days. "Let us go now, my daughters."

"Take my hand," Annabella said.

Angel beamed at her sister. "I told you all would be well once you talked with Quindarius."

Annabella forced a smile as frail as puddle-ice.

The streets were crowded with villagers, their faces tight with worry. There was not a child that Annabella saw that did not have a parent touching them or holding them. When they finally arrived in the courtyard of the Great Hall, the bellman stopped the bell's ringing and a low nervous murmur breathed from the people of Thorn.

The morning sun created long cool shadows as its light was obstructed by the Great Hall and the other larger buildings surrounding the courtyard. Every villager looked up to the platform in front of the Hall's entrance. There stood the village Elders along with Cyvilard and a troop of Tarrenbacks all with their crossbows slung around their shoulders. Also, up there with them was the Wheel—-the large cylinder that contained small leather straps each one containing the name of a child six winters and older from every household in Thorn.

"People of Thorn!" Quindarius called for order. "We know why we are here today. This morn, no matter whose name is called, all of us will have heavy hearts."

Annabella looked up to where Quindarius stood and felt a wave of disgust.

"Tis in moments such as these, that we should remember just how blessed we are to live in such a bountiful valley. That we all live most days in peace and abundance. That for generations we have lived not only as a village in harmony—-but as a large family. All of us extended fathers, mothers, children to each other outside of our own natural kin."

Quindarius paused. The old man's face strained. "But my brothers, sisters, and children of Thorn... such a rich life as we do have here in this valley does not come without cost. Our freedoms do not come without goodly sacrifice. We know that sometimes the good of the body politic must needs come before the good of the individual. And that is why we all come here today in submission for the greater good. Elder Cyvilard, you may proceed..."

"Angel..." Annabella turned to her sister. "Remember, we have a plan. And though they take you, we will come for you."

Angel reached up and took Annabella's face in both her hands and held her as if her sister's face was a baby fawn. "I know sister. All will be as it should be."

"Spin the Wheel!" Cyvilard commanded and one of the Tarrenbacks broke rank and turned the crank connected to the cylinder of names.

Every face in the massive crowd looked on the brink of complete terror. Except for Angel.

Cyvilard raised one hand from his cloak and the Tarrenback stopped his spinning. The bald elder opened the Wheel's gate and every villager gasped.

Cyvilard produced a leather strap and held it high in the air. "Fate has chosen our next savior," he said and then went through the show of reading the strap's name. "Angel, daughter of Vidgis!"

"No!" their father belted out.

"Here she be!" yelled a lady standing near them. The rest of the nearby villagers helped point Angel out.

"Here!" they pointed and hollered.

Four Tarrenbacks jumped down from the platform and rushed through the crowd to take custody of her. Two of them grabbed Angel by each arm while her father pushed his way through to fall in the dirt on his knees before his daughter. "Please," he said, sobbing. "Please let me say my peace to her, my Angel, before ye take her!"

One of them nodded. "Say yer peace, man."

"It's all right, father," Angel said. "You'll be all right."

"*Baa*," her father said in a loathsome burst of spit and snot. "Angel you're my love, my heart. I love ye, my own, my daughter."

Straining against the grip of her captors, Angel stretched her head forward and kissed her father on his head. Annabella then stood forward and put her hand on her father's shoulder and looked to her sister through her own tears.

"I'll take care of him," Annabella said.

Angel nodded and gave her sister a last grin and looked up to the Tarrenbacks. "I'm ready."

As they led her back toward the Great Hall, the crowd began to weep and call Angel's name. Droves of them drew in closer to her and the

Tarrenbacks and reached out hands to touch the hems of her skirt, to catch a graze of her hair.

"*Bless ye, child!*" they said.

"*The Angel that delivers us!*" they proclaimed.

Up on the platform, Quindarius and the other Elders quickly made their way inside the Great Hall, while Cyvilard stayed looking out to the crowd and finally resting his triumphant gaze solely on Annabella.

Annabella stared defiantly back. She noticed that under his robes he also wore a black shirt with a high collar, and under that collar must surely be the bruises she gave him in the aviary.

Cyvilard stared at her and was mildly surprised she wasn't more... *terrified* maybe? Or even more *grief-stricken* perhaps? But no matter, thought Cyvilard. Soon Annabella would fall again under his torments, of that he would make certain. And this time, he thought when he had finished his lusts with her, she would die. In fact, Cyvilard fantasized about it up there on the platform. In front of all of Thorn, he allowed himself to see visions of his future atrocities with Annabella.

A burst of laughter escaped his throat. And as he saw Annabella leaving the courtyard with her father at her arm, Cyvilard vowed to have her so.

13

"Hey! Look who it is..." Turner's dad goes. He watches Turner stride in through the front door. "My woebegone prodigal son. Back from his *Va-K* from the respectable part of town..."

Turner just looks at his dad all whatever and tosses his backpack on the couch.

He hears the toilet flush and Kevin Wilhelm from school comes out of the bathroom. "What's the motherfucking haps, crackerjack?"

"Aw—what the fuck?" Turner goes and turns to his dad. "For fucking real, man? What you got him here for?"

"Chill, dude." Kevin plops on the couch beside Turner's backpack. "I be taking over Kid T's spot."

"Oh the fuck you are. Dude, you don't even know what Kid T's spot really was. That wigger was on more than one payroll, you punk-ass—"

"Now stand down, the both of you," Turner's dad goes. "Relax, Jace. Relax. Kid T's still MIA, so K-Van here's gonna pick up the slack up with the schoolhouse rock, you know?"

"*K-Van?* What the hell's with you cabbies, man? You guy's gotta come up with your porno name before you can pimp the tweak, or what?" Turner grabs his crotch. "You know what, *K-van*? This here's *A-sac* and my little buddy's seen more action than—"

"Fuck you, dude—"

Turner's dad chucks a pillow from his recliner at Kevin's face and gives Turner a shove. "*Enough.* Christ—both of you shut the hell up. You guys fight like a couple of bitch-ass brothers."

"He aint my brother..." Turner goes and makes for the kitchen.

"True dat, but—" Kevin says and hauls out a short fat black and gray handgun from behind his belt and clicks out the clip and makes a big show of inspecting it.

Turner goes back to Kevin on the couch. "What is *that*?" he goes more to his dad than to Kevin.

"It's a Berretta Px4 subcompact, dog," Kevin goes and drives the clip back home with a click.

Turner smirks. "Well, thank you mister fucking *Guns & Ammo*. So what is this, Dad? Are all your cabbies gonna be packing hardware now? This part of the new 'crew' you putting together because of all that's been going down?"

"Jace..."

"But like I was gonna say, maybe I'm also here to protect your ass. Huh, *J*," Kevin goes.

"*What?*"

"All right, Kev," Turner 's dad goes. "Out. You got the package, right? Go pull the camel and call me if whatever, man. Otherwise, I'll see you tomorrow."

"OK, man." Kevin gets up. "You the boss, Pops..." he says and heads out the front door.

With Kevin gone, Turner's dad takes a closer look at his son. "Whoa—hey, Jace. You look good, kid. So what you been doing over there at that soccer kid's crystal palace, huh?"

"Sleeping. Look, you really tapping Kevin Wilhelm?"

Turner's dad falls into his recliner. Turner takes the cue and sits down on the couch.

"Look, Jace—Kid's been gone weeks now, and business has got to get back up and running here. If I don't get my shit together—and I mean like quick, chaos will reign here in the subs. And even though you're crystal and will *stay* crystal, you know if I don't get my shit together here, that means less flow for you too, son. I know you know that. So, I'm sorry if you don't like my choice of entry-level cabbies. And I know that's gotta make for some awkward shakes for you down at school because you know Kev and Kev knows you. But who the fuck knows? Maybe this thing with Kevin and some of his guys'll be temporary. Maybe—"

"Ah, fuck…" Turner hisses and covers his eyes with his hands for a sec.

"What?" his dad goes.

"OK. For one thing, Wilhelm's a major douche bag. He may know some people and be smart about how he parties and who he parties with—but he knows jackshit about the biz. And with him *carrying a piece…*"

"But—"

"Dad, the kid's gonna get pinched within a week. And what do you think he's gonna do? Where's that leave you? Where the fuck's that leave me?"

"No, *no*—it ain't gonna be like that with him, son. He knows the deal. He knows little blemishes on his record don't mean shit if he's ever gonna be a lifer. He ain't gonna burn me on a one-year stretch that he might only sit five months on. He knows burning me burns him for life in the biz where he knows the real money's at. And he's OK with being left in the dark about all my other shit. He gets that that's how you start in the biz."

"Hell's, dad. I get why you wanted me clear of your biz. I get it, man. But try as you might to shield me, make me crystal or whatever—I'm still so knee-deep in this shit, that I *know* your biz. I know how it works. The thick and the thin, man. And I *know* that Kevin kid will rat if he sees the right advantage, man. You can't trust him."

"Hey, you know Kid T going AWOL has put me in a spot. And I need movers like right fucking now. I need cabbies that can read but can't spell and those are goddamn hard to find. But this Wilhelm kid's close."

Turner just looks at his dad like *whatever, man.*

"Jace, there's—there's something else."

"What?"

"Couple days ago. You know Billy Ryan and Jacob Dugan, right?"

Turner shrugs. "Yeah, I guess. Billy's like been out of school for three years now and Duggy dropped out like last year. So what about a couple days ago?"

"Well, those two were found dead in a car out on the access highway by the interstate. It's been all over the news."

"Shit. Were they capped?"

"Shotguns. Damn near blew Billy Ryan's head off is the word."

"*Shit.* So you're thinking this is that Scotty tweaker from Lester's and that Maintenance Man guy? I mean, that doesn't even make any sense, man. Duggy and Billy smoked the shit but they ain't dealers."

"Hold up, because you ain't heard the best part," Turner's dad goes. "The car they were driving was fucking Kid T's Mitsubishi."

"The *fuck* you say?"

"I'm pretty sure they thought it was you. Those psychos clocked that Mitsu and laid in wait and just struck those boys with no hesitation."

"And they're still out there? The cops haven't picked them up yet?"

"As far as we know. In fact, I don't even know for sure that cops even got the tip it was those two."

"So—what the fuck then? Do those assholes know that wasn't Kid and me?"

"I don't know. There's like no way to know. Tweakers like that. Totally unpredictable and no way of knowing if they even checked, or cared, or even remember it very well."

"So you're telling me that there might be a couple hardcore glassholes rolling around out there, armed to the fucking teeth in shotgun shells, looking to blow me away on sight?"

"Maybe. But Jace, you gotta understand this is gonna be for like a limited time only. You know? If they are still roving around out there, there's no way sky-high idiots loaded with heavy muscle are going to last long before they get the attention of the cops. And then it's fucking *BANG-O!* You know what I mean? Because those two aren't getting arrested. It's gonna be *Donkey Kong* with shotguns a' blazing until enough cops show up and fucking execute those assholes for us. So relax, son—it's just a matter of time."

"Relax, huh?" Turner hops up from the couch. "Yeah, that's great, Dad. I'll just fucking relax then. Cheese and rice. Not even to mention what this means about Kid T."

"I don't know what this means about Kid," Turner's dad goes.

"What do you mean you don't know? Isn't it obvious? He's *dead*, Dad. Either he died of his wounds from that night, *or*—"

"Or what?"

"Or Dre's crew capped him. To shut him up and shut him down."

"I don't know, son. Just because they had his car, doesn't necessarily mean Kid's dead. I mean, if Dre did him, then how the fuck did Billy Ryan and Jacob Dugan get his Mitsubishi? It makes no fucking sense."

Turner stares at the turned off television screen for a bit. A never-ending collection of questions and fears ping around in his brain like a dropped box of BB's.

"Where you going?"

"My room, man. Gotta chill. Gotta think."

"It's gonna be OK, Jace. I'm not gonna let anything happen to you. You know that, right? *Right*?"

Turner closes the door to his bedroom and sits on the edge of the bed. He thinks. Every once in a while, he hears a car pass by out under the streetlight. He can't help imaging the Shotgun Brothers rolling by, staring up at his window pumping shells into their chambers.

He looks at his hands. Marvels about how steady they are. Amazing how just going a week without juice and junk can like totally re-boot your body's system.

He looks to the clock next to his bed. It's only seven o'clock. Dark but not late.

He gets up and goes over to clothes hamper. Man, it reeks. Pulls out the SIG from right where he left it and sits back on the bed. Just like Kevin had done, Turner clicks out the gun's clip and checks it. Full mag. He slams it back home.

He digs in his pocket for his phone. Texts Luke:

getting out of dodge for a few days maybe weeks

Throwing fresh clothes in his backpack Turner is freaking amazed when his phone tells him that Luke's texting back:

what's goin on?

Turner just lets out a weak laugh and texts:

fuck, what isn't, dude? i'll shout in a couple, ok?

After Turner tucks the SIG into his pack's side pocket, Luke's reply comes:

ok. Be careful, brosef. Read that letter yet?

"Fucking '*brosef*,'" Turner mumbles and shakes his head. He lifts up his mattress and pulls Rozzy's letter out. Taps the envelope on his chin a couple of times and shoves it into his backpack and zips it up.

getting to it. c-ya...

And hits send.

14

Someone flicks Erik Volgstaad's bedroom light switch on.

"Erik…" goes his mother's voice all urgent. She shakes him by the shoulders on his bed. "Erik, wake up…"

"Mom? What?" Erik goes all groggy. "What is it? What's going on?"

Her arms are crossed as she looks down on him; her face creased. "Ryan's downstairs and you need to go see him."

"What? Why?"

She steps back to the door and just says, "Get dressed."

After throwing on some jeans and a long-sleeve T-shirt, Erik charges down the stairs where Ryan waits for him by the door. Even Erik's dad's up standing next to his mom looking all concerned.

"Ryan?"

"It's Izzy's dad…" Ryan goes. "He just passed away a couple of hours ago. Coach called me. She's got a friend that works night shift at the hospital. He tipped her."

"Where's Izzy?"

"At home now. Luke just texted me. He thinks the three of us should go over there and you know, just be with him. You know—if he's up for that."

"Is that a good idea?" goes Erik's dad. "I mean, at this hour?"

"Well—we'll come straight home if it isn't," Erik goes and grabs a jacket out of the closet. "Mom, we'll—"

"Don't worry." Erik's mom gives him a quick hug. "Go be with your friend."

Outside on the driveway Erik's about to open the passenger door to Ryan's car when he's struck with a pain as if he had been shanked with an ice pick.

"*Erik*—" Ryan runs around to help him up.

Tears brake through Erik's eyes and run down his face. A huge sob takes over his breathing and he covers his face with one hand. "Sorry. I—*sorry*…"

Ryan puts a hand on his friend's back. "Hey—it's OK, man."

"I don't know," Erik goes but then stops to fight another wave of crying. "Ugh—I don't know where this is coming from. I—"

"It's OK, Erik. I love him too."

Erik takes in a big breath and looks back at Ryan through the shadows and the tears. "Let's go…" he says, and they both get in and take off down the desolate street.

15

Jason

So. Rozzy. I guess here it goes from the top.

After packing my shit, I creep downstairs where Dad's just cracking into a can of Miller after hitting his glass pipe and checking shit on his laptop. I can tell it's biz shit because he gets all secretive and stuff and tilts the screen closer to him. He goes, 'where you going?' and I go 'to Toe's for the night.' So anyway, he gets all suspicious like I knew he would and says how's he supposed to trust me when I been sneaking off to Luke's and not telling him and whatever.

So I act like I'm getting all pissed at him not believing me and I toss my phone to him and say, "Call'em. Check for yourself if you don't believe me."

He catches my phone and looks at me and then looks at the phone and I can tell by the way his eyes are glazing that he's starting to feel the crystal he just inhaled. "OK," he goes, "I think I will, you little bastard."

I tell him to tap my recents and he makes the call. "Hey Toe—it's me, Pop's. Yeah—hey, you got plans for Jace to come over tonight? All right. No. Yeah, thanks," he goes and then presses end. "I guess you're good. But Jace, you gotta understand why I gotta keep close tabs on you, right?"

But I just tell Dad that *hey*—maybe I'm safer at Toe's, Luke's, or wherever else than fucking here—especially if those fucking Shotgun Brothers figure out I'm like his son.

But he just shakes his head and goes, "Look, I'll see you tomorrow. Keep your eyes open. OK?"

Rozz, not like you don't already know this about my pops—but he can be such a stupid fuck-head sometimes. I mean he's still like my dad—but *fuck!* Can't tell sometimes if I love him or hate him or both in like equal measure, man. But cheese and rice can the guy be a ditz sometimes, man. I mean doesn't he even realize that Toe and I got each other's back enough to confirm whatever bullshit play the other makes—especially if like our parents start blindly investigating and shit? I mean fucking *duh*, man.

So I go squealing out of there in my piece of shit Civic and sure as shit go right past the turn to Toe's and keep heading back out to the interstate. I just go, Rozz. I mean I was thinking *fuck him*, man. Fuck sitting around waiting for those shotgun assholes to find me. And fuck having to sit there knowing that some cunt like Kevin Wilhelm thinks he's out there protecting *me* for chrissakes.

I was thinking might as well bounce all the way to Buffalo. Find my moms. Chill there for a few days—maybe weeks. See what she's up to. Fucking not have to worry about someone wanting to cap my ass. Was thinking maybe even get enough distance from all the bullshit here to get some perspective. Away from school, away from this town, away from Dad's biz. And even away from Luke's crazy ass—even though he just helped me get off the juice and junk.

So I'm hauling down the highway cranking tunes. We're talking fucking blaring, man. Smoking cig after cig too, Rozz. Figuring I could maybe even make my mom's and Aunt Laurie's by midnight if I cruised. So I just start grooving to my tunes, man. Finding the ones that really get me going. A few of your favorites too. I was thinking maybe after a good night's sleep at Mom's, maybe I'd finally open your letter and just sit and read and take it all in somewhere quiet with a cup of strong-ass coffee, man. I just kept thinking about you and how special you are/were compared to me. *Serious*, Rozz—I just bawled right there driving in the car.

Why, Rozz?

Why did you have Luke and I go to Bath and hear that old guy's story? I mean what the hell was with that? Questions about all that shit was like all I was thinking about after that, and I just started hoping that your letter would answer it all—but I was still so fucking afraid to open that thing up. Afraid of what you had to say. I'm *still* afraid, girl. Even now that I—but anyway…

So this little get away trip really started getting nuts once I pulled off the interstate to this shit-hole gas station right outside Niagara Falls and once I crossed back into the States. I'm filling up or whatever and it was starting to get chilly as a bitch. Like I could tell it had the feeling it was gonna snow soon, so I pulled my hoodie up while standing there minding the gas nozzle. Anyway this fucking late model Dodge Ram pulls up to the diesel pump and this big burly-looking guy jumps out of the cab and starts yelling to this other burly guy with an oil-stained softball cap and this chick in his cab. Telling them to *shut the fuck up* and some other shit I couldn't make out and could care less about, man. So, while he starts filling up, this skinny chick still in the truck squeals back at him giving him shit and then the guy pumping gas points his big-ass sausagey finger at her and then says to the other burly fucker on the passenger side to *shut that bitch up*. So the other hairy guy lunges over and slaps the chick across the face. Not hard, but she gets the point.

At this point, Rozz, I'm like *whatever* and put the nozzle back and head inside to pay and maybe grab another pack of cigs and some jerky.

On my way out I practically slam into the two guys from the truck as they're heading in the doors.

"Watch where you're going, kid," goes the fat ass with the sausage fingers. "Ya fucking piss-ant," he mumbles more to his buddy than to me. The guy behind me just laughs.

What a couple of douche bags. I just shake my head and walk to my car.

"*Hey*—" I hear a scrawny voice call out.

It's the skinny chick calling out from the Ram's rolled down window.

"Can I bum a smoke, dude?"

I'm not kidding, Rozz, I just stand there looking at her holding my car door open not saying a word.

"Come on, dude. Gimme some smoke," she goes.

I don't know what it is—maybe I feel bad cause she got bitch-slapped, or maybe because she's gotta hang out with those b.o. smelling trailer motherfucker's—but I go over to her and give her a cig.

"You need a light too?" I go.

"Yeah. Haven't smoked in like forever. Usually vape a Juul when I'm feening."

Rozz, this girl—when I get up close, I realize she's young. Like too young. Like thirteen or fourteen, you know? Fifteen at best, man. At fucking best. And I start getting this feeling like shit, man… those guys are gonna be coming out of that gas station in like two shakes and want to kick my ass and probably her ass too just for me giving her a cig. I just knew it. But I go ahead and take the time to give her a light anyway.

"Thanks," she goes and takes a drag. "Shit's getting colder out, huh?"

"Yeah," I go knowing full goddamn well I should be getting in my car now and getting the hell out of there. "Smells like snow," I say instead.

"What?"

"The air," I go. "It smells like snow."

She takes another drag and gives a crazy laugh. "Yeah."

I finally force myself to turn back to my car.

"Hey—where you heading?"

Cheese and rice, Rozz. I almost don't turn back around to answer her. *Almost.* "Buffalo," I go.

"Dude, take me with you."

"No."

"Seriously. Take me with you. I got an older brother in Buffalo. Dude, you can drop me off there. *Please*."

"What about these guys you're with?" I go.

"*Those* fuckers? C'mon—you saw Simon hit me, yeah?"

I just stare back at her.

"Well, they do that shit to me all the time. That and worse, dude. I mean, you don't even want to know. Should turn those assholes in to the *Five-0* is what I should fucking do."

"So why don't you?" I go.

She jumps out of the truck even though I still ain't said shit about taking her nowhere. "Because one's my stepdad and the other, Simon—that fuck who hit me—he's his brother." She opens my passenger door. "C'mon, dude. I promise you I won't take you too far out of your way. My brother might even pay you for your troubles when we get there."

Honest to fucking god, Rozz—she just gets in my car. And I'm just stuck standing there a second under the gas station's lit canopy, man. The hum of I90 traffic buzzing by on the overpass. And I just get these flashes, you know? Of like *you.* And then of that girl at Lester's house right after she got fucking showered with glass from that shotgun blast through the front window. I even get a quick flash of that Carver dude's sister, Olivia, from that older than hell black and white picture, all Scout Finch-looking lying dead on her living room table, man. And then I'm back to you again, Rozz. Like in my mind I see you asleep on my couch. Like it was just this morning I saw you there or some shit.

So, *fuck*—I get in and start it up. "Your brother," I go. "What part of Buffalo is he at?"

She grins all yellow teeth. "East side. Broadway and Fillmore, dude. You know it?"

"Yeah," I go and squeal out of the station and into the darkness. Hell's yeah, I knew it, Rozz. Because Fillmore Avenue ain't more than ten minutes from my mom's crib, man.

16

The funeral was held at the First Baptist Church on Haggard Street. Among the other extended family, Isaiah's uncle from the upper peninsula arrived in town the night before the visitation. A bunch of Izzy's dad's former co-workers from the power plant were there too, milling around the church's foyer and occasionally ducking out to the parking lot for a smoke. Isaiah had never seen many of them before in his life. There was also a smattering of other family friends as well as his grandparents from his mom's side. Gran and Pap's were the only guests that were invited to stay at the house. And finally, there was the soccer team. All of them. Coach Striden and Coach Vogel too. All decked out in black.

And Izzy was so, so glad they were there.

The minister got up and went on and on. Isaiah didn't really listen too much—he just sat and thought good things about his dad. Every time he looked at his uncle, Izzy couldn't help imaging in detail the hunting story with his dad and the trophy buck. Especially his dad wetting himself after tagging it with his bow. The memory of it made Isaiah smile.

Rows of pews away, Erik was fighting back strong tears the entire service. He still couldn't quite understand why he was getting so emotional. He'd never been a crier before—but ever since Ryan had come to pick him up at the house the other night, he just could not help himself from letting it flow. I mean, Erik hadn't even hardly cried at all when they lost at State. Just when he's finally got it back under control, he sees Isaiah sitting with his mom across the auditorium, smiling—and Erik just loses it again. Ryan put his hand on Erik's shoulder while Erik sat with his head down trying to ride out his sobs.

After the processional and burial out at the graveyard the whole crowd drove back to Haggard Street for a pot luck in the church's basement. The crowd of mourners moved in slow sloppy lines all laden with their conversations wandering past folding tables grabbing stuff from veggie trays and cheese platters, modestly filling their paper plates, and grabbing small cups of coffee or whatever from a couple of those old school metal urns.

Erik sat in a chair against one of the basement's painted cinderblock walls. He could feel the wall's coolness as he leaned back and took everything in. He took a sip of weak lemonade and watched Isaiah and his mother standing together greeting people, shaking hands, and accepting hugs from people in line. Erik was totally blown away with how brave Izzy was to keep his cool and be able to look normal at his own dad's funeral party. Erik seriously doubted he'd be able to act the same if his dad died suddenly, and he was almost seven years older than Izzy.

Erik stood up.

"Where you going?" Patrick Durning goes. Most of the rest of the team was huddled in the same area. They all look up at Erik.

"Just need some air." He looks at Ryan. "I'll be right back."

Erik trudges upstairs and then out to the church's front entrance. He sees Luke already up there sitting down on the concrete steps leading down from the door.

"Hey…" Erik goes and sits down next to him.

Luke just watches Erik sit.

The two just sit there, taking in the afternoon sun. They watch a couple cars roll by. A leafless tree's thin branches move a little bit all creepy-like with the chilly wind.

"Sucks for Isaiah, huh?" Erik goes.

Luke turns to him.

"I said, sucks for Isaiah, huh?"

Luke gives a nod.

They both sit there all quiet again for a while.

"Look, Luke—I gotta, I gotta tell you something."

Luke stares at Erik all unreadable.

"I *um*—I just—I been thinking a lot lately. About a lot of stuff. The past. And myself and how I am and how I—you know, operate with people and all…"

Luke says nothing.

"You see the thing is, I owe you an apology. From like back when we were younger, you know? I mean, we were friends back in the day, right? You know, before—before like everything happened with you."

Luke nods.

"Here's the thing. It's just that—I should've been there for you. The whole team should've—all of us. But mostly I'm talking about myself. *I* should've been there for you. When your mom and sister died, I didn't reach out at all. And then when you lost your hearing and all—I mean—I just wussed out on ever saying anything or reaching out in any real way like a friend should. I'm sorry, man. That was weak of me—you know? To just go on playing soccer with you and never acknowledge all that stuff. To ignore it and not reach out to you in any way that counts when you're supposed to care about somebody else. And I want you to know, I *do* care. I *care*, Luke. I'm so sorry for not stepping up and showing it. You know? I don't know what I was thinking. I was scared. But I'm trying. I just—"

Luke reaches over and grabs hold of Erik's shoulder.

Erik stops trying to talk, while another tear forces its way out of his eye and slides down his cheek.

For a second it looks like tears threaten to glisten Luke's eyes too, then with a face all a'light of freaking morning glory he mouths a *thank you* to Erik and squeezes his shoulder again with his hand.

Erik nods back as the two continue to just sit out on the church steps awhile as the occasional car rolls on by and the dull-dim sun slides down the November sky.

17

Jason

So I'm like blowing through traffic like big-time just in case those rednecks in the Dodge guess right and start chasing us towards Buffalo. The chick just sits there smoking in the passenger seat chattering on and on about all the models of cars we're passing, telling me which one's she thinks sucks and which one's rock and which one's she thinks are just OK. I ain't got the brain to really pay attention to all the bullshit she's blowing, because I'm way too busy thinking about how I should have my fucking head examined for basically kidnapping a fourteen-year-old-looking kid from her abusive stepdad in the first place. Honest to fuck, Rozz—what was I thinking?

Everything's a blur of taillights when I hear her go, "Nice fingernails, dude."

"Huh?" I go.

"Cause *you're* not a tweaker or anything." She takes a long glowing drag. "Only a serious toker's got fingernails like that."

I look right back at her real hard and puff out a laugh. "Well, takes one to know one, I guess."

"Yeah, well…" she goes and flicks some ash into the *dash*-tray.

"I'm off it though," I go.

"No shit?" she goes, actually looking genuinely impressed. "Just that *Christy* or the whole deal, dude?"

"All of it, man. The whole *sha-bang*. I'm clean."

"Good for you, dude. That's fucking tits, man. I'm thinking of going straight soon too. I mean, I ain't hooked on nothing yet. But I sure like to suck that sweet *Christy* when it's party time."

"Yeah, well I wasn't much of a glass man. I mean, I done it plenty of times and shit. But I was really into jamming coke and booze. Throw in a little weed sometimes to sleep."

She laughs. "Sorry, dude. The coke and weed I get. But who the fuck our age *drinks*? Party jocks maybe, but nobody down. I mean seriously?"

I was like laughing on the inside about her whole 'our age' comment. But I didn't say anything. You know how it is—when you're seventeen or eighteen, four or five years on either side of that is a big difference in a hell of a lot of situations. Just went back to paying attention to the road.

Seriously, Rozz—just by looking at her you could just tell this chick had already been through it, man. Shit—I know you had it as rough as anybody, but I couldn't help thinking this girl was on her way down too. One look and you just knew her whole line about not being hooked on anything was total bullshit. She had a tweaker's eyes and voice already. And that un-slept and un-showered funk all over her—but there was something else too. I could totally smell it now that I was in the car with her. I hate to say it, Rozz—but I think it was her snatch. Took a little while for me to figure out that's what I was smelling. At first, I just thought she had some regular nasty body odor going—but there kept being more to it with every whiff I got. And fuck-all if it wasn't strong, man. It's like she had many, many moons of dried periods still crusted between her thighs. Seriously, I couldn't help myself from thinking a big ass carp had swum up her vage and died.

And when I finally got over how gross it all was, I couldn't help feeling so sorry for her. I mean, what kind of parents don't teach their daughter she's gotta douche and clean up her business when she gets her period? And what kind of friends don't make a big deal that she's got stanky dugout so she goes and does something about it? Made me realize either she's hanging around peeps that don't give a shit about her or people that smell just as bad because they ain't got enough brain cells left to know no better either.

"What's your name?" I go, trying to get my mind off her reek and how sad I felt for her.

"Uh…" she shakes her head for a sec like I just asked a hard question. "Nicole. Yeah. *Oh no—wait*, wait. No call me Bella."

I stare over at her. "So which is it now? Nicole or Bella?"

"It's Bella, dude," and she smiles all nutso-looking.

"OK—whatever, kid," I go back to looking at the road over my steering wheel. "And my name's Jason. Oh, shit—wait. I mean, *Dickhead.* Yeah, my name's Dickhead. Yeah, for reals, dude."

Bella, or whatever, starts laughing. Which was probably good for both of us. I didn't press her anymore about names. I figured what would be the fucking gain, man?

"I like it, dude. I like it. Bella and Dickhead cruising down the road," she goes.

"Yeah—*Bella and Dickhead do Buffalo*," I go back, all screwing around, like it's a stupid movie title or some shit.

We just kept saying lame stuff like that for a while. Even though it was dumb, I didn't mind it. At least it made her smile.

We were finally heading into the heart of Buffalo and getting close to the exit for Broadway/Fillmore.

"Hey—you got a phone," she goes. "Can I use it? You know—call my brother? See where we could hook up."

I dig in my hoodie's pocket and give it to her.

"Hey, you got like three missed calls on here from your dad it looks like," she goes.

"Yeah, well, fuck him, I guess. Don't worry about it," I go.

She shrugs like *whatever* and then dials a number, waits, then groans all pissed.

"Fucker's not picking up," she goes, and hits redial. Same thing—dude doesn't answer, Bella gets pissed. She dials again. On the fourth attempt, the dude answers.

"Yo—Jesse," she starts. "No—yeah. I'm like in Buffalo like *right now*," she goes. "No, no, no—you gotta come pick me up then if we can't go to your crib. What? Some guy. No. He's just some guy I bummed a ride from in Niagara. He's cool. Nah. He's your age."

While she's talking, I pull off the interstate and start heading into the Broadway/Fillmore hood. It'd been years since I'd been here last to see my moms—but *damn* the place hadn't changed. Still run down to shit—not as bad as the worst parts of *The D*—but getting closer it looked like.

Bella hangs up and goes, "OK. Take a left up here and then go two blocks down to the light. We'll meet him down here aways."

"Why can't I drop you off at your brother's place?" I go.

She groans. "I don't know—some shit happening. It's Jesse, dude. There's always some weird drama with him. Who knows what's going on at his crib that he don't want me to see."

I didn't ask her anymore about it—but this whole thing got my *Spidey*-sense tingling. We're talking some serious sketch, man.

I followed her directions. The yellow streetlights and the fact that there were hardly any people out walking around gave the place a ghost town feel, like there had just been some kind of vampire apocalypse wiping everybody out or some shit like that. Like there were blocks and blocks of beat-to-shit and abandoned houses broken up by the occasional liquor store/deli-market or whatever businesses. Fucking plywood and tarp covering windows everywhere, man. Chains and padlocks on every other door. Graffiti too—like all over the place, Rozz. Saw a lot of gang signs, man. Like *GAZ* and *Tha 66* like spray-painted on every abandoned building.

"Pretty crazy hood, huh?" Bella goes.

"Yeah—you know—whatever. A lot like Detroit, man. Same shit—different city."

"You from Detroit, dude?"

"Round abouts. Pretty close, yeah."

Bella gets all impressed. "Damn. That's some hardcore shit. But I tell you, dude. The B-LO ain't no joke neither. Just look around. And every time I come around here it's getting worse."

Well, I wasn't about to get in no pissing contest about whose city was more ghetto than whose—so I just rode that comment out and finally she told me to make a couple more turns.

"Pull over. We're here," she goes, and I stop in front of this shut-down, fenced-off, construction equipment warehouse, all tin-sheet walls and rusting down to its rickety screws.

I light a cigarette and offer her another, which she takes, and we wait parked on the side of the street. No one was around. There's a steady flow of traffic on an avenue two blocks ahead of us—but no cars were coming down our street. Then out of nowhere this full-size van creeps to a stop behind us.

"That your brother?"

"Uh—yeah. That's Jesse," she goes. "Look, dude—stay put for a minute. OK? I'm gonna go talk to them a minute and see what's up. I still might need a ride if everything's not cool. OK?"

Out of the rearview I see both front van doors open and then the side doors flip out too and these four guys all get out. Cheese and rice, Rozz—I should've fucking known. They all look like wanna-be bangers too. Kicking it in ski jackets and long-ass shorts even though it's like practically winter now. Socks pulled up out of their high-tops. Three out of four got their baseball caps all twisted to the side and one of them with a doo-rag on his head.

"What are you talking about?" I say to her. "Why would I need to give you a ride if these are your people? The guy's your brother, right?"

Bella reaches across the car and touches my arm. Her eyes get as wide as a doll's. "Please, dude. Just hang one more minute. *Please*?"

Christ, Rozz—I'm such a sucker. "OK," I go, and she smiles all her yellow toker-teeth then bolts out the car.

The banger dudes walk closer, and I get a better look at them. Two of them are white, one of them's kind of brown-skinned I guess and the one in the doo-rag's definitely Asian. So a total mixed-bag which tells me for sure, they're not legit bangers because most legit bangers don't ride like that. Which means they still could be like low-level or freelance pushers—or just actually like a gang of legitimate buddies with like no official colors.

Bella skips up to one of the white dudes that I guess has gotta be Jesse and they all start talking making their words steam up in the cold air. I can't really make out what they're all saying but at that point I didn't really care because I was more focused on hauling my backpack out of the backseat to the front and unzip it enough to put my hand through and fish out the SIG. I keep the SIG in the pack but arrange it so it's right in grabbing distance if I need it.

By the time I look back at the rearview I see Bella climbing in the side doors of the van followed by the guy I think is Jesse and the brown-skinned guy. The Asian with the doo-rag and the other white guy then start walking up to my car.

"Shit…" I mumble.

The Asian strolls up and just taps on my window like he's a fucking traffic cop or something and I roll the window the rest of the way down.

"Hey, yo—" the guy goes. "What up?"

"Hey—" I go back and just wait to see what he's gonna say next. Takes a while though because it seems like the Asian doesn't really know what to say. He looks back to the white dude for sec and then turns back to me.

"So—like who are you, man?" he finally says.

Hmm, I think. I mean what do I go with here, Rozz? No real reason not to tell them my real name—but no reason to tell them shit either. I almost just tell him, *Hi! My name's Dickhead!* But then I think maybe I should just go with the old classic *A-Sac* in honor of Kid T. That of course makes me laugh.

The Asian steps back a bit and starts smiling himself and looks to the other guy, then back at me and goes, "What the hell, bruh? Did I say something funny? Hey, yo—check this dude out. Laughing and shit."

The white guy's not impressed though. "Guy's being an asshole, Ching. Guy's got no reason to be an asshole."

So Ching steps up closer to my window. "Naw, man—you're right. He ain't got no reason."

"Whoa, whoa, whoa," I go and put both hands up in front of the wheel. "Easy, yo. I'm not trying to be a dick here. I just thought of something random, and it made me laugh, OK? No offense. Look, I'm just a taxi right now. That's it."

Ching kinda rubs his bald-ass chin like he's considering shit and goes, "So how you know her?"

"I don't. Just picked her up tonight at a gas station in Niagara. I was heading this way anyway. That's all, man. Just dropping her off with you guys and her brother, I guess."

"Her *brother*?" Ching looks over to his white boy buddy again. "What you mean her brother?"

"Jesse, man. She said he was her brother."

Both of them start laughing hardcore, man. "Is that what that bitch told you? That's some funny shit, man" Ching goes.

I look back to the van. It's too dark for me to see anything of what's going on through the windshield. But I do see that the van is moving a little bit from side to side resting on its tires.

Rozz, I can't explain it. But in that moment, I just freaked out. I guess if I would've just slowed down and really thought about it, I would've been able to piece it all together from the top. No big deal. But like I said—I'm a sucker sometimes. And all I fucking knew then was that Bella might be in some danger. You know I've seen this shit before. I just flipped a switch, man. But unlike every fucking goddamn time this feeling happened like with you or any other time I pussed, I finally did something about it this time, man. Kind of like when I went off on Kid T in his Mitsu when I was getting him to spill about Dre's suspicion about my dad.

Like lightning fast, I reach into my pack and pull out the SIG and aim it at this Ching kid. His eyes get wide real fast and he like takes a big step back and I open the door and step out.

"Holy shit," the white guy goes, and I point the SIG at him for a sec too and then back to Ching.

"Over to your buddy. *Now*—" I motion to Ching, and he shuffles real slow over to the white guy standing in front of the van. "All right, both of you—*get down.* On your fucking abs."

They both go down. No questions. No hesitation. They must've been able to see it in my face—*I aint fucking around, man.* "Keep your heads down. No lie. You guys move or get up I'll fucking blast your brains all over this sidewalk."

I go closer to the van's side double doors and peak through the shaded window. Bella's hands are griping the arms of the custom van's two captain's chairs as she's bent over between them. She's still got her shirt on but she's naked from the waist down while this Jesse dude's in the back ramming her from behind. He's just banging back there, biting his lower lip—oblivious to whatever while she's thrusting her backside in rhythm like a donkey kicking at a swarm of bees, man. Meanwhile the brown-skinned dude's holding her hair out of her face with his shorts around his ankles, head tilted up with his eyes closed and mouthing words like he's praying or some shit while she blows him.

I'm such a sucker.

Well, that's it, Rozz. I'm stacking so hard with rage I just whirl around, step over the other two dudes on the sidewalk, plant my feet in front of the van, point the SIG and fire a round right into the driver's side headlight.

Ching and his buddy cower further into the pavement while the fuck-fest in the van gets seriously put on pause.

The brown-skinned guy's the first to peer out through the windshield, swearing—trying to figure out what the hell. I hear the side doors fling open and that Jesse guy comes running around yelling, "What the fuck? What's going—"

I point the SIG at him.

"Whoa—fuck," he raises his hand.

"What the hell, dude? What are you doing?" Bella runs around the van still zipping up her skinny jeans and ratty jacket all thrown back on.

"Get in the car," I tell her.

"You fucking crazy?" she goes, looking all nuts.

"Is this fuck a friend of yours? Is this your idea of a heist?" Jesse yells at Bella.

"No—this aint a fucking heist. He ain't here to rob your shit. So, Jesse, you just need to chill," Bella goes.

I keep the SIG trained on Jesse. "C'mon. Let's get out of here. I'll take you anywhere you want to go."

"You go with him you're fucking cut off from me for good," Jesse tells her.

Bella looks at him—looks at me and keeps breathing in and out like the world's running out of oxygen. "Get the fuck out of here, you bastard," she up and lunges at me all fists and spit. "You goddamn motherfucker!"

I didn't know how to react. Here I am—I got a gun and all and I'm the one blocking and dodging blows from some skeleton girl that don't weigh ninety-five pounds. Eventually I'm like *fuck it* and shove her down on her bony ass just to stop her psycho-bullshit.

"Ungrateful *bitch*—" I hiss and start walking back to my car.

"Damn, man—you didn't have to blow out my headlight, dickwad," Jesse calls after me. "Now my fucking van's just screaming to the cops, *pull me over! pull me over!* Thanks, ass wipe."

I wheel around and march back towards all those fuckers and they scurry away like rats from a fire. I raise the SIG and put three bullets right into the engine's grill. The shots echo like Thor's fucking thunder, man.

I run back to my car then, Rozz—because ghetto or no ghetto, cops are bound to show up anywhere if there's enough rounds going off. So, I throw the SIG back into my pack and squeal out of there big-time. I look in the rearview to see if I could see Bella one last time—I see the van, but she was gone—long gone—as if she'd never really been there at all.

Erif

X

The Scoundrel Prince did not make good time. Being saddled with stupefactions and mortifications about what had transpired between he and Annabella slowed his trod from Thorn considerably.

A two-day's walk had not even found him outside the valley of the Great Mountain yet—-which should have been plenty enough time for a young man of his vigor to easily walk out of well before a day and a half. Thoughts muddled and sprits dampened, Prince made his camp just before nightfall while still being very much under the colossal mountain and its Crack lording above him like a silent god.

He made his fire from long, gnarled branches he tossed to the ground and lit without the slightest thought concerning the quality of the fire's construction. The fire barely gave off light, let alone heat. But Prince didn't care; he sat and stared at it, nonetheless. He tried to chew his way through half a crusty loaf of cinnamon bread he bought off some pastry hag on his way out of Thorn, but lost heart and ended up tossing it into the fire.

Out in the trees before him, and in the tall grasses behind him, were the sounds of animals coming out for the night. He heard the call of a nightingale and some coyote yips but did not start—-he could've heard the roar of a lion and wouldn't have stretched up to look around him so rapt he was in his reverie.

Why did she say those things? How could she have treated me thus? It was just not fathomable that after all the things they had said to one another Annabella would turn so spitefully upon him. Did she distrust his intentions? Did she believe he would play her false? Prince was limed in his thoughts.

Admittedly, in all his travels from the high citadeled cities to the provincial villages, Prince had flirted and dallied with many a young lady. Blooming belles of the aristocracy, fresh and bonny milkmaids—-Prince was no stranger to exerting his wit and charms to woo and dance around with a variety of girls—-especially after a particularly splendid performance on the stage.

But with Annabella it had been different. *But why had it?* Prince thought, woodsmoke stinging his eyes. What was so different about her? Did he feel sorry for her? *No—-it had to be more than just that.* Was it purely because of her looks? *Maybe. Let's be honest, Annabella is fiery in all manner of her features.* Or was there more? Could it be that Prince really, truly, with all honor, actually meant every word of it when he told Annabella that he did like her?

There it is lad.

Prince let it sink in. *I love Annabella. For real and for certain.*

He finally broke out of his trance, uncrossed his arms and laughed.

The coyotes laughed back in their howling way.

"I love Annabella..." he let himself say out loud. It felt good to say it—-to mean it without jest—-to say it to himself, for himself. "I love Annab— " he started to say again louder when the sound of approaching hoof-beats thudding from the valley stopped him.

"Hail! You there—-by the fire," the mounted stranger called.

Prince stood and strained his eyes against the dark. It appeared to be a lone man on a horse.

"Are you the one they call 'Prince?'" The rider stopped just a few paces from the fire.

"Aye. I am." Prince readied himself for anything.

The rider dismounted and flipped down his hood. "I come at the sincere and urgent request of Annabella to give you word—-"

"What word?" The rider appeared to be no older than Prince himself—-nor less handsome.

"That Angel, through treachery, has been chosen by the Lottery. She is to be devoured by Erif as Thorn's annual tithe."

"Hail Hereafter!" Prince said. "Through treachery you say?"

"Aye. The lot was weighted against the girl."

"Tell me how."

Samuel introduced himself as a son of the village's chief elder and of how Annabella had come the night before to seek counsel with his father. Samuel went on to tell Prince, as best he could, that Annabella knew Cyvilard would make it so Angel would be picked because of some new grievance he had with her. Samuel went on to say that they believed that his father and the rest of the Elders would do nothing because they were all afraid of Cyvilard for dark and secret reasons. He told Prince about how Annabella had found him after her meeting with his father and begged him to track Prince down. At her request, Samuel saddled immediately and took to the road leading out of the valley.

"So, you didn't see Angel actually get chosen?" Prince asked.

"No," Samuel said. "I've been riding hard to get to you."

Prince shook his head. "Then how do you know Angel was chosen?"

"The Lottery does not alter. Ever. The child is chosen precisely at the same time every year."

"No—-I mean, how do you know that it really was Angel that was chosen?"

Samuel answered as though he were missing something, "Because Annabella said it would happen."

"And why do you believe her?"

Samuel took a few breaths. "She's very convincing."

"You mean very pretty." Prince narrowed his eyes.

"I don't deny the lass is a fair landscape for the eye to wander—-but *no—-*there's more to my belief in her than that."

"Then what is it? Have you two been long friends?"

"No. Sadly no, we're not longtime friends. But I do believe we share a bond. Prince, do you know what it's like to grow up in a place that seems to reveal itself, slowly, each day as something wholly and completely different than you thought it was when you were a young child?"

"Uh, no. Not really. I've always been a rover. Come up from a family of rovers."

"Well, let me tell you a truth," Samuel said, "it messes you up—-a day at a time. And these revelations just start out as feelings at first. Feelings that twist and turn inside your mind, telling you that things are not quite level. That things are not quite what you thought they were."

Prince listened. He put another couple of sticks on the fire to give them some light.

"There's something very, very wrong in Thorn. And it's more than just the dragon that lives above us. It is as if our village is rotting from the inside out. You can sense it in every house, in every corner, in every hushed conversation in Thorn. Some of the things Annabella told me about Cyvilard and my father I've never heard before. But I've *sensed* them my whole life. I sense she has more to tell me still. You ask me why I believe her, Prince? I believe her because she grew up here. Because she, like me, has survived this place. Thorn is a corpse, vile and unnatural in her motherhood—-and we are her children."

They went quiet for a while. Samuel tied his horse to a tree and fetched some oats from his saddlebag. The horse munched right out of his hand.

Prince sat back down by the fire, thinking. He looked up and saw stars barely glowing through the night with their celestial hinting.

"So, what's the plan?"

Samuel sat down too. "You are. I'll help you right now anyway I can—-but Annabella said you are Angel's only hope."

Prince groaned like he'd been hit with shovel in the gut. "So, it falls to me, then?"

"If you are good and right enough to undertake such a charge."

Prince looked up to the stars and made odd smacking noises with his lips. It was an odd tick to be sure—-but one he often did when putting serious mind to thought. "Just my luck to fall in love with a girl from a crazed village where the only way to actually prove my goodly love is to rescue her sister from the jaws of a fire-belching dragon."

"They make legends of such proofs of love," Samuel said.

"And epitaphs..." Prince smirked. "Samuel, come now—-let me have it straightaway. Have you ever wooed—-with words or with goodly lips—-my Annabella?"

It was Samuel's turn to smirk. "No, good sir—-I have not. My word, my oath."

"Well then, I rest easy, and the challenge is mine. Sorry for the plain speech, Sam. I needed to make sure my heart's aright before I forfeit all my wits on its behalf."

Samuel waved his hand at the apology as if he were shooing away a fly.

“Right then,” Prince straightened the V of his tunic. “So, this dragon of yours—-”

“Erif.”

“Yes, *whatever have you*—-this Erif. Is he real?”

“Quite.”

Prince leaned in closer to the orange glow of his meager flames. “So, he’s not just some smoke and hokum story? That there’s not actually just a merry band of rapists up there in the Crack who are the true winners of this depraved Lottery every year?”

“No merry rapists. Just the most diabolical dragon of all times. A slayer of thousands, maybe millions, depending on how ancient he really is.”

“And you, personally, have seen him?”

“Yes,” Samuel said. “He flies out from the Crack several times throughout the year. Every time he does it still creates a panic in the village even though we all know he’s not coming out to blaze us.”

“Well, what’s he come out for then?” Prince asked.

“To eat. Destroy other villages half the world away. Swoop down and murder other people and cattle of his whimsical choosing.”

“Oh...”

“You see, Prince, just because we offer up a child sacrifice to protect ourselves—-no other village or province does. Erif goes wherever he wills and takes whatever he wills.”

“I see--you are all resigned to atrocity and that there's nothing you can do about it,” said Prince. "Has your village ever thought of offering up thoughts and prayers to the families that have lost children? Or thought about getting some of your local shamans to set up huts where they might perform spells that sooth the mind upon those of the village traumatized by this sacrificial ritual?"

Samuel just stared back at Prince as serious as a stone.

"Or better yet," Prince continued, "Has your village once ever come together to perhaps, I don't know, *try* and come up with a plan to somehow rid yourselves of the child-killing dragon that lives above your home?"

"I feel your words' bite," Samuel finally answered. "No. Our parents nor our Elders will do it, so Annabella and I are hoping to break this wheel. With your help, of course."

Prince smacked his lips again. “All right, then. So how does this work? Where’s Angel? How much time do I have before she is devoured?”

Samuel straightened up. “Right now, she’s being kept somewhere in the Great Hall. At first light, she’ll be escorted by a troop of Tarrenbacks up to High Grove—-up there,” Samuel pointed to a final cluster of dense pines up on the mountain—-the last of the trees before the mountain became all rock and incline leading up to the Crack. “It will take them until nightfall to reach it. Once there, she’ll be turned over to the Rogni.”

“The *what*?”

"The Rogni. They're said to be a small guard of monsters loyal to Erif. They say they are as old as the dragon. It is the Rogni that will deliver the child to Erif the following dawn."

Prince nodded. "So less than two days."

"Aye," Samuel said.

"Then there's no time to waste." Prince stood and dusted off his pants.

"So, what is your plan?"

"Plainly, I have no idea. But I'm leaving for that grove now. With luck I'll be able to get there before dawn and intercept our Angel before she's turned over to Erif's monstered guard. Have you any weapons, Sam?"

"Aye. Two daggers and this—-" Sam pulled out a broad ornate sword from a sheath stowed behind his saddle.

"Impressive—-but I'll take just the daggers," Prince said.

"Do you want my horse?" Samuel offered.

"No. You need to ride back and help protect Annabella from Cyvilard."

"I'll do my best," Samuel said.

Prince took the daggers, kicked dirt over the coals of his fire and started walking back in the direction of High Grove.

"Prince..." Samuel called. "No matter what, save that girl—-even if all you can do is flee with her."

"And what will you all do if Erif comes down enraged?"

"I don't know. Stand. Fight. Die with honor," Samuel said. "But no matter what, it's time for this cursed Lottery to end. *Good Luck.*"

"The like to you," Prince called back and then broke into a sprint up the crag-patched mountain.

18

Jason

I must've been yelling *fuck* the whole way to my mom's house, huffing pissed off breaths like a fucking racehorse, hitting the dash with my fist like I was a righteous-to-hell judge slamming a gavel. I don't know what my deal was, Rozz. I didn't know this Bella chick from nothing. So why all the rage? Maybe it was because I just got played hard—but I don't think it was all that. I don't know, Rozz. Maybe I am still like getting waves of post-traumatic stress from everything with you.

Fuck if I know. All I really knew at that point was that I was blaring through Eastside Buffalo traffic and missed my turn to get to mom's. I like turn around and try to calm my nerves. It was going to be crazy anyway just showing up at her house at midnight out of the blue and it wasn't gonna help nothing to be all raging too. I pulled over at a corner market and got a pack of gum. I took a moment and smoked a cig while I just zoned out leaning on my car door watching cars cruise and people walk by.

Well, I got back in the car and pulled up Mom's empty driveway. There was a car in the garage, and I could see lights on in their little one-story house, so I got out and knocked on the back door. My Aunt Laurie opened totally surprised.

"*Jason?* What are you doing here?" she goes and gives me a hug and I follow her into the kitchen.

I tell her I need a break from Michigan and my pops for a while and that I missed her and my mom and wanted to surprise them.

"How long has it been since you were here last? It's gotta be ages. Look at you—all grown up," she goes and starts peeling back the years in her mind so's she can answer her own damn question.

"Three years," I go, trying to save her some time.

"Three years…" She repeats, I guess just to let the fact sink in or something. "Well, it's good to see you. Real good."

Rozz, I know you never met my mom or Aunt Laurie. I can't remember if I ever really told you anything about them other than they lived in Buffalo. Anyway, Laurie's my mom's older sister by like five years. Laurie was always the responsible one, I guess. The one of them that could keep a job anyway, maintain a house, keep up with the bills—all that grown up shit while my mom was always the hotter one—the wild girl—reckless and fucking fancy free. It always seemed to me that they fought constantly—but they kept on living together ever since my mom and dad got divorced.

Anyway, sitting there in the kitchen, I really was struck by how much older Aunt Laurie looked from the last time I'd seen her. Worry-line wrinkles all around her mouth and dragging eyes. Laurie's eyes always looked a little heavy, but man—they were worse now. She's got these thin, bony arms that come out of her T-shirt sleeves that look more like smooth dead sticks than arms. She was like late forties now which would make my mom like early forties, and *man*—did Laurie look it—even with her colored hair and caked-on make-up.

"So, where is she?" I go. "She upstairs asleep? Passed out?"

"No. She ain't here. She's out. She's gonna shit a cat though when she sees you're here."

"How she been doing?" I go.

Aunt Laurie just groans and shakes her head at that. "She ain't been good. Ain't been good at all. I had her going to AA there again for a while, but she jumped off that wagon about three months ago as you can see by the little mini-bar she's got all set up by my fridge."

I look over to a bunch of towering bargain bottles of gin and vodka and schnapps all on the counter next to the refrigerator.

"She been working at all?" I go.

"Oh, hell no—" Aunt Laurie starts laughing. "Not unless you call scamming off random guys at bars working. No sir—she's still riding your Aunt Laurie's train of charity. I'd kick her ass out but then I'd have nothing else to distract me from looking at my own miserable life."

She kept laughing, but *man*—I didn't see no humor in that. My Aunt Laurie's always been good to me—and most of the time I've enjoyed being around her, but she always put herself down. Like all the goddamn time. But she'd always say it like she was like half-kidding or something—but she wasn't. It got old after a while—you know? Well, it did for me at least.

The two of us just sat there and jawed for a while and I asked her if it was cool if I could stay there a few days—maybe a couple of weeks even and she said *sure.* She asked about my dad a little—about if the cops had busted him yet. I told her no but didn't go into any details about anything. I almost started talking about you, but I didn't know how to begin. I also knew if I started telling Aunt Laurie about you, she'd ask questions and be real concerned because she cares about me—and I knew if I really got going on you I didn't know if I'd ever stop—or could stop—and there I'd be bawling my eyes out in front of my aunt. I just didn't know if I wanted to go there yet—especially right then.

Then Aunt Laurie's phone started having a ping-gasm and she picked it up off the table. "What do you know—it's a text from your mom. Says, *not coming home—see you morrow.* Of course, she can't text for shit—every word's misspelled."

I was starting to think whatever, you know. Maybe it was best to see mom tomorrow anyway after we've both had some sleep.

But Laurie starts texting her back. "I'm telling her you're here. See if that changes her plans."

I almost say '*don't.*' That I'd really rather take a shower and just go to bed. But I didn't. I just sat there.

Took two shakes for my mom to text back, *no shit... tell him come out here.*

"Hey, it's your call if you want to do this," Laurie goes. "She's probably drunk off her ass. But then again you could be her safe ride home too if you do go."

I groaned. "Where she at?"

Laurie looked back to her phone—started texting. "Let's find out."

Mom texted back some bar called *The Waterbuffalo* out on Gerfaults Street. She followed up with another text that said, *tell him come.*

Well, shit—Rozz. I tapped up the route on my phone and then got back in my goddamn car. The fucking hope and plan was to just go in there, find Ma, have her go apeshit over me for a few seconds, and then haul her ass home.

Such a sucker sometimes.

First of all, I get there and have to like practically get down on my hands and knees to convince the guy at the door that my mom's in there and I'm here to pick her up. The bouncer looked like he wasn't gonna budge though on account of me being underage. I sold him though when I told him, "Look—if I don't come out here in like fifteen minutes with a middle-aged, blonde-out-of-a bottle chick—then it's only going to take you two seconds to find me and kick my ass out because everybody in there's like two decades older than me." The guy kind of grunts and lets me in. But cheese and rice what a production.

The whole place was like blue-collar white people, man. About half-filled—a few people drinking at the bar a few people gathered around some tables. Fucking *Aerosmith* playing through the speakers. It's always fucking *Aerosmith* in those places, man. Darts, pool table, a big flat screen replaying the week's NFL highlights. You know the deal, Rozz—adults and their dive-ass sports bars, man.

I'm scanning around and finally I see her. Sitting next to some guy with her elbows on the bar, leaning forward. Her shirt's all small and tight and you can see the lower part of her back all the way down a little past the seat of her jeans to the tiny thin black bands of her thong. Her *thong* for chrissakes, Rozz. Fucking should be a law against moms over forty wearing thongs, man. I mean, c'mon Congress—where's that legislation? It gets worse though because the guy reaches down and starts sliding his fingers over and under her thong straps.

Sick, man.

I can tell the guy is tall even though he's sitting, and broad shouldered. A beefy fucker—but not fat. He's got some whiskered beard thing going—like he's trying to do his best Aaron Rodgers impersonation, man.

They both are huddled in real close, almost leaning into each other—both their eyes all glassy from drinking.

"Hey mom—" I go, and she swivels her stool a little so she can face me.

"Hey! *Sweeeeet heart!"* she goes, all slow and slurry and then lunges out to hug me. "This is my boy. My little-little's," she goes I guess to the guy she's with. "It's been so long you little shit." She cradles my face in her hands. And before I could break free and back away, she goes, "Oh I could just eat you up like I did back in the day, eh? *Mmm—*" And she starts kissing me all over the face with these weird fucking yummy sounds till she finally got to my lips and then she just latched on and kissed me real hard on the mouth. The stench of her booze breath was like un-*fucking* believable, and I nearly vomited from that and from how sick it is she's fucking kissing me in the first place.

"Get the fuck off me. Goddamn, Ma…" I go and push away from her once I could breathe again.

"Whoa—that's some crazy shit, babe," the guy goes reacting all slow.

But she just laughs and keeps looking at me all swaggery like she could lose her balance any fucking moment but like she doesn't give a shit if she does.

Rozzy—I've seen her trashed many, many times through the years—but nothing like this. Beyond flushed skin. She looked like if you were to slice her arm with a knife, she wouldn't bleed so much as leak clear liquor.

"So…" she goes, kind of looking at me, kind of rolling her eyes up into her eyelids. "How's that shitty meth-dealing dad of yours, kiddo? Behind bars yet? Still charging blow jobs from all the young hotties hooked on his wares?" She runs her hand up through gelled and hair-sprayed supernatural blonde hair and then lolls her head toward the guy. "His dad's a fucking low-life drug dealer outside Detroit. Fucking left his ass years ago. But now my little-little's is come back to me."

"Huh. No shit?" Aaron Rodgers goes and takes another swallow of what looks like a whiskey sour.

I just stare at her all unbelievable. Rozz, I gotta say—standing there, looking at her at that moment I felt real fear, man. The kind of fear I haven't felt in a long, long time. The kind of bogeyman fear I thought I was done with now that I was older. I was jolted with the kind of fear I felt as little kid when my mom and dad would wake me up in the dead-all of night with their fighting. My dad yelling shit to her like, "You fucking drunk! You fucking dyke!" Fear that came from the sound of bottles crashed against walls and faces getting slapped—and those nights when my mom would come and lay down on my bed sometimes. Always drunk. How sometimes she'd just pass out there. Other times she'd curl up to me and stroke my hair or try to sing me some kind of lullaby but would always turn into drunken *mumbling*. And I could never trust her or relax when she came in because I never knew what she was gonna do. Where she was gonna touch. I just remember being fucking terrified. Just totally frozen, lock-up, no remedy terror.

I snap out of it and go, "Come on, mom. Let's go. I'll take you home."

She starts wagging her finger at me. "Hold on there, mister. I'm the mom and I say when it's time to go home. Now do you want a sip of mommy's little tottie? C'mon, Jacey… just for old time's sake?" She holds her glass of whiskey up and wags it in my face like she had with her finger.

"No. I don't want your fucking booze, mom. C'mon, let's go back to Laurie's and we'll get some sleep and get up in the morning and we'll have breakfast. You know—catch up. What do you say, huh?"

She suddenly just moans out and lifts her head up like she's fed up with me for being a killjoy or something. "Fine. Whatever, you little goodie, goodie. More for mommy then," she goes and downs the rest of her glass. "OK then. Run along, you little runt. Run along." She runs two of her fingers over my chest like they're little fucking legs. "Go back to that other goodie, goodie's house and wait for me. I'll be by tomorrow. But tonight, mommy's gotta get her needs met." And she all quick-like runs her fingers from my chest down towards my crotch.

"Sheesh, fuck!" I jump back.

She just grins back at me like a hyena in heat while the Aaron Rodgers-looking douchebag starts chuckling like her sick shit's funny. Then she reaches over and rubs her hand on his thigh and cruises it up to massage the bulge under the fly of his jeans. She just keeps grinning at me. Some people around us notice what my mom's doing and just stare. Rodgers starts humming this low fucking note—doing like the man-version of purring.

Fuck this, I think and just start backing away.

Fuck all of this.

I drive back to Aunt Laurie's house with my mind numb, man. I felt seriously so messed up. And not just because of Mom, I mean the whole night, man. Even before that going with Luke to that Carver guy's farm, man. Hearing that story about that psycho blowing up kids. Luke's mind games. All that bullshit at home with dad and Kevin Wilhelm for chissakes. The news about Kid T's car and those poor fucking druggies that got blown away in it. Even your letter, Rozz. I just felt just so messed with in the head, man. And it just felt like there was no place for some peace.

I pull into Aunt Laurie's driveway and come back in through the kitchen. The lights were still on. I called out for Laurie, but she didn't answer. So I walked through the house into the living room and see my aunt all passed out on the couch in front of the TV. Big bottle of vodka and an old, chipped coffee cup she's been drinking it out of sitting on the beat-up ottoman in front of her.

I just let her sleep. I picked up the bottle and the cup so she wouldn't knock them over and headed back to the kitchen. I put the cup in the sink and gripped the bottle's neck in my fist.

What the fuck is it with my family, man? I start thinking.

I pace around the kitchen still gripping the big bottle thinking and thinking. I just got so sad and so pissed the more I thought, Rozz. And that Bella girl—what the hell? Thoughts just kept swimming in my head like sharks—hungry and lethal, man.

I'm stone cold sober and my life's still a disaster, man. There ain't no way out of this shit, I'm thinking. No way. What's it matter if I'm high or if I'm sober?

I stop pacing. I look at the bottle in my hand. I unscrew the top and hold it up. I can smell that electric sour smell—like liquid decay. I took a sip, Rozz. One sip and then screw the cap back on. And just like that, I decide to leave. No waiting. No note.

Fuck you, mom.

I get back in my car and squeal out the driveway and down the street. Cruise through Broadway/Fillmore headed back towards the interstate. I take another swig of vodka. One hand on the wheel, one on the bottle. Fucking two in the morning and nothing but hours of road to look forward to.

19

We were nearly halfway through *Moby Dick* the week after Thanksgiving in Mr. Malory's *Great Works* class. And believe it or not, I was actually keeping up with the reading. On this particular day, Malory split us all up into small groups to discuss and respond to a number of prompts about some of the deep stuff in the book so far.

Anyway, I was pretty pumped too about who I got put in a group with.

Erik and Maddie and I all moved our desks together in a cluster while Mr. Malory set a note card with our prompt onto Maddie's desk. I was happy to be with them because since the game at State, I really hadn't talked to either of them that much. Sure—we all had class together every day—but that doesn't really mean you have a lot of opportunity to talk like you're hanging out or whatever. I mean, since I wasn't like technically friends with either of them yet, I hadn't really talked to them much other than little comments here and there and catching some of what they said briefly to each other.

"All right, boys—here we go," Maddie says looking at the note card.

"What's it say?" Erik goes.

"Uh, interpret Stubb's odd 'kicking dream' he relates to Flask in the chapter titled *Queen Mab*."

"Great. A real easy one. Thanks, Mr. M," Erik goes.

"Aw—it won't be that bad," I go. "I've actually been reading this—I even think I've been getting it. Well, most of it anyway."

"You know—I've been keeping up too," Erik goes. "And I'm surprised how much I think I actually like it."

"Well, great then. Between you two professors talking it out and my uncanny ability to write down from dictation, we've got these group points like in the bag," Maddie goes lifts her pen up ready to write.

"*Hey, hey*—O'Leary girl—you think you got it easy. Look who I got working for me here," Dallas calls from her huddled group all comprised of the brain trust of Gray Cahill and Greg Forsythe a few feet over.

"That's right. She's got her nerds working hard," Gray goes and shoves Greg's shoulder.

Greg looks back at Gray all unamused.

"But hey, girl—seriously, do you think I can bump a ride witchyou on Saturday?" Dallas goes leaning all closer towards Maddie.

"Yeah, sure. I got room in the Merc," Maddie goes.

"What's going on Saturday?" Erik says.

Maddie lowers her shoulders and leans down and Erik and I just both instinctively do the same thing like we're all going to share some big huge secret or something. "Kirk Wellington's brother is having a huge party at his house near campus in Ann Arbor. Like it's supposed to be lit. So, like a bunch of us are gonna crash it."

"Who's all going?" Erik goes.

"Like seriously, a ton of people. A bunch of my friends, Dallas, Dignan Cooper and his crew," she nodded to the back of the room where Peter Calloway and Philip Lukas's group were screwing around, "Peter and his girlfriend and a bunch of their friends I heard too."

"The pregnant girl? She's going?" Erik goes all astounded.

"Abby," I go. "That's her name. Abby Browne."

"Yeah, like I said. A ton of us," Maddie goes.

"Well, I guess Kirk and Dylan and all those guys would be going too, right? I mean, if it's Kirk's brother's party?" Erik goes.

"Well—*duh*—yeah, of course. I mean that kind of goes without saying," Maddie goes looking back at Erik all like whatever.

"So—I mean does it bother you that Dylan's going to be there? Are you guys so cool with stuff now you can hang out together after that kind of a breakup?" Erik goes.

"*That kind of a breakup*?" Maddie goes and looks at him all like, *seriously?* "Look, I'm not going to hang out with him or whatever. Like I said, it's going to be a big party, Erik. A lot of us are going and there's going to be like a million college kids there. I'm not even planning on talking to him. And even if I did, why do you care?"

Erik puts his hands up. "Hey—whoa. Hold up, I don't care. I was just being nosy I guess."

"Yeah—you guess…" Maddie goes and then smiles at him. "Anyway. That's what's up Saturday. Do you want to come? You know—the more the merrier? Will, you can come too, you know."

"No, I can't—I mean, I'd love to join your little army of preps, but I got a thing with me and my boys on Saturday," Erik goes.

"Uh—yeah," I go too. "I don't know if I'm quite up for a frat kegger or whatever—"

But before Maddie can respond to our separate refusals, a lot of loud laughter starts erupting from the back group.

"*Pequod?* Serious now—*The Pequod*? Should've called it the *The Cumwad.* Know what I'm saying, dawg?" Philip Lukas goes all loud and Peter Calloway cracks up even more than he already was.

"Uh—gentlemen, let's forgo the pornographic language for the time being and focus a little more on Melville's genius," Mr. Malory calls out from across the classroom where he's helping another group.

I love watching Mr. Malory during small group discussion sessions. He always gets so freaking giddy. Seriously, he just floats around the room hovering over each group like a literary angel of death listening in on the comments, swishing around his reading glasses in his hand like a little dagger, or conductor's baton as he gestures all through his devil's advocate devilry. It's ridiculous. I mean, when see him flip around the room like that, I totally get why so many people think most English teachers are *flaming* in the best sense of the word.

"Yo, like looky here, ya'll—like 'pornographic' is the right word for this stuff," Philip starts up again—this time a little quieter. "Like I can't even get through one chapter without laughing my ass off, yo. For reals, now. Funniest book ever. First off just look at the title, ya'll. *MO-BEE DICK.* Ha! *MO-DICK*, dawgs. *DICK.*"

"Grow up you, guys. Serious," Dallas goes.

"Hey, don't be hating on me. I didn't write it. Blame my boy *HER*-MAN here," Philip goes holding up the book.

"He's got a point. Not Philip's fault there's a lot of pervy stuff," Peter goes between giggles. "Come on—the whole book's loaded with *sea-men*—get it?"

"Yo, my nerds—check it out, see—it's all about sex and like gay sex at that, yo. Witchis cool, if that's your thing," Philip resumes his in-depth analysis. "I mean, when you boil it down, ya'll—ain't this mug all about a guy obsessed with chasing down dick? Serious, yo—does this Ahab fool want to kill this whale or hump it? Don't laugh, ya'll—I be serious here, yo. You see how many times the word 'hump' been used so far? What about how much they's been talking about *sperm*? 'Sperm' this, 'sperm' that. *Sperm, sperm, sperm.*"

"Yeah—no doubt. No doubt, dog—" Peter backs Philip up, laughing the whole time.

"Bunch of dudes sailing in the belly of they woman—aka the ship *Cumwad*—oops, I mean *Pequod*, yo. They all coming up from below decks, if you know what I mean, looking for the big white dick. Not to mention Ahab's hobbling around on the biggest, baddest, bone-dildo of all time for a leg, yo. And this Stubb dude's like having wet dreams about getting his ass beat with it. Witchis all cool—I don't judge."

This gets bursts of laughter from a number of boys in earshot and looks of disgust from most of the girls—certainly Dallas and Maddie included.

"If you would like a meaty companion read along with Melville," Mr. Malory starts belting from across the room and addressing the whole class—(who knows if he's heard a word of Philip's rant or not)—"then check out Cormac McCarthy's *Blood Meridian* for a contemporary novelist's spin on the style and themes presented here in Melville's classic. Of course, McCarthy's work is not for the faint of heart and most assuredly is banned from most school libraries—ours included, so you'll have to mine the shelves of the *Pub Lib* to find a copy…"

"What's he talking about?" Erik leans towards me.

"No clue. Honestly, I don't hear or get half the crap he's talking about. Sometimes I try though—sometimes I don't," I go.

"So—this thing you and *your boys* are doing this Saturday—" Maddie goes, bringing it all back, "what's that all about?"

Erik kind of shrugs. "Oh, just a bunch of us getting together at my rent's cottage. Just hanging out. *Shenanigans*, you know…"

"This going to be all your soccer chums?" Maddie asks.

"Yeah—mostly, but not all soccer guys. Dickie Schwartz will be there. Maybe even freaking Turner depending on if Luke decides to keep bringing him around."

"Is that not so nuts *he's* hanging around *Jason Turner*?" Maddie goes.

"Yeah—it's pretty crazy. But then again, it's Luke. Everything that dude does these days is pretty crazy."

"So, I guess they'll be no drinking then this time—huh?"

Erik snickers. "Yeah, well—let's just say there ain't going to be no kegger this go around."

Maddie smiles back. "Yeah, well—I hope you have fun. I'll try to think of you guys while we're surrounded by insanity in Ann Arbor."

"Yeah—you do that," Erik goes, smiling back, then turns to me. "Hey, you want to come hang with us then Saturday?"

I like totally hesitate. "Uh..."

"Come on, Will. Saw you at most of our games when hardly anybody else would go. You must like something about us. Come on—what'd you say?"

"Yeah—all right," I go all nonchalant and whatever. But inside I was freaking thrilled. This was my chance to see them *closer*. To try and put a finger on what was going on with them and with me. For me to try and figure out why I was so captivated with their story so far. Neither of them—Erik and Maddie both—had any idea how interesting I found them. Nor did I yet have a clue just how interested I would still become in them (and not just Erik and Maddie—but *all of them* that would have a hand in this). Interested to the point of obsession almost. By the end of it all, I would have notebook upon freaking notebook about each of them. Mountains of notes. Mountains of facts. Mountains of recollections through ridiculously exhaustive interviews. But enough of the obvious, huh?

I guess at this point it's enough to say I was stoked to be invited to chill with Erik, Luke and all their friends—and I had every freaking intention of being at the Volgstaad's cottage come Saturday night.

20

Jason

Couldn't drive back to Michigan through Canada, Rozz. I'd never make it. Not at two in the morning with fucking vodka on my breath. No way I was going to willingly go back through an international checkpoint at Niagara like this. So my only option was hooking up with East 90 in West Seneca and going around the Lake Erie horn. The whole thing was hours out of my way, but I didn't care at that point. This was the night from hell as far as I was concerned, man.

I ramped on to the pitch-black interstate and took another hard pull of vodka doing seventy-five mph. I just left the cap off and zoned out cruising east listening to the tires hum, man. Sober a week and now look at me: driving interstate swilling liquor with *fuck this* on repeat cycle running through my brain.

Didn't even turn no music on. Just drove, man.

Eventually the rage of the whole night started to die down—but not the confusion. Or the weariness. Looking out to the road I imagined I was starting to look like a dog does when he's laying down like by a warm fire or some shit all content, and he lifts his head up, but his eyes keep glazing over and shutting, then like barely opening and then shutting them again. And then I knew, man. Knew I wasn't gonna make it back home in one night. I needed to stop. To rest somewhere. But where? I couldn't very well get a room anywhere because that would like cost money and I couldn't just pull over and turn the car off because it was colder than a fucking witch's tit.

But fuck I needed to stop. I had only taken a few gulps of the juice, but it must've gone to my head extra quick on account of me not eating much or the fact I'd been off it for over a week.

I capped the vodka and exited at Pinehurst hoping to get to Old Lakeshore Drive. Everywhere I passed was dark and dead, man. Houses, buildings, streets, and fields. I was starting to get paranoid about cops too at this point. Those fuckers love to lay in wait in those small towns off the interstate after hours, Rozz. Hiding wherever with their lights off. Licking their chops. No lie. Like that's all those fuckers do and I wasn't about to give them myself on no silver platter, man. But damn I was getting tired, and it was starting to be a bitch keeping my eyes open.

Finally, I make it to Old Lakeshore and cruise along the massive shoreline of Lake Erie. And Rozz, I tell you what—they named that fucker right because it was *eerie*.... It was like I had the whole highway to myself passing by parking lots and beachheads, tourist shops, closed lakeshore inns and shit—even all the gas stations looked closed.

On the other side of the highway, I see headlights approaching and guess what, Rozz? A fucking Five-0 cruiser passes me. So, I have a little mini-heart attack right then and there and take the next right, which is basically like a trail road leading toward the shore. I see a sign for Center's Point in my headlights and hope for the best, man. The road peters out at this rest stop-like parking lot out on this peninsula with the lake suddenly on three sides of me.

No other cars in the lot. I turn off the headlights. *Fine*, I think—here's what I'll do: I'll just leave the car running for a couple of hours or so and get some sleep. No big deal. Lock the doors and hope no cops or fucking crazies show up and I should be OK. Even with the gas burning, it's still a hell of a lot cheaper than a motel or whatever.

So, I ease the seat back, Rozz. Close my eyes. I feel myself start to really conk out, but I suddenly feel even heavier somehow. Like somehow, I feel way drunker than I thought. And right before I totally pass out, I remember thinking like almost in a panic—*Wait—am I drugged? Did my mom drug me somehow?*

So, I like try to shake myself out of it—to fight this huge fucking sleep I got coming over me like a dark cape. I even slap myself in the face—or do my best to—and slobber globs out of my mouth and hits the window. I make all these like groaning sounds I guess, trying to stay conscious and the last thing I remember is seeing out my windshield—I swear to god, Rozz—this shape of a person fucking walking toward my car all zombie-like out of the fuck-all dark.

Then *BOOM*—BLACK.

And in the beginning, there was the musty smell of hay and shit. There's fucking stacks of baled hay, man. Hay on the floor with full nostril wafts of putrid drier-than-dust hay. Tied in twine, tied in twine. Old sunlight-see-through board planks to my right, to my left, and behind. Old boards of cedar—once painted—now parched, split, divided. Hot in here… hot like the devil's crack sweating a river flowing pain-ass streams… and all that fucking chicken shit too, all plastered and *mooshed* into the hay. I don't have many hens, but I got enough for a stench that's for sure, jack. Horses kicking hell in the barn but I'm in the coop. Horses neighing in the barn, boy—and I stuff it all with hay… Stack it full of hay. All you fucking bastards.

Stack the world full of hay.

Hate like a mongrel running around my head, tail on fire happy with howling. Chickens in the henhouse picking out pyrotol and I'm setting up those fuses like a finger spindly fool. Sweat baptizes my brow, work of the righteous and the furious stinging my eyes. Sting on—sting away. How do I know it's pyrotol? *Who cares*? Where did I learn to set fuse? *Don't worry about it*. What the hell is pyrotol? *You know. It's gonna bring the boom, boy. Gonna bring the boom…*

Monsters are made not born, jackass. Monsters are made not born. It's all marvy to me, boy. Stabbing pain down low beneath my fly. Put my hand to the rough cedar wall of the coop. Steady myself through the pain… splinters pin into my palm… a burning in my dick. Monsters are made not born, jack. I'm a fuse set to blow. Feel an itch, man—on my dick—so angry at them all—those bastards and bitches… bastards and bitches. *But my dick!* So angry—so pissed! It starts to move, man—starts to grow—got a mind of its own. Slither, slither. Hiss, hiss. Gotta real live python for a cock, man… I feel it down there in my trousers. (Why the fuck am I wearing dress shoes?) Stop wiring for a moment and lean my back against the bales of hay. I look to my fly. Underneath veins twitch like tendrils waking….

Horses getting more and more spooked… they kick and scream and kick like sodomy now against the planks adding their piss to the seeping smell of shit and hay. Yelling now… gotta finish setting the fuse, but I'm getting the boner of all boners, man. Where did I get these clothes? White button shirt… sleeves rolled up and wool trousers for fuck's sake. *You know where*—goes the mongrel voice— *that haberdasher in St. Louis. St. Louis*? The hell's a *haberdasher?* But that's right, I somehow know though. St. Louis and brogans for shoes. I see the shop… brown brogans for shoes… ties striped like peppermint… the guy with the slick hair-tonic-ed melon sells me everything thing I need while the old phonograph in the corner of the shop's playing fuck-all jazz ancient and scratchy from the needle off the vinyl. I buy three suits with cash that looks more like old worn napkins than real bills and put'em in a trunk, headed back to Michigan.

Grraah—but my dick! It burns, burns, burns to the mongrel's chorus through my cooking brains:

Fuck-Fire, Fuck-Fire
Burning in a Lake
Big Cock, Bigger Cock
Wrapped in a Snake

I can't take it. Looking down to an old guy's body that can't be mine and yet is still somehow mine anyway, man. Pulling my trousers down around my ankles… boxers too. There's a thick gut with dark-graying belly and cock hairs rousing. Below that an old man boner rises from my thicket and just keeps rising like the son of John Holmes or something. Growing up past my navel thick as a stovepipe—if the shaft's head reaches my chin, I get this quick fucked up thought I'll make out with it. That's right—just French lick the split-eye and lap like a kitty all vamped up for milk and lap and lap and lap.

Yeah—why not, dude? I look up and there's Bella sitting on a couple bales in the corner of the coop smoking a cigarette all zoney and whatever with her legs all sprawled out wide wearing just her jacket and mothy white panties spotted about her vage with near-black bloodstains. *Just go for it…* she puffs. *And when you're done with that, why don't you stick that tongue in me and go fish? Eh? See whatcha catch, dude…*

Growling, howling, I look back to my dick and its everfuckingrising. This can't be me, but this is me it is it is it is. Maybe I should grab it I think and then I grab it in my grubby-dry old man hands and it's so big and red by now swollen with rage and heat and veins. Horses still all brast from their tethers neighing and I can feel their froth fly through the planks on the back of my neck and a sick-white horse goober slides down under my collar while their terror screams like a murdering of infants but I've got fuses to finish I know I know—it's all gotta blow—all gotta burn down down down—but my dick comes first angry as it is so I take it in my hands. Bella's gone but what the fuck anyway—horses be damned while we're at it too. This is so *not* me, but it *is* me taking my old man dick in my hands. Rub and pump, rub and pump—but it don't feel good it's just rough and necessary like it needs the hurt, man. It's all hitting and stroking and pumping now. All violent and lusty like wife-beater slapping. The itch still stabbing just beneath my skin it feels like I'll need sandpaper to get to it and I wish so bad I had enough sandpaper there in my coop at that moment, man—to rub it down to the itch—rub it out, this blaze inside me glowing like a glass ball's ember… like a white-hot iron or a wire welding gun's blue-white arc.

Pump, man—pump!

The world's a barn… a coop… a basement. Jack… jack … pump!

Come for a smoke. Come for a show. Double-hand jack… I pump-pump…jack!

Pump to the rhythm pump to the chorus and even mongrel-boy's found some friends and they all go howl:

Fuck-Fire, Fuck-Fire
Burning in a Lake
Big Cock, Bigger Cock
Wrapped in a Snake

Over and over and over and over and over and over…

Thunderclap and horns. Trumpets blow a sudden doom outside the coop I fuck you not. *What the hell?* I stop and stagger to the door. A Thunderclap…and there—there—there and more—before me stretches a spine of orange lightning across the purpling sky. Like a knife of light was gripped by a god and ripped down the heavenly expanse of clouds and air like a blade through a canvas, man. I stagger all stupid out the coop to my yard and fields—my organ still hard… huge… raw… and inhuman—the length of a shotgun dripping… my white farmhouse to my left a couple of assholes darting around an oak tree giggling. One goes behind my tractor too.

Bang. A bullet whizzes past my head. Fuckers' are shooting at me trying to kill me dead. One behind the oak… one behind the tractor. They fire again, man. Such assholes! My rage—my loins. My dick is my gun… Lava o'death flowing acid and blood-lava all merge in my vein.

Pump. Jack. *Shoot.*

I fire a blast of hell-spunk at the oak. The tree bursts to splinters and flame. Dre of all fuckers, somersaults from behind it and rises firing yelling the whole time, *Lookey here Lil Pops—I got hell in my hands!*

Pump. Jack. Shoot.

My fire-glob sprays out of my dick-gun at Dre diving away, but my lava scorches his arm and skin, and muscle starts to melt away like fucking cheese in a microwave all bubbly disintegrating to the bone. Tagger comes up from out the tractor spitting Parabellums from his Glock. I turn my zooka-prick ripper at him and blast his leg off in a glory of blood and kill-spooge. Tagger screams so hard his nose splits and bleeds down seeping between his teeth and I step up to finish his ass off and he turns somehow into Kirk Wellington. Grinning the fucking mongrel grin, I go *Who's the cum belching faggot now?* and blast a rain of hell-spunk through his chest blowing out his back to splatter on the grass beyond. I turn to where Dre's trying to get away on the other side of my house but he ain't Dre no more he's Dylan now. Sorensen now with a look of well-deserved panic in his eyes for once as I jack another shell of lava-load ready to fire from my old man boner cannon. He's holding his melted-to-hell arm while he whimpers trying to scamper away and I can smell his Hugo Boss cologne through the pre-rain smell coming from the purple clouds. *Hey—Ass-fuck! Where you going?* I fire. My blast hits him hot and rips his head off with such a force it hits off the side of the house with the sick-ass thud of a deflated basketball.

Take that, bitch, I go, and more trumpets call with the thunder shaking me. The farmhouse looms. The fields around it are all on fire now blazing like a million witch burnings where naked people black as scorched marshmallows scream and run around the flaming corn. I hear unbelievable laughter and look up to see my dad sporting his leather jacket on top of the house sitting by the weathercock, twirling his chrome .45 in his fingers with his arms on his knees like he's taking a break from a hard-ass day of work. *It's your show now, son. Go get'em, Jace*, he goes and keeps on laughing and waves his arm like *carry on, carry on*.

A guy comes out of nowhere covered in blood so much I can't tell if he's wearing clothes or if he's buck-ass as all fuck and he comes up to me all frantic with huge eyes through the blood like Rambo emerging from a wall of mud and he grabs me by the arms and tries to tell me something but I just haul off and hit him twice on the head hard like my fist is a fucking sledgehammer. *Fucking dickhead*—I go and hear some sort of growling and roaring now from the fire-fields. Something's out there with the burning people chewing them up and ripping them to shreds because there's like flaming arms and legs and twisty bundles of guts looking like bloody cornucopias being hurled from the fire and landing all over my yard.

My yard for chrissakes. *How the fuck is this my yard?* But it is, man. I know it from my sagging balls to my fully loaded bone. This is my place. Mine.

The farmhouse looms but somehow a bunch of folks arrive all in frumpy dresses and suits—men with suspenders and ladies wearing make-up and the men all wearing more of that fucking hair tonic and they come up on my property like they got some right and all congregate around my old horse cart and just look at it like a bunch of dumb-founded dip-shits. *That's where he put her body to burn.... How awful! Brute! Monster! Poor Nellie...* I hear some of these idiots babble and a couple of them even have these old light bulb-flash cameras and are taking pictures of the cart like it's some kind of shrine for chrissakes. But then it's all over for them because the burning people start pouring out of my fire-fields and attacking the folks around the wagon and bashing their brains in with rocks or tackling them and holding them tight until they start on fire too and there's running and screaming everywhere around my yard and I see that bloody guy running around again too and consider for a second shooting him with my dick but then that ass, Truman—Hemingway's liaison officer— shows up and tries to help the folks by drawing his Glock and yelling *Everybody down! Everybody down!* And I just laugh and laugh at that shit and go *Hey Truman—good luck keeping this dam from breaking, you fucknut!*

The farmhouse looms but above it more lighting strikes out like a spiderwebbed-cracked windshield across the sky and one of the clouds is on fire while tons of children plummet from it trying to escape. Naked kids all dropping at least a thousand feet jumping from the cloud to escape the flames only to fall into the fiery waste of my field. I can hear their high screams a second before they hit the ground disappearing into the hell of my property and chuckle to myself all whatever. I turn again to my farmhouse but almost trip on my mom who's lying down on the grass right in front of me naked from the waist down and legs spread-eagled jabbing a bargain bottle of gin in and out of her loose hound-eared nethers. I hate her in that moment I hate her for all the nights when I was small and scared, and she'd come into my room all drunk and dead and curl up and get bad-lovey with me all soft but sad so many nights I wet myself I was so scared. Well, she looks up to me now and winks all spacey and bloodshot and wags her impossible Gene Simmons-injected-with-amphibian-hormone tongue and then I see she's got my dad's .45 in her hand, and she just raises to the temple of her head and pulls the trigger. Blood blows out a hole on the other side but somehow, she's still alive like a fucking booze-zombie or whatever and just keeps on doing herself with all the soul of an automaton, man. I just step over her and let her continue try to meet the bottomless pit of her own fucking needs.

That farmhouse still looms, man—and I know I gotta get there to regulate the rage—to complete the mission of my old man body—to finally sheath my dick of hell. I leave the fields and my backyard and the sounds of sex and slaughter and the trumpets of thunder and the plummeting of infants and get up the stairs to the farmhouse's back door. *Wait!* Goes the all-bloody dude from behind me but I am so done seeing that nut running around I just go in the house and shut the door behind me. I know what I'm after is in the kitchen ahead of me, but I look down to the cellar steps all dark and damp and the body part of me that's not my body but is, longs to go down there and I tell myself *just for a second, man— and then I'll finish it—finish what I came here to do…* and I follow the steps downward.

It's cold—so cold—and I can see faint swirls of my breath by the only ray of light that comes through the two small windows near the top of the cellar wall. All else is starless outer-space black around me. But in that dark, there's sliding movement all round me like someone's dragging a suitcase across a sandy floor in all four corners of the cellar. I feel its presence—this cold thing—I sense its coiling. The thing's eyes flash yellow like twin fog lights before me out of the cellar's abyss and a hiss slips out of its mouth and I realize I'm surrounded by it—this mammoth anaconda closing in making me walk closer to the center of the cellar. My eyes are adjusting, and the cellar shifts and changes like a living thing. The windows on top of the cellar wall are still there—still small—but at some point, they've changed to colored stained glass. I can make out a few stalactites fanging down from the ceiling and I nearly trip on a stalagmite rising up from the broken dirt floor.

I look up and there's a person bound with rope all tied up to a wooden chair in the middle of the cellar. The stained-glass ray of light reaches him making glow like a throb from a computer *power-on* indicator. His head is down—he looks tired—beaten—and I move closer and yank his head up by the hair to face me. *Fuck all! Fuck-all! Does the snake not hear me yell and scream? But do I yell and scream? How can I when I'm the one sitting bound in that chair? How can I when I'm gagged and it's me whose hair I'm yanking up?*

The old man body that's me but not me steps back confused—but still somehow willing—willing to proceed—to do what's necessary. The snake hisses behind my ear: *Do it. Do it Lil Pops….*

Do what? I think I say but it sounds like the words never leave the dome of my own skull and I turn around to those expanding yellow-jacket eyes and dark tongue hissing. *Do what?*

What you were born to do… comes the fucking hiss. *Come—let me show…* the anaconda goes, and I like feel this deep compulsion to get closer to it—fucking bend down and lie upon its massive scaly back—pressing my mega-dick on its muscled vertebrae.

And then I'm gone. Fucking whisked away—out of the cellar and screaming alone amid a tornado of flames and this wave comes—a fucking tidal wave of fire like from a nuclear blast—and blows into me melting my flesh and skin in a vaporous flash and I'm fucking suddenly skeletal—all bone and somehow taller like my bones have stretched to size of a fossilized baby T-Rex but I've still got my many knuckled boner bone sticking out like a curved stinger sharp as a scimitar, man. I see my monster skeleton outside myself—like I'm watching myself on a movie screen enjoying my goddamn Oscar-worthy performance. Blue flames crystallize in the eye sockets of my skull burning with rage and purpose and I got on this red cape clicked to a gold chain hanging around my neck and collarbones and this kick-ass crown upon my bone dome and like *here I am!* suddenly in the front office at Hemingway High, man—like I'm waiting in line to get a pass to class for coming in late in the middle of third period. There's like instant screaming when the other kids and office hags all see me coming in there looking like the epitome of Halloween and they bolt like I'm a huge bomb ticking down. *Hey…* goes a voice behind me so I swish around and see Cunter—fucking Cunter asswipe supreme and his iPhone on his tripod. *Hey, Lil Pop's—you try moving your ass a little to tha left?* the fucker goes.

You trying to direct me? ME? I AM the great I AM here—I boom back—*now OBEY!*

Yes—my master—Cunter goes and stops dicking around trying to film me. *Where do you want me?*

I step towards him—I have to crouch to keep my crown from stabbing the ceiling tiles I'm so tall in there. *Here… kneel before me, wretch…*

And Cunter does—he steps up and kneels down in front of me and I dip my femurs and other leg bones so that I can maneuver the point of my death-dick right in front of his face. *Open…* I go and this look of like submission I've never seen on Cunter's face before—not even when he's following Dre's direct orders, man—comes over him and he just opens his yap wide in front of my bone. I laugh and laugh and laugh savoring the victory then grab him by the back of his head with my skele-claws and ram my blade in his mouth bursting it up and out of his skull with a crack.

I let the fucker's corpse fall to the office's thin blue-gray carpet and hear screams of kids that can see me in the cafeteria through the office's wide windows. I feel a surge of unholy powers rise in me and I push the office double doors off their hinges out into the commons and cafeteria. Hundreds of kids yell and get up to bolt but before they can get anywhere, I raise my claw and a fireball shoots out blowing up half the caf, man—blowing bodies and tables into oblivion. My fleshless jaws stretch out even more as I belt out a celebratory roar and send another fireball to the other half of the crowded cafeteria. *BooM!* Then I just start napalming the fucking place floating down the hallways, cape-a-flowing with blue-eyes flaming, torching teachers and students alike running and screaming their last breaths before I hold out my claw and ash them, man—into dust and flames and little misting globules of blood before they totally disintegrate from the earth. One kid tries to hide behind his locker door and I just reach out my claw fingers and crunch the guy's locker like it was a fucking soda can while he just pisses himself and I open my jaws and a fireball comes out of my mouth this time and blows his head apart and I continue roaring through the hallways and eventually some of these poor assholes just stop running like its completely pointless and fall to their knees like they're in supplication and just take it—take the flames I offer—take the death I deal like they worship the coming of my doom and by the time I've cornered hundreds into the gymnasium they all bow down to me as I enter. My crowned skull roars glory and my teeth sharpen to saber-tooth fangs, and they bow humming their last tune and the flames whoosh out from my lightsaber-like eyes and infernal mouth blasting them away in an atomic shower of disgust and final resolution. I turn and fly back through the rest of the school completely obliterating it with flames out of my mouth like I'm a teenage Godzilla laying waste to my kingdom—first floor then second floor until the school's ceiling caves in under the flames and the whole building is rubble and smoke and ashen ghosts of the Hemingway faculty and student body rising in a pall of black plumes of smoke. Seeing nothing else of the school to destroy I turn on the neighborhood houses surrounding Hemingway, exploding them at will shooting out fireballs from my claws, mouth, blade, and eyes bringing Armageddon to everything in my path and then I blast off into the sky and fly above the town with my cape flowing like giant bat wings or whatever and start blowing away every building in town. People are running around like scared-ass squirrels shitting themselves in terror as I blow everything I see up. Every business. Every school. Every house. Every goddamn place and person that's made me so fucking sick of my sorry life every fucking day here—and I just yell goddamn victory, man—at every explosion—every murder—every scream of all the bastards and bitches and as I keep unleashing fireball after fireball and I feel a vibration in my bone-sword—it begins to hum like a musical note as I fly like a skeletal anti-God with my crown of gold screaming at the top of my see-through rib cage: *I be fucking weary o' the sun! And wish the whole world was fucking undone!*

And after I've burnt everyone and everything in town into a cinderfuck holocaust, I stop and hover over it like an evil Superman and take it all in for a sec and then burst out like a fucking fighter jet back towards my farm—my real home—I haul the fuck supersonic back to Bath and my fields of fire—soaring through the purple sky—all my bones throbbing power with every flash of lightning—I see it coming up below me just ahead—the farmhouse looms—my coop—and a huge fluffy-ass cloud of cherubim babies cooing and slobbering all naked and beautiful on this white cloud bound for fucking heaven *but not on my watch* I think and zoom right up to it—looking those infants right in their bright eyes and clasp my claws together sending a lighting pulse of devastation slashing into the cloud blowing that fucker into a shockwave of incinerating light and blast rings like the blowing of the Death Star, man.

Blink. I'm back in the cellar, the dark and small church windows glow the only light. I don't feel Cunter the Snake anywhere now—only damp drippiness in the dark and the kid that's me still all tied up in the chair. I look up from the chair to where I stand in front of me. I'm no longer in my King Skull form but back to the old man. My pants are back on again thank god. I leave myself in the chair all strapped and gagged and head back upstairs.

The wood creaks with each step up to the light of the mudroom where the Bloody Guy waits finally looking calm but naked under his gore. He keeps breathing in these huge huffs and looking at me like he's been waiting for me. I move to pass by him to head into the kitchen when I finally recognize the crazy sonofabitch. It's Kid T and before I can move all the way by him, he hands me this hatchet all old and heavy and dull. I take it and kind of nod to him, and he bows his head back to me like he's just done his majesty's great duty or something.

I let the hatchet dangle at my side all heavy with its death-weight and step into the kitchen past the stove and icebox, the sink and cupboards, the table I've been meaning to varnish all winter but just never got to before the spring. I know where I'm going. I am going to finish it.

She's in the next room.

Behind me I sense some sort of movement and just assume it's Kid T following me like some kind of bloody gimp but when I glance over my shoulder, I see Cunter move out from a dark corner in the kitchen. He holds his iPhone in one hand and puts a *shooshing* finger to his lips with the other and hits record. He follows me like a fucking shadow-ass cape ready to capture what will surely become *must-see* footage.

I go into our parlor and there she sits on that bare-bones oak chair at her sewing. Her back is to me all sitting upright and rigid, impeccable posture as always even in infirmity and I watch her head move slightly with the motions of her handiwork—her hair tied up in a brown and graying bun atop her skull thin as eggshell. I approach my wife till I'm right behind her—she's so oblivious to the coming oblivion. The *Kill Chant* kicks up again in my head and surely if I can kill all those Hemingway fuckers I can kill this bitch, this sweet bane o' mine, this canker on my crotch—my wife—sicker than shit anyway, always in and out of the hospital—a wheezing corpse refusing to realize her true potential; her every cough offends me.

Aw yeah—old man, Cunter hisses behind me. *She wants it, dawg. She beggin for it, yo— Best give it her quick, dawg. Then get back so's I can catch all her geyser flow.*

I try to ignore the asshole and just grip the hatchet like an anaconda. I loom above her as she just keeps on sewing and sewing like some clueless cow before the slaughter strike. I even hear her softly humming *Leaning on the Everlasting Arms* as she weaves and weaves and weaves…

I raise the hatchet high.

Do it, dawg… Cunter goes.

Monsters are made not born. Monsters are made not born.

I strike. The hatchet slams down and the whole room bursts up in a sick glop of blood from her head.

Whoa, shit now! Back up, back up, yo— Cunter yells out from behind me, but I just stand mesmerized at the inhuman eruption of fluid jetting out of Nellie's broken skull. The room spins with spell and haze and I feel myself losing my balance as the hole in Nellie's head becomes bigger and bigger like an expanding mouth sucking in all the light, all the air, everything as I stagger forward and fall into it, into black freefall only to reset back into the kitchen where I approach the chair again but it's Luke sitting this time, facing forward, eyes closed ready for his brain stroke. It's fucking Harper Lake all over again—but this time I just rush up and bash him. Bash the back of his head till there's shards of bone and lava of blood and other matter flinging out with each stroke but then I fall into a trance again, into a black hole behind my own eyes and I'm falling, now walking into the dark, and now there's the little boy Jason Turner again on a chair and now there's Nellie and Luke on their chairs, but they're facing me now, saying nothing but looking all bovine and sacrificial and I hear her say *turn around*, from behind me and so I turn around and there's *you*—Rozzy—laying on an alter of splinter-ridden wood and you call to me, *Do it, Jason. Do it to me.* I step forward. Your raven face looking all seductive and prettier than I've ever seen it I come closer thinking you want to kiss me, and I really want to kiss you but then I notice I'm still holding the hatchet and you moan, *Do it, Jason,* and then I realize what I have to do instead. I *have to*–no going back. No acting like a fool, a pussy, or some freaked out no-good loser who can't do anything for himself. So I step up and you keep moaning, *Do it. Kill me. Kill me, Jason.* Then you morph into Luke and the black hole that's in my head spins again and now it's Nellie on the table and I drunkenly try to raise the hatchet again. *Yeah—do it again, Lil Pops!* hisses Cunter's snake voice again from the dark but she morphs again back into you, Rozzy, and you're crying tears of blood down your dark\pale face just in a black bra and jeans laying down motioning me to stand above you. *Kill me, my love... Kill me*, you say, and I burst into tears, and you take my free hand while I raise the hatchet in my other and I know now's the time—now's the time to bring it all down. Bring death, seal the deal, seal my doom and the snake laughter is too much and your dead-cold touch makes me fall in love all over again as I weep and weep and it's just too much. And I bring it down with all the remaining strength I possess, man—I just bring it down but before it can connect and split your head in two it all goes black again like I've instantly shrunk to the size of a particle of dust and I'm spiraling down, down, down—to my death I'm convinced—impossibly down until I land and I open my eyes out of the darkness and find I lay in a soft cave, a cave carved into the side of great mountain it seems, because the rushing breezes claw in for me—I hear their airy howls outside and I stand up like out of a drunken stupor and stagger to the cave's entrance. At first it looks like I'm looking out to like this long range of mountains looking over valleys of deep canyons which blows me away because I've never been to the mountains before or anything. But then it dawns on me the mountains are all super *smooth*.... There aint no trees, no rocks or anything—just smooth forms of mountains stretching as far as my vision and then I see what at first seems to be a mountain stream flowing from the peak across the divide from my cave flow down to the valley below—but this river's red. And then it hits me: *it's blood.* I realize the mountains are smooth like flesh—because they *are flesh* and I remember the feeling of shrinking I had before I killed you with the hatchet and realize that the mountains are bodies, gigantic mangled bodies flowing with tidal rivers of blood from reeking wounds from their hacked flesh and I stand atop it all, King of All, the man who stands alone, the man impossible, responsible—the King of All and suddenly a truth as heavy as an old ship's anchor tugs, seems to pull down at my very soul, drags at all that I am, all that I was, all that I was becoming and I fall to my knees in bottomless shame on a bed of tongue in the mouth of the giant corpse that I fucking brought into being.

And then—

Light.

When I first came to, I didn't know where or who the hell I was, Rozz. I fucking swear. I was aware of my splitting headache though. But it was strange too—because it didn't feel like a hangover headache. My head wasn't thick or ringing like it usually is after I've gone too deep into a bottle and chased it with weed or glass or whatever. This pain was like precise, man. A stab in one central location in my brain. At first, I couldn't tell if my eyes were squinting because the sun was up or just because of the pain itself.

Then I noticed the car's front seat heater blasting a welcome furnace of hot air at my face. The only problem was I wasn't in *my* car, Rozz.

"Rough night—eh?" goes this guy sitting behind the wheel.

I'm not gonna lie, Rozz—it about scared the shit out of me right then and there realizing I was in someone else's car with some random stranger looking at me. And this guy—*jeez*.... He was just sitting there looking at me kind of wake up and realize my surroundings. He had on this plaid barn jacket and this crazy looking red winter cap—you know, the kind with those lame earflaps? Yeah, so anyway he just looked at me with this blank expression on his face.

"Hey, relax. It's OK," the guy goes and lifts his fingers off the steering wheel like *whoa*. "I came up on you not far before dawn. You was passed out in the snow in front of your car there. Booze bottle in your grip. I throwed that away. Hope you're not sore, but the bulls—see they patrol up and down this peninsula all the time. Didn't want you to get pinched with it. Didn't see no reason for you to get pinched and frostbit too to boot."

I didn't know what to say at first. I was still just so damned confused—you know? That dream, or nightmare, or whatever by itself was a lot to recover from, let alone waking up in some strange dude's car. It was a lot to process. And that dream—it felt like more than a dream, man. Just writing about it just then, didn't feel like natural writing either, man. Like a voice that wasn't mine was telling me what to write about it. It felt real. Fucked up but *real.* Maybe that's why I remembered so much of it. Still, nothing made sense. Why would I be out in the snow? Did I just stagger out there in a fucking stupor? And then I remembered the dark shape approaching me. Did I get dragged out there? I guess with all this crap going around in my head the guy was understandably cautious and obviously trying to send out a calm vibe.

"How long I been out?" I go, my voice all croaky.

"Dunno," the guy goes. "You been in my car here going on two hours now. No telling how long you were out there getting buried by snow. Couldn't have been too long though—" he swiped off his crazy hat and rubbed his static-*y* hair, "or you'd be in a lot rougher shape than you are I'd imagine."

I don't know what it was exactly about this guy, but Rozz, I'm telling you—he looked familiar, man. It was his face, mostly, I guess. Something about it that I recognized but almost as if I knew this guy when he was younger—when the deep lines of his face were smoother and the brights of his eyes were brighter maybe. I couldn't place it.

Well anyway, I was stabbing for a cigarette and pulled a pack from my jacket pocket. "You mind?"

"Go ahead," the guy goes. "Who am I to tell a body what bad habits they can and can't have? Just let the window go down a roll."

I rolled down and lit up and held the pack out to him. "Want one?" I go.

He shook his head. "I quit."

I took a few puffs and looked out to the big cold lake and the couple inches of snow that now covered all over the peninsula.

"You know, kid—" the guy starts in, "I know it ain't my place but—likely whatever it is you're running from aint gonna stop chasing you. Maybe it'd be best to just stop to turn and face it head on."

"What makes you think I'm running, man?" I go back.

"Dunno. Wild guess," the guy shrugs. "Can I show you something?"

I didn't say anything, but he must've took my silence has a 'yes' because he slipped his right arm out of his barn jacket and rolled up his sleeve. And talk about sick. The guy had a few of these little craters dotted all around his veins where he'd shot up. Fucking dope potholes, man. The *H-Train.* They looked all dark and unused for a while—but still, that shit doesn't ever totally heal up I hear.

"I guess I know running when I see it, kid. Because I been there. Like I said, ain't my place but I know facing tough shit head on hurts like a bitch, but at least you take your wounds in the front—and that's a whole lot better than taking them in the back."

"And why's that, man?" I go.

The guy let sprawl this weary grin. "Well, if for no other reason it's a lot easier to lie down and get some sleep, kid. And that's a fact."

I take another deep drag. "So what's your name?"

The guy slips his arm back in his jacket. "Maybe we should both just keep our names to ourselves for now, eh?"

I just look at him. "Yeah," I go. "Good call. Maybe we should." But the truth was I really wanted to know his name to see if I knew this dude from somewhere.

But whatever.

"Well, whoever you are, man—thanks for helping me and stuff. But I gotta go now," I say.

The guy turns to the wheel and nods. "Right-*eo, ho, ho,*" he goes.

I open the door and get out. I was about to slam the door shut when the guy suddenly leans over and calls out, "Kid—look, just remember what I said. You know, about facing your demons, OK? Cause if you don't, you're doomed to ricochet from now till the end of your days and then some. Believe you me, kid. Till the end of your days and then some…"

I didn't know what else to do or say to that, so I just nodded like I got what he was saying and closed the door. Then he backed up and pulled away down the peninsula heading for Lakeshore Drive.

I took another tug on my cig and watched him go.

What a fucking night, man. I just stood there for a bit, numb. I mean, I literally thought of nothing as I just stood there like fucking dumbfounded. I mean, shit—twenty-four hours ago I was driving with Luke to see that geezer in Bath. That seemed like fucking years ago. Like a lifetime ago, man. The day that never ended. When I finally snapped out of it, I looked all around making sure I was alone out there. The sun was rising higher now, and the morning was getting seriously bright. I took a step closer to my car and unzipped my fly to take a piss. Steam rose from where my pee hit the thin blanket of snow, exposing dead brown grass and rose up like some kind of thin smoke. I flicked the butt of my cigarette then got in my car and turned the key. She started up easy and I cranked up the heater full blast. The sun was blinding now. Light like glory shining off the lake, the snow. It was all beautiful, I guess.

I just sat there in *park* for a bit.

It wasn't gonna get any more peaceful than this, I remember thinking.

I reached over to the passenger seat and grabbed my pack. Unzipped the top zipper and grabbed your letter. Just stared at the envelope a while. Traced the lines of your handwriting with my finger and closed my eyes. Felt the warmth of the sun through the windshield. *Here we go*—I thought and tucked my finger under the gap at the envelope's top and ripped it open using my index finger as a knife. Holding the envelope upside down I pulled out your folded sheets of handwritten notebook paper.

And then I did it, girl. I read your letter.

21

Mr. Forrester remembers waking up to a strange clicking sound that at first made him think of rain pattering against the windowpanes. But as he became more and more lucid lying there in bed, he realized it wasn't rain at all. He registered that the sound was coming from downstairs, but he still couldn't quite nail down what it was exactly—only that it sounded familiar…

The next thing he was aware of was the smell of strong coffee brewing. He looked at his bedside clock. One-twenty-one in the morning. At first, he wasn't going to get up. It had been a long day at work, and he hadn't been sleeping well anyway the last couple of weeks. Truth was, he felt like he was dragging lately. So, he was thinking to hell with it, and he'd just roll over and try to ignore the racket Luke was making downstairs and try to get back to his much-needed sleep.

But the clicking just kept persisting and Mr. Forrester's curiosity got the better of him. He staggered up and put on some sweatpants to go with his V-neck T and shuffled downstairs.

His eyelids cringed at the light. It looked like all the lights downstairs were on. He stumbled down almost blindly following the clicking sounds into the dining room where a blurry Luke sat at the table typing. On an old school typewriter. Mr. Forrester recognized it at once. It was his wife's old Olivetti Valentine typewriter she kept from her mother. The thing was huge and heavy, a relic from the Sixties for crying out loud. Luke had hauled it out of storage from the basement. At first Mr. Forrester recalled a pang of nebulous anger at Luke for digging the old machine out—as if Luke had disturbed his wife's grave in some weird way. But he just as quickly got over it once his groggy brain added a little rationality. After all—it was just a typewriter.

"What are you doing?" he goes. Luke kept typing. He waved his hands a couple of times till finally his son looked up at him. "What are you doing?" Mr. Forrester repeated.

Luke grinned and reached all frantic for his pad.

Found it with some of Mom's old stuff in the basement.
It's great, huh?

"Yeah, but—what are you typing?"

Finishing my manuscript. Figured out how to end it! Had to go all the way to Bath to figure it out—but I got it now.

Luke's dad looked confused. "Bath? What were you doing in Bath?"

Took Jason there to see a guy. Long story.

Mr. Forrester didn't really know what to make of that. In fact, he was at a loss when it came to his son and his doings lately. Since the start of this school year when

Luke stayed home 'sick' supposedly for a few days he'd noticed a dramatic shift in Luke's behavior. A complete one-eighty turn with no warning or reason. At first Mr. Forrester thought maybe Luke was finally reaching out and making friends, you know, getting a social life. Then there was the whole weird incident where he turned himself in for drinking along with the rest of the team. Mr. Forrester briefly wondered if Luke was secretly continuing to party—what with his son's weird comings and goings and staying up late every night. *I mean when did the kid sleep?* Mr. Forrester remembers thinking. But the thing was, Luke never looked tired or hung-over in the mornings—like *ever*. In fact, to Mr. Forrester, Luke always looked quite the reverse. He looked like beyond refreshed. His son always appeared the very definition of *awake*. No, it was more than that even.

Luke was *scary* awake. And seemingly all the time now.

He just watched a moment while Luke kept typing frantically, fingers all a-blur on the typewriter's keys as his eyes scanned a sheet of his handwritten scrawl. There were handwritten pages scattered all over the face of the dining room table and one neat stack on Luke's right side next to the typewriter itself. His final draft.

Mr. Forrester shook his head. "Since when did you become Stephen King?"

Luke just kept on typing. Oblivious.

Mr. Forrester scowled a little and then turned to head back up to bed. A sudden thought occurred to him, and he turned back to Luke and waved his hand a few times to flag down his son's attention.

Luke finally looked up to his dad like *what?*

"Why the typewriter? Why type it out on that old thing?"

Luke just looked back at his dad a sec, processing the question, maybe. Then he quickly jotted on a scrap: *Because it was Mom's.*

Mr. Forrester nodded, and Luke barred back down and started pounding the keys again like a madman. Too tired to press any further, Mr. Forrester shrugged and trudged back up the stairs, again at a loss at what his son was up to but quietly glad too to see him looking so purposeful, so healthy, so alive.

Erif

XI

"Gragh!" Prince grunted with a burst of spit. He got particles of dirt and grit jammed underneath his fingernails with each knuckled grasp as he grappled up the steep wooded path decked with a sabotage of mountain scrub and brush.

He had been hiking, then climbing, feverishly for hours through the darkness towards, he hoped, the place Samuel had called High Grove, the place where he planned to intercept Angel from the Tarrenbacks before they turned her over to Erif's monster guard, the fabled Rogni.

Prince was almost free from the latest dense clump of pine trees; he could see the forest open to a moon-bathed clearing a mere twenty boot strides ahead.

But he paused, freezing stock still in a half crouch.

Prey-sweat trickled from his brow, his heart beating like a chase-crazed rabbit.

Eyes were upon him.

The youth had sensed this since entering this particularly thick alpine patch of forest, but now it seemed closer all shadowy and creeping.

Could it be the Rogni?

Were these mysterious creatures somehow already alerted to his presence? Stalking him, swords bared ready to strike?

Prince remained motionless. He held his breath. He knew if he was indeed being stalked, that whomever, or whatever, it would have to pounce on him before he left the darkness of dense pines. If he got out to the clearing onto open ground, the chance for an ambush would be lost.

He strained to listen.

Shattering the silence, a large owl burst out of a tree in a flapping panic and into the open night.

Is that it? Prince thought for a second, but then heard a great nostriled breath blow out behind him coupled instantaneously with the sound of a strenuous push.

Within the flash it takes for a thought to flicker into mind, Prince enveloped himself entire within a mystical glowing aura.

The airborne panther slammed into the protective force field less than a second later.

The animal fell to the ground with an awkward brokenness. White froth oozed and foamed from its mouth, the fluid the only thing visible in darkness other than the black outline of the panther's dark lump of a body. Prince heard what he guessed were the paws of the dying cat twitch and scrape against the rocky path. The panther had broken his neck.

He dissolved his protective aura. "*Sorry*—" he whispered and tore out into the clearing.

Prince looked up the mountainside. Before him lay an expanse of rock and scrub, broken only by another dark shadow of forest that seemed to curve about and connect with the woods behind him, making a horseshoe around the clearing he was now moving through. Farther up past this horseshoe were more cliffs and crags and above that, sat a last patch of trees that he knew to be High Grove—-and finally, lording above all, the mouth of the Crack—-Erif's cave—-looming, open, and dark just beneath the Great Mountain's summit.

The Scoundrel Prince trudged on, racing against the coming of dawn that surely would be within the next hour or so. As he ascended, he noted a faint diamond of flame against the black shape of trees. "What the devil...?" he hissed. Standing up straight, squinting at the distant light, Prince considered what to do. High Grove was there, clearly visible above him yet still at least another couple of hours of hard climbing away. The light near the forest was much closer, but was it worth the risk of investigating? *Could this light be that of the Rogni?* He wondered. Stumbling onto these 'monsters' unawares and outnumbered was not a prospect he particularly relished, but if yonder light *was* indeed a camp of Erif's monster guard, would it not be wise for Prince to seize the advantage by observing and/or attacking these beasts by stealth?

Crouching back closer to ground, he began creeping towards the light.

The night's dew dripped and glistened from the long blades of the highland grasses nearly soaking Prince completely as he crawled through them, moving closer to the tree line. Bobbing his head cautiously, creeping ever closer, he could finally make out the outlines of a small cabin, or big hut, and saw that the light he'd been drawn to was shining out from its open door, coming from a lantern or torch of some kind.

He crept closer a few more paces and went motionless. Nothing moved; nothing made a sound. Prince waited. Still there was nothing. All he could tell by looking past the threshold of the cabin was that the light sat on top of a rough boarding bench or table.

Slowly, Prince rose off the ground and scanned the darkness around him. Still nothing; no movement, no sounds—-not even a cricket chirp. He took a step closer to the open door. And another, and another. Each step so deliberate, so calculated, as if he were walking on a suspended tightrope towards the mysterious cabin.

He got to the threshold and poked his head in; on the table was cluster of candles all dripping wax sticking out from the lid of a low jar. A small cot of straw lay in one corner, a couple small embers glowed from the humble hearth with a cold pot and kettle hanging above it; on the walls hung a rough miniature tapestry with odd, almost primal looking painted symbols and embossed sigils of a kind Prince was not familiar with.

But despite these effects of habitation, there was no one inside the cabin.

"Hmph..." Prince groaned, trying to figure out what this all meant.

"*Turn around, lad...*" a voice all rasp and crackle called from directly behind him.

Prince's blood instantly turned cold along with a lone, piercing, and reflexive thought: *Aura...*

He stood that way for a moment—-protected but waiting for violence—-like with the rush of the panther. But nothing came. Prince dissolved his aura and then slowly, first lifting his palms from the cabin's threshold, turned around.

22

Jason

It was getting near late afternoon when I pull onto my street. And right away I notice, man. There's like five cop cars all parked on my driveway and on the street in front of my house. Two of them still got their red and blues twirling on top.

"Cheese and rice—" I go out loud.

Then I see the big front window's been all shot out and there was a big-ass blast hole in our front wall between the window and the front door. There was a whole bunch of our moron neighbors standing in and across the street, just fucking standing there with their thumbs up their asses gawking at the cops and the messed-up front of my house.

So I put together the two and two and start assuming that the Shotgun Brothers had shown up, blasted the house, and then barged in and shot my dad to death.

I pull the car up as close as I could get, grab my backpack, and get out of the car.

Dad's dead, I tell myself. Dad's dead, so get ready for the news. Here we go—accept it, man.

I step onto our front lawn and a cop immediately pulls away from where he was standing next to his cop cruiser and steps in front of my path.

"Whoa—hold up there," the cop goes. "Are you the son?"

The son? "I live here," I go. "This is my house, man."

"OK. Hold up a minute," the cop holds up one of his hands and with his other hand he pulls his walkie-talkie on his shoulder closer to his mouth. "I got the son out here."

"OK, bring him in," comes back this static voice from the walkie.

"All right. Here—come on," the cop goes and then starts to lead me to the front stairs of my own goddamn house.

The living room looked like a road-side bomb had blasted it. The couch was torn and shredded, our flat screen had been obliterated: a huge black burn mark on the wall where it used to hang, a large hunk of it laying on the floor. Glass and shit everywhere, man.

I started getting flashbacks of Lester's house all of a sudden.

I was thinking if this wasn't the Shotgun Brothers, I don't know anything, Rozz.

Dad's dead, Dad's dead—I keep thinking. *There's no way in hell he's not dead.* Should I be sad? Relieved? Jealous even? Pissed maybe because I wasn't the one to snuff him out? I didn't know what to feel, Rozz. I really didn't. So much shit was going through my brain, man.

The cop leads me back to the kitchen.

"Jace! Oh, thank God!" my dad like suddenly yells when he sees me come in. He like gets up from the table where he was sitting, jawing to two other cops.

Rozz, I'm not kidding, when I saw my old man alive and well, I totally went blank. Like blank from my mind all the way through to my soul, man. I was like paralyzed, man. Like a bite from a poisonous spider. I couldn't move, couldn't speak at all—I just stood there. Then he comes over and like gives me this hug right there in front of a bunch of pigs for chrissakes. A hug! Man, he hadn't done that in fucking years and now here he was putting his arms around me real quick like we start every day with that kind of father/son bullshit.

But I didn't do or say anything. I just stood there like a frozen jackass while he gave me this like limp dead-fish of a hug, man.

"Shit, boy—I been trying to call you on your phone for hours and hours, but you ain't been answering. What the hell's with that?" Dad goes.

"Phone died. Battery's gone to shit," I say and take a step back from him.

The cops got up from the table then too and told my dad they'd be leaving soon but would be sending a patrol car to cruise by once every hour for the next couple of days. One of the officers even gives my dad a card with a number on it to call if he noticed anyone or anything suspicious. He walks them to the door and keeps talking like a brown-nosing cheeseball thanking them and telling them he'd call if he got any more ideas about who could've shot up the house.

But the second the cops are out of the house Dad runs up and just hauls off and swaps me in the ear with his open hand.

"Ow! Goddamn! What the hell?" I go.

"Hey, fuck you right back. How about what the hell about last night?"

I didn't answer. Just hold my hand to my screaming-in-pain-ear, suddenly wishing like hell he *had* been killed by shotgun blasts.

"You know I'm getting pretty fucking tired of you running off and Toe always covering your tracks. Were you even there at all last night?"

"No! I wasn't—all right? And what the fuck do you care anyway?" I go.

"What do I care? What the fuck do I care, Jace? Seriously? People are trying to kill us! Trying to kill *you.* I know this might come as a shock to you, but I want to protect you from these assholes."

"Protect me? Oh yeah—that's fucking awesome, man. Protect me, huh? Well, you got a fucked up way of proving that by all the shit you done to me."

"What are you talking about? Riddle me fucking this then: why do I want to know where you are if it isn't to protect you? No, seriously, what the hell are you talking about?"

"I'm talking about smacking the shit out of my ear for starters," I yell back.

"Yeah well, I'm sorry about that but sometimes that's all I can do to get through to you, you know? You're so goddamn stubborn sometimes. I wish to hell I didn't have to rough you up, but you just don't get it—"

"So you *smack* me? So let me get this straight—the times that you go all psycho on me and shit is because you *have* to? That's such bullshit and you know it," I go. "You're my dad—you're supposed to be—"

"What?" he yells back. "*What?* What am I supposed to be? What am I supposed to do when you fucking say you'll be someplace and then fucking crankheads come pulling up at high noon and start blasting the house hoping to blow both you and me away and then I try and call and find you and then I get the fucking runaround leaving me to believe you're just bumbling around somewhere else—a sitting duck for those tweakers to blast if they come across you? What am I supposed to do then, Jace? What?"

"I don't know! Cheese and rice, man. Be a fucking normal dad for once. Don't hit me for starters. And how about acting like you care about me because I'm your son and not because there's fucking cops in the kitchen!"

"Hey—I'm sorry I wasn't your regular mini-van driving dad taking you to Little League every night or whatever, OK? And I'm sorry that you gotta have an old man that's in the biz and has to push the narco to every trailer junkie and party-kid in the subs. I know it's easy to say, *Dad, why can't you be crystal?* But you gotta understand I burned that bridge long before you were even born, Jace—and if I could change all that I would—you gotta believe that—I'd change it in a fucking second. But you can't get a real job in the world once you get pinched nickel and diming enough times like I done. And there ain't no way a man can make enough bank to support his family with the strikes I had and still stay crystal. There just ain't no way. There's no way I could've provided for you. And I'm sorry as hell too that your ma had to turn into a drop-dead drunk. If I would've known she'd be like that around kids, I never would've married that bitch in the first place. It's the truth, son. But just because you had it rough—hell, just because *we've* had it rough—don't think for a second I don't care about you. That I don't… *love* you, Jace—in my way. You know?"

"*Love?*" I say all fuming up. I felt this like furnace fire up from somewhere deep within me, Rozz. "Is that what you're calling it these days? Keeping me crystal? Rozzy and all that? Cozying up with big time dealers like Dre and fucking psychos like Cunter? All so you can make good bank to support me, huh? All this because you *love* me? Because I'm your son? Because I'm your family? All for your own flesh and blood—is that right? Because you *love* me. That's pretty fucking funny, Dad. Hilarious, man."

Dad just looks back at me like he's seeing me for the first time. It was weird, Rozz. If I didn't know any better, I'd almost say he looked stunned, like he was realizing something either about me, or himself, or about both of us maybe. But then again, maybe he just wasn't thinking anything at all. Maybe that was it—he just didn't have any response whatsoever to any of the shit I was saying. But then he goes all raspy like he should've cleared his throat first before speaking, but didn't: "Well, love *is* funny. It's fucking funny that way."

It got all quiet and awkward suddenly as we both stand there in the hallway between the kitchen and our blown-to-hell living room. And there was just something about standing there with him in that quiet while he just stared at me with that look I'd never seen before on him—and right then and there, Rozz, all I wanted in the world was to leave. To get out of the house again. To get somewhere. Fucking anywhere to get away from him. I just all of a sudden felt so low, so pissed, so everything aggravated and tired and wired and completely messed with. I was just suddenly *done*. You know? (Of course, you know, girl—like fucking 'duh' right?) Fucking done with my dad and his bullshit. Done with my moms and all her diseased nastiness. Done with crazy deaf kids with insane plots and plans and I was done with thunder-hell visions of massacres and farmhouses and never-ending canyons and mountains of bodies. Shit from Dylan and the jock-cocks at school. Fucking Dre and his missing backpack of glass. Cunter and his goddamn MOO-VIES. *Done.* Stick a fork in my ass *D-O-N-E.*

"I'm getting the fuck out of here—" I go and move to push past him to the front door. But he like comes to life all of a sudden and squares his shoulder into me, blocking my way.

"Where the hell you think you're going now?" he goes.

"Somewhere else," I snap back. "Now get out of my way."

"Oh no you don't. Not a fucking chance. There's no way I'm letting you go anywhere, mister," he goes and shoves me backward. "Did you just miss what the hell we've just been talking about? I can't believe this—"

"Believe it, man—" I go and push past him again. He shoves me again, this time harder. So I ram at him a third time.

"Goddamn it!" he goes and then hauls off and socks me in the face—*hard.* "What the fuck is wrong with you? See what I'm talking about? I tell you you can't leave—it ain't safe. But *no*—you gotta push it. See? See what I gotta deal with? Unfuckingbelievable, man—"

While he's yelling, I'm doubled over from his hit. I touch the back of my hand to my lip, and it comes back red, my blood smeared all over my upper knuckles.

Goddamn done.

I sling off my pack and rip open the top zipper and jam my hand down inside.

"I don't know how else to say it, Jace! Those hophead shotgun boys are gunning for you. Duh—fucking get it yet? Look what they did to the goddamn living room for godsakes! I don't care what it takes—you ain't— *What the fuck?"*

I put the SIG inches from his face.

"Where the fuck did you get that?"

"Get the hell out of my way," I go.

Then this like amused look goes over his face. Like this is funny. "Like hell I will. Look—"

"Get out of my way!" I go again and jam the barrel right under his eye. Rozz, I'm telling you at that moment I was surging with rage. It was fucking coursing through every vein in my body. Like after Lester's place when I pounded the shit out of Kid T to get the information I wanted out of him. And like the overfuckingpowering rage/joy I felt come over me in my dream. Here with me pointing the SIG in my dad's face, I felt all the sexy horror of my King Skull-self coming through. Just one trigger-squeeze away from seeing that geyser-flow of brains and blood burst out of my dad's head like a little sick mini-volcano or something.

Do it—I think I heard the Snake-Cunter voice hiss.

And I wanted to, Rozz. In that moment I really did.

"Do it, boy," Dad goes. "What are you gonna do—blow me away right here with the cops still outside?"

Seriously Rozz, on one hand it would've been so fucking cool to just go "Yeah, *dicklick*—that's what I'm gonna do—" and pull the trigger. BANG. The end of Dad. Pops is dead, long live the new Pops.

D-O-N-E.

But instead, I pull the SIG's barrel away from Dad's eye, take a big step back and point it up to the ceiling. "No—*I ain't* going to shoot your deserving ass. But if you don't get out of my way—and I mean like right quick—I am going to fire a round off so's those pigs outside come running back in here. Then you know what I'm gonna do, Dad? You want to know what I'm going to tell them while I got their fucking undivided attention? I'm going to tell them my own dad is the biggest fucking drug dealer in town with like serious connections to some heavies out of Detroit. And that ain't all, *Pops*—

that ain't all by a long shot, man. I'm going to tell them about how your boy Dre from Detroit has got himself some like serious *cartel* connections too or whatever and I'm sure that's going to sure as hell interest them enough to look into you like *ASAP*. So what do you think of that?" I go. "Should we take it *there*? Is that what you'd like, man? Or are you going to get the fuck out of my way now?"

You should've seen it, Rozz. That cocky grin that was on his face when I first held the SIG up at him was like long gone now and he actually looked more afraid of me squealing to the cops than the threat of me blowing him away.

"Don't you get it?" he finally goes. "The only thing, boy—the only thing at all keeping you safe from the thunder and lightning of Dre and his crew is me. *Me*—Jace—just me. You get out from under me, and word hits the street to that effect—then watch out, *Lil Pops*, because the juice's on then, man."

"Who's going to preach it to the streets though?" I go. "Fucking who? Because there ain't nobody who'd know outside of you and me right here and now unless *you* go and put it out there."

Dad just stands there with his hands on his hips, all military-looking, shaking his head slowly like I was his biggest disappointment piece-of-shit-son in the whole goddamn world.

"So's that what you gonna do? If I walk out that door right now, you're going to put it out, so Dre knows I'm out from under you and fair game for losing his shit or whatever at Lester's? *Huh*, Dad? Is that what you're going to do—put it out there on your own flesh and blood?"

"They'll hear it without my squawk, Jace…."

"So that's how it's going to be?"

"Don't play it this way, kid."

I snicker at the way he said *kid*. "You recognize the piece yet?" I go.

Dad nods, unimpressed. "Yeah. Took me a second to realize it was Kid's gat. Look, don't do this. Don't walk out that door."

I take a step toward the front door. Then another. Dad moves aside but keeps staring me down. I lower the SIG and stuff it back into my pack.

"Don't, son. Do not walk out that door."

He didn't say 'or else,' Rozz. He didn't say 'or don't ever come back,' or anything like that. But I felt a heaviness to my going. Like a *bigness* in this moment. Like there wasn't going to be a way back from this.

I turn the knob and swing the door open to the cold. I zip my pack and look back at him one more time. "Bring the thunder," I go and walk out.

That was a little over three weeks ago and I've been kicking it over here at Toe's ever since. Toe and his folks have been cool with it so far—they think my dad and I are just having like some serious issues and I'm pretty sure Toe's parents think Dad's been like beating me, which I guess is at least kind of true, but anyway. I think they'll still reach the end of their rope with me being here soon if there doesn't start like being some end in sight though. In the mornings I usually cruise around to the mall or someplace instead of going to school. I just can't handle that place right now. I know I'm like really putting my graduation hopes in jeopardy if I don't start showing up more and turning at least some of my homework in—but I just can't build up the energy to care enough right now.

Meanfuckingwhile, Luke's been texting me like crazy to hang out and I've been mostly just giving him the cold shoulder. Like he's been really trying to get me to make this thing that he and his soccer boys are doing out at one their parent's cottages. I don't know, Rozz. I'm sure I'll hang out with him sooner or later—in fucking fact, there's a bunch of shit I need to ask him about you and your letter.

Yeah—about that, Rozz. Your letter. I don't think I can talk about that yet. I want to and I will, but I gotta still think my way around it yet. I'm still lost in it and what you're saying. Is that OK, girl? Can you wait up for me a bit on that? I hope so…

I've been taking a lot of walks lately. By myself in out in the cold and snow—which is probably here to stay by the way, all winter long now. I mostly walk around neighborhood streets smoking whole packs of cigarettes and thinking about you and how it's all, my life and all that, gotten to this. Then I come back here and try to write you all the stuff that happened since I left for Buffalo and came back. The writing sometimes surprises me—you know, about like how much I can remember when I put my mind to it. It's like something else inside of me, like, takes over. The dream I had in the car especially. So freaked up, man.

Trying not to sleep so much. I used to crave dreaming earlier this year—after you took your exit—hoping I'd run into you in my brain's night spasms. But since that freak-out I had dreaming about that farm and blowing up the school that night in my car on the shore of lake Erie, I've been trying to avoid a return voyage if you get what I'm saying, Rozz.

The other night though I dozed off for a couple of hours I guess while watching TV alone in the dark on Toe's couch. In my dream I didn't dream of killing people or babies jumping out of burning clouds or any of that twisted shit, but I did see big Luke leaning up against the trunk of this big-ass tree on a goddamn sunny afternoon. Across the road from where we were standing was a two-story schoolhouse—and not just any schoolhouse, Rozz—fuck if it wasn't Bath Consolidated, the Belmont kids' alma mater before that Kehoe fucker made his atomic renovations.

Well hell if Luke's got that same amused, at-peace-with-every-fucking-thing-under-the-sun look he's always practically sporting. And then he just looks at me and says, (I kid you not, Rozz—says, like *out loud*) "Let rip the sky and let the glory fall."

Let rip the sky? That make sense to you? Sounds an awful lot like that poetry crap you liked. Just saying…

Anyway, that's it. That's all I remember. Is that just a kick in the nuts or what?

Just give me some more time, girl. And I'll talk to you soon…

23

Isaiah

I know that I can't let Mrs. Farris ever see this writing. If she does, she will make me do way, way, way more meetings because she'll be worried about me and probably get other doctors like her to talk more to me. She keeps saying that my writing in my journal is more important now than ever because Dad has finally died. And I *have* been writing more. And I think it's helped. Only probably not in the way she or my mom might like. That's why I think I've got to keep these pages to myself because I'm writing them for myself.

It all started a couple of nights after Dad's funeral. That's when I really started to *feel* weird things. *See* weird things. See things, but not see things, I guess.

I've not been sleeping much. I go up to my room all right though. It makes Mom feel better, I think, that I go up to my room at my normal bedtime without a fuss and don't cry too much in front of her. I think she's trying real hard not to cry too much in front of me too.

But anyway, like I said, I haven't been sleeping much. Instead, I like to stand by my window, in the dark and just stare out to the big empty soccer fields across the street. I just stare out there for a long time at night. Most of the time I look out there and think about Dad. Sometimes my mind wanders to soccer and the team and practicing with Luke out there this last fall, and sometimes my mind thinks about nothing at all, I just stare out there.

Last night I was standing by my window and looking out to the dark snow-covered soccer fields, and I started thinking real randomly about the planet Pluto. It was probably because of the snow glowing almost blue under the shine of the moon that got me first to think of it. We had been studying planets and stars and galaxies all this year in science and we learned how Pluto is covered in ice because of being such a long way away from the sun. While I was thinking, I started kind of pretending that the soccer field was planet Pluto with nothing on it but ice and snowdust blowing all over it. But I pretended there was more to it than that. I kind of started imaging this whole story in my head. A story about a spaceship full of astronauts in the future that get all the way out to the end of the galaxy to explore Pluto like those astronauts did on the moon way back long ago. Once they're there, the astronauts walk around and film stuff with like futuristic cameras and computers that don't exist yet and drive around on rovers and smaller ships they can fly around the frozen planet with and at first, they're all convinced about what every scientist has ever thought about the that far-off planet: that there's no life there. *But they're wrong.* See, sooner or later, I pretended that the astronauts find this cave. This huge dark scary cave in one of the big ice mountains on Pluto. And the astronauts go exploring deeper and deeper in this cave doing tests and chipping out ice chunks in the cave to study and stuff. When suddenly down there they see this regular looking human man coming walking up to them out of the darkness. Unlike the astronauts, this man has no spacesuit, nothing to help him breathe, no winter coat even to stay warm. This man is just wearing regular pants and a sweater like any normal middle-aged man would back on earth. Then one of the amazed astronauts falls on his knees when he gets a better look at this man coming out of the planet's dark. All of them are scared and shocked because a man is just walking around without a spacesuit and has been here before they all showed up. But the astronaut on his knees is shocked because of *who* the man is. The man is this astronaut's father—his father that died five years before his mission to Pluto. That's my story's whole thing—that either through magic, or maybe some black hole or something—some dead people get to jump to planet Pluto after they die where they wait there in the cave before they go to heaven or something. I haven't really thought of all of it yet.

While I was coming up with this whole story, looking out to the frozen soccer fields, I kind of came back to, I guess, and I noticed I'd been pretending so hard I had started slobbering on myself. It's kind of embarrassing, but I was slobbering out of my mouth, down on my shirt even. Like a baby does.

I've been coming up with a lot of stories lately for some reason. Stories, all kinds of them, keep popping up. That's never really happened to me before. I have never really been able to make up stories. At least not good ones, or ones that are as clear and thought-out feeling as the ones I've been making up since Dad died.

Anyway, last night after I came back from my story, I rubbed my mouth off, trying clear the slobber and looked back up to the field and saw Dad standing out there in the moonlight looking up at me through the window. It *was* Dad. And *not* Dad, I guess. I knew that he couldn't be *really* real. But I know that doesn't mean that I really *didn't* see him. It's hard to put into words, or to think about, in like a school kind of way. So that's why writing helps. But it's also why I can't turn these pages in with the rest of my journal. I don't want Mrs. Farris and especially my mom worrying about if I'm going crazy.

Dad stayed out there in the field staring at me for a while until I raised my hand to wave to him. Once I moved my arm he disappeared. *Whoosh.* He was gone. Unlike the astronaut in my story, I wasn't scared or shocked when I saw my dad. I knew it would be like this somehow. I knew I'd be able to see him like this, that he'd show up like good ghosts do in some movies or like in *Star Wars* when good Jedis die they become part of the Force and can talk to their living friends.

I only saw Dad once last night, but I know I'll see him again. Hopefully again tonight. But we'll see, I guess.

Of course, I think about him all the time though and all our memories together. And not just all the good ones—but all of them. Yelling fights, times where I got punished, or where he got mad at something else, I didn't want to be around him while he was cranky. Times where he and my mom would talk about stuff that I really didn't listen to because I was busy playing or watching TV or something, but they would laugh together or just have normal grownup talk. I try to remember everything. Stupid stuff like him jumping out of a closet once when I went for my winter coat to go outside to play. Or boring stuff like the time we were driving to Detroit for something, and we got caught in traffic and we sat still in our car for a long time not talking and listening to the boring news on the radio. I want to remember all of it and not lose one memory.

Or about the time a couple years ago when Dad didn't know he was so sick yet and he had a bunch of the guys he works with over to watch a Lion's game one night. They were all sitting on the couch and on the chairs in the living room by the TV yelling and groaning at the game and getting pretty into it like Dad used to back then. I was sitting on the stairs eating a paper plate full of chips and a couple of my mom's brownies and trying to get my cool *Spiderman* watch to tell the right time. I remember I was having trouble with it, trying to press the right buttons—which were really small, and my fingers were too greasy because of all the potato chips, so I was getting really frustrated about it. So, I went over to where Dad was sitting and tried to ask him to help me with it. Well, I asked him for help, but I guess he didn't hear me, or didn't hear me enough because he didn't say anything, just kept looking at the game. So, I moved closer to him and asked again and kind of held the watch up to his face. Well, he kind of blinked at the watch like he couldn't believe it was there right in front of him and, really quick and hard, took me by the wrist and slung me out of the way. I didn't know he couldn't see the TV with me in front of him like that. I was just really frustrated with my watch. That was all I was thinking about. But when he did that, I guess I looked at him like I was hurt or scared or something.

"Jeeze, Izzy! I'm trying to watch the game here," he said. But even while he was yelling at me, he missed another big play in the game. The other guys went wild and stood up off the couch because it was a Lion's touchdown and slapped each other high-fives. "What? What happened?" Dad turned away from me and started yelling too when he saw the replay on the TV.

They were being so loud, and it really surprised me when Dad yanked me out of the way that maybe I really was scared—you know? In a real little kid way, so I got embarrassed about it and just started walking out of the room, fast.

Dad saw me and called out, "Wait, Izzy—"

I turned back. I guess I had some tears in my eyes. He saw them, and real quick slapped his hands on his knees and hung his head and then looked back at me and got up from his chair.

"Come here," he said and took me back to the kitchen. Once we were there, he got down on one knee and put his hand on my shoulder. "Look—I'm sorry. Sorry that happened that way. I was just watching the game and—*you understand*?"

I nodded my head. I was getting a handle on the tears, but I wasn't sure I could talk yet without starting them up again.

"Now what is it? What do you need?" he said, and I got a whiff of his beer breath mixed with the flavored-out smell of his gum.

"Nothing. It's OK," I said.

"*Nothing*, huh?" he said and looked at me a long time before saying, "No, Izzy. It's *not OK*. I'm sorry. I was wrong to do that. You need to understand something. There ain't nothing—not one thing, not one catch, run, or touchdown, or one godforsaken moment of the NFL that I would trade for one hair on your head. OK? You got it? And if I ever act like I've forgotten that you have permission to hit me real hard on the head to remind me. OK?"

I nodded and he hugged me. I don't remember whatever happened to that watch though. But that's just it—all these kinds of memories keep coming to me over and over. Stuff that I never even realized I remembered. See, what I think is, I think Dad is still visiting me somehow. Or at least part of him is. Kind of like a ghost, but not a scary ghost. Like he's trying to make sure I remember certain things about him and about us before he leaves for good. Leaves for heaven, or maybe the caves of Pluto. Just kidding, I'm sure he's going to heaven.

Luke came over tonight. I guess he came over just to visit my mom and me and check on how I'm doing. Most of the time he comes with Ryan and Erik. But this time he just came by himself. Mom made us all mugs of hot chocolate with marshmallows, and we sat around the kitchen table and talked. Luke wrote his words on his pad as usual.

Mostly he asked about small stuff. Like how school was going for me now that I was back after being out for a week. And if Mom needed any chores done around the house. Luke even offered to shovel the walk or snow blow the driveway. But she said 'no' because Erik already volunteered to do it and all that.

Then he reached down into his backpack and pulled out this present, all gift wrapped for me.

I opened it up and it was this box and inside the box was this binder full of paper like a book. "What is it?" I asked him.

It's a story. Wrote it for you.

"For me?" I said. "Why? What for?"

I started it after I said you were a hero of mine.
It's about losing someone you care about. And being brave about it afterwards.
Kind of. It's about other stuff too.

I picked it up and flipped through the pages a little. "Just for me, huh? Cool…" I said.

Yep. But I kind of wrote for me too. It helped me understand
better about how I feel about my mom and sister. And it's kind of about our
world. How it's broken. And how we can fix it—if we're brave enough.

I swallowed hard. I had known a little about the plane crash that killed Luke's mom and sister. But we had never really talked about it much. Probably because Dad was still alive but dying. But I always knew part of why Luke hung out with me was because he'd lost family members too. That had to be why Mom and Dad both were always OK with me hanging out with Luke.

I can't wait to read it.

Before he left, he wrote down one more note and ripped it off his pad for me.

Don't turn off your soul, Izzy. I did. After I lost them.
But don't do it too. Keep your soul on.
Even when the pain comes
Keep it on.

Hope you like the story.

Erif
XII

He expected to be stabbed. Or for someone to *try* and stab him, with a dagger to the heart. Or a sword thrust perhaps, an attempt to gore him right through the tangle of his guts. But Prince turned slowly from the cabin door and faced nothing. Where he expected to find an assailant there was nothing but darkness.

"*On your knees...*" the voice called out again. It seemed close—-right in front of him, actually—-but that couldn't be possible. There was no one there. As impossible as it seemed to him, there was apparently no one there in the clearing with him in front of the cabin. Before he could think any more on it, the same rough sack-scrap voice croaked, "*Kneel now, boy*!"

Prince obeyed and tried to peer through the gloom past the clearing into the long grasses from where he had just come. Surely, he thought, that must be where they were hiding, crouched in the grass armed with a crossbow, no doubt, sighted in on his chest.

Prince aura-ed himself again. Just to be sure.

Then to his complete shock, Prince felt something singular and blunt strike him from behind between the shoulder blades. His face slammed cheek-down into the dirt. His aura inexplicably was gone—-popped-—blown apart from around him. He was aware of feet shuffling next to his body, someone standing over him, presumably with a club raised ready to brain him.

I'm dead, he thought.

And though he did not feel a blow, Prince lost consciousness.

A moist snail of a tongue squeezed into the recesses of Prince's ear. Another tongue lapped a papillary kiss on his lips. Still another couple of cold-nosed snouts huffed and blew around his face and head. Prince shook awake and pushed the furry mongrels around him back. "Grragh! What goes now?"

"*Hzzt, Hzzt—*" came some hissed command from somewhere nearby, and the four grey-backed wolves crowding around Prince scampered back into the shadows.

Prince shook his head as if jostling would clear his vision. The wolves retreated behind a hooded figure, slightly stooped, leaning on a crooked stick. "What's on here? Who are ye?" Prince said.

A cackly laugh—-an old woman's laugh, was the only response. The wolves tapped their paws to the ground repeatedly; one yawned and blew his nostrils clear of snot. Prince noticed that they were no longer in front of the cabin. They were out in another alpine clearing of scrubs and short grasses a few paces from one lone dead tree that looked perfect for a hanging gallows.

Prince drew one of Samuel's daggers and crouched up on one knee. "*Hark*—-I say again. What's on here?"

The figure pointed the walking branch at him, "Put yer toy away now, boy."

He held out his hand with the dagger and loosened his fingers from its hilt and let it fall free. Prince intended for the dagger to be encased in one of his auras—-but that didn't happen. The dagger fell to the dirt. "*What*?" he mumbled, stunned.

"Ya's got problems with yer balls, eh?" the old woman cackled again. "Baa! It won't go. Ye can't do it here, boy. Not'un now, anyways."

In vain, Prince tried to make an aura around himself and again he couldn't. "*How*?" was all he could utter.

"I turned'em off," the old woman said. Then kneeling closer on one knee herself in a surprisingly quick and fluid movement that caused Prince to shrink back, she continued, "Now, lad—-what else can ye do?"

Prince let himself fall back onto his buttocks. "Nothing. Auras are my only power."

"BAA! Young Yonderling! Then answer me thus: *where* did this late power come from?"

Prince strained his eyes to decipher the riddle of her face from the dark and shadow. He answered, "I don't know from where—-the gods, I guess."

"Ah... *gods.* Yes—-the gods in their wonderful heavens, ye guess now." She stood and removed her hood. Her hair was gray and tangled, her face grooved and leathery—-an old woman indeed. She looked the very archetype of the crone hermitess, thought Prince. Again, the old woman leaned down towards Prince's face and grinned with a surprising number of teeth for someone so ancient. "Do ye want to see something strangely now?"

Prince just stared dumb back at her.

And then a fury of things all happened at once: the woman's arms plumed out like wings of a bat, a flash of flame burst from where her chest should've been, the wolves erupted with shrilling howls, and the rest of the woman's form seemed to vanish into the air.

She was gone. The wolves then shot up and ran as a pack down the grassy slope. Prince, wide-eyed, clutched the dagger again and waited in the sudden silence.

"Up here..." came a voice, but it couldn't be the old woman's, thought Prince. No, this voice was softer, higher in pitch, sweeter—-*younger*. "Here," it said again.

He looked wildly around him in the full moonlight.

"In the tree."

Twisting around, he looked up at the dead tree just quick enough to catch something fall from what would be the hangman's branch. It fell and disintegrated on the ground into a dark formless hump. It must be her cloak, he thought. Then his eyes roved back up to the branch to indeed see a figure sitting upon it with legs dangling. But this person was no old woman—-or if she was, she was old no longer...

"What devilry..." Prince mumbled.

"*Devilry*—Baa! What unknown power—-Baa! Come, me lil' lad. Do you say you do not know me now?" said the female up in the tree, her voice still sweet and lilt, like that of a young woman.

Prince stayed dumb-still.

The girl vaulted off the branch to the ground and pounced back up with alarming speed and nimbleness. Prince redoubled his grip on the dagger, readying his hand as she bounded right up to him.

"There now, lad. Do ye recognize me now?"

"No—-" he blurted. She wore the strangest garb—-all tight but rugged and dark. Somehow, she looked not a winter older than Annabella with skin just as smooth and fair—-but raven hued with straight black lips and white eyes surrounded by the oddest circles of streaking shadow. She looked a corpse, but the most beautiful corpse Prince had ever seen. And yet here she was in front of him breathing, alive—-this old woman turned young, this illusion, this trick she-wolf in human form.

"Ah no matter then," she continued. "Because a friend of yours does."

"How now—-what friend? Speak—-witch," Prince demanded.

The girl put her hands together and placed her fingers to the cleft of her lips. Though the dark, Prince saw her eyes twinkle and glow like a cat's. She hummed a note and took one step back while continuing to consider him. "Look up to yonder moon, ye yonder boy... How now, what if that luminous orb weren't a moon a'tall, but an *eye*? An eye straight of your gods visioning from their noble realms. And that divine eye, what if it t'were to read ye and every brushpluck'n move ye made? Ha! And not only that, but saw into being whatever move it wanted ye to make next? What say ye to that now, lad?"

Prince boggled. "I—-I have not the wits for this..."

"*BAA*! Look ye up and harken the moon!" she barked.

Prince looked up to the moon's full magnificence and began to sincerely panic that this was not a sorceress before him but that something even more terrifying was afoot: that he was indeed alone on this mountain and going ear-bleeding insane.

The girl lurched forward and grabbed hold of Prince's hand and the two of them were whisked in a firestorm of white. Prince felt the exhilaration of movement, as if his present world and reality were drawn away as easily as a stage curtain revealing a dreamscape before them. He couldn't make out definite sights in front of him—-just shadows hiding from their flying brilliance warped in supernatural speed.

Prince tried to yelp with childish exultation of the mystery, but the sound lodged in his throat like a trapped songbird.

He felt fingers squeeze between his fingers. She was still there—-flying with him through the searing light—-holding his hand like a lover. Prince felt warm.

"Come to life, Prince. *Come to life...*" she whispered seemingly not in his ear but closer, somewhere from beneath his skull.

His eyes began to blur back to him. Light receded and shadows formed into shapes. Chaos coalesced into discernment.

They were in a room somehow, but not like any room that Prince had ever seen before in his life. He could see from the strange windows that it was night outside, but the light inside went well beyond the illumination of meager candles or the glow of a peasant's fireplace. A miniature sun seemed to hang from the immaculately white and smooth ceiling. Prince's mouth gaped stupidly at the perfection of such a room.

The air around them was full of the queerest clicking he had ever heard. *Click, click-click-click.* ZIP! *Click, click–*"

"Where? How–?"

"No, lad," the girl said and tightened her hold of his hand. "Stand fast. Ye watch now."

There in the center of the room was a young man sitting at a large wooden table, the shiniest and most unscraped that Prince had ever seen. On the table was some ornate box that looked to be forged from some thin metal and nailed together. The parts slid and moved with the unceasing clicking and zipping. The young man seemed to be manipulating the strange piece of smithwork with his busy fingers with much of the same dexterity and concentration that Prince had seen in many accomplished musicians with their instruments.

Overcome with the most itching wonderment, Prince was about to yell to the man-boy to ask him what he was about and to inquire about what this dreamscape was—-but before he could utter a word, the girl turned into him clasping Prince into a violent embrace. And there was light again.

Spinning and twirling through flames without heat it seemed, the both of them—-Prince and this witch, until all became a slowing, sliding and halting in yet another bright room. This one was different though, Prince noticed. It was still night outside the casement, and another solaris of light hung from this room's ceiling as well, but this chamber was more cluttered with the most alien of debris and knick-knacks. Prince saw that this room's lone occupant was a boy—-surely not more than twelve winters sitting on the softest and most luxurious of beds reading torn parchment pages from a book. But what a white were these pages! The boy seemed engrossed in his study to the point of looking dumbstruck.

Again, Prince felt the urge to speak to their sudden host, but again, the girl prevented him, this time by putting her finger up to his lips. Prince did not press the issue and nodded in submission.

They watched silently as the boy read a page, then another. It occurred to Prince that if this were a normal circumstance there was no way the boy could not be aware of his and the girl's presence. And yet he did not doubt the boy truly did not realize they were there. That's when Prince realized they must be invisible somehow—-or that the boy they saw before them was not truly real at all.

And then, with the speed of a swordstroke, the girl kissed Prince's mouth and the world fell into spin once more.

"Who were they?" Prince asked between big breaths.

"Your fabled gods, lad—-" she answered, but her voice had changed again. It was loose and croaky.

They were back on the cold mountain meadow by the hangman's tree. The moon was nearly fully fallen behind the peak of the Crack.

Prince looked up from where he was sitting on the grass. The girl was indeed the old woman again, complete with her cloak and crooked stick. Behind her he could see and hear the shapes of the wolves returning. He let out a sigh; he realized he could really do with some sleep.

"My gods, eh? A young man about my age and a boy reading on a bed?"

"Aye. They be ye gods a'right. One be yer creator, the other yer judge. The gods that know that rightly heard, all tales are one."

Prince was well beyond trying to understand all that, much less possessing the strength of will to press further, so he merely asked, "Then, good lady, do you be a god then too?"

The old crone thrust out a dagger of a laugh and a snort worthy of one of her yonder wolves. "Nah—-I be none, boy. But I tell ye true, they sent me to ye this night. To be yer oracle. To tell ye good warning of what ye undertake now."

"You know what I intend to do? You know of the girl, Angel?"

"Aye. But the real question, lad, is do *ye* know of Erif? Do ye really comprehend his power? His dark magnificence?"

Prince nodded. "I've been told of him. Of his Lottery, his ravaging, and of his Rogni."

"Then what mean ye? To steal this young Angel, the dragon's chosen Supper-Bride, and run off? To where might ye hide, lad? Ye must know Erif will not sit upon his scaly haunches and let yer heroics pass. He'll burn Thorn to cinder fer sure, but he'll not stop there, boy. Surely, ye know it? His wings'll darken the world over before he halts the hunt fer ye and yer Angel."

Prince looked down and tightened his jaw. "Content yourself. I know there can be no running. Old woman, I mean to slay the brute." He waited for the crone to burst out into more coughy laughter, but she issued none.

"Many, many winters ago, I saw King Mercurius and his whole army from the Northern Realms ascend this mountain to corner Erif in his cave up in yonder Crack. The devil burned'em all to hell, every one of them. Not a soul left alive, not even the cowards that tried to flee in the end. Erif trapped them all in rings of fire, waves of infernos up and down the mountain. Nothing was left of them, not their armor, not their shields, nor their bones. The crags and rocks ran oily with streams of the men's melted fat and grease. The ash of the slaughter hovered in black clouds down in the valley for more than twenty winters after."

Prince gave a dark chuckle. "So, was *that* your divine warning that you were sent to give me?"

"Ha!" the old woman barked into the night. "Laddy—what do ye think?"

"Methinks there's a reason my auras failed me here with you. This Great Mountain has magic that goes deeper and is older than my Yonderling gift, I know that now. So now, my dear venerable oracle, tell me—-if I go up higher, up to High Grove, and all the way to the Crack—-will I have my Auras, or no?"

"Oh now, good lad. That is not for me to make ye see or hear. But ye be right in say'n there's magic that can trump yer Auras if they're sensed ahead of time. Be wary of that truth. I can't tell directly on it though. But here's what I was above all else sent to say, my boy—-" the woman bent down to look Prince in the eyes. "I tell ye truly—-a death—-and a death only waits fer ye up in yonder Crack. Believe in me. Look to my eyes for ye know I blazon to be true. The only question there be fer ye to answer rightly now is this—-*do ye still go up to yer Angel anyways*?"

Prince nodded, soberly. He stood up and looked to High Grove and farther beyond up to the Crack. Turning back, he looked down to the vista of the valley and the dark speck he knew to be the sleeping village of Thorn and the expanse of the meadow next to it where he and Annabella and Angel had picnicked. The first mellowing of the morning sun was beginning to glow to the east.

"Do you think—-" he began and turned back to the old woman.

But she was gone. The wolves had vanished too.

Prince looked around stupidly for another moment and then went still, looking towards the dawn. "So be it..." he growled and put one boot in front of the other, ascending again, staring at his destination, High Grove, with each determined step.

24

Abby

So, the night of the "big" college party started with a bunch of us all hopping into Peter's mom's *Escalade* and heading out to Ann Arbor. A ton of other people were all riding out separately too and the plan was to all hook up at Kirk Wellington's brother's frat house or whatever.

Peter drove, of course, and his friend Nelson Tremblehall came with us and sat in the front seat while Gabby, me, and Jenna all sat in the back seat. I remember we were like starving, so I had Peter pull into *Taco Bell* for some nachos and sodas before we hit the interstate.

I remember Gabby was like non-stop talking the whole time while Nelson was constantly texting Kirk's car about where they were at, while Jenna was also like constantly playing around on her phone with other people in other cars that were rolling to the party too. The whole operation was like massive. A total *who's who* of the school apparently was going to this thing.

The whole thing just started to seem like a way bigger deal than it should be and as Peter pulled us onto the interstate, I remember like seriously second-guessing my coming along. I had been back and forth all week about whether to go to this thing anyway. I mean, I was pretty positive I would for sure be the only pregnant girl there. There could be basically no doubt about that, *right*? And even though I was wearing the kind of clothes that it would be harder to tell, I still felt like I was too bloated and self-conscious, and let's face it—too pregnant to be at a college party. But Gabby had been the one to convince me to go. Sure, Peter said he wanted me there too—but I could tell he would've been just fine if I sat this one out. I mean let's face it—what guy wouldn't be OK with his pregnant high school girlfriend *not* tagging along with him and a lot of his guy buddies to a college party sure to be packed with hotties of all stripes all over the place? I mean, for reals—*right?* But like I said, it was Gabby with her pouty, non-stop begging that I go, saying wouldn't it be great if we all—her, Jenna, and me—all ride along with Peter? So, I caved. I went along. The way I saw it, the whole party was like going to be my last bash before I went into total social hiding until I had the baby anyway.

"Dude, let's get our roll on," Nelson looks up from his phone at one point. "Dylan and Kirk and the boys just got there."

Peter was like *OK, OK.* He was pushing eighty and he said there was like no way he was getting a ticket while driving his mom's SUV.

"Man, this thing is such a cougar-wagon, dude. Your mom must get *MILF*-eyes from the guys all the time rolling around in these wheels."

"Shut up, Nelly. You're so stupid, man. You would think about my mom that way," Peter goes.

"Hell with that, dude. I'm not saying I want to *bang* her or whatever. I'm just saying this ride is pimp."

"Hey, you guys want to stop talking how sexy your mommas are and take the South State Street Exit," Gabby goes and looks up from her phone's GPS.

"Whatever you say, Gabstinence," Peter goes and looks back at her through the rearview.

"*Gabstinence?*" Jenna stops texting and looks up from her phone.

"Oh cute," I remember saying. "Since when did *he* give *you* a little pet nickname?"

Gabby just looks up from her phone again real quick and scrunches up her face in a bratty *Ha-Ha* expression.

I guess at the time I thought it was just weird for my own boyfriend to have a little inside name/joke with my best friend and that was about it. During the course of the night, and certainly later on, I would think more about it and think stuff like, *But why not call me Abstinence? Isn't that even funnier because my name is actually Abby? Or isn't even funnier on top of that because of how ironic it would be to call me Abstinence in my current condition?*

But all those questions would just have to wait, because like two seconds after Gabby gave me her dumb little face, Peter's phone rang. It was Dignan Cooper and his carload of guys wanting to know if we were there yet, and if we were, could we pin them the destination since they were now in the heart of *Wolverine* country. So, Peter was talking all loud and stupid with him and asking Gabby questions because she was still on her GPS app and Gabby was yelling back at him all loud and stupid too while Jenna and Nelson both chimed in every once in a while, making it way too loud to think anyway. Not to mention two seconds into all that I got a *WHASSUP* text from Luke and I wondered about responding or not responding to that the rest of the way to the party.

25

It took me awhile to remember the exact way with all the different turns—but I found it. I had forgotten just how many other cottages were back there and all the different winding little roads. Not to mention how places always look different in winter, especially when you've only seen them without snow. But like I said, I found it—I found Erik's cottage.

There were at least four different cars there by the time I pulled up. The light by the front door was on and so was the light that I knew to be in the cottage's kitchen where in the fall I had seen the team's goalie, Patrick Durning drink tight-end Nelson Tremblehall under the table. I knocked on the door twice and waited. There was no sound I could hear coming from inside. My breath rose to the light bulb as thick as if I were smoking a freaking stogie.

Finally, the door opens and Erik welcomes me in.

"Hey—Caxton! You made it, you little bastard. Come on, come on. We're all out back. Did you bring a hat? Some gloves?"

"No, I—"

"Hey, no worries," Erik opens his closet and tosses me this wool braided toboggan and some hefty mittens with what looked like rabbit fur lining. "They're my dad's. For ice fishing. Should keep your hands warm. We got a fire going but it still might get a little nippy, man. Come on."

I follow Erik through the cottage and out the back door to where they had a medium-sized bonfire blazing surrounded by several wooden lawn chairs and stools. A bunch of the soccer guys are already there and along with Dickie Swartz in his standard sombrero and blaze orange hunting coat.

"*Who dat*?" says one of them. After a second, I see that it's the freshman, Tristan Merigan, under a big fuzzy hat with a big scarf all wrapped around his neck nearly up to his mouth.

"Boys—this is Will. *Willy Boy Caxton*," Erik says as they all look up. "He was one of the only Hemingway students at most of our games *after* we all turned ourselves in for code and then got gay in the showers together. So, he's true blood. I don't have a clue why—but he's a good egg. He's also in my English class and's basically as clueless as I am."

"Welcome," Ryan Leone goes. "Grab a Dew from the cooler—or there's hot chocolate in that thermos over there near those cups. Grab some chips or cookies if you want and pop a squat."

I sit down on this empty wooden chair and see Luke Forrester right across from me in a big parka and tapping buttons on his phone. Next to him, smoking a cigarette and looking as freaking sullen and pissed off as ever is Jason Turner with shoulders all hunched in the cold and his hoodie coming up over his jacket and covering his head. I am kind of amazed to see him there, so I guess I stare at him a little too long. He notices too and stares right back at me like some weathered, but wild, wolf.

"Uh, *hi*—" I go.

"The fuck's wrong with you?" he snaps back with a question that's not really a question but more like a serious invitation to shut the hell up.

So… I shut the hell up and go get a Mountain Dew and then sit back down, making sure not to look back at him when I do.

26

Abby

"*No, no, no*—listen to me, stupid. Go *left* after the sign to Ray Fisher Stadium, not *right* after the sign," Gabby yells.

"Are you sure? I thought we were supposed to turn right on Westminster," Peter goes back. "I mean, we're looking for Westminster, *right*?"

"Yes, we're looking for Westminster, but not until after we take a left after the sign for Ray Fisher—get it?"

"But what street is that, then? Granger? You never said anything about Granger before, Gabby. It was just *Westminster, Westminster—gotta find fucking Westminster, Peter!*" Peter goes all mocking.

"I don't remember what I said like five minutes ago. It doesn't matter, you ass! My phone says right on Granger now, so that's what we take. Unless of course you want to drive around the Michigan campus all night looking at locked buildings."

"Guys, would you just knock it off? Enough bitching already," Jenna pipes up.

I was beyond annoyed with all of them at that point—especially both Peter and Gabby if you want to know the truth, and I was so ready to get out of his mom's *Escalade* even if that meant being at a huge college party in front of like a million people I didn't know and almost four months pregnant. "Peter, seriously—just turn around and take Granger like she said."

"OK. But don't all these avenues run parallel?"

"*Peter*!" I go, trying not to freak out too, but finding it hard not to.

"Christ, all right. All right. I'm taking Granger. Chill, everybody. Chill. Not my fault Gabby is like the worst directions-giver ever."

"Funny, asshole," Gabby goes in a voice that just didn't really sound sincerely pissed and then flips him off so he can see it through the rearview.

Nelson's just laughing up a storm next to Peter in the passenger seat.

"The hell you laughing at?"

"Nothing, man," Nelson goes. "Nothing. You're just fucking hilarious. That's all."

Like I said at that point, I didn't care anymore. I really didn't. I just wanted to get out. I put my head down for a while and rubbed the sides of my forehead in a little massage just like I'd seen my dad do like a million times when he's tired and over-stressed and is on the verge of no longer giving a shit.

Then the car stops. "We're here!" Peter yells all giddy in his voice like it's the Christmas morning of all parties.

27

"Dude—I cannot believe I'm missing this party. It's like the blow-out of the century and I'm freezing my butt off with you guys. I hope ya'll feel blessed, bitches—I really do," Dickey Swartz goes. His head bobs under his sombrero as he reads an incoming text. He strikes me as an oversized teddy bear, Dickey—all comedic the way he tries to work his phone in the bed of his huge mitten, wearing his stuffed-up blaze orange hunting coat.

"Seriously, Dick—I can't believe you'd rather be kicking it at some frat party in Ann Arbor, getting all sloshed trying to pick up chicks that you got no shot with and probably getting your ass beat in a fight with some Wolverine lineman because you looked at his girlfriend too long getting your perv on," Ryan goes, laughing at him.

A bunch of us start laughing too.

"Well, *whatever*—because apparently, I'd rather be here for some reason. But seriously, if I keep getting all these texts about how killer it is over there, I may have some serious regrets later, I'm not gonna lie."

"Who's texting you," Tristan goes.

Dickey looks up, "Well, Coop right now. He and his blokes just got there apparently."

Erik lets out a groan. "Aw man, freaking Dignan Cooper's a tool. I don't know why you hang with that guy sometimes, Dickey."

"Dude, Cooper's all right and you know it. The dude's pimp, and it's not like he's all mean like Sorensen and his a-holes. You're just all sour on him because he's been taking an interest in your *milady* O'Leary as of late," Dickey says and looks back at Erik grinning all hyena-like.

Erik brushes his hand in the air.

"Here—wait, wait, Volgs. I'll see what the stats are at with him and her tonight," Dickey goes and bites off his other mitten so he can finger-type.

"Look, I don't care what Dignan Cooper… I don't want to even—"

Dickey's phone chimes, receiving another text. "Oh, here we go! She's already there he says. She's looking '*presentable*' he says."

"He took the time to text the word *presentable*?" Tristan goes.

"Oh yeah," Ryan goes back, "all those smooth guys, they know how to use big words at the right times. Take notes. Vocab makes the mack, kid."

Dickey laughs up a riot-ball as he types in his next text.

"What are you writing, moron?" Erik yells.

Dickey holds up his phone and sticks out his tongue.

"What? What's it say? I can't read it from over here, genius."

Tristan leans closer to Dickey and reads aloud: "**are u gonna hit that?**"

Dickey hits send, the chime rings out.

"Are you freaking serious? Grow up, man" Erik goes. Practically everybody else howls laughter.

The chime rings again. Dickey reads Dignan's response and convulses with big jolly laughs and holds it up for Tristan to read again: "**if I can fit it in...**"

More laughter. More like guffawing, really. Erik gets up and stalks over to get another drink and grabs a bag of chips too.

"Whatever—you guys suck. The freaking lot of you." He sits back down, and Ryan gives him a shove and finally shakes a reluctant looking grin out of him.

"Well, he certainly gets attention from plenty of other girls too," I offer. For the first time that night everybody sitting around the fire circle (except for Luke of course—who still seems to be texting too by the way) looks over at me. "I mean, in English class once I overheard Dallas tell a couple girls, she thought Dignan was by far the hottest guy at Hemingway and that she thought he smelled like some kind of sexy moss."

"*Sexy moss*?" Troy Jensen repeats.

"What's 'sexy moss?' Is that some kind of body spray or something?" Tristan goes.

"She did not. No way she said that. That doesn't even make any sense," Erik goes.

"I kid you not," I go. "She had a hard time putting it into words, but she said he smells like a 'sexy kind of moss.' Like *earthy* but in a sexy way, I think."

"*Earthy but in a sexy way*? That's—I don't know what that is," Matt Glendening goes.

"Sounds like the very definition of dick if you ask me," Jason mumbles.

Patrick Durning sits up straighter. "Hmm—*sexy moss*, huh? That's how I would describe my pubic hair—you know, if I was *stupid*."

"OK. So obviously Dallas was thinking that was some kind of compliment though, right?" Erik goes. "But that's got to be like one of the worst compliments ever. Especially for a guy like Dignan who's supposed to have as much game as Dylan Sorensen or whatever. I mean wasn't he like dating some hot college girl earlier this year from Rochester? Seriously, saying some guy smells like sexy moss is like one step away from saying they smell 'spring fresh' or something. Which is like one step away from calling the guy like seriously douchey. I am I right, or what?"

Everybody laughs again which makes me feel pretty good and a part of things a little bit for just bringing up Dallas's weird observation—but then the laughing is cut off by this crazy beeping and siren-like sound. It takes a second to kind of zero in on where it's coming from when suddenly Luke stands up and holds out his phone and it becomes obvious that's where the sound is coming from.

"What the hell, Luke?" Dickey goes, asking basically the question all of us are thinking, when the beeping noises just cut off and get replaced by this crazy robot-like voice coming out of Luke's phone.

"AH-IGHT! Good evening, buttwipes—" the stiff robot voice goes. All of us kind of snicker but quiet down and look back to Luke and the face of his glowing phone that talks for freak's sake.

28

Abby

It takes all of two seconds once we're inside the huge castle-like house for us to just get enveloped into the sea of partiers. Without seeming to even take a step, Gabby, Jenna, and me get swept away like a receding wave from the space near the front door to one of the huge living rooms. The music booms a sonic pulse like it's vibrating out from the walls. People are everywhere. It's like not even funny how packed in everyone is. Seriously, you got people touching your back, your shoulders—everyone chatting, shouting, laughing—brushing up against each other just to move an inch it seems like.

I lose sight of Gabby just ahead of me and suddenly like a second later she's back and has a plastic cup of beer in each hand. She hands Jenna one. They both take sips and suddenly I feel like an idiot. I can tell Gabby like totally picks up on it and she suddenly looks all apologetic and goes, "Oh god, sorry. This guy he just like goes, 'need a beer?' and I was like 'yeah, a couple for my friends too' and he like just puts only these two cups in my hands. You want a sip? I mean, can you do that? You know, have just a sip? I mean, like one sip can't like cause major retardation, right?"

God, I wish she'd shut up already. Shut up about it, Gabs. I mean come on, *think!* Of course, one sip can't cause birth defects, you airhead. But you know that, you're just talking out of your butt right now because it's really awkward talking to your pregnant best friend while you got a beer in your hand chilling at a college party. But I just shake my head *no thanks* like it's no big deal and start scanning around if for no other reason than to change the subject.

All I see are college kids everywhere. I'm surprised not by how much older they look—which a lot of them do, not by much, but they do—but more by how much older they *feel*, you know? Almost as if they give off a different kind of body heat than we do. Not hotter than us, exactly. But different. It's hard to describe, but like a more *lived-in* kind of heat, I guess. Anyway, I know it's weird, but that's what I thought at the time. Everybody's got a drink, everybody looks cool—like they're all in on the same inside joke that's not that funny at all—but you really, really want to know what it is anyway.

I look at most of the girls here and it's unbelievable. Just about all of them look tanned and are like wearing designer tight T-shirts that just happen to perfectly creep up just over their waists even though it's the middle of winter. And even though this is not by any means a formal party, all of them are wearing nicer clothes and jewelry than you would ever see in high school. Like by far. And don't even get me started on their boobs. I mean seriously. Unbelievable racks. Yes, some are huge—but what gets me is that whether they're larger or smaller, all these girls seem to have absolutely perfect breasts for their body type. And it's not only that—they seem to all know how to like totally *accentuate* their body's positives without crossing over in awkwardness or trashiness like so many high school girls do. Looking around I feel like the ugliest, worst dressed girl here. But that's not the end of it. All of them seem to have perfected the art of makeup too. I feel like all of them should go into movies or modeling, they look so professionally done. It's like their faces are made up so much that they'd all be ready at a moment's notice to put on a bridesmaid's gown and stand up in a wedding or take everything off and star in a glam porn scene. And then it hits me: they're not girls anymore. All of us in high school are still *girls*—even those of us who've had sex—and even me who's freaking pregnant for crying out loud. But surrounded by these females, I still feel very much like a little girl. But they don't seem like women either. When I think of the term *women*, I think of my mom and moms in general; I think of other ladies who are independent and have careers too, and responsibilities and lead lives of respectability and importance. But all these college girls around me laughing, and drinking, and flirting and looking perfect in their hot-ness and seeing the way all the boys look at them and talk to them, I realize they're not girls or women at all. They're goddesses. *Hot as fuck. Goddesses.* And I touch my belly and just think *damn*—I'm only eighteen and I may never get to be one. At least not now anyway. Not tonight—that's for sure.

The guys all look like smarter, cooler versions of Peter and Nelson and even Dylan Sorensen. Standing around, laid back, looking clever and hungry and ruffled in all the right ways. The way they sip their drinks, shrug their shoulders, slowly nod their heads, or smile while they listen to the girls—they all look so smooth—so practiced. Not like most of the immature, jocky, *playa*-wannabes at Hemingway. These guys all look like real players. Guys with real money and real brains and real shady intentions—but all in a cool way.

This music I've never heard before, but know it's cool, keeps up its steady rhythm and bass. The very air around all these party people is ridiculously thick with damp heat and the smell of bodies and booze. I breathe in heavy perfume. I exhale strong cologne. It's all too much. I feel like I'm going to puke.

I finally catch sight of some Hemingway kids in the far corner of room. They're all pretty groupy looking with stars in their eyes as they scan all the college kids mingling. Then I see Maddie O'Leary and her uber-high-class friends, like Dallas Douglass and Thora Berkholder.

Maddie's all leaning in close to Dignan Cooper who looks like he's saying all sorts of stuff in her ear. Those two practically look like college kids themselves—both beautiful and golden. Almost as if this were the kind of setting people like them were born for.

Then I spy Peter and Nelson hooking up with Dylan and Kirk and their gang. They all yell curse words and howl at each other and guzzle their beers and then turn around to scope all the hot girls that are everywhere. I can't get over just how much Peter looks like he loves being here, in the thick of all this like he just fits right in with all of them.

I pull my phone out to check the time. At some point Luke sent me another text so I read it. He's all like *you there yet?* And I text back *oh yeah* and after like two seconds he's like, *how is it?* And I'm like, *already regretting it.* He goes, *why?* And I'm like, *tell you later. How's it going at Erik's? Cold,* he goes. *But fun. Wish you were here instead* I re-read that last part like five times. Where's the question mark? I feel like this warm stab in my belly that's got nothing to do with the baby or the nachos I had on the way over here. Does he mean do *I* wish *I* were there instead of this freaking party—or does he mean *he* actually wishes I was over there with *him* and the soccer team rather than here with Peter and million other people? I mean, if he had just put a question mark or a period clearly at the end of his text it would be a no-brainer, but without…*? Sheesh.*

I think this means he wishes I was there…

Text something back, Abby—I tell myself. He's gonna think you're spacing or getting weird about his question, or his statement, or whatever. But *I am* weirding out about it. Seriously, I go in my head—would I rather be with Luke Forrester right now?

Like a complete ditz I just text back, *Ha!*

A few seconds later he just texts something about having to address the troops or something and he'll talk to me later and I put my phone away and try not to be frustrated.

I turn my attention back to the party. I've totally lost track of Jenna and Gabby. A huge eruption of yells and hoots suddenly goes up from the next room and a wave of people push to get near the large doorway to it. At first, I think it's a fight which is pretty lame for a college party, but that's not it.

"Oh hey, yo—they're gonna get those dudes to play Twerk n' Jerk!" I hear some guy yell. I have no clue what that means, but I also have no choice but to move closer to that room since everyone is moving toward that part of the house.

"Abby!" I look up and see I'm like suddenly standing next to Jenna.

"Hey—where's Gabby?" I go.

"I don't know. She was talking to a couple of college guys while I was talking to Gracie Gutowski and a few other Hemingway people, and we got separated. What's going on?"

"No clue," I shout so Jenna hears me.

In this other room, the first thing I see above everybody's head are these two guys standing on top of this crazy/long Viking-size table. Then suddenly a bunch of people just start yelling, "Welly! Welly!" like super loud. I realize one of the guys standing on the table is Kirk Wellington from Hemingway and at first, I think everybody's yelling "Welly" for him. But they're not. Because then this other bigger guy stands up on the table too and has this bottle of whiskey or whatever and a couple plastic cups. And by the way they keep yelling "Welly" at this guy, I realize that he's Kirk's older brother. You know, one of the guys hosting the party and like the only reason any of us from Hemingway were even allowed to get in here. Kirk's brother pours the cups about half-full and hands one to his brother and the other cup to the guy I don't recognize at all.

"Can I get a toast for my kid brother before he gets his first University of Michigan education in the bioscience of Twerk n' Jerk?" Kirk's brother yells to the crowd. A bunch of people raise their cups too as Kirk and the other guy down their shot. Jenna raises her cup too and takes a drink even though she's as clueless as I am as to what's going on.

The DJ cuts off the music for a second and then he comes back on playing some funky/sexy sounding jam sounding all silky through the big speakers. For a second Kirk and the other guy just stand there all awkward in front of everyone, but these two rougher college-looking girls come out of nowhere and start dancing on these chairs in front of them. Everybody goes crazy again when the girls start moving their hips and twerking the air in front of Kirk and this other guy.

Kirk's brother climbs up the table again behind Kirk and pours another couple of ridiculous-sized shots. But before he can hand the cups to the guys though, the two girls reach over from their chairs and start unbuckling Kirk and the other guy's pants. The place just erupts in cheers and whistles as the girls tug the guys' pants down to their ankles and the boys just stand there in their boxer-briefs.

"Oh my god—are you serious?" Jenna goes.

I'm just standing there too, like totally speechless. I can't believe I'm seeing this.

Kirk and the other guy share this goofy look with each other like they can't believe they're actually doing this and down their shots. The girls start their dancing again, but now they've moved so they're on the table with the guys and they're close enough to grind on them a little bit. Both of these girls with fake-bake faces and tight jeans that are barely keeping their shapely asses from bursting out.

The two young women both pull off their tight T-shirts, revealing these tight, red, strapless bras.

"Oh my god, oh my god, oh my god. What's happening?" Jenna goes.

The women go back to grinding on Kirk and the other kid. They turn around and shove the boys' faces into their tanned cleavage.

The whole house comes alive with yelling and raising beer cups all frenzied and I'm glad to see I'm not the only girl in here that looks completely shocked and creeped out by what they're doing. But it's also crazed how many girls look just as excited as all the guys do.

"Yeah, it's a game. It's called Twerk n' Jerk," this random guy near us goes. "See, it's a race to see which guy can get hard first. The girls dance and shove their faces all up in their business to get the boys turned on. But the whole time they keep giving them massive shots of hard stuff. In a minute here the chicks will give them a dong check to see who's hardest."

"A *dong check*?" I go.

"Well, what do you get if you win?" Jenna goes.

The guy just shrugs and goes back to watching.

"Look! It's Little Welly!" some other guy closer to the table yells and a ton of people laugh.

"*Lil Welly*!" more people start to join in.

I just could not believe what I was seeing. It was all like something out of a stupid movie or some random, lame X-rated TikTok or whatever. Both the girls keep dancing and bouncing in front of everyone in their bras. More and more of the guys are yelling for them to take those off too, but they seem more concerned at the moment in turning the two guys on so they can keep uh, *racing*, I guess. Both Kirk's and the other guy's faces are getting red and flushed. And one of the girls grabs Kirk's waistband and yanks it down and the crowd—*uh*—goes *nuts*.

I mean, I went to elementary school with Kirk for crying out loud and now—*Surprise!* There's Kirk's hard dick right out there for everybody to see. There's no good name for them, I decided. You know—*penises*. No name that doesn't sound like some seventh-grade boy came up with it. Even the correct term 'penis' is awful. I mean, no matter what name you call them, every one of them just sounds so limp, so unserious and crass.

Everything seemed so ridiculous at that point. I mean, I fully realize I am no expert on male genitalia—I'd only seen one other one in my life—Peter's. But before I'm hit with total disgust, I start to notice the little differences between Kirk and Peter's you know, *business*. And it just made me realize how weird sex is and how it makes you think crazy and whatever. I remember Gabby telling me her first like *real* experience with a guy the summer before freshman year. His name was Travis something if I remember it right. Anyway, she had started to blow him in this lawn mower shed at the church both their families went to, but they had to stop because they almost got caught, or so she says. Anyway, Travis moved away before the start of school, and I remember thinking how convenient that was for her. No slut rumors for her to deal with, no awkward encounters with Travis in the hallways or anywhere else, but she still got valuable experience points. Another complete score for Gabrielle Altman.

But I shake out of it and can't look at this scene anymore. The whole party, the whole night, has lost its luster if it ever had any to begin with if you know what I mean.

"We're out of here," I go to Jenna.

"What? What are you talking about?"

I get out my phone and start texting Gabby I want to leave. She texts back 'why?' and 'where are you?' and whatever. I text her I'm getting Peter and then heading towards the front door where we came in.

29

"Whoa—how'd you get it to talk like that?" Pauly Thompson asks, and we all look at Luke and his phone.

Luke taps on his finger pad a bit and the phone goes, "A *Speak and Spell* app. You like?"

"That's one freaky voice, man," Dickey goes.

"No kidding," Tristan goes. "If I ever heard a voice like that wake me up in the middle of the night, I'd totally crap my pants."

"All right—listen up, ya'll. I think Luke's going to finally tell us why he put together this little shindig," Erik goes.

We all shut up. We all listen with our breath rising steadily above us in the firelight.

Luke starts off talking about what a great season it was and how grateful he feels just to be a part of it. He talks about how the whole thing was so much more than the big wins and making it to State, but also the bonding that happened between all of them. He calls them all his *freaking blood brothers* at one point. He goes on and on about the team's tightness. Their one-*ness* and how precious it is and all that. But he ends his rousing re-hash of the season with a question: "But now what? What do we do with our one-*ness* now? What are we going to do with *this*—our togetherness—now that the season is gone?"

Everybody's quiet for a bit. One of the logs in the fire cracks, sending tiny fiery shards of spark into the air.

"Well, why don't you tell us what we're gonna do, captain?" Erik finally goes. "You started this. So, what's next? I'm game."

"I think a lot of us are," Ryan goes.

I notice just about everybody nods in agreement, except for Turner who just keeps a steady gaze on the flames.

Luke taps into his phone. "I say we spread what we got. This *one-ness*."

"Spread it? To who?" Glendening goes.

"To whom," I mumble.

"To everybody at school," comes Luke's reply.

"What? How do we do that?" Patrick looks all skeptical.

"I don't know yet. I'm working on it. But I think we can do it. Try at least," Luke's phone goes.

"But remind me *why* we should try?" Erik goes. "I mean, I'm all for doing something together. Something real, something purposeful or whatever—but why would we want to reach out to the school in general, exactly? Especially when so many of them kind of hate us now, or won't associate with us at all because of the whole narc-ing thing?"

"Yeah, Erik's right. The season was great, and I love hanging with you guys—but sometimes at school I get weird vibes from people and I'm pretty sure it's still because of us turning ourselves in this fall," Troy goes.

"Yeah, I sense that too, dude," Glendening goes too. "A lot of awkward moments at school since then, fellas."

"For all of us—and I'm just a freshman," Tristan goes.

"That's what I'm saying," Erik continues. "We get ripped on all the time for turning ourselves in after that party. So many people have talked so much shit about us, it's freaking ridiculous. People I even thought were friends too. So why should we make an effort to all of those haters to make peace and spread whatever it is we got? I mean, if we waste time and try to get all of them to be like us, to join us, or whatever—I mean, Luke—don't you think that's going to make them laugh and rip on us more?"

"You know why they laugh?" Robo Luke goes.

Nobody answers.

"They're afraid."

"Afraid? Of what?" Erik goes. "Morehouse isn't afraid, I'll tell you that. He's pissed. He hates our guts now. I mean like *really* hates. I know for a fact he's the one that started that b.s. about all of us jacking off in the showers together."

"I don't think he's talking about Trevor, Erik," Ryan pipes up. "I think he's talking about everybody else at school. The *In-Betweeners*."

"The what?" Patrick laughs.

"The *In-Betweeners*. The one's at school caught in between the people that like us and the people that hate us."

Across the fire, I see Luke nodding at Ryan as if Ryan is on to something big. Luke hits a button, and the robotic voice continues, "They're afraid because they don't understand why we did it. Plus, we're up in grills. We're making a stand for something that no one wants to really talk about. Kids or adults." The raspy-metallic voice cuts off and Luke taps up a storm on his finger pad. The rest of us just look around at each other for what seems like an awkward forever. "Everybody at school is divided from everyone else in so many ways," he finally continues, "and some of that's natural. But some of it's not. Some of it's not healthy. It's just the way school is. The way it has always been. Broken. So, nobody ever tries to change it. Not for real anyway. We're all castaways self-stranded on our own islands with just our own little pockets of friends if we're lucky. If we're not lucky, we're just castaways by ourselves, surrounded by the sea of a thousand other kids. Seriously… do any of you have to think hard to see the faces of kids at school that barely got any friends?"

"So, what are you saying? That we're gonna try to be everybody's friend?" Erik goes.

"Hey—I'm everybody's friend. Everybody loves me," Dickey goes and laughs at his own comment.

Luke continues. "Not exactly. But I do think we can change the feel of the place. Take the edge off. Get people to think. And expand the circle."

30

Abby

"What are you talking about, Abby? I mean, we practically just got here," Gabby goes.

"I'm sorry. I really, really shouldn't have come in the first place—but I can't stay here—" Some guy totally bumps into us and spills some of his beer on my shoulder while he's yelling and raising his cup to the full-frontal craziness going on up on the table. "I got to get out of here, like *now*."

"Sweetheart, look—let's just go in back to the kitchen, or go look upstairs and see if we can find a quiet room or whatever for a little bit so you can get a break," Peter goes.

Ever since I texted them that I wanted to leave, both Peter and Gabby totally like converged on me and are spending many minutes trying like mad to convince me to just chill out and stay.

"Peter, I don't want to take a break. I don't want to go talk somewhere either. I'm sorry this is inconvenient as hell, but I need to get out of here, please," I go.

Peter shakes his head. "Inconvenient? It's selfish is what it is. You know how long we've been planning this? I mean, why didn't you just stay home like you talked about?"

"Why didn't I?" I nearly explode back. "I didn't stay home because you and Gabby like convinced me I should come." I glance at Gabby and she shrinks back but has this weird little condescending look on her face. I look back at Peter and he looks back at me saying nothing.

"So, you're not going to take me home?" I finally go.

He huffs and looks at me like he's really annoyed and pissed but won't let it all out. "I can't. I'm Nelly's ride and he's not ready to go."

"Well, let Dylan or somebody else take him home. He's just one guy. Somebody should have room for him."

"But what about me and Jenna?" Gabby goes.

"What?" I go. Surely, she must be kidding.

"Well, if you two leave, how are me and Jenna going to get home too then?"

"Gabby, are you saying you wouldn't leave with me? With us?"

Gabby makes this sickening subtle *duh*-face and goes, "Like I said, we haven't even been here an hour yet."

What. Ever. "Unbelievable. Seriously?" I go.

"Look—you need some time I think to just settle down or whatever, so I'm going to walk over there and let you two talk like the couple of adults that you are," Gabby goes.

I feel like grabbing her from behind by the hair and choking her as she starts walking away. Not going to lie.

Up on the table the two chicks finally take their bras off and it feels as if the whole house will crumble beneath the noise of the crowd. The random guy next to Kirk stands up and cheers too, flashing his semi at the same time. So many people have their phones out recording and taking pics you'd think it was a red-carpet event till you looked up on the table.

"Are you really *not* going to take your girlfriend home when she asks you?" I go.

Peter just kind of stands there a for a moment, not really looking at me, but like making a point of not looking at the topless girls bouncing and gyrating up by the pants-less boys either, even though I have this sneaking suspicion he really, really wants to.

"This is so unfair, Abby," he shakes his head. "Look—" he begins, and I can just tell. I can tell that whatever comes out of his mouth will not be *OK, let's go*. I can tell just by looking at his face, the way his jaw is so set, that all he's capable of offering me right now are delays, semi-heartfelt apologies, dead-stares, and restrained anger masked in his freaked-up idea of patience. Because in his mind, this is the party of the millennium. This is the night that will launch a thousand stories. This is his first glimpse of what college *could* be. His first night in the big leagues. An Ann Arbor frat house party—*for reals*. There's imported beer on tap, half-naked girls, and Kirk Wellington's dick. How could I, his pregnant teenage girlfriend, ever compete with *this*?

"Hey, excuse me for like interrupting—" cuts in a voice from out of nowhere, "but do you need a ride home?"

It's Maddie O'Leary and I'm in shock. Up to this moment, I can't think of two whole words we've ever spoken to each other at school or anywhere else and now here she is, totally cutting into an argument between me and Peter, at a college party no less, offering me what neither my boyfriend nor my closest friends will give me: *a ride out of here.*

"Could you?" It's Peter that answers her first. I'm too much in shock at how weird this all is.

"Sure. Especially if you're wanting to stick around. I mean, I know Kirk's one of your homeboys and it looks like it's turning out to be a *big* night for him—and I'm sure you're not going to want to miss any of it," Maddie goes.

"Yeah," Peter goes, not sure it seems if Maddie's being serious or not. I guess I'm not really sure for sure either. He turns to me. "Anyway, are you cool with going with Maddie then?"

It kills me how the magical appearance of Maddie O'Leary, and two of her friends standing next to her, have softened Peter's tone and facial expressions suddenly.

"Yeah, sure," I go. "If that's really OK? I mean, I don't want to make you leave just because, you know—"

"No—don't worry about it. It's all good," Maddie waves me off.

"OK," is all I can think of to say.

"Great. Thanks so much, Maddie," Peter goes. "Thanks, sweetheart," he says to me and gives me a quick peck on the cheek. "Call you later, OK?" He turns and doesn't even wait for me to mumble out an OK or whatever, he's in such a hurry to get into the other crowded room where all the drunken porn is happening on the table.

"Mmm. *Romantic*," Maddie goes.

"You don't know the half of it," I say.

"I bet I don't," she says with what looks to me like real kindness in her eyes. She turns to her friends. "Abby—Thora and Dallas."

I nod to the other two girls, and they smile back. Dallas I've at least had a class with, but I've never talked with Thora before in my life.

"Well, shall we?" Maddie goes and starts to push her way through the party.

As we get closer to the front door a couple of college guys are drinking and leaning up against a wall. "Hey, ladies. Where're you going? You're going to miss the climatic finish," one of the guys goes.

"I'm pretty sure we can all figure out how it's going to end, we all passed Health class in sixth grade," Maddie goes back.

"But you leave you won't know who wins."

"*Hmm.* But I already know who lost. See you boys," Maddie says and the two of them turn their heads to watch us go.

We make it out into the freezing night air. The house's massive front porch is packed with other partiers, mostly vapers in ski jackets and hoodies. As we walk down, we pass through the thick, undeniable smell of pot.

"Smells like Cheech is here," Thora goes and Dallas and Maddie giggle.

We get to the sidewalk and Maddie nods left. "We're parked down this way."

"I really appreciate this. I just hope I didn't cut your night shorter than you wanted in there," I go as we walk down the sidewalk.

"No worries, Ms. Browne. Besides, we made our appearance, and it was definitely time for us to make our disappearance. Clearly. There was getting to be too much beans and sausage in there if you know what I mean."

I start to laugh. "You mean Twerk n' Jerk wasn't your thing?"

"Honey, that shit shouldn't be anybody's thing," Dallas goes.

"No kidding. I mean, what was Kirk thinking? Does he not realize how many people will be posting his junk like within the minute or what?" Thora adds.

Maddie groans, "Oh, Kirk will be fine. In fact, he'll be more than fine. The guy's going to be a legend because of this. You just watch. Not going to hurt his rep at all. The fact that tons of people have vids of his junk will only make his legend even more ridiculous. But I guarantee you if it was a Hemingway *girl* that got de-pants-ed up there and people posted videos of it, she'd be done for years, ladies. For freaking years. I kid you not."

"So not fair," Dallas goes.

"She'd be called a skank in seconds and every guy at school'd be sharing pics and vids, tugging off to her boobies every night because they'd get so turned on even more than their usual porn they jack off to because they know her," Maddie goes. "And let's not even start to imagine all the smack she'd have to hear at school on top of all that."

"That's *beyond* not fair," Thora echoes.

"OK, but what's going to happen to those two—uh—*ladies* up there with Kirk? Aren't postings of them going to get them in trouble with the university or kill their reputations?" I ask.

"*Honey*—" Dallas goes, "those gals ain't civilians."

"They're not?" I go, not really getting Dallas's meaning.

"Those girls are on the clock," Maddie adds. "They're not college kids, they're strippers, yo. Frat parties hire them to do stuff like Twerk n' Jerk."

"*For real*?" I go.

"*Real*—" Dallas goes.

Maddie turns to me. "So—no worries, Abby. It was seriously time to make our disappearance. In fact, a perfectly timed disappearance is one of my rules when it comes to parties like that. I mean, it's just as important as making a perfectly timed appearance, if you want to know the truth."

"You have rules? For parties? Like for real?" I go. I realized she could be totally messing with me, but I couldn't help it. I was really curious if she really did have rules.

"Sure," she goes, pointing her key at her black Mercedes, unlocking it. *Rich kids,* I think. *How did I get this surrounded by them?* "A girl's gotta have rules to help keep her focused. Ahead of the game. Aint that right, ladies?"

"I hear that, girl," Dallas goes and opens a back door.

"*Word*," Thora goes and opens the one on the opposite side, leaving me the passenger seat. I get in and Maddie fires it up and we pull out onto the street. We pass by the house party again.

"See you gotta have rules, or places like that can get a girl in trouble. Like serious trouble," Maddie goes.

"So, like what are some of them?" I go.

"Well, most of the art comes in knowing when to show up and when to leave. Like I said. If you know it's going to be cool—make sure to show up, but don't ever be the first females to get there."

"You want to hit the club mid-stride," Thora chimes in from behind me.

"And never show up in less than a pack of three," Dallas goes. "Two's no good. Two can work for boys, but not girls. Like I said, it's so unfair."

"So, once you're there, how do you know when to leave?" I go.

Maddie snickers. "Well, obviously when you got topless girls and guys shamelessly showing off their meat next to them—*clearly*, it's time to bounce."

"*Word*," Thora goes again.

"But there are other signs too. Like when a couch is set on fire, or any piece of furniture really. Or when somebody shines a gun is a clear sign. Oh, and if there are any other drugs there other than your good old-fashioned alcohol, tobacco, weed, or X. Anything else shows up other than that, it's *goodnight, girls*. Stick with those tell tales, and you're golden."

"Wow," I go, fairly impressed, not so much with the actual rules themselves but the way Maddie presented them—or actually presented herself. She was so—I don't know what the word is—it's not confident exactly, it's more than that. But anyway, the point is, at that moment I could see why so many guys liked her. It's not just her looks—she's got serious personality. I know that sounds so dumb to say about a person, but in her case it really was true.

"You don't ever want to drink either," She keeps going. "I mean, you want to make everybody think you're drinking—but try not to."

"You don't like to drink?" I go.

"It's not that. I drink. I even like it sometimes, but I certainly don't do it at big parties anymore. I gotta have my sense in that kind of environment, you know?"

"See now though, this is where Maddie and *I* differ in our rules," Thora goes. "If a party's lively, I like a good buzz going. Especially if there's dancing."

"So, what were you drinking tonight? I saw you with a cup," I ask.

"That, my dear, was a cup of pink lemonade I got from the guy tending their little homemade bar they had going. They use lemonade for a drink they call a *Pink-Panty-Pulldown,* I hear. I got him to fix me one without the *Pulldown*. But that's the thing—everybody else in a place like that just assumes you're drinking."

"And fair game," Dallas adds. "To them playas you're *always* fair game."

"Thinking with they cocks, with they heads full of rocks," Thora sings in the back seat and the rest of us all giggle.

"Sorry for butting-in back there though," Maddie goes. "I wasn't trying to listen in on you and Peter or anything. It's just when Kirk and those girls started playing that game and taking off clothes, I was just looking for anywhere else to rest my eyes and I saw you guys and took a guess you wanted to leave, and he didn't."

"Well, I'm glad you did," I go. In my head I got a quick flash of Peter still at that party and it getting crazier and him getting drunk and talking to other girls. "I mean, what kind of guy refuses to take his girlfriend home from a party like that?"

Dallas and Thora both start laughing.

"Damn, girl! You serious? A guy that's surrounded by booze, tunes, and ladies taking off they clothes. That's what kind of guy!" Dallas goes.

"Just about every guy in the universe would play you the same way," Thora adds and keeps laughing.

"Well, just about every *straight* guy," Maddie goes and laughs too.

"Hey hold up, yo—a gay guy wouldn't want to leave too soon neither. Not with all that manhood sticking out and flapping all over the place. *No way*, girl," Dallas goes.

At first, I was kind of getting a little pissed because they were making fun of me but then I realized what I said was pretty ridiculous. Plus, these girls were laughing; nothing in their laughter felt mean, or sarcastic. So, I just start laughing with them.

"Maybe you should just dump Peter and hook yourself up one of those straight-edged soccer players. Most of them might have taken you home. They all took a pass on being at the party tonight anyway to chill all sober over at Erik Volgstaad's cottage, I hear," Maddie goes. "And you know those guys, right? I mean, don't you hang out with Forrester?"

I feel my face flush all red. "Uh, well—I wouldn't say we hang out, but we used to be good friends like a long time ago. We live on the same street."

"*Mm-hmm*, the same street you say," Dallas goes.

"You ever creep over in the dark and watch him change through his window? I hear he's got like UFC abs," Thora all leans up to my ear.

There's like no way I'm going to admit I was actually spying on the Forrester's house that one night earlier this year, so I just laugh.

"Now that's who you should be dating. Luke Forrester. He strikes me as the kind of guy that wouldn't do you wrong," Maddie goes, grinning.

I can't believe she just said that—even if she is kidding.

"That's who we *all* should be dating, Maddie-girl. A hot guy with muscles that don't talk," Dallas goes.

"No kidding. Sounds like the perfect guy. *Especially* if he takes his shirt off," Thora adds.

"Are you being cereal, Dally? Do you really think we should all be dating Luke rather than Monsieur 'Scxy Moss?" Maddie goes.

"*Sexy Moss*?" I go.

"Well, you know I love my Dignan, and after the way he was chatting you up tonight, I know for facts he got eyes on you—but Diggy's still a playa just like the rest of them," Dallas goes.

"Yeah. But Diggy's nice and everybody likes him," Thora goes.

"Sure, and Dignan know it too," Dallas nods. "*And wow*, do he know it. And he works it too, girls. But I'll give Luke this, Maddie—he's better for you than that other soccer fool you been flirting around with."

"Erik? You think, huh?" Maddie goes.

"Look—all of you better step off Forrester now. Because the more we talk about him the more I like the idea of him wrapping me up in those big strong arms of his," Thora goes.

I kept giggling all stupid and hoped they didn't realize how nervous and weirded out I was talking about this. And I wasn't sure I liked Thora's thick and honeyed way she talked about Luke at all—and yet I didn't know what to make of what that said about me at the time, and how I felt about Luke either. I suddenly remembered Luke's text too and the knots in my stomach returned. And there was something else. Even though none of them even mentioned it—I knew they all knew I was pregnant (I mean, everybody at school did by then, or could figure it out by just looking at my belly)—and even though they hadn't done thing one to make me feel weird about it, I suddenly got all awkward just the same.

31

Patrick looks confused. "Expand the circle? What circle?"

Luke makes a swirling motion with his finger and ends with a *ta-da* deal with both hands.

Now the rest of us sitting around the fire look confused along with Patrick.

Luke taps furiously to his phone's keypad; raises it back up. "Duh. *This* circle. Buttwipes. Our circle. Us," goes the robot voice. He does the *ta-da* thing again with his hands a couple times with his eyes bulging and this cheesy look on his face I've certainly never seen before.

"What's he doing?" Pauly goes.

"I don't know; this is crazy. It's a spaz attack, guys. I think Luke is finally going crazy. Like for *real* crazy," Glendening goes back.

"You guys are idiots. Fucking morons to the last man, I swear on my dead grandpa's rotting nuts. He means expanding *this*—all you guys. What you got going here. All this good-feeling, let's-be-everybody's-friend bullshit. *This…*" Turner barks and gestures to all of us sitting around the fire.

"He's right," Ryan goes. "Turner's hit it on the head, guys. That's exactly what Luke's talking about."

See, at the time I was sitting there—my butt going crazy/numb on a freezing lawn chair—listening to these guys, I couldn't help but feel something. Like, *Yeah—I think I want to be a part of this.* Finally, something's going on that seems *alive*, something that was socially risky but wasn't too dumb or totally done-to-death. Something I could belong to or to help me identify myself with. You know?

But that was about as far as my mind could take it at that point.

But now, having had the time to really look back on who I was—or what I was trying to be, who these guys were, what Luke was really talking about and touting—maybe now I can see things a little clearer.

The truth was—I mean if I really, really, focus—the truth was, at that point in my life I didn't know *who I was*. You know? Like *who* I was as a person. My *real* identity. I guess I had like a ballpark idea of who I was but nothing solid enough to really put into words. And anyway, I don't think it was all that common for high school kids to think about it in terms like that. You know? Not the kids I knew anyway. I mean, high school kids don't think in clearly defined slogans or mission statements—adults do—but not kids in most cases.

Anyway, I'm saying all this stuff to say that even though I wasn't sure what I was—at least I was pretty sure what I *wasn't*. I think that's how it starts out at first for all of us—we see something we're not, and we begin to identify ourselves by that. By what we're *not*. By what we don't want to be seen as. We get inspired first by avoiding becoming what we don't want to turn into—you know?

I'll be honest, every time I saw Jason Turner in the hallways, or even that night sitting across the fire, I always thought on some level: *no way—I ain't turning out like him. Stay away from drugs, dude. Say no to drugs*. That kind of stuff.

Or maybe a kid that isn't trans sees a kid that is—or might be—and goes *no way—no matter what, I know I ain't that.* Or maybe a kid that wants to be trans looks at themselves in a mirror and realizes, *no way—I'm not wearing this mask anymore.* Or how a stoner, or a hick, is like immediately adverse to anyone they see as a prep, and a prep-type is all *no way* about skater kids, or whatever.

I mean, you get my point, right? We know what we're *not* before we know what we *are*. And listening to Luke's crazy robot voice all coming through his handheld, I realized that I didn't want to be one of the millions and millions of high school kids out there that just didn't *care*. I realized, even though it was all crazy/nebulous and undefined in my brain at the time, that I wanted to be *on fire,* as Erik put it.

And I knew that these guys were on to whatever it was that I wanted too. I saw them as the key somehow, and Luke as their leader—their guide. And since I wasn't an actual soccer player, or their close friend like Dickey was, or uh… a hardcore druggie, I guess, like Turner was, I felt I needed to find a role with these guys. To earn my *fire* sort of speak. I needed a function.

So, I would document. I would watch. Ask questions. Join in when I could, but above all else, record *this*—whatever *this* was. You know—if they would let me, of course.

"Yeah! Expand the circle! *Rahhhhh*!" Erik up and yells and stands up shaking his fists.

"Whoa—hey, what are you doing, man?" Glendening goes.

"Duh, dude—getting up. Getting stupid. Getting excited. Following Luke, even though as usual, I don't have a clue why," Erik goes and starts laughing.

"Well, how are we going to do this, exactly?" Ryan goes, looking at Luke. "How do we *expand the circle*?"

Luke taps into his phone. "IDK. I'll come up with something. We'll figure it out."

"We'll figure it out! Expand the circle! Stand with me, brothers! Stand with Preacher Forrester!" Erik starts motioning for everyone to rise.

"Amen, brother Volgstaad. You can count on my steel!" Dickey yells and launches up, pulling young Tristan up with him.

Tristan looks seriously startled but still yells too, "Y-Yeah—expand the circle!"

Suddenly big Patrick roars and bolts up and draws Glendening and Troy and Pauly under his arms and moves forward towards the fire. Erik locks arms with Luke and suddenly all these guys are huddling up like they're back on the soccer field.

Ryan pulls me up and I join them along with Dickey and Tristan.

Everybody just starts howling into the night. Guys just start yelling *expand the circle*! We all start roaring and laughing.

"Everybody put your hand in," Erik yells and stretches his arm over the middle of the glowing fire. Without a second's hesitation, everybody does. And even though it's still considerably hot over the fire, I put mine in too.

"An oath, then," Erik goes, looking into all our eyes.

Luke is all smiles; nods his approval.

"To nobly expand the circle!" Dickey howls. We all laugh and howl with him. There's no doubt everyone's feeling some excitement here, but also, I can't help thinking that most of these guys have no idea what we're really vowing exactly, and therefore cannot really be taking this seriously.

Erik spies Turner still sitting, sulking on his seat. "Yo—Turn-dog! You in, or what?"

"*Hey—*" Turner springs to life and stands up clenching his hands into fists. "Don't you ever call me fucking 'Turn-dog' again. You got that?"

Everybody shuts up.

"Uh—yeah, man. No harm intended," Erik goes. "Just wanted to know if you're… *in*?"

Out of nowhere, Turner drops his scowl—and for the first time that I can ever remember, the kid actually grins. "*Am I in*?"

We all look at Turner.

He just looks at us.

He shrugs and goes, "Look, whatever. I'll stand right here while you guys hoot and holler if that gets your rocks off, but I aint putting my hand in, OK?"

Erik kind of frowns but nods his head like that's cool. I look over and see Ryan and Luke with big grins.

"OK," Erik goes. "I think we'll take it, right boys?"

We all howl.

"Expand the circle! *EXPAND THE CIRCLE! RAHHHHHH*!"

So this was it. If you've been wondering, this is how it came to pass that I became the teller of this tale—however, it must be said that I had no idea at the time what I'd stepped into. Like none at all. I had no clue yet just how much had already happened, all of what was happening with most of them at that moment, or what colossal events awaited us all just around the bend.

CANTO III

"Roll on, thou deep and dark blue ocean, roll!"

Byron

Erif
XIII

The afternoon sun glared down. Even under her canopy of shade, Angel felt its heat. She saw the sweat roll off the Tarrenbacks' brows in transparent miniature rivers and smelled the pitted odor of exertion from those that carried her carriage up the steep mountain path.

She spent most of the morning wringing her hands and trying not to look at anything, or anyone. They had come in to wake her before dawn—-the Great Hall's ceremonial attendants and an escort of Tarrenbacks. There was no need to wake her though, Angel had not slept a wink and waited for them sitting on her humble cot with her hands in her lap. They took her to the Hall's water chambers and the attendants stripped her naked. She let them gently bathe her in the stone fountain with the Tarrenbacks posting guard outside the chamber door. She was dressed in the white robes of the Chosen, prayed over by Thorn's seven holy Fathermen, taken and seated in her man-held carriage on the trail by fist light.

I will not cry. I will not show fear. I will not struggle or scream. Angel repeated to herself. And to her good credit her face never showed one bit of distress—-only placid, implacable calm. The only sign that this was indeed a child of the Lottery on her way to her dutiful death were Angel's small reddening palms and the white knuckles above them.

Her troop of Tarrenbacks took a long break just past midday and chowed down on a lunch of bread and dried meat. While the men ate and gulped water out of their bladder-bags, Angel was allowed out of her carriage to stretch her legs, provided she was in sight.

Angel closed her eyes and felt the mountain breeze play upon her cheeks. Her nostrils took in the deep smell of the mossy rocks and wildflowers that grew out from rich dirt between the crags. *Such a glorious day... The entire valley singing with life... Such a bittersweetness, on this, my last day.*

"Savioress—-" One of the Tarrenbacks approached her. "It's time to continue."

Angel looked up to him and nodded. She shifted her feet, preparing to follow him back to her carriage, but the man yet made no move to lead her. He had taken his helm off; his auburn hair lifted in the breeze. The man had a sincerity about his eyes that Angel hadn't seen with his helmet on.

"Savioress, while we have a moment—-I have something, a gift of sorts. Something the Fathermen wanted me to give you."

Angel looked confused. "What is it, sir?"

The man took a knee before Angel and reached underneath his breastplate, into his tunic. In his palm he presented a small crystal vial. "It's a strengthened draught of *godsmercy.*"

"*Godsmercy?"* Angel repeated. Although, in truth she could guess what it was for and why the Fathermen would want to give her the powerful wits-number.

"It is customary," the Tarrenback continued, "to give to the Chosen along the way to the Crack. For the moment you face Erif. Be careful with it Savioress. The crystal cracks easily enough. The best way I'm told is to merely set it between your teeth and press down and the potion will do the rest."

Angel took the vial in her hand. "Will it put me to sleep?"

"I don't believe all the way, miss. But it is very powerful. Swallow it not before the very moment you are given wholly to the dragon."

"*Wholly*?" Angel repeated. "You mean swallow it right before I am devoured, sir?"

"Take it. For the pain—-for the moment you enter the dragon's... Hide it on the side of your cheek when the time comes. Be mindful with it around the Rogni. Tis said that they present the Chosen to the dragon naked. I wish so much that this—-my Savioress, I—-"

Angel put the vial in the pocket of her robes and reached out to touch the man's cheek that knelt before her. "What is your name?"

The man seemed well beyond shocked, as if one of the yonder boulders had just asked him the question. "I am called Kylan, Savioress. I am a father of three children of Lottery age. I cannot—-"

Angel managed a frail smile. "Thank you, Kylan."

Kylan quickly bowed his head and then just as quickly rose to lead her back to the trail. Angel followed and made no noise, tip-toe-ing on the stones to get back under her canopy. A moment later, Kylan's helm was back on his head, the rest of the Tarrenbacks were on their feet with a fresh rotation of them picking up her carriage to trudge on.

By the start of sunset, the troop was into the steepest part of their journey yet. The four huffing and straining men laid down Angel's carriage.

"We all walk from here, Savioress," Kylan bent down to tell her.

Angel took his hand. "*Angel*—-good Kylan. I have been called Angel all my life, and it would seem silly to be called anything else now, please."

"Very well, *Angel*," he managed a smile and motioned to the steep path ahead of them.

She looked above and saw the rise of the winding path and the looming small forest, the unmistakable copse of High Grove. Angel did not let herself look up at it long, or the ever-expanding darkness of the Crack that opened seemingly just above High Grove.

Be brave. She took a step. *Be brave.* She took another.

The sun had finally dipped down behind the peaks and sharp shadows ruled in the crags between rays of red glow. More and more darkness gathered as the day continued to bruise into nightfall. The two Tarrenbacks in the rear stopped to light torches.

"Look lively, lads. The Rogni are just ahead," Kylan said. "They know you're scared of them—-so they'll play on that knowledge. Don't be rattled by it—-but be wary just in case."

Angel noticed that except for the Tarrenbacks with the torches—-all the others, Kylan included, walked with their crossbows drawn.

"Great gods—-" one of them muttered coming up to the trailhead into High Grove. Stationed to one side, was a cairn of human skulls piled high as Kylan's shoulders.

Angel let slip the quietest of shudders when she passed it and saw that some of the skulls still sported rough tufts of hair and patches of hardened skin.

"Whose heads are those?" one of the Tarrenbacks gasped.

"*Quiet*," Kylan commanded. "They are none of our Thornfolk, so it is not our matter. Eyes to yer front."

They entered the dead-still and full darkness of High Grove. Angel smelled the thickness of dense small trees, but also the smell of rot and death.

A low growl rumbled through the dark and the troop came to a halt. No one spoke. Barely did they breathe.

They saw a glow of torches appear first through the trees and then blaze on the path before them. Again, a chorus of low growls hummed as the Rogni approached. At first, they were just large, hunched shapes, but as they came nearer the full horror of the Rogni came into Angel's view.

They all were at least three heads taller than all the Tarrenbacks. Their bodies sprouted arms and legs like a man, but their heads looked more like that of a hideous wolf, with the addition of one rhinoceros-like horn atop their foreheads. Yellow eyes glowed from sockets just above their perpetually bared white teeth glistening of froth. They wore no clothes, making it easy to see their massive chests and muscles, more powerful looking than any men Angel had ever seen and covered in dark hair just shy of fur. In their left hands, many of the Rogni carried torches—-but their right was not really a hand at all—-more like a full claw set to tear, like that of a grizzly's rather than that of a wolf.

I will not scream.

Angel stood still, looking at them, wringing her hands till the veins in her hands bulged out.

The Rogni halted and fanned out in front of Angel and the Thornmen, seven in all. They huffed out big breaths from their snouts looking at Angel and the Tarrenbacks with what could only be described as menace.

After what seemed to Angel like forever, Kylan finally took a step toward them.

"Hark—-Stagfin. We bring you the Chosen Child of Thorn."

The Rogni known as Stagfin stepped to the fore and let out a sharp bark before speaking. "We hereby take the Dawn's Feast from you as our Lord Erif's yielded tithe."

"You can speak—-" Angel could not keep herself from blurting.

Stagfin's wolfish grin grew wider. "Aye, soft little Dawn's Feast. And that's not all we can do—-" he growled and put his claw over his large hairy groin and gave it a thrust.

All the other Rogni blew up in barks of laughter over that, even a few howls.

"Have ye had yer blood yet, child?" Stagfin bent his head down below his torch to get a better look at her.

Angel managed not to cower or shrink—-but to shake her head.

The Rogni leader stood up straight again. "Pity. Erif sometimes lets us ravage on the lasses a bit before he feasts, if they's already had their first moonsblood."

Angel felt the slightest nudge of Kylan's arm brush up against her back. She could not tell if this was a feeble attempt by him to comfort her in this dark hour, or if it was just pure accidental contact.

"Thornmen—" Stagfin addressed the Tarrenbacks. "Erif the Merciful thanks ye for yer pains and considers Thorn's annual tithe rendered."

Without a moment of hesitation, the Tarrenbacks began to back away out of High Grove. Kylan was the last to step away from Angel, but not by much.

"Swiftspeed, lads. See ye next spring," Stagfin growled.

Angel turned and watched Kylan walk backward, wordlessly, until he disappeared into utter darkness. She wiped the lone tear from her cheek and tensed as she felt the weight of Stagfin's claw on her shoulder, turning her toward him and the other waiting Rogni.

"Come, my master's Dawn's Feast. There are final preparations to be made." Stagfin seemed to hock up his words more than actually speaking them. "Try not to fret so. It'll all be over soon enough—you'll see."

She let him lead her and could feel the host of yellow eyes watch her every step as they parted to let her pass.

Every step was a challenge to keep her balance. Not because of the darkness of the path, but because of the near-paralyzing thoughts that tried to invade the throne room of her mind. Angel tried to think of nothing—-absolutely nothing as she put one foot in front of the other. She could hear the odd, heavy footfalls and bestial breathing of the Rogni behind her. Her hand snuck into her pocket to fondle the vial of *godsmercy* Kylan had given her. But *no*—-she thought. Now surely wasn't the time for that. Not with so many hours left before her devouring.

Be brave, she continued to think. *For sister, for father, for Prince—-for Thorn. To die can sometimes be an act of love. Mother knew this and met it so bravely. So be brave too, Angel. Be brave.*

It was not long before they came to a clearing lighted by more torches on staffs. Angel saw a rough building with a large steepled arch entryway jut out from the mountainside. To either side of the clearing were two more cairns much like the one of human skulls she had seen earlier, only that one cairn was a pile of grizzly skulls and the other mounded up from the heads of deer.

"Keep going. Inside's where ye'll get yer last morsel—-yer last cup of water," Stagfin growled.

Resigned, Angel continued to cross the clearing to the ominous archway followed by the seven Rogni.

There was a sudden odd noise; a commotion behind her. She turned and saw one of the Rogni inexplicably on his knees, his human hand at his throat and gouts of purplish blood pumping through his gnarled fingers.

The wounded Rogni tried to speak but only choked up a *vomitsplatch* of blood.

While they all looked on in shock, Angel thought she glimpsed something flash toward them from the woods out of the corner of her eye. But before she could give more thought to what it might've been, another of the Rogni let out an anguished bark and arched his back, staggering forward.

"Garesh!" Stagfin reached out, but Garesh's yellow eyes only glazed in terror as he fell forward revealing a dagger sunk to its hilt between his beastly shoulder-blades.

In a blink, Angel saw each of the remaining Rogni drop their torches and pull out a short-handled double-sided axe from some sort of lanyard around the backside of their waists that she had not noticed before.

The Rogni instantly made a perimeter around her and crouched into defensive postures.

Nothing. Stillness. There was no sound, no perceptible movement in the trees anywhere.

"Get her inside now. Once she's secured, we come back out and track' em down so's we can rip' em limb for limb," Stagfin whispered from the side of his snout.

The other four Rogni nodded.

One of them nudged Angel forward and she and her circle of monsters took a few more steps towards the building.

"*Wait*—-" one of the Rogni said and they all stopped again.

Angel turned back to the woods and saw Prince emerge from the shadows and into the torchlight.

"Yer as good as dead, boy," Stagfin said.

Prince said nothing.

"How many are ye?" another of the Rogni asked.

"Come find out," Prince said.

The Rogni all stood there looking at him, at the dark forest around them, gripping their axes, tensing their claws. Angel saw a thin string of drool ooze down out of Stagfin's mouth between his jaws.

"After we're done ripping and tearing ye," Stagfin called out, "I'm going to pulp yer heart and drink it from my goblet."

Prince put both his hands behind his back and raised his chin as if he were observing something amusing.

"*Raghhh!*" All of the Rogni roared and sprinted headlong toward Prince.

"No!" Angel yelled.

Prince brought his hands back from behind him and lifted his palms up. With the gesture, five small orbs of blue light rose from near his feet and up level to his chest in less than a heartbeat of time. He lowered his chin, looking like he was concentrating all his thought on the five beast-men baring down on him. With a push of his palms and a yell from his throat, he sent the five auras hurtling forward, fanning out directly in the paths of each of the oncoming monster guards.

Angel watched the Rogni and auras collide in a violent blur.

Stagfin and another Rogni were able to swing their axes in time so that they were able to save themselves at the critical moment that Prince dissolved the auras, unleashing their contents.

The three other Rogni were not so lucky.

Stagfin looked down to see three of his comrades stone dead on their backs, each with a sharpened branch buried into the socket where one of their eyes had been.

Stagfin and the other Rogni were simply able to knock their speeding wooden stakes away.

"*Yonderling*—-he's a yonderling," Stagfin realized. "The kid's an aura-maker!"

Angel saw Prince seem to fidget a moment and suddenly run back into the trees.

"*Thistleprick!*-—after him. But be wary of his little magic trick now," Stagfin ordered. The Rogni nodded and obeyed, chasing off into the darkness after Prince.

"Who is he? Yer brother? Baa! It doesn't matter." Stagfin grabbed Angel by the arm with his claw. "Into our house with ye—-"

A sharp yelp pierced the night. Both Angel and the Rogni looked back to the clearing. Nothing. Until Prince emerged out of the trailhead and back into the torchlight of the clearing. *Alone.* In one hand was a dagger, dripping purple with Rogni blood. In his other was Thistleprick's short axe.

Stagfin let go of Angel's arm walked out to meet Prince. "What's yer goal, youngsuck? Got grand schemes about slaying the dragon up in his cave whiles he sleeps, do ye?"

Prince approached as well.

Angel could tell by his face that Prince did indeed intend to battle with the monster on open ground. "Prince—*run*," she called out.

"Well, yer schemes are about to get as dashed as yer brains," Stagfin continued. "Because my master never sleeps. But what matters *that*? Ye'll never breathe again past yer next step!"

The Rogni lunged at Prince with a savage swipe of his axe that turned into a full arc and swipe with the other edge. It was all Prince could do to duck and shift out of the way of the swirling steel.

Stagfin followed his axe-stroke immediately with a back-and-forth swipe of his claw meant to tear Prince's throat out.

Again, Prince could only retreat and dodge. He made a token thrust at the beast with Samuel's dagger, but at the zenith of his arm's thrust Stagfin slashed down with his axe and cut Prince's hand off clean through the mid-forearm.

Angel screamed and ran towards them seeing Prince's blood spurt in heavy streams from his wound, reeling back from the berserker wolf-man.

He staggered and summoned up the strength to swing the axe at the oncoming Rogni, but Stagfin easily shifted away from the blade and struck it with his own, sending it spinning out of Prince's only hand with a sickeningly heavy *clang* sound. The beast took another big step towards his wounded adversary, kicking his foot out with all his body weight behind it. Hairy heel first. The blow connected solidly into Prince's sternum and sent him flying ten paces backward leaving him breathless and pumping gouts of blood from his severed stump with each heartbeat.

Angel tried to help him up, blood spouting onto her white robes, red slobber flowing from his open mouth, his terrified eyes threatening to curl into the back of their sockets.

"Step away, child," Stagfin stalked closer, nearly looming above them. "It'd be a shame to get any more blood upon yer sacrificial garb. This fool's errand must end as all fool's errands must."

1

Jason

My piece of shit car was slow to start this morning. I fucking thought for a sec that I'd have to ditch the whole deal, at least for a while. I mean, there was like no way I was going to wake up Toe's dad and ask to borrow his car, and anyway, even if I did wake him, I was in no mood to conjure up some elaborate bullshit about why I'd need his car practically the whole goddamn morning through afternoon, you know?

But anyway, after a lot of key-turning and dashboard slamming, the bitch finally started.

I left before Toe or any of his family even woke up. So fucking cold out, Rozz. You don't even want to know. Winter's here for real, man.

The tough bit was going to be sneaking into my own goddamn garage for fuck's sake. So I pull up and right away I see Dad's got like the new windows all up, of course, and the whole front of the house even looks like it's been power washed or whatever. No outward signs at all that the place'd been fucking nuked by shotguns a couple months prior at all. I park a couple houses down and hoof it back to our driveway and slide real close to the house just in case Dad, or anybody else for that matter, can see me from inside. Not that there's much chance of Dad being up this early. I mean, unless he's pulled an all-nighter and is still on a coke high or fucking cranking it or whatever.

But it looked like the house was dead. There was only his truck in the garage, and everything looked as still as shit.

So as I grab the auger from its huge hook, I suddenly get like all curious about how my dad's Christmas was without me. Did he have anybody over? Did he just say to hell with it and get fucking wasted and watch TV specials? Or maybe he just kicked it in Detroit with some of his hook-ups or clients or whatever. Bang a hooker, maybe? Who knows, Rozz. All I know is just as quickly as I became curious about all that, I just as quickly realized I didn't give a shit about my old man and whether or not he had a fucking happy holidays.

I buy a pack of cigs and a cup of coffee on the way out of town. I been smoking like fucking no tomorrow. *That's it*, girl. Nicotine is the next thing I'm quitting. Maybe I'll start with that gum shit next week or whenever I'm out of the rest of this pack. But anyway.

So I'm driving and I really like realize that since I've been all clean and sober or whatever, that I can't get enough morning, man. Like, I really think I'm a morning person. Go figure that shit, huh? I think it's because I'm calmest in the mornings. Everything's brand new and quiet. All untouched and unfucked up. I like it. I feel like I can get my shit together, you know? So, I guess that's probably why I wanted to run this little errand so early. Maybe I knew it would be better—mean more, I guess if I got an earlier start on it.

After a while I get out and can see Lake Erie all froze up and bright under the morning sun. The Great Lake's just this massive field of snow and ice as far as my eye can see. I think for a quick second that it'd be kind of cool to just walk out there, you know, hike all the way out to the middle of it till I couldn't see shore anywhere—I could just stand in the middle of a great white nowhere and just sit and think in peace with nobody anywhere nearby. But then I remember just how fucking cold it is out there and if I did hike out there, I wouldn't be able to think about anything at all except what a whore mother nature is and how bad my nuts hurt because I'm fucking freezing them off.

"We meet again, bitch," I mumble at the lake, driving north. There are barely any other cars I notice, which suits me fine. I settle in behind the wheel, crank some tunes, blow some more smoke, and sip more coffee.

I was like fully prepared to find the access road all snowed in and clusterfucked. That was why I had taken my big heavy snow boots out of the garage too. I just assumed I'd be hoofing it the last mile or so, man. So you can imagine my total shock, Rozz, when I get to the road and it was plowed.

The road and the woods all looked like way different, but so did the little lake too, of course, when I got to it and parked.

I put my wool cap on and tug my hoodie through my coat and pull it over my cap. I haul out the auger and get a little pissed because it got some black grime on my back seat upholstery.

The ice looks steady enough, I guess. There were no ice shanty's or anything else out there at the time, but it looked like someone had been driving out there at some point already this winter. Which made sense—I mean why else would the road to Harper Lake be plowed in the dead-ass of winter unless there were some people that wanted to ice fish on it every once in a while?

I walk past where Luke had fallen to his knees, where I was supposed to brain him but couldn't. I keep walking till I was on the ice, the crunch of the jagged-ass frost beneath me. Out near the middle of the lake the ice got all ice-skatey smooth and I really had to watch my footing and balance with the auger. But the trickiest part by far, man, was trying to get the thing started, pulling the ripcord. Came up with the bright idea way too fucking late that I should've just started the bastard on shore where my footing was steady or whatever and then come all the way out here to the middle. But whatever. The stupid thing finally buzzes to life, and I get her to bore through the ice in like less than fifteen seconds.

When I get the hole all made and cleared, I go down on my knees and sit on the heels of my feet for a little bit. Sure was peaceful out there. Like I said, Rozz I barely recognized the place from that night. It's amazing the difference a little sunshine makes. Well, that and some pure white snow. I mean, even the abandoned truck and trashed refrigerators and other shit out there didn't look half as shitty as they should've with a fresh blanket of snow on them.

After another moment or so of just looking around, I finally haul out Kid T's SIG from behind my belt. Time to do what I came to do. Press the release with my thumb and slide out the clip and lay it on the ice right next to me. Put the barrel of the gun just inches away from the hole and fire off the round in the chamber. Water splashes up and gets all over my jeans and I about piss myself at how loud the shot was, and I even knew it was coming for chissakes, Rozz.

I look back up towards my car and around the lake, but of course no one comes running, no cops pull up to see what the fuck, because no one was out there. That's why people probably liked to ice fish here, it's probably why other jackasses felt OK about dumping all their junk here and why Luke had picked this place for me to kill him and dump his body. Because Harper Lake's the place to dump things that don't get found.

I slid the SIG down into the hole. It made a little *plop* sound and sank. I took up the clip and dropped it in. Bullet. By. Bullet.

I had done the math. By my count I had pulled Kid T's piece on nine people since that night at Lester's. Including my own dad and even myself. You're right, Rozz. With the way things are going it'd only be a matter of time before I just up and shot someone. But no matter what, I do know I ain't going to make it any easier for that to happen. For better or fucking worse, I know if it does come to guns a'blazing, it ain't going to be me capping people. At least not with Kid T's SIG. I know that much, Rozzy. I know that much.

2

Erik could not believe he had an erection. Oh god, not now, he thinks. Not now of all times all mighty lord of lords, freaking hosts of heavenly hosts, thou art great and good and did bring forth the animals two by two. And the thing of it was, it was just one of those random erections guys get. Just blood flowing through the body, you know? It really didn't have anything to do with how absolutely beautiful, hot, sexy, voluptuous, and seriously delicious Maddie O'Leary looked to him. Honest—not at all.

But Erik realized the fact that he had a serious *jones* for her didn't really help him with his crotchtal crisis at that particular moment either, if you know what I mean. Let's face it—I've already told you she was his dream girl from way back before puberty. And now here he was, possibly on his first technical date with her and he didn't dare stand up from Isaiah's *waaay* too cushiony couch lest she notice his hard bulge and get majorly freaked out.

Everything leading up to this moment between he and Maddie had gone pretty great though. Erik couldn't deny it. I mean, he was nervous (he'd be the first to admit) when he decided to ask Maddie to help him do something at the end of Mr. Malory's English class one day. But he told himself, look if she even remotely likes you this is a pretty safe deal—it's low key, it's on a Thursday night (not a weekend for freak's sake), and it's like a totally nice thing to do for someone else. So, after asking her, she didn't give even the slightest impression that she thought it'd be a weird thing—helping him baby-sit Isaiah on some random weeknight in February. And after he had told her Izzy's whole background and about losing his dad, of course she thought it was like seriously cool that he was helping out in such a way.

Erik felt like a genius.

They both drove over together in his car. Mrs. Walker actually seemed excited that he had brought Maddie along and was really welcoming and chatty with Maddie before her friends showed up to take her on a well-deserved night on the town. And Maddie and Izzy seemed to hit it off just fine too. It didn't really surprise Erik that Maddie was so good with younger kids though. Maddie seemed to be great with like all people in general, but he thought it was still great to see her and Isaiah getting along so well. Erik was also like super-glad Izzy was minding his freaking manners (for the most part) too, since he had already confided to the little squirt that he liked Maddie and had already talked about her numerous times while hanging out at their house since Izzy's dad's passing. Although, the twerp did make that dumb comment to Maddie right before turning in—"I'm going to bed now so you guys can make out big time." But for the most part little Izzy stayed away from making too many googley-mush *Duh/Der—Erik's-got-da-hots-for-you* kind of dumb-ass statements.

But of course, as freaking usual, Erik was in the middle of perpetrating the biggest sabotage of the night *himself*, by sporting the most massive and unprovoked boner of his life while he and Maddie sat together on the Walker's new couch (sitting incidentally in the same spot where Erik always had known Izzy's dad's bed to lay) in the living room sipping raspberry lemonades, chatting about a million random things, but mostly hot gossip about their Hemingway classmates.

"So, you heard about Abby Browne like totally breaking up with Peter Calloway, right?" Maddie goes, sitting up on the couch, legs folded under her bottom, turned all towards him.

"Yeah. What was up with that?" Erik tries to subtly crush his wood with his forearm across his lap.

"What was up with that? *Serious*? He was like way more interested in seeing Kirk flashing in front of the whole University of Michigan rather than taking her home because she didn't feel well. I mean, duh? What did he expect? Your boy, Luke, must be pretty happy though, huh?"

"Luke?"

Maddie makes her duh-face at him again for like the millionth time that night. "Yeah, Luke. Doesn't he ever talk about Abby at all? I mean, everybody sees those two hang out in halls together all the time and stuff."

Erik shifts in his seat a little. "I don't know, you know? I mean, Luke doesn't really talk about that kind of stuff with all of us. With us he's more all about long weird stares, eyewinks, and like inspirational texts and post-it notes. Not really so much an open book when it comes to his love life if you know what I mean."

He lifts his arm off his bulging dong for second. *Yep—still hard.* In fact, he was (oh, what was that new word he'd seen surfing around looking at random comments and analysis online about *Moby Dick…*?)… *turgid.* That's it. That was the appropriate word. He was *turgid* with erection. Keep the conversation going, you freaking fool, Erik told himself. Must keep attention off my crotch. What are we talking about again? Oh yeah, Luke. Stay focused, stay focused.

"I mean, he might spill all his secrets like that with Turner who's like his new BFF—but not us. We're just his soccer minions."

"Hmm, yeah. Turner." Maddie gulps down the last of her lemonade till the ice slides down her glass and clinks her front teeth. "So, what's the deal with Luke and him?"

"Turner?" Erik goes. "I don't know. We didn't get a lot of info on that either. Luke just started bringing him around. Now he's like hanging out with us like all the time. I mean, sometimes we just forget he's chilling with us because he usually just sits off in a corner and like says zippo or is outside smoking in the dark somewhere. But yeah—something's going on there. We've noticed though that he's not as trashed anymore these days. He seems a little more with it in the eyes. So, I think Luke's helped him clean up or something. Made him take a shower every once in a while, you know."

"Don't be mean."

"I'm not. It's like a fact. Turner stinks way less—" Erik goes and almost giggles, but then he takes in Maddie's eyes. "Sorry. I just— you're right, I shouldn't joke about it. I mean, it's obvious to us. Ryan and I were just talking about it the other day. Luke's been like helping Turner with stuff."

"Well—he does look better. Like healthier. I mean from what I can tell just seeing him in the halls. You know? When Turner bothers to show up to school that is."

"Yeah," Erik goes.

They both fall into a little silence.

Oh no—my freaking fear realized. An awkward silence. Bad on so many levels. *Think of something to say!* Erik freaks to himself. He knows the longer the silence lasts the more Maddie'll stare at her empty glass, her hands, the room, his hands… and finally, his lap. It's inevitable. Say something and break the chain before it's too late!

"Uh—do you want some more lemonade?"

Maddie looks at her glass for a second. "Sure. Only about half a glass this time though. Thanks—"

She hands him her glass.

He takes it and sits there beyond stupid with a glass in each hand.

Not a very well-thought-out plan. She just stares at him while he sits there for a second.

Moron. You utter and freaking complete moron. So, you offer to get her more raspberry lemonade? Where's the freaking logic?

With no other foreseeable course of action to him, Erik slowly rises up, hoping beyond all hope that Maddie is temporarily struck blind, or somehow finds the Walker's turned-off flatscreen so interesting she won't notice his pork-pitched tent.

He makes it a whole two steps towards the kitchen before he hears her muffled gasp. He can't help it; he turns back to her to see what the matter is.

Her feet are all tucked up under her and she's staring at him with her hand over her mouth and her eyes all wide like she's just seen a serial killer pop out of the shadows in some cheesy horror movie. "Oh my gosh—do you… *do you have…?*"

Erik just groans and retreats into the kitchen. *Why yes, Madelyn—I do. I have an erection.* Almost robotically he goes about the business of filling each of their glasses and then putting the pitcher back into the refrigerator. Only before he picks up their glasses again, he ceremoniously bangs his head a couple times on the kitchen counter.

He can hear her trying to stifle her freaking giggles as he stands back up straight and takes the glasses in his hands.

Only now, now that shame and self-ridicule are falling so hard upon him, does he finally feel his manhood deflate and begin to shrivel. He slowly shakes his head at life's cruel irony and walks back to the living room.

"That's it, laugh it up." He hands her a glass half full. "It's only the most embarrassing moment of my life so far. But please, don't let that stop you from enjoying every last second of it. Seriously. You know, go ahead—I mean if you'd like to take a couple minutes real quick and Snap everybody, or take an Insta pic or whatever, be my guest."

"Sorry—I really am," she goes between giggles. "But come on—it's not that bad. It could be worse."

"*Worse?* How?"

"Well, at least you don't get periods. Do you realize just how many embarrassing moments 'nature's little gift' causes for girls? At least what your body does can kind of be taken as a compliment in some shape or form."

Erik frowns. "*In some shape or form?* No pun intended, right?"

Maddie bursts into real laughter over that. Full out *lemonade-through-the-nose* laughter.

Seeing her laugh at his little self-depreciating joke like that, watching the lines of her face crinkle up and eyebrows shift, and her eyes soften, feeling her hand come up and squeeze him, to brace herself on his arm—Erik's ready to marry her right then and there. Who cares if they're still just in high school?

It takes her awhile to calm down, but he doesn't mind. He laughs too. Totally all over his embarrassment now. Now, with his eyes so full of stars.

"I wasn't going to say anything about it at first," she goes. "I mean, while you were on the couch."

"You knew I had one while I was sitting here?"

"I thought maybe you did. You were sitting there so weird, you know? But I wasn't going to bring it up then. But when you got up so slow and all creepy, I knew it was for real. And you seemed to make like zero effort to hide it—"

"Zero effort? Man, all I wanted to do was hide. But I couldn't think of anything else to say other than ask if you wanted another drink. I panicked. *So* stupid."

"Well, when I knew for sure you had one, I thought maybe you wanted me to notice. I don't know. I didn't know what to think." She starts giggling again.

Erik laughs again too. "Well, I guarantee you I didn't want you to know. For reals. I was just a huge idiot for offering to get you another lemonade. It was all because of that freaking awkward silence after talking about Jason Turner."

"That's right. It's all Jason Turner's fault." Maddie tilts her head.

"It is. His fault for starting to look healthier."

"To Jason Turner then," Maddie raises her glass, ready to toast. "May he continue to be in good health."

Erik nods and clicks the tip of his glass to hers. "Jason *freaking* Turner. Yep. Whatever."

They gulp their lemonade.

"Well, I've had a pretty good time tonight," Maddie goes.

"Well, thank you for coming and helping me out with Izzy," Erik goes.

"Like you needed help. That kid loves you. He'd do anything you told him."

Well, I love him too—Erik thinks but doesn't dare say. Because he knows if he starts talking about Isaiah and how much the squirt means to him, he really will embarrass himself. And as embarrassing as the boner incident was, there's no way—not a freaking chance—he wants to cry in front of her. So, he just nods.

"You've really set the bar high as far as just hanging out. So thanks for asking me here. Really."

"What do you mean?" Erik takes another sip.

"Oh nothing," Maddie goes and leans back a little. "I mean, I've really had a good time here and it may be hard for other guys to show me as good a time. It's nothing. I'm just paying you a compliment."

"Oh, yeah. Sure, sure," Erik goes and swallows kind of hard. "But like—what other guys?"

"You know, like any other guys I might hang out with in the future," Maddie shugs. "You know?"

"Well, yeah. I mean—what? Like you got a hot date with some other dude coming up?"

"Erik—" she shakes her head. "I'm sorry. I shouldn't have said the whole 'set the bar' comment. I was trying to say I've had a good time. That's all."

"So, who are you going to be going out with? I can take it. I mean, it's not like we're going out or anything."

"You're right. We're *not*—" She goes and leans even farther back on the couch until she's on another cushion entirely.

Erik knows he's pushing it. He can tell that to keep up this line of questioning risks all that he's been building up to with her. But now that the conversation's turning here—he also knows he just can't help it. This is his chance to find out some of her thoughts (some of her *real* thoughts, not just rumors) about other guys.

"So—?" he goes.

Maddie barely just shakes her head.

"Is it Dignan?"

"He's been trying for over a month to get me to go out and do something with him. I said 'yes' to this Saturday before you even asked me to come do this, *OK*?"

"*This* Saturday? Like in two days Saturday?" Erik leans back himself now. "Wow. That's a pretty fast turnaround, isn't it?"

"Are you serious right now?"

"What? Am *I* being serious right now?"

Maddie stares at him. He can't tell if she's on the verge of fuming or not. He remembers he really doesn't know her that well. Half of him is furious as hell with the other half of him for freaking bringing up Dignan Cooper in the first place. I mean, he knows one of the major rules of *Being a Player 101* is never put a girl in a position where she's sticking up for some other dude. And here he is about to go on the offensive, setting the stage for her to defend poor little Dignan for asking her out too. As if *The Coop* needs any help at all from anyone in the *ladies'* department—especially with his looks, his personality, and all his freaking swagger.

"Sorry. I—I don't know. I'm not trying to come off all jealous. It's just—" Erik stammers, all backtracking. "Yeah—"

Her face starts to soften, thank god. She breaks her stare on him, which he's also thankful for. "Don't worry about it. I can understand why it probably sucks to be in your position," she goes. "But the thing is, I'm not really ready, or looking, to be somebody's girlfriend for a while. *OK*?"

Erik nods, reluctantly.

"I mean, I just want to hang out with interesting people. Have a good time. You know? Flirt around a bunch. Like this. *This* has been great. I'm not lying—I'm having a great time tonight. Awkwardness and all."

Erik gives a little snicker at that 'awkwardness' bit. She does too.

"OK—yeah, you know—OK. But aren't you the least bit worried about what some people might say about you if you're going out on dates with a new guy every night, or flirting around like all the time?"

"Well, first of all—I'm not going out on dates every week. And second of all—that's so stupid."

"What is?"

She leans up off the couch. "Like the notion that if a girl goes out with multiple guys like in quick succession or whatever, that she's easy or some kind of nymphomaniac or something."

"What? And if it's a guy that's going out with a different girl every night of the week he gets all hailed as a player? Is that what's so stupid?"

"Well, that *is* stupid—but that's not my main point. My point is that whether it's a guy or a girl that's flirting around, there's this weird vibe, or reputation that lands on the person with all these like sexual connotations to it. And maybe some of that's warranted if the person is honestly just looking to hook up—but if they're *not*? Doesn't that seem totally stupid and unfair?"

Erik shook his head real quick; he was getting the feeling like he was back in Malory's class again hearing her use words like '*connotations*.' "Hold up. So—what are you really saying?"

"I'm saying we're *young*. We're not married. It's like real life is just beginning, you know? Not *kid* life but like *adult* life. And it just seems to me we should be hanging out with as many different kinds of people as possible. We should be open to what's going on with other people and what's going on in ourselves. You know?"

"By 'we'—are you talking about *you* and *me*?"

Erik suddenly gets the impression that Maddie's looking at him like he's an idiot. "Yes. *You, me—everybody* at school. When I say 'we' I'm talking about everyone our age, basically."

"Sounds like you're talking about like *Woodstock*, or some kind of love fest."

"No, *no*. See—there you go again, bringing that whole sexual vibe back into it. *You're* the one who's making it sound like a creepy orgy or whatever. I'm talking about growing up, Erik."

He thinks about that a moment. He still wasn't sure he understood everything she was on about, but the growing up thing rang true for him somehow. In fact, Erik was suddenly struck by how much her words sounded like Luke's.

"OK. Forget sex. Sorry. No more sex stuff, I promise. But what about love?"

She looks at him. "What about it?"

"Well—" Erik goes. "What if you, or somebody like us—you know, our age—while in the middle of all this growing up suddenly, without warning, you know—falls in love?"

"Hmm. I don't know, I guess. You mean they like fall head over heels, like in big, huge, like out of the movies but *real*, love?"

"*Yeah*—like real-life thunder and lightning *real love*. Love that comes in and blows you away like a tornado out of nowhere. Takes you totally out of where you were and what you were doing all in a second and like tattoos your heart forever, man."

Maddie's eyebrows arch up while she considers the question in a way that makes Erik feel caught up in a magic that would make his knees buckle to the Walker's carpet if he were standing up.

"I guess that'd be a game changer, maybe. But I wouldn't know. I haven't honestly been in love yet. Not like *that*. Not like how you're talking. And honestly, I don't think many kids our age have either. Oh, I'm sure lots of them *think* they have, but I think they're just drowning in their hormones. Have *you*?"

But Erik doesn't have a chance to stammer out an awkward answer. Upstairs they both hear a weird heavy thud. They look at each other all *hey—did you hear that* for a second before they hear shattering glass.

As they both run for the stairs, a series of crashes shake the ceiling getting louder with each one. Once they get to the stairwell, they both stare horror-struck as Isaiah's body slithers on his back awkwardly down the stairs.

"Izzy! You awake?" Erik yells, climbing halfway up to grab the boy by his rigid shoulders.

Maddie gasps as she sees the blood pumping out of Isaiah's split forehead, streaming out in long, rich-red fingers down his face; pink ooze coming out of his mouth. His eyes nearly bursting with popped blood vessels.

"9-1-1. *Now*—" Erik yells as Isaiah's head starts to bob so violently, like he's trying deliberately to shake it off his body and send it flying down the stairs to Maddie O'Leary's feet.

3

Abby

All I know is that I *really, really, really* just wanted to talk to Luke. Not on the phone texting all awkward where I could totally misunderstand him, or he could misunderstand me. But talk to him live, you know, in person. Where I could look into his eyes, and he could look into mine.

I remember it was a Saturday morning in February. The day after I officially, finally, broke up with Peter. I was sitting in my room getting all ticked because I sent Luke a couple of texts about wanting to see him today and he wasn't responding. Well, I didn't want to come off as a psycho or something and send him a million texts before like noon, so I decided I'd just work up my nerve and just walk over to his house and see if he was home.

So, I gave myself a big pep talk, put on my cutest pair of sweatpants (and it was almost always sweatpants now these days. I just couldn't get into how I looked in the weird maternity pants that Mom and I had bought at the mall recently) said *whattup* to my folks and marched down to the Forrester's house.

The short walk was cold, but I liked it. It sharpened me up and gave me a chance to really think about what I wanted to say to him.

But once I got there, Mr. Forrester told me Luke wasn't home. I'm sure he saw the instant disappointment on my face. Luke's dad also didn't know why Luke hadn't texted back. He told me usually Luke's fanatic about keeping his phone on, but that I shouldn't worry too much about it.

"Look, Abby, if it's really that important, I can tell you where he is," he goes. "He spends most of his Saturday mornings at Mr. Darringer's place."

"The welding teacher?" I go all puzzled. "Why?"

Mr. Forrester gets this grin on his face and just shrugs. "Welding of some kind, I guess. Luke's not big on details these days. But there you go."

Well, he tells me he doesn't know for sure where Darringer lives exactly, just that it's just out of town someplace, but that he's pretty sure that's where Luke is. I thank him and tell him I'll try to find out directions from someone else. And after some calling and texting around, I get it figured out and borrow my mom's minivan still totally determined to talk to Luke.

It takes nearly half an hour to get out to Darringer's place. I mean the guy lives out in the freaking boon docks for crying out loud. I had to check my phone again just to make sure I had the right place pinned and then turn into his driveway. Turns out Mr. Darringer lives out of town a few miles in the country in this real old-fashioned looking two-story house with a garage out back that looks more like a small barn or something rather than a garage.

Anyway, I pull up and all I see is Darringer's Jeep parked there—no other cars. Crap, I think. Maybe it's possible that Darringer picked up Luke, but that didn't seem all that likely. I suddenly feel pretty stupid. Like the whole situation is weird and awkward anyway because Luke comes here for one thing, and now I'm about to make it even more awkward by just showing up now.

The front door opens, and Mr. D. comes out.

I actually half-think about just tearing out of there even though he's already seen me for sure—but don't.

Whatever, I go to myself. I already look like a huge dork, might as well find out where Luke is. And I open the door and slide out, pregnant belly leading the way and all, and start walking up to meet him.

"From Hemingway, right?" Darringer goes, sounding neither upset nor thrilled that I'm in his front yard.

I nod. "I'm Abby Browne. A senior."

"The *pregnant* senior," Darringer goes and then just looks at me all blank. He looks at me how Luke stares at you sometimes when you can't tell at all about what's going on in his head.

"Yeah—" is like all I can say, as everything immediately gets as awkward as I knew it would.

Suddenly Darringer pushes some of his long dark hair behind his ear. "It's OK. I know who you are. Luke talks about you quite a bit."

I kind of smile at that. "I came out here looking for him. Obviously…"

"Yeah. He just left."

"Did he say where he was going?" I go.

Darringer doesn't answer right away. Instead, he takes a real quick look behind him like somebody might be sneaking up on him or something. "Can I ask how you found me? Like where I live?"

"Snap," I go.

He kind of frowns. "I ain't on Snapchat, kiddo."

Maybe he is a little upset I just showed up here, I think. And then suddenly I kind of understand. I mean, here I am—a pregnant girl by herself from the high school where he teaches. And then there's Darringer himself—young teacher, single and who's already got like half of Hemingway's girls who have crushes on him. There are only about a million different ways this could be misunderstood by clueless people that should mind their own business. And even though I feel kind of bad for him that I didn't realize this and just showed up at his house, I'm also a little miffed he's getting a little snotty with me *and* he doesn't even realize how the freaking internet works.

"No. I know. I just mean I got your address from Gala Sarah."

"From Gala Sarah?" he goes.

"Yeah. Know her? Senior at school? In all the drama productions? Anyway, I put the word out I wanted to find you and she messaged back that her older brother delivers a pizza for you almost every week. She texted him then he texted your address which is in the pizza place's computer, which she sent me—and here we are…"

Darringer looks like I've just slapped him in the face or something. Again, he looks back at his house like he expects a hidden camera crew to burst out onto his front porch. "*Run from technology long enough, technology runs to you…*" he mumbles.

"What?" I go.

Darringer shakes his head. "Just my new slogan. Look, Luke's friend just got home from the hospital. Isaiah Walker—a middle school kid Luke sometimes hangs around. You know him?"

I nod. I mean, I knew who the kid was—I knew he was like the soccer team's manager and that the team all loved him and that his dad had died and all, even though I had never talked to the kid personally.

"Why was he in the hospital?" I go.

"Bad seizure, I guess. Happened last night."

"Well, I guess I'll go try finding him there," I said.

Darringer nodded. "Wow. You really want to find him right now, huh?"

Why is it that even seemingly bright and *with-it* adults can't help but say the ridiculously obvious sometimes?

"Yep. Well, thanks. Sorry to bother you," I go and step back.

"Not a bother, Abby. It's wildly inappropriate that you're here—alone, no less—but not a bother," he says.

"Sorry—and thanks again," I go and smile and wanting to get out of there before it gets even more awkward.

But before I can take another step towards the mini-van he goes, "Say—before you go—you know, since you're already here, do you want to see what Luke and I have been working on?"

"Sure," I go, like actually surprised at the offer. And I had to admit, as much as I kind of wanted to get out of there and finish my epic quest to find Luke and finally lay it out there and tell him just how much I liked him, I actually was curious about what the heck it was that he was doing out at Mr. Darringer's on Saturday mornings each week.

"Come on then," he goes. "It's in the barn."

As we were walking up the driveway to the barn though, I suddenly got this creeped-out feeling. Not *for real* creeped-out, but the whole scene just felt like a moment out of a thousand horror movies, you know? A vulnerable girl goes into a scary-looking barn with a seemingly trustworthy but mysterious guy. And then suddenly the guy opens the barn and instead of a bunch of pretty horses or whatever she thought would be in there, it turns out to be all these chains and tools the guy wants to slaughter her with.

I'm embarrassed about it now, but I really did have like sweaty palms and an urge to bolt as Mr. D. opened the barn door. But *whew!*—relief. No torture devices. Well, unless of course you count all the welding stuff and blow torches like everywhere. But anyway.

"C'mon—it's back here," Darringer goes and pulls this light switch and the whole barn instantly glows with light.

"Whoa—" I can't help but say—which is kind of weird because at the time, I had no idea what I was looking at, but also because I really had no idea what to expect either. Taking up nearly one whole side of the barn were these huge (and I mean *huge*) curving metal—uh, *things*. There were six of them all lined up neatly next to each other. They struck me as like massive metal toenails or something. Or like six separate steel teeter-totters, except they were artistic. Each one of them big enough that Mr. Darringer and I could each sit down on the ends of them and totter if we wanted to.

"What are they?" I go.

"Well to get any answer to that, you'll have to ask Luke," he says back.

"So—you'll show them to me, but won't explain to me what they are?" I go.

Darringer just shrugs and goes, "Luke's a pretty cool guy and I think I've been slowly getting to know him while we've been working on this *project* here. But I think it might do him good to open up a little more to other people. It's just a hunch I have. I know he likes you, Abby. And I'm pretty sure he'd probably trust you knowing about this. So, when you see him later, tell him I showed it to you. He might be a little ticked at me about it, but just tell him I think he's being a little too secretive lately and that it might be good for you to ask him questions about it."

"OK," I go. I didn't really know what else to say about all that. I mean, of course I already knew that Luke was a pretty closed-off guy. I mean, *duh*—up until this year, he hadn't talked to me, or hardly anybody at all since Angela and his mom died. And then he lost his hearing about then too. It was a lot. You could always tell by looking at him during those silent years that there was a lot going on inside Luke Forrester. And that's what made him so intimidating for so long to everybody. Even me. And even now, you know, senior year, he was suddenly plugging in and talking to people, it was great and a huge turnaround, *but*... It still wasn't like he was an open book. He was suddenly a nicer book, a kinder book, completely interesting, and I was becoming ridiculously, hopelessly attracted to him. But the boy's book was still a total mystery.

"Come on, I'll show you one more thing," Mr. Darringer goes and leads me to this long work bench with a massive tarp covering something big underneath it. With one big pull, he rips off the tarp, revealing this huge ultra-shiny piece of steel lying there on the workbench.

I'm sure my eyes were looking like they were going to bulge out of my head. I couldn't believe the size of this thing or how... *beautiful* it looked. I mean it looked like something out of some super high budget fantasy movie.

"Is that what I think it is?" I go to Mr. Darringer, totally blown away.

"Pretty cool, huh?" he goes.

And it was. It was the coolest, biggest, baddest, truly epic sword I'd certainly ever seen. It was so big that even if a hulking giant the size of Mr. Darringer's house came bursting in and roaring into the barn at that moment, even he might have a hard time picking that sucker up.

ERIF
XIV

Prince looked at the stump of his ghastly forearm. His lifeless hand lay on the ground a few feet away.

In that instant he could not yet feel the maximum pain of the wound, but he felt the nausea, the faintness, and saw the dim stars exploding behind his eyes. He could barely make out the sounds of Angel's screams standing above him, his blood squirting all over her white robes.

She was trying to help him up, but he couldn't find his balance enough to rise.

The wolf-man was stepping towards them and snarling out words too—-but Prince couldn't really make that out either. But he did hear the words of the old woman from the hangman's tree: *a death waits for ye...* whisper from somewhere in his skull.

A death... a death... a death.

This is it, thought Prince. *My death—-and I couldn't even save her...*

Angel was now trying to put something small and crystal in his mouth.

Godsmercy, he finally understood her to say and let her place the vial onto his tongue.

Godsmercy, he thought.

He gently moved the powerful wits-number to one side of his cheeks and finally stood up straight. It took all Prince's wits to keep himself steady though as he stood between Angel and the approaching Rogni. He tried once more to concentrate and conjure up another aura, but his Yonderling power failed him just like it had with the old woman, and right after he had used his magical orbs to kill the first five Rogni here in the clearing.

The last of Erif's guards snarled and frothed and stopped a few feet in front of him.

"A death then..." Prince mumbled, more to the old woman's voice in his head than to the Rogni or Angel.

"Oh yes, boy. A death ye have surely found." Stagfin let his small double-sided axe fall to his feet and raised his hand and claw. "I'm going to slowly choke ye while I rip yer heart right—-"

Prince roared forward while the brute was still speaking and jumped up, wrapping the beast as best he could in a desperate hug.

Stagfin welcomed Prince into his powerful arms and crushed the lad to his chest. Unable to resist such a devastating target, the beast opened his maw and savagely clamped down his jaws onto Prince's shoulder.

Prince heard his collarbones crack and snap. Flesh and blood ripped up from the tearing wound as Stagfin's teeth chewed deeper into his body.

Angel's screams once again filled Prince's ears as he freed his whole hand and took the *godsmercy* from his mouth. He gripped the vial in his fingers, and with Stagfin still going berserker into his shoulder, he summoned up his rage and the remainder of his strength.

Howling himself now, Prince slammed his hand down into the beast's eye like a hammer. The vial of the wits-number exploded into Stagfin's pupil, while Prince followed with a series of repeated bashings of his fist into the Rogni's now obliterated eye.

The fluid of the *godsmercy* mingled with the blood and humors of Stagfin's wound while Prince pressed as much of it as he could with his thumb back monster's eye socket and into his brain.

The beast stopped mauling Prince's shoulder and yelped in agony before throwing Prince from him to the ground. Stagfin clutched at his gory socket where his fearsome yellow eye had once been and staggered around, spitting out rage and horror.

Angel ran to Prince and helped him back up.

As horrible as he had been after losing his hand, he looked even worse now. In addition to his grievous wound in his arm, blood also now flowed freely from his ravaged shoulder.

Prince knew he only had moments before he would forever collapse from loss of blood. There was not a moment to lose.

"Back away, Angel. Let me finish..." Prince whispered and bent down to pick up Stagfin's axe.

"No, Prince—-let me," Angel squealed.

But Prince weakly pushed her back and staggered towards the wounded Rogni.

Stagfin was having problems of his own trying to stay upright. Prince could see the *godsmercy* had him in its grip. The wolf-man tried to speak, but his frothy tongue prevented speech, hanging out from his slimy mouth like a dead snake.

Prince hauled back and swung the axe into Stagfin's face with all he had. The beast reeled but did not go down. Prince swung again and connected with Stagfin's snout but again he did not go down. Prince hauled back for another thrust but fell backward himself to the ground.

"Prince!" Angel rushed again to him.

"We must kill him. Before he gets his wits back, Angel. We must. We must..." Prince could barely say.

Finally, Stagfin tripped down in his own delirium and writhed on the ground, moaning and growling but making no attempt to get up.

Prince realized he couldn't do it. He was just too weak to finish the Rogni off. He sat up as best he could and handed Angel the axe. "You must, Angel. Or...we're done...for."

Angel took the axe, looking unsure.

Prince could only nod her forward and watch.

She approached the drugged beast slowly, eventually making it to where his head lay.

Good, thought Prince. *She knows where to strike him.* Prince was certain he could pass out at any second, but he wanted to see her at least slay the brute before that happened.

She raised the axe but brought it back down and looked back to Prince.

Prince tried to nod her forward again. "*You must...*" he tried to say. *With all your might, lass.* He thought. *With all your might.*

Angel turned back and raised the axe again. She raised it high.

That'a girl...

With a yell, Angel brought the blade down, and Prince heard the unmistakable sound of the axe chopping down through a layer of flesh and bone.

Angel split the beast's jaw in half, separating Stagfin's upper teeth and skull from the rest of his mouth and body. She walked away from the corpse, her hands over her mouth, leaving the axe sticking to the ground and Stagfin's flesh like it was jutting, hilt-up out from a piece of cord wood.

Prince nodded approval and all went dark.

When regained himself, at least a little, it was in the grip of searing pain and the smell of burning flesh. *His* burning flesh.

He screamed and tried to see through the stinging sweat in his eyes. Angel was above him holding a hot iron to his wounded stump. His brain couldn't form words, so he just continued to scream.

All went dark again.

When Prince next came back to, he felt water pass through his lips and down his throat. He still couldn't talk, so he drank more. He felt nauseous and on the brink of passing out again, so he closed his eyes and just hovered there awhile. Hovered sweetly between life and death. Between extreme anguish and its release with each breath. He thought of the sea where he fished with his father as a child and the sounds of the waves at moontide.

He was aware of someone stroking his hair. *Angel*--he thought. He opened his eyes to a blur. He looked up from her lap to where he knew Angel's face must be as his vision began to focus. He saw her golden hair first. Her chin and her lips next. And then the eyes. Those beautiful eyes... *But her eyes.* He realized it was not Angel soothing him.

"Annabella..." he whispered. "I love..." he tried to say.

She smiled down, teary eyes beaming and put her finger to her lips. "*Shhh. You rest easy, my love. All will be love now. All will be love.*"

4

Jason

I don't know, Rozz—it must've been sometime near two A.M. when they busted into Toe's house and got me. I was fucking stone asleep on the couch, and they came right to me and wrapped a coat over my head and tied my hands behind my back with this plastic zip-tie before I could even fully come to or open my eyes.

Next thing I know they throw me into the backseat of a running car, and we go burning rubber down the road.

My heart's about to pump out on me I'm so scared. I'm just waiting to hear that CHH-CHH sound right before one of those Shotgun Boys blows my brains out. I'm like having this freaked out little conversation about it in my head—little voices screaming lightning fast about what's about to happen. Like: *they're gonna fucking shoot you right now, man! You got one more breath!* While the other half is like, no, man. No fucking way. Not while you're in the car. This aint fucking *Pulp Fiction*, asshole. No idiot just blows someone away in their car while they're cruising the streets in a fucking residential area no less.

I don't know though—goes the other part of me again. *These are the fucking Shotgun Brothers we're talking about here. These tweakers are capable of the stupidest shit of all time. You know that.*

Yeah—but hold up a sec. How'd they know to find me at Toe's? Not just at Toe's house, but like in Toe's house *with* my ass asleep on the couch? And what did they do? Search the whole place before they found me asleep? No way. They would've made a shitload of noise doing that. They either killed Toe and his whole family real quiet-like, like fucking ninjas or something—or they crept in and found me asleep. They had to be quiet breaking in and fast getting out. Which they were, Rozz.

But then all the suspense of whether I was about to get shot gunned right there in the backseat ended when a familiar voice up in a front seat goes, "Da hell, dawg? You been in the bath, yo? Why ain't you smelling how you usually do? All reeking like a junkie dipped in cheap whiskey piss?"

Sin Dawg. *Shit*, Rozz. Don't get me wrong, I was glad as hell on one hand that it wasn't Scotty or Maintenance Man—but still, *shit.* The fact that it was Sin talking to me, meant I just got jacked up by Dre's crew. Which meant this was all about the fucked-up camelback at Lester's and the missing backpack of glass these mother's felt I owed them.

Not good.

"What up, Sin. Dre in here too?" I go.

"Naw. Just me and Tag, see? We playing limo tonight."

I was scared, Rozz—not gonna lie. But I had to play this right. You know how it is with these guys. No matter what they got planned for you, show fear around them and it makes it ten times worse.

"So what the fuck about this middle of the night kidnapping shit? Why couldn't we just set up a meet at Pazzaro's or something? Sort this shit out over some fucking deep dish or whatever?" I go all trying to play if off that mainly I was just upset that I wasn't still asleep. I even look like I'm trying to hold back a fake yawn as I say it.

"Fucking *'deep dish*?' Yo, Tagger—you hear this muthafucker and his *'deep dish?'"*

"Yo—Lil Pops—you know we way past deep dish." Tagger goes in his ground-zero deep voice.

"So, we ain't headed to Pazzaro's, huh?" I go, getting more scared by the second.

"Naw, we ain't. Settle back, Lil Pops. This meet's going down in *The D*."

No fucking way, man. I can't be going to Detroit with these thugs. But I was trapped, Rozz. I was going into the dragon's lair, man.

Took me a second to realize I was shaking my head. I tested how tightly they had bound my wrists. If I could somehow get free, I could jump out of the car if I had to. It was getting to that level, Rozz. I shit you not I was ready to jump out of the speeding car if I could.

"Consider yourself lucky, Lil Pops. Up to me, we'd be taking your ass nightswimming," Tagger goes.

That pissed me off. Which was good. I needed a little rage to mix with the fear. "Is that what you did with Kid? Take him fucking 'nightswimming' that night after the park?"

Like out of nowhere this fist comes in and blasts me in the mouth.

"Not another word," Tagger booms. I can tell he's turned in his seat and is looming over me. Ready as shit to deck me again. "Every muthafucking word you breathe out from here to the city gets a fist, yo? Now shut the fuck up."

Blood was all in my mouth and running down my lips and I was starting to salivate like a bitch. I was glad for a second they had a coat over my face, because I knew I was crying a little and there was no way I could let them see that.

I didn't say nothing after that for a while, Rozzy. I just sat back and tried to think. Thinking my way out of this was going to be like my only way to survive this night. I just knew it.

It had to be over an hour later that we finally stopped. They dragged me out, bare-footed, and hustled me over what felt like a parking lot and through what sounded like some big doors into some kind of cold building. It sure as shit wasn't no house. It didn't take long before we walked into the room that sounded all *echo-y* and smelled like rat spunk and bags of trash. The floor was all squeaky and I was like a hundred percent sure we were walking through a basketball court. We head down a few stairs and then down a hallway and pass up a room that's got this loud mechanical chugging racket coming out of it. Sounded and smelled like a motorboat or something. Anyway, we finally make it to this room that was way warmer than the rest of the place so far. There was some classical music shit playing really low from speakers that seemed to be in every corner of the room. Either Sin or Tagger put their hand on my chest to stop me and then pull down on my shoulder to place me in a chair.

"Naw—not in the chair yet. Make'em kneel," goes this voice that I was expecting to be Dre's, but it's not.

They haul me off the chair, push me to my knees, and finally rip the coat off my head. I take in a breath and look at Cunter in front of me sitting all gangster in this big leather-looking office chair. Behind him is a long table with several laptops and screens all up and glowing. Above the table, little lights flash on other computer shit on shelves and the rest of room is lit up by a couple of tall lamps in the corners.

He scoots up his chair closer and grins all jackal-like. "Long time, no see—*boi…*"

What a Dracula motherfucker. Not enough this asshole's been like the fucking Freddy Kruger of my dreams lately, and now I actually have to come face to face with him in the flesh. A white guy that wishes to hell he was a black gangsta. Rozzy, I'm telling you—the first thing I thought when I saw him was, I picked a hell of a time to get rid of Kid T's SIG.

I just look back at him. His fucking face has not changed, Rozz. He's still as skinny-assed as ever, still shining those bulgy, cocky eyes out of that skeleton face of his. His tight fucking oily hair, and that crazy starfish birthmark on his left cheek, still pink, but looks redder than I remember it, probably on account of the lighting down here. And that raggedy-ass goatee. When is he gonna realize, nobody—fucking *nobody* wears a goatee no more? I mean, cheese and rice…

"*Aight,* boyz—we got chores. Tag, help Eddie and the fellas get set up above decks and Sin, Dre wants you to enter the day's traffic, yo," Cunter goes. "And I gots Lil Poppy here."

Tagger leaves and Sin crosses and picks up one of the laptops. On the computer's cover there's this strip of green tape. Then I notice that each of the laptops has a single strip of duct tape on backside of their screen. Each piece of tape is a different color.

"Hey, yo—change the gates this week?" Sin goes.

Cunter nods. "Yeah-yeah. Take the Bible with you, yo. You know the chapter and verse."

Sin opens up a drawer under the long table and lifts up a leather-bound book.

"Holy shit—you weren't kidding. That a real bible?" I go.

"Mind your own dick, dawg. Nobody telling you shit," Sin looks all pissed at me and then leaves too.

Cunter goes back to just staring at me. He looks thrilled to death, Rozzy, to have me right where I am—hands tied and all to himself. "Lil Pops. Poppy, Poppy, Poppy…" he goes with his voice coming very near the fucking hiss shit that he did in my Lake Erie nightmare.

"Sweet crib," I go, trying to stay tough, composed.

"Ha-ha, yeah-yeah. You likey huh, *boi?"*

On the wall opposite their computer shit, Cunter's got tons of his video equipment. You know, like video cameras, tripods, microphones, and a million different lights. All very high tech. Must be thousands of dollars of shit, Rozz. But maybe you knew that?

Were you ever here? Of course, you were. Fuck.

Anyway…

"So what's with the race boat engine going in the other room," I go and nod my head backwards to the door.

"Aw, now ain't you a curious fucka," Cunter laughs. "It's a generator, dawg. We got a bunch of them back there. This whole here establishment's off the grid, yo. See, Dre and I ain't gotta be distracted by no electric bill."

"More like you don't want to be distracted by the fucking meter-man," I go back.

He laughs again. "You a little shit-ass punk, but you always been a smart fuck. I'll give you that, *boi.*"

I nod up to a big poster of Al Pacino in *Scarface* on the wall ahead me. "That's fucking original. Please tell me Dre made you put that up."

"Yeah—I know. Every wannabe gansta's got Tony Montana up on they wall. *'Say hello to my little friend!'* all that bullshit. But what can I say? I love the classics…"

He holds up his hands a little like I was supposed to see something in the air and then I notice the classical music again drifting quietly out of the speakers.

"Say, Lil Pops—you wanna see something really cool, dawg?" He hops up from his chair and goes over to this metal double-door locker by the video equipment. Punches some numbers into the lock and pulls out this huge-ass assault rifle. "Yo, check it. This here be *Samuel.* Samuel, this here's Lil Pops," he goes and puts fucking Samuel's barrel an inch from my face. There's no clip in it—but *still.* "Sammy here is a sweet Heckler and Koch 416. Got it in a straight-up exchange from a client of mine in Amsterdam. Now, it ain't got a grenade launcher secondary barrel—but, if it ever comes to the Columbians coming over the mansion walls, this here's what I'll be making my stand with."

The thing looks like a seriously bad-ass machine gun wrapped in a meat grinder with a scope.

"You ever had to use it?" I go.

Cunter shakes his head looking all disappointed. "Naw. I wish, dawg. Nothing but a little target practice. Just waiting for some unlucky fucka to piss me off or have everything turn to shit where there ain't no way out. Cause if you gotta go down—gotta go down *blazin. Blazin!* Ain't that right, dawg?"

I try to chuckle a little bit to keep from seriously freaking out.

"But *no*, Lil Poppy, all poster and shit aside—*Scarface* ain't my favorite movie," He flops back into his chair and lays Samuel across his lap. "You ever see *Event Horizon*, dawg?"

I shake my head.

"Now that's some fun shit. It's this old horror movie that's all in space."

"You mean like fucking *Aliens*?"

"No—naw, nigga please—they ain't no fucking lame-ass aliens. It's like this spaceship breaks down that has this engine that creates this mini blackhole in order to move through space, yo. But the thing is, out of this blackhole seeps out the blackest spirit of voodoo-evil you ever seen, man—and it gets all up the ship's ass. Well, this evil makes the crew all go psycho-killa and they get naked and slaughter each other. It's fucking awesome. Guy's ripping they own eyes out and shit. A few of them turn cannibal and start eating each other and they just let theyselves get eaten. Some ho be letting a dude ram her cockpit from behind while she letting somebody else rip her guts out. I first saw it when I was a little kid and—*I mean it*, dawg—it was love at first sight. Inspired me to be what I am today. *Ha-ha, ah…*"

I just nod my head like I dig what he's talking about.

He hops back up all quick again and puts the huge rifle back into the locker. "But shit—*boi.* I could talk about my favorite guns and movies all day. Sadly though, the bizz-ness must intrude. *Yessir.* See here, Dre wants me to go over where we at witchyou and how shit's gonna play from here." Cunter sits back down and puts his hands behind his head. His eyes shine all cocky again.

"Where is Dre?"

He starts laughing again in a way that's not funny. "Oh, Dre is off getting all high and mighty with Mr. Sunrise. Making deals to take care of us all. Now don't you go worrying your ass over where Dre is. I be his proxy today, yo?"

Rozz, I was really starting to put together how much maybe Cunter didn't like working under Dre. I guess I had always thought before that they ran everything fifty-fifty. And even though it was obvious that Cunter carried more weight than Sin or Tag, and that Cunter definitely called the shots when it came to the crew's video business—it was Dre who handled most of the drug operations. It was Dre that oversaw all labs and distribution channels and shit. Cunter ran the vids, probably kept the books, and ran all the tech of their little empire—but it was still Dre at number one, Cunter at number two.

And I was maybe starting to see through some cracks in their operation. *Mr. Sunrise*. Gotta remember he said that, Rozz. Kid T had said some shit about a *sunrise* too when he spilled to me about Dre getting international connections. Fucking 'men in suits,' he had said when we were driving in his Mitsu.

"So, let's get down to it, *boi.* The pack full of glass you and Kid tried to biz at Lester's never surfaced, yo. We talked to every fucking trailer in the subs and couldn't hail no glass."

"Yeah—well, you find fucking Lester's buddy, Scotty? Or that Maintenance Man fucker? Cause they're the ones that got your product."

"Yeah, yeah. Your shotgun boyz? Naw, we ain't found them. Talked to some trailers that know'em and are convinced those boyz ain't long for this world. See deal is, we don't ever think we gonna get paid from them. They on an execution order from your pops *and* us. And that's probably as good any of us is gonna get from them."

"Yeah—but they're the ones that probably smoked the glass. It's sure as shit all been smoked and farted out their asses by now but *they're*—"

"Maybe, Lil Pops—but we don't know for sure. Lester's house was so hot after you all shot the shit out of it—Dre and I are more convinced that the cops got it in impound, yo? Which means somebody still got to pay and that falls to you, *boi.*"

"That's such bullshit. It don't even make any rational fucking sense, man. What about Kid?"

"Kid skipped out. He's gone."

"Where? Can't you fucking hail him?"

Cunter shakes his head. "The punk bolted rabbit and got free of it, we guess. Ain't no one seen his raggedy ass for months, yo."

Rozz, I could've just started yelling that maybe Kid took the backpack. Try and make him the scapegoat. Argue that *duh, maybe that's why he bolted—because he had the glass!* But I knew they wouldn't buy it. They had me by the nuts and it was clear they wanted to keep me by the nuts. And I can't help thinking that the real reason they were on my ass so hard, was not because of me and that fucking backpack at all, now. Maybe it's because of the friction between Dre and Dad. Because Dad was making moves and selling their high-end shit to the subs and turning around and selling someone else's low-end shit to the trailer-park, there-fucking-by saving him some cost on the manufacturing. And they were getting pissed because either they couldn't catch him at it—or they just needed his operation too much to sell their shit in the suburbs. And so now I get to be a pawn that may or may not get sacrificed.

"This is such bullshit," I go again.

"Hey—tell that to Pops. He the one cut you loose. That's right, bright eyes—you fair game now, muthafucka,"

I knew it, Rozzy. I knew he'd spill it that I wasn't under his protection anymore. That I wasn't crystal and could get squeezed. My dad who fucking loves me. Cheese and rice, man.

"So, this is how we gonna play it," Cunter laced his fingers together and leaned forward, scooting his chair close again. "The retail price of the glass was three-five large."

"Three. Dre told us to offer three-five, but if he dealed us down that was OK and we could sell it for three," I go.

"OK. Fine. Three. Doesn't matter, see—because Dre ain't gonna stick you retail. He gonna come down closer to discount, yo. Which means you on the hook for twenty-seven-fifty."

I roll my eyes. "Yeah, that's a great discount, man."

"Oh, we ain't done, *boi.* Ugh-uh. *No sir.* Because before he cut you loose, your old man paid five hundred of it. Now aint that something now?"

Fucking whatever. The hell's my dad thinking? Why not pay all of it? I know for a fact he's got a hell of a lot more than three grand stashed away somewhere. Or work some fucking business out with Dre that doesn't include me getting kidnapped in the middle of the night. It's like I'm caught in some lame passive/aggressive pissing contest between two fucks that want to fight each other but are smart enough and greedy enough to realize they'll both be out cash, so they both decide to just annoy each other instead.

And play a game of chicken with me.

"So—that puts us at twenty-two-fifty you owe us, Lil Pops."

"No," I go. "It's nineteen-fifty, final tally. Check your math, man."

Cunter rolls back a little. "How you figure?"

"The three hundred I was supposed to get from the camelback."

Cunter just chuckles. "Fuck that, the deal went to shit. You don't get paid for that. The fuck, dawg?"

"Kid T told me—hell, even Dre himself said three hundred guaranteed whether the deal went down or not. That's the whole reason I did the bitch in the first place. Call Dre on it, man."

You could see Cunter dim a little in his eyes. He knew I was right, which sucked for him. And—there was no way he was gonna call Dre in the middle of this shit. It would look like he couldn't handle stuff and take him down a notch with Dre.

"*Aight*—fuck it, whatever. Nineteen-fifty, final tally. You owe it. So, you got it?"

I laugh. For real this time. "No—*fuck* no, I don't got it. I'm a high school kid for chrissakes."

"Well, sell that piece of shit car you got for starters then. But be quick about it dawg, because the juice is fifteen percent each week, yo." Cunter drops the bomb.

"*Fifteen* percent? You kidding me, man?"

"That's standard, dawg. That's why you don't mixed up with no criminals," Cunter chuckles some more.

"There's no fucking way, man," I go. "I mean what if I can't pay it?"

"Oh—Lil Pops, we don't want to go there. At least not yet. Guess you need to get a job."

"What the fuck ever, man. I don't think flipping *Whoppers* weeknights is gonna quite cut it. And fuck if I'm gonna start knocking off liquor stores or whatever just to pay *you guys*."

Cunter sits all the way back in his chair. I can tell he's really enjoying this part. "Well, we gotta think of something, dawg. You know how's I get bank, right?"

My blood goes cold. I know he's not talking about the drug money part of their operation. "Yeah, I know."

"Naw, *boi*. That's not what I mean. I mean, have you seen any of them?" he goes, his eyes getting wider.

I shake my head.

"I tell you—I get me some bank for them vids, dawg. We're talking *cha-ching!* Especially the ones I cook up for my high clientele. Man, I tell you they's some sick rich muthafuckas up in this here world, bitch." He smiles wide and beams like most guys would talking about their sons if they were kick-ass athletes or whatever. "Yes sir—they's sure some hunger for my *MOO-VIES.* I mean, you probably know we got a lot of your beat-down gansta shit that sells. Every once in a while, we'll do some of that softer kind of shit you can see online. Then there's all the freaked-up crack sex. Oh, we'll do some that psycho porn shit, violent gang-bangs, you know. But for my high clientele muthafucka's—there's the shit that brings in the real flow. You know, the shit that gets sold and sent on a hard drive. Delivered by contract courier, yo. Not by them Fed Ex bitches. Private jet to Zurich ain't cheap, dawg. Best believe, now. Well, we got the means set up here to get some real freaky shit on film, Lil Pops."

I can't describe really what was going on with me there, Rozz. Part of me was so raged up at Cunter for what he is, and the shit I know he probably made you do. But I was also getting more scared sitting there by the second. I kept getting flashes of my nightmare. The part where I was both that psycho Kehoe fucker and me as a little kid strapped to the chair. This bottomless pit was opening in my stomach. I wanted to just get the fuck out of there more than anything else I've ever wanted in my life.

"Sometimes we pull off some S&M. Not that pretend whips and wax spank-a-jizz, or that kinky 'safe word' bullshit. No—the *real* fucking deal, dawg. Real blood and blades, *boi.* With real blowtorches, real gags and real screams, Dig, now? And of course we don't shy away from *snuff.* I guess you can say that's our specialty. Snuff be hauling in the flow. I mean, *shit*—does it ever, *boi.* This *one*—I kid you not, dawg—we had this crack ho all naked and strapped, drugged to the nines. Fucking got these brothers to cut off the bitch's arm with this saw. And then—this is the best part righty here now—they *rubbed her off* with that shit! Yeah—no joke, dawg! And she was so gone into the black, so on her way out and numb to the world, the bitch *actually* got off on it. You believe that shit? Yeah—she's like all writhing around and thrusting her gash up on it—going *ugh!-ugh—ugh!*—the whole time till she bled out. Fucktest shit you ever seen, dawg."

I could feel sweat popping up everywhere on my body. My lips were swollen up and throbbing from Tagger's punch and I think they were bleeding again. I looked at Cunter and tried to stay calm. I didn't want to fidget my leg, but I couldn't control it.

"So, how's about this Lil Pops? How's about I give you a job? You hold a light, or work a cam if you be showing some talent, eh? Or, who knows—you could even be an extra if you play your cards right, yo. Sound good? Good. Don't worry though—long as you're paying off your debt you won't ever have to be the *star.*"

I force myself to look him in the eyes. Big mistake, because they looked as bulged and evil as I've ever seen any eyes before—like they were coming out of their sockets to get me all by themselves, Rozz.

"Well—I take that back, *boi.* You gotta be starring in your first one. And Tagger's up getting the set ready to go *right now,* bitch."

5

Isaiah

I can't believe this is all happening. I'm home now after being in the hospital for a couple of days. Everything has been so crazy and scary. I think it's worst for my mom though. After losing Dad, I think if anything real bad happens to me, she'll totally lose it. They said at the hospital that I had a seizure. A pretty bad one, I guess. It happened the night that Mom went out with her friends and Erik and Maddie came over to watch me.

I had to stay in bed at for two days, while doctors kept coming in to check on me. Mom says we have to go back sometime this week for more tests too, so they can be sure what caused it. I have to have an MRI, I guess. Which is like some kind of test that checks your brain.

Anyway, it was great to finally come home. When I came through the door it was cool, because a bunch of the soccer guys were there to surprise me. Maddie was there too, which I was real glad for Erik about. He's got a crush on her, and I hope they start going out. Luke showed up too and later some other girl came by looking for Luke. She's going to have a baby. Which I really thought was weird. He's never said anything about any girl. Anyway, she looked real nervous the whole time—but seemed nice. When I get some time with Luke again, I'll ask him more about it. Maybe he's going to be a dad? But I don't think so.

The doctors are working hard on getting me medicine once they find out why this happened to me, so that it hopefully won't happen again. But I don't know. They asked me a million questions about what I felt like before it happened. And I answered most of them. But there was some stuff I just couldn't tell though. Like about all the weird things I've been thinking about and seeing in my imagination lately. I didn't want to tell them about seeing Dad hanging out down in the soccer fields when I look out my window at night. I didn't want them to think I was crazy and tell Dr. Farris and worry my mom more.

Plus, there's something about the stuff I imagined (well, the stuff I can remember anyway) the night I had the seizure that is pretty scary, and I haven't figured it out yet and I just don't want anyone else to know about it.

The night it happened seemed to be pretty normal for the most part. I had fun hanging out with Erik and Maddie, just talking and playing games and stuff. I really didn't feel tired at bedtime and really would've liked staying up later with them, but I knew Erik wanted to have a chance just to hang out with Maddie all by himself, so I didn't put up a fuss.

I went up to my room and turned off the light. I remember laying down for a while, but not really thinking I was sleepy. But then I just started kind of zoning out. I lost track of time there. Maybe I fell asleep for a bit, maybe not. Next thing I knew, I couldn't move. It felt like my arms and legs weighed a thousand pounds. My head felt heavy, like it was a bowling ball or something. I couldn't move it either or hold it up off my pillow. While I was trapped like that, suddenly, this slow wave of blue light started to like sparkle and pulse out in the air halfway between the floor and the ceiling. It rolled out and creeped over me, past the bed. Moving, like water sloshing in a bowl or something, from one side of the room to the other. It was so beautiful and scary.

I tried to call down to Erik and Maddie downstairs, but my voice wouldn't work. I think all I could do was moan and slobber.

Then the wave of light got brighter. And brighter, till the only thing I could see was a bluish glow above me.

Suddenly I no longer felt like I was lying down on my bed. But I didn't feel like I was standing either. I was *flying*. Flying through the blue wave. It felt so cool! It was kind of like being underwater on a sunny day, except without the heaviness of water. And oh, yeah—I could breathe too.

The light started to like clear away, I guess. Like it wasn't light I was flying in anymore, but fog. I don't know how else to describe it. Anyway, as everything cleared in front of me, I realized I was flying in outer space. It was so *amazing*. I think I started to cry it was so beautiful. The stars were everywhere around me. I didn't need a spaceship, I didn't need a suit, or oxygen. I didn't even need a coat! I felt perfect flying through the solar system.

Ahead of me I saw I was approaching a couple planets. It didn't take me long to realize it was actually Pluto and its huge moon Charon. I couldn't believe it! I hovered down closer and closer. As I glided past Charon, I began to hear this low rumble—like an old man clearing his throat before he talks or something—except it was super-loud and seemed to rumble the whole moon below and I could feel its booming in my chest.

And then I lost track again. The next thing I know I'm on the surface of Pluto on this never-ending field of ice. Everywhere was glowing in the night because of the Charon's huge glow in the sky that looks so close I could touch it.

A hand reached out behind me and touched my shoulder. It's this astronaut. One of my astronauts from my waking story. I tried to talk, but words don't come out. I couldn't see his face because his gold shield was down on his helmet, but it doesn't matter. I know he was glad to see me.

The astronaut led me off the field of ice and suddenly it's like we've fast-forwarded to the mountain. There were tons of other astronauts here at the base of the cave, and they all had their shields down so I couldn't see their faces either—but I know, just like the one leading me, they all want me here. Nobody seems to talk and they all kept up with their work. There was equipment and gear everywhere and these little space buildings they kept coming in and out of, which must be where the astronauts eat and sleep and run tests and stuff.

We entered in the cave. It was huge and dark. My astronaut handed me a flashlight. I turned it on and started walking forward. It seemed like I walked for a long time. I turned around and saw that my astronaut wasn't there anymore.

The rumbling began again. The same rumbling that came from Charon when I passed it. Except it was lower, louder and shakier here in the cave. I felt a groaning sound all the through my whole body and it made me want to pee. Probably because of all the shaking, but also because how afraid I was. But there was something else in me too besides the fear. Something else I knew but didn't really understand made me want to keep walking deeper. That's when the smoke started blowing in. I could see it all gray and thick coming up in big clouds from deeper in the cave. I knew that if I was back on Earth in this kind of smoke, I'd be coughing my head off, probably. But not here.

My flashlight started to flicker. I shook it, hoping that it would keep it on, but it didn't. Everything went dark. My whole body was like shaking with fear, but I felt I *had* to keep walking deeper.

Up ahead of me, I couldn't really tell how far, a tiny red light started to glow. Like a glowing coal from an almost dead campfire, or something. Then another appeared. Same size, same glow. Another, and another, until there were five of them. Spread out in the dark ahead of me, all red as glowing coals.

The rumble got louder, lower. It started to sound more and more like a growl than a groan. I know it's crazy, but then I thought it's *somehow Luke's dragon!* Like from his story he wrote me. *It's Erif!* At the time it made sense, I guess. That's when the five red lights started not just to glow, but actually started beaming out, like they were intense flashlights or lasers or something.

Those aren't just lights, I thought. *They're eyes... Dragon's eyes.* Five of them. They started to move towards me. It looked like the dragon's whole head was moving to get me. I couldn't move. I still couldn't force myself to yell or scream.

"Isaiah!" someone yelled behind me. My dad suddenly yanked me back with the same kind of strength he had before he was sick and wrapped me in his arms. He pressed my head to his chest, and I knew everything was going to be all right. I just knew it! My dad wouldn't let anything happen to me now.

And then I realize we were not in the cave anymore. *Just like that*, we were in a totally white room, sitting at a white table on black chairs. Somehow, I knew it was the inside of one of the astronauts' buildings. There was this humming noise like big computers and air vents running and stuff.

Dad leaned in close with his elbows on the table. It was so good to see he got his muscles back. A hot steaming white cup of coffee sat on the super-clean table in front of him. My dad loved coffee so much. But after he had gotten really sick, he wasn't able to drink it because it made him sicker. He took a sip of it now though. "I want you to listen to me very carefully. This is very, very important and we don't have much time here now. You can't come back here, Izzy."

"But Dad—this is great! This place is awesome and feels so real. You're *here!* And look like you used to. How can I *not*—" I said, but Dad cut me off.

"It's not safe here, OK? I'll come to you, son. When the time is right. Let me come to you."

"Is it because of the dragon?" I said, still not sure if I should obey him.

Dad leaned back in his chair. "He's more than a dragon. More than just a monster. He's *a man*."

"A man with *five red eyes*?" I said like somehow this wasn't possible in a place like this—a place where it seemed *everything* was possible. "Dad—can't you just—"

"*No, Izzy.* You must stay away from here. Stay away from Charon—"

Then *boom.* Everything disappeared in a blast of light. I don't remember anything that happened from there. I'm pretty sure some stuff did, but it's all too far into the back of my mind. Like when you know you had a dream and it was like a real powerful one, but you can't remember it.

The next thing I remember is waking up in the hospital. Erik and Maddie say I must've hit my head on my window—*hard.* Because they said it was all shattered after they found me. But I don't remember doing it.

I just know there's no way I could tell the doctors, my mom, or Dr. Farris any of the stuff I remember on Pluto, *well*, on *my* Pluto, anyway. If I started going off about guys with five red eyes, there's no way they won't think I'm crazy, and I won't do that to Mom.

As for what my dad said, I don't know what to make of all of that. I mean, I don't even know if I could imagine myself back there even if I wanted to. Part of me really does want to go back, though. Even to the cave. The whole thing was just so powerful and awesome. And I felt more alive there than anything that's happened around here. But here's the other scary part: *I know Dad is right.* I know that it's dangerous there somehow. Just like how I knew all the astronauts there were glad to see me—I know, without being able to explain how, and even though it makes no sense, I guess—I know that if I go back there, whatever, or whoever's in that cave *can* kill me. Like *for real*, in *this world*, kill me. I can't explain it, but I know it's true. I know it is.

So, what do I do? I wish I could talk to Dad again. I think about him all the time. So, what if I can't help it and I get another seizure and I think myself back there? And if that *thing*, or man, in the cave really can really kill me—and I do find myself back at the mouth of Pluto's cave—what if I can't *help* from going in?

6

Jason

Cunter hauls me up to the gym. Rozzy, I gotta tell you, I liked the place better with a coat tied over my head. Turns out there *is* a lot of fucking trash all thrown around, and you can bet there's more than one fucking species' shit on the floor too. Human included.

None of the gym's regular lights are on. The only light comes from some of these multiple lamps that one of Cunter's guys is fucking around with. The fact that this guy's having trouble turning on a light and looks like he was born in the clothes he's wearing tells me he's gotta be big time tweaker.

Tagger's up there too, standing next to another guy holding a cam that turns out to be Eddie. You ever meet Eddie, Rozz? If you didn't, then consider your ass lucky, because he's one fucked up and mean little dude. First of all, he's this short, fat but solid of sonofabitch. He looks like he's got a little bit of everything in him, like his mom got raped in a prison riot or something. Next, one of his ears had been chewed off. We didn't get enough time to chat for me hear that story, but anyway. And finally, he had this heavy brow line that seemed to come down like a fucking visor over his dim eyes.

The last guy up there is this sad looking white motherfucker wearing this shit-ass blue *Ford* stocking cap sitting on this beat-to-shit ice cooler. He's a big-time addict too—you can just tell—and he ain't doing so hot. Like he needs his fix like yesterday, and bad.

Cunter nods to Tagger, and Tag clicks out this pocket-knife and cuts my hands free.

"Play nice now, *y'hear*? Don't want to be having to shoot you in the leg first night out," Cunter goes and gives me a wink.

Tagger goes over to this body-bag size duffle and pulls out two roughed up baseball bats and rests them all crisscross across his shoulders, behind his head.

"A'ight—and listen up, bitches. This be the script. That's *Thing One—*" Cunter points to the junkie on the cooler, then points to me. "And that's *Thing Two*. Now these two fucks is going have theyselves a swordfight. Winner gets a pipe full of glass. How about that *fuckazzz*!" He starts clapping and then hits me on the shoulder. "I'm on Cam One, Eddie got Cam Two up in the bleach for the wides, Tag on props, and you can hit the floods, Sugar Tits."

"Cheese and Rice*...*" I can't help saying out loud. *Sugar* fucking *Tits*. Just when I thought my life couldn't get more weird, Rozz. A guy that goes by the handle Sugar Tits.

Tagger goes over and lays the two bats parallel on center court. "Yo—*Thing One*. You over here. Lil Pops—on that side. We about ready for tip off, yo."

I look back down at my bare feet. "You don't think I could borrow a pair of high tops or something?"

"Fuck that, Lil Pops. You be fine," Tagger goes and laughs.

All I'm thinking is that this can't be happening, over and over. I'm thinking I'd even love to see Dad right now—even though I know it would never happen. But to see him just show up through those gym doors, his big chrome .45 blasting bullets, taking these fuckers out, and saving my ass—would be beyond awesome. But then I remember, he knows I'm here. Or at least knows I could be, all because he cut me loose. And I know he won't show because he believes these assholes won't really kill me, because they need him. He's calling their bluff.

The junkie gets up from the cooler and walks all slow to his place at center court. Tagger crosses the court and stands up next to Eddie in the bleachers. Sugar Tits finally figures out the floods and the six big-ass, blinding lamps fill the court with light.

"OK, now—lissen up. When we got the cams all ready to go, Tagger's gonna give word, dawgs. When he do, you both hop for the bats and come up swinging. Got it? Remember don't be chasing each other all over the fucking gym. This ain't a track meet. This here's a *swordfight*, remember. So stay in the middle there as much as you fools can. Try not to be hitting in the head—this ain't snuff. *But, yo*—make it real though. Either of you don't come correct, we go real on you. *A'ight?* Fucking nod so I know you *boyz* get it, now," Cunter goes while he screws his little cam to a tripod.

Thing One nods, still looking serious and sadder than shit.

I look at Cunter. "I ain't doing it."

Cunter's nostrils flair and his dark eyes bulge out again, and he walks over to me like he's gonna bitch slap my ass. "Oh, you'll do it, *boi*," he hisses—Rozz, he hisses so much like in my nightmare, I almost shit myself. "Cause you don't, script changes so's the new movie'll be cutting off that muthafucka's head and then all us be putting on jerseys and playing a Game Seven with it, yo. You got it, now?"

I don't say anything.

"So think of it as saving that piece of shit's life. You gonna be doing this bitch a favor by cracking his ribs, yo. And don't be worrying about yourself. Ain't gonna let you get killed. If the fucka starts going psycho, either Tagger or me'll pull a gat and shoot his ass. Now get in there, like right the fuck, dawg."

Cheese and rice, Rozz—I walk over to the bats, my knees getting wobbly. My toes so froze I can't even feel them anymore. I look at the junkie, but he just looks down.

"Sorry about what's gotta happen, kid. It ain't personal, man," he goes still looking at the floor.

I take a closer look at the bats. They're wood, old and chipped. Each one missing huge strips on their ends, so that they have a more square shape to them now rather than round. Both with thick layers of stained athletic tape peeling off their handles.

A fucking *swordfight.*

"Go!" Tagger yells from the bleachers.

The junkie springs down, clutching his bat first. I barely duck down to my bat before he takes a swing. His bat swooshes over my head as I crouch and back-peddle a few steps.

"Not in the head, asshole!" Cunter shouts from behind his cam.

The junkie rushes to me ready to give me a two-handed backhand. I grip the bat with both hands too and thrust out to block.

Our bats smash and I can feel the vibrations all the way to my elbow.

He twists his torso ready to give me his best fucking forehand. I pull back, crouch and take a swing at his left thigh. The fucker easily steps back and rears his bat back ready to take a hard shot at my right side.

I see it coming but I still can't raise my bat fast enough to block it all.

He connects.

My bat takes the brunt of it, but he still gets me hard in the shoulder and I nearly fall to the floor.

Tag and Eddie laugh and start cheering in the bleachers.

I'm still walking backwards as the guy charges me again all yelling now. You can tell he can almost taste his next fix—it's so close if only he can finish my ass—so he comes in at me swinging like one of the Tigers for chrissakes.

All I can do is block, block, block, and step back with each clash of bats. The thunder of wood-on-wood echoes all over the gym, and Sugar Tits is on his feet holding some sort of microphone yelling; "Go, fucking *Thing One!"*

The junkie starts drooling with each hit showing no signs of tiring. His aim's getting wilder but each swing is also more ferocious than the last.

He's corralling me, forcing me back—and we inch closer to where Cunter's filming.

We get so close to his tripod, I can hear him say, "That's it, bitches. Come on in."

Again, all I can do is block it seems. So, I try to slow his hits down by blocking and maneuvering my bat to make him hold the clash.

But the junkie's having none of it. The dude just wants to keep hitting. He raises his bat away as soon as he can.

Finally, I get him to hold for a few seconds.

Sweat's pouring off this guy now like clear liquor, and I feel mine sting in my eyes as we hold our bats together. I quickly try to figure out which of us has the weight advantage. I couldn't tell before because we're both about the same height and frame and we're both wearing baggy clothes. But for the two seconds with our bats locked together, for the first time and I can feel the extent of his force. And then I know.

I got this lightweight, motherfucker.

I release my left hand from my bat and wrap it around the end of his.

He instantly looks at me all strained and stupid for a second like he can't figure out what just happened.

I drop my bat and quickly grab onto the end of this bat with my right hand too.

Now it's tug-o-war. We start yanking the bat back-and-forth.

"Whoa now—hey. What happened to my sword fight?" Cunter goes but keeps filming.

I realize this junkie probably hasn't had a meal in days. There's no doubt I can take him now. As we tug away, I have enough time to see my window. It ain't much of one, I know. But *hell*—it's worth a shot, I think.

I set my feet and finally pull with all my strength. The bat and the junkie both come into me, and that's when I push forward, shoulder first into the guy, and the dude goes flying off his feet and crashes on the court.

Tag and Eddie yell and cheer more, and Sugar Tits yells for me to *beat the fucking shit outta the guy.*

I grip the bat in my right hand and look down on the junkie. "No—*please…*" he whimpers, spit all over his mouth.

I raise the bat over my head.

This is my chance. "Hey, man—just want you to know, it ain't personal," I go.

Then I turn around and rush Cunter behind his cam. He's only got a second, and he uses it to give me this priceless look of *what the—?* before I baseball bat him in the side of the face, blasting him and his shattered camera down to the court floor.

I run. Big time.

Towards the doors I know they must've brought me in through.

All of them in the gym are yelling, and Tagger fires off a round from his gun. Whether it was just a warning shot to get me to stop, or he was really aiming at me, I don't know.

I sprint out of the gym and down a hall and come to these double doors that used to be glass but now are just wooden boards. I slam into them and—*thank god*—they bust open to a parking lot.

I bolt again. Keep in mind I don't know where the fuck I am—just in some hood in *The D.* It's gotta be getting close to four or five in the morning, but there's still at least like three hours to daylight.

And I'm still fucking *bare foot.*

I sprint across the parking lot and across the street and turn past the first corner I come to. I know those fuckers are going to be hot on my trail in like two shakes and I'm trying to figure which way I should sprint next. Not only was it cold as a bitch out there—but also *The D* is one of those cities where it's possible to actually freeze to death because you can't find a warm building in time that ain't locked.

"Hey there, *huny*. Hey there, kid," goes this voice in the dark ahead of me.

I like strain my eyes trying to see who's calling me from across the street.

"Come on over here. Quickly now. They's after you, kid?" It was an old lady, I think. All wrapped up in coats and a bunch of scarves around her head.

"Yeah, they're after me," I go, still trying to figure out who this is and how the hell she knows who *they* are.

"Come on—quick now," she goes and ushers me up to the door of this shitty looking camper trailer that must be where she lives.

I really fucking had no choice, Rozz. So, I climb in there and there's like two other people in there—both wrapped up like the old woman. There's a bunch of candles burning and a small flashlight shining up on this little table.

"Aw—now Thelma. What's this?" goes one of them sitting on the small bed.

But Thelma keeps pushing me forward to the back of the trailer. "Bernie—help me raise the bench."

The wrapped-up guy sitting at the table gets up and helps her clear away a bunch of grimy dishes and shit, and they lift up the wooden board that makes up the seat of the bench.

"Go ahead now, *huny*. Get in. We won't let'em find you," The lady goes.

So I get in, Rozz. What else was I supposed to do? I squeeze into this little coffin-like space, and they place the board back over the top of me. I can hear them stack magazines and the stack of dishes back on top of the bench.

Not kidding, like two seconds after they hide me in there, I hear Tagger's and Eddie's voices outside the trailer.

They start banging on the trailer door.

"Yo—open the fuck up," Tagger yells.

I hear the door squeak open and Tagger and Eddie start grilling Thelma and the others if they've seen a white kid in jeans and a T-shirt running around. Thelma starts giving them the runaround and I just wait, all crouched and still, to see if they'll buy it.

While I'm trying not to make a sound, I suddenly feel something start to crawl over my foot.

Tiny claw-like paws step onto my skin, and I feel slick fur.

It's all I can do not to freak out, Rozz—as a fucking rat starts walking all over my legs and feet. I feel its thin bald tail follow its creeping body like a smooth piece of rope. All I want is to kick at the fucking thing. Get it off me and jump out of this dark shit-hole of a space.

But I take it and stay still.

Tagger and Eddie finally leave, and Thelma and Bernie come over and lift the bench.

I burst up all pissed and freaked. "There's a fucking rat in here. *Look—*" I go, and the thing goes scampering through a tight hole on the trailer's floor. "The thing was crawling all over me, man."

The wrapped-up guy on the bed starts laughing.

I stare at him like he should shut up.

"Hey now, child. Rather be back in that rec center with them gangstas?" Thelma goes, and grins.

"No. No, I don't," I go. "Look, thank you. Those guys—they would've hurt me. Or worse."

"Oh, we know. We live here, so's we see some of the people that come in and out of there. We know they's some bad shit goin' down in that building," Thelma goes.

"Maybe you guys should call the cops or something?" I go, and the second I say it the guy on the bed laughs again. Bernie sits back down at the table and laughs too.

"*Huny*—cops don't come round here, see? This whole hood's abandoned buildings mostly. Only people here be junkies, or homeless like us. Or *them* assholes," Thelma goes.

I guess it made sense, Rozz. If Dre was going to have his HQ somewhere, it was clever to have it so far off the grid. The place wasn't a lab though. He probably had those in other buildings in different parts of town. Just like he had Pazzaro's Pizza and Al Skid's bowling alley back home. Still, as clever as it was—it had its risks, holding so much of your operation in such a derelict abandoned building surrounded by junkies that want your product. But I guess living with risk is all part of the gangster's trade—*ha, ha.*

"I gotta get home," I go.

They ask me where home was, and I tell them. They all laughed at that. They couldn't believe it. They acted like any place outside of *The D* was like being as far away as a distant planet or something.

Thelma digs out an old worn coat and puts it on me. The old guy on the bed—Lawrence, turned out his name was—he gives me socks and the boots right off his feet. I couldn't believe it. I mean, he was the one that didn't want me to come in the trailer in the first place. Bernie gave me this ratty pillowcase and part of a ripped-up sweater put over my head and face.

Thelma fished out some crinkly dollar bills from out of a plastic bag they had under their tiny dried out sink. She places them in my hands and tells me how to get to the nearest couple of bus stops. I try to give it back to her, Rozz. I mean, obviously they couldn't have had a lot of money—and this could be *all they had*, you know? But she tells me that the best chance for me to make it out of there alive is to get on one of those busses, and make it back to a safer part of Detroit. "Get your ass north of 8 Mile, now *huny*." She says she only wishes they had more to give me so I could take a bus or a cab all the way back home.

I was blown away, Rozzy. Blown away.

"I promise I'll come back. I'll pay you all back and then some. Bring back your stuff," I go.

They all just look at me.

"*Huny*, don't you never come back here, now. We don't see you again, it's a good thing. Means you safe," Thelma goes.

I think about that for a second.

"Are you all not *scared*? Living here like this?" I go.

They all smile these sad smiles. "We scared all the time. Every second of every day. It's what makes us *strong* though, child. Now, you go on now. You find one of them busses," Thelma goes.

I step out of the trailer and take one last look back at them. "Thanks."

They look at me real gentle-like and nod, and Thelma closes the door.

I walk. Down one deserted, crumbling street after another. Barely any of the streetlights giving off light. Most of them just shattered shells. Dark buildings on each side of the street. Not one window I see with glass. Some have a half-ass chain-link fence, but most don't. Some have plywood board and a chain lock on their doors, but most don't. Everything looks like some sort of plague came in, or fire, or wind, or whatever—and took every soul and glass window with it.

But then I hear someone cough from inside one of the buildings. *Man*, Rozz—for as empty as this place looks—it would be a big mistake to think there ain't no one here.

I only heard that one cough, but I swear I could feel eyes on me the whole time I was there. I seemed to be walking through and entire city of fucking haunted houses filled with real-life ghosts, silent—but full of flesh and blood.

I remember Bella's little comment about how maybe Buffalo was getting to be just as ghetto as *The D.*

No way.

Not a fucking chance. *Fuck* Buffalo. Detroit wins—*or loses*, depending on how you want to put it.

I got to a bus stop after over an hour of walking. Never been so glad in my life to see a bus either, man. I rode it as far south into the city as I could and searched for fucking ever to find a pay phone. You ever try doing that, Rozz? Find a fucking pay phone when you need one? Impossible. I had just enough change left over from Thelma's money to call Toe and give him a rough idea of where I was at.

He was beyond freaked—and so were his parents—about those guys coming in and taking me. They didn't know if they had just been some of my friends being crazy, and I went with them—*or* if I had been kidnapped. Toe's dad knew to wait about calling the cops, because he and Toe both knew my dad was a dealer.

Anyway, I had to calm him down and make sure he had the exact address of the gas station I was chilling at, because he couldn't call me to get more directions, on account of me not having my phone.

Well, like almost two fucking hours later, he finally pulls up all pissed and concerned and we drive back to his place. Toe's folks had like a million questions, and I basically tell them that those dudes came in and kidnapped me. They all freaked. Toe's mom wanted to call the cops again, and Toe's dad had to stop her. It was a fucking mess. So, I just told them I was moving back in with my dad until this whole thing blew over (which was bullshit, by the way. No way I'm ever staying under the same fucking roof with that bastard again). They made a good show of saying that wasn't a good idea either, but in the end, they let me go. Because let's face it—who keeps a houseguest that now has *two separate crews* with guns out to get him?

I knew only one person fucking crazy enough to keep me and be cool with it.

When Luke opened the door, he was eating a piece of pizza and looking like he didn't have a care in the world, man.

"OK—I'll join your little band of misfit pussies. Whatever your little schemes are, helping old ladies cross the street, or fucking putting together roller-skate parties for all the losers at school that ain't got friends—*I'm in*. If you let me crash here again—*deal*?" I go.

Luke just takes another big bite of pizza and opens the door wider.

"All right then," I step inside, "where's your dad? Because I got a couple more developments that you guys should be aware of first before you take my ass in again."

7

The night before we started it all, we all met at Luke's. Most of the soccer boys, Dickie, Turner—*and me*. We were all sitting in the Forrester's living room when Ryan read aloud Luke's first real idea about how to expand the circle.

"That's it?" Patrick goes. "That doesn't sound like such a big deal, really. I mean it's different from the way it works at school—but it's not as—I don't know… as *extreme* as I thought we'd go, maybe."

Pauly, Glendening, and Troy start nodding in agreement.

"I don't know," Erik pipes up. "It could be extreme though. I mean—I think people are going to notice this."

Moments before all the debate started, Luke had Ryan read his pre-written greeting and an outline of his first idea about how to reach out to Hemingway in general. He called it 'Project Lunch Box,' which everyone pretty much groaned at right away because of how freaking cheesy it sounded. But the gist of the plan was that every day at lunch, all of them would fan out all over the cafeteria and infiltrate other groups of people that they didn't know at all and have lunch *with* them. Luke explained that they weren't there to provoke so much as to kind of *forcefully* make these pods of other people include them in their lunch conversations.

"But hey—what if they don't want to talk to us? Or what if like what they're talking about isn't something you know about or have any opinion about, or whatever?" Tristan goes.

Luke shrugs. "Figure it out. Adapt," goes the digital voice from his phone.

Dickie just laughs. "Dudes, this is going to be ridiculous. I can't wait. People are going to think we're freaking high on something."

"They already do," Ryan goes.

"Well, when do we start this whole thing?" Glendening goes.

Luke taps into his phone. "Tomorrow."

Turner scoffs from his chair in the corner. "I'm out—"

Luke just looks over at him.

"All right. Tomorrow it is," Erik goes.

"And how long do you think we'll be doing this for?" Patrick goes.

"We'll know when we can stop," Luke's phone goes. "It'll be obvious by then."

The next day at school I came down to the cafeteria and had butterflies in my stomach the size of vampire bats. Don't get me wrong, I was like thrilled to be hanging with these guys now—but this whole task of going and sitting with random people at school I never talk to just felt so beyond me in some ways. Lucky for me though, I happened to fall in line with Patrick Durning just as both of us were heading into the main part of the caf.

"Hey," I go.

"Hey," he goes back. "You ready for this?"

"I guess. I'm about to freak out though."

"Yeah. Me too," he goes.

That caught me off-guard. I mean, walking next to him like that, I was totally reminded about how big and strong Patrick was. The guy was just as big as Luke, and maybe even a little beefier. I couldn't imagine Patrick being intimidated by anything. So, I guess it kind of floored me when he said he was nervous too.

"Hey," he goes again. "Look, since this is the first day of this and all, and since we don't really know each other practically at all either—you think it'd be OK if we go sit at some random table together with some other kids we don't know?"

"Yes. That's a freaking great idea," I said probably a little too fast—but I couldn't help it. I was so glad he was the one to come up with the idea.

We chose this table with a lot of drama-club-type kids. I knew most of their names in like a pictures-in-the-yearbook way but had never talked to any of them before in my life—*and neither had Patrick*, that's for sure. At first, I don't even think they noticed us much—they all were talking so loud and so fast at each other. Patrick and I didn't really talk to each other either—we just awkwardly started eating our lunch real slow and just listened to about seven of these drama-types talk. Then they started buzzing about the try-outs for the spring musical coming up and who among them had a real chance at the leads.

That's when Patrick cleared his like sizable throat and asked what the musical was going to be.

All of them at the table just stopped and looked at Patrick and I and then just as quickly looked awkwardly away.

"*The Pajama Game*," one of the girls finally answered. Her name was Gala Sarah. Like I said, I had never talked to any of these kids before—but I had seen them around plenty in the last four years. And Gala had always struck me as a particularly interesting girl. You know—from like afar or whatever.

"Um…is it like a good one?" Patrick goes, his voice as close to squeaking as Patrick's was ever likely to get this side of puberty.

Gala looks back and forth between Patrick and me like she's missing something. "Is it a good musical? Are you asking if it's a good musical?"

Patrick and I both nod our heads.

They're all looking at us again. I feel like such an idiot. Like we're suddenly elementary school children sitting at a table for middle-aged adults.

"Is this like for real, or what are you guys doing?" Gala asks—but it's obvious the rest of her drama crew's thinking the same thing.

Gosh, she's got great eyes. And her brown skin—so perfect-smooth, I think.

But what I say is this like mumbling mess while I turn to Patrick as he's turning to me and we're both making this same mumbling/stuttering sound, both hoping the other will snap out of it first and tell them what we're doing at their table.

"Um, no—we're real," Patrick goes.

"This is—yeah—happening here," I blather at the same time.

Gala and the rest of them were all giving us the most epic *whatever* faces of all time, so much so that the word *whatever* seemed to be floating right out of their foreheads and into the air, heading towards Patrick and I like a fleet of helium balloons all formed and twisted by some birthday party magician. Finally, they all looked away and went back to their conversation, giving Patrick and I both a second to take a breath before looking down again to our respective sandwiches.

What a mess, I think and turn to look around the cafeteria to see how the other guys were faring. I see that Ryan Leon was only two tables down eating with three guys that would be considered loser-*ish* types by most at Hemingway. You know, guys that look like *their entire lives* are wrapped up in the RPG's they play. Watching Ryan interact with them seemingly so naturally, made me feel ridiculously inadequate when I thought about Patrick and me with these drama kids.

Then I see Erik laughing and totally getting all flirty with a gaggle of preppy freshmen girls. *That so figures*. He would pick chicks. All young, *yes*—but all future cool. All good looking and seemed not to mind Volgstaad being there. Across from him Troy and Pauly had the same idea Patrick and I had and were all teamed up at a table of hicks and look just as out of place as I'm sure we do.

I scan around more and see Luke over with Gray Cahill and two other Ivy League hopefuls all leaning in and having what looked like a genuine conversation: Luke scrabbling away on his pad and Gray talking away all excited like. Who knows what they were talking about—but it had to be way better than me and Patrick's first attempt with Gala Sarah and her crew.

The real surreal moment of the day though comes when I look a few tables away and see Jason Turner sitting with three petrified looking girls. They were big reader types. You know, like the kind of mousy girls that are always lurking in the school library scarfing down the latest hit Young Adult book series or whatever. All of them in modest shirts and jeans that are nowhere near too tight. All of them with their shoulders hunched, not saying freaking word one, making no eye contact with Turner much less each other. It was like they suddenly felt the frost of the grim reaper among them or something and just put their heads down like some kind of submissive pack of puppies in the presence of a crazed alpha. And there's Turner, eating chips and all leaning back in his seat, apparently making no effort to put them at ease, or even explain to the poor girls why he's there. He scans around and we make eye contact. He puts another potato chip in his mouth and shrugs like *whatever*.

So that's the way it went for the next few days. It was all business as usual for us all: go to your classes, hang out with whoever you want to before and after school, no big deal—but at lunch we all spread out and picked some random group to eat with. For me, it never got less awkward. And I could tell there were plenty of the other guys that felt the same way. Pauly, Troy, Patrick, Glendening—they all seemed just as lost and out of their comfort zones as I did. But then there was Dickie who was like a walking party everywhere he went. For that first week, no matter what group he was with—freshmen, sophomores, juniors, hicks, emo kids, jocks, geeks, stoners (I mean, he even sat with Kevin Wilhelm and his band of increasingly shady characters) girls, guys, gays, straights, trans—it didn't matter. Wherever Dickie went, within minutes you could hear him *laugh, laugh, laugh* all over the cafeteria, talking and joking around with whomever. The chubby lug really was like one of the most popular guys in school. I mean, Dickie Schwartz was born for *Project Lunchbox*. No doubt about it.

And Ryan who seemed to have a gift for picking out all these pockets of invisible kids that usually spent their lunchtime quiet and alone or huddled over the small screens of their chosen hand-held devices. Kids whose postures seemed to be collapsing in on themselves like they were trying to *cave-in* smaller and smaller until they were practically as imperceptible to the rest of us as a discarded pencil on the floor. And it wasn't just that Ryan would approach these kids. No, from the looks of things he was also drawing them out. Having actual discussions with them, making them smile. It really was kind of—well… *awesome* to watch.

On the other hand, there was Turner who seemed to have the reverse effect of Ryan. Turner never looked lost or uncomfortable himself—but rather seemed to freaking *thrive* on making whoever he sat with feel uneasy. It was like you could see him almost getting off on the squirminess of others. One day I saw him go over to Gala's table and my guts got tight just watching him freak most of the drama kids out. But to my total surprise, by the end of that lunch they were talking to him, and he was talking back, and they all seemed to be cool with the interaction. But anyway—by and large Turner was still creeping a lot of people out.

And of course, Luke was fine with it too. He had no issues pulling up and sitting with anyone. But I will say that sometimes he kind of gave people the creeps too. Now, *no*—it wasn't the same kind of creeps as Turner probably. But to those who were not used to communicating to a guy of Luke's size, through either his system of post-it notes, or his weird-sounding robot voice on his phone—it was kind of a bit much sometimes for some kids.

But the real problem would start with Tristan. The freshman had really taken to *Project Lunchbox* right out of the gate. For being the youngest of our group, he showed no signs of timid-ness, or fear of sitting with any of his older peers at all. In fact, he really was a lot like Turner, in that Tristan seemed to get a bang out of making others feel awkward or confused. And unlike Turner, Tristan was picking people to sit with that were likely to get provoked or react in a way that could escalate the tension. Like take for instance the day that Tristan sat with the starters of the Hemingway basketball team. There's Tristan sitting among team captain Phil Lukas, from my Great Works English class—Mr. *Mo'Dick* himself, with near seven footers' Wade Garner and Ty Redding towering over him like a couple of mountains. Well, it didn't take long of course for Lukas to start running his mouth, making jokes about the little ninth grade soccer player being lost and whatever.

So, by the first week of March, Tristan found himself gravitating over to where Turner sat during one of our meetings over at Luke's house. The two were like joking around about which stuck-up group would be the most fun to mess with at lunch, and they both agreed it was time someone sat down with Dylan Sorensen and all the ultra-preps at his table.

"OK, I'll do it. I'll take that dare. I'll sit with them. You don't think I will?" Tristan goes.

"OK, then, man. I want to see it. Tomorrow. You go park your bony ass at their table and we'll see what happens from there," Turner goes.

"OK—but you got my back then when things turn freaking postal?"

"Aw yeah, man. I'm all over it," Turner goes, all smiling.

"Whoa—hey look, nobody's going to be making anyone go postal," Ryan goes, catching Turner and Tristan's escalating conversation from across the room. "Especially since some people are starting to take notice—and in a positive way no less."

"Pump positivity up the ass—let's shake things up," Turner goes.

"Yeah—well, I don't know about pumping stuff up the butt—but he's right. We've been doing this for weeks. Is this *Lunchbox* thing all we're going to do? Well, if it is, then we should be shaking things up," Tristan goes too. "I mean, are we just playing around here, or do we really want some things to change?"

"Hey, I'm all for change too, but I'm with Ryan here," Erik pipes up. "We're not doing this to start a riot. I mean, you sit by Sorensen and Wellington and the rest of those dudes—the whole lunchroom might blow."

Well, Turner and Tristan *seemed* to have dropped it after that, and the rest of us thought they would let it lie once they got back into the cafeteria too. But that wasn't going to be the case.

The next day Tristan comes in with his lunch tray all stacked high with garlic bread and pizza dippers and starts moving towards Dylan's table. He looks over and sees Turner, who's sitting at a table with a group of Hmong girls talking a mile-a-minute and raises his chin like he was the shit.

Turner motions back with a palm-up hand like, *after you, my fine friend*, inviting Tristan to carry through with his promise.

Most of us of *Project Lunchboxers* were in the caf by then and could see what was potentially afoot, watching with interest.

Tristan passes Ryan on his way, and Ryan catches him by the arm. *"Don't."*

The bold freshman looks at him a sec and then moves ahead. But to all of our surprise, he doesn't sit down at Sorensen's table. Instead, Tristan moves across the aisle and plops himself down right in the space between former Hemingway soccer stars Trevor Morehouse and T.J.

"Oh *schiiizz..."* Erik hisses.

It takes about five seconds before Morehouse, T.J., and Linus, on the other side of the table, are all up and yelling at Tristan to rethink his choice of seating.

"Get the hell out of here, you little turd," Morehouse starts going off. "You think you're big stuff because you took my spot after I wouldn't narc? And now even that bs isn't enough, you guys all gotta be floating around creeping everybody out and getting them all pissed."

Suddenly the whole caf quiets down and looks over at Morehouse.

Erik stands up. "Hey, not everybody's pissed, Trevor."

Morehouse looks away from Tristan over to Erik. "Oh yes they are. Just look around, you asshole."

Erik groans. "OK, yeah—they might be creeped out because—yeah, people tend to get creeped out when something's going on around them that they don't understand. But *you're* the only one pissed."

"No, he's not!" T.J. pipes up.

"Yeah, yeah—OK, I mean just *you guys* are pissed," Erik goes.

Morehouse starts to walk closer to Erik. His whole posture tenses like he's coming in for a mixed martial arts match. "Oh, we're beyond pissed. You sold us out, Volgs. Stabbed us in the back."

You can feel everyone in the caf get all electric at the possibility of a fight breaking out. Some are just frothing for it, you can tell.

Luke stands up and goes over behind Erik. Getting Erik's back.

T.J. rises. The whole thing's turning into a stand-off.

You can just sense most kids in the cafeteria watching hard, *willing* someone to throw the first punch.

Across the aisle from Dylan's packed table, Peter Calloway suddenly jets up and gets right in Luke's face. "Back up. You read my lips? Back up. You think you can just swoop in on my girl? Write up some lame poems about how cool it is to be deaf or whatever and steal her, huh?"

Wow—everyone must be thinking. *Peter's taking it there.* Jealous rage suddenly on display. Most of us totally aware that knocked-up Abby broke it off with Peter with most people buzzing that it was because Luke Forrester had stolen her away. And now the whole school was getting to see the fallout.

Could this get any better? everyone must be thinking.

Patrick Durning gets up and gets behind Luke, which prompts Nelson Tremblehall to fall in behind an increasingly red-faced/clenched-fist, Peter Calloway.

I look around for the teachers on lunch duty—*how could they be missing this?*

"*Peter*—" Abby calls out from a couple tables away sitting with Maddie O'Leary and her crowd now.

"Shut up, Abby. You know it's true. This deaf freak butted in and turned you against me. Screw it, for all I know he's been banging you the whole time we were together. Maybe that baby you got swimming in you right now ain't mine at all, maybe—"

"Oh *whatever*—" Maddie suddenly stands up and blurts. "If somebody's guilty of cheating it's *you.* I mean look around, *Petey Pete.* People know. You're the one who technically cheated on *her.* You're the one that hooked up with Gabby in your mom's SUV in Ann Arbor that night after Wellington's house party—"

"*What?*" Abby goes.

"Oooo *snap!*, ya'll," Dickie Schwarz's the first one to gasp in trash-delirium as the whole cafeteria brakes out all in raised eyebrows and shocked smiles.

The air in the caf goes static.

"Sorry, Abby," Maddie goes. "I just found out and was going to tell you as soon as I—"

"You *bitch*!" Gabby lunges all rabid out of her seat from Sorensen's table, past all the battle-stance boys and slaps Maddie across the face.

Ka-bang.

We have total drama detonation.

Everywhere cheers blow up and yells and beating fists on the tabletops. Teachers and lunch-aides finally descend at a dead-sprint upon Gabby and Maddie as everything whips way out of control and the Hemingway cafeteria gets as close as it's ever going to get to a full out prison riot.

I see Ryan hide his face in his hands, shaking his head in apparent disbelief. Patrick pulls a bemused-looking Luke away from the downright stupefied Peter Calloway, while Erik hauls Tristan out of his seat and forces him into a quick retreat, leaving his untouched pizza dippers right there on the table.

Two teachers haul a still-screeching Gabby Altman to the office, while Maddie holds her cheek and gets escorted to the nurse as kids all over the caf get away with yelling *anything* and *everything* inappropriate and even throwing some food.

Still sitting at his table, leaning back in his seat, Dylan Sorensen is all laughs. He looks like life couldn't get any more entertaining. He and Kirk almost seem to be patting each other on the back like they're congratulating each other for just being here to see such chaos. "This is *awesome*," Dylan was heard to say. "Seriously, this is like the greatest year of all time. And we got that lip-reading dick to thank. Since week one he's been making this place fucking bonkers."

I guess I had to agree with Dylan, at least in part. Luke really *was* the major cause of most of this weirdness. It couldn't be denied—even with what little I knew then. But it wasn't all Luke though. There was Rosalind Howard. She *was* the one that really got this year off on a surreal note. Rozzy and her .38 revolver. And once my mind turned to her, I couldn't let her go. I mean, really—*who was Rosalind Howard?*

8

Jason remembers the first time he met her. It was sunset. Late September. The streets were all lined with wet piles of sopping dead leaves. He was in seventh grade, stickman skinny, stuck with a voice squeakier than a rusty playground swing and sporting new armpit air still too new to curl. He was rolling home on his skateboard after hanging out with Toben, before the faux-hawk, and Jacob Duggan, who was older than him and Toe by a year. They had been out with some cans of spray paint Duggy had gotten from somewhere tagging concrete walls underneath a shitty overpass on Toe's part of town.

His earbuds were blasting some of that hard-ass shit he was prone to jamming to non-stop back then as he rolled down the street zoning out, mindlessly taking all the turns that would lead him home, when like out of nowhere an empty plastic pop bottle whizzed by, almost clocking him in the head.

"The fuck?" he had said, or something of the like, taking out his buds and looking around to see who threw it.

"Hey—*faggot,"* goes a voice and then a couple of snickers. Jason saw Kevin Wilhelm and Brian Legget—two guys in his grade he knew but had never hung out with. He had always kind of thought they were assholes and now here was the proof.

"Hey, come here—" Kevin goes, and Brian laughed again.

Jason just stared at them.

"Come on, don't be chickenshit. Come back here with us," Kevin goes and then he and Brian stepped back into this overgrown lot turned into a jungle of bushes, tall grass and small trees fountaining out branches from the ground. The rest of the street was all cramped tight with small houses, except this one wild lot, and Jason could see like four or five little trailheads heading into the thick shrubs where kids had trampled into it many, many times. "Come on, you douche. We got some cool shit back here," Kevin goes again.

"Yeah. We'll share, yo—" Brian goes too and laughed yet again.

Jason thought for a second. He really didn't like these guys, but it wasn't like he was in a hurry to get home. All that waited for him there was his drug-dealing pops and a cold bologna sandwich for supper. And that's if he was lucky. Plus, even though these guys were jerks, he really didn't think they were seriously going to try and beat him up. *Besides*, Jason thought, *if they try anything stupid, I'll smash their skulls in with my board.*

So, he went across the street and followed them into the overgrowth. As they walked and dipped through the thicket to the middle of the lot, Jason could smell a lit cigarette which meant someone else was in there because neither Kevin nor Brian had one. They came to a small, trampled clearing just big enough for all four of them, because sure enough, there she was—sitting on this small pile of bricks holding a lit Camel between her fingers and taking a swig of some kind of liquor in a brownish pint-sized bottle.

Sure, he knew her name was Rozzy—but he'd never actually talked *to* Rosalind Howard before. It wasn't that he either liked her or didn't like her—he didn't think about whether he thought she was good looking or not good looking. She just hung around a bunch of kids Jason didn't know at school and therefore, he never really thought too much about her until now, as she held the bottle out to him.

"It's Jägermeister. I lifted it off my folks."

Turner reached down and took the bottle from her. He knocked back a small swig. A really small swig and fought back a grimace. He couldn't help it; he had never tried Jägermeister before.

Rozzy scooted over a little on the brick pile. "Pop a squat, kid. Stay awhile," she goes.

So, he sat down next to her.

Jason didn't talk all that much after that. Just listened mostly to Brian and Kevin talking stupid about all the stupid stuff they had done or were into. Listened to them basically flirting with Rozzy by making fun of her. But they weren't funny, Jason thought. Anyway, he could tell that all three of them were way drunker than he was—but he sipped from the bottle whenever it was passed to him and took a pull from a cigarette when they gave him that too.

He noticed Rozzy didn't say much either. She looked mostly bored in fact, but pretty content to just sit there and chill.

After about five minutes, Jason was kind of ready to leave because he found the guys so annoying, and he didn't want to drink too much in case his dad smelled it on him. But then Rozzy's thigh brushed up against his—denim on denim—but he could still feel her flesh underneath. It was such a little thing. Probably she didn't even mean anything by it, the contact a total accident. But he must've liked it—because he stayed another five minutes just sitting there basically listening to Brian and Kevin just yap, yap, yap a bunch of bullshit.

But then he started feeling awkward again and realized he really was on the verge of getting too drunk—which would piss off his dad big time for some reason—and got up to go.

"What's the *hurry, Mr. Scurry?*" Rozzy goes looking lazily up at him.

"Uh, I just, I think I gotta get back," Jason stammers.

"Aw, man—get back to what?" Kevin goes. "We're just getting started back here, you puss."

"Yeah, you gotta stay till we at least finish the Jäger, hey," Rozzy goes.

And while he was just standing there dumb, Brian told Kevin about this nasty used condom that he saw at the other end of the lot and how it was like totally overloaded with spooge and Kevin just couldn't believe just *how much spooge* Brian said there was, so the both of them hiked back there to check it out. They of course extended the invite to Rozzy and Jason too, but Rozzy took a pass and Jason just stood there saying nothing, still trying to decide if he was staying or going.

She had a raven, soft-looking face, with a nose he found both childish but kind of sexy at the same time. The really Halloween-*ish* amount of mascara around her eyes didn't completely obliterate how pretty they were either in Jason's opinion. Sure, they were kind of spacey, her eyes—but they were alert too—in a sneaky way he thought. Jason felt a little uncomfortable, as if she knew what he was thinking on some level. It was hard to explain. He couldn't help noticing she was mostly flat-chested. He tried hard not to look at her breasts—the tips of her chest pressing up the fabric of her tight black tank-top. I mean, why was she wearing that? It was chilly enough as it was and getting chillier with dark coming on. She must've been cold. Was it that she didn't have a jacket? He could tell on sight that Rozzy wasn't the kind of girl that came from a rich family, let alone a well-off one. Or was she *trying* to get all their attention by nipping out in front of them? Well, no matter what the reason, Jason was trying not to look. For some reason at that moment, he wanted to be better than that. But it was hard.

"So yeah, I've seen you at school," Rosalind goes and sucked in some smoke.

"Yeah," Jason goes back.

"That place sucks, huh?"

"Yeah. Rather skate all day than be there, man."

She coughs. "Rather be anywhere. You ever see the ocean?"

"What? Like the Atlantic or whatever?"

"Yeah," she goes, "the Atlantic, the Pacific—the ocean. You ever see one?"

"Hell no. You?"

She shakes her head. "They say Lake Erie looks like the ocean sometimes."

Jason shrugs. He shifts his butt a bit on the brick pile. Then a thought hits him. "You seen Lake Erie before, right?"

Rosalind takes a swig of Jager and passes the bottle to him. "I ain't been nowhere."

Behind them through the thicket, they can hear Kevin and Brian screwing around with the condom. "*Ugh! Faggot! Don't fling that shit on me!*"

"What a couple of fuck-ups," Rozzy mumbles. "Hey, do you mind sticking around till the bottle's gone? It's just that when I get hammered with those two, they get all horny sometimes and beg me like non-stop to blow them. But they'll keep it in their pants if you're still around. I know they will. So could you—you know, stick around?"

Jason just stares at her for a second. "Yeah. Sure," he goes, talking on the wrong side of a breath, his voice all strained and wheezed.

She looks at him and smiles. He feels his stomach jump. Just to have something else to do with his face and hands, he brings the bottle up to his mouth for a drink. In his nervousness he takes in a little more Jäger than he intended and fights off a serious gag reflex. Forces a shot of burning bile back down his throat. I mean seriously, the last thing Jason wanted right then was to freaking puke in his lap after he had just taken on the role of Rozzy's protector for the very first time.

9

Later that night (the night after the big Hemingway lunchroom drama) Turner remembers he and Luke found themselves up late, shooting the shat up in Luke's bedroom. Luke lounged back on the large pillows of his immaculately made bed, while Turner sat on Luke's wooden desk chair that he'd hauled over to the window so he could smoke. They had mostly been going over the craziness in the cafeteria, recounting all the drama and all the stuff they heard other kids buzzing over later in the afternoon.

Turner seemed way more impressed with the amount, and the juiciness, of chatter than Luke.

"I mean, that was fucking crazy, man. Crazy," Turner goes for close to the millionth time and takes a greedy drag on his cashed cigarette. "I gotta fucking quit these things…" he goes and flicks it out into the chilly darkness. "It smells warmer out there—like it's gonna rain intead of snow, man."

Luke rips off a sheet from his pad and extends his arm out.

Turner just looks at the note and shakes his head. "Hey, man—why don't you use your phone? I mean, come on—I'm way over here and don't want to be crossing the room every time you got something to say, man."

Luke jiggles the little note in his hand.

Turner stares. "Fine," he huffs and finally goes and scoots the chair close to the bed. "Stubborn fucker…" and snatches the note.

Why don't you?

"Why don't I what?"

Luke puts an imaginary cigarette to his lips.

"What? Fucking finally quit smoking you mean? Like instead of just sitting here and bitching about it like I been doing for the last month?"

Luke smiles; nods.

"OK, you're on, bastard. I'm done. That's it. You're looking at the fucking definition of cold turkey here. How's that? Now how about a cup of coffee? You game? I gotta have something bad to put in my system and looks like caffeine's all I got left, man. Who needs sleep anyway?"

Luke nods.

They tiptoe past Mr. Forrester's bedroom, where Turner can hear him snoring through the door. Down in the kitchen they scrounge around for the coffee. Luke grinds the beans while Turner pours the water from the carafe into the coffee maker and puts down the filter. While they busy themselves with their separate tasks, Turner thinks about Abby Browne—the pregnant girl down the road. Abby Browne—the reason for the greatest bitch-slap in Hemingway High history. Abby, who's been here to see Luke three out of the last five nights and seems to text the big guy every waking hour.

"So—" Turner goes, once they're sitting down at the dining room table, a couple steaming mugs and Luke's notepad between them, "You really screwing her or what?"

Luke just stares at Turner and takes a sip of Sumatra blend.

"Sheesh. Fucking *at ease*, private. I'm only messing," Turner goes.

Luke grins only slightly and takes another sip.

"OK. But you like her, right? Abby. I mean she's only over here every other day now for chrissakes."

Luke grabs his pen.

You're here every day now too. Are we screwing?

"All right, all right. *Douche-ay*, my friend. OK, so the chick's a sensitive topic. I get it. But for the record, I think she's nice, man. I could definitely see you two together, even with her being, you know—knocked up and all."

She's giving the baby up for adoption.

"Oh, I know. Everybody knows, man. What do you think everybody at school buzzes about when they're not freaking about me hanging out with you soccer assholes, having lunch with every random kid at Hemingway? Abby the Pregnant Prep, man. That's who. She's a rare species, you know? Seeing her is like seeing a falling star in the hallways. Then add all the drama with Calloway and that Gabby skank stabbing your girl in the back? *Whew-we*, man. Believe me, everybody knows. She's all anybody's talking about now. I'm just asking what's the stats between you two. That's all. You know like one friend to another. I mean, isn't that what *friends* do? Talk about chicks they like or don't like or whatever?"

Tell you what. I'll spill about Abby if you start spilling about Rozzy.

Turner's face hardens. He takes a sip of coffee and is quiet for a while. It's in moments like these that Turner really wonders what it is he's actually doing with Luke Forrester. Like with so many things in his life, his relationships with everyone—from his dad, his mom, even Toe (*hell*, even Rozzy herself when she was alive)—there's this back and forth feeling of whether it's even worth it to ever try and explain yourself to anybody. Why did being with people have to be so much goddamn work sometimes? Even people you *actually* wanted to be around—or felt you should be around for whatever reason? Seriously, sometimes when he really thought about it—when he realized how far he'd come with Luke—it made him laugh. A WTF-laugh, you know? Really, what the hell was he, Jason Turner, doing living in Luke Forrester's house? Hanging out with Luke's soccer buddies? Going along with all these weird-ass schemes that they were always baking up to 'bond' with all their fellow classmates? But then Turner thinks about what the alternative would be. Home. Alone. Getting ripped on all kinds of shit up in his room while his dad ran the town's drug trade downstairs. Turner knew where all that ended. It ended with a barrel in your mouth running out of reasons not to pull the trigger. But *this*—living with Luke—staying clean—hanging out with these soccer dudes that seemed to be not just from another neighborhood than him, but like from a completely different planet than him... Well, Turner had no idea where this road ended. Freaking uncharted waters, man. And as weird and sometimes awkward as it felt being in these waters with Luke, Turner also had to admit it was pretty goddamn liberating too.

Fuck it, he thinks.

"OK, man. Whatever. I'll start spilling how abouts. So yeah. I write to her sometimes. Rozzy. At night mostly. I tell her all the fucked-up things I got going on in my head. All the bullshit that's been going down between me and my dad. With Cunter and Dre and all the drama about the missing glass. You know, a lot of the shit I've talked to you about now."

Luke listens.

"Well, she wasn't my girlfriend, if that's what you're wanting to know. At least, not really. I mean, it's no secret I guess, that I liked her—but you know, she just never let us take it there. It was always complicated with her, you know?"

How long were you friends?

"We hung out once in seventh grade. We got drunk together in this old, abandoned lot. But nothing for a while after that. I mean, we saw each other in halls and said 'hi' a couple times, but we never hung out again till sophomore year. She was in that circle with Kevin Wilhelm and his crowd of heavy druggies Kid T sometimes used as small-load cabbies at Hemingway."

Kid T? From the meth-house shoot-out?

"Yeah. Anyway, Wilhelm introduced Rozzy to Kid and Kid liked her and used her sometimes to drop off baggies and pills at Hemingway. Which all led to me coming home one afternoon and seeing her in Kid's Mitsu waiting for him while he was inside the house bizzing with my dad. Her and I got to talking again and before you know it, we were hanging out more and more. She was the first Hemingway kid, other than Toe, that my dad let into our house."

Turner takes a swallow of coffee. "She was already a big-time addict by then. I mean, I was drinking and coking by then too—*but Rozzy…* She was just on another level, man. She just flat-out needed the shit. Like *really* needed it. Like fucking oxygen. And as thankful as I was to get to know her, you know—be with her, get close to her and all that. I can't help thinking that I led to her downfall too though, man. Because hanging out with me and Kid T, and then being around my dad, she got mixed in with Dre and Cunter and those guys. She needed her fixes so bad and didn't always have the money to feed them, you know. So, she felt she had to get all social with those guys. And I don't know what their angle was to hook up with her—maybe because she was so outside their norm. You know, teenage girl—a down trash girl from the trailers. I don't know. She didn't always tell me about what happened when she hung out with them, but I knew some hardcore shit was going down with her and them sometimes. She'd like disappear for a whole week and I didn't know if it was because she was on a nuclear tweak run, or bizzing with Kid, or fucking trapped with Dre's crew in Detroit—or if it was just all of the above, man. All of the above. She just didn't talk about that part much. And I guess I was just too chickenshit to ever ask much either.

"And I'm still scared, man. When it comes to Rozzy, I'm still like terrified."

Scared of what?

"Scared to really deal with the fact I was partly responsible for her death for starters. That I didn't do enough to save her. And then there's her letter. Yeah, I read it by the way. Once. I can't bring myself to read it again. I fucking near shit my pants when I think about trying to."

Luke looks all *well, what about the letter, man…*

"Well, let's just say she has expectations of me, for one thing. And for another, I think she believed in—I don't know how to put it—like some kind of magic, or power or something. I can't put my finger on it. But it comes through in that letter. You know—that like she believes her suicide somehow is serving some major destiny or higher fucking purpose or whatever. And I don't think I believe it. I don't think I *want* to believe it."

Luke sips some coffee; starts scribbling a note.

You believe in life after death?

"I don't know, man. *Ugh*—I want a cigarette already. Fuck. Maybe not, I guess."

But you write Rozzy?

"Yeah. And at first, I really kind of wanted to believe she really was listening. That maybe she was *up there*—or a ghost hovering or like maybe my letters just crossed over the darkness to wherever her soul was at. But I think that was just wishful thinking, man. Or the drugs and booze. I mean, I still write her—but I don't *really* think she's reading it. When it comes down to it, I guess I just don't want to believe there's some spiritual or magical connection between me, you, that Carver dude up from Bath, and that crazy whatever-the-fuck vision/dream I had coming back from my mom's."

Then how are you here? Rozzy wanted this. You and me.
She wanted us in Bath with Carver. How did she pull it off?
Get three strangers to go along with it?

"Coincidence. She got lucky with the timing maybe. But it wasn't magic, man. So she wrote three guys letters telling them to meet. Big deal. That don't make her a witch or something. Man, this is all just random horseshit. The dreams. The letters. It's just your mind tricking itself into believing that your spirit, or God, or whatever, is telling you it's OK, all this pain, all this unfairness in the world, all this bad shit the bastards of this world perpetrate—that it all will work out in the end when all our souls will eventually rise up and let rip the sky and let the fucking glory fall." Turner chuckles and twirls his fingers. "Or however the hell you said it."

How I said what?

"What? I don't—oh, yeah. Sorry, man. Yeah, you said that in one of my dreams. That was a freaky one too."

What did I say?

"*Let rip the sky*, man. I dreamed we were in Bath. By a tree in front of the school before it got blown up. The fuckiest thing about it was that you actually *spoke* the words. I like dreamed your voice, dude."

Luke grins.

"Hey, look. I know you ain't no virgin to all this. I mean, I know my little tragedy of losing Rozzy has a long way to go with you losing your mom and sister in that plane crash. So it's cool if you don't agree with me. But since we're talking here, like for fucking reals, this is how I feel. And the way I see it, is just because I had the bitch-all of Halloween nightmares dreaming I was that crazy school-bomber and then an all-powerful skeleton king, don't mean that the ghost of Rozzy Almighty or the power of sweet Jesus or whatever is shining down and giving meaning to everything."

Turner sits back in his chair. "But I don't know. It could just be that I'm scared that if Rozzy *did* know what she was talking about, then I gotta take that letter seriously. And like I said, I don't know if I'm capable of what she dreams for me, man."

Luke just keeps looking at Turner.

"Well, what do you think? You got an opinion on this? I mean, what do you believe here?"

Luke starts writing.

I believe in Rozzy.
I believe she started something real, something important.
Regardless of how she started it.

Turner shakes his head. "But why? You didn't even know her."

Because I choose to.

"I don't get it. I don't get it at all, man. She wrote you even though you didn't know her. She dies and then you start following what she wrote? It doesn't make sense. Not just Rozzy's faith in you, but just *you* in general. I mean, honestly—what is your deal? How do you… how did you get this way? Plane crash, going deaf, you don't talk to nobody for years and now all *this*…? You and some dead girl you never even met before changing the world?"

It killed me, Jason. The plane crash. My dad and I were both sitting in the kitchen when he got the phone call. Mom and Angela—gone. Just like that. Killed my soul. Broke my dad's heart in half. I turned into a screw machine. Screw everything. Screw everyone. Except soccer. I became a robot. I didn't think. I didn't talk. Then I lost my hearing. I was glad, Jason. Going deaf made it easier to shut it all down. People leave you alone when you're deaf. Except for soccer. Soccer zombie. That was me. Lost myself in it. In so many ways I wasn't even alive anymore.

And then Rozzy. First day. I get home and there's a letter waiting for me. On good old-fashioned paper. Handwritten. Her letter. She wrote that by the time I read this she'd be dead. She wrote how she would do it and where. It was crazy. I had to keep re-reading it and I still couldn't understand what was happening. She said she dreamed about me. That she had seen me before in the halls, but that she knew me from her dreams. Knew I was the only one who could do something very special for her.

Turner looked up from the notepad. "What was it?"

Save you.

"Save *me*? From what exactly?"

She didn't say. She just said to save you.

Turner scoffs. "OK. So random dead girl tells you to save my wasted ass, and then you do. But why? Why would you? Why *did* you, man?"

Because it wasn't just the letter. I dreamed about her too. That first night. It was the craziest, most vivid thing I ever dreamt. Rozzy and I were underwater. Just hovering with an entire ocean of dark blue water around us. But it was like we could breathe. She started talking to me. I could hear her plain as day. She told me this was my last year to live. She told me to breathe and act wisely, that time would quickly go. Then she floated close and took me in her arms and whispered, 'And live so ever—or else swoon to death.'

And that was it. She kissed my cheek, and I woke up.

"And that was enough, huh?" Turner goes. "And then you *believed* it? Just like that?"

I believe because I <u>choose</u> to believe.

Turner slams his hand on the table. "You really *believe* you're gonna die soon? That's great, man. That's why you were so good to go with Harper Lake then?" He grips the top of his coffee mug like he might throw it. "Fuck. You crazy, fuck. You have any idea how close I came—" Turner starts to tear up. "You *fuck*, you *fuck*… you *fuck*," he whispers.

Luke looks at Turner. Looks him in the eyes.

"You know she had mental issues, right? She had epilepsy too for crying out loud. Had meds she was supposed to take. Had seizures from time to time. Some of them bad. Made her lock up like a vice or flop around like a suffocating fish all over the place. And add the fact she was a heavy meth-head on top of that—I mean, damn Luke—what were you thinking?"

No guts, no glory.

Turner turns away, looks to the living room instead. He shakes his legs under the table for a bit humming on his adrenaline and caffeine. He breathes. He turns back to Luke and his pad. "It's not that I'm not grateful, man. For everything. You and your dad. It's just that I don't get what's going on here. I don't understand your kind of faith and commitment. I don't get it. It just seems to me, that whatever's guiding you and whatever guided Rozzy is based on like bullshit and insanity. And it worries me. It scares me. Because I just don't think I can go there, man. Even if I wanted to. It's too far, you know? It's just too far."

Luke reaches over and puts his hand on Turner's shoulder. Turner remembers instinctually feeling the need to pull away. But he fights it. He takes the awkward friendship Luke offers.

Luke lets Turner go and reaches for his pen.

> I think you should talk to Carver again. I think he's got more he can tell you about Rozzy and why she wanted us to go to Bath.

"Carver… great, man," Turner goes. "Definitely what I need—more of that old turd."

Luke just looks at Turner.

"What?" Turner goes. "Oh whatever, man. We'll see, I guess. We'll see."

ERIF
XV

Annabella walked directly toward the two Tarrenbacks watching post at the Great Hall's shadowed back entrance. The same entrance Cyvilard had used to escort her to his aviary two nights ago.

The guards saw her and tensed—-one raising his crossbow, the other his hand in warning.

"Hold now, las," one of them said.

Annabella smiled—-a come-hither smile with fetching eyes—-but continued moving forward.

There were no torches at this entrance, but the darkness was beginning to gray with the coming morning; Annabella saw the Tarrenbacks slacken a bit at her approach, maybe supposing that this lithe budding young woman posed them no threat, only a welcomed distraction from duty.

The one dropped his crossbow to his side and the other grinned. "Hey now—-so what's on, girl? You lose yer way? The Vigil'll be starting on the Hall's yonder side."

The still smiling Annabella slid her hand behind her and slipped the blowgun from her dress's drawstring.

Whap.

She blew the dart in the first guard's neck.

Whap. Whap.

Two more darts blew in from behind her, tagging the other guard in the cheek and ear.

The drug took immediate effect. The Tarrenbacks slumped to the ground without so much as a grunt.

Annabella swooped down to pluck the dart out of the guard's ear. After all, she didn't want to kill him.

"Well done," Samuel said, running up out of the shadows behind her.

"You too," she said.

"It wasn't me. Denisen and Paulus took the shots," Samuel nodded to his mates, both breathless from their shots and the short sprint to catch up.

"Grab their crossbows. I'll get the key," she said and searched the Tarrenbacks' belts and pockets. It didn't take her long to come up with the gnarled iron key and open the heavy oaken door.

She looked back to her fellow conspirators. "For Thorn."

"For Thorn," the boys all repeated and followed Anna.

The hope and the plan was for no one to die but Cyvilard. The four of them had talked it all out hours ago in Samuel's chambers—-after Samuel's return from his meeting with Prince.

They all agreed. They had to do something. And it had to be now. If nothing else, that snake, Cyvilard, at least had to be exposed for the villain he was and taken out. All else might follow after that.

So now, here they were—-Annabella and Samuel and his friends—-storming the Hall in the moments before the Vigil—-looking for Cyvilard, village Elder, the Head of the Tarrenbacks, and Minister of the Lottery—-so that they might expose him before the whole of Thorn for what he and his vicious Lottery had become.

They took the stairs two at a time.

Their way was clear all the way up the spiraling staircase, up to the aviary door.

They paused to steady their breathing. Annabella looked to Samuel who nodded back and stepped up to the door.

He pressed the latch slowly with his thumb and grinned. The door was unlocked.

Denisen and Paulus raised the Tarrenbacks' crossbows, ready for the assault.

Annabella dropped another dart into her blowgun. A dart laced with an instantly lethal poison. Cyvilard's dart. She nodded back to Samuel.

Sam drew his small sword and kicked the door open.

They all burst in, fanning out immediately, hoping to maximize their advantage of surprise.

The room was empty, save for a ring of blackbirds perched on the rail circling above the room.

Annabella shivered at seeing the room's table—-at smelling the old bird droppings and parched paper.

They all shared a moment of stunned indecision. The birds fidgeted and looked down on them. One of them let out a croaky squawk.

"What now?" said Denisen.

A sudden thought pierced Annabella like a dagger in the stomach. "The birds. Shoot the birds!"

She raised up the blowgun and tagged one of them through the breast feathers. It dropped to the aviary floor as flightless as a statue.

Denisen and Paulus raised their crossbows to kill more when Samuel heard the footsteps charging up the staircase.

"It's too late! They're coming!" Samuel said. His friends whirled around and followed Sam back down the stairs.

Annabella looked at the bird she'd slain and cursed it. She loaded another dart into her gun and followed the others. As she descended, she heard struggle: the sound of steel, of crossbows being loosed, of shouts and groans.

By the time she caught up to her fellow conspirators, she could also see their grim handiwork as well. Three dead Tarrenbacks. Two with bolts sticking out of their bloody necks and one with a heart shredding stab wound under his arm made by Samuel's sword.

Samuel looked up to Annabella and wiped the sweat from his brow and flung the blood from his dripping blade.

The hope and the plan was for no one else to die, save Cyvilard.

So much for that.

They heard more troops ascending the stairs.

Denisen bent down and took a quiver of bolts from one of the Tarrenbacks. Paulus did the same.

Annabella threw down her blowgun. "Samuel," she said, "Hand me one of those crossbows."

Sam tossed her one of the fallen Tarrenback's bows. Without another word, Annabella drew the taut string back till it caught and slid the bolt in place.

I'm coming, Cyvilard—-she thought. *No matter what the cost in Tarrenback blood, I'm coming.*

10

OK. So, everything went ape-nuts after *Project Lunchbox* and Gabby bitch-slapping Maddie. I mean totally ape-nuts. The whole school was all flurry, flurry, flurry. Gabby was suspended for two days and a bunch of us got hauled into the office for questioning—but nobody else got punished.

But wow—were people talking. Talking about *The Slap*, obviously, and the Peter/Gabby hook-up thing, Abby and Luke, and the soccer cult that seemed to be winning more and more people to their side.

Turns out Erik was mostly right when he told Morehouse that the bulk of Hemingway kids were only kind of creeped out by the whole *Lunchbox* thing rather than pissed. And most of the creep-factor was like he said: because most kids just didn't understand it. But now as people buzzed more and more about it, it became obvious that a lot of people thought it was actually kind of cool what we were trying to do.

Which all led to a few brave souls even approaching us to let them be in on whatever else we were planning to do, *you know—if you were planning on doing something else like that...*

Which we were.

And so that's how by the beginning of March, all of us met again at Luke's house trying to figure out what to do next, but this time we had newbies Maddie O'Leary, Dallas Douglass, Abby Browne, future valedictorian—Gray Cahill, along with Gala Sarah and two other drama dudes.

I could not believe it. I mean like suddenly half of Mr. Malory's *Great Works* class was here... When I said, 'hey' to Gala I felt my heart jump-roping my intestines. But enough.

The added members of *whatever this was* infused our meeting with like a whole new energy. Especially having the girls. I mean, it was *loud.* It was energetic. Oh, we definitely had energy before with just us guys—but this was different. And for how loud everyone was talking now—throwing out ideas this way and that—these new people gave us a focus that we were kind of lacking before.

We had expanded the circle all right. And I, as I sat back happy to watch everyone else get excited, I looked over and saw Glendening and Patrick look at each other with these raised eye-browed looks, looking clearly overwhelmed with what this was becoming.

The Slap had changed things. And things were about to get serious up in here.

So in the middle of all this fevered brainstorming, Ryan Leon stands up. He starts talking about this idea he has. He says he's been thinking about it for weeks now and that maybe now is the time to come out with it. As he tells us the gist of his plan the room gets quieter and quieter—soon Luke's living room that was so full of voices and laughter and ridiculous gesturing is all ears, all eyes, and stillness.

As far as a focused endgame for the whole thing, Ryan's a little fuzzy—and he admits the details need a little fleshing out. But as I listen to him and look at the faces of everyone else listening to him—there's not a doubt. This is our next *big deal.* This will be our next attempt to expand the circle. But *wow*—there's about a million ways something like this could go wrong.

When he's done, I'm blown away about Ryan's courage. The real heavy lifting of this plan is going to be all on him. But I'm not the only one. Once they get over the initial shock, everyone else seems to think Ryan's brave and also maybe a little bit nuts.

Even Turner says something about Ryan's *balls* that's got nothing to do with his actual testicles.

I look over to Erik, who also is moved and inspired—but there's something else there too, something that looks a little like betrayal.

He didn't know, I remember thinking.

"I'll be in charge of the T-shirts," Maddie offers. "I'm in good with a couple of guys that work over at Sporty's Apparel."

Abby turns to Maddie. "I'll help with the designs."

"OK. But keep it simple," Ryan goes.

There's a short discussion about all the things that must be done. Luke jots down the list. One by one all the soccer guys seem to come up to Ryan and give him a word and meaningful high-five or a stiff, arm behind-the-shoulder, guy hug. Not Erik though, I notice.

People start to head for the door—off to get to their homework or dinner with their families or whatever. I wave to Gala as she leaves with her two friends (OK—one's name was Jordan and the other one was Keith—but anyway). She waves back, and I'd like to think she flushes a bit in the face when she does so—but I can't really tell for sure with beautiful skin like hers. But enough.

"Listen up though—" Erik pipes up as people start to leave. "Nobody says anything about anything until it's time. Nobody. Got it? Dallas, got it?"

Dallas looks pretty offended. "Hey now, why you gotta be pointing me out? I look like a blabbermouth to you? *Nuh-uh*—no, I know how to keep my mouth shut so's I don't get slapped."

"Real funny," Maddie goes standing behind Dallas.

"Oh girl—you know I'm just playing," Dallas goes.

Before Abby takes off, I see her pull Luke aside and whisper something to him. Her eyes are all sparkles. Exactly how I'd like to think Gala might look at me soon.

But enough.

I'm about ready to take off myself, but then I realize that Gray's still here. Tell you the truth, I was beyond shocked anyway that Gray showed up here at all—*period.* But now, with him obviously, awkwardly hanging back… I hung back too.

At this point the only people left are Turner and Luke, of course, and Ryan and Erik. And me and Gray.

"Now that they're all gone, can I talk with you guys a second?" Gray goes mostly to Erik and Ryan, with respectful glances at Luke.

I knew he wasn't really meaning Turner and me too. He wanted to talk to the big-wigs. The dudes in charge. But regardless, he must've felt comfortable enough with us there to continue.

"Sure. What's up?" Erik goes.

Gray all fidgets with his metro-looking glasses with a Clark Kent-type flourish. "Well, first let me just say I wanted to be here tonight because of what you guys did with that whole cafeteria thing. Which, you know, to me felt like the first real meaningful experience to happen at Hemingway in like *ever…* Look, it's no secret: I hate high school. And I'm usually pretty cynical when it comes to the motives and behaviors of my fellow classmates. I mean, mostly it seems that kids treat school as a contest to try and make themselves look as good as they can in everyone else's eyes before they graduate. But they don't ever seem to realize it's a contest you can't ever win, and it doesn't amount to anything anyway."

Both Erik and Ryan kind of patiently nod as Gray talks, while Luke watches his face. I gaze back behind Gray to where Turner lounges on the sofa. We make eye contact and Turner makes an exaggerated jack-off motion with his fist.

"Anyway, my point is—I'm all in with this plan and I have a few ideas about how to document as many of the reactions this is going to get as possible."

Ryan looks confused. "What do you mean 'document?'"

"I mean," goes Gray, "I think we could set it so we could pull in a ton of posts, IG's, tags and texts from people after we pull this off and post it up somewhere for all to see. The good, the bad, the ugly—you know?"

"You mean, get their raw reaction?" Erik goes.

"Yeah—and then post it with their name attached to it so they own it. As long as they post it electronically," Gray goes.

"You collect it and post without them knowing about it?" Luke's robot phone voice goes.

Gray shrugs. "Well, technically if they post it, it's public. So… The only thing we're doing is taking it and putting it on an even wider forum than they intended. We're just gonna make it all go *mini*-viral."

"But not if it's just a straight up text from one person to another though—right?" I butt in.

"Well, mostly no on those—but if we network the right people, we could still get a slew of private texts too."

Gray goes into all how he could do it. Getting people we trust to just simply forward any response they get on their social networks or texts on their phones to us. He says it would only take about twenty well-placed people to spill everything they get sent to them to canvas most of the school.

"Especially with all the friends that Dallas and Maddie are sure to fish in posts from—I think we could get a pretty huge database of reactions," Gray goes.

"This sounds risky…" Ryan goes. "We can't really be sure of what people will think about *everybody* knowing what they think."

"Well—yeah. There's a lot of shady area here. But I can set all this up," Gray goes, "you know—if we want to take it there."

"I like it," Luke's handheld goes. "It is risky, but it's good risky. It'll make people think. It'll make them think about their part in the whole system. Even more than *Lunchbox* did."

"Man," Erik chimes in, "I just wish there was some way to set up mics all over the school to catch everybody's whisperings in the halls about it."

"Yeah, especially somebody like Dylan Sorensen and his pals. They're gonna be freaking unmerciful on me I bet," Ryan goes.

Gray bursts a snicker over that. “Well, get me alone with Dylan’s unlocked phone for like two minutes and I can get you that.”

We all look at Gray.

“What do you mean?” Erik goes.

“I mean, I can turn his phone into a live microphone that I can tap into from my laptop.”

We all boggle. “Are you serious?” I go. “You really know how to do that?”

Gray smirks. “Sure. But hey—fellas—I’m kinda kidding around here about doing it though. I mean, unlike the other shady stuff we’ve been talking about—this is like *for sure* illegal if we get caught. And besides, I don’t see any way I could ever get access to Dylan’s phone. I mean, *duh*—right?”

“I can get his fucking phone for you,” Turner barks from the couch.

“Whoa, whoa, whoa—thanks for the offer, but the last thing we need is a half-assed pickpocket attempt,” Erik goes.

“Screw you, Volgsdick. That ain’t what I’m talking about.”

The rest of us start sniggering.

“What’re you laughing at?”

“Um—he just called you *Volgsdick,”* I go.

“Whatever,” Erik goes and turns back to Turner. “OK. So, what are you talking about?”

“I’m saying,” Turner goes, “I know how to get boy genius here some quality alone time with Sorensen’s phone without any fucking fuss whatsoever, man.”

“We’re listening…” Luke’s phone goes, and Turner looks over at him, and Luke’s got this out-of-nowhere goofy look. He looks like he’s totally screwing around and Turner grins for a second getting the joke.

“OK. What’s the safest place in school to stash stuff?” Turner goes.

“What? You mean like bad stuff?” Ryan goes.

Turner laughs at him. “Sure. *Bad stuff.* Shit you don’t want anyone knowing you got, but you got it at school. Where’s the best place to put it?”

“Your locker?” Ryan goes.

“Car?” I guess.

“Uh, *on* you,” Erik goes, “like in a secret pocket or something?”

Turner just shakes his head all unbelieving at all of us. “A fucking *secret pocket*? Seriously?”

“Sorry the rest of us aren’t like seasoned criminals or whatever,” Erik goes, getting louder.

Luke reaches out his hand from where he’s sitting and touches Erik’s arm. Gives him an *easy* look.

“You don’t need to be a seasoned criminal to figure this out—you just gotta stop being a douche and think…” Turner goes. “Look, you got something at school you don’t want to be caught with, you don’t ever—I mean fucking *ever*— want it to be on your person, or in your locker, or car where you can easily be searched, and slammed red handed for it. So, what are the two places in school that everyone has access to but don’t have cameras or constant teachers eyeballing you up?”

“Bathrooms,” Gray goes.

Turner nods. “*And*?”

"Locker rooms," Ryan goes.

"See Volgsdick, it ain't that hard—you just gotta stop being a douche and think."

I don't know how he does it, but Erik just frowns and holds his tongue.

"OK. But what does the fact that the locker room is the safest place to keep stuff have to do with getting at Sorensen's phone?" Gray goes.

"I'll tell you. See, it's still not good enough to hide shit in your gym locker—I mean it's safer than your regular locker—but your gym locker can still get searched, and then you're on the hook for it because it's assigned to you. So—ideally, it'd be better to have access to another gym locker that ain't yours—"

"You mean like hide stuff in somebody else's locker?" I go.

"Oh, no way, man—" Turner goes, "you're just asking to get narced out if you do that. No. Think about it. There's always more gym lockers than there are kids that need one…"

"An *empty* gym locker…" Gray says, starting to piece it together. "Yeah. It's perfect because no cameras, teachers don't like to stand and monitor it, and most guys keep their eyes pretty much on their own stuff, so they don't get accused of checking out another guy's business. There's just one hitch—"

"How do you get an empty locker's combination?" Erik butts in.

Turner grins at Erik. "There you go again. Doing some of that thinking shit. Wasn't that hard, was it?"

I swear Erik's eyes are telling Turner he can F-*off.*

"Well, make that two hitches," Gray corrected. "Even if I had access to Dylan's phone, I'd need his password to unlock it."

Erik grins all devilish. "I bet Maddie knows it. Bet she'll tell us if she knows what it's for."

"Well, text her, genius," Turner goes, and Erik goes to work on his phone.

Gray raises his hand like he's in class.

"What?" Turner goes.

"How you going to get Dylan's gym locker combination?"

"OK. What if I told you I knew of this guy who used to go to Hemingway like three years ago or so. And this kid worked for the biggest drug dealer in town. So, selling Hemingway kids little baggies of shit was part of his job and bringing a little contra to school was just part of the occupational hazards."

All of us are listening pretty hard, saying nothing.

Turner continues. "So anyway, this kid figures out if you have it on grounds, boys' locker room in an unused locker's the way to go. But where do you get the combination? The kid starts thinking. Realizes there's one person in the school that's sure as shit going to know where to find any locker room *comb* at a moment's notice, man. The athletic director, dudes. So, the kid drops into Steinholz's office. Makes up some BS about forgetting his own gym locker *comb*, even though that doesn't make sense because it's like halfway through the semester and *combs* at that point are like etched in your brain. But Steinholz doesn't even think twice about it, reaches up to this shelf and pulls down this binder with the word LOCKERS written across it. The kid tells Steinholz his locker number and then he gives the kid his 'forgotten' *comb*. So now he knows where all the precious combinations are kept, but how to get at them? *Hmm…?* So later that week, as fate would have it, some asshole in a COVID mask and a hoodie pulls the fire alarm while the kid hides in a toilet stall in the bathroom just outside the A.D.'s office. And guess what? The clueless athletic director doesn't lock his office when he leaves for what he believes is just another routine fire drill. And why would he? It's not like he keeps cash in his office. Just stacks of physical cards, eligibility forms, and a thousand other boring pieces of paperwork. So, our little dealer sneaks in, hauls down the binder and makes photocopies of all the boys' locker *combs* and tears out of there before anyone's the wiser.

"When this kid is able to study the photocopy later, he sees that every locker rotates around the same six combinations changing each semester in a sequence. And by matching where his current combination was, he was able to figure ALL the combinations, no matter what the semester or year, because he knew the sequence."

"And you're telling us this because you have this photocopied sheet?" Ryan asks in a treading lightly voice.

Turner recoils. "Hell no—I don't have the sheet. But here's what I do have: I know as a stone-cold fact that Dylan Sorensen's got second hour gym. I know this because my boy, Toe-Faux's got gym second hour too. And it ain't gonna take *Mission Impossible* to find out which locker's Dylan's."

Turner turns to Gray. "Four-eyes, what you got second hour?"

"Uh—I volunteer as a tutor in the student center," Gray goes.

Turner smiles. "*Fuckn-A*. Yeah—you're gonna be late getting there in a couple days then."

Gray looks suddenly terrified. "OK. But whoa—I still don't know if—"

"Wait—" Erik goes, "hold up, you said you don't have the sheet though…"

"So?" Turner goes.

Erik scoffs. "Well, so—how you gonna get the combo? I mean do you still know the kid that took it?"

Turner shakes his head. "That kid's long gone, man. Long gone. No, I'm gonna get the sheet from the asshole who took the first dealer kid's job."

11

Jason followed Kevin Wilhelm down the hall in between third and fourth periods. Kevin wasn't the wiser, strutting like he was a total burnout badass. As they were passing a row of math rooms, Turner tossed a crumpled ball of loose leaf sending it bouncing off the back of Kevin's head.

"Hey, man. Hey K-van, dude," Turner goes all loud. "You know where I could score a little weed? Or what about one of those kiddie-sized baggies of psychos? Or you know what? I'm feeling a bit cranky today—how's abouts hooking me up with an eightball's worth o'glass?"

"Shut the fuck up, you drunken asshole," Kevin hisses to Turner, murder in his eyes.

"We need to talk," Turner goes. "*Now.* Or I'm gonna keep this bullshit up, but louder so even teachers understand what I'm talking about."

Kevin turns and charges into the nearest bathroom. Turner follows. Two other guys are blow drying their hands and checking themselves out in the mirror.

"All right, clear out, bitches," Kevin barks at them. The boys leave, no hesitation.

Kevin faces Turner and crosses his arms. "OK. What?"

"You got something I need and your gonna spill it," Turner goes.

Kevin rolls his eyes. "Well *Lil Pops*, that totally depends on what you want, dude."

Turner takes a step closer. "Don't call me that."

Kevin smirks. The bell goes off. "Are you gonna get to the point? Because I'm late for Graphic Arts, and you know I love me some Graphic Arts."

"Kid T's combination sheet for the Boys' Locker room. I know my dad gave it to you when you started bizzing for him. I need the combo for one of the lockers."

"No way, dude. You get caught breaking into someone's locker and you narc me, we all got serious problems. Your dad will have serious problems," Kevin goes.

Turner shakes his head. "Won't happen. I'm not taking anything. Nothing's gonna get reported because nothing's gonna go missing. And besides, I could never spill you because you could spill my dad and that gets me dumped hell knows where."

"You're already dumped, asswipe," Kevin goes. "Or did you not get the message? Pop's is done with you. We ain't even got to look out for the Shotgun Methheads no more because you're fair game."

"Yeah, yeah—whatever," Turner goes. "Stay with the point. I need that combo. You are going to give it to me. Like right the fuck, get it?"

Kevin lifts his head to the ceiling tiles and just laughs. "I don't have to do shit for you, man. I don't have to impress your dad anymore. I don't have to worry about offending Rozzy anymore when I talk shit about you. I ain't under Kid T's asshole anymore either. So, I'm finally free to say and do as I please. So's here's what I got to say: you're a fucking *cunt,* Jason. I always hated your guts. And I ain't gonna help you because I don't feel like it, yo?"

Turner just stands there, stares at him. Tries to do his best Luke Forrester impression. "Fine. All right. I'll just go on down to officer Truman's office and tell him to search locker number C012 down in the locker room. I got nothing to lose anymore—and like you said, I've been dumped by my dad anyway."

"You're bluffing, asshole," Kevin says and wags his finger. "But even if you aren't, there ain't anything in C012 today anyway. It's clean and clear right now, bro. And you know what? Even if they did call me into the office for questioning, I'll just turn all their suspicion back on you. Because right now you got nothing but your tale, so it's your word against mine. And you know they're gonna take mine over yours any day of the week. Because you got all the wrong kind of history down there in that office—and I ain't been busted for shit my whole time here. So go ahead."

Turner sighs. "Ah… *K-Van, K-Van, K-Van…* I'm almost glad—you know? Glad you decided to go this route," and out of nowhere Turner kicks Kevin in the nuts. *Hard.* Like lift you off your two feet hard.

Wilhelm crumples to the bathroom floor and Turner winds up and smashes his right fist to Kevin's left cheek. Before Kevin can fully collapse, Turner follows the punch with a left-footed laces kick to the right side of Kevin's face catapulting him backwards, towards the toilet stalls, blood now running down his face from both blows.

Kevin scrambles in a backward crab to the bathroom's back wall. Turner takes a couple steps toward him, fists clenched. Kevin's right-hand swipes behind him, over his shirt, under the belt of his jeans and comes back up gripping his Barretta.

Turner freezes.

Aiming the gun, Kevin slides himself up the bathroom wall. "You fuck—"

"You stupid bastard, carrying a piece in school…" Turner goes.

"Got to these days. It's the fucking wild west out there right now. But *fuck* you. I'm gonna pistol-whip you into my bitch right now for that."

"Like hell you are," Turner takes another step closer.

"Back the fuck up!"

"Been practicing your draw in front of your mirror, haven't you?" Turner goes. "I know how it is. I been there. Only thing is—I ain't no mirror looking back at you."

Kevin keeps the gun trained on Turner's chest. "Stay *back…*"

Turner slowly raises both hands. "I'm gonna put my hand in my pocket now."

"The hell you are!" Kevin shifts side to side.

Turner stands still. "It's OK. I don't have a gun. I don't have a knife," his voice is calm. "You know you're not gonna shoot me. Not right now in a bathroom *at* school." Turner slowly reaches into his pocket.

"What the fuck are you doing?" Kevin goes. "*Stop it—*"

Out comes Turner's hand with his phone.

"What are you going to do, *call* somebody?"

"No," Turner goes and raises it up; presses a button. The familiar *click* sound comes from the phone.

"What *the—*" Kevin goes.

Turner turns the phone so Kevin can see the screen: a pic of himself holding the Barretta straight toward the camera, the familiar Hemingway boys' bathroom tiles in the background.

Kevin stares back up to Turner. "What do you—"

"OK. This is how it's gonna go," Turner goes and starts hitting more buttons. "*I'm* texting you the locker number, and *you* will text me the combo by tonight. If you don't—*K-Van*—I send this pic to the office and the cop shop. And your mom, if I can find her number. Your family's in the phone book, right?"

Kevin still doesn't look like he knows what just happened.

"Or—I guess you can blast me away right here in the bathroom… Look—what I'm asking for's got nothing to do with the *biz*, or you, or my dad, in any way whatsoever. Giving me that combo is no skin off your nose, Kevin. *Or* don't give it to me and I can burn you with this pic and you can take the full rap for it. So take your pick. Because we both know you're not gonna take option C—which is to go to prison for the rest of your meaningful life for shooting me in a Hemingway shitter. I mean, am I right or what?"

ERIF

XVI

"Help me lift this one up," Samuel yelled.

Annabella put her crossbow down on the stairs and helped Samuel raise the slain Tarrenback up. Some of the dead man's blood smeared on her arm.

For Thorn, she repeated the mantra in her head, staring at the red streak. *For Angel,* she added.

"Denisen—-you—-Paulus—-pick that one up," Samuel commanded.

"Shields then?" Paulus asked.

Samuel nodded and gripped the dead man by the back of the belt.

Annabella heard men's voices below them just beyond the stairway's spiral. There was no way to tell how many Tarrenbacks, but it sounded like there had to be more than three for sure. Samuel had the dead man firmly gripped and held in front of them, so she picked the crossbow back up.

"Denisen and I will hold the bodies. Alternate shooting bolts at them," Samuel said.

She and Paulus nodded and readied their crossbows. Samuel and Paulus and their corpses began to shuffle down the stairs in grunts and huffs. The yelling of the Tarrenbacks below was getting louder; more of them were amassing.

Annabella's heart pumped blood beyond a pace she had previously thought possible. She tried to summon her courage, her nerve, her rage. It was odd—-but had she had enough time to really think about how scared she was at that moment, she might have realized that this was the most consumed she had ever been with fear. Even more than the first time she and Angel came into their house to find their father in the darkest realms of drunk after their mother died, even more than when she truly realized she would have to be like a mother to Angel, or even worse—-when she realized that Angel's maturity was beyond hers in so many ways. And somehow this fear on the staircase was even more piercing than the fear she felt strapped to that hideous table in Cyvilard's aviary. Because then, she was almost resigned to her fate and that her sacrifice would free Angel—-but then of course her rage took over. And that's what she wanted now—-for the rage to take over. To overthrow her fear. Her fear—-not so much of death—-as much as that she would die before *doing anything.* Anything that would avenge her sister—-that would change Thorn and its barbaric Lottery. That her death would be for nothing. That's what the sound of the massing Tarrenbacks meant to her. A death without meaning. Death without victory. A defeating death—-meager and stupid—-befitting the worthless and foolish girl she always feared she was. That their family would only amount to a mother dead too early, a blind-drunk father, Angel shat out from the bowels of the dragon, and herself made a riddle of bolts on the Great Hall's spiral staircase.

They rounded the spiral and saw the mass of Tarrenbacks at the foot of the staircase.

The Tarrenbacks roared and opened a volley of bolts, arrows piercing the chests and thighs of their dead comrades, while some whizzed over Samuel and Annabella's heads.

Paulus peeped over Denisen's shoulder and fired a bolt of his own into the huddle of Tarrenbacks, scoring one in the stomach. The wounded man howled and doubled over—-his comrades grabbling him by the elbows and dragging him backward out of the fray.

Annabella yelled and shot one high over their heads and careening off the stone wall behind them next to a torch stand.

Still more bolts came at them, ripping into their fleshy shields, the blood of the dead men running down and making slick the stairs. The storm so steady now that Samuel and Denisen could no longer move forward against it.

Paulus poked up and shot another bolt, screaming when an arrowhead grazed off his head, slashing a torrent of blood from under his hair flowing down into his eyes.

They crouched and hunkered as best they could, still holding up their dead shields. Bloodlust roars came from the Tarrenbacks as they inched closer—-some casting aside crossbows and drawing their swords.

And still the bolts came, slamming home into their dead fellows and ricocheting off the narrow walls of the staircase—it barely mattered to the Tarrenbacks to aim now, just keep the barrage coming. Clearly, they wanted to just keep the kids pinned down until their swords could finish them off.

Paulus continued to wail, clutching his gash, and wiping the blood from stinging his eye. Annabella dropped her crossbow and screamed herself—-sensed this was the end—-until she felt Samuel yank her by the arm.

"Up and grab his belt!" he yelled. She saw him jiggle the dead Tarrenback. "Hold him just for a few seconds!"

She rose and grabbed the man's belt with both hands, leaned his weight against her and straightened her back. She held him upright—-but knew she couldn't support him for long.

Samuel crouched, pulling a slimy cloth from a bag tied to his belt with his leather gloved hand. With his other hand he pulled a flintstone from his boot. Placing the cloth near the stair, he struck the flint off the stair, flashing into a spectacular spark, the cloth igniting into a perfect green flame. Raising with a yell, Samuel threw the green fire ball into the cluster of Tarrenbacks approaching, swords drawn. Three men ignited instantly. The flame was blinding. Samuel knelt again and ignited another slimy cloth. This fireball he lobbed over the first row of Tarrenbacks into the row behind them still firing crossbows. More men burst into flames. The green fire spread amongst the closely filed ranks. Within moments, most of the Tarrenbacks were on fire or fleeing from those who were.

Annabella and Denisen let the corpses fall. Samuel descended the stairs, picking up a fallen man's sword and roaring, entered the fiery mass cutting at any body part the flaming men offer in their consumed staggering. Denisen did likewise, while Annabella turned to Paulus.

"I'll be fine," he pushed her hands from his face and stood up, his white eyes showing through a horror-curtain of blood. "Let's help them!" Both he and Annabella picked up crossbows and began systematically shooting flaming and fleeing men—-in the head, backs, and chests. Men screamed and died—-most collapsing to the ground to let the unquenchable green flames consume their robes and flesh and mail completely.

Samuel and Denisen were chopping heads, one by one—-sending them like loose fireballs into the air to crash and roll hideously to the corners of the hall.

Samuel had told them he knew where his father hid three small vases of the outlawed *dragonscorch*—-Erif's slobber-drool sometimes fallen from his jowls in flight back up to the Crack and collected from boulders where it cooled enough to harvest. But their intention had been to burn down the Great Hall itself if they needed to—-it was never the plan to use it to burn any Tarrenbacks alive.

When all the men in the hall were slain, Samuel and Denisen let their swords and arms droop with exhaustion. Paulus let himself collapse and put his hands again to his wound.

Annabella looked around at the savagery of their work and tears flowed out of her eyes but without sobs, without sound.

"Come—-we can't tarry here—" Samuel croaked. "The Vigil will be starting. The dais is only down another hall and up a small stone ramp. Cyvilard and all of Thorn are waiting. These fires will burn out once their flesh and bones are consumed."

Slowly, they all staggered behind Samuel. Paulus threw down his crossbow for a sword. Annabella threw down her crossbow but picked up nothing.

"You OK?" Samuel asked her.

"I'll kill no one else, save one," she said. "And for Cyvilard my weapon will be my words, and my shield, truth. And when all of Thorn hears it, they will rise and tear him apart with bare hands and barred teeth."

"Let us hope you are right," Denisen said.

"Come then. Let's finish it," she said. "Let's take back our home."

12

Turner remembers the exact moment he fell in love with Rosalind Howard. Not when he first liked her, or wanted to have sex with her, or whatever. Like real *this-is-it* love. It was a morning, the summer before their senior year—about month before her death—and Turner was coming home from a night of partying with Toe Faux. He came in through the back kitchen door and opened the fridge to snag a swig of milk. On his way upstairs he saw her lying on the living room couch. It was pretty customary to see his dad all passed out on the couch, even though he usually preferred the EZ Boy, but he was nowhere to be found this morning. Just Rozzy. She was passed out and naked except for what looked like just a T-shirt wrapped close around her chest and a couple of couch pillows covering her belly and lap. Well, and she also had her socks on. They were white ankle-highs. Probably cheap Walmart's.

Turner bolted upstairs to get a blanket from his room and poked to see if his dad was sleeping in his room. Nope. Dad was M.I.A...

Kneeling down by Rozzy, he took in the full extent of how rough a shape she was in. There was a sprawling fresh bruise on the side of her face which could've meant she was hit, or she had one of her bad seizures. Before he draped the blanket over her, he swept the pillows away. He couldn't help noticing she looked painfully swollen and there was even a little blood smeared on her thigh.

There was no doubt she had been totally banged. Probably raped. The guy, or guys who did this would probably say she was consenting, but Turner knew she was probably completely wasted, but still… He knew she had probably had sex with Dre for glass before—maybe even had to bang his whole crew. Which made Turner so pissed he could hardly stand it sometimes. But Rozzy never wanted to talk to him about it. Never complained. Probably because she had her habit that she always seemed determined to maintain. To hell with the cost.

After she was covered, he scanned around for her clothes. Zippo. Which made no sense. *Whatever*, he thought. He would give her some of his till he could get her home.

When she started to come to, he went and got her some water. He held the glass to her lips, and she drank some but then gagged and started to cough. She sat up and started wiggling one of her front teeth and it fell right out in her hand.

"Holy shit," she goes and held it up to him. "I think I'm gonna be sick—"

Turner ran and got a bowl from the kitchen that his mom used to put apples in on the table back when she lived there and held it under Rozzy as she retched. A clearish fluid roiled out of her, mixing with spit and maybe a little blood. He held her with one arm, still holding the bowl at the ready, while she rocked in her sea-sick motion, spittle dripping out her gaping mouth.

He laid her back down on the couch, sitting down himself, putting her head in his lap. She seemed dozy, but calm. The coughing and the retching seemed to be past her.

Turner stroked her hair.

She moaned a little and seemed to smile, her eyes half closed. Her head nestled into his lap, and she pulled his hand down to kiss it. She released it just as quick, and he continued with her hair.

"Darkling, I listen—my night—" She whispered.

"What? Your *night*—you mean last night? You wanna tell me—"

"No. No," she weakly tried to shake her head. "You're my night…"

"I don't…"

She opened her eyes and Jason fell in love.

"In shining armor, stupid. You're my *knight*."

Turner managed a smile, but inside his soul was soaring/plummeting. "Your knight?"

She nestled into him again and closed her eyes. "My knight…*my knight…*"

They stayed that way until she was asleep. Then Turner slipped from under her and ran back up to his room to pace the floor. He loved Rosalind Howard. But Rozzy was in trouble. Trouble that Turner had no way he could think of to free her from. Lunging to his dirty clothes hamper, he pulled out his bottle of Jim Beam and took four huge gulps and wiped his chin. All he wanted at that moment was to take her away. Hide her and keep her safe. Hold her and kiss her and keep all the darkness away.

Forever.

But how? Turner just couldn't figure how. His hands trembled. He took another massive pull of bourbon and it seemed to slide down to his heart. He loved her but he was so freaked out about how hopeless it all seemed. *Save* her? From his dad and the biz? From Dre and Cunter? From the meth? Not to mention from herself?

That morning it was all too much for him.

It was just too much, so he gulped more bourbon.

13

OK—you know in comics when people think and stuff, and artists draw those thought-bubbles with the people's thoughts inside? Yeah—well, when I think back to that day in March when we came out with Ryan's plan, if I were trying to tell this story like a comic book instead of just like prose or whatever, I would've drawn this sweet panoramic picture of the school building of Hemingway. And above it would be all these little thought bubbles starting to rise all over the place above the school. All small at first—but many—like the hundreds of little fizz bubbles that rise when you pour some soda pop into a glass. And all of them rising—this armada of bubbles and baby balloons—to merge into one massive collective thought above the school, expanding all freaking YAWP-like in its potential energy and girth—coalescing into one three-letter acronym: *WTF?*

That's what it was like in those opening hours of school that morning. Kids were catching random glimpses of some of us and didn't get it—but still realizing something was up. Something weird. Something big.

But of course, by the end of second hour, thoughts turned into freaking fevered whispers and under-the-desk texts, and then to all out chatter in the hallways between classes.

WTF?

Reportedly, there were repeated phrases like *'I knew it!'* and hissed refrains: *'Fags!'*

It's so funny—you know when you really think about it. That T-shirts could stir up so much buzz and controversy. I mean sometimes that's all it takes: a few words across a cotton shirt. See, it didn't matter if they saw Ryan first or any of the rest of us. They wouldn't get the full picture until they saw both shirts: *Ryan's* and *ours'*.

On the front of Ryan's shirt were the words: HI, I'M HOMOSEXUAL. And on the back:
CALL ME *FAG* IF YOU MUST,
BUT WHAT THEN SHOULD I
CALL *YOU*?

Ryan Leone is one of the bravest guys I've ever met. His courage that day blew me away. I mean, Hemingway is a *suburban* high school. Not west coast, not northeast coast. Sure, we got Detroit a few miles away, but this is still the Midwest, baby. Midwest family values, Midwest family fears. How could any of the rest of us not wear our shirts after knowing he was wearing his?

So, for the rest of us, *Circle Expanders*, we wore HI, I'M HETEROSEXUAL on the front, and
BUT I GOT A FRIEND
WHO AIN'T. on the back.

That's right. Welcome to *Awkward Day* at Hemingway High.

By the time the bunch of us that got to Malory's *Great Works* class, you could tell the whole school was thoroughly a'buzz.

"Yo—you soccer freaks…" Phil Lukas goes, kind of laughing/kind of not, before the bell rings, "at it again."

"And what the hell's with the rest of you?" Peter Calloway goes all sour to Dallas, Maddie, Gray, and me who are all sporting our shirts too. "I mean, I expect nothing less from Volgstaad here, and the rest of his soccer fairies. But not all of *you.*"

Maddie turns in her seat to face them. "And what exactly, Peter, do you think it is we're doing? Why don't you just say out loud what you think about this?"

"Yeah," Gray goes all slyly, "We'll even quote you on it…"

"*Whatever*—look, you guys are all messed up. You're just trying to get everybody all hyped up and freaked out because you guys need attention or something. Stupid thing is, everybody knows this is all that big fuck's idea, and you leeches are just playing along. I bet you Leone's not even gay. I bet Luke got him to do this just because it'd make a stir."

Phil just starts laughing again. "Naw, naw, naw, now, Petey. No, I think our boy Leone's gay all right. Lot of them soccer fairies are now. And it's OK—it's even cool now. Wouldn't be surprised if more of them be coming out the closet now Ryan has, yo."

"Or maybe some of your basketball buddies," Erik shoots back.

"Hold up, Volgs. Ain't no chance any my ballers be puffs now. Gotta come correct on that. This here be a soccer thing, yo."

"Oh—I see," Erik goes. "It's by sport, huh? Homosexuals just naturally flock to soccer and not like *basketball*, or *football* even, right?"

Phil starts nodding his head, "For reals now, son. There you be. I mean, fairies probably in tennis and cross-country or whatever. It's all good though. And we know a bunch gotta be out for swimming, *feel me, now*?"

"Can I quote you on that?" Gray cuts in, smiling.

Phil keeps giggling. "Yeah, dawg. *Hell.*"

But before it can continue, Malory flies in and passes out our copies of *Frankenstein*, which the title alone prompts more stupid jokes from Phil and Peter in the back. I notice though that every time Peter and Phil say something gay-bashing, Dallas and Maddie and Gray are all writing it down on their notepads.

I look up at Erik and he's just smiling. He leans over to me and whispers, "These bastards don't know what's about to hit them."

I grin too.

That afternoon everyone met up at Luke's. We were jazzed up and giving high-fives and hugs, especially to Ryan. He beamed and said the whole experience was basically indescribable and he was just so thankful all of us were there to back him up. The craziest day of his life, he said.

Luke gave Ryan a massive bear-hug and slipped him a small note between his fingers.

You're a hero of mine.

Ryan grinned, clasping Luke's shoulder. "We are brothers—you and me. Brothers."

Then we immediately got about the business of turning the Forrester's home into a command center of texts and tweets and posts. Gray was in the middle of it with his laptop and pad. Dallas, Maddie, Abby, and Gala were all over their phones, collecting every comment they could get their hands on.

It was unreal. Like well beyond cray/ridic if you know what I mean. The whole thing was like something out of a spy flick. The girls were tapping their handhelds, sending Gray all sorts texts and posts from all the peeps they were linked with. And *SCHH-POW!,* man. There were so many! It seemed every kid at Hemingway was chiming in with a take on our day's business. And most of it was scathing. (I mean the worst by far was the stuff Gray recorded from Dylan Sorensen's hijacked phone—but more on that later…) So, like I said by and freaking large, the talk was mostly pretty harsh gay-bashing BS.

We were kind of surprised not all of it was. There were still plenty of kids we were picking up comments from that actually thought what we did was pretty cool—or close to cool anyway. And most of these people thought that Ryan was unbelievably brave too.

Anyway, our little command center kicked into gear. Gray was the freaking man, cutting, posting, streaming, linking. He had constructed this site: *hemingwayownit,* a few days before, and now it served at a massive poster-board where he blasted every straight-up quote and comment ALONG with the name of the person who either said, texted, or posted it. And Gray put it all up there too: the good, the bad, and the butt ugly. He and Erik and Patrick did most of the posting work on three different computers; each of them chugging coffee and Red Bulls till their eyes went bloodshot and their hands trembled.

Eventually the girls all went home, (Abby lingering with Luke in the kitchen a little longer than the others until eventually splitting to her house down the street) and a few of us guys stayed and crashed on the floor or couch, except for Turner and Luke who eventually staggered up to their rooms—while Gray, Erik and Patrick soldiered on till dawn.

ERIF
XVII

They ran through the long corridor that led up to the stage and main entrance of the Great Hall. They could hear the whole village begin to sing the Old Song. Voices young and old alike began to rise and swell.

Samuel got right up to the short staircase that led to the stage and crouched. The rest of them did the same. Denisen and Paulus both rested their crossbows across their laps, while Samuel pointed his up and took a deep breath.

Annabella alone was weaponless now. She wanted this all to be over. To convince Thorn of Cyvilard's treachery and malice and to have the village elders order his imprisonment.

She looked up to the sky through the arched doorway. Dawn had broken, the sun was all new with its morning glowing. The Old Song's heartbreaking melody continued. Hundreds of voices, the voice of Thorn, sang out the old lyrics of sacrifice and healing and triggered memories in Annabella of singing the song every year with her family. She remembered the sound of her mother's voice and clinging to her waist, thinking about how awful it was about another child's sacrifice morning. She remembered the first time she and Angel and her father came to the morning Vigil after the passing of her mother. Holding Angel's hand so tightly it hurt and weeping openly about giving unto Erif what must be rendered unto Erif. Then her thoughts turned to Angel. Was she alive? Or had this terrible morning already claimed her life? Was that cursed dragon chewing on her bones this instant? And what about Prince? Had he made it to her? Was he dead too? Such a hopeless plan, Annabella thought. All of it.

Annabella shook out of it and was aware she was on the brink of tears. She looked at Samuel and saw on his face he was thinking similar thoughts. She reached over and squeezed his hand.

"It's time," she said.

He nodded, resolved. He looked to Denisen and Paulus. "Ready?"

Denisen nodded back, while Paulus wiped a slow-moving trickle of blood from the slash on his forehead and muttered an 'aye.'

"For Thorn," Samuel said and stood.

"For Angel," Annabella said.

They all stood to rush up to the stage, when suddenly Denisen fell forward, making no attempt to keep from falling on his face. A crossbow bolt stuck out from his back.

They wheeled around and saw two Tarrenbacks heading toward them. Paulus let loose his bolt and it stuck deep into one of the Tarrenback's neck.

The other dropped to his knee and shot his bolt into Paulus's chest.

"Paulus!" Annabella said.

The Tarrenback rose, drawing his sword, and ran at them.

Paulus fell to his knees, blood leaking through his shirt, but managed to pull Denisen's crossbow over to himself and shot the oncoming Tarrenback in the gut, felling him on the spot to groan and clutch the wound.

"Go..." Paulus managed to say and coughed up a gout of blood and fell dead.

Samuel lunged up the stairs and onto the stage where all the Elders and Cyvilard were standing. Annabella ran after him.

"Cyvilard! You will not move!" Samuel thundered up onto the stage and boldly aimed his crossbow at the bald elder.

The people broke their singing and grunted and guffawed in wonder at the sight of Samuel and Annabella up on stage. A few of the women even screamed.

"Behold!" Cyvilard said, pointing a gnarled finger at the approaching Samuel. "Here is the very face of insurrection and treason!"

"Samuel!" Quindarius erupted. "Do not do this, son!"

"Quiet, father," Samuel hissed. "I'm merely doing what you should've done years ago. People of Thorn! It is time for all to know the deeds of this man, this robed snake that hides behind his Tarrenbacks and his title as our village protector. It's time that all should know the depths of his treachery!"

"Baa! Enough sniveling boy!" Cyvilard snarled. "Put down your weapon and surrender. It's your only chance to survive this day."

The three Tarrenbacks on the stage trained their crossbows solely on Samuel while Annabella stood a few paces behind him.

"Stay back—-" Samuel said to them. "I swear, even if you nail me in the heart with your bolts, the last thing I do before I fall is shoot mine into Cyvilard's eye."

The Tarrenbacks said nothing, keeping their crossbows on Samuel.

"What goes here?" yelled a man at the front of the crowd. Hundreds of Thorn villagers then cried out at once, all confused and by this turn in the Vigil ceremony.

"People of Thorn! This elder here—-Cyvilard, has rigged Lottery countless times, or threatened to rig it to manipulate others to his dark designs," Samuel bellowed.

"It's true," Annabella said. "The reason my sister was chosen to die this morning was not due to the randomness of the Lottery, but Cyvilard deliberately called her name because I would not lie with him."

"Whore's lies!" Cyvilard spat. "Do not listen to these anarchists whose only wish is to supplant the Elders and let Thorn burn to ruin."

"You're the *whore*, drunk on your lust for power. Taking the already vile practice of the Lottery and corrupting it further," Samuel said and stepped even closer to Cyvilard and then looked to all the Elders standing nearby whose looks of deep mortification and shock were etched all over their faces. "And you all *let* him!"

"Samuel—-it is not that simple," Quindarius said, taking a step towards his son.

"I do not want to hear it, father! How long? How long have you been in his clutches? How long have you full known of his black heart and his yonderling powers?" Samuel said and several villagers recoiled and swooned.

"*Samuel*..." Quindarius pleaded.

"Enough of this drivel," Cyvilard said with a face beaming extreme malice. "Prepare to die, boy..."

Cyvilard suddenly vanished. He turned into a blackbird in the blinking of an eye and soared up to the top of the Great Hall's roof.

In the crowd there were yells and gasps and a few screams from the women.

Samuel lowered his crossbow, dumbfounded, and Annabella was struck by the realization that with Cyvilard off the stage, Samuel no longer had any leverage to keep the three Tarrenbacks from shooting him with their crossbows.

The Tarrenbacks and Quindarius appeared to have realized this at the same instant as Annabella.

"No!" Quindarius yelled and darted in the space between his son and the Tarrenbacks just in time to receive the three zipping bolts into his chest.

"Father!" Samuel said and darted down to raise his dying father's head up. Annabella fought back a sob as she looked down at the ghastly amount of blood flowing out of Quindarius and onto the wooden planks of the stage. The poor man's eyes rolled back in their sockets as he seemed to struggle to stay conscious.

Cyvilard swooped down from his perch and re-formed into his robed human body as fast as a lightning flash right behind Samuel and dying Quindarius.

"Your mother..." Quindarius groaned. "...Not *your* mother..."

"*What*?" Samuel said, still holding his father's head.

Out from the sleeve of his robe, Cyvilard pulled his curved dagger. Annabella couldn't scream quick enough, as the bald Elder crouched down and slit Samuel's throat wide.

The crowd erupted in horror and disbelief while Annabella jumped from the stage into their midst. The dumbstruck villagers parted for her. Fighting back her tears, she sprinted to a horse that stood tethered to a post by a leather strap. Before the horse's owner could pipe up in protest, Annabella unsheathed a sword that was strapped to the saddle, mounted the horse, and cut the strap.

"Seize her!" Cyvilard shouted and then moved to finish his grim work, stabbing Samuel in the heart as the boy clutched his bleeding and gurgling neck. After the son was dead, Cyvilard turned to the father.

Quindarius, with half-closed eyes still huffed with breath right up until Cyvilard plunged his dagger between the old man's ribs.

The other Elders could only watch in ultimate terror. The three Tarrenbacks shook off their own bewildered looks and reloaded their crossbows.

To navigate the animal, Annabella had to hike her dress up while the reigns grasped in one of her hands, a short sword in the other. She was a sight to see, like some kind of warrior princess from a distant and savage land, and the villagers all gave her a wide berth.

"Do you not see, *now*? With your very eyes? Come, look upon this Elder in black robes and know the very face of evil!" Annabella addressed the crowd. "Did you not see him slay a boy and his father right here before all our eyes? And the *father*? None other than our Elder Quindarius!"

"Those I slew were traitors to our common good. Quindarius betrayed our ancient justice the moment he stepped into the line of fire. That boy, as you call him, was on the verge of slaying me on this stage in the name of insurrection," Cyvilard barked. "How dare you come here to confront me. Damn and blast you! It is I, and our Lottery alone, that keeps Erif and his Rogni from slaughtering this entire village for good and all."

Cyvilard whirled around to face the remaining Elders. "You all know me. You know my undying love for Thorn. I wish to preserve this home we've built here for all times. But to do that, you all know what is required. As terrible as it is, you know and accept the price to remain here."

"Children of Thorn!" Annabella spun her horse in a slow circle, trying to take in as many of the crowd's faces as she could. "This way of life, this wretched Lottery, this evil man's grip on our souls—-all of it—-it's all ending. Right now—-as of this breath. Erif be damned. The murders, the terror. It all ends *now*. All we must do is rise, hang this devil for his crimes and move to places of peace and start over. Join me! Join me now!"

"Baa! Dissembler thou! Whereto would we move? Think you not that Erif would not track every one of us down and burn us to dust just for spite?" Cyvilard thrust his bloody dagger at Annabella. "People of Thorn, join me in dragging her down this instant from that horse and crush her head under your boot heels! If you want to keep your homes, there's no keeping with rebel whores!"

Annabella looked upon the people. "Rise! Take to the stage! Let us take him now! For your children! Rise all!"

"Men—-slay her," Cyvilard turned to the Tarrenbacks. "Shoot her where she sits, *slay now*!"

The Tarrenbacks looked at each other, terrified. As did the Elders. Annabella couldn't believe it: no one moved, no one spoke. Hundreds of people, motionless and silent. Only she and Cyvilard stirred and railed for action, but no one moved.

"How can you not?" Annabella's heart suddenly filled with loathing, with an ultimate hopelessness. "How can you not do *anything*?"

They all looked away from her.

"Slay her! *Slay* her! *Slay, slay, slay*!" Cyvilard called to everyone. When still no one moved, he began to stride over to the Tarrenbacks to either slay all of *them* or take a crossbow so he could kill Annabella. But before he could make it across, one of them fired a bolt at her tagging her in the thigh.

She howled and clutched the bolt sticking out of her flesh. Realizing no one was coming to her side, she wheeled the horse around and took off at a sprint through the lane. Villagers parted for her while another crossbow bolt whizzed past her head.

14

"All right, moment of truth, boys," Gray goes. Those of us that had stayed the night at Luke's house all gathered around Gray and his laptop. "The site's already up and running, and all I have to do to activate our hack into Hemingway's system is click right here." Gray looked back at us. Looked to Luke. "We still want to do this?"

Turner rubbed some sleep out of his eyes and answered. "Hell yeah, man. Fucking *yes* with a capital Y. Cyber-bomb the shit out of this mother. Blow it all right the fuck."

I looked at everybody's faces. You could tell we were all nervous, all amped.

Luke nodded to Gray, and Gray clicked it.

"Let there be light, dudes," he goes.

We went to school. Well, OK, most of us went home, showered, put on some new clothes told our parents our little slumber party at Luke's was fun and all that, and then we went to school and waited for the place to blow. It didn't take long.

The first flash of hemingwayownit simultaneously flickered to life on all fifteen of the school's hallway flatscreens in the passing time after first period. Within an hour, the site had hundreds of hits from kids checking it out on their phones.

The buzz got downright eerie. Kids were pissed, some were scared about what was on there, and more than a few just cut out and left for the day because they couldn't handle it. It was crazy—it was like people wanted to both talk about it and totally ignore it and pretend it didn't exist at the same time. And even though a bunch of us were responsible for it, the brunt of the anger seemed to fall mostly on Luke, Erik, and Ryan. The really pissed off kids stared daggers at them.

The site itself was pretty bare bones—it had no pictures, just tons and tons of comments in quotation marks followed by the names of the people that said it or posted it or texted it. That's all. But that's all it took for the school to go on complete social lockdown.

At first, all the teachers and office staff couldn't really tell what was going on—they just suddenly sensed that all the students were basically going batcrap to varying degrees. Until they noticed the hacked flatscreens. Once the school district tech guy couldn't figure out how to get the hemingwayownit off the flatscreens, finally one of the counselors decided to check out the full site in her office. Well, apparently it only took her about thirty seconds before she got up and stormed over to Principal Carter's office and got him online. Then it really started to hit the fan after that. But before the principals could start hauling us in, Gray let loose the big guns right before lunch.

From his handheld, Gray launched the first sound bite he had sniped from Dylan Sorensen's tapped phone. It was crazy. We were all walking either to class or to first lunch, when suddenly Dylan's voice comes over the school's PA system: "Hey, I told you those guys were all butt-pirates."

Everywhere throughout the school, kids and teachers alike all froze and lifted their eyes to the ceilings where they speakers were like we were hearing the voice of God or something.

You could hear the super-loud giggles of Kirk Wellington too as Dylan continued. "Dude, I bet Leone just spreads his ass and Forrester and the whole team lines up with their diseased dicks out ready to fudge pack him."

Everyone's eyes about popped out of their heads and looked around at each other with the same *did-that-just-happen* looks on their faces. And for those of us that knew it was coming, we answered those looks in our heads: *Yes*, oh yes, that *indeed* just happened.

By the time I got down to the cafeteria, it was like a freaking creep zone. It wasn't loud or as chaotic as when Maddie got slapped by Gabby Altman—but it was just as intense, if not more so. The whole caf had this crazy static kind of energy. Almost like when you get the first whiff that you're near something dead on a hot summer's day. People were sitting down and huddling in little safety circles or standing off in the corners. Then Dylan himself stalked in and went straight up to where Luke and Turner were sitting. Like immediately, Turner stood up and met Dylan halfway and it looked like they were gonna start throwing down like big time. But they just started yelling at each other.

Mrs. Burlington was the first teacher on lunch duty to try and get between them—but you could tell she was scared to get in there.

"Oh, at ease, Mrs. B—ain't nobody going to be fighting here," Turner goes. "No, this is just all going to be about the truth here. Ain't that right, Sorensen—the truth, right?"

Dylan looks all disgusted back at Turner. "Truth? Whatever. Lies. That's all you guys have been spreading all day. Pure lies."

"That's rich coming from you," Turner shoots back, then looks around to the crowd of students that are gathering. "OK. Let's talk lies. Let's talk bullshit. So if I were to just ask everyone right here, right now, how many of you have every heard Mr. Sorensen here ever say anything that was a dis, or lie, or just complete bullshit about someone else here at school—I mean, how many of you could raise your hands and say 'yeah'?"

A few kids actually put their hands up. A few even say 'yeah!' Then you can see Assistant Principal Henderson come out of the main office and start to walk over to where Dylan and Turner are squaring off.

"I mean, we've been hearing truth all day, right? I mean, even before we heard this gay basher over the PA, yeah? I mean, let's be honest here people," Turner goes and keeps looking around to everyone. "We've been hearing his voice and other voices like Dylan's all year long—some of us all four years long, hearing that voice calling us pussies, faggots or skanks, or worse—just because you thought you could get away with it or thought it could make you look tougher by lording your swagger over some of us. Well, that's done, man. This week's all about serving notice, asshole. To you and anybody else that thinks it's all good to be a royal-ass douche and think you get a bully-card for free just because you're cool and know how to do it all on the down-low so adults won't want to believe it's you. Well *F*-that, man. We're shutting that shit down."

And, unbelievably, some kids are cheering Turner. Granted, mostly the one's cheering are gothy and misfit types—but there's plenty of preppier-looking Hemingway kids that aren't cheering, but they're nodding. And some of them just stare at Dylan.

Dylan looks around. He looks stunned. More stunned than any of us ever thought Dylan could ever look. Like some Greek god watching in slack-jawed disbelief as the walls of his Olympus begin to crumble.

"All right, whatever's going on here, it's enough," Assistant Principal Henderson finally makes it to the crowd, but people are all breaking away and Turner's already stepped back closer to Luke and well away from Dylan.

"It's over, man," Turner says maybe to Henderson, maybe to Dylan.

Henderson looks all flustered. "Well, in any case I need to see…uh—Mrs. Burlington, who do I need to see?"

Poor Mrs. Burlington looks completely overwhelmed. She just holds her palms out and shrugs.

Dylan narrows his eyes and practically hisses at Luke and Turner, "This isn't over…" and turns to stalk off.

"Uh, Mr. Sorensen, Principal Carter and I need to see you in the office," Henderson calls out after Dylan.

Dylan keeps walking for the front doors. "Yeah, you can talk to me once I tell my dad what's going on here and he gets our lawyer."

Some bold skater-looking kid calls "*Asshole*!" to Dylan as he walks out the door.

I turn around and see Gray, Erik and Ryan all slink up to where Luke and Turner are standing all defiantly.

Gray just leans in and goes all quiet, "Oh boy, this isn't good… I think we're all going to jail…"

Turner smiles and glances back down to Gray and goes, "Well, I'm sure you'll be really popular there, four-eyes…"

ERIF
XVIII

After stirring awake and opening his eyes for real—-not opening them while still in the grip of delirium and hallucination—-Prince realized that he was alive. He also realized he had never felt worse though. He was aware of an ever-sharpening pain where his arm had been severed and where Angel was forced to burn his flesh to stop him from bleeding out. Then there was his broken collarbone along with the ragged wounds in his shoulder where Stagfin had set his jaws on him. So, Prince lived, but he suffered and was weak and fevered.

He looked around and saw they were still in the Rogni's hall. "How long was I out?"

"A few hours. It's nearly dawn," Angel said. She helped him sit up and held a ladle of water to his lips.

"I thought I had died, and I was with your sister in the afterlife," he said.

Angel gave a frail smile. "That sounds like a good dream." She watched him try to grin back at her but raised his stumped arm up to lightly touch it with a probing finger, triggering a wince across his face. "I'm sorry I had to do that. Put the iron on it."

"You saved my life by doing it." Prince gave a grim chuckle. "I came up here on the slim chance I could save your life and you ended up saving me..."

They both sat silent for a while.

"Last night, after you fell asleep, I took a torch and found the trail that leads up to the Crack. It's almost dawn, Prince," she took his good hand, "I need to go up there soon or Erif will fly out, see what we've done to his Rogni, burn Thorn..."

"No," Prince said. "Look on me, Angel. I came up here—-your sister, Samuel, they sent me up here to try, *try* beyond all hope, to save you. And I have a plan. It's slim, but I have one."

"What is it?"

He took a breath and explained. Angel listened, her blue eyes thoughtful; she asked him a few questions and made a few concerned nods.

"There's just one botch though. Since I've been on this mountain, my power, my auras—-sometimes I can make them, sometimes I can't. Last night I was able to use them to start my attack on the wolf-men, but..." he snapped his fingers, "then I couldn't. Quick as a whisp—-they were gone, and I couldn't hail them. And now with me this injured, weak—-my fear is that the dragon's lair, or his magic, will counter my abilities, leaving me helpless."

"Leaving us helpless," Angel said.

She helped him rise to his feet. This was no easy task since Prince's balance was off, and he was so nauseous and weak. Once they had staggered outside, Angel found a sturdy branch for Prince to use as a crutch so he could traverse without leaning on her. The darkness was melting away and the sky was chilled and gray before the rising of the sun. They both looked out one last time to the clearing where they could see the still and ghastly heaps of the slain Rogni. The small axe handle still stuck up from the earth where Angel had slain Stagfin.

They started their slow climb. It was treacherous, many times Prince slipped, sliding slowly back down the path causing small avalanches of rocks and shale shards. Each time Angel would take his hand and pull him painfully back up till she could reach under his un-injured arm to stand him back up.

Above them loomed the dark gape of the Crack. It seemed the cave's entrance was a living thing, a mouth expanding wider and wider till it could encompass the whole sky with its blackness.

They smelled it before they actually saw it, the smoke billowing out like a sick gray pall, reeking of sulfur and decay. The breath of the dead. It got so thick that Prince had to rip two shreds of his tunic so that they could tie the cloth around their mouths to breathe easier. And then they could hear the dragon's low moaning, or sustained growl so awesome in its terrifying intensity that its rumble seemed to be shaking the whole mountain from underneath.

And yet the boy and the young girl continued to climb towards it. Continued towards the dragon.

15

Well, we didn't all go right to jail. But some of us did immediately get hauled down to the office. Taking in Luke, Erik, Ryan and Turner was like a total no-brainer for Assistant Principal Henderson there in the cafeteria. Then more of the soccer dudes got hauled in—and why not, right? Start with the soccer guys because they're the ones who got this school year rocking like the freaking *Cuckoo's Nest* in the first place, the principals were probably thinking. So—Tristan, Patrick, and Glendening got hauled in too—even though Tristan and Glendening barely had anything to do with the planning of hemingwayownit other than knowing it was going to happen. I mean, they even called in Coach Striden who had like zero clue about any of this just because she was their coach.

Well, that left Dickie, Gray, and me to scramble over to Gray's house to swipe the site down and try and delete all traces of where Gray had hacked into Hemingway's system.

Meanwhile, back in Principal Carter's office, an epic pow-wow was ensuing about what just the hell happened here today.

"What?" Erik goes, one of the only three other people, other than the principal himself, to manage a seat in Carter's *standing room only* office.

Carter's stone face sours. "What do you mean, '*What?*' I want to know what's going on here. I want to know why there's adds for a website filled with profane quotes *by* and *about* Hemingway students all over our building's flatscreens. I want to know why there was a sudden burst of profanity-filled hate speech that got broadcast building-wide right before lunch. And I really, really want to know *how you* did all this not to mention *why?*"

"That's BS, man," Turner goes with his arms crossed from the back of the room. "How do you even know it was us anyway?"

"Are you saying none of you were involved with today's activities?" Carter goes.

"Man, we ain't gotta to tell you shit," Turner snaps back.

"*Language*, Mr. Turner," Carter goes and sighs.

"OK, whatever—but point is you got any proof we did this?"

Carter sits back into his chair behind his desk and scratches behind his head. "Coach Striden, do you have any idea here?"

Striden goes all palms up looking surprised not only that's she's in this meeting in the first place, but that she's suddenly being called upon. "Um, no. I don't know what's happened here, obviously. Is that what you're asking me?"

"Elizabeth… I'm asking if you know what *might* be the best way of finding out the truth of what these boys know about this present situation?"

"Look, I don't even know if what these guys—or whoever did all this—did was really all that bad. Now I understand, Principal Carter, why you would be very concerned about *how* they did this. But that kid's right. First you have to establish that they *did* do this. At least on some level."

"Well, for starters—boys—there's your behavior earlier this week with your, uh—*T-shirt day* concerning Mr. Leone here," Carter goes.

"So what?" Erik goes. "Just because we did that, doesn't necessarily mean we hijacked the flatscreens or the PA."

Carter boggles a bit. "Well, it sure looks like it could be construed that—"

"Why?" Turner cuts him off. "Why the hell would these guys run a clip through the whole school saying they're a bunch of fudge packers? Why would anyone in their right mind do that to themselves if they're not? The way I see it, this all could be payback *for* the T-shirt thing."

"I guess that's another way to look at it, but uh…" Carter trails off.

"The thing is, sir, you're going to have to *prove* that we did this," Ryan goes.

Carter exhales a breath that seems to age him about another ten years right in front of all of them. "I don't get it, fellas. Last fall you all come rolling in here and you turn yourselves in for drinking. You display a tremendous amount of maturity and accountability to get back your honor, as you put it. But now you're sitting here before me *denying* that you had anything to do with this?"

Everybody's quiet.

"Sir," Coach Striden pipes up. "You might get further if you just ask their leader, directly…"

All eyes in the room glide to the big kid slouching in the chair right across from Carter himself, sitting there with this very calm, but very amused face.

"Well, Luke," Carter finally goes, "Are you denying involvement?"

Luke just keeps staring right back at Principal Carter as if he has no clue what's being said around him, then he circles his ear with this finger and then just grins as if he's saying *hey, look I'm kinda deaf here, so you know—whatevs!*

Tristan and Turner both immediately burst with laughter. I mean they're suddenly both crying, almost pissing their pants laughing so hard.

"Well look at that," Patrick goes, grinning leaning on the opposite wall. "Guess he's decided to actually act like a real deaf person today."

Of course, this explodes into a new round of laughs from the other guys, while Coach Striden shakes her head. Luke just grins. Carter continues to look in no mood. No mood whatsoever.

"Look, sir—" Ryan tries to talk above the laughing, "we turned ourselves in because we had signed an oath and broke the oath. It wasn't really because we drank so much as it was because we had broken our word. Get it? Well, we didn't sign any oath specifically outlining that we *wouldn't* do whatever it was that was done here today. And I don't think any of us really feel like admitting to anything right now."

"Well, this is a slippery slope you're on then, boys," Carter goes.

"You're on it too, sir," Ryan goes back.

The principal lets out a chuckle. "What? How so?"

"These people that did this today—*whoever they are*— I mean, what did they really do when it comes down to it?"

"They broke the law by getting into our system—"

"Cheese and rice, man. There you go again all obsessed with the fucking *how*," Turner cuts in.

"*Language*—" Striden reminds him.

"I think what my *friend* here is trying to say is—let's forget about the how for a minute here. I'm sure you'll get back to that. But let's just concentrate now on what the end result is. In the end, what did they really do?" Ryan goes.

Carter leans back in his seat again. "There's no way for me to know those quotes on that site were real, or what their context was, or if Sorensen's sound bite was authentic."

"True. I get that, and I know that's important for you, sir," Ryan goes. "But for just right now, let's say that the quotes are all valid and true to their sources and that really was Dylan's voice today…"

"Then, given all that, I would have to admit that today's events shed a light on a lot of hurtful and inappropriate things being said by and about Hemingway students," Carter goes.

"Then would you agree that shedding that light might, or could actually lead to some sort of positive change to some students' behavior?"

Carter looks back at Ryan for a long moment. "Maybe…"

"So that's how you could be on that slope too, sir. You're in the position where you may feel you need to catch these people, then punish them accordingly—when in the end, the results of what you're punishing them for are mostly positive, or even desperately needed around here."

"Yeah, man—" Turner cuts in, "you might want to crank a little brain on how much you want to push this shit and where—"

"Is it just me, or does this kid swear more than any other person on the planet?" Striden goes and the other guys all shrug and nod.

There's a knock on the door and one of the office ladies pokes her head in to tell Carter the site is gone.

"Gone? What do you mean gone?" Carter goes.

"It's just not there anymore when you try to get on it. Linda even tried getting to it by going back on the site history, but still it won't come up. Off the flatscreens too," the lady goes.

"Hey, don't look at us," Erik goes.

"Well, did you print it out like I asked?" Carter goes.

"Maybe Linda got a few pages, but then there was a paper jam, or something…"

"You didn't get screen shots first?" Carter asks.

"You said to print hard copies."

"Excuse me," Carter goes and takes off with the lady. He comes back like five minutes later and announces to everyone, "OK. Things are about to get even more complicated. The Sorensen's are here and meeting right now with Henderson in his office and they've brought their lawyer in threatening to sue *everyone*."

ERIF
XIX

From that height, so far up nearly to the entrance of the Crack, it seemed to Prince that he could see the world entire. It was full dawn. He could just see the haze blue of the sea beyond the range and on the other side, far, far off, he fancied he saw the tips of the towers of the high kingdom of Cambia. The dragon's smoke continued to billow, but a morning breeze had thankfully raised it up to find the jet stream above the peak and out of Prince and Angel's faces.

How unjust, Prince thought. How cosmically sinful in fact, that it was Erif Sky-Foul that was afforded this majestic, even holy, view every morning. How can it be? That such beauty and such wanton evil could so commingle up here at the throne of the world? It was now the most vile joke Prince knew.

A loud puff and snarlburst of flame shot out of the darkness of the Crack. A myriad of low noises echoed out, freezing Prince and Angel shock-still. Something heavy and very much alive was stirring in the yonder cave.

"Angel," Prince pulled her down to kneel behind a rock mere paces from the Crack's terrible entrance. "Listen to me. Listen. Forget our plan. I want you to leave now. I will confront him alone; you need not be here. Hide yourself best you can. And should you hear the sounds of my-—"

"No Prince. It shall not be. We're here. It's time. It will only further incense Erif if I'm not with you at all. He's likely to rush out and burn Thorn first and then return to the mountain for us."

"But?"

"*No.*" Angel grasped his tunic. "No matter if our little plan works or not—-understand. I'm willing to lay down my life. I lay it down, Prince. Just as countless children of Thorn through the countless years have done before me. And do you know what their thoughts were? *Here*—-at the Crack—-at the end? Their last thoughts were not only of fear. In fact, their fear was outweighed."

"Outweighed?" Prince said with true fear pulsing in his eyes. "How is that possible?"

"Fear of meeting their death gave way to the thoughts of their families. They saw the faces of their brothers and sisters that would live. They saw their parents. They saw the fields of wildflowers outside the village where they played in the summer. They saw Thorn alive with lights during the Mayodon dances. And you know how I know this, Prince? I know this because these are *my* thoughts too."

He shook his head, wild-eyed with tears starting to stream out. His hand trembled. "I don't—-I don't know if I can stand to see it. If it happens. Him devouring you. I *can't.*"

She took his hand into her smaller one. "The day my mother died. The day the fever took her. It was so awful. But what overshadows all about what happened and what I felt and still feel about that day... is not sadness. Not anger. Not even loss. It's *love*. That's what I'm filled with more than anything else when I remember that day. When I remember her life. Her memory. My love for her, her love for me and my father and sister. Our love of our lives together, despite death. Love as big and warm and as blinding as the sun. Prince, there *can* be love in death. If you invite it in, it will overpower all else, and it is that love that makes all of life worth it. Do you believe me?"

Prince looked at this girl through his tears, through his sobs, in awe. "I so very much want to."

"And if it is written that we should die this morning—-then let us die with love, Prince. *With love.*"

"I would die for you, Angel."

"And I you. I love you."

"I love you too—-"

She put her hand up to wipe his cheek. "Then my dear Prince, what have we to fear?"

16

Jason Turner sits at a kitchen table. The table's wood is unvarnished and the first thing he is aware of is the way it slightly moves under the pressure of his fingers. Next to his hand is a mason jar of water. Half-filled, he stares at it. It's a bright morning that's shining through the lace curtains from the window over the long-basin sink where the dishes from breakfast wait.

As he sits, he looks down and sees that he is also wearing a dress. Cream-colored with yellow paisleys. He considers the dress a moment with no real opinion about it—other than it appears ridiculously old-fashioned. But then he sees that he also seems to have breasts, woman's breasts underneath the dress. Jason then gets a vague notion that he should not be a woman with breasts wearing a dress. That really, he should much rather be a *boy*. Wearing jeans and a hoodie.

And what's the deal with this kitchen?

Is it his kitchen? He thinks probably *no*.

There's wallpapered walls. He tries to think if he's ever seen real wallpaper before in a real house.

Yes, he has. In Rozzy's trailer house. But who's Rozzy again?

The wallpaper. Light orange with small white diamonds in a pattern that just repeats and repeats and repeats…

Till Jason's eyes get to the clock. It's an old clock, wooden; it hangs there on the wall and ticks.

Eight-Forty-Three.

It's morning.

Wait, Jason thinks. I know this place. No, I do—I *know* this place.

There's an incredible boom. The house shakes. The clock flies off the wall. The window by the sink shatters. His mason jar of water topples over on the old wooden table and splashes across his bare legs.

Jason scrambles up to run out the kitchen door.

But now he's looking out to a field of wildflowers. A bunch of teenage girls are all hunched—it looks like they're collecting wildflowers. The girls all freeze for a second where they're at and look past where Jason watches them—to some place beyond him.

They scream.

Or at least he thinks they're screaming. Jason can't actually hear them. He sees their mouths open, and it sure looks like they are straining the hell out of their vocal chords.

Jason looks up. Hey, look at that—he's under a tree. Oak tree, a big one. Perfect leaves. He looks down. Good, I'm not a woman anymore, he thinks. He's got on boy's clothes and a big boy's body.

Hmm… but is it *too* big?

Yep. It is. I really don't know exactly who I am—but I know I'm not this tall, or this buff.

Jason almost starts laughing. But then he remembers the screaming girls and turns around to see what they're screaming at.

Oh yeah—I forgot. *I know this place.*

Then it hits Jason all at once. Bath. May 18th. 1927.

He's there. He's *here.*

Through a shroud of grit and dust the school's front is obliterated and collapsed just like in Carver's photograph. Smoke is pouring up from the basement where Jason knows Kehoe's bombs went off. As the fog clears a bit, he looks over and sees from the church across the street, the high school boys that were playing football running over to start a panicked rescue. Other uninjured kids are starting to climb out of the blown walls of the school.

It's chaos. But Jason still can't hear a thing. He whirls back to look again at the oak tree. He steps back until he can see the tree in front of him *and* the bombed school behind it.

Then he knows. He still puts his hands on his bulging pectoral muscles and confirms it.

He's *not* himself.

Jason lifts his head up to the blue sky and says the words even though he can't hear himself say it.

He turns back to the school and says it again.

Let rip the sky and let the glory fall.

Jason sees Carver's brother, Clem, and Clem's buddy start to haul away debris looking for survivors. Sprinting across the street, Jason feels a rush of air into his lungs, the likes he's never known before. His feet blaze as he sprints up to Clem and just starts helping, flinging red-hot bricks and rubble away.

Clem stops to look all crazy-amazed at Jason and says something, but Jason can't hear it. So, Clem just gets back to it.

He can't believe this strength. Jason throws heavy brick and mortar, massive shards of iron and wood desks like they were cardboard. And he—*never. Loses. Breath.*

I'm fucking *Superman!* he thinks and then sees a child's bloody arm. Frantically, Jason moves away as much as he can and grabs the kid's arm. He pulls, slowly at first, but the buried kid grips Jason's hand back, and firm too. So, Jason pulls up faster until the kid's whole-body slithers free!

The kid looks to be about ten years old, covered in dirt and soot and he's bleeding from about a thousand cuts and scrapes—but he's *alive.* Jason sets him down safe on the grass and the kid's just crying and looks like he's saying, 'thank you,' over and over to Jason—but Jason can't tell for sure and is about to get back to digging when he looks up and sees Bella from Buffalo wandering around among the survivors like some sort of helpless zombie.

She's wearing her ratty jeans and a black tank-top and she's got what looks like a big cut on her forehead.

"Bella! *Bella!*" Jason hopes he's shouting, but he still has no clue what it sounds like since he's got Luke's body on loan.

She turns to him and seems to recognize him—which is crazy he knows because he looks like Luke—but he's not sure. Till she raises her hand and goes, "There's my Dickhead!"

Jason laughs—and it hits him. He can *hear!* He looks back down his body—but's still very much Luke's. He checks out his bulging biceps from all the lifting and marvels and what it must be like to be Luke Forrester 24/7.

Then he remembers Bella again and looks up to call her over, but she's gone. Instead, he looks up and sees Scout Finch. Wait, no. "*Olivia*!"

I can save her! he thinks. "Olivia!"

She looks to him, looks a little confused. A little out of it, which is understandable. She's so beautiful, he thinks, and a quick glimpse of her dead up on her dining room table flashes into Jason's mind in black and white.

"*No*," he says. "Not today. Not this time."

But Olivia's gone.

In fact, so is Jason.

He's not in front of Bath Consolidated School anymore. He's in a truck. An old truck of course—huge stick shift. Double clutch. Moving down a small-town street on the same beautiful morning.

But the exhilaration of Luke's body is gone.

"Shit."

Jason looks down at himself. "*Shit, shit, shit*!"

He knows this body. Middle-aged and a little overweight. Underneath this button-down shirt and suspenders, he knows he's got graying belly-hairs around his navel. He's been here before. *He knows this place.*

He *is* Andrew P. Kehoe.

Hands still on the wheel, he turns to the truck's backseat.

Sees a shitload of pyrotol and dynamite.

But as bad as this is, Jason also realizes this is not like before. This is not like when he last dreamed that he and Kehoe were one. When they *both* seemed to have control of *their* body.

No—it's only Jason now that has complete control of Kehoe's body, just like how Jason had control of the woman in her kitchen—like how he had control of Luke's body.

Jason realizes the possibilities.

What if I just stop this car right now and sit here? Wouldn't that save Olivia right there? But wait.

He reaches inside his jacket pocket.

Yeah there it is, man—and Jason pulls out Kehoe's .38. What if—he thinks—what if I just shove this fucker in my mouth—*Kehoe's* mouth—and just pull the trigger? I won't be the one who's dead, right? It'll be him. *Yeah*, Jason thinks, that ought to save her for sure.

With the .38 clutched in his hand he slams the truck to a halt in the middle of the street and rams the barrel of the gun onto the bridge of his/Kehoe's nose. It cracks and bleeds through a snaggled laceration.

Jason grins through the pain. He felt he owed Kehoe at least that much before he blew his brains out.

He raises the tip of the barrel to his mouth. Straight past the teeth with gold fillings.

Not today... he thinks with his mouth full.

And his finger presses the trigger.

But then Jason's out on the street. Running for some reason. Out of breath. This is not Luke Forrester's body either. He sees the truck there stopped all eerily there in the middle of the road, sees the dazed lump of Kehoe sitting in the driver's seat touching the edges of his newly broken nose through the fingerhold of the .38 revolver, in some kind of detached amazement.

I can still do it. I can still get the fucker. And that'll save her. Jason looks down to the gravel street. His eyes scan along the road's edges and sees what he's looking for. Bending down, he clutches a stone about the size of a plump crabapple—you know, to give his fist a little weight when he decks Kehoe in the fucking jaw—and starts striding over towards the mass-murdering monster in the driver's seat.

Kehoe shakes his head like he's trying to clear a fog from his brain and spies Jason. "…What the hell? *Clem*?" But then Kehoe looks at the rock and tries to get the truck started again.

Impatient, Jason hauls off and chucks the rock at Kehoe, pegging him on the side of the head. Kehoe howls. Jason runs towards the truck but veers to the truck's rear when Kehoe points the gun out the window and fires off a round.

"You sonofabitch!" Kehoe yells, revolver in one hand, the other holding the side of his head.

Jason clings to the tailgate, breathing heavy. *Hey, he called me Clem*, he remembers. Of course, Clem left the school *after* they found Buddy to help Mr. Grogan get supplies at his store downtown and then his jalopy broke down.

The engine ignites and the loud clank of gears shifting fills the air. The truck's tires start to pull away.

Left with no choice Jason hauls himself into the truck bed where Kehoe's filled it with metal scraps all sharp and heavy. He spies a rusty crankshaft and wheels it through truck's back cab window in hopes of hitting Kehoe.

"Goddamn it!" Kehoe erupts. The truck grinds to a stop again and Kehoe blazes out with his .38 leading the way.

Wasting no time, Jason tears out of the truck bed and into the first front yard by the street and just makes it around the side of the house before another gunshot rings out and a bullet zips past him into the grass.

"I know what you did, you fucker!" Jason calls out with Clem Bellington's voice from behind the house. "You murdered those kids, asshole—and I'm going to fucking tear your head off, man."

Kehoe laughs. Through his angry huffs of breath, he just laughs. "Not in this life, you little shithead," he goes and turns around, hopping back in his truck and speeds off again down the street.

Olivia. Jason sputters to his feet and sprints back to the street. He doesn't need to follow Kehoe's truck to know where he's going: a huge plume of black smoke rises like a massive and airy anaconda from where Bath Consolidated school is.

Olivia. Can I make it? Did I slow that fucker enough? Jason doesn't know—he just sprints. He rounds the next corner, and he can see the church, the school, the bodies being lined up—all of it.

Kehoe pulls his truck right in the center of it all like he owns the place.

Jason sprints while Clem's lungs threaten to burst.

Superintendent Emory Hyuck moves across the lawn to Kehoe's truck.

Jason sees Olivia walking past the truck, unaware.

"Olivia! Olivia! Over here!" he tries to shout, though he's out of breath.

Olivia looks across the street and sees him sprinting. She half-raises her hand in response, like she wants to acknowledge her big brother but doesn't understand his meaning.

"Come now! *Now!*" Jason yells only a hundred feet from her now. But he sees Emory step away in horror from Kehoe, realizing that fucker's true colors and Jason knows there's no time.

"You should know when you're bested..."

"Get down!" he yells to her.

Olivia tilts her head with the innocence of a puppy.

Boom. The truck explodes into oblivion, taking Emory with it.

Jason is blown back in a terror-wave of light and heat. Both feet lift off the ground and he seems to float ten feet back from where he was running. His lips feel as if he's just kissed the sun. He's deaf again—but just like before, it doesn't last long before he starts to hear again—mostly voices and screams of horror but like they're coming from the other side of an apartment wall.

He rises off the ground, slowly at first, then urgent—and realizes he's still Clem. Over a few yards away lies Olivia, a piece of scrap metal sticking out of her chest a foot long. Jason curses and runs to her. Puts her head up in his lap and tries to comfort her. Her blood's everywhere; her eyes glazing while the rest of her body trembles in her final throes. Jason can't speak—he just weeps. Weeps uncontrollably, like that night at Harper Lake when he couldn't kill Luke. He wants so much to tell Olivia *sorry*. Sorry I couldn't save you. Sorry I couldn't stop this even though I knew it was coming. But he's crying too hard.

But then out of her terror, Olivia's face turns serene. She reaches up and puts her small hand on his face. "It's OK," she says. "It's OK, Clem."

Jason swallows hard and wants to tell her the truth—that he's not Clem, but before he can think how, Olivia's face and body change. He realizes that he's really holding Rozzy there on that lawn. Her tears are blood, but her eyes still beautiful through her smudged mascara.

"It's OK," she repeats Olivia's words. "I know what you wanted, Jason..."

More tears erupt in sobs out of Jason, but he manages to say, "To save you... To *be* with you..."

Rozzy's eyes close with a trace of a smile. *"Not today, my knight... Not today..."*

As she breathes her last breath there in his arms, Jason looks up to blue sky and roars his lament. Just roars it and wonders how the sky can be so perfect—with clouds white and majestic as beds for angels and the rest so blue it looks like the realm of heaven itself—when such horror can happen under it?

Looking back down to Rozzy, Jason sees she's wrapped completely in white bandages, so he lies her down on the grass. A few yards away, he sees shreds of Kehoe's and Hyuck's bodies. Others who witnessed the truck's explosion are now braving to get closer to the wreck to get a better look. Jason gets up and walks along a roadside ditch filled with body parts till he comes to a chunk of Kehoe's head. Part of his face still intact, free from anything else, lies there in this grisly taunting half-grimace.

Looking at this *scrap* of Kehoe fills Jason with such a rage his vision seems to sparkle, like when you're not getting enough oxygen during the heat of the day. He looks away from Kehoe's face and sees Clem off in the distance holding the real corpse of Olivia in his arms. He looks down at his body and sees his familiar self. Jeans. Hoodie.

He's back.

Now Jason looks back to the chunk of Kehoe's face and feels the anger rise again. He steps forward and considers smashing it with the heel of his shoe. But no. Not now.

Instead, he spits on the long grass just to the side of the face and tightens both his fists. And for some reason, somehow—he *knows*—knows that this fight ain't over.

17

It was late March and things began to happen very, very quickly. I was in middle of it then, it's true—but not until much later was I made aware of all that was going on—all the dynamics at play, you know? Also, even though I was hanging out with this gang, I wasn't there for everything. I wish I could've been—it would've made this job a lot easier for sure.

But whatever, I guess. One of the events that was huge, and that I wasn't there for, was right after most of the soccer guys and Turner had been suspended for the hemingwayownit prank, even though the office couldn't prove they were behind it. What happened was that Dylan and his parents told Principal Carter they'd be satisfied if Luke and company were just suspended for a few days. If Carter would do that, then they wouldn't take any legal action against the school or anybody, and just drop the whole affair.

Carter agreed, I guess, and the guys got a three-day suspension.

After everyone's parents freaked, a bunch of them decided to spend some of that suspension time at Volgstaad's cottage, which led to Luke, Erik, Ryan, Turner, and Patrick all cruising out there one night in Patrick's dad's Suburban. Tristan, Pauly, and Glendening were all going to meet them out there the next day, and poor Gray, me, and Dickey were still stuck in school along with the girls because we weren't even suspected by the office of being involved with any of this.

"Freaking suspended," a few of them remember Patrick saying from behind the wheel. "I can't believe it."

"Hey, whatever, dudes—we're getting off easy, remember?" Ryan goes. "Gray said if they really pressed invasion of privacy with Dylan's phone, we'd be cooked. So, a three-day suspension's a piece of cake compared to that, right?"

"But they could never get us with the privacy charge till Dylan admits that was his voice we played through the school. I mean, if he won't admit that's him saying that shit—then there's no way they could ever charge us for tapping his phone. So, suspending us for something they can't prove is still total BS," Erik goes.

"Yeah, it's BS, but my point is, it could still be worse," Ryan goes.

"Well, who cares now," Patrick cuts in, "it's over. The question now, dudes, is what's up next? Aw crap—it's starting to snow."

"Snowing? That's a bitch, man," Turner goes but keeps his eyes on his phone, texting.

"C'mon—I mean, it's almost freaking April for crying out loud," Erik goes.

Turner scoffs. "I've fucking lived in Michigan all my life and I swear the winters are getting longer, man. Fucking whoever came up with that global warming theory's full of shit."

Sitting in the front passenger's seat, Luke's phone vibrates in his hand; he opens Turner's text: **dreamt I was in bath again last night. in 1927. it was fuckt.**
Luke: **it feel real like the others?**
Turner: **yep.**
Luke: **call Carver yet?**

Turner: **yeah, yeah. getting to it, yo.**

"So, like I was saying, what's next?" Patrick asks again.

"I don't know—let's ask the genius," Erik goes and reaches from the back seat to tap Luke on the shoulder. When he turns, Erik goes: "What do you think, eh? Patrick wants to know what's next?"

Luke just smiles and shrugs.

"Yeah, well—no rush. We got three days at the cottage to think of something."

The snow picks up even more and Patrick turns on the wipers to see the road ahead of them. "It's like turning into a total blizzard."

"Hey Pat—turn on your brights," Erik goes. Patrick flicks them on and the night ahead of them explodes into an ocean of flashing white snowflakes. "Cool. Looks like we're zipping through space."

Patrick flicks his brights off. "Yeah, but I can barely see when I got them on like that."

"Whoa, man—" Turner goes, and holds up his phone. "What's the deal? My phone just lost all its bars."

"Yeah—that happens to mine too. There's like a dead spot out here once you get out of town. Can't get a signal or something. Don't worry though. It only lasts for about ten miles or so," Erik goes.

"I got another idea about what we can do next," Ryan goes.

"I don't know, man. Look where your last idea got us. We do another one of yours, we're all likely to get expelled before we can graduate," Turner goes, and grins. They all do.

"No seriously, I got an idea. My church has been talking about setting up a soup kitchen somewhere in Detroit for the homeless. They got people who would make the food, they've just been needing people to get it set up and find a location. We could—you know—volunteer to head that up. What you guys think?"

"Church group?" Patrick goes. "Hey, after you coming out like you did, I'm surprised you even still go to church. Don't they kind of frown about how you're—uh, you know—*wired?*"

"Well, what are they going to do—kick me out of church? Wouldn't that completely defeat the purpose of what they're supposed to be about? No. I talked with my pastor after I had talked to my parents, and he's cool with me. If that Jesus guy was anything, he was an ally. I'm sure there's plenty of people there that totally disagree with me and my being there—but just like at school, they'll never say anything to my face."

"Hey man—I'm in. In fact, I know exactly what neighborhood to put the kitchen in too."

Everybody looks at Turner.

"You serious?" Erik goes.

"Shit, man—yeah. I got me some friends that live in a beat-up trailer past 8 Mile that could really use some warm meals. So yeah—let's get it set up, wonder boy."

"*Wonder boy?* OK. Well, I'll call Pastor Mike tomorrow and get the ball rolling. You got a street name?" Ryan goes.

Turner shakes his head. "No. But we'll check out a map online when we get to the cottage, and I'll show you where."

"What the crap is with this guy?" Patick goes, glaring at the car behind them in the rearview mirror. "He was lagging behind us for miles, but now he's riding our ass—"

Turner, Ryan, and Erik all turn around to get a look at the car behind them, but before they can get a good gander, the driver flicks on his brights and fills the back of the Suburban with light.

"What an ass," Erik goes, and he and Ryan turn away.

But Turner holds his hand just above his eyes and keeps staring. Out of the passenger side window he sees what looks like the shadowy torso of a man emerge. And then he knows. "Get your heads *down!"*

The shotgun blast is deafening, even inside the Suburban, even before shards of the blast *thunk* in all over the Suburban's back door and shatter the right back window.

The big Chevy fishtails a bit before Patrick steadies the wheel and straightens the vehicle.

"Slow down a little and then pull off-road, now—" Turner yells.

The shotgun blasts again and the Suburban's right back tire blows out just as Patrick pulls the vehicle to the right, up and over the snowy ditch and rolling onto a barren farm field.

The car slows down too and follows them onto the field. Another shotgun blast comes but misses the Suburban completely.

"Go, go, go, go—" Erik yells to Patrick while the sick sound of the blown and flapping back tire fills the vehicle.

"Why are they doing this?" Erik roars.

"Because of me, man," Turner goes and looks at Luke. "They're after *me*."

ERIF
XX

She rode hard to the village gate and then out into the field of wildflowers. Breaking off the trail, she rode through the high grass to the small bend in the brook where she and Samuel had stashed her quiver and bow and a few supplies just in case they had to make a hasty retreat like she was doing now. Annabella flung herself off the saddle and grimaced at the pain in her thigh when she landed, the crossbow bolt still sticking out of her flesh.

Curse them. Curse them all, she thought.

Reaching into the knapsack of supplies, she pulled out a knife and cut off a length of cloth from her dress. She then put the knife down on the grass next to her and slowly pulled the bolt out of her thigh. The pain was overwhelming, and Annabella screamed as she pulled it out. Stepping into the shallow brook, she let the cool water run over her bleeding wound till it finally numbed a little; then after she got back out, she took up the cloth and wrapped it around the wound and blood immediately began to seep into the fabric. Exhausted, she laid down for a moment catching her breath, while the horse put his head down and began to munch on the tall grasses.

The morning sky was glorious.

Then Annabella let it all in, and she started to cry in great powerful sobs. Samuel was dead. Denisen and Paulus. And Quindarius. All those Tarrenbacks were dead—-some by her own hand. And for what? She turned her head a little and saw the Crack atop the mountain and thought of Angel being devoured by Erif. And what of Prince? Had he made it up there too, only to die some awful death? It was too much for her and she wept. She thought of her father and imagined him drunk beyond thought, sitting alone by their hearth and miserable.

Was this it? She thought through her tears. Was this all that her life could offer her? And it was in that moment that Annabella prepared herself for death.

Back at the Great Hall, Cyvilard had assembled the last remaining Tarrenbacks. There were not many—-just shy of a dozen. And he knew Kylan and the ones that went as escorts to Angel would not be back for a few more hours yet.

But it would be enough, he thought. Certainly, more than a match for that bitch daughter of the village drunkard.

Cyvilard led his Tarrenbacks through the village to the gate, while all the people of Thorn scurried back to their homes to quake in fear after what they had just witnessed on the Great Hall's stage.

Striding down Thorn's main road, with his brow down and determined, Cyvilard grinned at the fear he commanded from the

Thornsfolk, and even from the Tarrenbacks themselves. Now he was certain that they were all so weak and afraid that they would never oppose him, no matter what—-and that maybe he should even thank Annabella, before he killed her, for confirming how strong his grip was on Thorn.

At the gate they all came to a halt. One of the Tarrenback's pointed to where he saw the girl's horse grazing in the field.

"Should we seize her?" the Tarrenback asked.

"No," Cyvilard said. "Stay here. I will take her alone." And with that, he changed into a raven and took to the sky. Now that everyone knows of his Yonderling power, why not change right in front of them? Cyvilard knew that his power would now only instill more fear and obedience.

From high above the field, the Elder saw his prey; he saw Annabella lying in the grass with her hands over her face, weeping, and the rough bandage on her leg.

Ripe for the taking, he thought. *Ah, yes—-I will have thee indeed, Annabella. And now will it be so much the sweeter as I possess your body in the open daylight so close to the village gate!*

Cyvilard lifted his black head and cawed out in victory and hoped even Erif himself, presumably picking his teeth after his sacrificial breakfast, could hear the glory of it.

18

How did they find me? Turner thinks. They must've found out that I was staying at Luke's and then somehow those fucking tweakers used some restraint, which is a miracle unto its fucking self, and then clocked us tonight when we went over to Patrick's to pile into his Suburban.

And *now* they strike. Gotta hand it to them, he thinks—Scotty and Maintenance Man might be some crazy-whack tinas, but they ain't the stupidest crazy-whack tinas of all time neither.

"We're not going to be able to go much further. We're riding on a bare rim back there—" Patrick yells.

"Try to get to that farmhouse!" Erik goes.

"You know who lives there? Somebody with a gun?" Turner goes.

"No, it's abandoned, but maybe we can hide—"

Patrick feels Luke tug on his shoulder. Luke points to the big run-down looking barn behind the farmhouse.

"Yeah—try to get there," Turner goes too.

Patrick veers hard toward the barn and comes to a sliding stop on the snow-covered ground.

"Oh my god—we're gonna die," Ryan blurts.

"Run! Run to the other side of the barn!" Turner commands and they all burst from the Suburban and book it around the corner of the barn.

Then Scotty and Maintenance Man get out of their car—but take their time now, now that they got their prey cornered and totally out-gunned. "*AAAA-SAAAC—*" one of them hollers. "Oh, *AAAA-SAAC*! Or should I say Pops' little fucker—Come on out, pussy, and get what you got coming!"

The boys all huddle a sec behind the barn in the dark and snow. "Look—we need to split these fuckers up," Turner goes. "Best way to do that is have some of us in the barn and some in the house."

"I'll run to the house," Patrick goes.

"I'll go with you," Erik says.

"OK. We'll take the barn. Look, if they both come together at either building, then the others make noise to see if we can split them. OK?" Turner goes, then Erik and Patrick tear off towards the dark house, while Ryan, Luke, and Turner move around to one of the barn's side doors.

Little beams of light cut and scan across the property. The Shotgun boys got guns and flashlights. "Come on out, Turner. Why draw it out?"

Both men start laughing this giddy-ass pipe smoker laughter. "Yeah, no—*hey!* You other preppy assholes! You want to live, just shove that piece of shit on out. And we promise not to blow y'all to Jesus. All right?"

They both move around the barn. From inside the ruined kitchen of the house, Erik remembers seeing the shapes of both men—each holding a shotgun, but one gun was way shorter than the other. Turns out the gun had no stock and the barrel had been sawed off too. The guy with the sawed off held a flashlight in his other hand. The other guy had a full size twelve-gauge.

"We gotta make noise," Patrick whispers.

Erik remembers not wanting to do that at all. But he also didn't want to see his friends get murdered right in front of him either.

Patrick knocks out one of the kitchen's widows with his elbow.

Immediately both guys wheel around to face the house. Patrick and Erik hit the deck as the flashlight sweeps the room through the busted window. Scotty and Maintenance man start walking to the house.

From the barn, Luke and Turner look out from a crack in the door, while Ryan quietly freaks out behind them.

"Hey, fuckheads!" Turner calls out.

The two men stop in their tracks and turn back to the barn. Turner can just imagine their mouths gaping all stupid with their snaggled and brown teeth, looking at each other in the dark.

Finally, the one with the sawed-off and the light goes, "You stand here and keep watch on that house. I'll go in the barn and russle'em up."

As he starts walking towards the barn, Luke, Turner, and Ryan scatter into the dark of the barn. There's old, rusting farm equipment everywhere: a decommissioned tractor, balers, old half-assembled furniture—you name it. Turner and Ryan stick together and hide by a stack of old tires, but they lose track of where Luke is.

The guy steps into the barn and points the flashlight from wall to wall. "After I'm done blowing you to hell, you know what I'm going to do, kid?"

Fucking Scotty, Turner can tell by the voice. "See my boy out there, he's got this saw in his trunk for cutting off thick-ass tree limbs. And see, we gonna saw your head clean off your body, boy. Then take it to your double-crossing old man. Throw it in his lap before we blast his heart right out of his chest, see—"

Double-cross? So, he *did* have a deal with Lester, Turner thinks.

Scotty slowly starts to walk deeper into the barn, checking the nooks and crannies with the light, holding that sawed-off just ahead of him, ready to fire. "We almost had it. Lester and me. A fucking sweet set-up. We got us a lab started. We were gonna be piping to your pops. And he was gonna start paying us a righteous cut. A *righteous cut*, man. But that first cut don't come after our first delivery, and then you and that Kid T fuck come in all guns a blazing—and fucking blew our world apart."

Scotty gets closer to the tires.

Ryan grips Turner's hand, either as a call to rise and attack, or just out of fear—Turner can't tell. "But you fuckers are gonna pay. And before we pop Pops, he gonna tell us where his lab is, and we gonna take over these subs!"

What an idiot, Turner thinks as Scotty gets within two steps of their hiding place. *He's got no clue my dad ain't got no lab. He gets his shit from Dre. And they have no clue.*

Turner realizes that his dad was going to use them as his "cheap" lab. Dre was right to be suspicious. Dad needed them to cook his Walmart glass for all the trailers in town, while he kept feeding the middle-class subs with Dre's shit from Detroit. *So why did Dad stiff them?*

Scotty clicks off the flashlight.

Turner thinks Scotty's gotta be just standing there because he hears zero movement. *Where the fuck's Luke*, plays across his mind, while Ryan keeps gripping the shit out of his hand.

"Yo, Scotty, man?" Maintenance Man calls out from the yard, which they all can hear because of a huge hole in the barn's wall where a board is missing. "Speed it up. My ass is freezing out here."

Still silent—but Turner thinks he hears what could be movement.

"C'mon, man. *Scotty—*"

"Would you shut the *fuck* up?" Scotty yells from the dark. Turner can tell Scotty's moved away from them, back closer to the center of the barn. "I'm stalking 'em out here. Just wait and blast anyone that steps out that ain't fucking me. Got it?"

Even though Ryan's pulling on him to stay down, Turner raises up to chance a peak. His eyes have adjusted to the dark as much as they're going to, and he can faintly see the shape of Scotty by the glow coming through the hole in the wall.

Scotty steps almost even with the hole, and Turner can make out Scotty's skinny frame and the menacing shape of the sawed-off shotgun in his right hand. But then Turner sees something rise seemingly up from the floor of the barn and poke out the hole in the wall.

It's glowing. At first, he can't believe what he's seeing. It's Luke's phone. It's Luke's phone and Luke is waving it out the hole towards Maintenance Man.

"Holy shit! Scotty—" Maintenance Man yells.

Turner can see Scotty start to turn towards the hole.

"*Scotty—*" Turner yells and Scotty wheels back towards him and points the sawed-off at his chest. But before Scotty can fire, hell and earth comes pummeling out of Maintenance Man's barrel, blowing even more of a hole into the barn, blasting buckshot and splintering wood that rips into the upper half of Scotty's body.

As what's left of him sloshes to the floor, Scotty triggers the sawed-off up in the air and a god-freaking-Genesis-light explodes in the barn. A blinding flash, then back to darkness.

You can hear Maintenance Man pump another shell into the chamber outside and Turner dives to the floor looking for the sawed-off.

"Scotty, man! Did I get him? Did I get the fucker?" Maintenance Man runs up and sticks his head through the new and improved hole in the barn's wall. So eager he is to see if he's shot Turner—or whoever the hell was waving that phone at him—that he doesn't really consider that someone like Luke Forrester is waiting for him against the wall, holding a massive rusty table-saw bench up above his head, ready to bring it down if anyone would ever be stupid enough to walk in under it.

So, the second after Maintenance Man pokes his head through, Luke brings the bench down *hard* on his head.

At first, Ryan thought Luke's blow must have freaking decapitated the guy. I mean, surely. But he was a little relieved when, after picking up the flashlight and clicking it on, he sees—*no*, the guy still has his head, and he appears to be breathing—but barely.

Luke reaches down and takes the twelve-gauge up off the floor and stands over Maintenance Man like some kind of colossus.

"You crazy sonofabitch—" Turner goes and comes storming over to Luke and starts shaking him by the shoulders. "What the hell, man? You could've been killed pulling a stupid stunt like that, man."

Luke stands there and Turner barely sees that Luke's smiling.

Turner keeps a firm hand on Luke's shoulder. With all this darkness, Turner can't even tell if Luke can tell what he's saying, but he still says anyway, "Yeah—I get it. You're all in. You balls-out Chris Hemsworth motherfucker. You ain't dying today, Luke. *Not* today, brother."

"Ryan! Turner!" Patrick and Erik yell from outside. "You guys OK? You in there?"

"Yeah. Come on in," Ryan runs over to the hole shining the flashlight. "It's over. Uh—Luke pretty much took out the bad guys."

"You kidding?" Erik comes running. "How'd he do that?"

"Come see," Ryan goes, helping pull Erik and Patrick in the barn. The three of them hug each other, just like they did when they had scored a goal on the field, and then they hug Luke, and finally a somewhat resisting Turner too.

"Holy crap, is that guy dead?" Patrick goes looking at Maintenance Man sprawled out on the ground.

"Naw, he ain't. But *that* fucker is—" Turner says, and Ryan shines the light over to canvas what's left of Scotty.

"*Whoa…*" both Erik and Patrick go.

"Guys—we need to call the cops," Ryan goes.

Turner raises Scotty's sawed-off and pumps another shell. "No. We don't," he goes and steps through the wall outside.

The other guys stand there a second more and then follow Turner out.

It's still snowing hard as they crunch over to where the two vehicles are parked.

"Patrick—the Suburban's got a spare, right?" Turner goes.

"Yeah. I've never put one on before—but I know it's got one."

"Good," Turner goes and walks up to Scotty's car and blasts the two front tires on the driver's side to freaking smithereens.

"Jeeze! What'd you do that for?" Erik goes.

"Look. I can't go to the cops with this. It would end up causing me even more trouble trying to explain why these dudes were after me. I'm sorry as hell you guys had to go through this, I really am, but—"

"Are you freaking *serious*? Then what are we going to do?" Erik goes.

Turner looks over to Luke who's still got the twelve-gauge. "Well, we're gonna put that spare tire on Patrick's ride for starters. Then Luke and I are going to wipe our prints off these shotguns before we toss them, and then we're gonna get the hell out of here."

"This is insane. What about those guys in the barn?" Ryan goes.

"Fuck'em. What do we care?"

"What about my dad's Suburban? I mean, how am I going to explain a blown tire and a shotgun blast on the back door?" Patrick goes.

"Your dad isn't expecting you back for at least three days, right?"

"Right."

Turner grins in the dark. "Well, tomorrow we're gonna take your ride into *the D* to see one of my dad's friends who's got a garage that specializes in custom work—especially bullet-hole repair. Real discreet if you know what I mean."

Erik just starts laughing. "Freaking *gangster…*"

Patrick's still not sold though. "Yeah—but how am I going to pay for that?"

Turner laughs. "Relax, man. I'm going to hook you up. See, it ain't gonna cost you a dime, man. My dad's got a tab there. Get it?"

Patrick just nods his head with his eyebrows raised in what looks like awe.

"Good," Turner goes. "Now let's get to it."

ERIF
XXI

Angel stepped into the Crack alone. The smoke had stopped, she noticed as she continued inside. Erif knew she was here—-he must, she thought, and now he was lurking in the darkness, just obscure from her sight, watching her. She could feel him, feel his enormous presence there just ahead in the shadow of the cave, hear the huffs of his breath, feel the heat radiating off him like a thousand hearth fires at once.

Sweat streaked from her brow and thirst began to gnaw at her throat. She turned to take one last look at the daylight behind her and the glorious valley below and tried to steel herself at the trial that had come to her at last.

My life for theirs, she thought. *My life for Annabella, for father, for Prince. For Thorn. My life for theirs...* thinking their names in cycles, over and over as she walked further into the cave.

No matter what, Angel decided, she was willing to do what would be necessary to save them—-whatever happened next.

"Pray—-come you now, child, without my Rogni?" the dragon's voice lulled low out of the shadows and the great beast moved forward, finally into Angel's view.

She stifled a scream and killed it there in her throat as she took in Erif's terrible image: his greenish, impenetrable-looking scales, long torsional neck, muscular legs and powerful claws, his snout tipped with puffing-black nostrils, and mouth that housed his gray and hungry jaws.

Erif dipped his great head closer to where Angel stood and fixed his red eyes upon her.

Angel was trembling now but summoned the courage to speak. "Your Rogni are dead."

"Is this so?" the dragon said and did not move, nor blink. "And how did their slaying come to be, child?"

"They killed each other over me. They wished to ravage me and fought over who would be first."

"Bah," the dragon laughed puffs of black smoke. "So, the truth of it I may never know, eh? And yet here you come up my mountain yourself to complete your destiny..."

Angel swallowed hard. "I come to pay Thorn's price."

Erif stopped his chuckling. "And so you have, child. You have come to me."

For Annabella, for father, for Prince...

The dragon raised his head. He was still for many moments and seemed to be looking past Angel, to the Crack's wide entrance.

"Step forward, my sly friend, for I know you are there," Erif boomed.

Prince slid out from the cover of the outside rocks and entered the Crack. His hobbled steps were slow; his good hand holding the stump of his other arm.

"Your friend, child—-seems to carry wounds of battle. I wonder if you would care to revise your tale of my henchmen's demise?"

Angel stood before Erif and said nothing.

The dragon reared his head up and groaned. "Bah. It does not matter now. You have come seeking death and death ye both shall receive."

"*Please*, Oh great and powerful Erif—-" Angel began.

"Child! Do not petition so. His life is wholly mine to take now. This is not the hour of pardons. Look at the young man's face. He knows this. Knows deep that this is his end as well."

"Why?" Prince said. "Why do you do this here? Why the children?"

Erif answered, "A child's blood and gristle... nothing so soothes my soul as their young flesh torn and rendered in my maw. It is my whim and my ecstasy. And my *right*. A few moments from now, I shall tear this child before me and consume her body, bones and all. It is her destiny to have this done and my destiny to do such to her. Any other outcome than this now would upset the very order of our creation."

Contempt swept across Prince's face. "*How* did the gods ever allow for such as *you* to exist?"

Erif let out a chuckle. His whole neck and frame shook with it. In his mirth, Prince and Angel now could see the full arsenal of his teeth and Angel's hands knotted into nervous fists.

"How little you know of gods, boy. How small your grasp of the universe. Know you now that the gods are but a word, and I too was born upon the creation of this word—-my egg broke ope, unmothered, upon the first rays of life's dawn. My birthright here is as ancient as the ocean's claim. These mountains are not my father, but my brothers." Erif lifted one of his claws and pointed a talon at his head. "Every holy book resides here. No words, no parchment, there are no wisdoms this world has ever spawned that I have not consumed. This is right and just and holy, what we are about to perform here today. For how could it not be? Am I not dragon? Am I not Erif of the Strong Word—-Erif of the Crack? And all the gods say amen to my chosen deeds."

"I've seen the gods," Prince said. "I've seen the Creator and the Judge!"

Erif arched his dragon's brow at this. "You've been with the old witch, then?"

"Aye. And she showed me these gods."

"Hmm. The old witch... Boy—-you may very well have seen them—- but I'll venture my hide you do not understand them."

Prince did not answer that, just continued to look defiantly at the dragon.

Erif turned his attention back to Angel who stood before him. "You are a brave lass. You need only be brave a little longer."

Angel took in a big breath and exhaled it as slowly as she could to calm herself down. The fear was there—-she could feel in the base of her stomach—-but the love was too. She latched onto it. Forced her heart to swell with it. Cleared her mind of all and took a step toward the dragon. She lifted her face to him, looked at him with clear eyes, and waited.

"Listen now, child—-my Dawn's Feast—-and follow my instructions entire. In a moment, I will lay my head to the ground and open my very mouth to you. You must then step into it freely and lay your body across my mouth's tongue. I will savor you there for a time and then I will slowly bring my jaws down upon you to crush and tear you. Do not attempt to avoid my teeth. It is your willing death I require—-and only your compliance will save Thorn from my wrath. When I have pierced and pulverized your body sufficiently, only then will I swallow and consume you. And there's your end. Then I shall rise and burn your friend to ashes with my fire for his trespass, and for the slaying of my Rogni. This is just and good. Only when your deaths have gone thusly will I honor a year's safety for your village and your loved ones. Do you understand me now?"

"I understand," Angel said. "I'm ready." She turned to Prince. "Are you ready?"

Prince bowed his head to her.

Erif's neck moved snake-like and glided to the cave's rocky floor. The dragon opened his cavernous mouth wide, cradling his forked tongue for her at the bottom of his mouth.

"*Love,* Prince," Angel said and then walked to Erif's maw and stepped into it through his bottom jaws and obediently laid her body down.

Annabella's back was starting to get sore. It was uncomfortable to lie this way—-but she also knew it would all be over soon. Just like she also knew that the raven flying and cawing cravenly above her was Cyvilard. It had to be, she thought. She watched him soar around, circling her. She waited as she lay there looking up, seeing his little black shape stain the otherwise luminant sky. She willed him to come closer. To come and finish it. "Come, you devil," she finally said aloud, gripping the arrow by her side. "This is what you want, isn't it? My body. Then come on down and take it."

Then, as if he actually heard her from those heights, Cyvilard tipped his wings into a dive, heading right for her.

Slowly, Erif closed his mouth around Angel, enfolding her in his moist darkness. And true to his word, the dragon raised his neck and looked to

Prince like he was indeed *savoring* the sensation of having the young girl upon his tongue.

It was the moment Prince had been waiting for.

He took his good hand from holding his stump, extended his arm towards Erif and splayed his fingers wide. Spreading his feet in a bracing battle stance, Prince concentrated and felt the Aura form. Even without seeing it—-he felt it there. *Strong.* And within his complete control. He felt it conforming around Angel's body. He concentrated on keeping it small, so as to not alert Erif too early.

Erif snapped out of his reverie of pleasure and glared at this Prince's baffling new posture. But before the dragon could speak his displeasure, Prince stepped forward and with his Yonderling mind forced the Aura that held Angel to the back of Erif's throat.

The dragon's eyes widened with surprise and maybe even with a little fear.

Prince pushed the Aura farther, into the beast's windpipe and it began to slowly slide down Erif's neck.

Erif furiously began to retch and cough, trying to spit Angel back up—-but it was too late. He staggered and bellowed like a drunkard and smashed his bulk into the rock wall of the Crack.

"You want to talk of birthrights!" Prince shouted to the writhing beast. "The birthright of every child born today till the end of time will be to live in a world without *you.* Without fear of your terror. Your Lottery. The time of Erif is done. I swear it. You'll be nothing but a bad bedtime story. And that brain full of holy books you were bragging about? *Gone.* Because tonight the carrion crows will pluck it out of your skull!"

And with a surge of will, Prince pushed Angel and the Aura down Erif's neck and into the well of his stomach.

With his throat cleared, Erif seemed to regain himself and stomped towards Prince, intent on crushing him.

Prince spun and ran as fast as his beaten body would let him out of the Crack where he tripped and fell down the mountain path. The dragon emerged from the Crack and spread his gigantic wings and roared.

Prince raised his hand again to Erif and concentrated on the Aura in his belly. Slowly, Prince made the Aura around Angel a perfect ball. Then, he began to expand its radius, making it bigger and bigger.

Erif started to feel the ball growing in his gut and abandoned going after Prince. He flapped his wings and lifted his body into flight.

As Cyvilard's raven form swooped down upon her, Annabella rolled off her longbow, notched her arrow to the bowstring, extended the bow with one arm, holding the string with the other—-and aimed.

The bird had no way to stop mid-air or even evade, he was diving so fast.

Annabella let loose.

The arrow shot up true and ripped into the meat of Cyvilard's feathered breast. The Yondering turned back to a man and free-fell, shouting until he landed on the earth through the grass and wildflowers.

Annabella reached for another arrow out of her quiver. But before she could make it to where Cyvilard lay, she gasped at what she saw soaring in the sky.

Erif was loose and flying wild circles above Thorn.

Prince climbed back up to the Crack and looked at Erif flying panicked above the valley. He had saved her. Well, nearly—-there was just one thing left to do. *A death... And a death only waits for you at yonder Crack,* the old crone had said. Prince smiled. And what a death it will be, he thought. Closing his eyes, he focused on his Aura inside Erif. There in his mind, he saw Angel safe within his Yonderling cocoon—-and with his will he continued to expand it within the doomed dragon.

Erif felt his stomach start to burst from the inside. The beast had never, *never* known pain like this. He roared and flailed through the sky as his stomach stretched to the limit and ripped apart with lancing agony. The strange expanding was now pressing against his heart and pushing on the vertebrae of his back. His skeleton was beginning to creak and crack. Erif's eyes radiated his terror—-his mind emptied of all thought other than his tortured sensations and that somehow *he*—-Erif Ever-Present—-was now on the very brink of oblivion.

She found his smashed and bleeding form lying in the grass. Incredibly, Cyvilard was still alive—-but looked unable to speak, choking as he was on gurgles of his own blood. His eyes widened when he saw her. Annabella looked at her arrow that stuck out of the Elder's chest.

"Now look to where your treacherous ways have brought you. You'll dine in hell tonight," she said. "And if there's any justice there, something will dine on *you.*"

Cyvilard struggled to speak—-but just couldn't manage it; he stretched out his hand in what looked to Annabella like some kind of appeal.

High above, Erif roared a final deafening scream, his wings spread to their limit. Then there was a loud crack and a rip, like a deep peal of thunder, as the great dragon blew fantastically apart in the air. His head and neck separated from his body proper, and big chunks of his back and belly ripped away and fell as they would.

Annabella gasped, and choruses of cries and cheers came from the village, from the many others that must've witnessed Erif's destruction.

But Annabella had little time to ponder, for the dragon's head looked to be plummeting straight for where she stood. She took off in a sprint hoping she could clear the area of certain impact. She did. The thud of Erif's head shook the ground under her feet. When she turned to survey the carnage, she saw that the beast's head and neck had landed completely on top of Cyvilard, surely pulverizing him to a meaty squelch. She imagined what his final moment must've been like seeing that awful mass bearing down on him—-and thought, *yes—-maybe there is justice in this world.*

It was only when Annabella looked up again that she saw that something else was descending from the height where Erif perished. But this thing was not plummeting—-it was floating down. At first it looked like a soap bubble hovering down, but she knew better than that. She knew this was one of Prince's Auras—-that it was how he'd done it. How Prince had slain the dragon. But what she saw next immediately brought her to tears, and as the Aura gracefully landed on the grasses and popped out of sight, *there*—-standing among the flowers, and now running to her—-was Angel.

The sisters collided with one another and embraced, kissed, and embraced again. They wept and took in the sight of each other. And with gentle thumbs they wiped each other's tears.

"And Prince?" Annabella said.

Angel nodded and pointed up to the Crack. "He's there. I'm sure he'll join us soon. He did it! He did it, sister! He's saved us all."

And up atop the great mountain, up at the mouth of the Crack, exhausted but smiling, Prince let himself fall to the ground. Angel was safe down below. He could feel it. He had seen Erif blow apart and had willed his Aura down. And now he imagined her running to find Annabella. He imagined the joy the sisters would feel once reunited. He thought of the village of Thorn, finally delivered from the horror of the Lottery. Visions of them dancing in the streets and singing at the Great Hall filled his head. And he thought of how they would receive him—-Prince the Auramaker. Prince the Dragonslayer.

"*Hero...*" he mumbled; his eyes closed. But as soon as he said it, Prince felt how hollow it was, and then realized that he didn't feel altogether like a hero at all. In fact, deep down—-even though it didn't make any rational sense—-he felt, or rather *knew*—-knew right down to his soul, that it was Angel who was the hero. Why had his Aura succeeded? How could it have been strong enough to rip through a dragon? It was her love that sustained it, he knew. Angel's love, overwhelming even in the jaws of death, that prevailed. It was Prince's final thought before falling into a well-needed slumber, that it wasn't an Aura at all that had defeated Erif.

The dragon was defeated by love.

CANTO IV

"But Death is only a launching into a region
of the strange Untried; it is the first salutation to the
possibilities of the immense Remote, the Wild,
the Watery, and the Unshored..."

Melville

1

Abby

I just couldn't seem to keep my thoughts focused on one thing at all that day. It was like impossible. Like how I get when I'm in like a really cool shop and can't stay looking at one outfit too long because there's so many other ones that are just as interesting/distracting.

We had started the day, my mom and me, going to the hospital for my latest pre-natal check-up. Another ultrasound and they checked all my parts, and everything seemed pretty normal. And, you know, except for like my gargantuan size—I was finally feeling way better than I had in months. I felt like I had my energy back.

After the hospital, Mom took me to the store to get another bottle of cocoa butter lotion, I had been putting on my belly like religiously every night. (I was so afraid of getting stretch marks after, that I was reading up all the time on the best preventative skin care and cocoa butter was supposed to be the *schizz.)* Anyway, it really did make my tummy feel smooth. Well, after we picked that up, we had lunch, and then headed over to the adoption agency to have another meet and greet with the adoption parents and everybody's lawyers. This meeting took up all afternoon—so, yeah—I didn't make school that day.

Which was fine with me. Because Hemingway was all like freaking out anyway. I mean this was right after we pulled off the website thing and Gray's hack into the school's system so he could play Dylan's vocal bit, and then the guys' suspensions—so it was pretty crazy. Luke and the boys were all at Erik's cottage too, so I didn't mind being out a day at all.

This was the second time I'd met the Klinger's. Rob and Emily. I mean, don't get me wrong, nice people. Both in their early thirties. Rob was like some engineer-type at Chevrolet and Emily said she worked at some theater house in the city. I mean, they looked like they would have plenty of money and stability to raise a child. No doubt. Emily was pretty with reddish hair and looked like some actress that I just couldn't place. And like I said, they were like beyond nice.

I didn't know what it was though, but something did seem just a little *off* to me about them. After I first met them, I was trying to tell Luke about this feeling and he had written something like, *yeah—of course you feel something's off. You're giving these people your child.* He smiled after he wrote it, and maybe he was trying to be a little funny—but I think I understood what he meant. This whole adoption thing—even if it's a good idea—still isn't ideal. Just like me keeping this baby wouldn't be ideal either. Single mom in high school who had a daughter with a guy she no longer loves. A guy who cheated on her with her best (former best) friend. Not ideal.

Anyway, while the agency people were steering the whole meeting in their conference room, our lawyer was talking to the Klinger's lawyer, and they were constantly going over endless legal documents. That gave me a lot of time to zone out to the million things going on in my head too.

Like Luke—*always* Luke and his strange ways. I had told him like months ago that I thought I might be falling in love with him. I told him after I had tracked him down to Isaiah's house after Izzy had his big seizure. I got him to go out with me to Starbucks after. We found a little quiet table in the back, and I told him. He smiled and took my hands all while those eyes just beamed at me. He didn't say it back. He never said it back in the months since. But that evening when we got in our cars, he took me in his big arms and kissed my head.

I'd only brought up loving him one other time since then, and he reacted all caring then too—but still never said it back.

I didn't push him. I took the affection he gave me in return, and we started texting and hanging out more and more. Even though it did get a little awkward when I'd go to his house and there'd be Jason Turner—like *living* there—watching TV with his feet up on the couch or smoking on the back porch before he quit or whatever. It never bothered Luke that I was pregnant, and I would spill everything I was feeling about being pregnant and how self-conscious I was like all the time, how I worried how this might affect college next year, and telling him when there was tension at home, or all the weird feelings when I, and practically the whole school, found out that Peter had screwed Gabby and all that. And Luke would never look judgmental or bored, and always seemed to care and give good advice—and just *be there*, you know? And even though we'd hold hands, and he'd let me put my head on his shoulder or hug him, we never kissed. You know, kissed like *for sure* romantically.

But like I said, I didn't push it. I didn't make a big deal of it. Because how could I? How could I press him about kissing and falling in love when we were together, all while I was carrying some other guy's baby? I knew it wouldn't be fair of me to do that. But also—I just didn't want to blow it, you know? Like Luke was this perfect miracle of mystery that everyone was now seriously interested in. Yes, he was devastatingly good looking—but he was also this guy that *did stuff* now. Everyone knew he was the one planning all this weird school-bonding stuff. They all knew, or acted like they knew, he was the leader of our underground movement. People were dying to ask him a million questions—but they were also afraid and crazy-nervous to say anything to him. And besides Turner and other soccer guys—I was the only other person he was talking to. *Me*. The only girl for the most part he was seen with. Just pregnant old me. And I was not going to wreck that by asking a million needy-girl questions of him. No way. I wasn't going to do it. Instead, I was content to analyze every conversation, every handhold, every long stare he gave me, for signs of feelings on his part.

He's waiting till after the baby, I told myself. Waiting till the Klinger's take custody of my baby girl. Then... *Then*.

That's what I tried to tell myself.

While I was sitting there still very much all lost in my thoughts, my mind drifted from Luke to a few nights before when I was hanging out at Maddie's house with her and Dallas. We had been watching some lame movie, but we turned it off—all of us just wanting to talk about all the stuff going on at school and the schemes the guys were coming up with.

Eventually, the conversation turned to love and freedom. And were these two kind of the same thing or were they more like opposites? Like once you love someone do you lose your freedom in a lot of ways? Or was it totally the opposite? Meaning, once you began loving the right person, you were suddenly free, like truly free from all sorts of things that do people harm in this world. That by loving someone, you were truly free to be yourself?

It was a pretty heated debate—but not one of us took like any kind of rigid side. I would say Dallas and me both leaned heavy on love being true freedom—with like the major stipulation being that you loved the right person (but there was a huge side debate about what the "right person" means too, but anyway…). And Maddie definitely was leaning more towards you have to sacrifice freedom for love.

"Come on, doesn't it make sense," I remember her saying, "that if you go out with someone in a serious way—or like marry them—then you totally give up a lot of freedom about what you want and what you'd like to do?"

But Dallas and I tried making the case that maybe in that instance what you gain in that kind of relationship should outweigh what you lose.

But Maddie stayed mostly unconvinced. She asked me if I had truly loved Peter right when we got pregnant. I told her I thought so. But obviously Peter hadn't been the right person, which totally got us back to who's the right person then.

But anyway, I kept thinking. Was Luke the right person? I didn't know. Maybe Maddie was right. Maybe there's hundreds, maybe thousands of right people out there for everyone—it just comes down to the choices we make and the timing.

I was caught in these thoughts when I finally snapped back to the meeting and noticed my mom handing some photos of me across to the Klinger's. Last time we met they had asked if they could see some childhood pics of me that might give them a better idea of what my little girl would look like. Mom gave them a few of my baby pictures and a couple pics of me at like ages two through four, and a couple of me at like eight or so.

One of the pics of me at eight gave me a jab of butterflies.

"Could I see that one please," I said.

Emily slid the photo across the table towards me and she and Rob grinned at the others while saying all sorts of nice stuff about how cute I used to be.

I pulled the picture over.

It was one of Luke and me in second grade. We were standing side by side outside my house after just coming home after school.

That's how we'd met. Our moms got together just before we started kindergarten and thought it would be a good idea if Luke and I walked the three blocks to and from school together since we were the same age and lived so close to each other.

Both our little-kid selves smiled. Hard to believe we were both the same height back then. Back before Luke turned into the towering inferno.

I was totally hit with a memory of one time when Luke and I were running home after school had been let out early because of an approaching blizzard. We were excited, like all the kids were, to be suddenly let go out of school early and running free into the winter afternoon. There were already high snowbanks everywhere and kids were all talking about how super-deep the snow would be after the blizzard. A lot of kids were hoping we'd be out of school the rest of the week.

Luke and I bundled up and I said goodbye to my friends, and he met me at my coat hook and cubby, and we took off.

We talked more than usual that day, I remembered. I tried to recall the sound of his voice back then, back when he still spoke. I couldn't remember everything we talked about, I just remembered how happy we were. We played a game. We started running up on the snowbanks between people's driveways, and when we came to the edge, we'd slide down and jump up to the next bank. We'd throw our backpacks ahead of us and pretend they weren't full of homework and folders, but full of mountain survival gear. It was all Luke's idea, but I went along. We said we were lost in the mountains and if the blizzard caught us, we'd die. So, we ran and slid and jumped and ran again in the snow. From snowbank to snowbank. Till we were both totally tired and laughing. If one of us was slow to get up, the other would pull them. A few times we both would just collapse on each other laughing then say something all dramatic about how we had to keep going. *We* had to make it. I'm not leaving you! I'll never leave you behind!

"Abby—" Mom tried to snap me out of it.

Emily asked if they could keep a few of the photos and Mom said she had printed them up just for them so feel free.

They were both pretty pleased with that and that's when Emily said, "You know just the other night we think we decided on a name and now these will help us put a name with a face."

"Oh, well what name did you decide?" Mom goes.

Both Rob and Emily gave each other this quick cute grin.

"Charlotte Gray," Emily goes.

My mom said that was a pretty name and—*I don't know,* maybe it is. But I remember suddenly getting hit with this flash of my kid photographs up on the Klinger's fridge with the name *Charlotte Gray!* I felt this stab that I just hadn't felt about this decision since I made it last fall. I certainly didn't say anything about it there at the meeting, and I didn't try to explain it to my mom on the way home. But it suddenly was becoming real to me. Did I really want the child from my own body to grow up as Charlotte Gray Klinger and never know me?

Because that's where this all was headed. I had always known that, but now that knowledge was becoming ice cold in its reality. But really, what other option looked better at this point?

Ugh. I was in knots that day. All I knew was I wanted to talk to Luke again. To lay these feelings all out. To read his notes. To feel the warmth of his arms.

I thought of the blizzard again. I thought too of the day we heard that Luke's sister and mom had died. I cried so hard when my parents told me. Cried so hard for little Angela. I cried for Luke. Afterwards, we got a card, and my mom made some cookies. I told Mom that I wanted to give them to Luke and his dad by myself. Tears started coming as I started to walk, so I put the big plate down and wiped them off and then picked the plate back up again.

I rang their doorbell. I knocked at the door. No one came. But Mr. Forrester's car was in the driveway. I left the cookies and stepped out in front of the house and looked up to Luke's bedroom. He was standing up there looking down at me, but his face was nothing. No tears, no smile, just quiet seriousness. Then he walked away.

I cried to Mom that I didn't understand, and she said the Forrester's just needed space. I didn't see Luke the whole summer. He didn't talk to me once school started. Then he went deaf. I couldn't believe it. Then it seemed he didn't talk to anybody.

But all that was before his note, before he came up out of nowhere, seeming to want to pick up being friends just like that. When I most needed him back.

That night after coming back from the agency, I went right to my bed and cried. About my unborn daughter and what was going to happen. About Luke. About my life and everything that had led it to this point. All my mistakes. Peter. Gabby. What was happening at school. All the nasty things people had said, mostly about Ryan and Turner and the rest of the soccer guys—but also about the stuff they said about me. And it all swirled in my brain while I wrapped my covers around myself and my unborn child till it all just numbed, wanting Luke to be near me, his silent and strong body lying next to mine.

2

"Carver?"

"What? Can't sleep, kid?"

"Yeah—I—sorry it's so..."

"Don't worry about it. I'm up at four most mornings anyway. The way I'm wired. Been waiting for your call."

"How the hell's that?"

"Luke. He wrote a couple weeks ago. He's written me three times in fact since you boys came over last fall."

"Really?"

"Really, kid."

"Well, how..."

"*Yeah...*?"

"How much did you really know about Rozzy, man? I mean, like how much did you know about what she was into or what the fuck was going on with her?"

"Well to be honest, I didn't know a lot about that stuff. I guessed she had had a hard life. Was *living* a hard life. But since the get-go, we talked mostly spiritual stuff. And a lot about my family. About Bath Consolidated School. What I knew about the bombing."

"So, you didn't know she was a meth addict?"

"I suspected drugs, but I didn't know for certain. I knew she was epileptic though."

"She took the shit to help with that—but it only fucked her up more in the end. She had her regular meds too, I guess. But she said the pills were too weak. Didn't stop her seizures. Not the big ones anyway."

"Well, I knew all about her meds. I got epilepsy too, kid. We talked a lot about that."

"No shit? I didn't know that, man."

"I believe it was one of the portals that connected us. Helped draw her to me. It's hard to explain to someone like you."

"Well, I guess that's why I'm calling, man. My brain's itching about what's going on here. Like how Rozzy's got you and Luke working together, doing stuff—all when neither of you actually fucking met her. While I—*you know*, one of her closest friends, am stuck here trying to figure out all this shit after the fact."

"Jason. Just tell me. What is it you want to know?"

"Did you know what was in my letter?"

"No, kid. You want to tell me?"

"She said she killed herself partly because she was spent. Her habit and her seizures were getting worse. Also, what she had to do to support her habit was getting to be too much. She believed she could never quit the junk. Like ever, man. But there was something else. She was having more and more visions. Not from the drugs so much as from the seizures she thought. Seeing the future, she said. But also seeing the past. In the letter she said she'd been to Bath many times—in her visions. But she'd also seen her future. Well, not one future, but two of them, man."

"Two futures?"

"Yeah, man. Both of them different. She wrote about one where she lived until she saw herself *O.D.-ing* when she was twenty-six. She was alone in some shitty tweaker house with other glass-zombies hitting their pipes into oblivion. She wrote that she stood over herself, spazzing in a fit of convulsions, vomit erupting from her mouth until she was dead on the ratty carpet."

"And her other future?"

"*Jason…?*"

"She wrote about *this one*, man. One where she killed herself early. One that she could prepare for. One she could try and make matter. A future where her life and her death might actually mean something rather than be some statistic used in an anti-drug campaign. She said this future could only happen if she could get the right help. She didn't write about you and Luke like by name. But I'm guessing you're who she meant."

"She also might've meant you too."

"Yeah, *maybe*. It's just—I don't know what to believe, man. Part of me really wants to believe that she's not totally gone. That she's watching over, like some kind of ghost or something. But another part of me knows it's bullshit. But then too, I've been having crazy-ass dreams, which is nuts because I ain't loaded no more, and as far as I know, I don't have epilepsy. And then there's Luke acting out, doing all sorts of crazy stuff all because of Rozzy's prediction for him—"

"He *told* you that? Rosalind's prediction for him?"

"Yeah. He said she told him he wouldn't live out the year, man."

"Luke didn't tell you she said that in her letter to him, did he?"

"No. He said it was in a dream he had after she shot herself."

"But he said he *believes* it?"

"Uh, yeah. I think he believes it all right. He acts like someone who definitely has got nothing to lose."

"Yes sir, that's interesting."

"But hey, man. Stay focused here. You really think because she had epilepsy that gave her some kind of power or something? To see the future? Or like to get in people's dreams or whatever?"

"No, kid. Not exactly, anyway. I think through the ages some of us have had more of a sense of the great connection than most. And that sometimes, the falling sickness can be a side-effect of that connection."

"*The great connection*?"

"The great tremors of things, boy. The earth shakes beneath us and all things upon it share in the movement."

"What?"

"Either everything's connected—by some strand—in some way. Or it's not."

"*Everything*? You talking like every, single, thing?"

"I am. Everything and every single person. By the threads we weave or the ones that are woven around us. A great spider web of relevance."

"Or it's not?"

"Right. Or it's not. Then the whole of life is formless, meaningless, and unrelated. Probability and coincidence. It all comes down to if the world is intentionally constructed and has meaning, or if everything is just coincidence that we're here and everything's arbitrary."

"And you think *it is* then, right? That there's meaning and we really are all connected?"

"Yes. Of course, I do. From Olivia to Lindberg, to Rosalind, all the way down to you. Then on down the line *from* you. On and on it goes, crisscrossing with other strands."

"I don't know, man. I just don't fucking know."

"Think about it now. I'm not alone here. Think about our human need to identify. By identifying, we connect. We form narrative, we reach for meaning. We have a drive for this, *yes*?"

"*Hm...*"

"The ocean's full of waves, kid. There's never the same one twice—and yet they're all part of the same ocean, all waiting their time, rising, and falling in their given turn. I think Rosalind was trying to get you to see the connection between yourself and what happened here so long ago."

"And so, *what* exactly am I supposed do with that connection *if* there is one?"

"When faced with questions of the soul, a person either embraces that connection we share—sees it—learns from it—maybe even wields it. *Or*—a person doesn't. Instead, you ignore it. Discredit it. Or you blunt yourself until you're so incapable of understanding and empathizing with all the humanity around you that you might as well strap a bomb to it all and blow it up."

"So what the hell, man? If you don't believe in this connection thing, you turn evil and kill people? And if you *do* buy it, you're suddenly a good guy?"

"No, Jason. I didn't mean it that way. Remember I'm not talking about destiny—I'm talking about connection. I'm saying that for most people, whether you see a grand connection is not a tipping factor if a body's going to be good or evil. See, for most folks how they come down on this will have a bearing on where their mind will, or won't, find coherence in this world. But for those few—like Kehoe and maybe even yourself, how you fall on it *may* result in profound acts of good or evil upon the world."

"*Man,* I am barely with you here. I mean, you do remember who you're talking to right now—*right*, old-timer? I mean, I'm pretty fucking sure if I were to take a philosophy class, I'd flunk it due to napping and truancy."

"They are twin brothers from the same mother—this good and evil. I believe that when there arises a great evil, a stealthy but ancient presence of good rises as well, right next to it. And vice versa. And all this rising and falling of the terrible and the beautiful doesn't just happen in continual circular flux in the world—but ebbs and flows inside everyday folks, I believe. Hell, I more than believe it. I've seen it. There can't be but one without the quick pursuance of the other."

"You're talking about what went on after the explosion. How people came together."

"Yes. Sure. But not just here in Bath. This pattern's everywhere, kid. Open your eyes, now. Take this—here's what's going to happen. Someday a nuclear bomb will detonate in the United States. It's just a matter of math, of probability. It *will* happen. But you know what else will happen right alongside such horror? On the day that bomb goes off, some people will rise and be at humanity's best. Heroes will emerge. Babies will still be born somewhere that day, and someone will fall in love. That's the story. It's *our* story, Jason."

"*Jeeezusss*— Really? You believe that?"

"And we're all connected to it."

"Damn if you don't sound like a fucking old man version of Luke right now."

"Oh, I don't know about that. He and I ain't the same, kid. I think we got different takes when it comes down to it. I suppose I'll leave it to him to explain all the little differences if he cares to. But I will say at least *Captain Pragmatic* and I are on the same team."

"Hm. *Pragmatic*?"

"See, the main difference between your large friend and myself is that he seems to me to be all *will* and very little *belief.* I could be wrong—Rosalind's prediction for him aside. But from our correspondence, I think I'm right. As for me, I'm all belief and much too old to harness a will anything near the radiance of Luke's. It really all comes down to this, kid. Rosalind is what I believe in. This plan you talk of—this future she chose—that's what's left of her now—a *belief.* Me? *Well*, I'm the believer. Luke is the do-*er*. The planner. Rosalind chose well. She found a guy that's determined to make all this happen through the power of his bare hands and the might of his mind. And then there's *you*."

"*Me…?*"

"Yes. You. You're the wild card, Jason. You've come so far. All of us—I think we're just all waiting to see what you're going to do *now*."

"What *I* do, huh?"

"Of course. She asked you to do something right?

"*Right?* Are you there?"

"Yeah. In the letter, man. But it's hard. You know—to know what she means."

"Why is it hard?"

"She…she wants me to save someone."

"Well, *who?*"

"I'm not sure. Like I said, it's hard because she's vague about it. She wrote 'someone.' And I don't know if that means a *he* or *she*, or *them*. But the kicker is, I think I know who she wants me to save them from."

"And who's that, kid?"

"*Kehoe*."

3

Hemingway was changing. You could feel it as you walked in every morning now. Something was missing—or maybe not quite missing but starting to fall away. A molting of sorts might be more accurate, I guess. Maybe the feeling was intensified by the coming of April and true spring, but it wasn't just because the snow melted to puddles and the puddles turned into green grass. It wasn't just the trick of seasons. It was something more.

The awkward anger, shame, and embarrassment of *hemingwayownit* had faded, and in its place was this subtle, widespread—*I don't know*—period of reconciliation. Maybe most of us first noticed it in what kids were saying to Ryan. It started with Dan Pamenter coming up to him after school in the halls and apologizing outright for what he had said about Ryan after *T-shirt Day*. "I was way out of line," Dan goes, "I don't really feel that way. It was stupid. I only said it because I thought you'd never know. I would've never said that to your face because it's so mean. *Sorry*."

Dan wouldn't be the last to tell Ryan something similar. Even kids Ryan never knew came up to him with stuff like that. Even some of the other guys like Erik and Luke got a few people coming up wanting to make it right.

And Turner? *Sheesh*. He got almost as many people coming up to him as Ryan, saying they were sorry for *all* the crap they said about him through the years. You could tell it made him feel super-awkward, like they had put a couple of slimy eels tripping on crack down his shirt. He told the rest of us anytime it happened, he half-wanted to just turn around and run away and half-wanted to punch them in the face just to make them shut up about it.

But this new feeling wasn't just directed towards some of us—kids started directing it to each other, like *en masse*. I mean, there weren't like mass group hugs in the halls between kids that usually hated each other's guts. You should eliminate any hippie-love fest images right now, and for the record, there were still plenty of people that were still too cool or mean. But there still was a collective *harshness*, I guess for lack of a better word, that seemed to be receding or whatever, from our hallways, our classrooms, the caf and commons.

We could all feel it.

And maybe that's why there were so many kids we were able to recruit to help with the soup kitchen Ryan Leone was able to set up in Detroit. More and more kids seemed to want "*in*" on what we were doing now.

Ryan's pastor had worked with the city and located an abandoned, but not yet rundown, elementary school to serve from in the neighborhood Turner had pointed out to Ryan. City Hall was pleased at the offer but told Pastor Mike they were a little surprised since that whole area of the city had been legally vacant for nearly three years. But they approved the church's request.

An army of us showed up to spruce up the school's bathrooms, kitchen area, and cafeteria. Most of Ryan's youth group was there of course, but so were a lot of us—and our numbers had grown. Maddie and Dallas and a few more of their friends were there to be servers, Gala Sara came bringing along a few more of her drama kids, even Dickie

Schwartz was able to pry away a few friends he had in common with Dignan Cooper. (Diggy himself was a no-show though. Maybe all this still wasn't cool enough for him. But *whatever*.) Then there were the rest of us standards: Abby and Luke, Erik and most of the team, Turner, not to mention Gray and me.

While most worked hard preparing the food and cleaning up the cafeteria, a gang of us also went out into the deserted streets nailing up flyers for the weekly kitchens on telephone poles, most of them with no cables or anything connecting to them. Anybody we did see walking around didn't come close while we were tagging them up, but we saw them gather behind us to read them when we started heading back.

By the time we opened the doors, there was a line down the street. Our little elementary school was the only building with lights for blocks and blocks. There were no streetlights. No cars other than our own parked in the school's teacher lot.

The tables filled up fast and before the end of the first hour, we had to set up some folding chairs to give all the residents a seat.

"Where'd they all come from?" Tristan whispered to me, but I think we all were wondering the same question too.

"Well, they sure didn't all come from 8 Mile," I said.

After combing his eyes through the seemingly never-ending crowd coming in through the doors—finally, Turner saw them. Just as he hoped, they had all come together, bundled up in some of the same clothes he remembered, except for maybe the hats and scarves. He waited until they had been served and seated before coming up to them.

"Hey, take your time, ya'll. And dessert is on me."

Thelma looks up from her steaming bowl and full plate. "Oh now, that you *huny*?"

"Yes ma'am. Good to see you fellas too," he nods to Bernie and Lawrence and then shakes their hands. "I was hoping you'd show."

"*You* put all this on?" Bernie goes and waves his hand all around.

"Me and my friends. Mostly my friends, though. But yeah. Hey—I got something for you guys." Turner bends down and digs Lawrence's boots out of his backpack and places them by Lawrence's chair. Fishes out two twenty-dollar bills and slips it to Thelma.

"Nuh-uh now. You don't need be doing that. We sure didn't give you that much," she goes shaking her head.

"Oh yes you did," Turner goes. "You all gave me more than I could ever repay."

4

Sleep these days for Alan Forrester was either deep and cavernous or twitchy as rabbit ears making him roll in his bed every five minutes it seemed. *Yes*, it was due in part to the stresses at work, as always, but then there were also the strange comings and goings of the two teenage boys he had living under his roof. And don't even get him started on the group meetings Luke and Jason would have with their friends where twenty kids would be down in his living room, all of them yakking at once planning god knows what—or the time they pulled that all-nighter with the computers and then were freaking unilaterally suspended afterward for vague reasons by Hemingway administration.

All of that, Alan would have to admit, also contributed to his very uneven sleep regimen. But what could he do? His son, even with all his erratic energy and happily dodgy demeanor, was doing wonders with the Turner boy. There was no doubt about it. Alan had seen the state of Jason earlier in the year. And to see the kid now—lucid, full of color and life, even smiling and laughing. Heck, Jason did half the cooking and cleaning lately. And Luke had more than come alive too. All year Alan had been in silent wonder. His son had always been secretive, yes—to almost a disturbing Nth degree. But he was *alive*—interacting with people, and even with his own father, in ways that he hadn't in years. For the first time since the crash, Alan really did wish his wife, Cynthia, could see their son now—not sullen and brooding like he had been all through high school—but this young man: silent, but vibrant, steely, but warm. And he couldn't be sure whether the Browne girl was Luke's girlfriend or not—and he sure as hell wasn't going to ask now—but he thought his wife would be surprised and pleased that their son and Abby were hanging out as much as they were (her present condition aside). The point was, Alan wasn't about to come down hard on rules now—not with Jason doing so well and Luke practically out of the house for good. Less than three months. Then Luke would choose a college and be gone—and Alan somehow knew even then, his son would never come back. Well, not to live anyway.

So why hassle? Let the boys *do*. Try to enjoy this, he thought. Time enough for all the quiet in the world come the middle of summer.

So that's why he didn't make such a big deal when his sleep schedule was completely out of whack. Anytime he couldn't sleep, he'd just roll with it. For instance, one late April night or early morning, Alan remembers stirring awake and finding his stomach rumbling. He got up and went downstairs to make a sandwich from some of that shredded buffalo chicken they had eaten for dinner. Down in the kitchen, the first thing he noticed was the strong smell of coffee. This was nothing new. Since Jason came back to live with them, the Forrester's expenditure on good coffee skyrocketed. It seemed lately that Luke and Jason (mostly Jason now) seemed to run more on French and Italian roast than actual food.

Alan looked and saw the coffee maker's burner was still on. He turned around. The rest of the house was dark, and it looked like no one else was awake, so Mr. Forrester moved to turn the burner off. That's when he noticed the backyard light on.

Creeping to the back window, he could see Jason sitting out on one of the Adirondack chairs, a coffee cup sitting on one arm steaming. He was hunched forward with his elbows planted on his knees; hands folded together slowly rubbing his thumbs together. From the look on Jason's face, Alan could see the boy was lost in thought. But as to what he was thinking on so hard, Alan couldn't hazard the remotest of freaking guesses.

Let the boy be, Alan thought and returned to his midnight snack. After slowly munching on the sandwich with a side of tortilla chips and a beer, watching the last half of some godawful monster movie on TV, Alan went back to the kitchen to put his plate in the sink. The light in the yard was still on and Jason was still there. No longer sitting, but pacing. Alan almost thought he should go out there to see what was troubling him but stopped himself. It clearly wasn't angst on the boy's face—it was something else. Alan had seen this kind of look before on his own son many times through the years. Usually when Luke was trying to figure out a new video game, or the way he would construct his Legos or like how, up until a few months ago, he was up all-night writing on his mother's old typewriter. Alan knew this look and backed reverently away. It was the look of genesis, of creation. Jason was building something there in the backyard while his coffee continued to sit, chilling on the Adirondack's arm. So, Alan left Jason to his construction.

5

Isaiah

It's great in the mornings again because Luke is back working out at the soccer fields now that the snow's gone and it's not so chilly in the mornings. The other day though it was different because Luke had jogged here rather than taking his car, and he had Jason Turner jogging with him. They both had these backpacks with their school stuff in them and Jason was breathing so heavy when they got to the fields, and he looked like he was going to puke. But Luke just unstrapped his ball from his pack, and I already had mine, and we started to work on our moves like usual.

The whole time we practiced, Jason just took a nap on the wet grass with his head on his backpack like a pillow and groaned every once in a while. Luke just laughed and slipped me this note that said this was Jason's first time working out and not to worry about him.

When we were done, I was about to go into the house for breakfast and Luke asked if I wanted to hang out a little after school. He said he was sorry he had been so busy lately with other stuff at his school that he hadn't really done too much with me, which I said was OK and I understood. Well, I was pumped that he wanted to hang out, so I said sure, and he came by the house again that afternoon after I got home from school on my bike.

We went to *Twisty's* first to get a couple of chocolate shakes and play a few games of air hockey. While we were having our shakes, I told him I finished his story about Prince and the dragon. He asked me what I thought about it, and I told him that I really, really liked it. But some of it was kind of confusing. He asked me what parts and I told him, and he sort of explained them telling me what some of the parts meant to him. Then he told me some of the stuff that he wrote with me in mind, which I thought was cool and I think I like it even more now.

When we left *Twisty's,* I asked if it would be all right to go visit Dad in the graveyard and he nodded sure. It was sunny, but I still needed my jacket out there while Luke stood off aways looking off to the forest at the edge of the graveyard while I had some time alone by my dad's stone.

I still think about him every day. Think about him when he was alive here with us and I thought about my dad and how I've been seeing him since. In my thoughts and dreams. How I see him out my window in the night.

After a while I went over to where Luke was. I told him a little about my dreams and some of the stuff I see and don't really see sometimes. He told me to keep going, so I did. Telling him everything about flying through space all the way to Pluto. The astronauts, the cave, the man with five red eyes. And about how my dad said never to go back there because the man could kill me. I told Luke how I still felt the urge in my mind to still go back there anyway though.

I asked Luke what he thought, and he sat down there in the grass and really did seem to think about it for a while. He took out his pad and wrote me a note. It said: *Part of growing up is sometimes doing what you think you need to do, if you really believe you have to. Even if that means doing something against your father's wishes. Doesn't mean we don't love our fathers any less. But at some point, we sons gotta figure out for ourselves what's the right thing to do.*

We sat there for a while more till the sun started coming down behind the tall trees and all the gravestones made long shadows across the grass and paths. I put the note in my pocket.

When we got back to his car, he took out his phone and made it say, "Hey you want to see something cool? Something nobody other than Abby's seen?"

I said sure and *wow*, I'm so glad I did—

6

The next week we were all back serving over at the soup kitchen at the end of the earth. Believe it or not, there were even more homeless than the week before, and we were all bustling to keep up. It was a good thing Pastor Mike had recruited a bunch more adults from his church to help—most of them recently retired folks, or people with children that were out of the house.

Again, Turner kept a lookout for Thelma, Bernie, and Lawrence. When he saw them come in, he got Tristan to cover his post manning the beverages and went over. He pulled up a seat this time and ate with them, which they all seemed to get a real kick out of. When they finished, Turner helped clear their dishes away and escorted them out the door and into the street. The line into the school still stretched down the block, so Turner walked with them a while down the dark sidewalk.

"Listen," he goes. "I want you guys to take this—"

"Well, what's that?" Bernie goes, as Turner hauls something out of his hoodie pocket.

"It's a phone."

"Who for?" Thelma goes.

"Well, for ya'll. For you to use however you need. Look, it's already activated. Here's my number too."

"Oh, *huny* now—you don't need to be giving us no phone. You done enough—" Thelma goes, and Bernie and Lawrence start mumbling in agreement.

"No, no. You don't understand," Turner goes, "I also want you to do me a favor with it."

"What's that?"

"I need you to keep watch from your trailer about the coming and goings in that rec center across the street."

"Aw, now you best leave that alone now," Thelma goes.

"Ain't no good come of that," Lawrence agrees.

But Turner's firm. "I appreciate that—but I know what I'm doing. I ain't asking you to go near it or stick your neck out any more than you already are by living near it. *OK?* All I'm asking is to keep track of what cars come in, how long they stay, when they leave, and how long it is when it looks like there ain't no cars there. Got it? I'll call every so often to get the low down and that's it. Meantime, you can call me if whatever, and you got a phone for emergencies or to call people you know, or whatever you want. *OK*?"

Well, all three of them still hemmed and hawed a little, but finally Thelma took the phone. Turner showed them how to use it and they all said they'd see him next week at the soup kitchen. Satisfied, Turner went back into the school.

All the eating and cleaning finally wound down at about nine, and Pastor Mike announced the total number of people served and we all kind of cheered and whooped at our good work. It was a Thursday night, but there wasn't school tomorrow because of a teacher workshop day or something, so everybody was breaking off into little groups, making plans about where to head to next.

You could tell, the way he was flirting and laughing with Maddie over in the corner of the cafeteria, that Erik really, really wished he could just take off somewhere very quiet and cozy with her—but he couldn't. He and Ryan had to split off together because Monday was the deadline for most of the college scholarships they both were applying for—and as of yet, Erik hadn't done squat as far as his applications. *Ryan* on the other hand, had already filled out a bunch and knew what he was doing, so Erik was getting him to come over to help him out, you know, with the whole process. Erik would be buying the pizza.

Abby was not feeling well, so she hadn't come—basically leaving Luke to run some errand that Turner was saying they had to do together. Just the two of them. So, *whatever*—the rest of us took the hint.

Gala ran off with her drama hordes before I really got a chance to see what she was up to, which was a shame for me. But I tagged up with Gray and most of the team who were all going over to Dickie's house to watch a movie and basically just chill.

Well, we all took off , and I found out much later that Dallas, who had been Maddie's ride over, couldn't take Maddie back because she was under strict orders from her parents to meet the rest of her family over at her grandparent's place over in Dearborn once things were done at the kitchen. Which totally left Maddie high and dry because she just thought she could hook up with Abby afterwards, or even Erik, but both those options were shot now.

Which basically left her with Pastor Mike. *Or—*

"*Hey guys*—hold up a sec!"

Turner hits the breaks. Luke rolls down the passenger window.

"Can I hitch a ride with you? I kind of got stranded here. Bad planning, I guess," Maddie goes.

"Uh, sorry," Turner goes. "Love to help you—but we got some serious shit to take care of—"

But Luke arches his eyebrow and nods her to the back seat.

She smiles and hops in.

Turner slaps Luke's arm. *What the hell?* he mouths.

Luke shrugs.

"Uh—thanks. Thought I'd have to bum a ride with Pastor Mike or one of the church grannies in there. *Whew...*"

Turner says nothing and pulls out.

Luke holds his handheld up. "Don't mention it," his robot voice goes. "But Jason and I are on a date."

Maddie laughs. "Oh *well*—sorry for crashing then. Forgot, no school tomorrow and I know three's a crowd. But there's always prom..."

Turner scoffs. "That's it. That'll be us. Hanging out in double tuxes, playing goose the sausage while slow dancing in the middle of the fucking gym floor."

Luke reaches over and puts his arm behind Turner's head.

Turner bats him away. "Get the hell off me—cheese and rice, man—"

Maddie laughs again and Luke pulls his arm back, grinning.

"You love this, don't you?" Turner goes to Luke. "Yeah—*hilarious,* man."

"So—what's this uh, *serious shit* you boys got going down tonight. Huh?" Maddie goes.

"It's classified as far as you're concerned, sweetheart. Now where exactly do you live?" Turner goes, looking at her through the rearview.

"*Sweetheart*, huh? What are you my grandpa? I live over in Briarside Pointe."

"*Briarside Pointe?* Christ—I should've known," Turner groans.

"Why all the fuss? Seriously, where are you two going?"

"Al Skids," Luke goes by his handheld proxy.

"Well, that's off the Interstate. Can't you do what you need to and then take me home? How long do you need to be there?"

Luke gives Turner a loaded stare.

"No. No. No," Turner goes back to him. "No way. We're not bringing her along. You know why."

"Why?" Maddie goes. "You guys planning on laser bowling till dawn or something?"

"Not exactly," Turner goes.

"Twenty-five minutes to get to Briarside. Then twenty-five minutes to get back to Al's. We should do this with her. Save time," Luke's handheld goes.

Turner grips his steering wheel a little harder. "OK. But you both stay in the car. Got it?"

Luke gives him a quick mockery of a salute.

"*Got it?*" Turner repeats, looking back at Maddie again.

Maddie stiffens up a bit. "Uh—yeah. Got it or whatever." She taps Luke on the shoulder, and he turns so he can see her face. "He always this much fun?"

And Luke gives her a *thumbs up*.

7

League play ended the first week of April, so the only people showing up at Al Skid's Bowling Alley on Friday's now were mostly recreational bowlers and eighth graders with nothing better to do. And also, of course, your occasional player in the local drug scene.

The parking lot was a little less than half full when Turner pulled in and the alley's lights glared alongside the neon sign for Pazzaro's Pizza, whose establishment jutted out from the alley's west wall like some kind of swollen sore.

"*Oh, please* can we bowl? I haven't bowled since like the fourth grade—"

Turner shakes his head. "No. You stay in the car. *Remember?*" He shoots a pleading look at Luke. "Remember—*right*?"

Luke looks back at him. No expression.

"Look, this'll take like five minutes, tops. That's it. I just gotta go in and talk to a guy and I'm out. So there's no reason for all of us to go in there."

Maddie leans forward from the back seat. "*Then*—there's no reason we can't just wait right there at the front of the alley either. If it's just for five minutes, what's the big deal?"

Turner shakes his head and groans. He turns to Luke. "You gotta opinion on this?"

Luke holds up his handheld. "It's just five minutes."

The three of them go in through the glass double doors and the full aroma of late-night Skid's hits them all at once. Rough thirteen-year-old boys are holding dominion in the arcade area while some serious local sketchers are all sitting at the bar while the *rock'em sock'em* of crashing pins rumbles in from the lanes.

"*Wow*—I always wondered who it was exactly that kept this place in business. And *now* I know," Maddie goes.

"You have no idea, man," Turner goes. "Look, you two stay put. I'll be back in like two shakes."

Luke nods and Turner takes off towards Pazzaro's. As he stalks past the lanes semi-packed with mostly burned-out middle-aged adults and lost causes in their twenties, Turner gets flashes of his last outing here with Kid T. And then it suddenly hits him. What if—like on a fucking lark—he goes blowing into the pizza joint and Dre and his crew are there? *Cheese and rice*—what if Cunter's with them?

The thought nearly turns Turner's bowels to marble. But by the time he gets to Pazzaro's doors, he's over it.

Except for the douchey-looking guy with a mullet sitting by himself in a booth helping himself to a slice with what looks like some serious double-cheese—the joint's totally empty of customers.

Turner feels a wave of relief and then marches up to the counter.

"Can I help you?" a guy with a white apron and a tired voice asks.

"Maybe," Turner goes. "If I wanted to get a message to Dre, would you be able to deliver it?"

The guy just looks at Turner a hard second and then looks at the one guy chowing down in the booth. "No way. Not me. Only Jeff can do that."

"Well. Where's Jeff, man?"

"Ain't here. Be back in a little bit though. He had to go home and let his dog out. Said he'd be right back after."

"Cheese and rice. How long ago was that?"

"I don't know. Twenty minutes ago."

"How far away does Jeff live?"

The guy stares at Turner a second. "I ain't telling you where he lives, kid."

"That's great because I ain't asking where he lives. How far away in minutes is it? You know, so I can get some kind of read on when he'll be back. *Yo*?"

The guy's face relaxes a bit. "Just a couple. He lives in the trailer park back behind the alley."

"All right. Whatever. I *might* be back in five minutes," Turner goes and is about to leave, but then turns back to the counter. "Hey, you need to take any kind of test to work here?"

The guy shakes his head. "No. Just fill out an application. Why? You want one?"

"No," Turner goes. "But thanks though."

He doesn't see them until he's halfway through the alley, but once he does, he can't believe it. But there they are. On freaking lane number eight, wearing those gross beat-up bowling shoes. She looks like she's talking without breathing while he's punching in their names on the scoring keyboard.

"What the *fuck* are you guys doing?"

"*Jason*—you're in, right? Of course, he is," Maddie looks down at Luke, "Just mark him down."

Luke starts tapping Turner's name. Above, it pops up on the screen right next to theirs.

Did you do it? Luke holds his handheld up so Turner can read it. It was too loud to hear Luke's robot voice, and apparently, he forgot his pad.

Tuner shakes his head. "The guy I need to talk to was out. He might be back in few minutes though."

Luke starts tapping his handheld. Then let's bowl! No harm.

"Yeah, yeah," Turner goes and plops down in a seat behind Luke.

Maddie's the first up. Not that Turner's a bowling god or anything, but he knows enough to see Maddie doesn't have a freaking clue. In his opinion, the only thing she does right is bend over a little and stick her butt out.

She knocks down four pins and wheels around excited. She knocks three more with her second and it's suddenly high-fives all around.

Luke gets up, picks up his ball, steps up to the lane and zooms it down the lane without even aiming. The ball hits the pins, and they blow back like they were hit with a grenade. What's left is an impossible two-pin split, but Turner notices that people from four lanes over are peering down to see who flung such a violent ball.

Maddie just starts laughing. "What are you doing? You just rolled it and turned. You didn't even *see* what you did."

Luke's still just smiling and waves his hand down like *whatever*. He whips it down just as hard the second time and somehow knocks one of the pins into another lane.

Even Turner laughs at that. Some lane-jockey kid is out there fishing it out a few moments later, but what makes it funnier is that Luke turned away so quick again and sat down, he never saw the pin knock impossibly out of their lane.

"You're up, tough shit—" Maddie goes to Turner.

"I don't think so," he goes standing up. "No way I could follow that anyway. I'm gonna go check and see if the dickhead I need to talk to is here yet. Then we can get the hell out of here."

"Well, good luck, soldier," Maddie goes and then scoots into the seat next to Luke.

Turner peaks into Pazzaro's enough to see the guy he talked to mopping up the dining area floor. When the guy looks up, Turner calls out to him, "Hey—he here yet?"

The guy shakes his head. "Should be any minute now though—"

Turner turns back to the alley and thinks about what to do next. If they left, then he would have to come back later, and he really didn't want to take that chance. No matter what, when this Jeff guy finally did get back, he would know that Turner had been here and would surely tell Dre that some kid had been looking for him. Dre, of course, would realize it was Turner—but wouldn't know why. *No*—Turner thinks. Better to wait a few more minutes if he needed to and get it done right. *Gotta keep the plan moving forward.*

Even though the city-wide smoking ban had been in effect for decades, the freaking ordinance still couldn't vaporize the vast pre-ordinance decades of smoking that clung to every fiber of Al Skid's—and that burnt-pubes aroma was driving Turner psycho for a cigarette. His fingers were actually shaking he noticed. So, he opted for chocolate and caffeine. Turner would've killed for a Starbucks right there at that moment but that was pure *Pinocchio*-level wishful thinking, so he settles for a vending machine Hershey's bar and large fountain Coke.

On his way back to Maddie and Luke, he finds them sitting at the double scoring seats, facing each other. Her talking, and then him typing on his handheld, and then her hunched over reading.

Turner sits down on a seat right behind them and they carry on as if he isn't there—which was fine with him so he can devour his snack in peace—but he realizes it isn't just him—that to Luke and Maddie it's as if the entire bowling alley's walls had dissolved and blown into the night along with everyone and everything else, leaving the two of them in a place as peaceful as a nightsfield of crickets and fireflies.

Maddie finishes reading whatever was on Luke's handheld, her face looking all contemplative and then turns to look him in the eyes. "Yeah—like, I thought about that a lot, actually. I mean, my family's not super-religious for the most part, but we're not like hardcore atheists either. So, I would think, *hey*—if there's a god and an afterlife then *great!* You know? But if there's not—*then what*? I mean, if there's no after-death incentive, if there's no difference if you live with morals or not—what then? It used to freak me out a lot trying to really think what I thought about that. But *you*—wow. I just never heard an answer like yours. *Well...* Not till now at least."

Luke goes back to texting, and Turner takes a long tug on his Coke. When Luke's done, he shows Maddie his handheld and she nods some more and giggles.

"Oh—I know, *right*?"

Turner watches Luke tap more on his handheld and after she reads it, Maddie grabs Luke by the wrist, like it was involuntary, and agrees all hands-down with whatever it was he just wrote. At first Turner thinks this has got to be an act. Maddie's just another chick agreeing about some bullshit point in some supposedly deep bullshit conversation, all because she's talking with a hot guy. But by the time he finishes his candy bar, and slurps down the rest of his Coke, Turner's not so sure anymore. He's guessing they've been talking about life being so fragile and whatever, and how people really don't *live* all the time how they really wish they could. And they both go on about how normal that is and that it's OK to get discouraged when you catch yourself getting lazy and falling off track with how you wish you could be. I mean, nobody can be their best selves all the time, *right*? But it's what you do though *from there* that's truly important.

Maybe some of what they're saying is cheese-ass bullshit, Turner thinks, but maybe some of it's not. And maybe some of this is just a ridiculously hot guy flirting with a ridiculously hot girl—but then again, maybe there's more to it than just that, he thinks. But no matter what, Turner is pretty sure (even though he's not really privy to what Luke's writing) that these two sitting, facing each other before him, really *believe* in what they're talking about. It makes Turner think about what Carver had said about Luke. About how Luke's different than Carver. And as he sits there watching Luke, he thinks he can sense maybe what Carver was talking about—but certainly can't put his finger on it. Not yet anyway.

He gets up and doesn't even bother to tell them that he's going back to check if Jeff's here. He tosses his paper cup and wrapper into the trash can and looks back. Luke and Maddie are still just like they were—him typing away, Maddie reading and talking.

Whatever. And Turner heads back to Pazzaro's.

"Hey, *I'm* Jeff. You looking for me?" this graying pudge-bodied guy goes with a toothpick sticking out of the side of his mouth. He's wearing the same mostly-white apron as the other guys in Pazzaro's, except he's got this nifty blue pin sticking to his chest that says *Manager*.

"Yeah," Turner goes. "I want you to give a message to Dre."

"What do I look like, huh? A fucking *mailman*?"

"Nah. You look like a fucking ex-con trying to pass as a *pissant* pizza manager."

Jeff glares at him. "You got some mouth on you."

"Look," Turner tries to change up his tone, "I ain't looking to be an ass, I just want you to pass it to Dre that Lil Pops dropped by to say he almost has your money. Tell him I'll drop word soon about a pick-up through you. *Got it*?"

"And you're Lil Pops?" Jeff goes.

Turner audibly exhales. "*Yeah*, I'm Lil Pops. Give Dre the word. I'll be by in a week or so to have you give word about a pick-up."

Turner waits till Jeff nods that he understands what's going on. "So, Jeff—*you* need to pass a test to be manager here?"

Jeff's eyes narrow. "Get the fuck outta here. I'll give Dre your damn message. *Punk.*"

By the time Turner gets back to lane number eight, he sees Maddie and Luke are no longer in a frenzied discussion, but quiet and motionless. They're still sitting in the same seats, facing each other—but now all they're doing is looking at each other. Looking into each other's eyes like some kind of staring contest that he's just come in the middle of.

They're not touching, not even really in each other's personal space either, but Turner can't describe what they're doing as anything other than *intimate*. Looking at Maddie's face looking at Luke, Turner can't help but think back to how Rozzy used to look at him. When she would look at him, it was intimate too—it was like Rozzy was looking into him and seeing everything that was true about him. He felt so vulnerable with her when she did that, but he also felt so... *seen*. Even though he was embarrassed about how vulnerable Rozzy had made him feel sometimes—it was good to be *seen* like that, Turner thought. And even though the way Maddie looks right now is similar to what he had experienced with Rozzy—Maddie's look is different. It's something in the eyes. And that's when he notices it in Luke too. Their eyes—both Luke's and Maddie's—they're so *huge*. So open.

Surprised, Turner thinks. They both look surprised. Christmas morning eyes on faces that clearly know there's no such thing as Santa Claus and yet they still can't help but glow. They were not Rosalind Howard eyes, not the eyes of sad knowing, but the eyes of epic sunrise possibility. Jason thinks he might've been a little jealous of them both at that moment.

"Uh..." he mumbles. "I, um—saw the guy... *Sooo,* you guys ready to *go*?"

"We're ready," Maddie answers but still not taking her eyes off Luke.

And just like that, they both stand up and walk with Turner past the bustling nightlife of the alley and back into the parking lot.

They were all pretty quiet on the way to Maddie's house, with Maddie giving Turner the occasional cue to turn. Turner couldn't help muttering a *cheese and rice* once they entered Briarside and see all the *McMansions* lined up the curvy streets of the neighborhood. They pull up to this one with a Byzantine arch and columns on the freaking façade.

"That's me," Maddie goes and opens the door. "Jason, it's been a true pleasure rolling with you this evening. I hope you talked to all the dickheads you needed to tonight. And thank you so much for the ride." She reaches up and surprises him with a squeeze on his shoulder. "*Seriously.*"

He looks over at her. "Don't mention it. *Sweetheart.*"

Smiling, she gets out of the car and leans down to Luke's rolled down window. "And *you*—"

Luke looks up at her saying nothing.

"I feel like we just started a never-ending conversation," she goes and gives him a kiss on the cheek and rises to walk up her sloped driveway and through a door into the garage.

Turner and Luke sit there a minute with the car in idle. "I sure hope you know what the hell you're doing," Turner goes.

Luke turns back to the windshield and flings his index finger forward in a *let's drive* motion.

"Whatever you say, man." Turner puts it in reverse and presses the gas. "Whatever you say."

8

Jack Darringer, Hemingway welding teacher in the fall through spring, and certified hyperbaric welder aboard freighter ships in the summers, recalls the night when he and Luke finished the massive sculpture. It was the last day of April. All that was left was buffing and polishing. Lots and lots of buffing and polishing. The both of them went at it for nearly five hours straight that Saturday in Darringer's shop. The giant sword was the last piece they polished and that took two hours alone.

It was dusk by the time they finished, and they sat looking over the darkening yard toward the house on a couple of wooden chairs discarded from Hemingway several years ago. Darringer handed Luke an ice-cold glass bottle of root beer, while he uncapped a cold beer for himself. The two of them sipped their beverages all quiet and looking out at the lightning bugs zapping to life in the evening haze ahead of them. *My life's great work*, Luke had written, Darringer recalled at the start of the year when the big senior had come in to see him. It suddenly seemed like a thousand years ago.

After Luke had explained just what it was that he wanted Darringer to help him with, it took the teacher a whole week to think it over. But once he had said *yes*—Darringer was all in and realized there would be no way to complete a project like this without letting the kid work on it out here at his own place. And so just about every Saturday Luke would show up and faithfully work on this beast and Darringer couldn't help but admire both the boy and his work.

And even though Luke proved to be more and more mysterious the more he got to know him, Darringer had to admit he did have a true sense for the kid, the intangibles anyway. He remembers replaying this mental montage in his head while sitting there drinking his beer. He remembers drawing up the plans with Luke. Every minute detail. Collecting all the metal—a lot of it donated from Darringer's friends and acquaintances willing to part with quality steel for a good cause. And he remembers the work, bit by bit. The night's when they were done working where Darringer would tell Luke what it was like being at sea. Yeah, about the job of course—putting on the scuba gear, diving under the hull, seeing incredible sea life and all that. But also telling him about the sunrises. The sunsets. Darringer even let Luke in on his secret love of poetry, and how he would pack away volumes of Wordsworth, Yeats, Dickinson, Whitman, Byron and Keats, and of course his favorite, Tennyson—all of them and read them aloud when he was up on the deck at sunset after dinner. Darringer remembers helping Luke pick out the perfect piece of verse to go at the sculpture's base, and when he and Luke hugged like brothers at the last weld.

Darringer took another sip of beer and looked over to Luke. The boy was leaning back in his chair nursing his root brew and smiling back at him too. "I set up a meeting with Henderson for the week after next so we can discuss it."

Luke nodded.

"I'll let you know when he confirms," Darringer said.

Luke fished out his handheld and typed something in and then held it out to the teacher. **I need one more favor…**

Darringer laughed. "Why not? Shoot—"

Can I borrow a blowtorch for a couple weeks?

Darringer stopped smiling. "Why? This isn't for some lame senior prank, is it?"

No. Something noble. I promise.

"Oh, why not," Darringer said and took another swig. "Don't make me regret this, OK?"

Luke laughed; started to type. **Have you regretted anything we've done yet?**

"I guess not. Not yet," Darringer said. And he hadn't. He didn't say it then, but he remembers thinking at that moment, that this year had been the most rewarding in his whole teaching career, and Luke had been a big part of that. Darringer remembers thinking then that it was totally unfair to continue to think of Luke as a boy, or even as a kid, even in the most advanced sense of the word. Luke didn't look it. Certainly, he didn't talk it. Didn't act it. He realized for all intents and purposes this was a *man* sitting next to him and made a conscious decision then and there to always think of Luke as such.

He raised his bottle. "A toast—"

Luke tucked his handheld away and lifted his root beer too.

"To your life's great work. And what a piece of work it is."

They clinked bottles and chugged to the good toil of their hands.

9

Jason

OK, Rozz. It's been a while. But let's just put aside for a sec that you're dead, and I know you're fucking dead, and that I ain't got no more fucking delusions about how you can't actually hear me. It's just been a while and I miss writing to you. As I got more and more sober, I realized it was bullshit—you know, that you could hear me—but I still liked doing it. Liked writing it all out. It helped; you know? It helped to get it all out. To be able to see it on paper and make sense of all the fucked-up drama that was going on around me. And really—I guess that's why I'm writing right now—because the drama's still here like a motherfucking bitch that won't go away. And it might just help me to piece some of what I got going in my head out—in words and see if they gel. So let's just keep pretending a bit longer. OK? That you can hear me, and I can feel you, hovering right near me as I write this. You game? *Good.*

First off, I've been trying to run with Luke in the mornings. It's a real bitch, I ain't gonna lie. Ever since I dreamt I was in his body, I realized just how out of shape I am. And since I ain't smoking no more I figured what the hell? But fuck does it *suck!* My lungs and legs just burn when I'm doing it. I basically run with him to the soccer fields and take a nap while he plays fairy-ball with Isaiah, then I barely make it back to the house to shower before we gotta leave for school. But I gotta tell you, Rozz—once we're riding to school and I got a cup of coffee in my hand, this relaxed feeling comes over me. It's like ten times better than cigarettes. Luke just grins at me the whole time we're driving, because he must know this feeling because the bastard's worked out his whole life. But I gotta admit, girl—I feel fucking fantastic.

But it's not just my body lately that seems to be feeling better—it's my mind too, Rozz. It's ridiculous really. Like it's waking up from having this fuck-all mental nap and now my mind's totally wide-eyed, you know? It like tells me things now. Shows me details I'd been missing. Lines them all up so I can see everything all neat and fucking orderly, man. Like how I remember my moms lining up her shot glasses back when she lived with us. Before she got started in the morning. A row of three. Pour, down, repeat. Pour, down, repeat. On and on while I sat on the couch and watched kiddie videos on YouTube or whatever. That's how my thoughts are now, Rozz. But with me it's fucking two or three rows of three, man. Fucking orderly.

I think I finally figured out each piece about what went down this year between Dre and my dad. All except one. But anyway. Here's what it all boils down to close as I can figure it. Pops had been bumming out all last summer, I remember, about how Dre's price was like fucking immovable. It was too high. And Dre was always threatening to raise the price, not lower it. Which sucked for my dad because he had tons of low-rent junkies feeling the pinch and were seriously thinking of turning self-chef rather than pay top dollar for Pop's overpriced *christy*.

I remember Dad bitching about it out loud to himself and to me then, even though at the time, I didn't really know what he meant and really didn't give a shit either. You probably knew a lot more about the hard times with the traffic than I did, Rozz. In fact, I know you did, because you didn't hide it from me how it was getting harder and harder to scrape by as the summer went on.

Then, that two-way door, Kid T, let slip to me about *Sunrise*, and how Dre was making some big-time deals with some heavy-hitting cartel or mafia motherfuckers, which I've realized now couldn't have been to buy extra glass, because his price and supply seemed flat-lined. So the big deal had to be for the party psychos. It had to be for major shipments of premium X and shit like that. *Diversify*, Dre had said. Shit that sold in the subs all over Michigan—not the trailers. *Fuck* the trailers, Dre must've thought. At least the trailers in Dad's neck of the woods. So a huge chunk of Dad's clientele starves, while Dad's sitting on too much product he keeps having a harder and harder time moving.

So my dad courts Lester and his Shotgun Brothers. He fronts their home-lab and the tweakers cook up a shit supply of glass for the shit-end of his customer list. That was the plan anyway. But something got fucked up, Rozz.

That's the thing about two-way doors. Sooner or later, they slam shut and leave someone's ass out in the cold. Kid T sold Dad out. Had to have. He let Dre know what my dad had cooking with Lester, and when Lester put in a monster order—Dre sent in Kid and me, with Kid on orders to waste the fucker.

But Dad knew all about Kid T going turncoat on him. So my dad's the one who calls Lester in the first place and tells him to order the thirty eight-balls. Tells Lester to fucking blow Kid away in a shotgun ambush. Except my dad had no clue Dre would have Kid T *bring me*.

Cheese and rice, Rozz. Both of them—Dad and Dre—two clever, backstabbing, motherfuckers. And poor Kid was fucked no matter what.

And the rest is fucking history. Lester gets wasted and his deal with Dad gets wasted with him. Scotty's left thinking my dad screwed him and wants my fucking head on a plate because I was there when his house became the fucking *OK Corral*. Meanwhile, Dre and Dad have both shown each other a couple cards with the rest of the hand still left to play.

My only question is, Rozz—if you're Dre, why even waste energy trying to play with Dad? I mean, I know Dre's got product to move here, and Dad can move it—but what the hell? Dre can set up someone else to do that. Shit, Jeff from Pazzaro's could do it if they taught him and threatened to break his legs if he didn't do it right. So, why not take out my dad, like they probably took out Kid T, when he outlived his usefulness? Yeah, so—they kidnapped *me*, but they didn't maim or kill me to make their point—which Dre and Cunter both have the heart for. Instead, they just used me like some lame calling card threat.

See, Rozz—the only thing I can figure—the only thing that makes any fucking sense—is that Dad's got something on them. Ironclad with some heart on it. Something that Dre and Cunter both are afraid that, even if they take Dad out, it's still going to burn them.

Dad's got a failsafe somewhere. And it's just like him, Rozz. A smart, slimy, backstabbing, motherfucker. And whatever it is—it's the only thing that's been keeping him and me alive since this all blew up at Lester's.

Anyway, you would've loved today at school, Rozz. Your old pals, Kevin Wilhelm and Brian Legget both stepped up to me in the halls today after school. I was like surprised because I didn't think Kevin would have the balls to say jackshit to me anymore after our little 'moment' in the boy's bathroom a couple months ago. Yet here they were, two of my dad's high school caddies, thinking they're tough shit, stopping my ass in the hallway.

"Yo—Pops is done with you, man," Kevin goes.

"Yeah, no shit *K-van*. You told me that yourself like two months ago. Or are you having a flashback right now? Hitting your own product a little hard these days—"

"Yo, shut the fuck up. I know what I said. No asswipe—he's done *for real* now. We can fuck you up if we want. Hell, I can do more than that. Pops said he don't care if you get a Parabellum in the head after the shit you pulled."

"What are you talking about?" I go.

"You take a Suburban to get outfitted out at Ortiz's Garage?" Kevin goes.

I just start laughing, Rozz. "Why? My old man finally get the bill?"

"Yeah, fucking laugh, asswipe. Let's see how funny it is when someone comes to break your legs, or worse."

"Well, you boys know where to find me."

"Yeah," Kevin grins wide. "And so does Dre and his crew."

"You know Dre now?" I go.

Both he and Brian start chuckling now like a couple of cocained dogs. "Yeah, man. Your Pops called them direct and told them when it comes to you now, he ain't your blood no more. The hand of god's been lifted from your ass. You got no protection from anyone now."

"*Hand of god?* My dad ain't no god." No kidding Rozz, I take a step right up into their grills and put my best game face on. "If you two are smart, you'll walk out of school right now and quit the biz today. Like right the fuck. And go find yourself a lake to throw that pussy Baretta you're packing into. Because you better believe the hand of god ain't gonna be lifted up—*no*, it's coming down. And it won't be looking to protect nobody's ass when it hits."

It was priceless, Rozz. They just look at me like I'm nuts, and I walk past them. But hopefully what I told them about the hand of god does turn out to all come true. Because I got a plan, Rozz. And I'm carrying it out. Wish me luck, girl. Because it's all for you.

10

Hemingway's prom is always the first Saturday in May. And despite the cries from the kids with rich parents always wanting the dance to be moved to the large banquet hall at Indian Village's country club, prom is always held in Hemingway's gymnasium decked out to the hilt with all the sparkle and posh the student council budget can afford. And this year's prom was no exception in those regards.

But where it was different is that there was a bigger chunk of the HHS population that *didn't* go—or went but left way earlier—than normal.

So where was this missing piece of the usual prom-going demo of the Hemingway population?

Well, I can't speak for everybody else, but there were tons of us that basically said screw it to prom and all the after-parties and headed out to Volgstaad's cottage one more time for an alterna-prom blowout. It all started when Abby told Luke she just didn't think she could handle showing up to the dance, all ready to pop at any moment with tons of people snapping photos all over the place after he'd offered to take her. Then a few days later, Maddie shocked most of us—especially Dallas—by saying she didn't feel much like going either and why not hold a party of our own? Well, that's all Erik needed to offer his cottage again, so everybody started brainstorming ideas—and the whole event was born.

The big soiree kicked off with about fifteen of us gathering around the table of Vogstaad's screened-in porch feasting on a bunch of pizzas from DiNoto's after we had set up the cottage's back yard and grounds for the festivities. Volgstaad made a toast and we all held up our red plastic cups of Coke or Mountain Dew or whatever—while Turner held up his coffee cup. Most of us that had been involved since *hemingwayownit* were all there, except for Gala Sarah and her crew who opted to hit prom first and then swing by later—so I was bummed, but not too bummed since they were just all going as one big group and she didn't really have a like real 'date' per say.

At dusk, Erik and Ryan got the bonfire going and Tristan, Turner, and me went around with lighters and lit up the fifty or so Tiki torches staked out in the woods in and around the pond. The whole place looked like a magical elfin grot on the freaking cheap. But no matter what you thought of Tiki torches, you couldn't say the place wasn't atmospheric. There had been talk about lugging Dickie's huge speakers out there and pumping the place with jams—but it got nixed in favor of a more low-key and eerie vibe.

It seemed the moment night fell, the cars started showing up. There were no real invitations that got sent out or anything—but word had spread anyway—which was fine, because I think we all wanted the event to be pretty open. I remember I wasn't the only one curious about who would show up out there if it was freaking all *carte blanche* about who wanted to come or not. Most of them were kids that had helped so far over at the soup kitchen, but there were also a bunch that had just recently thawed towards us and what we'd been doing at Hemingway the last few months. Others were probably just hangers-on, looking for the next good time—but whatever. They came around from parking their cars in front to join us in the back. The fire circle became a small swirl of souls; bodies and faces around the orange glow. Some of them actually brought bags of chips or drinks or whatever and put them on the folding table Erik had fished out from underneath the cottage's carport and set up back there. There was no beer, no booze—nada on the weed and pills too. Well, *almost*—on my way to get a refill and some food I did catch a peek of a couple of guys tipping some airplane-sized rums into their sodas. But all that was kept down low out of respect for the soccer guys, I guess, and their well-known adherence to the school's activity code.

On my way back to the fire circle, I noticed Abby pulling Luke along going into the trees in the direction of the pond.

"So, when's she actually due? Anybody know?" Tristan goes as I sit back down.

"June first," Turner goes.

"Man, that's like in just a couple weeks," Tristan goes.

"Yeah—*duh*, dude," Patrick goes and laughs at him.

"Shut up, man. All I'm saying is that she's close. Like she could have her baby like any day. That's like major."

"Yeah, it's like *major*, Tristan," Dallas goes, rolling her eyes.

"So—she really gonna give it up for adoption?" Tristan continues.

"*Her*. It's a girl. And *yes*, Tristan—she's really going to put her up for adoption. She's already met the parents and everything," Maddie goes.

Tristan starts munching on a chip. "Man. I can't imagine. You think she ever has second thoughts? Like maybe what if she keeps it—I mean *her*—and, I don't know, like marries Luke or something?"

"*Dude*—" Patrick shakes his head.

"What?" Tristan goes.

"Look here, youngen—that's like all Abby's business, see?" Dallas goes. "You don't need to be sticking your nose into it. Just sit back, eat your little chips, and support her like we all doing and see how it all plays out. *OK*?"

Erik stands up and looks down at Maddie. "You want to go for a walk?"

"Hmm," Maddie goes. "How long have you been sitting there working up the courage?"

"Don't flatter yourself. I thought of it just now."

"*Whatever*," Ryan mumbles and Dallas raises an eyebrow.

"Well, why not?" Maddie goes and then holds out her hand so Erik can help her up. We all watch them disappear into the woods behind the line of Tiki torches.

"So now—" Ryan goes. "I wonder who else is going to hook up tonight?"

"*Oh, I think you'd be surprised…*" I hear Turner whisper.

"Why? You wanna go on a walk with me?" Patrick goes.

Ryan laughs. "Nah. Sorry, dude. You're not my type."

"That's OK. I know you got a serious jones for Dickey here," Patrick goes as Dickey comes bounding up carrying a cardboard box.

"All right guys—it's time, man!"

"Time for what?" Dallas goes.

Dickey plops the box down. "For glow-in-the-dark-tag! Let's get it on!" He opens the box up and starts handing out these necklaces of glowsticks tied with string and a glowing super ball with a hole drilled in the middle of it.

"Aw cool!" Tristan goes.

"No. *Not* cool. What are we? In the second grade again?" Gray goes.

"Oh, come on—it'll be fun," Dickey goes.

"What the hell—why not?" Patrick goes and slings a necklace around his thick neck. "Come on everybody, let's do this or Dickey'll never shut up about it."

Within minutes there's suddenly like thirty kids running around all berserk in the dark with their glowing necklaces all slinging around. I had to admit, it did look pretty fun. But I wasn't out there. I was still sitting next to Turner around the fire, with him sipping at his coffee, looking at the flames, while I took a swig of my soda looking over at him.

"So what did you mean before?" I go.

"What do you mean, *before*?"

"Like about being surprised about who would hook up."

Turner just starts grinning. "Man—appearances can be deceiving. That's all. Except maybe in your case."

That caught me off guard. "What's that mean?"

"Come on, Caxton. I know exactly why you're sitting here when I know for a fact you'd love to be frolicking out in the woods there with your glo-buddies."

"And why's that?" I go.

"Well, I'd wager that you're waiting around for a certain someone of the female gender who has luscious brown skin and's got a face that makes you look embarrassed every time you're in the same room with her."

I immediately get embarrassed, of course, and shrug.

"Don't even try to deny it, man. But it's OK, you know. Ain't nothing wrong with liking a girl. Especially somebody as cool as Gala," Turner goes.

"Well. Thanks, I guess. I just want to be here when she gets here, you know…" I go and turn around and check for like the hundredth time.

"Hey, man. I understand," he raises his coffee cup. "Good luck with that."

What Erik remembers doing as he and Maddie walk off into the dark trees, is trying to muster up the sac to take her hand. But before he can, she goes, "So, how far are we going here?"

Erik swallows. "Uh, you mean in the woods?"

"Uh, yeah."

"Here's good," he goes. He knows what he wants out of this. Part of him still can't believe he's gotten even this close to her. His Holy Grail of girls. His life-long crush of crushes. The thunder and lightning of his heart. Even with her here in the dark, where he can just make out the stubborn of her chin, he knows he's snared by her aura—her beauty.

Raucous shouts and laughter start coming from everywhere. Erik turns and sees scattered green-glowing necklaces sprinting and stumbling all through the woods and around the pond.

"What is *that* all about?" Maddie goes and laughs, further intoxicating Erik in the shadows next to her.

"*Dickey*. It's all Dickey and his games."

Every hormone in Erik's raging body is telling him to make his move, while his mind is telling him not to push it. To savor everything about this moment with her. To play it slow. Be mature. Be the man Maddie could fall *in* love with. But he catches a trace of her perfume mixing with the moist pines, and he just can't take it anymore. As she's still giggling at some poor glow-in-the-darker tripping and probably face-planting in the woods just ahead of them, Erik leans over and kisses her cheek.

"Well, *hi*—" she turns to him. "So, you're taking it there, huh?"

"I guess so. If that's OK."

"Maybe. I guess it depends on what you do next…"

"Do you like me?" Erik goes.

"Of course, I like you."

As much as he likes being out with Maddie in the dark, Erik can't help thinking at this moment that he wishes he could see her face as she says this.

"Do you *like* me like me?" he goes.

"Wow. That's a little point blank, isn't it?"

"Yep. Go for broke. Cards on the table. Hauling out the big guns. Take your pick what to call it."

"Well, I don't know about hauling out the *big guns*—"

They both laugh at that, but Erik hast to fight this urge to just ask Maddie outright about how much sex she actually had with Dylan Sorensen. Did she really *do* him? If *yes*—how many times? Is it really true you let him do you up the, uh…um, up the you-know-what before you broke up?

But he knows he would tank it all if he asked such a thing now. Only an idiot would go there. *Not. My. Business.* So, with a super-human will, he stuffs all that away and tries to stay focused.

"So, I take it you really *like* like me, huh?" she goes.

Erik nods in the dark and moves his face closer again. "*Caught*."

"You've felt this way for a while now, haven't you?"

"You have no idea…"

"Before high school even?"

"Before middle school even. You should remember."

Erik feels her hand on his cheek. "You poor boy…"

"Yeah. That's me," he goes.

She takes her hand away. "One question though. What was with drilling me with that snowball in fifth grade then?"

"Ugh—*that*? I'm so damn sorry about that. In my defense though, you should've never let Sabrina Dostel read my card. She was brutal to me that day."

"What are you talking about? What card?"

Erik goes rigid. "What do you mean *what card?* My Valentine's Day card. The one I revealed my feelings for you in."

"Oh my god," Maddie goes.

"What?"

"That's what she did. Sabrina Dostel. That Valentine's Day, she came over to my house and I caught her rifling through my Valentine's box after I had left the room to go to the bathroom. She had this weird vibe about her after I came back too. I always thought she took some of my cards that day. I was pretty sure I was missing some from a few boys."

Erik boggles. "You mean—you like never—I mean, never, saw my card?"

"I am so sorry. Yep, not ever. I had no idea, Erik. I mean, Sabrina told me later that you had told some boys you wanted to hump me behind the school, but I didn't really believe that. I mean she was always telling me which boys wanted to hump me behind the school. She was always lying just to start something."

"That little *bitch…*"

"So, you pelted me with that snowball because you thought I was just ignoring your note?"

"And that *you* were the one making fun of my feelings. Not just Sabrina," Erik goes.

Maddie just starts laughing. "After all these years…"

Erik laughs too. "I guess…"

"So, what did it say?"

"The card?"

"Yeah. What did you write me?"

Erik shrugs. "I don't remember."

Maddie hits him on the shoulder. "Oh yes you do, you're just trying to hide it. Come on—why be all coy and bashful about it now? What did it say?"

Erik, of course, remembers it exactly. He remembers every moment he spent agonizing over what to write up in his room the night before. And now, finally—here was his chance to get it right.

"It said, *Dear Maddie, I think you're OK. Maybe even better. Erik.*"

"*OK, maybe even better*, huh?"

"Yep."

And then she's quiet. Erik remembers the shouts of the others going more distant, the sight of their glowing horde moving farther away from them. He sees her form step closer to him. He feels her lips peck his cheek.

"You poor boy," she coos.

Erik can fight it no longer and moves in with his mouth seeking hers. He finds it and locks their lips while wrapping her in a frail embrace. She doesn't resist, but he will only realize later that he can't remember her escalating any intensity. But that doesn't matter to him now. His whole world becomes their kissing, and he feels the years of longing begin to break and the promise of that longing's release surges upon him. He kisses her deeper. Brings his hand from her left shoulder to the top of her chest and slowly, but inevitably moves it down to her breast.

And she slowly pulls a step away.

Erik stands there breathing in all shallow panting, not knowing if he should feel ashamed or overjoyed over what just happened.

Maddie steps forward again and takes his hand. "Do you want to be here with me?" her voice a whisper.

"Yes," he goes.

"Then be here with *me*. Not just my body. But with *me*. Can you do that?" she goes.

"I can. I know I can."

She raises his hand back to her shoulder and steps into his arms. The side of her head cradles into his face. Erik nearly swoons from the smell of her hair upon his cheek.

An aromatic rush of sun-dried apples, sugar cookies, and maybe a dash of waterfall. *Easy tiger*, he says to himself.

He hears a huge splash in the pond but makes no move to try and see which glowing moron cannon-balled in there, because at this moment of moments, Erik simply does not care. Not when he's finally got Maddie O'Leary in his awkward arms. Let them all jump into the pond if they want, buck naked, if need be, but Erik Volgstaad isn't moving.

"I've named her," Abby goes, the Tiki torches light flickering across her face.

Luke nods slowly and waits for her to tell him the name.

"Clara. Clara Lynn. What do you think?"

Luke put his handheld away and reaches to his back pocket to haul out his notebook.

Clara Lynn Browne?

At reading the note, Abby is hit with waves of emotions. She suddenly feels all over the place. Her insides a sea roiling with all sorts of uncertainty and nebulous guilt. Tears streak from her eyes as she looks at Luke and is unable to say anything, only quiver and cry.

Luke moves over on the bench they're sitting on and holds her for a while as they look over the dark water of the pond made seemingly blacker by the reflection of the Tiki torches.

"I just… I can't decide, you know?" she's finally able to mutter. "For months and months, I was fine with it. It wasn't a big deal. Once I decided I wasn't going to have an abortion, it just seemed so settled in my mind that I would carry her, and then I would give her to some good people and that would be it. *But—*" her lower lip begins to quiver. "But somewhere, at some point it just all changed. I don't know how it changed. But it did. It changed and I don't know if I can give her up. *Luke*—I don't know. I don't know if I can—"

He held her some more. After a while, he tried to dry under eyes with the palm of his hand.

It's up to you. You can still do whatever is best.
Best for yourself. Best for Clara. It's not too late.
Your family. Friends. We're gonna love you no matter what.

Abby can feel the tears welling up again but fights them off and nestles into Luke. Luke puts his pen and pad down and takes her hand.

"It's so *heavy*," she goes, "this decision. I just feel the weight of it all. Just how big a deal it is. And it's worse because all I have to do is look down at myself and I'm reminded that I'm a ticking time bomb. I feel the literal *weight* of it all in my body. My feet. My hips—oh my god, Luke—my *hips*—"

Luke suddenly stands up and looks down at her and then looks at the pond, then back to her.

"*What?* What are you doing?"

He grins and then leaps, fully clothed into the pond. Abby moves her feet to keep from being splashed. Luke's upper half emerges from under the water in a splash almost as big as the one he made jumping in.

Matt Glendening stops his glo-sprinting to gawk at them. "Whoa—Hey, Luke's going swimming? Pond party?"

Luke spits the water dripping onto his lip and extends his hand to Abby to join him.

"Uh-uh. No way."

He takes a big splashy step towards her and keeps his hand out, a little more demanding.

Abby just keeps shaking her head. "Are you crazy? I'm not getting in there. It looks cold. Besides I'm super-pregnant, not to mention I have no change of clothes here."

Luke apparently doesn't care about her protests because he just ups and grabs her and picks her up, pregnant belly and all and carries her screaming back into the pond.

Abby seriously considers hitting him in the face at this point, but then she notices the look he's giving her—which isn't all mischievous which she was expecting—but more calm and even affectionate. And then he stuns her by actually mouthing words to her. She couldn't make it out at first, but then she repeats, "*lie back*?"

Luke nods.

She can feel the cold water now that smells like mud and grassy frog stuff, but she decides to trust him and allows herself to lie down in his arms. She can feel his strong arms under her, straightening her out. She begins to get used to the chill of the water. It's crazy, but it begins to feel relaxing. The water laps her ears. This bothers her at first, but then it actually starts to have a calming effect. She wonders fleetingly if being deaf is like trying to hear while being a few feet underwater. Abby sees the moon all full in its glory. And then, as if they had all been secretly waiting for this moment for her to be lying in the pond like this with Luke, Dickey Swartz lights the first round of his fireworks. The sky above them bursts alive with sparkling red and goldspark weeping willow streams of fire-glitter. She moves her head slightly so she can see Luke's face. He smiles down at her while another round of fireworks lights up his eyes. She half-hears the cheers and voices of the kids out in the woods and by the fire circle with each coming and going of the pond's tiny waves against her ear.

And then she realizes what he's done.

Happier tears now christen her cheeks and run down to join the pondwater.

"Thank you," she whispers to him. "*Thank you*—"

And even if it doesn't last, at least for a while, there—in the Volgstaad's pond—Abby Browne feels *weightless*.

11

The Monday after prom was the last soup kitchen in Detroit. Well, at least until August. Pastor Mike said it had something to do with getting their permit re-issued with the city or something like that. So, a lot of us made it out to serve and say goodbye to some of the kitchen regulars that we had gotten to know. It was kind of a bittersweet deal, you know? It also had a weird feel to it too because it was the only time that Luke wasn't at the kitchen. Abby wasn't feeling too good that night and she asked Luke to stay behind to keep her company. Everybody understood, I guess. I mean we all knew she could totally go into labor like any day, and it probably wasn't a good idea for her to be stranded way out here in the most dangerous part of Detroit when she did.

But because of Luke's absence, I guess that's why Turner texted me and asked if I wanted to ride out there *with* him—which totally took me by freaking surprise. I was even more surprised when we picked up Tristan and Gray too. I guess we'd all been noticing it though. You know, Jason Turner *changing*, I guess. Somewhere along the line he seemed to soften that edge he always seemed to have around us. It was weird, but I think all of us started thinking of him less and less as just Luke's pet project or whatever, and more and more as our *friend*. I know. It was crazy. Jason *freaking* Turner.

Anyway, once we get there, I see Jason make a freaking b-line for his favorite ghetto old timers. But as Jason makes his way across the room, he makes eye contact with a skeletal white dude wearing a blue stocking cap. Jason recognizes him immediately from that night in the rec. center. Cunter's sword fight. Thing One. Jason just nods to him, the junkie nods back. Water under the freaking bridge between them, I guess.

"Well, look what the wind blew in," Bernie goes as Jason takes a seat at their table.

"Hey at ease, guys. Don't let me keep you from your pie there," Jason goes.

"This is some good eating tonight. Tell you what. Your pastor friend done pull out all the stops. I ain't had good barbeque in years now," Lawrence goes as he shakes Jason's hand.

"Well, you best eat your fill now, because they won't be no more for a while to hear the pastor tell it," Thelma goes. "They's shutting this all down till the end of summer."

"Yeah—I heard," Jason goes. "Look, I want to thank you for all the texts and all the spying you guys have been doing for me."

"Well, for being a bunch of thug drug dealers, they's sure run office hours over there. I never noticed it till you had us looking—but they's like clockwork," Thelma goes.

Jason nods. "Well, that's what I wanted to know."

"Lawrence," Bernie goes. "Go on now—tell him. Tell him about the other cats and the cars."

"What *cats*?" Jason goes.

Lawrence leans in closer. "They come every week. On Tuesdays. At eight o'clock in the morning."

"Tell him about the cars," Bernie goes.

"They roll in a caravan of three vehicles now. Two of them are these black GMC Yukon Denali's. They look brand new right off the lot. They got one Yukon in front and one rolling in the back."

"What do they got in the middle?" Jason goes.

"Oh, they got their bossman. And his driver. And they's rolling in style. Jaguar XK. I believe they call it cobalt blue. *Whew-wee*—a V8 engine to make you drool, if you're into that kind of thing," Lawrence goes. "See, the first Yukon pulls up right there in front of the rec. center and these five guys get out. They fan out all over the place like they's the marines or some shit. Two guys even go across the street behind a building over there. I don't know if they're looking out for cops or what. But one thing's for sure—ain't *nobody* going to be creeping up on these boys."

"What do they look like?" Jason goes.

"*Aw*—they white, but they don't look American. They speak some thick-sounding language too."

"Spanish? Portuguese?"

Lawrence and Bernie snicker. "Not that I would understand one goddamn thing in Portuguese, son—but if I had to bet, I'd guess these guys are from Europe. Like Serbia or Russia or something."

Jason nods. So, they're *not* cartel. Well, I guess Kid T knew less than he thought, Jason thinks. "OK. So, what do the other guys do?"

"The two guys in the Jag are wearing suits and sunglasses. They go in to see your buddies Dre and Cunter. I know this because those other two—"

"Sin and Tagger—"

"Yeah. Sometimes they's there, sometimes they ain't."

"That figures. It's Dre and Cunter that are in charge."

"Yeah, so—the two suits go in with these other four guys out of the other Yukon. And those guys haul out these three big metal boxes. Hefty suckers. I wouldn't want to carry them."

"How long are they in the rec. center?"

"Ten minutes tops. Then they come back out with the same boxes, load back up and peel out in that same caravan formation," Lawrence goes.

"You reckon they's picking something up—or dropping something off?" Bernie goes.

"*Both*," Jason goes. "My guess would be both."

"They's something else, son. All's them out of the Yukons had automatic weapons slung under their jackets," Lawrence goes.

"You know what types?"

"You mean the guns?"

"Yeah," Jason goes.

"*Shit*. I know cars not guns. But who cares? Even I can tell they's got heavy *muthas*. Huge clips, son. All gangstas and cops better beware," Lawrence goes. "Point is—these are some big hitters with muscle from outside the country which means they smuggling."

Jason thinks for a second. "They always roll with eleven guys each time?"

Lawrence nods. "Every Tuesday. Always the same eleven too from what I can tell."

"You ever hear any of them call the suit *Sunrise*?"

Lawrence shakes his head. "Already said. I can't understand what they's saying."

"Look now, how much longer you wanting us to be doing this for?" Thelma goes.

"Just for a couple more days. And then that'll be enough for me," Jason goes.

"Now *huny*—you're not thinking of going over there at all—*are you*? Because those boys be like to kill you on sight now."

Jason pats her hand. "*No*, I'm just curious that's all. I just wanted to know what I almost got messed up in. Just see how big it was. Now I know."

"Well, I hope so, son. Because you know now what curiosity did to that cat, right?" Lawrence goes.

Jason stands up and gives them a smile. "No worries, Lawrence. Besides, you know I ain't no pussy cat."

As Jason heads back to help Dickey with breaking down the beverage containers, Maddie O'Leary comes and walks along beside him.

"*Hey*."

"Uh, hey," he goes back.

"Can you do something for me?"

He groans. "Don't tell me you need a ride home again."

"No. Dallas and I are staying late to help Pastor Mike clean up anyway. I need you to do something else. It's painless, I promise."

"It better be. What is it?"

She hands him a small envelope. "It's for Luke."

"You know he's hanging out with Abby right now, right?"

"Of course, I know that. Can you just give it to him, *please*?"

Jason sighs and holds it up with a little shake.

She smiles at him. "Thanks," she goes and starts walking away.

"I don't get it," he calls after her. "Why don't you just text him?"

Maddie turns. "Luke and I don't text."

Whatever, Jason thinks.

A while later, after the cafeteria was all clear of diners and most of the students and volunteers had cleared out, Dallas and Maddie were almost finished scrubbing these big Nemco food warmers while Pastor Mike and a couple of retirees mopped the floors. The place had to be spotless before they locked it down or vermin would likely home in on it before they re-opened it in August.

By the time Maddie and Dallas were finished, said their goodbyes to Pastor Mike, and finally headed out to Maddie's car in the elementary school's parking lot, it was nearly eleven o'clock. And from there, here's what we know for sure. We know that Maddie unlocked her mom's jade Mercedes sedan hybrid and they both got all the way into their seats before the guy showed up. We know the guy was white. He was wearing a flannel shirt and had an old blue stocking cap on that had *Ford* printed on it. Dallas remembers his face being almost like a skeleton, but with tight blotchy skin and rotting teeth. (Jason later will be ninety-nine point nine percent certain this is the same tweaker he crossed baseball bats with at the rec. center that night.) He approached the driver's side and said something that Dallas couldn't make out. Then he pulled out the snub nose .38 and yelled for them to get out of the car.

At this point both the girls screamed.

Maddie threw her purse out at the guy's feet and told him to take it. But that apparently made the guy furious according to Dallas because he yelled "Are you stupid, bitch? I said, *get out of the car*," while saliva dripped out of his mouth.

Maddie screamed again and said, "No—it's my *mom's!*"

And then he hit her. That first blow with the revolver split her scalp at the top of her skull and likely rendered her unconscious. That's what we all hope anyway. Because that was just the guy's warm-up. It was the second, third, and fourth blow where the guy was really feeling the adrenaline.

But right after Maddie took that first hit, that's when Dallas likely saved her own life and got out of the car and started sprinting back inside the cafeteria. While she was running, the guy yanked Maddie's body to the pavement and unloaded three blows to the left side of Maddie's face, caving it in just below her eye. He drove off in the Mercedes before Pastor Mike made it outside with a mop still in his hands.

Maddie's funeral would be closed casket.

12

Isaiah

I went with the guys to Maddie's funeral today. The church was packed with people—even more than for my dad's funeral. It seemed every kid at Hemingway was there. I figured somebody like Maddie would be popular. I mean, anybody that nice has got to have a lot of friends. But *wow,* I just didn't think there would be that many people there. Some even had to stand in the back or off to the sides against the walls. I recognized so many of their faces from soccer games or hanging out at Luke's a couple times. So many nice big kids. It was sad to see them now in mourning for their friend.

I feel so bad for Erik. I know he loved her so much. I know he wanted her to be his girlfriend. Maybe even his wife someday. He had tears in his eyes the whole time. I sat with him on one side and Luke on the other. Most of the team sat together, just like they did at my dad's, but Jason was there with us too, and in the row ahead of us was Abby and Dallas and a bunch of these new people that are always hanging around the guys now.

Abby's going to have her baby soon. She moves so slow. She looks like a mom already now. She looks older—but in a good way. She sat next to Dallas who was just bawling the whole time too, sometimes so loud I thought she would break apart. Abby put her arm around her and held her head to Dallas's. It was so sad and beautiful seeing them like that.

When the service was over, everybody kind of took their time leaving. There were a lot of sad hugs and hushed talking. Maddie's family followed the casket outside to go to the cemetery for their final goodbyes, and Ryan told me that the graveside service was for family only and that we would go home soon.

As we were making our way through the crowd, Erik saw this tall preppy guy, whose name that I found out later was Dignan Cooper. Anyway, Erik got real ticked for some reason at this guy and started saying real quiet but real intense, "That prick. Who's he think is? She was *never* his. He probably thinks she died having a crush on him. That *freaking—*"

"Knock it off," Ryan said, trying to pull Erik back.

"Don't tell me to knock it off. I can say what—" Erik said, but then Luke reached over and grabbed his arm, *hard*. Erik looked all mad at Luke then for a little, but Luke just kept staring at Erik and then Erik seemed to loosen up and drop whatever it was he was so mad about with that Dignan guy.

Erik said he needed to go home and pushed his way out of the church. I started to chase after him since he and Ryan were the ones that brought me, but Ryan held me back.

"Hey—Jason," Ryan said while keeping his hand on my shoulder. "I'll go look after Erik. Can you guys take Izzy home though?"

"Yeah," Jason said. "No problem."

I got into Jason's beat up back seat and me, him, and Luke started driving home. None of us talked as Jason rolled us through town. The sun was going down and it was still warm. The whole day had been so beautiful really, I mean, as far as weather goes. I guess it happens a lot in life. Bad things happen. People you love die. But the sun still comes up. Your life can get turned upside down, but there will still be summer. Still be blue skies and pleasant breezes sometimes.

I was thinking this stuff in the quiet of Jason's car when I noticed Luke's shoulders kind of moving up and down over and over in the seat in front of me. At first it just looked weird to me, like Luke was screwing around or something, but then I heard him sniff and then I knew. He was crying. I guess I don't know why I was so surprised really. For some reason, I guess I thought guys like Luke were just too tough to cry. Or too big, maybe, even though that sounds so dumb now.

I looked at Jason and he just kept looking straight ahead on the road. But I knew he knew Luke was crying too. I mean, he *had* to know. He was sitting right next to him.

I unbuckled my seat belt and put my hand on Luke's shoulder just to let him know I was there. That I cared, I guess. He didn't turn around to face me. Maybe he didn't want me to see him like that, I don't know. I didn't know what else to do, so I just stayed that way—leaning forward in my seat with my hand on his shoulder.

"You're a good kid, Izzy," Jason said, still looking out at the road.

I didn't know what to say to that, so I just stayed quiet.

"The best of us if you ask me," he said and then I felt Luke's hand pat my hand on his shoulder. I got this thought then, like maybe, just maybe, I was finally doing something for Luke like he'd been doing for me all year. It made me feel good. Made me finally feel useful.

I guess I just had no idea that Luke and Maddie had been real good friends too.

13

The night of Maddie's funeral I went to school. I was almost certain it would be all closed and locked up—but I really wanted a notebook I had left in there. I had already begun taking notes—well, I thought of them as journals really, on some of these people—my friends—and all the stuff I had written on Maddie was in that notebook in my locker.

Well, I got freaking lucky. The school was open. Turns out there was some big school board meeting or something going on, so I was able to slip up to the second floor. I got my notebook and was all set to leave when, kind of on a lark, I peeked down one of the hallways. I saw that Mr. Malory's door was open.

When I poked my head in, I saw him at his desk reading some sheets of loose-leaf paper.

He suddenly looks up at me all startled. His eyes are red with tears. "Oh, Will. Sorry, I didn't know you were there."

"Sorry. I'm leaving. I just came to pick up a notebook. I saw your door—"

He swipes one hand over his eyes and straightens up into his chair. "No—come in. Since you're here, you might as well see something. Saw you at the funeral today."

"Yeah," I go.

"It's a record for me," he goes, and I roll up a chair from his computer station.

"What is?"

"Two student funerals in one year. I hope it never gets broken."

"Who was the first?"

"Rosalind Howard. You remember her, right? At the start of the year?"

Well, *duh*—I think and feel like kicking myself for sounding so moronic asking him who the first was.

"I had Rosalind as a junior all last year. She was smart as a whip, that one," he goes and flashes me this sad smile. "She just had so many *problems*... I only wish... I don't know. I do not know, Will. It's easy to sit here and wish in times like these."

"So—how was Rozzy's funeral?" Again, I realize the moment I say it, what a stupid question. *Sheesh.*

Mr. Malory just looks at me a second and goes, "Well, it was fine—I suppose. As fine as a funeral can be when it's in memory of someone who was so tragically young. But Rosalind's was a bit *different* than our Madeline's today."

"How so?"

"Let's just say Maddie's was better attended and leave it at that."

He was right of course. I couldn't think of anyone I knew other than Jason maybe that had gone to Rosalind Howard's funeral. Practically everyone I knew was at Maddie's.

"So, what do you want to show me?" I go.

He looks down to the two sheets of paper on his desk. Both handwritten, but with different scrawls. "Rosalind loved poetry. She rarely did any of her assigned reading—but was voracious in her consumption of extracurricular classics. She would come in sometimes going on and on about this and that poet she looked up online and ask questions about them and their poems. She'd grill me on my interpretations, and I would play devil's advocate and ask her about her own. I loaned her books. She said she would much rather read good poems out of a *kick ass old-school hardcover* than online if given a choice. She said the Internet sucked the souls from the verses. I just happen to agree with her on that score, so I gave her volumes from my own collection. Hardcovers, leather bounds. Old, tan, parched paper. Dusty covers, that sort of thing. She loved it. And the one she loved the most was Keats. Do you know Keats, Will?"

I shook my head.

"Well, looking back on it now, Keats probably wasn't the healthiest reading material for Rosalind. Given Keats's renowned love affair with death. But I had no idea then. I was just happy to have a student so hungry—so *alive* for poetry. The teacher in me couldn't do anything but foster her passion for the art." He looks down at his hands and splays his fingers over the two sheets of paper. After he stretches them to their limit, Malory closes his knuckles tight, making two fists.

"I'm such a fool, Will."

"No, you're not," I go. "You couldn't have known she'd do that to herself. There's no way."

He looks at me and the calm returns to his eyes. "I know that. I really do. It's just—I don't *feel* that."

"Yeah," I go.

"This right here is a note that Rosalind gave me the morning she killed herself. I had loaned her a couple of books over the summer, and she came in early that morning and returned them," he goes and then holds up the sheet. "I didn't find this until about a week later when it fell out of my volume of Keats when I opened it up."

"What's it say?" I go, unable to keep myself from asking.

"It's a *thank you* note. She also told me not to feel guilty. That her decision was not inspired by any poem and that her death would serve a greater purpose in time. Whatever *that* means."

Malory reaches down to pull on his glasses. He holds Rozzy's note up and reads aloud, "*I've been ripped apart in this life it seems. My mind and spirit seem torn too. I'm not complaining. Some of this I deserve. But even though the horrors I deal with are very much mine, I'm not the only one here suffering. Look around, Mr. Malory—there are kids everywhere that are suffering just as bad as me—kids—all of us, every kind of us—it doesn't matter our skin, our money, our friend-status, whether we're gay or straight, cis or trans—I see all of us, I see myself—we are legion in our fucking melatonin-induced zone-states caught in our never-ending swipe and scroll screen-scapes, all of us drowning in a dysentery ocean of worry, worry, worry. While inside us an alien of anxiety bursts through our chests and swims away from us with what's left of our hearts in its acidic jaws.*

And yet.

And yet I believe…

This world and everyone in it are worth saving.

My condition has given me a glimpse at my part. On one hand, it's horrible and terrifying. But some peace would be nice. It would be nice to think and dream, but not like I do now. It's a sleep I go to. A sleep that all of us will find eventually. And yes, maybe the place I'm off to will be dark ahead. But my heart tells me, Mr. Malory, that it won't be an eternal darkness though. It won't be like sitting forever in a lightless and silent room. I think where I'm finally going, there will be poetry. And dreams. Dreams exploding with every color.

If it exists, I bet my soul on it.

Your faithful student,

Rozzy Howard."

"Wow. *That's—*" I go. "...*Wow.*"

Malory puts the paper down. "It is what it is. Now. I want you to read this on your own," he picks up the other sheet of paper.

"Whose is *this*?"

"*This*—Will, is Maddie's in-class writing assignment on *Frankenstein*."

I look at him and narrow my eyes. "Uh, you want me to read her homework?"

Mr. Malory takes off his glasses and rubs his temples a little. "I can't tell you why, exactly. I can't seem to even trust my own thoughts on this, *but—*" he sighs. "But I *feel*—or rather, *sense* a symmetry here between these two young ladies. I just can't put a finger on it and it's, along with some profound grief, been eating at me all day."

"*Symmetry?*"

"Look, Will—just read it and tell me what you think of it."

"Is this all of it? I mean it seems—"

He shakes his head. "No. You don't need to read the beginning. I just gave you the good part. She gets on a roll right here."

I sit back in my chair a little and I start to read Maddie's words.

All of these seemingly little rips and tears in our behavior. Moments where we forget ourselves. Little bursts of anger, or sarcasm, or annoyance. Our lies—even our little ones—even the comforting stuff we should say but don't—not because we forget, but out of spite or fear. Every cold, indifferent glance we share, every little prejudice we let slip, every middle finger, every 'fuck you,' every 'slut' and 'faggot,' every time we callously complain aloud in class about somebody's b.o.—every moment we create awkwardness, every time we focus on ourselves blatantly in the face of an obvious opportunity to help others, every time we dip our heads down and shove our faces into our phones pretending we're looking at something because that feels more comfortable than actually looking up at each other, every time we feel so entitled to vent to everyone about how unfair our own self-inflicted drama is—or inwardly blame, blame, blame whatever for whatever. God, every time we get into the negativity all never-ending... All our beliefs we take too far into someone else's space. All these things are small by themselves, seemingly nothing—little turds of thought and behavior that we do so quickly and seem to quickly recover from–we all do this stuff, these micro- forgivable sins, in different degrees and ratios, I guess— and I guess it's real easy to think that these fleeting soiled thoughts and deeds just slip away and evaporate in the air and become nothing—our forgotten whatever's.

But I think this stuff doesn't evaporate, you know? I think that's part of Mary Shelley's point. This stuff–our bad stuff–doesn't evaporate. All these little pieces from everyone go and slither and hide in some dark room–for a while. All our little sins go in there together and we don't even notice. They go in and merge and stitch, stitch, stitch themselves together and amass. And in time, they become a monster even bigger than

Victor Frankenstein could've ever imagined. This is our true enemy. Our true monster—and we are all its true creator.

It's this beast of our own making that murders us, terrorizes us, that drives us, abuses us, that pushes us to suicide and madness. It drags us back into the dark places where we cluelessly gave it birth.

So how do you deal with such a monster?

Mr. Malory, my friend Luke was right. You don't run and hide from it like Victor did and then try and go back and try to make it right with all these lame half-measures after the fact. No. You look it in the eyes the moment it appears. You speak softly. You listen to IT. Let IT teach you. You realize what parts of IT are from you. Which parts ARE you. And through your tears, you ask IT for forgiveness—then quietly take your pieces of IT back and go and make each one of them as right as you can make them.

14

"That is all well and good, Mr. Darringer and Mr. Forrester, that you have already constructed this, uh—*thing*. And judging by these fine photographs, I have no doubt in your craftsmanship. It looks spectacular, no question. But maybe you can both appreciate why I have reservations here about having such a massive sculpture on campus."

"Principal Carter. I get that you don't want this to be seen as a memorial to a suicide that took place on campus. Believe me, as an educator, I understand the dangers in setting that kind of precedent. But that's not what this is. There will be no names on this thing. None. Only the Tennyson line. That's it. At the unveiling, if there is one, there won't be one word said about this being dedicated to Rosalind's suicide, or even Maddie's murder for that matter. This is all supposed to be a symbol of the resiliency and forward hope of our kids here. A symbol that will embody something positive for all Hemingway students—past, present, and future."

Principal Carter sighs and sits back in his chair, obviously thinking. Luke and Mr. Darringer sit in two seats on the other side of the principal's desk and wait for the man to speak again.

Today's the big day. Today is the day that will determine if the gargantuan steel sculpture Luke and Darringer took the whole school year to build will find a permanent home at Hemingway. At some point Luke told Jason he got the idea for the sculpture shortly after his watery dream premonition where Rozzy hinted at his imminent death. He wanted to build it *first* and then offer it to Carter, thinking that if he just told Carter about it before he built it the principal would just flatly tell him not to bother. But by already having it made and ready to go—he and Darringer were both hoping it would be a lot more difficult for Carter to say no.

"There's one more issue," Carter finally goes.

"What's that, sir?" Darringer asks.

A weary grin plays across the administrator's face. "Well, how about the fact that the thing's a giant weapon, Jack?"

Luke and Darringer both look at each other for a second and then turn back to Carter.

"It's a *sword*—" Darringer goes.

"Yeah—I know. That's what I'm talking about."

Darringer groans. "Come on, Larry. Seriously, how many schools in our own conference have mascots that are brandishing either a sword, a spear, or an axe?"

"An *axe*?" Carter sits up. "Oh, now that belongs to a lumberjack and is *not* a weapon and you know it."

"Oh jeeze—you're kidding me, right?" Darringer turns to Luke. "Hey—can you step outside for just a little bit? Give us a minute alone."

Luke nods and gets up and goes out the door.

Once Luke's gone, Darringer remembers calming himself down a little and looking right into Principal Carter's eyes.

"Larry, listen to me. This is it. You know? What we do here, what we want these kids to do, how we want them to be like. More than anything else. More than rocket science level test scores even. It's right *here*. They're on the verge of it, Larry. God, you gotta see that, *right*?"

Carter reluctantly nods. "I see it."

"This has been a beast of a year here. On all fronts. I mean, I don't have to tell you that. You *know*. I know you know. All the challenges, all the conflicts. I mean, they've really let each other have it this year. But I also know in these last couple months, there's been *growth*. You know? Like real growth. And it's not just a couple of kids—it's *widespread*. And this kind of stuff's rare, right? I've certainly never seen a student body turnaround like it. I mean, you can see it too, can't you?"

Carter nods.

"Then let's *honor* it, Larry. Let's stoke this fire." Darringer puts his finger on one of the photographs on the desk. "I know you're always on the lookout for the next PR nightmare, and I'm sympathetic about why you'd be really cautious with this. I do, Larry. But now is not the time to be timid. The kids know that. And you better believe Luke Forrester knows it. It's time to be bold. So, let's be bold too. Trust me. Trust *him*. And let's take the training wheels off."

15

Jason got the text from Erik a little after nine that night. He thought it was odd—not just that Erik wanted to meet him out at the soccer fields, but that Erik wanted him to come alone. Without Luke. Jason gave a moment's thought to just telling Luke anyway because nothing about this *felt right*, you know? But he decided against it and hopped in his Civic and headed over there.

Erik was sitting up in the bleachers on the main field right across from Izzy's house. Jason mumbled some graphic curse words I'm sure once he realized Erik was sucking down the third can of a six pack of beer.

"What up, *brother—*" Erik goes as Jason sits down beside him. "Wanna beer?"

"Sure I do. I also want a baggie of cocaine and a bottle of bourbon to wash it down with. But I hear sometimes it's best not to get what you want, man."

"Yeah. *Well—*" Erik goes and takes another gulp.

They sit there like that for a while. Jason notices the light's on in Izzy's room. Wonders for a minute what the kid is up to. Hopes he doesn't look out and see them there.

"Why is it that all good things always fall apart?" Erik goes and hangs his head between his knees.

"I don't know, man."

Erik picks his head up. "Did you love her too?"

"What?" Jason goes. "*Maddie*?"

Erik shakes his head. "No. Rozzy. Luke wouldn't tell me, and I was always too afraid to ask you. Well, I guess until now. *So…did you*?"

Jason looks at Erik a long time. Looks him in the eyes. "Yeah. I did."

"She love you back?"

"I think so. I think she'd say that," Jason goes and puts his elbows to his knees. "Her's was different though. From mine."

"Love?" Erik goes.

Jason nods and brushes a hovering mosquito from his face.

Erik puts down his beer. "I don't think Maddie loved me. Not like how I loved her. She just never got the chance to catch up with my feelings, I guess. Now she never will."

Besides the mosquitoes being so bad out there, Jason also remembers feeling pretty sorry for Erik at that moment. Not just because he was so heartbroken over Maddie's death—but also because the poor guy had no clue about how much Luke and Maddie probably liked each other. *Hell*, Jason thinks—even *he* didn't really know how deep that rabbit hole went and Luke sure wasn't spilling about it. I mean, who knows what that letter said that Maddie gave him to give to Luke.

"So why me, man?" Jason goes. "Why call me out here?"

Erik shifts on the bleacher. "I was hoping to use some of your gangster skills, *homey*."

"Yeah—how's that?"

"I was thinking maybe you could tell me a good way to corner Dylan Sorensen nice and good so I could fuck him up," Erik goes.

"What the hell good would that do, man?" Jason goes.

"I can't stand it, Turner! That arrogant asshole is probably the one that popped her cherry. For all I know maybe he's the *only* one she had ever been with like that. Every time I see him, I just think how freaking unfair the universe is. Stupid, rich pretty-boy. I just want to deck the guy in the face and kick his balls in."

"And again, I say—what the hell good would *that* do? Then what would you want to do next, huh? Go fucking kick the shit out of Dignan Cooper because he and Maddie went out on a date once? What are you going to do—*beat up* every dude that had an impure thought about her?"

"I wish," Erik goes.

Jason stares down at Erik and just starts laughing.

"What?"

"I never noticed it before," Jason goes, "but you and I are more alike than I thought, man."

"How's that?" Erik goes.

"Well, let's just say you and I should never get really truly trashed together."

Erik smiles a little at that, but it fades a moment later. "You know, screw Dylan and Dignan. If you really want to know the truth, what I want more than anything else is to burn the druggie bastard that killed her in the first place. But I know can't. I mean, even the cops will probably never find that needle in the haystack."

"What if," Jason goes and scoots closer to Erik, "I told you I have a way where you could fuck that bastard's shit up for real."

Erik's face sobers up. "You *serious*? How?"

"Well, do you know why the guy didn't take Maddie's purse and was just interested in the car?"

"I don't know. It was a Mercedes, man," Erik goes.

"Yeah," Jason nods, "But take it further, man. Why hasn't the junkie been picked up driving it around? Why hasn't the car been found like at all?"

"Uh—he *sold* it?"

"And *who* in their fucking right mind, buys a hot Mercedes sedan from a meth-head when pics of that *very car* and license plate are splashed across every local news channel in the state in connection with a homicide of a homecoming queen from the suburbs? I mean, who buys it from him?"

Erik looks totally lost. "Somebody *dumb*?"

"*No*. Somebody really smart," Jason goes. "Somebody not too far away from that soup kitchen that can give that tweaked bastard two hundred bucks for it—*if he's lucky*—and has the means to move and flip a hot car somewhere else and make some serious bank on it. Then our murdering addict has enough flow for his week's fix of glass. It's fucking commerce, man."

"So—my gangster friend," Erik goes. "How does knowing all that get to us messing this fucker's shit up?"

Jason gets up from the bleacher. "I'll tell you how. In every detail. But *first*—"

"First what?" Erik goes.

"First, you gotta toss the rest of that beer and we need to split back to Luke's house. We'll take my car. Besides, we better book before Izzy sees we're here. You don't want him seeing you like this. *Yeah*?"

Erik gets up and grabs what's left of the sixer. "You're right, man. Let's go."

16

My mom shows Jason up to my bedroom door. He does the rest by pounding the crap out of it.

"Jason?" I go, my heart punching my rib cage.

"Caxton, let's go. We need one more."

"One more *what*?"

He grabs me by the shoulder and starts pulling me through my own house for godsakes. "Come on. I'll explain on the way."

This has to be the darkest street in the city of Detroit. We are surrounded by emptiness. The only person we see is someone a couple blocks back covered in rags, no telling whether they were male or female, limping in the shadows next to one of the abandoned and condemned apartment buildings heading god knows where.

The Suburban's headlights are the only light anywhere around us. There simply are no streetlights in this part of town. A hybrid smell of mold, rot, and rust come in through the Suburban's vents.

"Whoa—hold up," Jason goes to Patrick. "Pull over right here for a second. Kill the lights but keep the motor running."

Jason sends a quick text. With the Suburban's lights off, the blue of his phone's screen is the only light.

We wait. I turn to my left and then my right. I can barely make out the shapes of Ryan and Erik on either side of me. Luke sits with a box of gear in the seat ahead of us—but I can't see him—I'm just going on faith he's still there.

Jason's phone lights up again. "All right. We're on. Thelma says they're all gone. They took the bait."

"What bait?" I ask.

"These assholes think they're meeting me right now in a park. They think they're gonna get money from me for a camelback that turned into a bloodbath," Jason goes, grinning like a fox.

Patrick flicks the lights back on and eases the clutch back into drive. I feel Ryan's knee moving rapidly up and down and it does nothing to calm my own freaking nerves.

"There it is—" Turner points out and Patrick pulls into the rec. center's empty parking lot.

But let's back up a little bit.

After basically dragging me out of my house and pretty much kidnapping me, Jason drives me over Luke's house and down into this weird room in the basement with blue carpet all over the floor and walls. The other four guys are waiting for us there. The first thing I notice is the black Under Armour compression long sleeve T's. They're all wearing them. And these black polyester warm-up pants. Which isn't that weird for the soccer guys—but even Jason's wearing them. I mean they all kind of looked ridiculous together. Like a team of jock-ninjas or something.

But then they start talking. They brake me in by asking me if I had heard anything on the news about that shootout a couple of months ago at an abandoned farm just outside of town. I say *sure*—it rang a couple bells. Something about two guys shooting each other over drugs in a blizzard, right?

Then they tell me what really happened. I think they might be kidding at first. But then I realize they're not. But it doesn't make sense, I say. I mean, if what you're saying is true, then how did the second guy—this *Maintenance Man*—how did he get shot too like how it was reported in the news?

But then Jason gives me his two cents worth. About how after *Maintenance* wakes up and realizes his bro Scotty is dead and their car was toast. It was probably getting as cold as a witch's teat by then. So not being all that bright anyway, and now having a massive head wound also clouding his suspect judgment, the dude in all likelihood grabbed what was left of their glass in the car, crawled back to the barn, smoked it, or ate it or whatever, and blew his own headcheese out with Scotty's sawed-off when he was done. And who knows why they didn't report it as a murder-suicide in the news. The cops probably just left out that tid-bit to test any unlikely tips they might get on the case, Jason guesses.

So, what's all *that* got to do with right now? I ask. And what's with the *back in black* you guys are wearing?

Well, if we can survive something like the Shotgun Brothers, Jason starts telling me—then we all feel we can handle what we're doing tonight. Then Erik tosses me a black long-sleeve and a pair of warm-up pants. And maybe you can too, Will. If you're up for it, he goes.

Patrick pulls the Suburban right up to the chained and bolted double doors of Dre and Cunter's rec. center. From the front passenger's seat, Jason turns back to us. "OK. Deep breaths, boys. Everybody crystal on what we're doing here?"

Nobody says anything, but we all nod back.

"All right, then. Rock n' roll," Jason goes, and we all put on our rubber gloves, jump out of the Suburban and sling empty backpacks on our backs. We make way for Luke, who pulls his goggles down over his eyes and strides up to the door and takes a knee. He cranks the head of the valve and strikes the igniter. It takes less than a minute for Darringer's blowtorch to hiss through Dre's chain and we're *in*.

We jog down the skuzzy hallway in two single-file lines of three—one led by Jason, the other by Patrick. Luke's last in line with me after tossing the torch back in the Suburban. It gets darker as we go.

"Flashlights," Patrick goes, and we all reach in and take our small black LED's out and click'em to life and point them down as we jog so we don't blind one another. We hit the gymnasium and Jason tells us to watch our step. "I'm serious there's shit all over. Don't *trip*—"

Our footsteps and our breathing are the only sounds as we creep across the gym floor to the stairway leading down to what we came for. After getting down the stairs, we hear the rumble and hum and smell the oily reek of the generators Dre's crew has running down here. We keep going forward now, towards the hazy red and slightly greenish lights in the room just ahead of us—when a man steps into the doorway.

"What the *fuck*?" the man goes and starts to reach behind his back for something.

But the guy never gets a chance to shine it out, because Patrick decks the guy right into the left side of his jaw and neck, and he goes down like a puppet free from its master's hand. Patrick follows the blow with a cracking kick to the guy's ribs.

"Holy crap, Patrick!" Erik goes and reaches down to pull the gun from the back of the guy's pants.

The guy groans all doubled over, still moving.

Jason looks to Erik. "Clock him once on the back of the head with that thing."

Erik nods and slams the butt of the gun down behind his head. Erik's eyes go all berserk as the guy stops moving and making sounds. Erik starts to raise the gun again.

"*No—*" Jason barks at him. "Once is enough, man. Now give it here and get to work."

Erik loses his wild eyes and hands Jason the firearm.

"What's the deal?" Ryan freaks. "I thought your people said they were *all gone*."

"Well, looks like Thelma missed one," Jason goes as we all step over the guy. I stop and shine my light down on the guy's face and Jason laughs. "Guys—meet *Sugar Tits*."

We all have a quick chuckle about that, but then it's back to work as we all yank off our backpacks and zip them open. We start unplugging and loading up every laptop, device, hard drive, and flash drive we see. *All of them.* And stuff them into our backpacks. In less than a minute, we clean the whole room out.

"See those two video cameras over there?" Jason goes to Ryan and me. "We need their hard drives. Grab those too."

"We good?" Erik goes to Jason as he slings his full backpack on his back.

Jason raises his finger up and then goes over to the big desk and riffles open the top drawer. He reaches in and pulls out this huge book all leather bound and grins. "*Now* we're good. Let's go! Everybody out now—"

I'm pretty sure I'm sweating right through both the Under Armour and the butt-crack of the warm-up pants as we bounce back up and out through the gym. Jason tosses Sugar Tits's gun across the soiled basketball court, and we follow the skuzzy hallway back out into the night and Patrick's Suburban. We slam into our seats and buckle up as Patrick wheels us out there and we're flying, doing fifty mph till we finally pass under a lit streetlight.

17

As we cruise back to the world of stoplights, other cars, lighted businesses, and public transit, Jason flips through Cunter's *bible* and smiles wide. And just as he had suspected, there ain't no gospels in there—but encryption codes, rotations and rotations of passwords. Numbers and symbols all compacted together in passwords of twelve characters or more forming the keys to unlock their criminal empire. The top of each page is tagged with a marker-streak of a color that Jason's willing to bet corresponds with the laptop with the same color strip of duct tape across its top. Just like Athletic Director Steinholz with his binder marked LOCKERS containing every combination just sitting out in plain sight—Dre and Cunter were banking that no one would ever be clever or stupid enough to just walk right in and take their most prized secrets from them.

Within an hour, we're back at Luke's house where we unload the rec. center payload into Turner's Civic. We all give each other amped up hugs and high-fives and freaking see-you-tomorrows and Patrick gives the rest of us a ride home, while Luke and Jason get in the car to complete the night's business.

They park two houses down from Jason's dad's house and kill the engine. The house is all dark from the front, which they take as a good sign.

Jason turns to Luke. "All right. I'm going in. Text me if anybody shows and I'll bolt out the back and meet you on the next street over, OK?"

Luke nods and gets out and takes the driver's seat while Jason creeps closer to the house.

He goes up the driveway to the back door and finds it locked. Fishes out his key from his chain and it works. *Hmm—he cuts me loose and never thinks to change the locks,* Jason thinks. In the kitchen he clicks his LED on and scans around as he creeps through the house. No one downstairs. No surprise. Upstairs he checks his room for the hell of it and finds nothing odd, the bathroom and then finally into his dad's room. All clear. Now to his dad's big lockbox. Jason dials his own birthday as the combination. The lock clicks and the door swings open. The .45's gone, which isn't a big shock—but his father's biz laptop is there as it usually is.

Jason snags the computer out, sits on the edge of his dad's bed and powers it up. The password lock screen comes up. He types **POPS**. No access. He types in their last name. No access. Jason types in his birth date again. Nada entry. He types in his dad's birthday and gets nothing.

"*Come on—*" Jason hisses.

He knows that it's not entirely essential to have access right now to his dad's hard drive. Somebody down the line will be able to hack into it. I mean, freaking surely—*right?* But the longer it sits warming on his lap, the more he just wants to bust this bitch open right now and see her secrets come spilling out.

He takes Dre and Cunter's bible out from where it's tucked behind his back. Turns on his dad's bedside lamp and starts rifling through pages of elaborate passwords for all their computers.

Why would Dad's password be in here with theirs? he thinks.

"It wouldn't," he answers himself. He slams the *bible* shut and whips it on the bed next to him. "*Goddamn it—*"

Jason puts his head in his hands and kicks the bed frame with his heel. He thinks. He stares all absently at the laptop's screen and then his eyes rove back to the leather-bound book on the bed. Why can't you just have one of *those*, you old prick, Jason thinks. And another thought hits him.

He scrambles off the bed and investigates the safe again. There's an envelope of cash, the title to his dad's truck—and a small black journal-looking type book.

"Get the fuck *out*, you unoriginal bastard—" Jason goes and opens it up. It's all blank except for the first page where there are what looks like three lengthy pass codes.

He types the first one in.

No access.

Jason types in the other two and still gets nothing. *But of course*—he suddenly realizes.

The passwords in the journal are probably for files his dad's got on his hard drive. They're way too freaking cumbersome to keep as your initial login. He'd pick something he's got on his brain all fast and furious like every normal person does.

Which dumps Jason right back to square one. Or does it?

"Sonofabitch—why didn't I think of it before?" And Jason types in his dad's username for every email account he's used ever since Jason can remember.

lyon_luvrrr

His dad loves the Detroit Lions. But so do a million other Michiganites for some godforsaken reason, which meant Mr. Galen Turner had to resort to being a *lyon luvrrr* instead. Jason remembers how his dad always thought the triple *rrr*'s at the end were actually kind of cool. *Like a lion roaring or something*, his dad always said.

Kaa-bing. The laptop screen zips to the desktop. After that it takes Jason all of three minutes to break into the detailed numbers of his dad's drug traffic. He even refers to each of the drugs he's buying and selling by their actual names—*methamphetamine*. *That*, along with his various account numbers alone would be enough to put him in the slammer for twenty years if they got in the right hands.

But Jason isn't satisfied. He's got to confirm one more thing. He searches the hard disk for video files. Two come up. He clicks to view—but another password request comes up. Jason types in the last password from the small black journal.

And *there she is…*

Rozzy's there, naked in his living room laid out awkwardly on the couch. Dre and Tagger are both naked too—Dre behind her and Tag standing by her mouth. Jason can hear Cunter calling out direction from behind the camera, giggling all sinister.

Then rocking on the EZ boy recliner, coming in and out of frame rhythmically is Jason's dad taking in the show with that half-drunk, half-high look he gets on his face when it's party time.

Rozzy's eyes aren't quite right—Jason can tell she's tweaked out too as she does who she needs to do to get her fix.

Then Dre starts in with his stupid porn-talk between his thrusts like, "*Yeah*—dirty, trailer, stank-ho. Take my black cock for your rock now."

And they all laugh and talk shit while Tagger backs off and Dre just keeps banging away.

Rozzy doesn't say anything and doesn't move her body in anything that looks like pleasure or pain—just a freaked-up zoned-out stare—when all abruptly her eyes flash wide and her pupils roll behind her eyelids. Her backbone zips up in a curve. Her skinny arms fix all rigid to her sides as her whole body seems to lock up at once. A frothy drool foams and oozes out the sides of her mouth.

"Aw shit, ya'll—" Tagger yells.

"Bitch be *spazzing,* yo!" Dre goes and backs away from her.

Rozzy then starts writhing around on the sofa like she's got the devil in her insides giving her the voodoo shakes and Cunter up and hops out from behind the camera and backhands her across the mouth with his knuckles. Rozzy's knocked to the floor, out of view as Cunter turns to face the camera and goes, "Now *that's* how we do tweaked baby-*ho's* up in here—yo!"

"*Failsafe*," Jason says through his clenched jaw and glides the cursor up to the second video file and clicks play.

This video is grainier—probably taken with the laptop's built-in cam. It's set up here in his dad's room, positioned to face the very bed Jason's sitting on.

Rozzy lays on the bed, still naked and seemingly unconscious. The camera angle fidgets a little and someone turns on the bedside lamp to improve the image. Jason's dad's head emerges into view as his upper body glides, snake-like, up even with Rozzy's face. Turner's dad plants a sloppy unreciprocated kiss onto her gaping mouth, and then he rears up to peel off his T-shirt and toss it behind him. He moves his hands down to start *unbuckling his belt and—*

Jason clicks the video off. He powers it down and folds it up. He grabs the two password books and shuts off the bedside lamp and heads back down to the kitchen where he flicks the switch to turn on the light above the sink. He puts both hands on the sink counter and sways a second like he might get sick but doesn't. Instead, after a moment, he takes out his phone and texts Luke:

want coffee?

18

He thinks maybe he made the coffee a tad too strong, maybe a bit more intense than even Luke cares for. *But then again*—I mean, it's nearly three a.m. and Jason's dad still hasn't come home, and they have no intention of leaving until he shows. Who knows? They could be here past dawn.

Jason sits on the concrete steps of his front stoop, takes another sip, and thinks, *fuck it.*

Leaning against the car's passenger door, parked right in front of the house now, is Luke with his arms crossed with a cup of coffee in his hand. Every few seconds or so he takes a sip from his steaming mug and looks across the front yard at Jason with a slight gleam in his eye.

Since Jason brought out the coffee, the two of them haven't even attempted to communicate.

They just wait.

Jason finishes the last gulp of his dregs, and he sets his mug down on the concrete at his feet. He reaches over to the landscaped shrub bed next to the stoop and picks up a rock and drops it in the mug. It makes a tinging sound.

Luke takes another sip and watches him.

Jason reaches down and drops another rock in. As he picks up a third, he realizes for being basically manufactured decorative rocks, they carry an unexpected amount of heft. More than he would've thought anyway. He puts in a few more. Fills the mug to the top with these jagged sparkly rocks.

Finally, they see the bright lights of a truck break the street's dark stillness. It pulls in slow onto the driveway, stopping before getting even with the house.

Luke puts his empty mug on top of the Civic and starts to loosen up his shoulders.

Galen "Pops" Turner gets out of the truck looking mostly sober—but probably more than a little confused as to what Luke and Jason are doing here—and *why* they're both dressed alike in what probably looks to him like black spandex.

Jason can see by his dad's face that they've thrown him and he's trying to figure out how to play it. Galen's eyes soften and he puts on a strained grin.

Great. He's gonna try to play the dad—Jason thinks and stands up. He takes his mug.

"Hey, *Jace*—what's up?" his dad gives Luke another glance too as he crosses the yard. "You guys just getting back from—"

But he doesn't finish whatever his dad's dumb joke was going to be. Because Jason steps up and smashes his coffee mug of rocks right into the side of his dad's forehead. The mug shatters in a mini explosion of ceramic shards and landscaping stones while his dad hits the grass open-mouthed as a dumbstruck child.

Knocked. The freak *Out*.

Luke takes out a couple large plastic zip ties from his pocket and he and Jason bind Galen's feet and hands and then dump him in the back of his own truck.

Jason grabs the keys out of his dad's leather jacket and fires the truck's V8 back up. Luke opens the passenger side door of the truck and starts putting all the backpacks full of computer gear in.

When Luke's hauled the last bag in, Jason goes, "Which one's got the password books?"

Luke unzips one of the bags and shows Jason the tops of the bindings.

"And what about my dad's laptop?"

Luke digs it out from underneath one of the backpacks and hands it to Jason, who then puts it up on the dash.

Luke holds up his handheld. "You sure you don't want me to come too?" goes the robot voice.

Jason grins. "No, man. You done enough. I think I got it from here. Look, don't wait up for me. No telling how long they may keep my ass in questioning with all this shit."

Luke closes the truck door and backs up a couple steps. He gives Jason a mock farewell salute.

Jason salutes back and pulls the truck out of the driveway loaded with its incriminating cargo. And even though it's like freaking three in the morning, and even though Luke Forrester's deaf as that proverbial doornail, Jason still gives his dad's horn a big double-honk as he rides that beast down the street, headed for the police station.

19

The day after Turner's dad was charged on numerous drug trafficking counts, and sexual assault on an incapacitated minor, they set the recreation center on fire. They torched the whole place—which made our whole rubber gloves thing moot, but Jason had a hard-on about not leaving any of our paw prints around just in case the place *did* in fact become a viable crime scene for the police. He told us the cops also found an unidentified incinerated body down in Cunter's computer room—which very well may have been Cunter himself—but Jason said his money was just as likely on it being Sugar Tits as the one who got country-fried. He had a theory that *Tits* was the crew's watchdog and probably hardly ever left the recreation center, which was why Thelma, Lawrence, and Bernie had missed him when we all went in to pull the big heist the other night.

The next day warrants were out for Dre, Cunter, Tagger, and Sin Dawg. Jason figured not only did they have them on whatever goods were on the laptops, but he was also pretty certain his dad had flipped on his former partners. Like hard-core.

That night they got Sin in a car bomb explosion right outside his sister's house in Sterling Heights. Word was he was all packed up and ready to blow town when his ride fire-balled in every direction upon ignition.

The next morning, they found Tagger and Dre. They were left together right outside the burning recreation center. Tagger was hung up by his neck on a telephone pole with his intestines hanging out and reaching down and coiling on the sidewalk. It was later reported that every bone in both his feet were broke.

What was left of Dre was laid out on the street next to Tagger's gut pile. It was just his two hands and his severed head. Each of the hands had five nails sticking out of them, while his roughly and newly shaved head had a lot more than that poking out all over the dome of his skull. Apparently, someone had gone to work on him with one of those high-powered nailing guns. Oh, and his tongue was cut out.

It was Thelma that called the fire in, on the phone that Jason had given them.

Within forty-eight hours of us taking their computers, Mr. Sunrise and his Yukon Denali crew had wiped Dre and his gang from the face of the earth. Jason said it sure looked like Tagger and Dre were tortured for information before they were killed. Sunrise and company probably wanted very specific confirmation on just what kind of information that led back to them, was on those hard drives and just *how much*—if anything—this *Pops guy,* who was already in custody, knew about them.

"Holy crap. I mean, holy crap, *right*?" Ryan goes.

"You mean, because of what we did, those gangsta guys all just got like, *obliterated*?" I go too and lean back on Luke's sofa there in his living room.

"Hey—that was the plan, guys," Jason goes. "Don't suddenly get all soft for these assholes. This is exactly what they deserved. Do not for a fucking second forget that it was these guys' glass the junkie who killed Maddie was going to buy. I guarantee it. And it was *these* assholes that were supplying every organized ounce of meth or coke and every pill of x that got fed into our school and town. Not to mention probably every other sub around Detroit. By taking Dre and my dad down, in one night we pretty much shut down all heavy drug traffic in our town and the surrounding areas. Don't forget, man. These guys were murderers. Rapists. Makers of fucking snuff films, man. And we shut them down. Permanently, dudes."

"Yeah, but—" I cut in. "Won't somebody else just take their place eventually?"

Jason looks at me. "Sure. Eventually. Yeah. But it won't be *these* dudes."

"The only thing I regret," Erik goes. "Is that they all didn't get tortured. The asshole that got car bombed and the dude that got incinerated got off too easy if you ask me. I wish those Russians, or Serbians, or whatever the hell they are, would carve up that murdering junkie that killed Maddie too—"

Luke reaches out and pats Erik on the arm.

"So, what about this Cunter guy then?" Patrick goes. "If that wasn't him in the fire, where's he at?"

"If he ain't dead," Jason goes, "then either he's out of town, or he's scrambling like a shit-scared rat trying to *get* out of town. Getting out is his only option. With Sunrise's death squad and the heat from the cops all around, he can't show hide nor hair anywhere in Michigan. So the way I see it, if he ain't already dead—and that's a big *if*, man—we'll either hear of his ass's grisly demise tonight on the nightly, *or* he's skipped with whatever rainy day cash he could gather, and we'll never see that motherfucker again."

20

So, here's what we know about what happened that afternoon on Tuesday, May twenty-eigh[th], that spring.

We know Edwin Mueller took his meds per usual. He took his Enoxaparin faithfully that morning just as he had every day since having it prescribed to him after his first heart attack. Besides the meds, Edwin had also been advised by his doctors to change his diet, which he did, begrudgingly, for over a year. But according to family and friends, in the recent months leading up to that day in May, Edwin had fallen off the wagon. He was a widower in his seventies who lived alone and was still highly functional, so it was hard for his adult children and his friends to *tell* headstrong Edwin what to do—much less monitor his risky binges on KFC, or cheeseburgers from various vendors. We're not really sure what set off his dietary revolt. His closest loved ones never could come to a consensus on it. But what is widely known, was Edwin's *zeal* for hot wings. While out to dinner at Duggan's Pub with a couple buddies after taking in a Tiger's game at the end of April, Edwin chowed down twenty wings lathered in bleu cheese dressing. With a side of fries and pint of Stout. By *himself*, to the dismay of his friends.

Upon clearing out his house afterwards, family members were horrified to find his fridge and freezer crammed with all sorts of culinary contraband.

But what's that old freaking adage? *Sometimes the heart wants what the heart wants…*

We know Lisa Ann Belfry got pregnant at fifteen. She had been going with DeMarcus Alrich, a boy in the grade ahead of her that lived in one of the high rises a couple of blocks over from hers. He said they would get married after they graduated high school, but that didn't happen. She and her daughter, Linsey, continued to live at home with Lisa's parents when she got pregnant again at age twenty-one after a one-night stand with some businessman she met at a bar downtown.

Her parents gave her never-ending grief about that second one. Another daughter she named Leslie. If her life was stressful before, it was even more so now. Trying to keep up two part-time jobs, caring for a willful six-year-old girl and a baby, all while having to endure living under her parents' supportive, yet disappointed, roof.

About the only time Lisa Ann found peace of mind was on her long walks she took with Leslie in her stroller every afternoon. Baby Leslie would munch on her pacifier and doze while Lisa Ann would walk past all the small houses and over the river and then along the stretch of the park path where there was space, and trees, and grass and where the river's never-ending current stretched out like some kind of freedom she feared she would never know.

We know that Abby's final check-up before her due date was set for four-thirty at the hospital. Luke had taken her to her last couple of check-ups and had offered to take her that afternoon after school. Jason got a ride back to the Forrester house from Patrick, and Abby set off across town with Luke.

The Macklin Avenue Bridge was the oldest of the three such bridges in town. The bitter irony that it was to undergo major reconstruction in less than two weeks escaped no one. They think that Edwin's second heart attack began right before he and his Buick started on the bridge. His pacemaker just couldn't keep pace with this cardiac tremor, and Edwin was probably well dead before final impact. In any case, when his heart gave out, his body slumped forward on the wheel—the bulk of his upper half keeping the wheel surprisingly straight for the first few moments, while his foot went heavy on the accelerator.

Lisa Ann didn't even notice Edwin's car, going close to fifty miles an hour now, veering off towards her and baby Leslie in time to scream. She only remembers her hands griping on the stroller's handle out of bodily reflex, preparing for impact.

We have no idea what Luke's thoughts were the instant before it happened. All we really know is that he didn't hesitate. Even with Abby on board—*he just didn't hesitate.* In all likelihood, he saw Lisa Ann and her baby, saw Edwin's speeding Buick, and Luke's instincts kicked in. The interesting thing—to me anyway—were his instincts. I think most human beings, on seeing an oncoming car swerving into your lane—threatening a head-on collision—would instinctively apply brakes and try to turn out of the oncoming car's path. Whether there were pedestrians like Lisa Ann in the car's path, or not. Self-preservation first, then, if you can, save others. It's like in our DNA, right? But those weren't Luke's instincts.

Some of us are just made of sterner stuff, I guess.

Well, *that*—and the fact that most of us don't live everyday with the conviction that we are not going to live through the year because some dead girl in a dream told us so.

That too, was likely a factor.

Luke sped up just past Lisa Ann and Leslie and turned *into* the path of Edwin's car. The front grill of the Buick plowed into Luke's driver's side and sent both vehicles through the bridge's guard rails and plummeting over thirty feet into the river.

Just before the collision, just before the sickening merging sounds of shattering glass and crunching metal and the thick smells of exhaust and burnt rubber, of broken concrete and gasoline, before watching in horror, two cars blast off the bridge right in front of her and fall all the way to the river and bob just a bit before starting to sink, just before all of that, Lisa Ann heard Abby's unforgettable scream.

Jason was sitting on the couch flipping through channels when the phone rang. At first, he paid little attention as Mr. Forrester answered it and listened to whoever was speaking on the other end. But when he heard Luke's dad's voice break, "No—oh god, *no*—" he sat up.

And watching Mr. Forrester put his hand up over his mouth while he listened to the terrible news through the phone he held in the other—Jason Turner didn't need to be told anything else. Even though he didn't know *exactly* what had happened, Jason remembers in that instant knowing *precisely* what had happened.

21

Isaiah

The night I found out about Luke and Abby I cried until I fell asleep. I hadn't cried like that since Dad. Mom was worried about me, of course, and the next morning she said I didn't have to go to school if I didn't want to. It was strange, but I actually wanted to go. I guess it was because I just wanted to be around people. The thought of just staying home and thinking about Luke and Abby's accident and how terrible it all was, was just too depressing.

So, I ate a little bit of cereal and went upstairs and got dressed. I looked out at the soccer fields and got even more sad. No workout with Luke. And really—we would never get to have a morning workout together again. I scanned down the street to see if Jason was jogging by. (He didn't just lie down anymore while Luke and I would train. He was getting in better shape, so he'd just turn around and run all the way back to Luke's house.) But no Jason either. I remember wondering if he'd even go to school today either.

I took my bike. I cried a little as I rode, but by the time I got to school and locked my bike on the rack, I was fine. By second period my head started to ache. At first, I just thought it was from all the crying and not sleeping much, but then it got worse, and I could feel that it was an aura coming on. I didn't want to have a seizure. Not on that day. Like I said, I didn't want to go home and be alone with my thoughts either. So, I just sat with my head swimming like that and hoped that when it came it would be just one of those quick zoney seizures and nobody would ever know I even had one but me, and then it would be gone.

It hit in third period Health class, which was good since we were watching the *Miracle of Life* video and that meant nobody would probably notice, I was hoping.

I felt it creep into me. I felt my saliva go all clear and runny. Blue waves started to roll in the room in front of me. My classmates all looked like they were sitting at their desks underwater. Health Class *20,000 Leagues Under the Sea*. I thought I heard the constant note from a violin that I sometimes hear when I'm about to seizure. I felt my eyes flutter. Everything waved blue and *then*—

The stars and space. The snow and ice. A starry night on Pluto.

I was there. I was back. The huge white mountain was in the distance, and I was standing on the ocean of ice with the moon of Charon reflecting off its surface. I took it all in—the night, the mountain, the huge frozen ocean—took in how beautiful it was, how peaceful and how real.

And about how my dad told me never to come back here.

I turned around to the vastness behind me and saw two weird-looking shapes on the ice. I walked toward them and realized they're like glass coffins, like out of *Snow White* or something. Then I realized who the bodies were. In the first one was Luke, laying down with his eyes closed and wearing his soccer uniform. In the other coffin was

Abby—but before she was pregnant, wearing a pretty dress, like the kind girls wear to church.

"They haven't woken yet," a girl's voice said behind me.

I turned and saw a thin girl wearing a black robe or dress, with black lips and dark eyes. In her hand was a flickering lantern.

"You're *the one*—" I stammered. "The one who, who *died*. The one that Luke—and Jason—"

"That's right, Izzy. My name is Rozzy," she said and put her lantern down on the ice.

"What are you doing here?" I said and moved closer.

"I've been waiting. Waiting for you to return. Waiting for you to come back so that you can choose."

"Choose?"

"Yes, Izzy," came another voice out of the darkness. "You have a very important decision to make."

"*Maddie*?" I said as she walked into the lantern's circle of light, her hair nearly glowing, her smile outshining the moon. She wore a dress very much like Rozzy's except that Maddie's was white.

Rozzy held out her hand and Maddie took it, and they knelt together by the light between the coffins.

"Join us, Izzy—" Rozzy said, and held out her hand to me and I took it and knelt with them.

They bowed their heads and said together in unison:

All in all the enormity of all,
These icy depths that ever lie
and beneath all
these waters
to bless all the souls they do harbor.

They raised their heads and Rozzy took Maddie's face gently into both her hands, looked into her eyes and whispered, "Until we are one."

Maddie kissed Rozzy's forehead and repeated, "Until we are one."

They turned and then looked at me with such—I don't know how else to put it—*love* in their faces. Their looks were just like the look my dad gave me the day he told me the story about the stag in the rain. I can barely stand such looks. I blushed and asked finally, "What choice do I have to make?"

"The *cave*, Isaiah," Rozzy said.

"It's always the cave, Izzy," Maddie said.

"It all comes down to whether you choose to see what's in the cave," Rozzy said.

Then we were no longer on the ocean of ice. But on the mountain overlooking the astronauts' worksite. There were hundreds of them now in their white space suits—all over their equipment like ants. The gold shield visors of their helmets again hiding their faces from me. I could see all the buildings down in their valley and wondered if my dad was in one of them, in one of those white rooms, drinking his coffee.

I turned to Rozzy and Maddie. "But my dad told me not to, you know. He told me not to come back here."

"Like we told you, it will be an important decision. It may be difficult for you to make, Izzy," Rozzy said.

"He told me," I said, nerves shaking my voice, "that if I went back there, that *thing* in the cave will kill me. Like *for real* kill me."

Rozzy reached out and touched my cheek. "That very well may happen. If you choose to go in—I hope it doesn't. But that is something for you to weigh. I know it's hard. Trusting this kind of thing. I had a hard time too—believe me, kid. It sucks, you know? Letting go."

"We all die, Isaiah," Maddie added. "But *why*, and *how*, and for *whom*? Sometimes we have a choice."

I looked again down at the astronauts' worksite and then turned and looked up to the cave's entrance. I heard what I thought was the low rumblings of the beast.

"What is *that*?" I asked.

"He's Charon," Maddie said.

"He's *man. Monster. Myth.* He's our outer darkness. Our inner terrors," Rozzy said.

The rumbling came again, but this time the whole mountainside shook under our feet. I felt I peed myself a little. Below, I saw the astronauts begin to scurry and point up to the cave.

Then, above us, above the mountain peak, stars began to streak across the sky in such a dazzle that I almost forgot how terrifying the tremors were just a few seconds ago. Rozzy and Maddie looked up at the falling stars and smiled too.

"The universe," Maddie said, "it's getting ready too."

"Ready for what?" I asked.

Rozzy turned her gaze from the sky and looked directly at me. "For our final report card. *Come*."

And then we were in one of the white rooms. One with a white table and chairs. Just like the one my dad took me too last time. There was the same kind of window with the same horizontal white slat blinders looking out to the worksite. But the view was different from the one I had been in with Dad.

Rozzy and Maddie were already sitting together on one side of the table. I sat opposite them.

"But why?" I asked. "Why would I willingly go into the cave with Charon?"

"*Now* you're asking the right questions," Maddie said.

"If you go and confront Charon, you'll *save* them, Izzy," Rozzy said.

"Save who?"

Maddie got up and put the blinds up so I could see them. They were all there, the astronauts, all standing in front of our room, packed together tight. I stood up, Rozzy did too, and we all looked out at them.

Then one of the astronauts in the front took a few steps closer to the window. He slowly brought his hand up to helmet and must've touched some button, because his gold shield rose from his mask so I could see his face.

It was Erik!

Then all the astronauts behind him raised their shields and I saw them all. Ryan. Jason. Tristan. Patrick. All of them, the team, Coach Striden, Dallas, all the faces of the kids I knew at Hemingway, from the games, from State, from Maddie's funeral. Hundreds of them. They were all there smiling at me through their helmets.

"If you go, you can save them, Izzy. Save them from Charon," Rozzy said.

Then all of Pluto shook. Shook more violently and longer than the first time.

"We're running out of time, Izzy," Maddie said.

"Will you do it?" Rozzy asked. "Will you go?"

I looked out to my friends who now had real fear on their faces.

"*Yes*," I said. "I'll do it. I'll go."

We were suddenly back out on the ocean of ice, next to Rozzy's lantern and Luke and Abby's glass coffins. They were both still *sleeping*, I guess. After being on the shaking mountain, the silence out here was unbelievably calming.

Then, just outside the lantern light, I saw shapes coming closer from the dark expanse of the frozen ocean. Into the circle of our light came a girl, a little younger than me—a girl with dark-haired bangs wearing an old-fashioned white dress. On her hip she held a toddler, a boy. The girl and the boy smiled at me, *but their eyes*... their eyes spoke of a justice delayed, eyes of heartbreak and yearning—eyes unblinking, watchful for an overdue reckoning. Behind them more and more kids walked into the light encircling me and Rozzy and Maddie and the caskets. Kids of all ages, hundreds of them, elementary school kids, kids my own age, high school kids even—all with the same *unkillable* stares.

My hands began to tremble. "Who are they?"

Rozzy put her hand upon my shoulder. "They are the children of Thorn."

I felt the ember of a new courage glow within me. "What do I have to do once I find him?" I asked, my hands still shaking. Tears were streaking down my cheek I noticed.

"Merely do whatever it takes to draw Charon forth from the darkness—and then *he* will take care of the rest," Rozzy said.

"What? Who's *he*?"

Maddie and Rozzy both motioned for me to look just out onto the dark ice ahead of the caskets.

It began to crack, small at first, then bigger. The ice ahead of us groaned and then split with a sound like thunder and I saw the tip of Luke's giant sword begin to poke majestically up through the huge hole in the ice. The sword continued to push up until it was fully out of the ocean and a giant blue hand came up out of the water, gripping the massive sword by the hilt.

Rozzy smiled at me. "The one who will rise. *He'll* take care of the rest."

And then I was alone in the dark. By the sound of my steps and the wet, rocky smell, I knew I was already deep in the cave. The growling rumble started again. I felt the closeness of Charon. Then just ahead, out of the shadows, I saw the red beam again zip out like it was seeking me.

I'm going to save them. I am going to save them, I kept repeating in my head. *No matter what, no matter if I die, I will not back away,* I told myself.

Charon roared. I felt the blast of his rotten breath blow back my hair and burn my eyes.

But I kept walking forward. "I'm not afraid! I'm not afraid of you!" I yelled.

My life for theirs. My life for theirs. My life for theirs.

Another red eye appeared before me. And another.

I made myself see an image of my father laughing in my head. I quickly thought of Angel stepping into Erif's mouth. I thought of Rozzy's and Maddie's prayer by the lantern. I remembered the infinite Children of Thorn massing on the ice with so much determined love in their eyes pleading me to give them a reckoning. I saw the Hemingway kids in their space suits, and I saw them hugging each other through their tears in the church at Maddie's funeral.

My life for theirs.

I was close enough I could spit in the beast's eyes and by their red light I suddenly saw it *was* a man. *A man with five red eyes.*

I woke up back in Health class and that's when I realized IT WAS REAL.

And who it was I saw. And *where*. And *when*. And that it was all happening *right now*.

22

Isaiah jumps out of his desk and runs out of the classroom, leaving his teacher and classmates stupefied. He runs out of the school, unchains his dirt bike, and hits the street. He pumps his legs and rides his bike as fast as his wiry thirteen-year-old body can.

Passing the parking lot now. *All you must do is round one more corner and you'll be at the rows of doors at the front.* The office is just inside, kid. They'll know what to do. If there's still time, that is.

He rounds the corner and sees the front doors of Hemingway High School. He's not too late. *No*, Isaiah Walker is about as *on time* as you can get. Precisely there when he needs to be there, when someone needs to be there to do what he intends to do.

My life for theirs.

Because, just as Isaiah gets there to the front of the school, they are there too. Two of them, just ahead of him, going for the front doors.

Isaiah sees the taller, skinnier one turn in his direction. Sees his big bulging eyes covered by a red-tinted goggled mask, like the one's SWAT teams or Marines wear in combat. He sees the small cameras strapped to each of the guy's shoulder straps, each with their little red light beaming indicating they are recording. Then Izzy sees—as the guy turns fully toward him and his bike—the guy's got the biggest machine gun that Izzy's ever seen in real life. A machine gun with a red laser scope that beams up into his eyes for a split second when the guy raises the weapon up in his direction.

Isaiah stops his bike and straddles it with his feet planted on the concrete and screams defiantly, "Hey! *Haaaay*!"

Some of us students in the cafeteria right by the doors are in an open study hall. Some kids remember hearing Izzy's yells right before it all started.

Then Cunter goes, "Hey, fuck you *kid*," and rips a volley of gunfire at Izzy with his Heckler and Koch 416.

Before Cunter's buddy, Eddie with the chewed-up ear, can blast through Hemingway's front glass doors and spray the cafeteria with ammunition from his own AR-15 rifle, most of the kids are up and running because of Isaiah drawing the initial fire.

It later will be noted that if Isaiah had not done what he had done, the death toll—however horrifying it was that day—would've been significantly more. There's absolutely no doubt about that.

Some of us are made of sterner stuff.

"Everybody! Out! Come on, this way!" Dickie Schwartz yells to everybody in the cafeteria. It's a big study hall, like close to a hundred kids during third period—the class before lunch.

Kids run towards Dickie and out of the caf into the hallway that separates the cafeteria and the gymnasium. Even Mr. Hebert, the study hall advisor, is running with them by the time Eddie gets through the door and open fires in the direction everyone is scrambling to.

There's suddenly bullets everywhere. You know how they use the word "spray" sometimes regarding automatic gunfire? The word makes it sound like bullets—these hard metal killing devices—are, you know, liquid-like. Like *water*. I used to think it was a poorly used word in that context. Made bullets seem less harmless. But not anymore. *Spray* is the perfect word.

Eddie sprays the cafeteria with bullets. Amazingly, freaking miraculously, he only hits four students, and kills no one on this attempt. If he chases the study hall kids, he could kill them all probably, but before he can, Cunter comes in.

"Hey, yo—" Tristan hears Cunter yell to Eddie as Tristan waits in the far hallway behind a wall with Dickey. "We gotta fuck up the office first, dawg."

Hemingway's main office is right across the hall from the main doors. As soon as Cunter shot at Izzy, Gretta Lutz, the school's receptionist, picked up the phone and dialed 911. When Eddie came in and fired at the study hall kids, the other office ladies all hit the carpet and screamed. Principal Carter bolted out of his office and headed for the public address system.

This is when Cunter and Eddie open fire on the main office, exploding the glass windows and ripping apart the tops of the desks and blowing up the computer screens. They tag Gretta at the base of her neck while she's still on the line with the 911 operator. She gurgles blood and dies a few seconds later.

Principal Carter stands up and grabs the public address walkie. "This is a Code Red emergency. I repeat a Code Red emergency. All students and staff are to—"

Instead of firing another clip of ammo into Carter, Cunter elects to pull one of the six URG-86 grenades he has strapped to his utility belt. He pulls the pin and lobs it through the shattered office windows in the direction of Principal Carter at the back. The grenade detonates the instant it hits the carpet, and the body of Carter disappears in a blast of smoke and shrapnel.

Cunter takes another grenade, pulls its pin, and whips it through one of the front door windows where it explodes magnificently and blasts the metal door out and breaks up some concrete on the school's façade.

"Yo—*Eddie*," Cunter yells above the school's warning sirens, "You go that way and try to find him. I'll go this way. We'll meet on the second floor yo." Cunter goes.

Tristan and Dickey hear Eddie go, "Yo," and run off.

Three of the four kids that Eddie shot are still lying on the cafeteria floor, crying and writhing.

"Come on," Tristan goes. "We gotta help them."

Both he and Dickey run back into the cafeteria and start to drag their wounded classmates back into the hall. The last one they grab is Gabby Altman, who clutches at the bleeding hole in her leg crying hysterically.

"It's OK, Gabby," Dickey tries to sooth her as they both pick her up and take her around the corner. "You're gonna make it, Gabby. You're gonna make it."

Trevor Morehouse comes running up to them. "We got everybody else from the caf study hall out to the parking lot. They're safe."

"Great," Dickie goes. "Help us with these guys then."

"Wait," Tristan goes. "What if they come back this way?"

"That's why we gotta go, man," Dickie goes.

"I got an idea first," Tristan goes and runs back into the cafeteria.

"What the hell, Tristan. We gotta go," Dickie says but follows him. Trevor comes too.

Tristan goes to one of the long cafeteria tables and tries to raise it at the joint in the middle. "Help me," he goes, straining. Dickie and Trevor help him lift the table up until it forms an A shape standing about ten feet tall.

"Now help me move it front of the doors," Tristan goes.

"I see," Dickie goes. "Like a barricade."

"It'll slow them down if they come back. Might even convince them coming this way ain't worth it," Tristan goes.

"Here. Get on the other side, you guys," Tristan goes.

"What about you?" Trevor goes after he and Dickie cross the threshold back into the hall.

"Get Gabby and the others to the parking lot. I'll find another way," Tristan goes and then moves the large table in front of the doorway and turns back to the empty cafeteria. His eyes instantly scan the blood smears on the floor and then up to the eerily quiet, smoldering office.

Tristan hears more screams and gunfire, above the continual warning sirens in the distance somewhere, deeper into the school and has an urge to run to it, but just as quickly realizes he would be helpless if he did. Instead, with his heart pumping like a jackrabbit, he runs through the blasted front doors and outside.

That's when he sees the bike and a body lying next to it. Tristan runs to him and calls out his name, "Izzy—*Izzy*!"

The moment they can hear gunfire, just about every teacher puts their classroom in lockdown. Even before Principal Carter's final PA warning. Most Hemingway kids and teachers live out the horror huddled in their classrooms with the lights off behind a makeshift barricade of desks. The lucky ones, I guess. It's those of us that were in the cafeteria, or Ms. Striden's lecture room study hall, or in the upstairs library and classrooms that were still in harm's way.

And then there's Kevin Wilhelm. If only he had just stayed holed up in Mr. Becket's classroom. But *no*. As soon as he hears the rata-tat of Cunter's HK, he whips out his Baretta right there in class. A few kids like immediately scream and back away from him. Mr. Becket just freezes while Kevin bolts up to the front of the room.

"All of you just stay here," he goes.

"What are you doing with *that*?" Becket finally speaks.

"The fuck does it matter, *now*?" Kevin goes. "Just sit tight while I go save your asses."

In the first-floor lecture room, Coach Striden pokes her head out into the hall. She sees Cunter at the end of the corridor of flashing strobe lights, approaching. "Jason Turner! *JAY-SON TURN-NER!*" he yells and blasts a few rounds up into the ceiling tiles.

Striden turns back to the thirty-seven kids she has in study hall. "We gotta move, *now*, people! *Erik*—you take the lead," she goes, and Erik moves to the front of the room but not before giving Ryan a terrified stare.

"It's Cunter," Ryan goes. "It's gotta be."

"Lead them out the west exit to the staff parking lot, OK?" Striden goes. "If you see a shooter duck into the nearest classroom if they'll let you. Run if you must."

Erik nods and looks back to his classmates. "OK. Let's go!"

As Erik leads them at a brisk pace out and around the corner, Striden grabs Ryan, "Help me keep everyone safe at the rear."

"OK," Ryan goes.

As the school's sirens keep blaring on and on, Striden and Ryan are the last to leave the room while Cunter sees them from down the hall.

"Hey you fuckers! Ya'll seen my *boi*, Jason Turner? *No*? Well, fuck you then!" he goes, and fires tagging the floors and lockers on the walls. The study hall group gets split in two: the group following Erik to the west exit and a group of thirteen with Ryan and Striden.

"Up the stairs! Up the stairs!" Striden screams and the kids change course and sprint up the stairs while Cunter keeps firing at them. A bullet *thwaps* into Dignan Cooper's head, fragging half of it and sending hair and bone and viscera upon his classmates and the stairwell. Dignan's body slides down a few more steps and lies still.

A bullet skips up off the stairs and imbeds into Striden's knee. She falls with a yell and Ryan turns to grab her. With a grunting effort and surging adrenaline, they both somehow get her to make it all the way up the stairs before she collapses.

For whatever reason, Cunter does not follow them. He keeps up his sweep of the first floor on his quest for Jason.

The remaining study hall kids all huddle around Striden who's leaned up against a wall by the staircase.

The kids are all crying, except for Ryan who tries to examine Striden's shredded knee.

"Ryan—listen to me," She goes. "You have to leave me here."

"No way—" Ryan goes.

She grabs his arm. "You *have* to. You gotta get everybody out of this building. And you have to do it now."

Ryan knows she's right. They hear separate smatterings of automatic gunfire coming from different parts of the school. Thora Burkholder starts to seriously freak and starts pulling her hair out. Ryan grabs her hands and makes her look at him.

"Hey—*hey!* You're not going to die, Thora. We're getting out of here," Ryan goes and then looks again at Striden.

"That's right, Thora. Ryan's going to get you out of here. *All of you*," she goes.

Ryan stands up and looks at them all. "All right. Everybody stay close and let's *go*."

Mr. Darringer runs into liaison officer Truman in the hallway. Truman's got his Glock drawn and sweat streaming down his bald brow.

"You know where they're at?" Truman goes.

"Not exactly. I heard gunfire down both these hallways," Darringer goes.

Truman groans. "Multiple shooters. You should be in a classroom or evacuating kids."

Darringer shakes his head. "I'll go with you. You might need help. They have *explosives* for godsakes."

Truman nods *OK,* and the two of them go jogging down the hall towards the west exit. They see Erik and a mob of kids sprint around the corner and make for the exit's double doors when Cunter rounds just behind them and lifts his weapon up ready to mow them down from behind.

Truman's training tells him not to open fire, even though he's a skilled marksman, he knows there's still too much of a risk he could hit one of the kids behind his target. So, he yells and fires a round into the ceiling to get Cunter's attention.

"*Take cover—*" Truman hisses to Darringer as Cunter turns to face them and levels the HK 416 at Truman. Behind Cunter, Darringer and Truman see the last kid make it out the exit and into the sunshine. Truman fires his Glock.

Darringer ducks into the enclosed doorway of a locked down classroom and hears the screams of the kids inside.

Cunter ducks Truman's fire and jogs in a zigzag while he spits the HK's full auto at the officer and scores a line of hits up Truman's leg and into his groin, blowing apart his femoral artery.

Truman howls and collapses in his own expanding arterial pool and expires in Darringer's arms while Cunter sprints away in the opposite direction heading for a staircase.

Eddie's already made it to the second floor but doesn't see anyone until he rounds a corner and sees one solitary kid at the end of the hall. "Hey—hey, *kid!* You know Jason Turner? You know where he at?"

Kevin turns around and sees Eddie all the way down the hall with his AR-15 in his hands.

"I won't hurt you if you tell me, man," Eddie goes and starts walking closer.

Kevin grips his Baretta in his left hand behind his back.

Ryan, Thora, and their gang round another corner and start jogging toward Kevin on the other hallway to his left.

"Yo, man—Dre *send* you?" Kevin shouts to Eddie.

Eddie cracks a grin. "*Dre?* What the fuck, man? What you know about Dre? *Hey*—you behind the times, *homes*—if you be asking about Dre."

"Oh my god!" Thora yells as they get closer to Kevin. "He's got a *gun*!"

Kevin sees Eddie squint, like he might've heard what Thora said, so he whips his Barretta out to try and get the drop on the thug.

Eddie crouches low just as Kevin blasts two rounds and then fires his rifle down the long hallway.

They both miss their target, and Kevin ducks behind the corner where Ryan, Thora and about eleven other kids are crouching.

"What are you *doing?*" Ryan yells.

"Yo—shut it, dickwad," Kevin goes. "I'm trying to save you dumbasses."

"Then, forget going that way and let's turn around and book it back around to the other staircase. Striden's shot and needs help. You could escort us—give us cover," Ryan goes.

Kevin shakes his head. "*Fuck* that. I'm gonna waste this asshole right here. You know this is all Turner's fault. These guys are here to grease him for narc-ing out his pops."

Ryan fights the urge to tell Kevin he doesn't know the half of it.

"Should waste the fucker myself when I'm done here, man," Kevin goes and stands back up straight. "Stay down."

Instead of changing his Baretta over to his right hand and just sticking the Barretta out to fire a covering shot, Kevin keeps the gun in his left and slides his whole body around the corner against the wall.

Exactly the kind of stupid, novice move Eddie is waiting for. The second Kevin's body is exposed, Eddie pops out from a doorway triple-taps three rounds across Kevin's chest.

Eddie probably knows the kid is dead but approaches the body anyway. Maybe he wants to trash-talk his corpse. Who knows? Once he's up close, he kneels next to Kevin's body and inspects the bullet holes through the blood saturating Kevin's T-shirt.

But what Eddie doesn't expect is what he sees once he turns his head down the left corner, because right before it all goes dark, Eddie sees Ryan crouching right across from him holding the Barretta level to his forehead.

"*Fuck—*" Eddie whispers.

Ryan pulls the trigger.

Eddie's skull fragments and brain matter blow right out the back of his head and slimes the base of the locker behind him.

Thora screams and Ryan stands up straight, gripping the Barretta in his hand. He tries not to look down at the man he just killed and reaches down for the AR-15. Ryan turns back to Thora and the rest of his huddled classmates, "*Go—*down those stairs and out the back doors. I'll cover your back if anyone comes."

Thora rises and steps closer to Ryan. "What will you do after we leave?"

"Find a place to hide these until the police come. Then I'm going back to Coach Striden and getting her out of here. *Go*, Thora, go with the others. You're gonna be OK."

Right before the shooting started, Patrick Durning and Dylan Sorensen were in Physics class together. Being the two strongest boys in class, their teacher, Mr. Lewis, had them go across the hall to the Science storeroom so they could haul these two big boxes of gear back for the lab Lewis had planned for class.

Once they were in the storeroom, it all began. They stayed locked in that room, the two of them as they heard all the screams and gunfire, heard Cunter's grenades explode.

But now, Patrick can't take it any longer. "We've gotta do something. We can't just sit here."

"What are you talking about?" Dylan looks at Patrick like he's nuts. "What the hell can we do against any of *that*? Those were *explosions*. Whoever these psychos are, they got bombs!"

Patrick shakes his head. "You know what else I'm hearing? *Screams*. Screams from our classmates, man. Our friends. *Look—*this storeroom has doors that connect to two different hallways. I'll stand watch out this one and you stand at the one in back. If any kids run by with nowhere to go, we can have them slip in here."

"OK," Dylan goes.

Not long after they're standing by their doors, Dylan peeks out the crack and sees Cunter striding down the hallway calling out Jason's name. Dylan watches as Cunter fires into one of the locked classroom doors. Blows the door's handle off. The kids start screaming inside and Cunter just starts to laugh as he moves to step inside.

But then Dylan sees Patrick's gone out of the storeroom from his door and yells, "JASON TURNER!"

Cunter wheels around and Dylan shuts his door.

Patrick runs back into the storeroom from the back door, panting heavily.

"What are you doing?" Dylan whispers.

"After he passes by your door," Patrick goes. "Yell out '*Turner*' so that he goes back. Then you run back here out this door."

"Then what are *you* going to do?"

Patrick clenches his fists. "I'll rush him from behind."

Dylan can barely believe that Patrick's serious, but still puts his ear to the door. He can hear Cunter's heavy boots walking past the big steel door.

Five seconds later, Patrick can hear Cunter walking around the corner near his door, and he motions to Dylan to call out.

Dylan opens his door and bellows out, "*THERE'S TURNER*!"

"Ya'll best not be fucking with *me*!" Cunter yells and doubles back towards Dylan's voice.

Patrick bolts out his door and creeps around the corner. He's wearing his Adidas running shoes and approaches Cunter as quietly and quickly as he can from behind.

Dylan tears across the storeroom and follows Patrick out. He sees Patrick's almost there. Sees him raise his fists.

But he's not quick enough. Somehow Cunter senses him, or hears him—and he spins around, firing the HK the whole time spreading a line of fire across the lockers, the ceiling, and finally, into Patrick.

The first bullet to hit Patrick is a ricochet off a locker that blows into his jaw. Another four burrow into his chest.

"*No*!" Dylan yells and falls to the floor.

He sees Patrick's watery eyes glaze over and sees the horror show of what's left of Patrick's jaw and his pooling black blood that seems to be everywhere now.

Cunter steps over Patrick and releases his spent clip as he does it. He grabs another clip from the right side of his utility belt and clicks it into place. He stands over Dylan and looks down on him.

Dylan just weeps, still looking at Patrick.

"Now that there," Cunter goes and nods back to Patrick's body. "That one was one brave, *sumbitch*. You can tell the news people that when they get here, *yessir*." Then he reaches down and pats Dylan once on the head and starts walking in the direction of the library.

Jason Turner *did* come to school that morning. He showed up for basically the same reason that made Isaiah decide to go to school. After what had happened to Luke and Abby, Jason just wanted to be with people too. He was supposed to be with the rest of his Psychology class in their classroom doing their final research projects, but he saw Gala and me sitting at one of the tables in the library and snuck over to talk with us. Of course, all that any of us wanted to talk about was the accident and how terrible it all was. We were all grieving over it.

Then the shooting started. Principal Carter's Code Red. The blasts. The warning sirens and the strobe lights. The librarian, Mrs. Plimpton, put the large gate down at the library's entrance. She yelled for us all to hide behind the bookshelves.

"Are you serious?" Jason yells. "That's the *plan*?"

"Yes, yes, yes! Now get between the shelves! All of you! Away from the windows and the gate!"

Gala, Jason, and me all crouch behind the same shelf and I hear Jason mumble, "That gate's not going to do too much good against an automatic rifle."

"You think that's what the shooter has?" I go.

"Sure sounds like it," Jason goes.

We hear more gunfire and screams. Kids in the library start crying, freaking out, calling 911 and their parents on their phones. Other kids start filming as they crouch, terrified.

"It sounds like more than one gun," Gala goes.

We wait out the agonizing minutes, knowing nothing. All sounds start to slip in a nightmarish pattern of silence, then distant screaming, followed by gunfire. There must be over a hundred of us huddled here among the bookshelves and along the back of the library's walls. A few teachers and Mrs. Plimpton too, but mostly its kids.

And then we hear him. "*JAY-SON TURN-NER*! Come out and fucking play!"

"*Cunter,*" Jason hisses between his teeth.

"You serious?" I go, the enormity of what that means washing over me.

And then we can see him just outside the library gate. "*AH-HA-HAA*! I can smell you kids pissing yourselves in there."

Cunter puts his pale and goggled face right up against the gate. "*Lemme in*. Or I'll fucking *huff—*"

I look around and see all these terrified faces. All these kids with real terror in their wide eyes, and they're all looking at Jason. Probably all thinking the same thing.

What are you waiting for, Jason? You're the one he's after.

I look at Jason too as he looks down at the floor and slaps his hand on his forehead a few times. "*Think—fucking think*," he hisses.

Cunter rips off one of his grenades and backs away from the library's gate. We lose sight of him.

We see the grenade roll to the gate.

"Oh, my *god—*" Gala goes and buries her face into me.

The grenade blows and the gate blasts at least thirty-five feet into the library, plowing over tables and chairs and a huge art display.

It's the loudest sound I've ever heard in my life. Every kid in there starts to scream.

Cunter walks in looking like some kind of *soldier of fortune/angel of death* and fires a torrent of bullets into the ceiling above the bookcases where he can easily tell we're all hiding.

"*WHERE IS JASON FUCKING TURNER*?" he goes and takes a few more steps forward.

"*I'M HERE*," Jason roars back. "*Motherfucker*. I'm here."

"No," I whisper to Jason. "He'll kill you."

Jason grabs my arm hard and puts his face right into mine. "I'm walking out there. When I do, you turn around and lead everyone out the fire exit."

Suddenly we all hear a lobby of gunfire just on the other side of the fire exit door.

"There's shooting out there!" I go. Besides, when we open that door the alarm's gonna go off and he'll hear it."

"You're gonna have to risk it, Caxton."

"*What?*"

"Now *go*." He lets go of me, rises, and walks out from behind the bookshelf.

"Yeah now—looky here..." Cunter starts grinning. "There's my bitch. Hey, Lil Poppy—long time no see, *brutha*. Yeah. Come on out here, so's I can getta good look at you. That's it, dawg."

Cunter slings his rifle over his shoulder and peels off his red-tinted goggles. "Hey—you like my get-up here, man?"

Jason just stands in front of Cunter and spits. "You look how you always look. Like *shit*, you googly-eyed pasty bastard."

Cunter raises his eyebrows. "Charming to the mutherfucking end. I'll give you that, *boi*. You gotta mouth and a pair of tanks. Just like your pops. Speaking of Pops, how's he doing down in lock-up about now? He done singing like the rat-bitch he is?"

"Well, why don't you surrender right now? Maybe you'll get locked up with him. Then you can find out anything you want to know," Jason goes.

Cunter laughs, un-slings his rifle back into his hands. "*Yessir*. You'd like that shit, huh? But that ain't on my *agenda* today."

"What exactly is your agenda today? Why are you even here, Cunter? Why the fuck didn't you get out of town, man?"

"*WHAT?* AND LET YOU GO, LIL POPS? LET YOU *WIN*? No way that's going to happen, dawg. You fixed it real good, didn't you? Fixed it so's my life ain't worth shit. Won't ever be worth shit. Say I skipped town. What's my ass going to do? *Huh*, Lil Pops? There's more to life than just breathing, dawg. And there's more to death than just *not* breathing, yo. See—you and me, we be going out in fucking style, man. See these cameras here—" he taps each cam on his shoulder straps with the tip of his rifle barrel. "Say, '*hi*,' dawg. We gonna be stars for weeks, yo. We got a live feed online right now. Highlights of this are gonna be on news worldwide tonight. Best believe, dawg. And you know why?"

Jason doesn't answer, just stares back at him.

Cunter coughs out a laugh and takes a step closer. "Because people *love* this shit. Pure and simple. Since the fucking dawn of time. We're just animals drawn to the scent of fresh drawn blood, *boi*. Truth, yo. *Now get on your knees*."

I do as I was told. While Cunter and Jason talk, I lead them all back to the fire exit. The second I open the door, the alarm goes off and everybody looks back to see if

Cunter will come running. But I usher them all out. Even Mrs. Plimpton follows me as I lead them out of the library, past a dead body of a man with blood splatter all over some lockers, and down the stairs to the doors leading out to the loading docks behind the school. I even hold the door open as they all file out.

"Come on. What are you doing?" Gala goes.

"I gotta go back. I can't leave him up there," I go and tear back up the stairs and run back to the library through the fire exit. I get low and can still hear Cunter talking, telling Jason to get on his knees. I frantically look around me for anything that might be useful as a weapon. I think maybe I could rip one of the metal racks off the of bookshelf. But how could I do that without making a ton of noise?

But then I peer out at the library and see something that makes it all irrelevant.

Jason goes down to his knees. He's got no choice really. But he decides he won't look down. *No*. He'll look Cunter in the eyes till the end. As if Cunter were Kehoe himself. Look at him with no fear. No tears. No begging. No terror. Not even hate.

Just defiance black as balls.

Cunter stands just a few feet away and points the long barrel of his HK 416 right at Jason's head. "You know what I'm gonna do after I blow your head into that stack of books back there?"

Jason says nothing.

"I'm gonna find out where Eddie's at and we gonna kill every kid left in this school till SWAT comes in full breach. And then I gonna have me some fun with my last three grenades. Best *believe*—"

"Shut up already," Jason goes. "*Yap, yap, yap*. I don't care what you do, man. It still won't change the fact that you *lost* and I *won*. You should know when you're bested, man."

The grin falls off Cunter's face. "Fuck that, man. Open your mouth." He rams the rifle's tip into Jason's tight-closed lips. "Open up and see if this shit takes like *victory*—"

Jason sees Cunter's eyes widen even more with rage, but suddenly there's a bang and a jolting *crack*—and the thinnest gleeking squirt of blood sprays out of Cunter's right eye before his body slacks and falls dead to the floor.

Just behind where Cunter stood is Darringer, eyes wide and breathing heavy, still holding up Truman's thinly smoking Glock.

23

Abby regained consciousness the night of the shooting. The first thing she remembered was the feel of the IV and the strong smell of sanitizer. Her parents were at her bedside watching news coverage of the shooting up on the flatscreen, but Abby really didn't register that yet. Her mind was still foggy for a few more moments as she tried to digest her surroundings. She realized she was in a hospital room. And then she was hit with it. All of it, all at once, it all came back to her, and she gripped the flab of her stomach through her hospital johnny robe.

She realized Clara wasn't there. Wasn't inside her anymore.

Abby looked wild-eyed at her mom whose eyes were already brimming with tears.

"*The baby. Mom*? My *baby*?"

Her mother reached out for her and clutched Abby's head to her chest. "I'm so sorry, Sweetie. I'm so sorry."

"*No, no, no, no—* " Abby began to weep.

"She didn't make it, Sweetheart. *I'm sorry—*" her mom said, still clutching.

A long and deep draught of sobs took hold of Abby's whole body. When she finally drew a breath again it was only to spit it back out in the most sorrowful of wails.

Abby's father could only watch a few feet away, helpless, while his wife held their daughter as Abby's bruised heart finally broke apart all together, washed away by an agony of tears.

CANTO V

"I never saw a moor,
I never saw the sea;
Yet I now know how the heather looks,
And what a wave must be."
Dickinson

1

Eight dead. Six wounded. Statistically, in the whole unforgivable American history of mass violence, it didn't seem like the most sensational shootout of all time in the least. The whole incident was over in less than five minutes. Down somewhere in some scorching corner of hell, maybe Kehoe was managing a sneer and calling Cunter a lightweight. Of the Hemingway dead, three were adults and three were students. Even split. Of the six that were wounded, Coach Striden was the worst off. She would lose her leg. She'd eventually get one of those spacey-looking prosthetic legs and continue coaching. But for weeks after the shooting, she was stuck in the hospital to recover.

Miraculously, Isaiah wasn't killed either. Cunter tagged Isaiah in the shoulder, ripping through his deltoid muscle, in the opening salvo, but missed his vital areas. Izzy was itching to get out of the hospital after only three nights, and they let him.

The funerals quickly followed. Each grieving family held their own private services and (except for Hemingway's receptionist, Gretta Lutz, and Kevin Wilhelm) they all had a public service too, giving the town and the students of Hemingway a chance to pay their respects.

The media absolutely frenzied over memorializing Carter, Truman, and Patrick as great American posthumous heroes. Whole portions of Principal Carter's funeral were even nationally televised and streamed. You might even remember the President spoke at the event. I think there were two main reasons why the media, and the public (including you too, probably) stayed with the story for so long. The first being that Hemingway had very distinctive heroes. *Sure*—our story didn't have the death toll, but we did have the heroes—*like all over the place*. We were one of the few mass shootings where the shooters got taken out by the people who were supposed to be their victims. Here at Hemingway, the gunmen didn't meet their deaths on their own terms like so many of these dark souls had done through all-too-recent memory. (Even Kevin Wilhelm had a MAGA-moment as a Second Amendment martyr. Forget the fact that he was a drug dealer and would've probably shot Jason on sight in the chaos. And *whatever,* I guess, about how Kevin obtained a firearm illegally and brought it to school every day. And *whatever* too that it was actually Ryan Leone that killed one of the shooters in self-defense.) The second reason everybody stayed with it was because of Cunter's live streaming of the events. Footage from the cameras strapped to his chest went out through multiple platforms, and enough people recorded it live, and then *Bam!*—it went unkillably viral, baby. I mean, you've probably seen some of that footage, right? So even though only eight people died, the world obsessed over Hemingway, because they *saw* it. Cunter put you there, in our hallways like a first-person shooter game. Anyone with a device could hear the grenades and screams, see the bullets and the blood, and feel just how true Cunter's words were: *"People love this shit."*

Shame on us all.

Forget the fact that the media missed all sorts of details about what really happened and why. They were caught up with the images and politics. So many news outlets twisted and turned the whole tragedy in whatever way fit their own angles and narratives they wanted to present. Every Left-Winger and Right-Winger talking head had plenty to froth about for months. But still nothing changed. Like the village of Thorn, maybe we had learned to live with a dragon in our midst—as long as we only sacrificed a few children at a time. A large population of the media even served it up like it was this *huge victory*—while all of us went to our friends' funerals and tried to cope with the greatest trauma of our lives.

Classes were suspended for the year. The school itself was closed off as a crime scene until August. Any student that needed to turn in outstanding class work could make arrangements with their teachers but other than that, grades would remain as is. Three days after the shooting though, Darringer's welding buddies brought Luke's sculpture to Hemingway and erected it on a grassy area by the front parking lot.

After an emergency school board debate, the unveiling ceremony was scheduled for two days later. Carver Belmont came over from Bath just to be with Jason. Most of us students were in attendance too. We all wanted to be together you could tell. We had just attended all the same funerals—so why not a dedication of some colossal, welded sculpture? I suppose we were all hoping for some sort of ceremonial closure we'd never get. We all stood in the parking lot in front of this massive metal sword Luke had built. Surrounding the sword was an encompassing metal circle that formed this kind of omega around it. It was pretty amazing. On the base of the structure were the last lines from a poem by Lord Alfred Tennyson: *TO STRIVE, TO SEEK, TO FIND, AND NOT TO YEILD*—a poem that Darringer had shared with Luke.

Up at the podium, Mr. Darringer says a few words and sits down. Then Jason Turner walks slowly up to the microphone.

Erik nudges my shoulder. "Did you know he was going to do this?"

I shake my head.

"Did you?" Erik asks Ryan.

"Yeah. He told me at Patrick's funeral that Darringer had asked him to," Ryan goes.

"Hey," Jason goes and backs up a step. "This is not really my thing, but whatever I guess." His eyes rove, and for a split second I get this stabbing fear that he's drunk. But no, I think—he can't be.

Jason steps back up to the microphone. "It's hard—it's all hard, this life. It shouldn't be me speaking here today. If I could trade places… if I could… But I *can't*, you know? And whether it's fair or unfair—damn it—I'm the one here. *We're* the ones here. Right?" Jason looks over to where Carver's standing next to Isaiah with his arm in a sling. Carver beams up at him like the grandfather Jason never had.

"A friend of mine once told me we are beset by evils all around. That we never shake full clear from them. That they're never far, these evils surround us—or lie within us—or at least it was something like that." Jason clears his throat and continues. "He told me it comes down to a choice really. So, what do we do when the darkness comes closer? Do we kneel before it? Do we hide? *Or*—do we *strive*, do we *seek* like it says up here? Well, as for me, *man*—I know my choice. And I sure as hell know in whose name I make that choice."

Jason fidgets with the mic stand and just stands there a moment looking out to us.

I feel tears flood my eyes into a blur. I don't seem to be able to control my bottom lip, and in the moment, I don't care.

"In the name of Rosalind Howard. In the name of Maddie O'Leary. In the name of Dignan Cooper, of Gretta Lutz, of Principal Larry Carter, of Officer Howard Truman. In the name of Patrick Durning. In the name of *Luke*—" Jason catches his voice on the brink of a sob himself.

I wipe my eyes with my palms. I look around and see everyone's eyes all gleaming and red too.

"*Never yield*," Jason's voice is all brittle—all raspy whisper into the microphone. "*Never yield. Never—yield.*"

Darringer and Jason step off the podium. There's no applause but I turn and see people all around us hugging and crying even more than at the recent funerals. I hug Erik and Ryan. We pull in Tristan and Gray, Dickie, Gala and Dallas. After a bit I look up and catch glimpses of those in the crowd. I see Dylan Sorensen and Philip Lukas with some friends and there are tears in their eyes too, I see Trevor Morehouse and T.J. hugging Thora Burkholder, and I make eye contact with Mr. Malory across the parking lot and he nods back with a solemn smile on his lips. I see Jason walk off with Isaiah and Carver. I break away from our group to follow—I want to tell Jason how much his words meant to me, but before I get close enough, I see the three of them going out onto the football field. Out to the fifty-yard line. I just let them go. Instead, I just watch from the chain link fence as they amble out and huddle close.

At that point I had no idea who Carver Belmont was, but I knew enough about Isaiah and Jason to know that something *holy* was going on here. They bow their heads like they might be praying, and they stay that way for a long time. I finally give them their peace and walk away back to the rest of our group.

Nearly a year later, when I was deep into my interviews, I asked Izzy once what the three of them were doing out there that day. He got really quiet for a moment then said, "We said goodbye."

"To whom, exactly?" I asked.

"To all of them."

2

Later that night, Jason goes to the hospital. When he gets to the room, he sees Mr. Forrester snoozing on the chair by the window while some talking heads debate teachers having guns in school for the millionth time on the flatscreen.

The machines surrounding Luke beep and hum, and the bruises on his face seem to have gone down some since Jason had last seen him. The tube sticking into Luke's raw mouth still shocks Jason though every time he sees it.

"Hey, sleeping beauty," Jason says to Luke, and Mr. Forrester flutters his eyes.

"Oh—*hey*," Mr. Forrester goes. "Didn't hear you come in."

"Here to take my shift. Why don't you go home, Mister F. and get some real sleep. I'll call if you know, whatever."

"That's all right. I think I'll just go get some coffee though. Have a walk to stretch my legs," Mr. Forrester goes, and stands up and arches his back.

Jason moves over to the seat just below the flatscreen. "See you in a bit, man."

"You got it," Mr. Forrester smiles and walks out.

Jason sits there a bit while the debate's intensity goes up a notch on the TV. "*That's right. Just keep yapping*—you bag of douches," Jason groans and reaches up and clicks the flatscreen off.

"Want some company?"

Jason looks up and sees Abby at the door. He smiles all weary. "Come on in. Pop a squat."

Abby crosses the room and sits. She looks at the monitors all blipping and beeping out Luke's vital signs, she seems almost tranced by them. Jason looks at her and thinks if he didn't know any better, he'd say Abby looked like she just hit a bong load of weed.

"So—the doctors say when he *might* wake up?"

Jason shakes his head. "Could be days, could be weeks, could be *never*. That's a coma for you."

She seems to zone out again looking at the monitors; when she finally speaks again, she doesn't look at Jason at all.

"I don't know what to feel right now."

"That's probably all right," Jason goes.

"I mean—I don't think I'm *capable* of feeling anything. You know? I think I'm all *felt out*."

Jason just nods.

"My parents—my mom, really—doesn't want me seeing Luke at the moment. She thinks he's basically to blame for—you know—*everything*. That he made a choice. A choice he had *no right* to make."

"Is that what you think?"

"I don't know. Part of me doesn't want to think about it either. And with the whole shooting thing on top of it all? With the whole town—the whole country going crazy over it? It's just all too much. I say screw thinking or feeling for a while."

Jason says nothing, just tries to look like he understands.

"I was going to keep her," Abby goes. "My baby."

"He told me you were thinking that."

"He tell anybody else?"

"Probably not."

"You two are really that close, huh?"

"Abby –" Jason goes. "I'm sorry about your baby. I wish *like hell—*"

She raises her hand for him to stop. "*Don't—*"

"OK—" Jason holds his hands up and sits back. Another long interval passes as they sit in silence. But Jason speaks up again. "You know. Back at the start of the year, back when I was wasted all the time, he offered himself to me."

"Offered?" Abby goes.

"Yeah. Offered to let me kill him. I was so full of hate and rage that I was crazy with it. And I almost did it, Abby. God damn me to hell, I almost *did it*. But somehow, he knew. Luke knew exactly how far down into the pit he'd have to go to get my attention. *Christ*—I thought he was just suicidal. I thought he was tired of life and being deaf and just wanted to die. That's what I thought. But I was so wrong. He was willing to dive into my raging river of shit and grab the last little part of me that was still decent and worth something, and then he pulled it up to the surface and into the air. And now I can't stop breathing. Because of *him*, I can't stop breathing. He ain't my friend. He's my brother. He's *family*. I still think he might be crazier than shit—but he's family, and there's nothing I wouldn't do for him."

Abby just stares over at Jason with calm, sad eyes—Rozzy eyes. "I love him too," she says, "but it's just that, you know… he killed my daughter."

The fire alarm starts going off. Out in the hallway the fire alarm sounds all loud and piercing. Abby and Jason both get up and investigate the hall right outside Luke's room. Nurses and orderlies are scrambling. Other visitors start poking their heads out of other patient's rooms to see what's the matter.

"We need you two to make your way downstairs," a nurse goes and starts leading Jason and Abby to the emergency stairway.

"Hey, what the hell?" Jason goes as he and Abby are swept along with a wave of other visitors. "What about my friend back there? He's in a coma."

The nurse keeps them moving towards the exit. "The staff. We'll take care of him. Don't worry. We'll get them all out if this is for real."

Other nurses help lead the charge and corral the horde of visitors down to the hospital's main foyer. The alarm suddenly shuts off and there's a collective sigh. A moment later a voice comes over the hospital's public address that it was a false alarm and that everyone may re-enter the hospital.

Jason moves closer to a security guard by the revolving front entrance who is listening to another guard on his walkie-talkie. The guard on the other end says something about some asshole up on fifth tried smoking a cigar in one of the rooms and didn't even open a window.

Jason and Abby run into Mr. Forrester by the hospital's café, and they make their way back up to Luke's room. But once they open the door, they see Luke's *not* in his bed.

"That's not right—" Alan Forrester goes. "If the staff had evacuated them, they would've wheeled Luke out on his bed. *Look*—his tube's out—"

All three of them go back out in the hallway and begin to fan out looking for where Luke might be. They stop every nurse and security guard they see, but everybody seems clueless in all the mayhem. Starting to get truly pissed, Jason stalks the hallways of the floor and pokes his head into every room that isn't locked.

He runs into Abby a few minutes later coming down the opposite end of the hallway.

"Anything?" she goes.

Jason shakes his head.

They both walk around another corner and peak into a small waiting area. Inside the little enclave is a flatscreen on mute, an old woman nodding off on one of the chairs, and *Luke*—standing with his back to them, looking out the window into the night's darkness, swaying in his long johnny robe.

Jason and Abby call out his name and move towards him. But before they can touch him, he turns to face them. His body still sways a little, like he's drunk or something, and his eyes are spacey—but bright.

And then he speaks. Clear and distinct, even if a little raspy. He says one lone word to them, in a man's voice neither of them has ever heard before—not even in Jason's dreams.

"*Water*—"

3

We roll up in two vehicles. Six of us in Erik's mini-van and four of us in Jason's *Civic*. We stash our stuff in Izzy's uncle's hunting cabin and waste no time finding the trail that leads to the lake. The trail quickly breaks out of the trees and opens into this sprawling wonderland of sand dunes and sparse long yellow grasses. I had never seen anything like it in my life—it was like being on another planet—a second Earth or something. The sky glories in blue with white clouds above us while we walk through the sand, each step revealing more and more of the massive expanse and greenish-blue haze of Lake Superior spreading out before us. By the time we crest the last dune and look down to this white beach of fine sand and smooth pebbles, and look out to the seemingly endless water, we all get the feeling we are not just on the final shore of Upper Michigan, but on the final shore of the world itself entire.

A gull glides out above us and pierces the azure; we take the bird's soaring as a call to charge down the deep bank, and most of us plunge forward, heedless—yelling and laughing as we do. Dickie trips into a graceless barrel roll the last twenty yards of the descent and I nearly wet myself laughing at him. Ryan picks Izzy up after completely biffing it in a spectacular face plant. Once the guys all make it down, they all immediately begin picking up pebbles and tossing them into the lake. We have come between the tides, and the immense surface is calm as the Volgstaad's pond water. I lag behind a little to help Gala down and she shakes her head watching the boisterous frolicking of Izzy, Ryan, Tristan, Dickie, Erik, and Jason. *Boys*, she says. I tell her she's brave for coming along. She nods back up the dune where Abby's with Luke, and says she only agreed to come because Abby would be here too. There's no way she'd be the only girl hanging around a weekend like this otherwise. I tell her I understand.

Jason must have wearied of tossing rocks, because he tears his shirt off and runs into the clear chilly water without hesitation. He plunges under the surface and swims out a few yards underwater. When he comes back up, he yells and shivers. *Get out here, ya pussies! This is great*—he goes and dives back under. Isaiah is the next to follow and soon all of them are splashing and shouting. Jason hoists up Tristan and tosses him over his shoulder, both laughing.

But I don't join. I was content to sit this one out and lean against a piece of driftwood with Gala. I wasn't aware of it at that moment, but I was on the brink of having my crush on Gala begin to fade. She wanted more than anything to follow her passion with acting, and I had this crucible beginning to burn inside me to write—to write about all of this and see what sort of horizon lay at the end of it. By the time she left to study theater at NYU that August, I was already over it and wishing her well. But sitting there with her against that driftwood that day, watching the rest of them gleefully horse around in that lake—I took her hand in mine and felt a contentment—deep and wordless—a contentment I would later realize that can only come from merging with something much larger than yourself…

Still up above the beach, Luke and Abby sit down on the cliff of the dune and look out to the water. They sit there a long time watching. On the four-hour ride up, Abby had chosen to ride in Erik's mini-van, not Jason's car with Luke. In truth, she did not decide until very late to even come up here at all.

Her dry and motionless face and eyes take in the expanse of the nature around her. The sun's rays feel warm on her bare arms; the water tries to give peace with every little subtle rise and swell—but as Abby looks on, she feels she has absolutely nothing left to give back to it. They both sit there so still. She can't help but think that her stillness is due to her hollowness, her emptiness. Like a husk. But Luke's stillness seems different, she muses. His is borne not out of emptiness—but out of sheer *weight*. If she is a husk, Luke is a living statue, a breathing monument.

But then again, is that really accurate? Is that really fair to think? Maybe not. *Maybe I don't really know anything*, she will remember thinking.

"The third day," she turns to him and starts to speak. "After the accident. The mother—Lisa Ann Belfry—she came to see me. With her two daughters. The baby and a six-year-old too it turns out. Did you know that?"

Luke shakes his head.

"She came to see you too, of course. But it was still real touch and go with you at that point, so—*yeah*. She just saw me. She didn't make it a minute before she was just bawling. Saying she was sorry about my baby. About how awful it all was. How she'd been praying for *us*. For you and me, and Clara."

Abby looks away from Luke and back out to the lake. She sees the guys jumping out into the lake and hears their yells. She turns back to Luke.

"She never actually said *thank you*—but you could see it all over her face. I think she wanted to, but she was also sensitive enough to know how that would sound. What their lives had cost me. I'll always be grateful to her for that, I think."

Abby closes her eyes and tries to concentrate for a moment on the gentle breeze across her face. Keeping her eyes closed she continues, "I think that's something she will want to say to you though. If you ever get to talk to her."

The guys' aquatic roughhousing gets louder down below, and Abby opens her eyes again and looks down the far stretch of beach. "Can't get over how much it looks like the ocean."

Luke looks outward too, his eyes wide, his face relaxed but unreadable. After a while, Abby tugs on his arm.

"I read your dragon story. Isaiah gave it to me a few days ago. He and I got discharged from the hospital on the same day, and he gave it to me."

Luke makes a face that says, *And...* more or less.

Abby exhales. Tries to conjure up the words. "Um—it was *vivid*."

Luke shrugs.

"But I got to say," Abby goes. "I don't know if I really liked the ending."

Luke looks at her and waits.

"I mean I get it. I guess it's fantasy and it should probably end happy, *but*—" she trails off.

Luke just waits for her to go on.

"There are no *Auras*. Sometimes in real life there's not any protection from the worst thing ever happening to you, or the people you love. And right now, I just don't find that kind of magical *the-good-guys-get saved*-type ending comforting. I'm glad Izzy does—and he's who you wrote it for. So that's great, I guess."

Luke reaches for his notepad. Pulls out his pen.

"But I'll tell you what—there may not be such things as *Auras*, but there are sure as hell such things as dragons," Abby goes and gives a bitter stare back out to the silent lake.

Luke writes. He hands her the note.

In the end, maybe what's important
isn't so much if we can protect them from the dragons.

Abby chokes up. "I couldn't protect Clara. Nobody could protect Maddie. And the school? Patrick? All this death. All this screaming and horror, how can *anyone* even… *My sweet baby—*"

Luke hands her a final note.

Maybe it more just comes down to this:
Can we love them more
than we fear the worst thing
in the world happening to them?

Abby stares at the note a long while. One of her tears falls on it, dampening the paper. When she finally looks back up to the great lake, another tear forms in her right eye, slowly, and glides down her cheek. She neatly folds his note, making precise lines as she does and tucks it into her short's pocket. All the truths of the world's harsh realities swimming around in her head. She turns to him and thinks about this man/boy, this colossus, this beautiful, but ultimately indecipherable enigma in front of her.

"Who are you, Luke Forrester? Of *what* matter are you made? Because clearly you are not of this earth, my friend," Abby goes and takes Luke's hand, not as a lover she finally knows, but as a true friend. "Clearly not of this earth. *Clearly*."

Luke squeezes her hand back, and looks back into her eyes and smiles, his eyes all wide and glistening, but gives her back not a word, neither written nor spoken.

THE INFINITE SEA

Meaning is magic.

Or so says Carver Belmont of Bath.

OK, I say. How so?

You want to name a seemingly infinite sea? First you gotta hem it in with shoreline. You want to know the contours of the apparently endless prairie? Look down on it from a border of mountains. You want make a map of the boundless expanses of outer space? Well, find a sun and start emanating rings.

Do you want solve the riddle of a tragedy? Then zoom in close enough to see every breath of those who lived it and died it, then pull back away from its epicenter and view what horror looks like from among the stars.

Is it still a horror?

Or is it something else entirely?

Mr. Malory seems to agree.

He says to understand anything through writing, you have to give it a page one. Start anywhere—it doesn't matter where. But start it. Do your grappling, page after page. Grapple, grapple. And then end it. Somewhere, anywhere.

Give it the old THE END. And then you've got it. Seemingly out of thin air. It's confined. Cover to a cover. A start to a finish. Now you can take it with you anywhere—it's moveable, consumable. Read it on an airplane if you like. A subway, in a park. Give it to someone else. Contaminate or illuminate their brain with it. Whichever, whatever.

Maybe it is a kind of sorcery. You know, this context I've created. This meaning from the madness. This magic.

But *truth?*

Hmm... I think this is that part where I say, *you tell me*.

The truth is, it's been three years now. Nearly to the day. Three years since the world was introduced to Hemingway. The Hemingway Shootout. Not the Hemingway Shooting, not the Hemingway Massacre. Thanks to Cunter and his guns and his grenades and cameras, thanks to Ryan Leone and Mr. Darringer for shooting back. Thanks to Isaiah, and Jason, and Patrick. It's The Shootout. Three years now—and closer to four years since Rozzy took her own life. A year bookended by bullets and blood.

Well, somewhere along the way I started smoking cigarettes. Don't ask me why. I keep telling myself that I'll quit them once this is all done but we'll see, huh? I'm smoking one now in fact. Malory never told me how much of a hazard writing could be to your health.

I'm holed up here in a roadside inn off Lakeshore Drive. Not too far from where Jason had his *Finnegan's* nightmare about Kehoe's farm and becoming King Skull. I can hear Lake Erie lapping right outside my door in fact. I pay for my room by the week with my credit card and pizza boxes stack the corner by the door. Near empty two-liter Coke bottles are perched here and there about the place and I write mostly at the circular table by the window, but sometimes I write like I am now, with my laptop on my lap, sitting on the floor with my back against the stucco wall. I've been here for three months, I think. Wait—scratch that. It's been four. They gave me a room with two queens. I sleep on one and my mountain of notebooks, and other scattered writing debris, sleep on the other.

I take walks a lot. I bought a coffee maker at Walmart in town and walk and smoke and drink bitter Italian roast at dusk. I usually refill and reload and write for a few hours and then walk the shoreline again sometime after midnight to clear my head.

In case you haven't guessed, I didn't go to college. I plan to start this fall though, maybe. Once I decided to write this, there was no looking back. I spent the first year just collecting my notes. I interviewed everybody (well, almost). I visited all those that went to college, and I interviewed those two out in Colorado. I went and stayed a week with Carver in Bath. I talked endlessly with these people on the phone and online. I collected journals from Izzy and Jason. I was even able to get a hold of Luke's story too, of course. I recorded, I jotted. I amassed and amassed, like a deep-sea fishing rig out in the Atlantic casting its wide net till I was so heavy I was nearly tipping.

The second year I started writing. It went slow at first. My parents freaked. They didn't understand what I was doing. I spent some of the money they had set aside for my college fund so I could eat and travel around. I wrote and wrote. I interviewed more and amassed more. I grappled and grappled.

OK. Stop it already. I can feel you out there. I know what you must be thinking. I'm trying to imagine you out there reading all this wondering how much of this is total bull crap and how much might actually be true. I can feel you thinking about Rozzy and Izzy and Carver and Luke. And maybe you're even thinking about Jason's visions and where they came from and all that would-be mystical stuff. I realize you may be struggling with what to make of it all.

I know, because I've had to struggle with all of this myself. I've had to struggle with the enigma that is Rosalind Howard and the distant monolith that is Luke Forrester more than you'll ever get to fully appreciate. But I still imagine you sitting there thinking, well—isn't there *anything* more you can tell me?

Well—I guess I could tell you what it was like visiting Rosalind's trailer home and the twenty minutes I spent there trying to talk to her mom who was too drunk and sick to even form a complete sentence and how the whole trailer seemed the saddest enclosed four walls in the world.

I could tell you about how Ryan Leone couldn't sleep for nearly year because of how traumatized he was from taking Eddie's life and how he was haunted by the sight of Patrick when he came upon his body in the hallway. I could tell you about how he withdrew his spot at NMU and moved out to Colorado Springs to work construction with his uncle and how, on a lark it seems, he invited Jason Turner, who went with him.

I could tell you about how last year, after both going to the University of Michigan, Erik and Abby started dating and about how they are the kind of couple that holds hands in parking lots and are comfortable together in long silences.

I could tell you about how before he left to go with Ryan to Colorado to work construction, Jason gave me his notebooks—his letters to Rozzy. He handed them all to me and told me to make good use of them. He said for me to go ahead and tell it. Tell it all. The good, the bad, the *fugly*. He said that he had written the last one that very morning after his run before packing.

In his final letter he wrote:

Rozzy—

This is the last time you'll be hearing from me. At least for a while. I just got back from my morning run and I'm about to pack up what little shit I got here in a bit and head off with Ryan Leone to Colorado.

For weeks now my head's been trying to wrap around everything that's happened. I don't know how you did it. How you reached out to so many people. I still don't know what I believe about it. I still don't know what to think of Luke half the time either, other than I owe him and you everything. I owe you my life. I'm so sorry I wasn't ready to do more for you when you were here, Rozz. My fuckup's have caused so much pain, for so many, it still overwhelms me sometimes.

But I also know, I've tried to do good. I've tried to live up to what you wanted me to do. So, I guess you did it, girl.

This morning I was out running (I'm getting in such good shape now, you'd be impressed). Anyway, I ran from town all the way out to the cornfields west of town. By the time I got to my turnaround point, I saw all these storm clouds gathering all pissed off looking. They were nearly black they were so thick. Then there was this lightning strike—I'm not kidding, it looked like it struck ground a few yards ahead of me—and then the rain hit. Fucking pouring, man. I ripped out my ear pods and tried to tuck it all under my T-shirt. I know—it seems like the worst jog ever, right? But it wasn't, Rozz. I ran through the soaking blankets of rain, my feet fucking sopping heavy, and I just yelled my head off like an idiot I was so happy. So, I'll keep running and breathing till I get far enough, live enough, do enough. Till I rise high enough or dream enough that the lightning that connects you to me becomes a never-extinguishing flash, a fucking forever light linking us till we come closer and closer, till there is no more breath, no more me, no more you—only us—full. Like you told Izzy in his dream. Till we are one.

The sky's ripped, girl, and the glory's falling.

Until we are one.

Always your knight—

And what about Luke? What could I tell you about *him*?

Well, Carver would have you believe that Luke's the greatest, most benevolent liar that ever lived. *But as for me…*

If you were to ask me to tell you about what I knew about Luke Forrester at the beginning of senior year, I wouldn't have had a lot to say. I mean, there would've been an awkward silence and then I probably would've stuttered out an "*uh…*" And then I would've told you that Luke Forrester is the big deaf kid that's really good at soccer and that would've been about it.

But like I said, that all changed. *Everything changed.*

Luke didn't go to college either. That first year he went out to sea with Darringer as Darringer's apprentice. After the shooting, the welding teacher resigned and made plans to resume his underwater and sea welding full time. When he offered the apprenticeship, Luke wholeheartedly jumped at the chance.

Despite my many attempts to contact him, Luke has never responded. In fact, it wasn't just me—he barely returned any text or message of any kind from any of us, as far as I know. Even his own father just got the occasional snail mail postcard.

At the end of the year, Luke didn't come back stateside with Darringer on the freighter they had been commissioned on. He quit the company when they had taken port off Yarmouth, Nova Scotia. Darringer said the last he had seen of Luke; Luke had just spent a sizable chunk of his pay on a long sea kayak and a load of gear. He told Darringer he planned to '*just paddle around awhile*.' A little less than a year later, Luke's dad would get another post card from Saguenay, Canada, followed by a few pictures in an envelope of Luke smiling through a beard and a calm sea in the background.

As far as I know, that's the last that anyone's heard from Luke in a while, leaving us all to wonder and imagine in those quiet moments when we dare to.

As for myself, I like to imagine Luke still kayaking—I see him in a red one for some reason, long and true and packed tight for a lengthy journey—out in the North Atlantic within sight of Nova Scotia's wild and rocky shore. He paddles these smooth arcs near a sunset without the sun, only clouds massing like half-drunk rioters into a creaking stadium. The water's as still as it's ever going to get and looks cool and clean enough to dip your chalice in and drink and drink and drink.

I imagine the only sound is the awesome hum of empty space and the rhythmic wheel of his paddling—and maybe, just a barely audible rumble of thunder.

I picture Luke's face looking as peaceful as the metallic gray-blue ripples surrounding him while his eyes sparkle with an unfathomable hope—*hope* inexplicable—looking to the blackening clouds before him, spreading forever untethered like never-ending dragon's wings across the sky.

I would know such peace.

May *you* know such peace.

Made in United States
Cleveland, OH
26 November 2024

10936817R00302